D0897036

Fredric Brown

Night of the Jabberwock

The Screaming Mimi

Knock Three-One-Two

The Fabulous Clipjoint

ZB

A Black Box Thriller from Zomba Books

FIRST PUBLISHED IN GREAT BRITAIN IN 1983
BY ZOMBA BOOKS, ZOMBA HOUSE, 165–167 WILLESDEN HIGH
ROAD, LONDON NW10 2SG

© ESTATE OF FREDRIC BROWN, 1950, 1949, 1959 & 1947

ISBN 0 946391 11 4 (pb)
0 946391 12 2 (hc)

Phototypeset by Input Typesetting Ltd, London
Printed by Richard Clay (The Chaucer Press)
Cover Design by John Gordon
Cover Painting by Robin Harris

Production Services by Book Production Consultants, Cambridge
General Editor Black Box Thrillers: Maxim Jakubowski

FIRST EDITION

Introduction
By H. R. F. Keating

There are some books, apart from the thundering great classics, that deserve to live as long as people read. Two of Fredric Brown's, perhaps more, to my mind fall into this class. They are his first, *The Fabulous Clipjoint*, and his most popular (though it does have a flaw in it), *The Screaming Mimi*.

Yet in Britain, where Fredric Brown is probably better known as a writer of science fiction, the crime novels which are his main legacy are little read, and even in his native America he is not a writer who, a decade after his death, makes a particularly impressive impact. There are many possible reasons for this neglect, even down to the ill-luck of his being called that almost anonymous Brown. (The only Brown to have made the least mark in British literature is one John Brown, a nineteenth-century Scottish essayist described as "a blameless and attractive character".) Not even our Brown's Fredric without the e or the k seems to be enough to mark him out in the torpid public mind.

Other reasons for this loss of status are perhaps more meaningful. Brown's having written in two distinct modes, crime and science fiction tells against him, however ridiculously. But a yet more powerful count is that he wrote what to the unsuspecting might seem to be merely straightforward tough pulp fiction and which, in paperback, was generally presented as just that, in decidedly lurid, cheap covers. Indeed, the notorious Mickey Spillane, a writer of brutish pulp if ever there was, hailed Brown as his "favourite writer of all time". Something of a kiss of death.

Brown's books have, too, been described by the American critic, Newton Baird, who made a study of them, as "easy-to-read entertainments" and thus they might be thought of as easy to forget. Easy to read they are. Brown's prose is a model of direct straightforwardness. The sentences are never long and very seldom complex. They seem simply to be laying down the information the reader needs. Yet the people he puts before us in this easy language are by no means simple, all black-or-white figures. Describing the wife near to divorcing her husband in *Knock Three-One-Two* he says "she did love him at least a little". There is the to-and-fro changeability of a real human being all in eight words, nine syllables. So the books are easy entertainment but at the same time something a great deal more.

In fact, Fredric Brown began writing precisely for the pulps, those cheap wood-pulp paper magazines that from the 1920s on revolutionised American crime writing with contributors as distinguished (later) as Dashiell Hammett and Raymond Chandler. Brown came to the field after these pioneers, selling his first story in 1936 when the was 30 at much the same time as he left a humdrum office job (years later writing his only straight novel, *The Office*, he put in a murder) to take up work more suited to his basically raffish temperament, as a proof-reader and later reporter on the *Milwaukee Journal*. Though he attended the University of Cincinnati, the city where he was born, and Hanover College, Indiana, he had taken no degrees and as a writer he was altogether self-taught.

But his long apprenticeship in the pulps – he produced more than 300 short stories in his lifetime – paid off. His first novel, *The Fabulous Clipjoint*, was the Mystery Writers of America first-book 'Edgar' for 1948, and deservedly. It is a remarkable feat. No wonder it remained his favourite of all the 23 crime novels he wrote and the half-dozen others.

Besides the virtues it shares with all the books in this volume, the iron-grip story, the direct masculine writing, the click-into-place plot, it is marked through and through with Brown's characteristic, and difficult to achieve, mix of the realistic and the romantic. The romantic comes in the character of the narrator-hero, young Ed Hunter. Brown chose just the right age for him to be, a boy on the verge of manhood, capable of a man's actions (even to going to bed with a gangster's moll), fired with the hopes of youth.

He is an earlier – by four years – Holden Caulfield of J. D. Salinger's *The Catcher in the Rye*, hearteningly alert for the phoninesses of the adults' world. He is a later Jim Hawkins, of R. L. Stevenson's *Treasure Island*. Like Jim he seeks something important, the name of his father's slayer rather than a golden hoard. Like Jim, though fearful he can rise to a heroism or toughness he did not know he possessed, as in the scene where he helps break down the crooked bar-owner Kaufman and rises to the height of quick improvisation in using his forefingers as an imaginary gun barrel. Like Jim he can bravely but stupidly disobey orders and, in place of single-handedly re-capturing the ship Hispaniola, he single-handedly tackles the floozie, Claire Raymond.

The reality in *The Fabulous Clipjoint* comes from the setting, Chicago. In its unvarnished brutality, and simple squalor.

*Guys who take ten-cent beds or two-bit partitioned rooms
in flophouses and in the morning somebody shakes them to
wake them up, and the guy's stiff, and the clerk goes quickly
through his pockets to see if he's got two bits or four bits or
a dollar left, and then he phones for the city to come and get
him out. That's Chicago.*

And Fredric Brown describes Chicago as it is, or as it was, coolly
and without exaggeration. The mark of a real writer. Nor is that
all. In the final charged pages of the book we learn what its odd
title means. Chicago is the clipjoint ('club', says my dictionary
sternly, 'charging exorbitant prices'), but it is a fabulous clipjoint,
its squalor can be lit by a light that comes from an unearthly source.

Two years and three books later Brown produced *The Screaming
Mimi*, a title as odd and intriguing as his first book's. It proved his
greatest success, eventually being made into a film (plot altered, of
course,) with Anita Ekberg and Gypsy Rose Lee. It is a variation
on the theme of fairy-story Beauty and the Beast, though who
turns out to be the beast in the end is a more than startling reve-
lation, (whether that shock finale is adequately prepared for is a
moot point: the flaw to my mind in an otherwise tremendous book).

The book's curious, pick-it-up title is admirable for more reasons
than its attractiveness. To begin with, the Screaming Mimi, a small
statue of a girl, plays a key part in the whole plot, besides echoing
the then popular American expression 'having the screaming
meamies' equivalent in Britain to 'the screaming abdabs', a phen-
onenon of that urban living which by quiet implication the book
criticises.

But, as well, the exotic and unlikely phrase shows us the typical
working of Fredric Brown's mind. It seems at first sensational, and
even ridiculous. He bangs it out at us, and we accept it, if only
just. But then, after a due wait, Brown calmly explains it in the
most sensible manner. The statuette was thus named, he says, by
a store-keeper because it was in sequence Catalogue No. SM1 and,
so as to remember which number went with which product, the
fellow had the habit of inventing appropriate names linked to the
initials.

This movement, from the extraordinary and irrational to the
explained and sensible, from high romance to everyday reality, is
something Brown does again and again. The whole of *Night of the
Jabberwock* is an example. Its events seem at first to be sheer
fantasy, odd mysterious activity tying in time after time with Lewis
Carroll verses. But no, get to the end and you learn that the whole
business is simply and plausibly rational.

Not for nothing is one of Brown's best short science fiction stories
– it's beautifully written – called *Paradox Lost*. Beginning with
something absurdly paradoxical and moving into something sharply

real was the way he thought. It comes out again in his bold use of his heroes' dreams. Two of the books in this collection, begin with the words "In my dream . . ." and *The Screaming Mimi* starts with the hero in the grip of a reality-annihilating drunken spree. Note, too, how real that is: the hang-over it produces lasts more than half-way through the book. And how well described it is. None of your 'bottom of a parrot's cage' clichés so beloved of inferior hard-boiled writers. Instead, "The coffee seemed to be swishing around in his guts like bilgewater inside a leaky ship – tepid, brackish bilgewater filled with little green algae." Wow!

There is a little more that should be said about *Night of the Jabberwock*. It is a conspicuous example of Brown's skill with plot. His widow, in a short memoir she wrote of him, tells how he would pace the room when plotting and, so as not to be disturbed at any particularly tricky point, would at such times don a red denim cap. Then silence had to reign. Sometimes even pacing up and down failed to shake out a tangle. Then he would take a night trip by bus, equipped with pencil and flashlight.

But, however achieved, his plots are first-rate – he contributed the chapter 'Where Do You Get Your Plot?' to the *Mystery Writer's Handbook* published in New York in 1956 – and *Night of the Jabberwock*'s is among the best of them. But plotting is, when all is said and done, a mechanical thing and Fredric Brown's books are alive. For one thing he sees with the utmost vividness whatever he chooses to describe, though he has a swift contempt for over-much description. "So, if it interests you," he says in *The Screaming Mimi*, "William Sweeney was five feet eleven inches tall and weighed a hundred and sixty-three pounds. . . ." But it is the character of William Sweeney or of Doc Stoeger in *Night of the Jabberwock* that is what he wants to tell us about; what makes the man think the way he does, act the way he does and fail to act.

Most of Brown's heroes have a good deal in common. They are first of all decent men. They are not overly brave, but in a crisis not cowardly. And, though generally sober enough, they are capable of letting go, sometimes in a spectacular way, sometimes with an almost modest gesture like young Ed Hunter finally deciding to go along with his vagrant Uncle Am and join the touring fairground, the carney (as Brown himself did in his youth) and, incidentally, to become the hero of six more books. "Sons of bitches must have more fun," Brown says in *Night of the Jabberwock*, and in the end his heroes side with the hellraisers. But never to the point of becoming out-and-out sons of bitches.

Between *Night of the Jabberwock* and *Knock Three-One-Two* in 1959, Brown wrote ten other books and four more before his death in 1972. Most of them do not rise to the heights, but *Knock* is well worth reading, especially for its excellent plot and the high last-pages tension it generates. It moves the reader boldly into looking through the eyes of character after character as it tells its realistic Chicago story with rather fewer forays into the romantic than elsewhere.

Perhaps it was because Brown was at this time also writing science fiction that he felt less keenly the need to mix reality and romance, and thus less often achieved his characteristic magic. But magic Fredric Brown could and did produce. It was his lasting gift to the world he left behind, and you will find it in plenty in the novels between these covers.

Night of the Jabberwock

CHAPTER ONE

'Twas brillig, and the slithy toves
Did gyre and gimble in the wabe:
All mimsy were the borogoves,
And the mome raths outgrabe.

IN my dream I was standing in the middle of Oak Street and it was dark night. The street lights were off; only pale moonlight glinted on the huge sword that I swung in circles about my head as the Jabberwock crept closer. It bellied along the pavement, flexing its wings and tensing its muscles for the final rush; its claws clicked against the stones like the clicking of mats down the channels of a Linotype. Then, astonishingly, it spoke.

"Doc," it said. "Wake up, Doc."

A hand—not the hand of a Jabberwock—was shaking my shoulder.

And it was early dusk instead of black night and I was sitting in the swivel chair at my battered desk, looking over my shoulder at Pete. Pete was grinning at me.

"We're in, Doc," he said. "You'll have to cut two lines on this last take and we're in. Early, for once."

He put a galley proof down in front of me, only one stick of type long. I picked up a blue pencil and knocked off two lines and they happened to be an even sentence, so Pete wouldn't have to reset anything.

He went over to the Linotype and shut it off and it was suddenly very quiet in the place, so quiet that I could hear the drip of the faucet way in the far corner.

I stood up and stretched, feeling good, although a little groggy from having dozed off while Pete was setting that final take. For once, for one Thursday, the *Carmel City Clarion* was ready for the press early. Of course, there wasn't any real news in it, but then there never was.

And only half-past six and not yet dark outside. We were through hours earlier than usual. I decided that that called for a drink, here and now.

The bottle in my desk turned out to have enough whisky in it for one healthy drink or two short ones. I asked Pete if he wanted a snort and he said no, not yet, he'd wait till he got over to Smiley's, so I treated myself to a healthy drink, as I'd hoped to be able to do. And it had been fairly safe to ask Pete; he seldom took one before he was through for the day, and although my part of the job was done Pete still had almost an hour's work ahead of him on the mechanical end.

The drink made a warm spot under my belt as I walked over to the window by the Linotype and stood staring out into the quiet dusk. The lights of Oak Street flashed on while I stood there. I'd been dreaming—what had I been dreaming?

On the sidewalk across the street Miles Harrison hesitated in front of Smiley's Tavern as though the thought of a cool glass of beer tempted him. I could almost feel his mind working: "No, I'm a deputy sheriff of Carmel County and I have a job to do yet tonight and I don't drink while I'm on duty. The beer can wait."

Yes, his conscience must have won, because he walked on.

I wonder now—although of course I didn't wonder then —whether, if he had known that he would be dead before midnight, he wouldn't have stopped for that beer. I think he would have. I know I would have, but that doesn't prove anything because I'd have done it anyway; I've never had a conscience like Miles Harrison's.

Behind me, at the stone, Pete was putting the final stick of type into the chase of the front page. He said, "Okay, Doc, she fits. We're in."

"Let the presses roll," I told him.

Just a manner of speaking, of course. There was only one press and it didn't roll, because it was a Miehle vertical that shuttled up and down. And it wouldn't even do that until morning. The *Clarion* is a weekly paper that comes out on Friday; we put it to bed on Thursday evening and Pete runs it off the press Friday morning. And it's not much of a run.

Pete asked, "You going over to Smiley's?"

That was a silly question; I always go over to Smiley's on a Thursday evening and usually, when he's finished locking up the forms, Pete joins me, at least for a while. "Sure," I told him.

"I'll bring you a stone proof, then," Pete said.

Pete always does that, too, although I seldom do more than glance at it. Pete's too good a printer for me ever to catch any important errors on him and as for minor typographicals, Carmel City doesn't mind them.

I was free and Smiley's was waiting, but for some reason I wasn't in any hurry to leave. It was pleasant, after the hard work of a Thursday—and don't let that short nap fool you; I *had* been working—to stand there and watch the quiet street in the quiet twilight, and to contemplate an intensive campaign of doing nothing for the rest of the evening, with a few drinks to help me do it.

Miles Harrison, a dozen paces past Smiley's, stopped, turned, and headed back. Good, I thought, I'll have someone to drink with. I turned away from the window and put on my suit coat and hat.

I said, "Be seeing you, Pete," and I went down the stairs and out into the warm summer evening.

I'd misjudged Miles Harrison; he was coming out of Smiley's already, too soon even to have had a quick one, and he was opening a pack of cigarettes. He saw me and waved, waiting in front of Smiley's door to light a cigarette while I crossed the street.

"Have a drink with me, Miles," I suggested.

He shook his head regretfully. "Wish I could, Doc. But I got a job to do later. You know, go with Ralph Bonney over to Neilsville to get his pay roll."

Sure, I knew. In a small town everybody knows everything.

Ralph Bonney owned the Bonney Fireworks Company, just ouside of Carmel City. They made fireworks, mostly big pieces for fairs and municipal displays, that were sold all over the country. And during the few months of each year up to about the first of July they worked a day and a night shift to meet the Fourth of July demand.

And Ralph Bonney had something against Clyde Andrews, president of the Carmel City Bank, and did his banking in Neilsville. He drove over to Neilsville late every Thursday night and they opened the bank there to give him the cash for his night shift pay roll. Miles Harrison, as deputy sheriff, always went along as guard.

Always seemed like a silly procedure to me, as the night side pay roll didn't amount to more than a few thousand dollars and Bonney could have got it along with the cash for his day side pay roll and held it at the office, but that was his way of doing things.

I said, "Sure, Miles, but that's not for hours yet. And one drink isn't going to hurt you."

He grinned. "I know it wouldn't, but I'd probably take another just because the first one didn't hurt me. So I stick to the rule that I don't have even one drink till I'm off duty for the day, and if I don't stick to it I'm sunk. But thanks just the same, Doc, I'll take a rain check."

He had a point, but I wish he hadn't made it. I wish he'd let me buy him that drink, or several of them, because that rain check wasn't worth the imaginary paper it was printed on to a man who was going to be murdered before midnight.

But I didn't know that, and I didn't insist. I said, "Sure Miles," and asked him about his kids.

"Fine, both of 'em. Drop out and see us sometime."

"Sure," I said, and I went into Smiley's.

Big, bald Smiley Wheeler was alone. He smiled as I came in and said, "Hi, Doc. How's the editing business?" And then he laughed as though he'd said something excruciatingly funny. Smiley hasn't the ghost of a sense of humour and he has the mistaken idea that he disguises that fact by laughing at almost everything he says or hears said.

"Smiley, you give me a pain," I told him. It's always safe to tell Smiley a truth like that; no matter how seriously you say you mean it, he thinks you're joking. If he'd laughed I'd have told him where he gave me a pain, but for once he didn't laugh.

He said, "Glad you got here early, Doc. It's damn dull this evening."

"It's dull every evening in Carmel City," I told him. "And most of the time I like it. But Lord, if only something would happen just once on a Thursday evening, I'd love it. Just once in my long career, I'd like to have *one* hot story to break to a panting public."

"Hell, Doc, nobody looks for hot news in a country weekly."

"I know," I said. "That's why I'd like to fool them just once. I've been running the *Clarion* twenty-three years. One hot story. Is that much to ask?"

Smiley frowned. "There've been a couple of burglaries. And one murder, a few years ago."

"Sure," I said, "and so what? One of the factory hands out at Bonney's got in a drunken argument with another and hit him too hard in the fight they got into. That's not murder; that's manslaughter, and anyway it happened on a Saturday and it was old stuff—everybody in town knew about it—by the next Friday when the *Clarion* came out."

"They buy your paper, anway, Doc. They look for their names for having attended church socials and who's got a used washing machine for sale and—want a drink?"

"It's about time one of us thought of that," I said.

He poured a shot for me and, so I wouldn't have to drink alone, a short one for himself. We drank them and I asked him, "Think Carl will be in tonight?"

I meant Carl Trenholm, the lawyer, who's about my closest friend in Carmel City, and one of the three or four in town who play chess and can be drawn into an intelligent discussion of something beside crops and politics. Carl often dropped in Smiley's on Thursday evenings, knowing that I always came in for at least a few drinks after putting the paper to bed.

"Don't think so," Smiley said. "Carl was in most of the afternoon and got himself kind of a snootful, to celebrate. He got through in court early and he won his case. Guess he went home to sleep it off."

I said, "Damn. Why couldn't he have waited till this evening? I'd have helped him—Say, Smiley, did you say Carl was celebrating because he *won* that case? Unless we're talking about two different things, he lost it. You mean the Bonney divorce?"

"Yeah."

"Then Carl was representing Ralph Bonney, and Bonney's wife won the divorce."

"You got it that way in the paper, Doc?"

"Sure," I said. "It's the nearest thing I've got to a good story this week."

Smiley shook his head. "Carl was saying to me he hoped you wouldn't put it in, or anyway that you'd hold it down to a short squib, just the fact that she got the divorce."

I said, "I don't get it, Smiley. Why? And *didn't* Carl lose the case?"

Smiley leaned forward confidentially across the bar, although he and I were the only ones in his place. He said, "It's like this, Doc. Bonney wanted the divorce. That wife of his was a bitch, see? Only he didn't have any grounds to sue on, himself—not any that he'd have been willing to bring up in court, anyway, see? So he—well, kind of bought his freedom. Gave her a settlement if she'd do the suing, and he admitted to the grounds she gave against him. Where'd you get your version of the story?"

"From the judge," I said.

"Well, he just saw the outside of it. Carl says Bonney's a good joe and those cruelty charges were a bunch of hokum. He never laid a hand on her. But the woman was such hell on wheels that Bonney'd have admitted to anything to get free of her. And give her a settlement of a hundred grand on top of it. Carl was worried about the case because the cruelty charges were so damn silly on the face of them."

"Hell," I said, "that's not the way it's going to sound in the *Clarion*."

"Carl was saying he knew you couldn't tell the truth about the story, but he hoped you'd play it down. Just saying Mrs. B. had been granted a divorce and that a settlement had been made, and not putting in anything about the charges."

I thought of my one real story of the week, and how carefully I'd enumerated all those charges Bonney's wife had made against him, and I groaned at the thought of having to rewrite or cut the story. And cut it I'd have to, now that I knew the facts.

I said, "Damn Carl, why didn't he come and tell *me* about it before I wrote the story and put the paper to bed?"

"He thought about doing that, Doc. And then he decided he didn't want to use his friendship with you to influence the way you reported news."

"The damn fool," I said. "And all he had to do was walk across the street."

"But Carl did say that Bonney's a swell guy and it would be a bad break for him if you listed those charges because none of them were really true and——"

"Don't rub it in," I interrupted him. "I'll change the story. If Carl says it's that way, I'll believe him. I can't say that the charges weren't true, but at least I can leave them out."

"That'd be swell of you, Doc."

"Sure it would. All right, give me one more drink, Smiley, and I'll go over and catch it before Pete leaves."

I had the one more drink, cussing myself for being sap enough to spoil the only mentionable story I had, but knowing I had to do it. I didn't know Bonney personally, except just to say hello to on the street, but I did know Carl Trenholm well enough to be damn sure that if he said Bonney was in the right, the story wasn't fair the way I'd written it. And I knew Smiley well enough to be sure he hadn't given me a bum steer on what Carl had really said.

So I grumbled my way back across the street and upstairs to the *Clarion* office. Pete was just tightening the chase around the front page.

He loosened the quoins when I told him what we had to do, and I walked around the stone so I could read the story again, upside down, of course, as type is always read.

The first paragraph could stand as written and could constitute the entire story. I told Pete to put the rest of the type in the hellbox and I went over to the case and set a short head in tenpoint, "*Bonney Divorce Granted*," to replace the twenty-four-point head that had been on the longer story. I handed Pete the stick and watched while he switched heads.

"Leaves about a nine-inch hole in the page," he said. "What'll we stick in it?"

I sighed. "Have to use filler," I told him. "Not on the front page, but we'll have to find something on page four we can move front and then stick in nine inches of filler where it came from."

I wandered down the stone to page four and picked up a pica stick to measure things. Pete went over to the rack and got a galley of filler. About the only thing that was anywhere near the right size was the story that Clyde Andrews, Carmel's City's banker and leading light of the local Baptist Church, had given me about the rummage sale the church had planned for next Tuesday evening.

It wasn't exactly a story of earth-shaking importance, but it would be about the right length if we reset it indented to go in a box. And it had a lot of names in it, and that meant it would please a lot of people, and particularly Clyde Andrews, if I moved it up to the front page.

So we moved it. Rather, Pete reset it for a front page box item while I plugged the gap in page four with filler items and locked up the page again. Pete had the rummage sale item reset by the time I'd finished with page four, and this time I waited for him to finish up page one, so we could go to Smiley's together.

I thought about that front page while I washed my hands. *The Front Page*. Shades of Hecht and MacArthur. Poor revolving Horace Greeley.

Now I really wanted a drink.

Pete was starting to pound out a stone proof and I told him not to bother. Maybe the customers would read page one, but I wasn't going to. And if there was an upside-down headline or a pied paragraph, it would probably be an improvement.

Pete washed up and we locked the door. It was still early for a Thursday evening, not much after seven. I should have been happy about that, and I probably would have been if we'd had a good paper. As for the one we'd just put to bed, I wondered if it would live until morning.

Smiley had a couple of other customers and was waiting on them, and I wasn't in any mood to wait for Smiley so I went around behind the bar and got the Old Henderson bottle and two glasses and took them to a table for Pete and myself. Smiley and I know one another well enough so it's always all right for me to help myself any time it's convenient and settle with him afterward.

I poured drinks for Pete and me. We drank and Pete said, "Well, that's that for another week, Doc."

I wondered how many times he'd said that in the ten years he'd worked for me, and then I got to wondering how many times I'd thought it, which would be——

"How much is fifty-two times twenty-three, Pete?" I asked him.

"Huh? A hell of a lot. Why?"

I figured it myself. "Fifty times twenty-three is—one thousand one hundred and fifty; twice twenty-three more makes eleven ninety-six. Peter, eleven hundred and ninety-six times have I put that paper to bed on a Thursday night and never once was there a really *big* hot news story in it."

"This isn't Chicago, Doc. What do you expect, a murder?"

"I'd love a murder," I told him.

It would have been funny if Pete had said, "Doc, how'd you like three in one night?"

But he didn't of course. In a way, though, he said something that was even funnier. He said, "But suppose it was a friend of yours? Your best friend, say, Carl Trenholm. Would you want him killed just to give the *Clarion* a story?"

"Of course not," I said. "Preferably somebody I don't know at all—if there *is* anybody in Carmel City I don't know at all. Let's make it Yehudi."

"Who's Yehudi?" Pete asked.

I looked at Pete to see if he was kidding me, and apparently he wasn't, so I explained: "The little man who wasn't there. Don't you remember the rhyme?

> *I saw a man upon the stair,*
> *A little man who was not there.*
> *He was not here again today;*
> *Gee, I wish he'd go away."*

Pete laughed. "Doc, you get crazier every day. Is that *Alice in Wonderland*, too, like all the other stuff you quote when you get drinking?"

"This time, no. But who says I quote Lewis Carroll only when I'm drinking? I can quote him now, and I've hardly started drinking for tonight—why, as the Red Queen said to Alice, 'One has to do *this* much drinking to stay in the same place.' But listen and I'll quote you something that's really something:

> *'Twas brillig and the slithy toves*
> *Did gyre and gimble in the wabe——"*

Pete stood up. "*Jabberwocky*, from *Alice Through the Looking-Glass*," he said. "If you've recited that to me once, Doc, it's been a hundred times. I damn near know it myself. But I got to go, Doc. Thanks for the drink."

"Okay, Pete, but don't forget one thing."

"What's that?"

I said:

> *"Beware the Jabberwock, my son!*
> *The jaws that bite, the claws that catch!*
> *Beware the Jubjub bird and shun*
> *The frumious——"*

Smiley was calling to me, "Hey, Doc!" from over beside the telephone and I remembered now that I'd heard it ring half a minute before. Smiley yelled, "Telephone for you, Doc," and laughed as though that was the funniest thing that had happened in a long time.

I stood up and started for the phone, telling Pete good night *en route*.

I picked up the phone and said, "Hello" to it and it said "Hello" back to me. Then it said, "Doc?" and I said, "Yes."

Then it said, "Clyde Andrews speaking, Doc." His voice sounded quite calm. "This is murder."

Pete must be almost to the door by now; that was my first

thought. I said, "Just a second, Clyde," and then jammed my hand over the mouthpiece while I yelled, "Hey, Pete!"

He *was* at the door, but he turned.

"*Don't go*," I yelled at him, the length of the bar. "There's a *murder story* breaking. We got to remake!"

I could feel the sudden silence in Smiley's Bar. The conversation between the two other customers stopped in the middle of a word and they turned to look at me. Pete, from the door, looked at me. Smiley, a bottle in his hand, turned to look at me—and he didn't even smile. In fact, just as I turned back to the phone, the bottle dropped out of his hand and hit the floor with a noise that made me jump and close my mouth quickly to keep my heart from jumping from it. That bottle crashing on the floor had sounded—for a second—just like a revolver shot.

I waited until I felt that I could talk again without stammering and then I took my hand off the mouthpiece of the phone and said calmly, or almost calmly, "Okay, Clyde, go ahead."

CHAPTER TWO

"Who are you, aged man?" I said.
"And how is it you live?"
His answer trickled through my head,
Like water through a sieve.

"YOU'VE gone to press, haven't you, Doc?" Clyde's voice said. "You must have because I tried phoning you at the office first and then somebody told me if you weren't there, you'd be at Smiley's, but that'd mean you were through for the——"

"That's all right," I said. "Get on with it."

"I know it's murder, Doc, to ask you to change a story when you've already got the paper ready to run and have left the office, but—well, that rummage sale we were going to have Tuesday; it's been called off. Can you still kill the article? Otherwise a lot of people will read about it and come around to the church Tuesday night and be disappointed."

"Sure, Clyde," I said. "I'll take care of it."

I hung up. I went over to the table and sat down. I poured myself a drink of whisky and when Pete came over I poured him one.

He asked me what the call had been and I told him.

Smiley and his two other customers were still staring at me, but I didn't say anything until Smiley called out, "What happened, Doc? Didn't you say something about a murder?"

I said, "I was just kidding, Smiley." He laughed.

I drank my drink and Pete drank his. He said, "I knew there was a catch about getting through early tonight. Now we got a nine-inch hole in the front page all over again. What are we going to put in it?"

"Damned if I know," I told him. "But the hell with it for tonight. I'll get down when you do in the morning and figure something out then."

Pete said, "That's what you say, now, Doc. But if you *don't* get down at eight o'clock, what'll I do with that hole in the page?"

"Your lack of faith horrifies me, Pete. If I say I'll be down in the morning, I will be. Probably."

"But if you're not?"

I sighed. "Do anything you want." I knew Pete would fix it up somehow if I didn't get down. He'd drag something from a back page and plug the back page with filler items or a subscription ad.

It was going to be lousy because we had one sub ad in already and too damn much filler; you know, those little items that tell you the number of board feet in a sequoia and the current rate of mullet manufacture in the Euphrates valley. All right in small doses, but when you run the stuff by the column——

Pete said he'd better go, and this time he did. I watched him go, envying him a little. Pete Corey is a good printer and I pay him just about what I make myself. We put in about the same number of hours, but I'm the one who has to worry whenever there's any worrying to be done, which is most of the time.

Smiley's other customers left, just after Pete, and I didn't want to sit alone at the table, so I took my bottle over to the bar.

"Smiley," I said, "do you want to buy a paper?"

"Huh?" Then he laughed. "You're kidding me, Doc. It isn't off the press till tomorrow noon is it?"

"It isn't," I told him. "But it'll be well worth waiting for this week. Watch for it, Smiley. But that isn't what I meant."

"Huh? Oh, you mean do I want to buy the *paper*. I don't think so, Doc. I don't think I'd be very good at running a paper. I can't spell very good, for one thing. But look, you were telling me the other night Clyde Andrews wanted to buy it from you. Whyn't you sell it to him, if you want to sell it?"

"Who the devil said I wanted to sell it?" I asked him. "I just asked if you wanted to buy it."

Smiley looked baffled.

"Doc," he said. "I never know whether you're serious or not. Seriously, do you really want to sell out?"

I'd been wondering that. I said slowly, "I don't know, Smiley. Right now, I'd be damn tempted. I think I hate to quit mostly because before I do I'd like to get out one *good* issue. Just one *good* issue out of twenty-three years."

"If you sold it, what'd you do?"

"I guess, Smiley, I'd spend the rest of my life not editing a newspaper."

Smiley decided I was being funny again, and laughed.

The door opened and Al Grainger came in. I waved the bottle at him and he came down the bar to where I was standing, and Smiley got another glass and a chaser of water; Al always needs a chaser.

Al Grainger is just a young squirt—twenty-two or -three—but he's one of the few chess players in town and one of the even fewer people who understands my enthusiasm for Lewis Carroll. Besides that, he's by way of being a Mystery Man in Carmel City. Not that you have to be very mysterious to achieve that distinction.

He said, "Hi, Doc. When are we going to have another game of chess?"

"No time like the present, Al. Here and now?"

Smiley kept chessmen on hand for screwy customers like Al Grainger and Carl Trenholm and myself. He'd bring them out, always handling them as though he expected them to explode in his hands, whenever we asked for them.

Al shook his head. "Wish I had time. Got to go home and do some work."

I poured whisky in his glass and spilled a little trying to fill it to the brim. He shook his head slowly. "The White Knight is sliding down the poker," he said. "He balances very badly."

"I'm only in the second square," I told him. "But the next move will be a good one. I go to the fourth by train, remember."

"Don't keep it waiting, Doc. The smoke alone is worth a thousand pounds a puff."

Smiley was looking from one of us to the other. "What the hell are you guys talking about?" he wanted to know.

There wasn't any use trying to explain. I levelled my finger at him. I said, "Crawling at your feet you may observe a bread-and-butter fly. Its wings are thin slices of bread-and-butter, its body a crust and its head is a lump of sugar. And it lives on weak tea with cream in it."

Al said, "Smiley, you're supposed to ask him what happens if it can't find any."

I said, "Then I say it would die of course and you say that must happen very often and I say it *always* happens."

Smiley looked at us again and shook his head slowly. He said, "You guys are *really* nuts." He walked down the bar to wash and wipe some glasses.

Al Grainger grinned at me. "What are your plans for tonight, Doc?" he asked. "I just might possibly be able to sneak in a game or two of chess later. You going to be home, and up?"

I nodded. "I was just working myself up to the idea of walking home, and when I get there I'm going to read. And have another drink or two. If you get there before midnight I'll still be sober enough to play. Sober enough to beat a young punk like you, anyway."

It was all right to say that last part because it was so obviously untrue. Al had been beating me two games out of three for the last year or so.

He chuckled, and quoted at me:

" *'You are told, Father William,' the young man said,*
  'And your hair has become very white;
And yet you incessantly stand on your head—
  Do you think, at your age, it is right?' "

Well, since Carroll had the answer to that, so did I:

> " 'In my youth,' Father William replied to his son,
> 'I feared it might injure the brain;
> But now, that I'm perfectly sure I have none,
> Why, I do it again and again.' "

Al said, "Maybe you got something there, Doc. But let's quit alternating verses on that before you get to '*Be off, or I'll kick you down-stairs!*' Because I got to be off anyway."

"One more drink?"

"I——think not, not till I'm through working. You can drink and think too. Hope I can do the same thing when I'm your age. I'll try my best to get to your place for some chess, but don't look for me unless I'm there by ten o'clock—half past at the latest. And thanks for the drink."

He went out and, through Smiley's window, I could see him getting into his shiny convertible. He blew the Klaxon and waved back at me as he pulled out from the kerb.

I looked at myself in the mirror back of Smiley's bar and wondered how old Al Grainger thought I was. "*Hope I can do the same thing when I'm your age,*" indeed. Sounded as though he thought I was eighty, at least. I'll be fifty-three my next birthday.

But I had to admit that I looked that old, and that my hair was turning white. I watched myself in the mirror and that whiteness scared me just a little. No, I wasn't old yet, but I was getting that way. And, much as I crab about it, I like living. I don't want to get old and I don't want to die. Especially as I can't look forward, as a good many of my fellow townsmen do, to an eternity of harp playing and picking bird-lice out of my wings. Nor, for that matter, an eternity of shovelling coal, although that would probably be the more likely of the two in my case.

Smiley came back. He jerked his finger at the door. "I don't like that guy, Doc," he said.

"Al? He's all right. A little wet behind the ears, maybe. You're just prejudiced because you don't know where his money comes from. Maybe he's got a printing press and makes it himself. Come to think of it, *I've* got a printing press. Maybe I should try that myself."

"Hell, it ain't that, Doc. It's not my business how a guy earns his money—or where he gets it if he don't earn it. It's the way he talks. *You* talk crazy, too, but—well, you do it in a nice way. When he says something to me I don't understand he says it in a way that makes me feel like a stupid bastard. Maybe I *am* one, but——"

I felt suddenly ashamed of all the things I'd ever said to Smiley that I knew he wouldn't understand.

I said, "It's not a matter of intelligence, Smiley. It's merely a matter of literary background. Have one drink with me, and then I'd better go."

I poured him a drink and—this time—a small one for myself. I was beginning to feel the effects, and I didn't want to get too drunk to give Al Grainger a good game of chess if he dropped in.

I said, for no reason at all, "You're a good guy, Smiley," and he laughed and said, "So are you, Doc. Literary background or not, you're a little crazy, but you're a good guy."

And then, because we were both embarrassed at having caught ourselves saying things like that, I found myself staring past Smiley at the calendar over the bar. It had the usual kind of picture one sees on barroom calendars—an almost too voluptuous naked woman—and it was imprinted by Beal Brothers Store.

It was just a bit of bother to keep the eyes focused on it, I noticed, although I hadn't had enought to drink to affect my mind at all. Right then, for instance, I was thinking of two things at one and the same time. Part of my brain, to my disgust, persisted in wondering if I could get Beal Brothers to start running a quarter page ad instead of an eighth page; I tried to squelch the thought by telling myself that I didn't care, tonight, whether anybody advertised in the *Clarion* at all, and that part of my brain went on to ask me why, damn it, if I felt that way about it, I didn't get out from under while I had the chance by selling the *Clarion* to Clyde Andrews. But the other part of my mind kept getting more and more annoyed by the picture on the calendar, and I said, "Smiley, you ought to take down that calendar. It's a lie. There *aren't* any women like that."

He turned around and looked at it. "Guess you're right. Doc; there aren't any women like that. But a guy can dream, can't he?"

"Smiley," I said, "if that's not the first profound thing you've said, it's the *most* profound. You are right, moreover. You have my full permission to leave the calendar up."

He laughed and moved along the bar to finish wiping glasses, and I stood there and wondered why I didn't go on home. It was still early, a few minutes before eight o'clock. I didn't want another drink, yet. But by the time I got home, I would want one.

So I got out my wallet and called Smiley back. We estimated how many drinks I'd poured out of the bottle and I settled for them, and then I bought another bottle, a full quart, and he wrapped it for me.

I went out with it under my arm and said "So long, Smiley," and he said "So long, Doc," just as casually as though, before the gibbering night that hadn't started yet was over, he and I would not—but let's take things as they happened.

The walk home.

I had to go past the post office anyway, so I stopped in. The mail windows were closed, of course, but the outer lobby is always left open evenings so those who have post office boxes can get mail out of them.

I got my mail—there wasn't anything important in it—and then stopped, as I usually do, by the bulletin board to look over the notices and the wanted circulars that were posted there.

There were a couple of new ones and I read them and I studied the pictures. I've got a good memory for faces, even ones I've just seen pictures of, and I'd always hoped that some day I'd spot a wanted criminal in Carmel City and get a story out of it, if not a reward.

A few doors farther on I passed the bank and that reminded me about its president, Clyde Andrews, and his wanting to buy the paper from me. He didn't want to run it himself, of course; he had a brother somewhere in Ohio who'd had newspaper experience and who would run the paper for Andrews if I sold it to him.

The thing I liked least about the idea, I decided, was that Andrews was in politics and if he controlled the *Clarion*, the *Clarion* would back his party. The way I ran it, it threw mud at both factions when they deserved it, which was often, and handed either one an occasional bouquet when deserved, which was seldom. Maybe I'm crazy—other people than Smiley and Al have said so—but that's the way I think a newspaper should be run, and especially when it's the only paper in a town.

It's not, I might mention, the best way to make money. It had made me plenty of friends and subscribers, but a newspaper doesn't make money from its subscribers. It makes money from advertisers and most of the men in town big enough to be advertisers had fingers in politics and no matter which party I slammed I was likely to lose another advertising account.

I'm afraid that policy didn't help my news coverage, either. The best source of news is the sheriff's department and, at the moment, Sheriff Rance Kates was just about my worst enemy. Kates is honest, but he is also stupid, rude and full of race prejudice; and race prejudice, although it's not a burning issue in Carmel City, is one of my pet peeves. I hadn't pulled any punches in my editorials about Kates, either before or after his election. He got into office only because his opponent—who wasn't any intellectual heavyweight either—had got into a tavern brawl in Neilsville a week before election and was arrested there and charged with assault and battery. The *Clarion* had reported that, too, so the *Clarion* was probably responsible for Rance Kates' being elected sheriff. But Rance remembered only the things I'd said about *him*, and barely spoke to me on the street. Which, I might add, didn't concern me the slightest bit personally, but it forced me to get all of my police news, such as it is, the hard way.

Past the supermarket and Beal Brothers and past Deak's Music Store—where I'd once bought a violin but had forgotten to get a set of instructions with it—and the corner and across the street.

The walk home.

Maybe I weaved just a little, for at just that stage I'm never quite as sober as I am later on. But my mind—ah, it was in that delightful state of being crystal clear in the centre and fuzzy around the edges, the state that every moderate drinker knows but can't explain or define, the state that makes even a Carmel City seem delightful and such things as its squalid politics amusing.

Past the corner drugstore—Pop Hinkle's place—where I used to drink sodas when I was a kid, before I went away to college and made the big mistake of studying journalism. Past Gorham's Feed Store, where I'd worked vacations while I was in high school. Past the Bijou Theatre. Past Hank Greeber's Undertaking Parlours, through which both of my parents had passed, fifteen and twenty years ago.

Around the corner at the courthouse, where a light was still on in Sheriff Kates' office—and I felt so cheerful that, for a thousand dollars or so, I'd have stopped in to talk to him. But no one was around to offer me a thousand dollars.

Out of the store district now, past the house in which Elsie Minton had lived—and in which she had died while we were engaged, twenty-five years ago.

Past the house Elmer Conklin had lived in when I'd bought the *Clarion* from him. Past the church where I'd been sent to Sunday School when I was a kid, and where I'd once won a prize for memorizing verses of the Bible.

Past my past, and walking, slightly weaving, toward the house in which I'd been conceived and born.

No, I hadn't lived there fifty-three years. My parents had sold it and had moved to a bigger house when I was nine and when my sister—now married and living in Florida—had been born. I'd bought it back twelve years ago when it happened to be vacant and on the market at a good price. It's only a three-room cottage, not too big for a man to live in alone, if he likes to live alone, and I do.

Oh, I like people too. I like someone to drop in for conversation or chess or a drink or all three. I like to spend an hour or two in Smiley's, or any other tavern, a few times a week. I like an occasional poker game.

But I'll settle, on any given evening, for my books. Two walls of my living-room are lined with them and they overflow into bookcases in my bedroom and I even have a shelf of them in the bathroom. What do I mean, *even*? I think a bathroom without a bookshelf is as incomplete as would be one without a toilet.

And they're good books, too. No, I wouldn't be lonely tonight, even if Al Grainger didn't come around for that game of chess. How could I be lonesome with a bottle in my pocket and good company waiting for me? Why, reading a book is almost as good as listening to the man who wrote it talking to you. Better in one way, because you don't have to be polite to him. You can shut him up any moment you feel so inclined and pick someone else instead. And you can take off your shoes and put your feet on the table. You can drink and read until you forget everything but what you're reading; you can forget who you are and the fact that there's a newspaper that hangs around your neck like a millstone, all day and every day, until you get home to sanctuary and forgetfulness.

The walk home.

And so to the corner of Campbell Street and my turning.

A June evening, but cool, and the night air had almost completely sobered me in the nine blocks I'd walked from Smiley's.

My turning, and I saw that the light was on in the front room of my house. I started walking a little faster, mildly puzzled. I knew I hadn't left it on when I'd left for the office that morning. And if I *had* left it on, Mrs. Carr, the cleaning woman who comes in for about two hours every afternoon to keep my place in order, would have turned it off.

Maybe, I thought, Al Grainger had finished whatever he was doing and had come early and had—but no, Al wouldn't have come without his car and there wasn't any car parked in front.

It might have been a mystery, but it wasn't.

Mrs. Carr was there, putting on her hat in front of the panel mirror in the closet door as I went in.

She said, "I'm just leaving, Mr. Stoeger. I wasn't able to get here this afternoon, so I came to clean up this evening instead; I just finished."

"Fine," I said. "By the way, there's a blizzard out."

"A—*what*?"

"Blizzard. Snowstorm." I held up the wrapped bottle. "So maybe you'd better have a little nip with me before you start home, don't you think?"

She laughed. "Thanks, Mr. Stoeger. I will. I've had a pretty rough day, and it sounds like a good idea. I'll get glasses for us."

I put my hat in the closet and followed her out into the kitchen.

"A rough day?" I asked her. "I hope nothing went wrong."

"Well—nothing too serious. My husband—he works, you know, out at Bonney's fireworks factory—got burned in a little accident they had out there this afternoon, and they brought him home. It's nothing serious, a second degree burn the doctor said, but it was pretty painful and I thought I'd better stay with him until after supper, and then he finally got to sleep so I ran over here and I'm afraid I straightened up your place pretty fast and didn't do a very good job."

"Looks spotless to me," I said. I'd been opening the bottle while she'd been getting glasses for us. "I hope he'll be all right, Mrs Carr. But if you want to skip coming here for a while——"

"Oh, no, I can still come. He'll be home only a few days, and it was just that today they brought him home at two o'clock, just when I was getting ready to come here and—That's plenty, thanks."

We touched glasses and I downed mine while she drank about half of hers. She said, "Oh, there was a phone call for you, about an hour ago. A little while after I got here."

"Find out who it was?"

"He wouldn't tell me, just said it wasn't important."

I shook my head sadly. "That, Mrs. Carr, is one of the major fallacies of the human mind. The idea, I mean, that things can be arbitrarily divided into the important and the unimportant. How can anyone decide whether a given fact is important or not unless one knows *everything* about it—and no one knows everything about anything."

She smiled, but a bit vaguely, and I decided to bring it down to earth, I said. "What would you say is important, Mrs. Carr?"

She put her head on one side and considered it seriously. "Well, *work* is important, isn't it?"

"It is not," I told her. "I'm afraid you score zero. Work is only a means to an end. We work in order to enable ourselves to do the important things, which are the things we want to do. Doing what we want to do—that's what's important, if anything is."

"That sounds like a funny way of putting it, but maybe you're right. Well, anyway, this man who called said he'd either call again or come around. I told him you probably wouldn't be home until eight or nine o'clock."

She finished her drink and declined an encore. I walked to the front door with her, saying that I'd have been glad to drive her home but that my car had two flat tyres. I'd discovered them that morning when I'd started to drive to work. One I might have stopped to fix, but two discouraged me; I decided to leave the car in the garage until Saturday afternoon, when I'd have lots of time. And then, too, I know that I *should* get the exercise of walking to and from work every day, but as long as my car is in running condition, I don't. For Mrs. Carr's sake, though, I wished now that I'd fixed the tyres.

She said, "It's only a few blocks, Mr. Stoeger. I wouldn't think of letting you, even if your car was working. Good night."

"Oh, just a minute, Mrs. Carr. What department at Bonney's does your husband work in?"

"The Roman candle department."

It made me forget, for the moment, what I'd been leading up to. I said, "The Roman candle department! That's a wonderful phrase; I love it. If I sell the paper, darned if I don't look up Bonney the very next day. I'd love to work in the Roman candle department. Your husband is a lucky man."

"You're joking, Mr. Stoeger. But are you really thinking of selling the paper?"

"Well—thinking of it." And that reminded me. "I didn't get any story on the accident at Bonney's, didn't even hear about it. And I'm badly in need of a story for the front page. Do you know the details of what happened? Anyone else hurt?"

She'd been part way across the front porch, but she turned and came back nearer the door. She said, "Oh, *please* don't put it in the paper. It wasn't anything important; my husband was the only one hurt and it was his own fault, he said. And Mr. Bonney wouldn't like it being in the paper; he has enough trouble now getting as many people as he needs for the rush season before the Fourth, and so many people are afraid to work around powder and explosives anyway. George will probably be fired if it gets written up in the paper and he *needs* the work."

I sighed; it had been an idea while it lasted. I assured her that I wouldn't print anything about it. And if George Carr had been the only one hurt and I didn't have any details, it wouldn't have made over a one-inch item anyway.

I would have loved, though, to get that beautiful phrase, "*the Roman candle department*," into print.

I went back inside and closed the door. I made myself comfortable by taking off my suit coat and loosening my tie, and then I got the whisky bottle and my glass and put them on the coffee table in front of the sofa.

I didn't take the tie off yet, nor my shoes; it's nicer to do those things one at a time as you gradually get more and more comfortable.

I picked out a few books and put them within easy reach, poured myself a drink, sat down, and opened one of the books.

The doorbell rang.

Al Grainger had come early, I thought. I went to the door and opened it. There was a man standing there, just lifting his hand to ring again. But it wasn't Al; it was a man I'd never seen before.

CHAPTER THREE

How cheerfully he seems to grin,
How neatly spreads his claws,
And welcomes little fishes in
With gently smiling jaws!

HE was short, about my own height, perhaps, but seeming even shorter because of his greater girth. The first thing you noticed about his face was his nose; it was long, thin, pointed, grotesquely at variance with his pudgy body. The light coming past me through the doorway reflected glowing points in his eyes, giving them a cat-like gleam. Yet there was nothing sinister about him. A short pudgy man can never manage to seem sinister, no matter how the light strikes his eyes.

"You are Doctor Stoeger?" he asked.

"Doc Stoeger," I corrected him. "But not a doctor of medicine. If you're looking for a medical doctor, one lives four doors west of here."

He smiled, a nice smile. "I am aware that you are not a medico, Doctor, Ph.D., Burgoyne College—nineteen twenty-two, I believe. Author of *Lewis Carroll Through the Looking-Glass* and *Red Queen and White Queen.*

It startled me. Not so much that he knew my college and the year of my *magna cum laude*, but the rest of it was amazing. *Lewis Carroll Through the Looking-Glass* was a monograph of a dozen pages; it had been printed eighteen years ago and only a hundred copies had been run off. If one still existed anywhere outside of my own library, I was greatly surprised. And *Red Queen and White Queen* was a magazine article that had appeared at least twelve years ago in a magazine that had been obscure then and had long since been discontinued and forgotten.

"Yes," I said. "But how you know of them, I can't imagine, Mr.——"

"Smith," he said gravely. Then he chuckled. "And the first name is Yehudi."

"No!" I said.

"Yes. You see, Doctor Stoeger, I was named forty years ago, when the name Yehudi, although uncommon, had not yet acquired the comic connotation which it has today. My parents did not guess that the name would become a joke—and that it would be particularly ridiculous when combined with Smith. Had they guessed the difficulty I now have in convincing people that I'm not kidding them when I tell them my name——" He laughed ruefully. "I always carry cards."

He handed me one. It read:

Yehudi Smith

There was no address, no other information. Just the same, I wanted to keep that card, so I stuck it in my pocket instead of handing it back.

He said, "People *are* named Yehudi, you know. There's Yehudi Menuhin, the violinist. And there's——"

"Stop, please," I interrupted. "You're making it plausible. I liked it better the other way."

He smiled. "Then I haven't misjudged you, Doctor. Have you ever heard of the Vorpal Blades?"

"Plural? No. Of course, in Jabberwocky:

> *One, two! One, two! And through and through*
> *The vorpal blade went snicker-snack.*

But—Good God! Why are we talking about vorpal blades through a doorway? Come on in, I've got a bottle, and I hope and presume that it would be ridiculous to ask a man who talks about vorpal blades whether or not he drinks."

I stepped back and he came in. "Sit anywhere," I told him. "I'll get another glass. Want either a mix or a chaser?"

He shook his head, and I went out into the kitchen and got another glass. I came in, filled it and handed it to him. He'd already made himself comfortable in the overstuffed chair.

I sat back on the sofa and lifted my glass toward him. I said, "No doubt about a toast for this one. To Charles Lutwidge Dodgson, known, when in Wonderland, as Lewis Carroll."

He said, quietly, "Are you sure, Doctor?"

"Sure of what?"

"Of your phraseology in that toast. I'd word it: To Lewis Carroll, who masqueraded under the alleged identity of Charles Lutwidge Dodgson, the gentle don of Oxford."

I felt vaguely disappointed. Was this going to be another, and even more ridiculous, Bacon-was-Shakespeare deal? Historically, there couldn't be any possible doubt that the Reverend Dodgson, writing under the name Lewis Carroll, had created *Alice in Wonderland* and its sequel.

But the main point, for the moment, was to get the drink drunk.

So I said solemnly, "To avoid all difficulties, factual or semantic, Mr. Smith, let's drink to the author of the Alice books."

He inclined his head with solemnity equal to my own, then tilted it back and downed his drink. I was a little late in downing mine because of my surprise at, and admiration for, his manner of drinking. I'd never seen anything quite like it. The glass had stopped, quite suddenly, a good three inches from his mouth. And the whisky had kept on going and not a drop of it had been lost. I've seen people toss down a shot before, but never with such casual precision and from so great a distance.

I drank my own in a more prosaic manner, but I resolved to try his system sometime—in private and with a towel or handkerchief ready at hand.

I refilled our glasses and then said, "And now what? Do we argue the identity of Lewis Carroll?"

"Let's start back of that," he said. "In fact, let's put it aside until I can offer you definite proof of what we believe—rather, of what we are certain."

"We?"

"The Vorpal Blades. An organization. A very small organization, I should add."

"Of admirers of Lewis Carroll?"

He leaned forward. "Yes, of course. Any man who is both literate and imaginative is an admirer of Lewis Carroll. But—much more than that. We have a secret. A quite esoteric one."

"Concerning the identity of Lewis Carroll? You mean that you believe—the way some people believe, or used to believe, that the plays of Shakespeare were written by Francis Bacon—that someone other than Charles Lutwidge Dodgson wrote the Alice books?"

I hoped he'd say no.

He said, "No. We believe that Dodgson himself—How much do you know of him, Doctor?"

"He was born in eighteen thirty-two," I said, "and died just before the turn of the century—in either ninety-eight or nine. He was an Oxford don, a mathematician. He wrote several treatises on mathematics. He liked—and created—acrostics and other puzzles and problems. He never married but he was very fond of children, and his best writing was done for them. At least he *thought* he was writing only for children; actually, *Alice in Wonderland* and *Alice Through the Looking-Glass*, while having plenty of appeal for children, are adult literature, and great literature. Shall I go on?"

"By all means."

"He was also capable of—and perpetrated—some almost incredibly bad writing. There ought to be a law against the printing of volumes of *The Complete Works of Lewis Carroll*. He should be remembered for the great things he wrote, and the bad ones interred with his bones. Although I'll admit that even the bad things have occasional touches of brilliance. There are moments in *Sylvie and Bruno* that are almost worth reading through the thousands of dull words to reach. And there are occasional good lines or stanzas in even the worst poems. Take the first three lines of *The Palace of Humbug*:

> *I dreamt I dwelt in marble halls,*
> *And each damp thing that creeps and crawls*
> *Went wobble-wobble on the walls.*

"Of course he should have stopped there instead of adding fifteen or twenty bad triads. But '*Went wobble-wobble on the walls*' is marvellous."

He nodded. "Let's drink to it."

We drank to it.

He said, "Go on."

"No," I said. "I'm just realizing that I could easily go on for hours. I can quote every line of verse in the Alice books and most of *The Hunting of the Snark*. But, I both hope and presume, you didn't come here to listen to me lecture on Lewis Carroll. My information about him is fairly thorough, but quite orthodox. I judge that yours isn't, and I want to hear it."

I refilled our glasses.

He nodded slowly. "Quite right, Doctor. My—I should say *our*—information is extremely unorthodox. I think you have the background and the type of mind to understand it, and to believe it when you have seen proof. To a more ordinary mind, it would seem sheer fantasy."

It was getting better by the minute. I said, "Don't stop now."

"Very well. But before I go any further, I must warn you of something, Doctor. It is also very dangerous information to have. I do not speak lightly or metaphorically. I mean that there is serious danger, deadly danger."

"That," I said, "is wonderful."

He sat there and toyed with his glass—still with the third drink in it—and didn't look at me. I studied his face. It was an interesting face. That long, thin, pointed nose, so incongruous to his build that it might have been false—a veritable Cyrano de Bergerac of a nose. And now that he was in the light, I could see that there were deep laughter-lines around his generous mouth. At first I would have guessed at his age at thirty instead of the forty he claimed to be; now, studying his face closely, I could see that he had not exaggerated his age. One would have to laugh a long time to etch lines like those.

But he wasn't laughing now. He looked deadly serious, and he didn't look crazy. But he said something that sounded crazy.

He said, "Doctor, has it ever occurred to you that—that the fantasies of Lewis Carroll are not fantasies at all?"

"Do you mean," I asked, "in the sense that fantasy is often nearer to fundamental truth than is would-be realistic fiction?"

"No. I mean that they are literally, actually true. That they are not fiction at all, that they are reporting."

I stared at him. "If you think that, then who—or *what*—do you think Lewis Carroll was?"

He smiled faintly, but it wasn't a smile of amusement.

He said, "If you really want to know, and aren't afraid, you can find out tonight. There is a meeting, near here. Will you come?"

"May I be frank?"

"Certainly."

I said, "I think it's crazy, but try to keep me away."

"In spite of the fact that there is danger?"

Sure, I was going, danger or no. But maybe I could use his insistence on warning me to pry something out of him. So I said, "May I ask what *kind* of danger?"

He seemed to hesitate a moment and then he took out his wallet and from an inner compartment took a newspaper clipping, a short one of about three paragraphs. He handed it to me.

I read it, and I recognized the type and the setup; it was a clipping from the *Bridgeport Argus*. And I remembered how having read it, a couple of weeks ago, I'd considered clipping it as an exchange item, and then had decided not to, despite the fact that the heading had caught my interest. It read:

MAN SLAIN BY UNKNOWN BEAST

The facts were few and simple. A man named Colin Hawks, living outside Bridgeport, a recluse, had been found dead along a path through the woods. The man's throat had been torn, and police opinion was that a large and vicious dog had attacked him. But the reporter who wrote the article suggested the possibility that a wolf—or even a panther or a leopard—escaped from a circus or zoo might have caused the wounds.

I folded the clipping again and handed it back to Smith. It didn't mean anything, of course. It's easy to find stories like that if one looks for them. A man named Charles Fort found thousands of them and put them into four books he had written, books which were on my shelves.

This particular one was less mysterious than most. In fact, there wasn't any real mystery at all; undoubtedly some vicious dog had done the killing.

Just the same something prickled at the back of my neck.

It was the headline, really, not the article. It's funny what the word "unknown" and the thought back of it can do to you. If that story had been headed "Man Killed by Vicious Dog"—or by a lion or a crocodile or any other specified creature, however fierce and dangerous, there'd have been nothing frightening about it.

But an *"unknown beast"*—well if you've got the same kind of imagination I have, you see what I mean. And if you haven't, I can't explain.

I looked at Yehudi Smith just in time to see him toss down his whisky—again like a conjuring trick. I handed him back the clipping and then refilled our glasses.

I said, "Interesting story. But where's the connection?"

"Our last meeting was in Bridgeport. That's all I can tell you. About that, I mean. You asked the nature of the danger; that's why I showed you that. And it's not too late for you to say no. It won't be, for that matter, until we get there."

"Get where?"

"Only a few miles from here. I have directions to guide me to a house on a road called the Dartown Pike. I have a car."

I said, irrelevantly, "So have I, but the tyres are flat. Two of them."

I thought about the Dartown Pike. I said. "You wouldn't, by any chance, be heading for the house known as the Wentworth place?"

"That's the name, yes. You know of it?"

Right then and there, if I'd been completely sober, I'd have seen that the whole thing was too good to be true. I'd have smelled a fish. Or blood.

I said, "We'll have to take candles or flashlights. That house has been empty since I was a kid. We used to call it a haunted house. Would that be why you chose it?"

"Yes, of course."

"And your group is meeting there tonight?"

He nodded. "At one o'clock in the morning, to be exact. You're sure you're not afraid?"

God, yes, I was afraid. Who wouldn't be, after the build-up he'd just handed me?

So I grinned at him and said, "Sure, I'm afraid. But just try to keep me away."

Then I had an idea. If I was going to a haunted house at one o'clock in the morning to hunt jabberwocks or try to invoke the ghost of Lewis Carroll or some equally sensible thing, it wouldn't hurt to have someone along whom I already knew. And if Al Grainger dropped in—I tried to figure out whether or not Al would be interested. He was a Carroll fan, all right, but—for the rest of it, I didn't know.

I said, "One question, Mr. Smith. A young friend of mine might drop in soon for a game of chess. How exclusive is this deal? I mean, would it be all right if he came along, if he wants to?"

"Do you think he's qualified?"

"Depends on what the qualifications are," I said. "Offhand, I'd say you have to be a Lewis Carroll fan and a little crazy. Or, come to think of it, are those one and the same qualification?"

He laughed. "They're not too far apart. But tell me something about your friend. You said young friend; how young?"

"About twenty-three. Not long out of college. Good literary taste and background, which means he knows and likes Carroll. He can quote almost as much of it as I can. Plays chess, if that's a qualification—and I'd guess it is. Dodgson not only played chess but based *Through the Looking-Glass* on a chess game. His name, if that matters, is Al Grainger."

"Would he *want* to come?"

"Frankly," I admitted, "I haven't an idea on that angle."

Smith said, "I hope he comes; if he's a Carroll enthusiast, I'd like to meet him. But, if he comes, will you do me a favour of saying nothing about—what I've told you, at least until I've had a chance to judge him a bit? Frankly, it would be almost unprecedented if I took the liberty of inviting someone to an important meeting like tonight's on my own. You're being invited because we know quite a bit about you. You were voted on—and I might say that the vote to invite you was unanimous."

I remembered his familiarity with the two obscure things about Lewis Carroll that I'd written, and I didn't doubt that he—or they, if he really represented a group—did know something about me.

He said, "But—well, if I get a chance to meet him and think he'd really fit in, I might take a chance and ask him. Can you tell me anything more about him? What does he do—for a living I mean?"

That was harder to answer. I said, "Well, he's writing plays. But I don't think he makes a living at it; in fact, I don't know that he's ever sold any. He's a bit of a mystery to Carmel City. He's lived here all his life—except while he was away at college—and nobody knows where his money comes from. Has a swanky car and a place of his own—he lived there with his mother until she died a few years ago—and seems to have plenty of spending money, but nobody knows where it comes from." I grinned. "And it annoys the hell out of Carmel City not to know. You know how small towns are."

He nodded. "Wouldn't it be a logical assumption that he inherited the money?"

"From one point of view, yes. But it doesn't seem too likely. His mother worked all her life as a milliner, and without owning her own shop. The town, I remember, used to wonder how she managed to own her own house and send her son to college on what she earned. But she couldn't possibly have earned enough to have done both of those things and still have left him enough money to have supported him in idleness—Well, maybe writing plays isn't idleness, but it isn't remunerative unless you sell them—for several years."

I shrugged. "But there's probably no mystery to it. She must have had an income from investments her husband had made, and Al either inherited the income or got the capital from which it came. He probably doesn't talk about his business because he enjoys being mysterious."

"Was his father wealthy?"

"His father died before he was born, and before Mrs. Grainger moved to Carmel City. So nobody here knew his father. And I guess that's all I can tell you about Al, except that he can beat me at chess most of the time, and that I hope you'll have a chance to meet him."

Smith nodded. "If he comes, we'll see."

He glanced at his empty glass and I took the hint and filled it and my own. Again I watched the incredible manner of his drinking it, fascinated. I'd swear that, this time, the glass came no closer than six inches from his lips. Definitely it was a trick I'd have to learn myself. If for no other reason than that I don't really like the taste of whisky, much as I enjoy the effects of it. With his way of drinking, it didn't seem that he had the slightest chance of tasting the stuff. It was there, in the glass, and then it was gone. His Adam's apple didn't seem to work and if he was talking at the time he drank there was scarcely an interruption in what he was saying.

The phone rang. I excused myself and answered it.

"Doc," said Clyde Andrews' voice, "this is Clyde Andrews."

"Fine," I said, "I suppose you realize that you sabotaged this week's issue by cancelling a story on my front page. What's called off this time?"

"I'm sorry about that, Doc, if it really inconvenienced you, but with the sale called off, I thought you wouldn't want to run the story and have people coming around to——"

"Of course," I interrupted him. I was impatient to get back to my conversation with Yehudi Smith. "That's all right, Clyde. But what do you want now?"

"I want to know if you've decided whether or not you want to sell the *Clarion*."

For a second I was unreasonably angry. I said, "God damn it, Clyde, you interrupt the only really conversation I've had in years to ask me that, when we've been talking about it for months, off and on? I don't know. I do and I don't want to sell it."

"Sorry for heckling you, Doc, but I just got a special delivery letter from my brother in Ohio. He's got an offer out West. Says he'd rather come to Carmel City on the proposition I'd made to him—contingent on your deciding to sell me the *Clarion*, of course. But he's got to accept the other offer right away—within a day or so, that is—if he's going to accept it at all.

"So you see that makes it different, Doc. I've got to know right away. Not tonight, necessarily; it isn't in that much of a rush. But I've got to know by tomorrow sometimes, so I thought I'd call you right away so you could start coming to a decision."

I nodded and then realized that he couldn't see me nod so I said, "Sure, Clyde, I get it. I'm sorry for popping off. All right, I'll make up my mind by tomorrow morning. I'll let you know one way or the other by then. Okay?"

"Fine," he said. "That'll be plenty of time. Oh, by the way, there's an item of news for you if it's not too late to put it in. Or have you already got it?"

"Got what?"

"About the escaped maniac. I don't know the details, but a friend of mine just drove over from Neilsville and he says they're stopping cars and watching the roads both sides of the country asylum. Guess you can get the details if you call the asylum."

"Thanks, Clyde," I said.

I put the phone back down in its cradle and looked at Yehudi Smith. I wondered why, with all the fantastic things he'd said, I hadn't already guessed.

CHAPTER FOUR

"But wait a bit," the Oyster cried,
"Before we have our chat;
For some of us are out of breath,
And all of us are fat!"

I FELT a hell of a letdown. Oh, not that I'd really quite believed in the Vorpal Blades or that we were going to a haunted house to conjure up a Jabberwock or whatever we'd have done there.

But it had been exciting even to think about it, just as one can get excited over a chess game even though he knows that the kings and queens on the board aren't real entities and that when a bishop slays a knight no real blood is shed. I guess it had been that kind of excitement, the vicarious kind, that I'd felt about the things Yehudi Smith had promised. Or maybe a better comparison would be that it had been like reading an exciting fiction story that one knows isn't true but which one can believe in for as long as the story lasts.

Now there wasn't even that. Across from me, I realized with keen disappointment, was only a man who'd escaped from an insane asylum. Yehudi, the little man who wasn't there—mentally.

The funny part of it was that I still liked him. He was a nice little guy and he'd given me a fascinating half hour, up to now. I hated the fact that I'd have to turn him over to the asylum guards and have him put back where he came from.

Well, I thought, at least it would give me a news story to fill that nine-inch hole in the front page of the *Clarion*.

He said, "I hope the call wasn't anything that will spoil our plans, Doctor."

It had spoiled more than that, but of course I couldn't tell him so, any more than I could have told Clyde Andrews over the phone, in Smith's presence to call the asylum and tell them to drop around to my house if they wanted to collect their bolted nut.

So I shook my head while I figured out an angle to get out of the house and to put in the phone call from next door.

I stood up. Perhaps I was a bit more drunk than I'd thought, for I had to catch my balance. I remember how crystal clear my mind seemed to be—but of course nothing seems more crystal clear than a prism that makes you see around corners.

I said, "No, the call won't interrupt our plans except for a few minutes. I've got to give a message to the man next door. Excuse me—and help yourself to the whisky."

I went through the kitchen and outside into the black night. There were lights in the houses on either side of me, and I wondered which of my neighbours to bother. And then I wondered why I was in such a hurry to bother either of them.

Surely, I thought, the man who called himself Yehudi Smith wasn't dangerous. And, crazy or not, he was the most interesting man I'd met in years. He *did* seem to know something about Lewis Carroll. And I remembered again that he'd known about my obscure brochure and equally obscure magazine article. How?

So, come to think of it, why shouldn't I stall making that phone call for another hour or so, and relax and enjoy myself? Now that I was over the first disappointment of learning that he was insane, why wouldn't I find talk about the delusion of his almost as interesting as though it was factual?

Interesting in a different way, of course. Often I had thought I'd like the chance to talk to a paranoiac about his delusions—neither arguing with him nor agreeing with him, just trying to find out what made him tick.

And the evening was still a pup; it couldn't be later than about half past eight so my neighbours would be up at least another hour or two.

So why was I in a hurry to make that call? I wasn't.

Of course I had to kill enough time outside to make it reasonable to believe that I'd actually gone next door and delivered a message, so I stood there at the bottom of my back steps, looking up at the black velvet sky, star-studded but moonless, and wondering what was behind it and why madmen were mad. And how strange it would be if one of them was right and all the rest of us were crazy instead.

Then I went back inside and I was cowardly enough to do a ridiculous thing. From the kitchen I went into my bedroom and to my closet. In a shoebox on the top shelf was a short-barrelled thirty-eight calibre revolver, one of the compact, lightweight models they call a Banker's Special. I'd never shot at anything with it and hoped that I never would—and I wasn't sure I could hit anything smaller than an elephant or farther away than a couple of yards. I don't even like guns. I hadn't bought this one; an acquaintance had once borrowed twenty bucks from me and had insisted on my taking the pistol for security. And later he'd wanted another five and said if I gave it to him I could keep the gun. I hadn't wanted it, but he'd needed the five pretty badly and I'd given it to him.

It was still loaded with bullets that were in it when we'd made the deal four or five years ago, and I didn't know whether they'd still shoot or not, but I put it in my trouser pocket. I wouldn't use it, of course, except in dire extremity—and I'd miss anything I shot at even then, but I thought that just carrying the gun would make my coming conversation seem dangerous and exciting, more than it would be otherwise.

I went into the living-room and he was still there. He hadn't poured himself a drink, so I poured one for each of us and then sat down on the sofa again.

I lifted my drink and over the rim of it watched him do that marvellous trick again—just a toss of the glass toward his lips. I drank my own less spectacularly and said, "I wish I had a movie camera. I'd like to film the way you do that and then study it in slow motion."

He laughed. "Afraid it's my one way of showing off. I used to be a juggler once."

"And now? If you don't mind my asking."

"A student," he said. "A student of Lewis Carroll—and mathematics."

"Is there a living in it?" I asked him.

He hesitated just a second. "Do you mind if I defer answering that until you've learned—what you'll learn at tonight's meeting?"

Of course there wasn't going to be any meeting tonight; I knew that now. But I said, "Not at all. But I hope you don't mean that we can't talk about Carroll, in general, until after the meeting."

I hoped he'd give the right answer to that; it would mean that I could get him going on the subject of his mania.

He said, "Of course not. In fact, I *want* to talk about him. There are facts I want to give you that will enable you to understand things better. Some of the facts you already know, but I'll refresh you on them anyway. For instance, dates. You had his birth and death dates correct, or nearly enough so. But do you know the dates of the Alice books or any other of his works? The sequence is important."

"Not exactly," I told him. "I think that he wrote the first Alice book when he was comparatively young, about thirty."

"Close. He was thirty-two. *Alice in Wonderland* was published in eighteen sixty-three, but even before then he was on the trail of something. Do you know what he had published before that?"

I shook my head.

"Two books. He wrote and published *A Syllabus of Plane Geometry* in eighteen sixty and in the year after that his *Formulæ of Plane Trigonometry*. Have you read either of them?"

I had to shake my head again. I said, "Mathematics isn't my forte. I've read only his non-technical books."

He smiled. "There aren't any. You simply failed to recognize the mathematics embodied in the Alice books and in his poetry. You do know, I'm sure, that many of his poems are acrostics."

"Of course."

"All of them are acrostics, but in a much more subtle manner. However, I can see why you failed to find the clues if you haven't read his treatises on mathematics. You wouldn't have read his *Elementary Treatise on Determinants*, I suppose. But how about his *Curiosa Mathematica*?"

I hated to disappoint him again, but I had to.

He frowned at me. "That at least you should have read. It's not technical at all, and most of the clues to the fantasies are contained in it. There are further—and final—references to them in his *Symbolic Logic*, published in eighteen ninety-six, just two years before his death, but they are less direct."

I said, "Now, wait a minute. If I understand you correctly your thesis is that Lewis Carroll—leaving aside any question of who or what he really was—worked out through mathematics and expressed in fantasy the fact that—what?"

"That there is another plane of existence besides the one we are now living in. That we can have—and do sometimes have—access to it."

"But what kind of a plane? A through-the-looking-glass plane of fantasy, a dream plane?"

"Exactly, Doctor. A dream plane. That isn't strictly accurate, but it's about as nearly as I can explain it to you just yet." He leaned forward. "Consider dreams. Aren't they the almost perfect parallel of the Alice adventures? The wool-and-water sequence, for instance, where everything Alice looks at changes into something else. Remember in the shop, with the old sheep knitting, how Alice looked hard to see what was on the shelves, but the shelf she looked at was always empty although the others about it were always full—of something, and she never found out what?"

I nodded slowly. I said, "Her comment was, 'Things flow about so here.' And then the sheep asked if Alice could row and handed her a pair of knitting needles and the needles turned into oars in her hands and she was in a boat, with the sheep still knitting."

"Exactly, Doctor. A perfect dream sequence. And consider that *Jabberwocky*—which is probably the best thing in the second Alice book—is in the very *language* of dreams. It's full of words like *frumious, manxome, tulgey*, words that give you a perfect picture in context—but you can't put your finger on what the context is. In a dream you fully understand such meanings, but you forget them when you awaken."

Between *"manxome"* and *"tulgey"*, he'd downed his latest drink. I didn't pour another this time; I was beginning to wonder how long the bottle—or we—would last. But he showed no effect whatsoever from the drinks he'd been downing. I can't quite say the same for myself. I knew my voice was getting a bit thick.

I said, "But why postulate the *reality* of such a world? I can see your point otherwise. The Jabberwock itself is the epitome of nightmare creatures—with eyes of flame and jaws that bite and claws that catch, and it whiffles and burbles—why, Freud and James Joyce in tandem couldn't have done any better. But why not take it that Lewis Carroll was trying, and damned successfully, to write as in a dream? Why make the assumption that that world is real? Why talk of getting through to it—except, of course, in the sense that we invade it nightly in our dreams?"

He smiled. "Because that world *is* real, Doctor. You'll hear evidence of that tonight, mathematical evidence. And, I hope, actual proof. I've had such proof myself, and I hope you'll have. But you'll see the calculations, at least, and it will be explained to you how they were derived from *Curiosa Mathematica*, and then corroborated by evidence found in the other books.

"Carroll was more than a century ahead of his time. Doctor. Have you read of the recent experiments with the subconscious made by Leibnitz and Winton—the feelers they're putting forth in the right direction, which is the mathematical approach?"

I admitted I hadn't heard of Liebnitz or Winton.

"They aren't well known," he conceded. "You see, only recently, except for Carroll, has anyone even considered the possibility of our reaching—let's call it the dream plane until I've shown you what it really is—physically as well as mentally."

"As Lewis Carroll reached it?"

"As he must have, to have known the things he knew. Things so revolutionary and dangerous that he did not dare reveal them openly."

For a fleeting moment it sounded so reasonable that I wondered if it *could* be true. Why not? Why couldn't there be other dimensions beside our own? Why couldn't a brilliant mathematician with a fantastic mind have found a way through to one of them?

In my mind, I cussed out Clyde Andrews for having told me about the asylum break. If only I hadn't learned about that, what a wonderful evening this one would be. Even knowing Smith was insane, I found myself—possibly with the whisky's help—wondering if he could be right. How marvellous it would have been without the knowledge of his insanity to temper the wonder and the wondering. It would have been an evening in Wonderland.

And, sane or crazy, I liked him. Sane or crazy, he belonged figuratively in the department in which Mrs. Carr's husband worked literally. I laughed and then, of course, I had to explain what I'd been laughing about.

His eyes lighted. "The Roman candle department. That's marvellous. The Roman candle department."

You see what I mean.

We had a drink to the Roman candle department, and then it happened that neither of us said anything right away and it was so quiet that I jumped when the phone rang.

I picked it up and said into it, "This is the Roman candle department."

"Doc?" It was the voice of Pete Corey, my printer. It sounded tense. "I've got bad news."

Pete doesn't get excited easily. I sobered up a little and asked, "What, Pete?"

"Listen, Doc. Remember just a couple of hours ago you were saying you wished a murder or something would happen so you'd have a story for the paper—and remember how I asked you if you'd like one even if it happened to a friend of yours?"

Of course I remembered; he'd mentioned my best friend, Carl Trenholm. I took a tighter grip on the phone. I said, "Cut out breaking it gently, Pete. Has something happened to Carl?"

"Yes, Doc."

"For God's sake, what? Cut the build-up. Is he dead?"

"That's what I heard. He was found out on the pike; I don't know if he was hit by a car or what."

"Where is he now?"

"Being brought in, I guess. All I know is that Hank called me"—Hank is Pete's brother-in-law and a deputy sheriff—"and said they got a call from someone who found him alongside the road out there. Even Hank had it third-hand—Rance Kates phoned him and said to come down and take care of the office while he went out there. And Hank knows Kates doesn't like you and wouldn't give you the tip, so Hank called me. But don't get Hank in trouble with his boss by telling anybody where the tip came from."

"Did you call the hospital?" I asked. "If Carl's just hurt——"

"Wouldn't be time for them to get him there yet—or to wherever they do take him. Hank just phoned me from his own place before he started for the sheriff's office, and Kates had just called him from the office and was just leaving there."

"Okay, Peter," I said. "Thanks. I'm going back downtown; I'll call the hospital from the *Clarion* office. You call me there if you hear anything more."

"Hell, Doc, I'm coming down too."

I told him he didn't have to, but he said the hell with having to; he wanted to. I didn't argue with him.

I cradled the phone and found that I was already standing up. I said, "Sorry, but something important's come up—an accident to a friend of mine." I headed for the closet to get my coat. "Do you want to wait here, or——"

"If you don't mind," he said. "That is, if you think you won't be very long."

"I don't know that, but I'll phone here and let you know as soon as I can. If the phone rings answer it; it'll be me. And help yourself to whisky and books."

He nodded. "I'll get along fine. Hope your friend isn't seriously hurt."

That was all that I was worrying about myself. I put on my hat and hurried out, again, and this time seriously, cussing those two flat tyres on my car and the fact that I hadn't taken time to fix them that morning. Nine blocks isn't far to walk when you're not in a hurry, but it's a hell of a distance when you're anxious to get there quickly.

I walked fast, so fast, in fact, that I winded myself in the first two blocks and had to slow down.

I kept thinking the same thing Pete had obviously thought—what a hell of a coincidence it was that we'd mentioned the possibility of Carl's being——

But we'd been talking about murder. Had Carl been murdered? Of course not; things like that didn't happen in Carmel City. It must have been an accident, a hit-run driver. No one would have the slightest reason for killing, of all people, Carl Trenholm. No one but a——

Finishing that thought made me stop walking suddenly. *No one but a maniac* would have the slightest reason for killing Carl Trenholm. But there was an escaped maniac at large tonight and—unless he'd left instead of waiting for me—he was sitting right in my living-room. I'd thought he was harmless—even though I'd taken the precaution of putting that gun in my pocket—but how could I be sure? I'm no psychiatrist; where did I get the bright idea that I could tell the difference between a harmless nut and a homicidal maniac?

I started to turn back and then realized that going back was useless and foolish. He would either have left as soon as I was out of sight around the corner, or he hadn't guessed that I suspected him and would wait as I'd told him to, until he heard from me. So all I had to do was to phone the asylum as soon as I could and they'd send guards to close in on my house and take him if he was still there.

I started walking again. Yes, it would be ridiculous for me to go back alone, even though I still had that gun in my pocket. He might resist, and I wouldn't want to have to use the gun, especially as I hadn't any real reason to believe he'd killed Carl. It could have been an auto accident just as easily; I couldn't even form an intelligent opinion on that until I learned what Carl's injuries were.

I kept walking, as fast as I could without winding myself again.

Suddenly I thought of that newspaper clipping—"Man Slain by Unknown Beast." A prickle went down my spine—*what if Carl's body showed*——

And then the horrible thought pyramided. What if the *unknown beast* who had killed the man near Bridgeport and the escaped maniac were one and the same. What if he had escaped before at the time of the killing at Bridgeport—or, for that matter, hadn't been committed to the asylum until after that killing, whether or not he was suspected of it.

I thought of lycanthropy, and shivered. *What* might I have been talking about Jabberwocks and unknown beasts with?

Suddenly the gun I'd put in my pocket felt comforting there. I looked around over my shoulder to be sure that nothing was coming after me. The street behind was empty, but I started walking a little faster just the same.

Suddenly the street lights weren't bright enough and the night, which had been a pleasant June evening, was a frightful, menacing thing. I was really scared. Maybe it's as well that I didn't guess that things hadn't even started to happen.

I felt glad that I was passing the courthouse—with a light on in the window of the sheriff's office. I even considered going in. Probably Hank would be there by now and Rance Kates would still be gone. But no, I was this far now and I'd carry on to the *Clarion* office and start my phoning from there. Besides, if Kates found out I'd been in his office talking to Hank, Hank would be in trouble.

So I kept on going. The corner of Oak Street, and I turned, now only a block and a half from the *Clarion*. But it was going to take me quite a while to make that block and a half.

A big, dark blue Buick sedan suddenly pulled near the kerb and slowed down alongside me. There were two men in the front seat and the one who was driving stuck his head out of the window and said, "Hey, Buster, what town is this?"

CHAPTER FIVE

When the sands are all dry, he is gay as a lark,
And will talk in contemptuous tones of the Shark;
But, when the tide rises and sharks are around,
His voice has a timid and tremulous sound.

It had been a long time since anyone had called me "Buster," and I didn't particularly like it. I didn't like the looks of the men, either, or the tone of voice the question had been asked in. A minute ago, I'd thought I'd be glad of any company short of that of the escaped maniac; now I decided differently.

I'm not often rude, but I can be when someone else starts it. I said, "Sorry, pal, I'm a stranger here myself." And I kept on walking.

I heard the man behind the wheel of the Buick say something to the other, and then they passed me and swung in to the kerb just ahead. The driver got out and walked toward me.

I stopped short and tried not to do a double-take when I recognized him. My attention to the wanted circulars on the post office bulletin board was about to pay off—although from the expression on his face, the pay off wasn't going to be the kind I'd want.

The man coming toward me and only two steps away when I stopped was Bat Masters, whose picture had been posted only last week and was still there on the board. I couldn't be wrong about his face, and I remembered the name clearly because of its similarity to the name of Bat Masterson, the famous gunman of the old West. I'd thought of it as a coincidence at first and then I realized that the similarity of Masters to Masterton had made the nickname "Bat" a natural.

He was a big man with a long, horselike face, eyes wide apart and a mouth that was a narrow straight line separating a lantern jaw from a wide upper lip; on the latter there was a two-day stubble of hair that indicated he was starting a moustache. But it would have taken plastic surgery and a full beard to disguise that face from anyone who had recently, however casually, studied a picture of it. Bat Masters, bank robber and killer.

I had the gun in my pocket, but I didn't remember it at the time. It's probably just as well; if I'd remembered, I might have been frightened into reaching for it. And that probably would not have been a healthful thing to do. He was coming at me with his fists balled but no gun in either of them. He didn't intend to kill me—although one of those fists might do it quite easily and unintentionally: I weigh a hundred and forty wringing wet, and he weighed almost twice that and had shoulders that bulged out his suit coat.

There wasn't even time to turn and run. His left hand came out and caught the front of my coat and pulled me toward him, almost lifting me off the sidewalk.

He said, "Listen, Pop, I don't want any lip. I asked you a question."

"Carmel City," I said. "Carmel City, Illinois."

The voice of the other man, still in the car, came back to us. "Hey, Bill, don't hurt the guy. We don't want to——" He didn't finish the sentence, of course; to say you don't want to attract attention is the best way of drawing it.

Masters looked past me—right over my head—to see if anybody or anything was coming that way and then, still keeping his grip on the front of my coat, turned and looked the other way. He wasn't afraid of my swinging at him enough to bother keeping his eyes on me, and I didn't blame him for feeling that way about it.

A car was coming now, about a block away. And two men came out of the drugstore on the opposite side of the street, only a few buildings down. Then behind me I could hear the sound of another car turning into Oak Street.

Masters turned back to me and let go, so we were just two men standing there face to face if anyone noticed us. He said, "Okay, Pop. Next time somebody asks you a question, don't be so God damn fresh."

He still glared at me as though he hadn't yet completely given up the idea of giving me something to remember him by—maybe just a light open-handed slap that wouldn't do anything worse than crack my jawbone and drive my dentures down my throat.

I said, "Sure, sorry," and let my voice sound afraid, but tried not to sound quite as afraid as I really was—because if he even remotely suspected that I might have recognized him, I wasn't going to get out of it at all.

He swung around and walked back to the car, got in and drove off. I suppose I should have got the licence number, but it would have been a stolen car anyway—and besides I didn't think of it. I didn't even watch the car as it drove away; if either of them looked back I didn't want them to think I was giving them what criminals call the big-eye. I didn't want to give them any possible reason to change their minds about going on.

I started walking again, keeping to the middle of the sidewalk and trying to look like a man minding his own business. Also trying to keep my knees from shaking so hard that I couldn't walk at all.

It had been a narrow squeak all right. If the street had been completely empty——

I could have notified the sheriff's office about a minute quicker by turning around and going back that way, but I didn't take the chance. If someone was watching me out of the back window of the car, a change in direction wouldn't be a good idea. There was a difference of only a block anyway; I was half a block past the courthouse and a block and a half away from Smiley's and the *Clarion* office across the street from it. From either one I could phone in the big news that Bat Masters and a companion had just driven through Carmel City heading north, probably toward Chicago. And Hank Ganzer, in the sheriff's office, would relay the story to the state police and there was probably better than an even chance that they'd be caught within an hour or two.

And if they were, I might even get a slice of the reward for giving the tip—but I didn't care as much about that as about the story I was going to have. Why, it was a story, even if they weren't caught, and if they were, it would be a really big one. And a local story—if the tip came from Carmel City—even if they were actually caught several counties north. Maybe there'd even be a gun battle—from my all too close look at Masters I had a hunch that there would be.

Perfect timing, too, I thought. For once something was happening on a Thursday night. For once I'd beat the Chicago papers. They'd have the story, too, of course, and a lot of Carmel City people take Chicago dailies, but they don't come in until the late afternoon train and the *Clarion* would be out hours before that.

Yes, for once I was going to have a newspaper with *news* in it. Even if Masters and his pal weren't caught, the fact that they'd passed through town made a story. And besides that, there was the escaped maniac, and Carl Trenholm——

Thinking about Carl again made me walk faster. It was safe by now; I'd gone a quarter of a block since the Buick had driven off. It wasn't anywhere in sight and again the street was quiet; thank God it hadn't been this quiet while Masters had been making up his mind whether or not to slug me.

I was past Deak's Music Store, dark. Past the super-market, ditto. The bank——

I had passed the bank, too, when I stopped as suddenly as though I'd run into a wall. The bank had been dark too. And it shouldn't have been; there's a small night light that always burns over the safe. I'd passed the bank thousands of times after dark and never before had the light been off.

For a moment the wild thought went through my head that Bat and his companion must have just burglarized the bank—although robbery, not burglary, was Masters' trade—and then I saw how ridiculous that thought had been. They'd been driving toward the bank and a quarter of a block away from it when they'd stopped to ask me what town they were in. True, they could have burglarized the bank and then circled the block in their car, but if they had they'd have been intent on their getaway. Criminals do pretty silly things, sometimes, but not quite so silly as to stop a getaway car within spitting distance of the scene of the crime to ask what town they're in, and then to top it by getting out of the car to slug a random pedestrian because they don't like his answers to their question.

No, Masters and company couldn't have robbed the bank. And they wouldn't be burglarizing it now, either. Their car had gone on past; I hadn't watched it, but my ears had told me that it had kept on going. And even if it hadn't, I had. My encounter with them had been only seconds ago; there wasn't possibly time for them to have broken in there, even if they'd stopped.

I went back a few steps and looked into the window of the bank.

At first I saw nothing except the vague silhouette of a window at the back—the top half of the window, that is, which was visible above the counter. Then the silhouette became less vague and I could see that the window had been opened; the top bar of the lower sash showed clearly, only a few inches from the top of the frame.

That was the means of entry all right—but was the burglar still in there, or had he left, and left the window open behind him?

I strained my eyes against the blackness to the left of the window, where the safe was. And suddenly a dim light flickered briefly, as though a match had been struck but had gone out before the phosphorus had ignited the wood. I could see only the brief light of it, as it was below the level of the counter; I couldn't see whoever had lighted it.

The burglar was still there.

And suddenly I was running on tiptoe back through the areaway between the bank and post office.

Good God, don't ask me *why*. Sure, I had money in the bank, but the bank had insurance against burglary and it wasn't any skin off my backside if the bank was robbed. I wasn't even thinking that it would be a better story for the *Clarion* if I got the burglar—or if he got me. I just wasn't thinking at all. I was running back alongside the bank toward that window that he'd left open for his getaway.

I think it must have been reaction from the cowardice I'd shown and felt only a minute before. I must have been a bit punch drunk from Jabberwocks and Vorpal Blades and homicidal maniacs with lycanthropy and bank bandits and a bank burglar—or maybe I thought I'd suddenly been promoted to the Roman candle department.

Maybe I was drunk, maybe I was a little mentally unbalanced—use any maybe you want, but there I was running tiptoe through the areaway. Running, that is, as far as the light from the street would let me; then I groped along the side of the building until I came to the alley. There was dim light there, enough for me to be able to see the window.

It was still open.

I stood there looking at it and vaguely beginning to realize how crazy I'd been. Why hadn't I run to the sheriff's office for Hank? The burglar—or, for all I knew, burglars—might be just starting his work on the safe in there. He might be in a long time, long enough for Hank to get here and collar him. If he came out now, what was I going to do about it? Shoot him? That was ridiculous; I'd rather let him get away with robbing the bank than do that.

And then it was too late because suddenly there was a soft shuffling sound from the window and a hand appeared on the sill. He was coming out, and there wasn't a chance that I could get away without his hearing me. What would happen then, I didn't know. I would just as soon not find out.

A moment before, just as I'd reached the place beside the window where I now stood, I'd stepped on a piece of wood, a one-by-two stick of it about a foot long. That was a weapon I could understand. I reached down and grabbed it and swung, just in time, as a head came through the window.

Thank God I didn't swing too hard. At the last second, even in that faint light, I'd thought—

The head and the hand weren't in the window any more and there was the soft thud of a body falling inside. There wasn't any sound or movement for seconds. Long seconds, and then there was the sound of my stick of wood hitting the dirt of the alley and I knew I'd dropped it.

If it hadn't been for what I'd thought I'd seen in the last fraction of a second before it was too late to stop the blow, I could have run now for the sheriff's office. But——

Maybe here went *my* head, but I had to chance it. The sill of the window wasn't much over waist high. I leaned across it and struck a match, and I'd been right.

I climbed in the window and felt for his heart and it was beating all right. He seemed to be breathing normally. I ran my hands very gently over his head and then held them in the open window to look at them; there wasn't any blood. There could be, then, nothing worse than a concussion.

I lowered the window so nobody would notice that it was open and then I felt my way carefully toward the nearest desk—I'd been in the bank thousands of times; I knew its layout—and groped for a telephone until I found one.

The operator's voice said, "Number please?" and I started to give it and then remembered; she'd know where the call came from and that the bank was closed. Naturally, she'd listen in. Maybe she'd even call the sheriff's office to tell them someone was using the telephone in the bank.

Had I recognised her voice? I'd thought I had. I said, "Is that Milly?"

"Yes. Is this—Mr. Stoeger?"

"Right," I said. I was glad she'd known *my* voice. "Listen, Milly, I'm calling from the bank, but it's all right. You don't need to worry about it. And—do me a favour, will you? Please don't listen in."

"All right, Mr. Stoeger. Sure. What number do you want?"

I gave it; the number of Clyde Andrews, president of the bank. As I heard the ringing of the phone at the other end, I thought how lucky it was that I'd known Milly all her life and that we liked one another. I knew that she'd be burning with curiosity but that she wouldn't listen in.

Clyde Andrew's voice answered. I was still careful about what I said because I didn't know offhand whether he was on a party line.

I said, "This is Doc Stoeger, Clyde. I'm down at the bank. Get down here right away. Hurry."

"Huh? Doc, are you drunk or something? What would you be doing at the bank. It's closed."

I said, "Somebody was inside here. I hit him over the head with a piece of wood when he started back out of the window, and he's unconscious but not hurt bad. But just to be sure, pick up Doc Minton on your way here. And hurry."

"Sure," he said, "Are you phoning the sheriff or shall I?"

"Neither of us. Don't phone anybody. Just get Minton and get here quick."

"But——I don't get it. Why not phone the sheriff? Is this a gag?"

I said, "No, Clyde. Listen—you'll want to see the burglar first. He isn't badly hurt, but for God's sake quit arguing and get down here with Dr. Minton. Do you understand?"

His tone of voice was different when he said, "I'll be there. Five minutes."

I put the receiver back on the phone and then lifted it again. The "Number, please" was Milly's voice again and I asked her if she knew anything about Carl Trenholm.

She didn't; she hadn't known anything had happened at all. When I told her what little I knew she said yes, that she'd routed a call from a farmhouse out on the pike to the sheriff's office about half an hour before, but she'd had several other calls around the same time and hadn't listened in on it.

I decided that I'd better wait until I was somewhere else before I called to report either Bat Masters' passing through or about the escaped maniac at my own house. It wouldn't be safe to risk making the call from here, and a few more minutes wouldn't matter a lot.

I went back, groping my way through the dark toward the dim square of the window, and bent down again by the boy, Clyde Andrews' son. His breathing and his heart were still okay and he moved a little and muttered something as though he was coming out of it. I don't know anything about concussion, but I thought that was a good sign and felt better. It would have been terrible if I'd swung a little harder and had killed him or injured him seriously.

I sat down on the floor so my head would be out of the line of sight if anyone looked in the front window, as I had a few minutes before, and waited.

So much had been happening that I felt a little numb. There was so much to think about that I guess I didn't think about any of it. I just sat there in the dark.

When the phone rang I jumped about two feet.

I groped to it and answered. Milly's voice said, "Mr. Stoeger, I thought I'd better tell you if you're still there. Somebody from the drugstore across the street just phoned the sheriff's office and said the night light in the bank is out, and whoever answered at the sheriff's office—it sounded like one of the deputies, not Mr. Kates—said they'd come right around."

I said, "Thanks, Milly. Thanks a lot."

A car was pulling up at the kerb outside; I could see it through the window. I breathed a sigh of relief when I recognized the men getting out of at as Clyde Andrews and the doctor.

I switched on the lights inside while Clyde was unlocking the front door. I told him quickly about the call that had been made to the sheriff's office while I was leading them back to where Harvey Andrews was lying. We moved him slightly to a point where neither he nor Dr. Minton, bending over him, could be seen from the front of the bank, and we did it just in time. Hank was rapping on the door.

I stayed out of sight, too, to avoid having to explain what I was doing there. I heard Clyde Andrews open the door for Hank and explain that everything was all right, that someone had phoned him, too, that the night light was out and that he'd just got here to check up and that the bulb had merely burned out.

When Hank left, Clyde came back, his face a bit white. Dr. Minton said, "He's going to be all right, Clyde. Starting to come out of it. Soon as he can walk between us, we'll get him to the hospital for a checkup and be sure."

I said, "Clyde, I've got to run. There's a lot popping tonight. But as soon as you're sure the boy's all right will you let me know? I'll probably be at the *Clarion*, but I might be at Smiley's—or if it's a long time from now, I might be home."

"Sure, Doc," He put his hand on my shoulder. "And thanks a lot for—calling me instead of the sheriff's office."

"That's all right," I told him. "And, Clyde, I didn't know who it was before I hit. He was coming out of the back window and I thought——"

Clyde said, "I looked in his room after you phoned. He'd packed. I—I can't understand it, Doc. He's only fifteen. Why he'd do a thing like——" He shook his head. "He's always been headstrong and he's got into little troubles a few times, but—I don't understand this." He looked at me very earnestly. "Do you?"

I thought maybe I did understand a little of it, but I was remembering about Bat Masters and the fact that he was getting farther away every minute and that I'd better get the state police notified pretty quickly.

So I said, "Can I talk to you about it tomorrow, Clyde? Get the boy's side of it when he can talk—and just try to keep your mind open until then. I think—it may not be as bad as you think right now."

I left him still looking like a man who's just taken an almost mortal blow, and went out.

I headed down the street thinking what a damn fool I'd been to do what I'd done. But then, where had I missed a chance to do something wrong anywhere down the line tonight? And then, on second thought, this one thing might not have been wrong. If I'd called Hank, the boy just might have been shot instead of knocked out. And in any case he'd have been arrested.

That would have been bad. This way, there was a chance he could be straightened out before it was too late. Maybe a psychiatrist could help him. The only thing was, Clyde Andrews would have to realize that he, too, would have to take advice from the psychiatrist. He was a good man, but a hard father. You can't expect the things of a fifteen-year-old boy that Clyde expected of Harvey, and not have something go wrong somewhere down the line. But burglarizing a bank, even his own father's bank—I couldn't make up my mind whether that made it better or worse—was certainly something I hadn't looked for. It appalled me, a bit. Harvey's running away from home wouldn't have surprised me at all; I don't know that I'd even have blamed him.

A man can be too good a man and too conscientious and strict a father for his son ever to be able to love him. If Clyde Andrews would only get drunk—good and stinking drunk—just once in his life, he might get an entirely different perspective on things, even if he never again took another drink. But he'd never taken a drink yet, not one in his whole life. I don't think he'd ever smoked a cigarette or said a naughty word.

I liked him anyway; I'm pretty tolerant, I guess. But I'm glad I hadn't had a father like him. In my books, the man in town who was the best father was Carl Trenholm. Trenholm—and I hadn't found out yet whether he was dead or only injured!

I was only half a block, now, from Smiley's and the *Clarion*. I broke into a trot. Even at my age, it wouldn't wind me to trot that far. It had probably been less than half an hour since I'd left home, but with the things that had happened *en route*, it seemed like days. Well, anyway, nothing could happen to me between here and Smiley's. And nothing did.

I could see through the glass that there weren't any customers at the bar and that Smiley was alone behind it. Polishing glasses, as always; I think he must polish the same glasses a dozen times over when there's nothing else for him to do.

I burst in and headed for the telephone. I said, "Smiley, hell's popping tonight. There's an escaped lunatic, and something's happened to Carl Trenholm, and a couple of wanted bank robbers drove through here fifteen or twenty minutes ago and I got to———"

I was back by the telephone by the time I'd said all that and I was reaching up for the receiver. But I never quite touched it.

A voice behind me said, "Take it easy, Buster."

CHAPTER SIX

"What matters it how far we go?" his scaly friend replied.
"The further off from England the nearer is to France.
There is another shore, you know, upon the other side.
Then turn not pale, beloved snail, but come and join the
dance."

I TURNED around slowly. They'd been sitting at the table around
the el of the tavern, the one table that can't be seen through the
glass of the door or the windows. They'd probably picked it for
that reason. The beer glasses in front of them were empty. But I
didn't think the guns in their hands would be.

One of the guns—the one in the hand of Bat Masters'
companion—was aimed at Smiley. And Smiley, not smiling, was
keeping his hands very still, not moving a muscle.

The gun in Masters' hand was aimed at me.

He said, "So you knew us, huh, Buster?"

There wasn't any use denying it; I'd said too much already. I
said, "You're Bat Masters." I looked at the other man, whom I
hadn't seen clearly before, when he'd been in the car. He was squat
and stocky, with a bullet head and little pig eyes. He looked like
a caricature of a German army officer. I said, "I'm sorry; I don't
know your friend."

Masters laughed. He said, "See, George, I'm famous and you're
not. How'd you like that?"

George kept his eyes on Smiley. He said, "I think you better
come around this side of the bar. You just might have a gun back
there and take a notion to dive for it."

"Come on over and sit with us," Masters said. "Both of you.
Let's make it a party, huh, George?"

George said, "Shut up," which changed my opinion of George
quite a bit. I personally wouldn't have cared to tell Bat Masters to
shut up, and in that tone of voice. True I *had* been fresh with him
about twenty minutes before, but I hadn't known who he was. I
hadn't even seen how big he was.

Smiley was coming around the end of the bar. I caught his eye,
and gave him what was probably a pretty sickly grin. I said, "I'm
sorry, Smiley. Looks like I put our foot in it this time."

His face was completely impassive. He said, "Not your fault,
Doc."

I wasn't too sure of that myself. I was just remembering that I'd vaguely noticed a car parked in front of Smiley's place. If my brains had been in the proper end of my anatomy I'd have had the sense to take a quick look at that car. And if I'd had that much sense, I'd have had the further sense to go across to the *Clarion* office instead of barging nitwittedly into Smiley's and into the arms of Bat Masters and George.

And if the state police had come before they'd left Smiley's, the *Clarion* would have had a really good story. This way, it might be a good story too, but who would write it?

Smiley and I were standing close together now, and Masters must have figured that one gun was enough for both of us. He stuck his into a shoulder holster and looked at George. "Well?" he said.

That proved again that George was the boss, or at least was on equal status with Masters. And as I studied George's face, I could see why. Masters was big and probably had plenty of brass and courage, but George was the one of the two who had the more brains.

George said, "Guess we'll have to take 'em along, Bat."

I knew what that meant. I said, "Listen, there's a back room. Can't you just tie us up? If we're found a few hours from now, what does it matter? You'll be clear."

"And you might be found in a few minutes. And you probably noticed what kind of car we got, and you know which way we're heading." He shook his head, and it was definite.

He said, "We're not sticking around, either, till somebody comes in. Bat, go look outside."

Masters got up and started toward the front; then he hesitated and went back of the bar instead. He took two pint bottles of whisky and put one in either coat pocket. And he punched "No Sale" on the register and took out the bills; he didn't bother with the change. He folded the bills and stuck them in his trouser pocket. Then he came back around the bar and started for the door.

Sometimes I think people are crazy. Smiley stuck out his hand. He said, "Five bucks. Two-fifty apiece for those pints."

He could have got shot for it, then and there, but for some reason Masters liked it. He grinned and took the wadded paper out of his pocket, peeled a five loose and put it in Smiley's hand.

George said, "Bat, cut the horseplay. Look outside." I noticed that he watched very carefully and kept the gun trained smack in the middle of Smiley's chest while Smiley stuck the five-dollar bill into his pocket.

Masters opened the door and stepped outside, looked around casually and beckoned to us. Meanwhile George had stood up and walked around behind us, sliding his gun into a coat pocket out of sight but keeping his hand on it.

He said, "All right, boys, get going."

It was all very friendly. In a way.

We went out the door into the cool pleasant evening that wasn't going to last much longer, the way things looked now. Yes, the Buick was parked right in front of Smiley's. If I'd only glanced at it before I went in, the whole mess wouldn't have happened.

The Buick was a four-door sedan. George said, "Get in back," and we got in back. George got in front but sat sidewise, turned around facing us over the seat.

Masters got in behind the wheel and started the engine. He said over his shoulder, "Well, Buster, where to?"

I said, "About five miles out there are woods. If you take us back in them and tie us up, there isn't a chance on earth we'd be found before tomorrow."

I didn't want to die, and I didn't want Smiley to die, and that idea was such a good one that for a moment I hoped. Then Masters said, "What town is this, Buster?" and I knew there wasn't any chance. Just because I'd given him a fresh answer to a fresh question half an hour ago, there wasn't any chance.

The car pulled out from the kerb and headed north.

I was scared and sober. There didn't seem to be any reason why I had to be both. I said, "How about a drink?"

George reached into Masters' coat pocket and handed one of the pint bottles over the back of the seat. My hands shook a little while I got the cellophane off with my thumb nail and unscrewed the cap. I handed it to Smiley first and he took a short drink and passed it back. I took a long one and it put a warm spot where a very cold one had been. I don't meant to say it made me happy, but I felt a little better. I wondered what Smiley was thinking about and I remembered that he had a wife and three kids and I wished I hadn't remembered that.

I handed him back the bottle and he took another quick nip. I said, "I'm sorry, Smiley," and he said. "That's all right, Doc." And he laughed. "One bad thing, Doc. There'll be a swell story for your *Clarion*, but can Pete write it?"

I found myself wondering that, quite seriously. Pete's one of the best all-round printers in Illinois, but what kind of a job would he make of things tonight and tomorrow morning? He'd get the paper out all right, but he'd never done any news writing —at least as long as he'd worked for me—and handling all the news he was going to have tomorrow would be plenty tough. An escaped maniac, whatever had happened to Carl, and whatever—as if I really wondered—was going to happen to Smiley and me. I wondered if our bodies would be found in time to make the paper, or if it would be merely a double disappearance. We'd both be missed fairly soon. Smiley because his tavern was still open but no one behind the bar. I because I was due to meet Pete at the *Clarion* and about an hour from now, when I hadn't shown up yet, he'd start checking.

We were just leaving town by then, and I noticed that we'd got off the main street which was part of the main highway. Burgoyne Street, which we were on, was turning into a road.

Masters stopped the car as we came to a fork and turned around. "Where do these roads go?" he asked.

"They both go to Watertown," I told him. "The one to the left goes along the river and the other one cuts through the hills; it's shorter, but it's trickier driving."

Apparently Masters didn't mind tricky driving. He swung right and we started up into the hills. I wouldn't have done it myself, if I'd been driving. The hills are pretty hilly and the road through them is narrow and does plenty of winding, with a drop-off on one side or the other most of the time. Not the long precipitous drop-off you find on real mountain roads, but enough to wreck a car that goes over the edge, and enough to bother my touch of acrophobia.

Phobias are ridiculous things, past reasoning. I felt mine coming back the moment there was that slight drop-off at the side of the road as we started up the first hill. Actually, I was for the moment more afraid of that than of George's gun. Yes, phobias are funny things. Mine, fear of heights, is one of the commonest. Carl is afraid of cats. Al Grainger is a pyrophobiac, morbidly afraid of fire.

Smiley said, "You know, Doc?"

"What?" I asked him.

"I was thinking of Pete having to write that newspaper. Whyn't you come back and help him. Ain't there such things as ghost writers?"

I groaned. After all these years, Smiley had picked a time like this to come up with the only funny thing I'd ever heard him say.

We were up high now, about as high as the road went; ahead was a hairpin turn as it started downhill again. Masters stopped the car. "Okay, you mugs," he said. "Get out and start walking back."

Start, he'd said; he hadn't made any mention of finishing. The tail lights of the car would give them enough illumination to shoot us down by. And he'd probably picked this spot because it would be easy to roll our bodies off the edge of the road, down the slope, so they wouldn't be found right away. Both of them were already getting out of the car.

Smiley's big hand gave my arm a quick squeeze; I didn't know whether it was a farewell gesture or a signal. He said, "Go ahead, Doc," as calmly as though he was collecting for drinks back of his bar.

I opened the door on my side, but I was afraid to step out. Not because I knew I was going to be shot—that would happen anyway, even if I didn't get out. They'd either drag me out or else shoot me where I sat and bloody up the back seat of their car. No, I was afraid to get out because the car was on the outside edge of the road and the slope started only a yard from the open door of the car. My damned acrophobia. It was dark out there and I could see the edge of the road and no farther and I pictured a precipice beyond. I hesitated, half in the door and half out of it.

Smiley said again, "Go ahead, Doc," and I heard him moving behind me.

Then suddenly there was a click—and complete and utter darkness. Smiley had reached a long arm across the back of the seat to the dashboard and had turned the light switch off. All the car lights went out.

There was a shove in the middle of my back that sent me out of that car door like a cork popping out of a champagne bottle; I don't think my feet touched that yard-wide strip of road at all. As I went over the edge into darkness and the unknown I heard swearing and a shot behind me. I was so scared of falling that I'd gladly have been back up on the road trying to outrun a bullet back toward town. At least I'd have been dead before they rolled me over the edge.

I hit and fell and rolled. It wasn't really steep, after all; it was about a forty-five degree slope, and it was grassy. I flattened a couple of bushes before one stopped me. I could hear Smiley coming after me, sliding, and I scrambled on as fast as I could. All of my arms and legs seemed to be working, so I couldn't be seriously hurt.

And I could see a little now that my eyes were getting used to the darkness. I could see trees ahead, and I scrambled toward them down the slope, sometimes running, sometimes sliding and sometimes simply falling, which is the simplest if not the most comfortable way to go down a hill.

I made the trees, and heard Smiley make them, just as the lights of the car flashed on, on the road above us. Some shots snapped our way, and then I heard George say, "Don't waste it. Let's get going," and Bat's, "You mean we're gonna——"

George growled, "Hell, yes. That's woods down there. We could waste an hour playing hide and seek. Let's get going."

They were the sweetest words I'd heard in a long time.

I heard car doors slam, and the car started.

Smiley's voice, about two yards to my left, said, "Doc? You okay?"

"I think so," I said. "Smart work, Smiley, Thanks."

He came around a tree toward me and I could see him now. He

said, "Save it, Doc. Come on quick. We got a chance—a little chance, anyway—of stopping them."

"*Stopping them*?" I said. My voice went shrill and sounded strange to me. I wondered if Smiley had gone crazy. I couldn't think of anything in the whole wide world that I wanted to do less than stop Bat Masters and George.

But he had hold of my arm and was starting downhill, through the dimly seen trees and away from the road, taking me with him.

He said, "Listen, Doc, I know this country like the palm of my foot. I've hunted here often."

"For bank robbers?" I asked him.

"Listen, that road makes a hairpin and goes by right below us, not forty yards from here. If we can get just above the road before they get there and if I can find a big boulder to roll down as the car goes by——"

I wasn't crazy about it, but he was pulling me along and we were through the trees already. My eyes were used to the darkness by now and I could see the road dimly, a dozen yards ahead and a dozen yards below. In the distance, around a curve, I could hear the sound of the car; I couldn't see it yet. It was a long way off, but coming fast.

Smiley said, "Look for a boulder, Doc. If you don't find one big enough to roll, then something we can throw. If we can hit their windshield or something——"

He was bending over, groping around. I did the same, but the bank was smooth and grassy. If there were stones, I couldn't find any.

Apparently Smiley wasn't having any luck either. He swore. He said. "If I only had a gun——"

I remembered something. "I've got one," I said.

He straightened up and looked at me—and I'm glad it was dark enough that he couldn't see my face and that I couldn't see his.

I handed him the gun. The headlights of the car were coming in sight now around the curve. Smiley pushed me back into the trees and stood behind one himself, leaning out to expose only his head and his gun hand.

The car came like a bat out of hell, but Smiley took aim calmly. He fired his first shot when the car was about forty yards away, the second when it was only twenty. The first shot went into the radiator—I don't mean we could tell that then, but that's where it was found afterwards. The second went through the windshield, almost dead centre, but, of course, at an angle. It ploughed a furrow along the side of Masters' neck. The car careened and then went off the road on the downhill side, away from us. It turned over once, end for end, the headlight beams stabbing the night with drunken arcs, and then it banged into a tree with a noise like the end of the world and stopped.

For just a second after all that noise there was a silence that was almost deafening. And then the gas tank exploded.

The car caught fire and there was plenty of light. We saw, as we ran toward it, that one of the men had been thrown clear; when we got close enough we could see that it was Masters. George was still in the car, but we couldn't do a thing for him. And in that roaring inferno there wasn't a chance on earth that he could have lived even the minute it took us to get to the scene of the wreck.

We dragged Masters farther away from the fire before we checked to see whether or not he was alive. Amazingly, he was. His face looked as though he'd held it in a meat grinder and both of his arms were broken. Whether there was anything wrong with him beyond that we couldn't tell, but he was still breathing and his heart was still beating.

Smiley was staring at the flaming wreck. He said, "A perfectly good Buick shot to hell. A fifty model at that." He shook his head sadly and then jumped back, as I did, when there was another explosion in the car; it must have been the cartridges in George's pistol going off all at once.

I told Smiley, "One of us will have to walk back. One had better stay here, on account of Masters' still being alive."

"I guess so," he said. "Don't know what either of us can do for him, but we can't both walk off and leave him. Say, look, that's a car coming."

I looked where he was pointing, toward the upper stretch of road where we'd got out of the car before it made the hairpin turn, and there were the headlights of a coming car all right.

We got out on the road ready to hail it, but it would have stopped anyway. It was a state police car with two coppers in it. Luckily, I knew one of them—Willie Peeble—and Smiley knew the other one, so they took our word for what had happened. Especially as Peeble knew about Masters and was able to identify him in spite of the way his face was cut up.

Masters was still alive and his heartbeat and breathing were as good as they'd been when we'd got to him. Peeble decided he'd better not try to move him. He went back to the police car and used the two-way radio to get an ambulance started our way and to report in to headquarters what had happened.

Peeble came back and said, "We'll give you and your friend a lift into town as soon as the ambulance gets here. You'll have to make and sign statements and stuff, but the chief says you can do that tomorrow; he knows both of you and says it's all right that way."

"That's swell," I said. "I've got to get back to the office as soon as I can. And as for Smiley here, his place is open and nobody there." I had a sudden thought and said, "Say, Smiley, you don't by any chance still have that pint that we had a nip out of in the car, do you?"

He shook his head. "What with turning off the lights and pushing you out and getting out myself——"

I sighed at the waste of good liquor. The other pint bottle, the one that had been in Bat Masters' left coat pocket, hadn't survived the crash. Still, Smiley *had* saved our lives, so I had to forgive him for abandoning the bottle he'd been holding.

The fire was dying down now, and I was getting a little sick at the barbecue odour and wished the ambulance would come so we could get away from here.

I suddenly remembered Carl and asked Peeble if there'd been any report on the police radio about a Carl Trenholm. He shook his head. He said, "There was a looney loose, though. Escaped from the county asylum. Must've been caught though; we had a cancellation on it later."

That was good news, in a way. It meant that Yehudi hadn't waited at my place after all. And somehow I'd hated the thought of having to put the guards on him while he was there. Insane or not, it didn't seem like real hospitality to a guest.

And the fact that nothing had been on the police radio about Carl at least wasn't discouraging.

A car came along from the opposite direction and stopped when its driver saw the smouldering wreckage and the state police car. It turned out to be a break for Smiley and me. The driver was a Watertown man whom Willie Peeble knew and who was on his way to Carmel City. When Peeble introduced us and vouched for us, he said he'd be glad to take Smiley and me into Carmel City with him.

I didn't believe it at first when I saw by the clock dial on the instrument panel of the car that it was only a few minutes after ten o'clock as we entered Carmel City; it seemed incredible that so much had happened in the few hours—less than four—since I'd left the *Clarion*. But we passed a lighted clock in a store window and I saw that the clock in the car was right after all, within a few minutes, anyway. It was only a quarter after ten.

We were let off in front of Smiley's. Across the street I could see lights were on at the *Clarion*, so Pete would be there. I thought I'd take a quick drink with Smiley, though, before I went to the office, so I went in with him.

The place was as we'd left it. If any customer had come in he'd got tired of waiting and had left.

Smiley went around back of the bar and poured us drinks while I went to the phone. I was going to call the hospital to find out about Carl Trenholm; then I decided to call Pete instead. He'd surely have called the hospital already. So I gave the *Clarion* number.

When Pete recognized my voice, he said, "Doc, where the hell have you been?"

"Tell you in a minute. Pete. First, have you got anything about Carl?"

"He's all right. I don't know yet what happened, but he's okay. I called the hospital and they said he'd been treated and released. I tried to find out what the injuries had been and how they'd happened, but they said they couldn't give out that information. I tried his home, but I guess he hadn't got there yet; nobody answered."

"Thanks, Pete," I said. "That's swell. Listen, there's going to be plenty to write up. Carl's accident, when we get in touch with him, and the escape and capture of the lunatic, and—something even bigger than either of those. So I guess we might as well do it tonight, if that's okay by you."

"Sure, Doc. I'd rather get it over with tonight. Where are you?"

"Over at Smiley's. Come on over for a quick one—to celebrate Carl's being okay. He can't even be badly hurt if they released him that quickly."

"Okay, Doc, I'll have one. But where were you? And Smiley, too, for that matter? I looked in there on my way to the office—saw the lights weren't on here, so I knew you weren't here yet—and you and Smiley were both gone. I waited five or ten minutes and then I decided I'd better come across here in case of any phone calls and to start melting metal in the Linotype."

I said, "Smiley and I had a little ride. I'll tell you about it."

"Okay, Doc. See you in a couple of minutes."

I went back to the bar and when I reached for the shot Smiley had poured for me, my hand was shaking.

Smiley grinned and said, "Me too, Doc." He held out his hand and I saw it wasn't much steadier than mine.

"Well," he said, "you got your story, Doc. What you were squawking about. Say, here's your gun back." He took out the short-barrelled thirty-eight and put it on the bar. "Good as new, except two bullets gone out of it. How'd you happen to have it with you, Doc?"

For some reason I didn't want to tell him, or anyone, that the escaped lunatic had made such a sap out of me and had been a guest at my house. So I said, "I had to walk down here, and Pete had just phoned me there was a lunatic loose, so I stuck that in my pocket. Jittery, I guess."

He looked at me and shook his head slowly. I know he was thinking about my having had that gun in my pocket all along during what we thought was our last ride, and never having even tried to use it. I'd been so scared that I'd completely forgotten about it until Smiley had said he wished he had a gun.

I grinned and said, "Smiley, you're right in what you're thinking. I've got no more business with a gun than a snake has with roller skates. Keep it."

"Huh? You mean it, Doc? I've been thinking about getting one to keep under the bar."

"Sure, I mean it," I told him. "I'm afraid of the damn things and I'm safer without one."

He hefted it appraisingly. "Nice gun. It's worth something."

I said, "So's my life, Smiley. To me, anyway. And you saved it when you pushed me out of that car and over the edge tonight."

"Forget it, Doc. I couldn't have got out that door myself with you asleep in it. And getting out of the other side of the car wouldn't have been such a hot idea. Well, if you really mean it, thanks for the gun."

He put it out of sight under the bar and then poured us each a second drink. "Make it short," I told him. "I've got a lot of work to do."

He glanced at his clock and it was only ten-thirty. He said, "Hell, Doc, the evening's only a pup."

I thought, but didn't say, *what a pup!*

I wonder what I'd have thought if I'd even guessed that the pup hadn't even been weaned yet.

Pete came in.

CHAPTER SEVEN

"It seems a shame," the Walrus said
"To play them such a trick.
After we've brought them out so far,
And made them trot so quick!"

NEITHER Smiley nor I had touched, as yet, the second drink he'd poured us, so there was time for Pete Corey to get in on the round; Smiley poured a drink for him.

He said, "Okay, Doc, now what's this gag about Smiley and you going for a ride? You told me your car was laid up and Smiley doesn't drive one."

"Pete," I said, "Smiley doesn't *have* to be able to drive a car. He's a gentleman of genius. He kills or captures killers. That's what we were doing. Anyway, that's what Smiley was doing. I went along, just for the ride."

"Doc, you're kidding me."

I said, "If you don't believe me, read tomorrow's *Clarion*. Ever heard of Bat Masters?"

Pete shook his head. He reached for his drink.

"You will," I told him. "In tomorrow's *Clarion*. Ever heard of George?"

"George Who?"

I opened my mouth to say I didn't know, but Smiley beat me to the punch by saying, "George Kramer."

I stared at Smiley. "How'd you know his last name?"

"Saw it in a fact detective magazine. And his picture, too, and Bat Masters'. They're members of the Gene Kelley mob."

I stared harder at Smiley. "You recognized them? I mean, before I even came in here?"

"Sure," Smiley said. "But it wouldn't have been a good idea to phone the cops while they were here, so I was going to wait till they left, and then phone the state cops to pick 'em up between here and Chicago. That's where they were heading. I listened to what they said, and it wasn't much, but I did get that much out of it. Chicago. They had a date there tomorrow afternoon."

"You're not kidding, Smiley?" I asked him. "You really had them spotted before I came in here?"

"I'll show you the magazine, Doc, with their pictures in it. Pictures of all the Gene Kelley mob."

"Why didn't you tell me?"

Smiley shrugged his big shoulders. "You didn't ask. Why didn't you tell *me* you had a gun in your pocket? If you coulda slipped it to me in the car, we'd have polished 'em off sooner. It would have been a cinch; it was so dark in that back seat after we got out of town, George Kramer wouldn't of seen you pass it."

He laughed as though he'd said something funny. Maybe he had.

Pete was looking from one to the other of us. He said, "Listen, if this is a gag, you guys are going a long way for it. What the hell happened?"

Neither of us paid any attention to Pete. I said, "Smiley, where is that fact detective magazine? Can you get it?"

"Sure, it's upstairs. Why? Don't you believe me?"

"Smiley," I said. "I'd believe you if you told me you were lying. No, what I had in mind is that that magazine will save me a lot of grief. It'll have background stuff on the boys we were playing cops and robbers with tonight. I thought I'd have to phone to Chicago and get it from cops there. But if there's a whole article on the Gene Kelley mob in that mag, I'll have enough without that."

"Get it right away, Doc." Smiley went through the door that led upstairs.

I took pity on Pete and gave him a quick sketch of our experience with the gangsters. It was fun to watch his mouth drop open and to think that a lot of other mouths in Carmel City would do that same thing tomorrow when the *Clarion* was distributed.

Smiley came back down with the magazine and I put it in my pocket and went to the phone again. I still had to have the details about what had happened to Carl, for the paper. I still wanted it for my own information too, but that wasn't so important as long as he wasn't seriously hurt.

I tried the hospital first but they gave me the same runaround they'd given Pete; sorry, but since Mr. Trenholm had been discharged, they could give out no information. I thanked them. I tried Carl's own phone and got no answer, so I went back to Pete and Smiley.

Smiley happened to be staring out the window. He said, "Somebody just went in your office, Doc. Looked like Clyde Andrews."

Pete turned to look, too, but was too late. He said, "Guess that's who it must've been. Forgot to tell you, Doc; he phoned about twenty minutes ago while I was waiting for you over at the office. I told him I expected you any minute."

"You didn't lock the door, did you, Pete?" I asked. He shook his head.

I waited a minute to give the banker time to get up the stairs and into the office and then I went back to the phone and called the *Clarion* number. It rang several times while Clyde, apparently, was making up his mind whether to answer it or not. Finally he did.

"This is Doc, Clyde," I said. "How's the boy?"

"He's all right, Doc. He's fine. And I want to thank you again for what you did and—I want to talk to you about something. Are you on your way here?"

"I'm across the street at Smiley's. How about dropping over here if you want to talk?"

He hesitated. "Can't you come here?" he asked.

I grinned to myself. Clyde Andrews is not only a strict temperance advocate; he's head of a local chapter (a small one, thank God) of the Anti-Saloon League. He'd probably never been in a tavern in his life.

I said, "I'm afraid I can't, Clyde." I made my voice very grave. "I'm afraid if you want to talk to me, it will have to be here at Smiley's."

He got me, all right. He said stiffly, "I'll be there."

I sauntered back to the bar. I said, "Clyde Andrews is coming here, Smiley. Chalk up a first."

Smiley stared at me. "I don't believe it," he said. He laughed.

"Watch," I told him.

Solemnly I went around behind the bar and got a bottle and two glasses and took them to a table—the one in the far corner farthest from the bar. I liked the way Pete and Smiley stared at me.

I filled both the glasses and sat down. Pete and Smiley stared some more. Then they turned and stared the other way as Clyde came in, walking stiffly. He said, "Good evening, Mr. Corey," to Pete and "Good evening, Mr. Wheeler" to Smiley, and then came back to where I was sitting.

I said, "Sit down Clyde," and he sat down.

I looked at him. I said sternly, "Clyde, I don't like—in advance—what you're going to ask me."

"But, Doc," he said earnestly, almost pleadingly, "*must* you print what happened? Harvey didn't mean to——"

"That's what I meant," I said. "What makes you think I'd even think of printing a word about it?"

He looked at me and his face changed. "Doc! You're not going to?"

"Of course not." I leaned forward. "Listen, Clyde, I'll make you a bet—or I would if you were a betting man. I'll bet I know exactly the amount of money the kid had in his pocket when he was leaving—and, no, I didn't look in his pockets. I'll bet he had a savings account—he's been working summers several years now, hasn't he?—and he was running away. And he knew damn well you wouldn't let him draw his own money and that he couldn't draw it without your knowing it. Whether he had twenty dollars or a thousand, I'll bet you it was the exact amount of his own account."

He took a deep breath. "You're right. Exactly right. And—thanks for thinking that, before you knew it. I was going to tell you."

"For a fifteen-year-old, Harvey's a good kid, Clyde. Now listen, you'll admit I did the right thing tonight calling you instead of calling the sheriff? And in keeping the story out of the paper?"

"Yes."

"You're in a saloon, Clyde. A den of iniquity. You should have said, 'Hell, yes.' But I don't suppose it would sound natural if you did, so I won't insist on it. But, Clyde, how much thinking have you been doing about *why* the boy was running away? Has he told you that yet?"

He shook his head slowly. "He's all right now, in bed, asleep. Dr. Minton gave him a sedative, but told me Harvey had better not do any talking till tomorrow."

"I'll tell you right now," I said, "that he won't have any very coherent story about it. Maybe he'll say he was running away to join the army or to go on the stage or—or almost anything. But it won't be the truth, even if he thinks it is. Clyde, whether he knows it or not, he was running *away*. Not toward."

"Away from what?"

"From you," I said.

For a second I thought he was going to get angry and I'm glad he didn't, because then I might have got angry too and that would have spoiled the whole thing.

Instead, he slumped a little. He said, "Go on, Doc."

I hated to, then, but I had to strike while the striking was good. I said, "Listen, Clyde, get up and walk out any time you want to; I'm going to give it to you straight. You've been a lousy father." At any other time he'd have walked out on me on that one. I could tell by his face that, even now, he didn't like it. But at any other time he wouldn't have been sitting at a back table in Smiley's tavern, either.

I said, "You're a good man, Clyde, but you work at it too hard. You're rigid, unyielding, righteous. Nobody can love a ramrod. There's nothing wrong with your being religious, if you want to. Some men *are* religious. But you've got to realize that everybody who doesn't think as you do isn't necessarily wrong."

I said, "Take alcohol—literally, if you wish; there's a glass of whisky in front of you. But take it figuratively, anyway. It's been a solace to the human race, one of the things that can make life tolerable, since—damn it, since before the human race was even human. True, there are a few people who can't handle it—but that's no reason to try to legislate it away from the people who *can* handle it, and whose enjoyment of life is increased by its moderate use—or even by its occasional immoderate use, providing it doesn't make them pugnacious or otherwise objectionable.

"But—let's skip alcohol. My point is that a man can be a good man without trying to interfere with his neighbour's life too much. Or with his son's. Boys are human, Clyde. People in general are human; people are more human than anybody."

He didn't say anything, and that was a hopeful sign. Maybe a tenth of it was sinking in.

I said, "Tomorrow, when you can talk with the kid, Clyde, what are you going to say?"

"I—I don't know, Doc."

I said, "Don't say anything. Above all, don't ask him any questions. Not a damn question. And let him keep that money, in cash, so he can run away any time he decides to. Then maybe he won't. If you change your attitude toward him.

"But, damn it, Clyde, you *can't* change your attitude toward him, and unbend, without unbending in general toward the human race. The kid's a human being, too. And you could be, if you wanted to. Maybe you think it will cost you your immortal soul to be one—I don't think so, myself, and I think there are a great many truly religious people who don't think so either—but if you persist in not being one, then you're going to lose your son."

I decided that that was it. There wasn't anything more that I could say that couldn't weaken my case. I decided I'd better shut up. I did shut up.

It seemed like a long, long time before he said anything. He was staring at the wall over my head. When he answered what I'd said, he still didn't say anything. He did better, a lot better.

He picked up the whisky in front of him. I got mine picked up in time to down it as he took a sip of his. He made a face.

"Tastes horrible," he said. "Doc, do you really *like* this stuff?"

"No," I told him. "I hate the taste of it. You're right, Clyde, it *is* horrible."

He looked at the glass in his hand and shuddered a little. I said, "Don't drink it. That sip you took proved your point. And don't try to toss it off; you'll probably choke."

He said, "I suppose you have to learn to like it. Doc, I've drunk a little wine a few times, not recently, but I didn't dislike it too much. Does Mr. Wheeler have any wine?"

"The name is Smiley," I said, "and he does." I stood up. I clapped him on the back, and it was the first time in my life I'd ever done so. I said, "Come on, Clyde, let's see what the boys in the back room will have."

I took him over to the bar, to Pete and Smiley. I told Smiley,

"We want a round, and it's on Clyde. Wine for him, and I'll take a short beer this time; I've got to rewrite a paper tonight."

I frowned at Smiley because of the utterly amazed look on his face, and he got the hint and straightened it out. He said, "Sure, Mr. Andrews. What kind of wine?"

"Do you have sherry, Mr. Wheeler?"

I said, "Clyde, meet Smiley. Smiley, Clyde."

Smiley laughed, and Clyde smiled. The smile was a bit stiff, and would take practice, but I knew and knew damned well that Harvey Andrews wasn't going to run away from home again.

He was going, henceforth, to have a father who was human. Oh, I don't mean that I expected Clyde suddenly to turn into Smiley's best customer. Maybe he'd never come back to Smiley's again. But by ordering one drink—even of wine—across a bar, he'd crossed a Rubicon. He wasn't perfect any more.

I was beginning to feel my own drinks again and I didn't really want the one Clyde bought for me, but it was an Occasion, so I took it. But I was getting in a hurry to get back across the street to the *Clarion* and get to work on all the stories I had to write, so I downed it fairly quickly and Pete and I left. Clyde left when we did, because he wanted to get back to his son; I didn't blame him for that.

At the *Clarion*, Pete checked the pot on the Linotype—and found it hot enough—while I pulled up the typewriter stand beside my desk and started abusing the ancient Underwood. I figured that, with the dope in the fact detective magazine Smiley had given me for background, I could run it to three or four columns, so I had a lot of work ahead of me. The escaped looney and Carl could wait—now that the former was captured and now that I knew Carl was safe—until I got the main story done.

I told Pete, while he was waiting for the first take, to hand set a banner head, "TAVERNKEEPER CAPTURES WANTED KILLERS," to see if it would fit. Oh, sure, I was going to put myself in the story, too, but I was going to make Smiley the hero of it, for one simple reason. He had been.

Pete had the head set up—and it fitted—by the time I had a take for him to start setting on the machine.

In the middle of the second take I realized that I didn't know for sure that Bat Masters was still alive, although I'd put it that way in the lead. I might as well find out for sure that he really was, and what condition he was in.

I knew better than to call the hospital for anything more detailed than whether he was dead or not, so I picked up the phone and called the state police office at Watertown. Willie Peeble answered.

He said, "Sure, Doc, he's alive. He's even been conscious and talked some. Thinks he's dying, so he really opened up."

"Is he dying?"

"Sure, but not the way he thinks. It'll cost the state some kilowatts. And he can't beat the rap; they've got the whole gang cold, once they catch them. There were six people—two of 'em women—killed in that bank job they pulled at Colby."

"Was George in on that?"

"Sure. He was the one that shot the women. One was a teller and the other one was a customer who was too scared to move when they told her to lie flat."

That made me feel a little better about what had happened to George. Not that it had worried me too much.

I said, "Then I can put in the story that Bat Masters confesses?"

"I dunno about that, Doc. Captain Evans is at the hospital talking to him now, and we had one report here that Masters is talking, but not the details. I don't think the cap would even bother asking him about that stuff."

"What would he ask him, then?"

"The rest of the mob, where they are There are two others besides Gene Kelley, and it'd be a real break if the cap can get out of Masters something that would help us find the others. Especially Kelley. The two we got tonight are peanuts compared to Kelley."

I said, "Thanks a lot, Willie. Listen, if anything more breaks on the story, will you give me a ring? I'll be here at the *Clarion* for a while yet."

"Sure," he said. "So long."

I hung up and went back to the story. It went sweetly. I was on the fourth take when the phone rang and it was Captain Evans of the state police, calling from the hospital where they'd taken Masters. He'd just phoned Watertown and knew about my call there.

He said, "Mr. Stoeger? You going to be there another fifteen or twenty minutes?"

I was probably going to be working another several hours, I told him.

"Fine," he said, "I'll drive right around."

That was duck soup; I'd have my story about his questioning Masters right from the horse's mouth. So I didn't bother asking him any questions over the phone.

And I found myself, when I'd finished that take, up to the point in the story where the questioning of Masters should come, so I decided I might as well wait until I'd talked to Evans, since he was going to be here so soon.

Meanwhile I might as well start checking on the other two stories again. I called Carl Trenholm, still got no answer. I called the county asylum.

Dr. Buchan, the superintendent, wasn't there, the girl at the switchboard told me; she asked if I wanted to talk to his assistant and I said yes.

She put him on and before I'd finished explaining who I was and what I wanted, he'd interrupted me. "He's on his way over to see you now, Mr. Stoeger. You're at the *Clarion* office?"

"Yes," I said, "I'm here now. And you say Dr. Buchan's on his way? That's fine."

My stories were coming to me, I thought happily, as I put the phone back. Both Captain Evans and Dr. Buchan. Now if only Carl would drop in too and explain what had happened to him.

He did. Not that exact second, but only about two minutes later. I'd wandered over to the stone and was looking gloatingly at the horrible front page with no news on it and thinking how lovely it was going to look a couple of hours from now and listening with pleasure to the click of the mats down the channels of the Linotype, when the door opened and Carl walked in.

His clothes were a little dusty and dishevelled; he had a big patch of adhesive tape on his forehead and his eyes looked a little bleary. He had a sheepish grin.

He said, "Hi, Doc. How's everything?"

"Wonderful," I told him. "What happened to you Carl?"

"That's what I dropped in to tell you, Doc. Thought you might get a garbled version of it and be worried about me."

"I couldn't even get a garbled version. No version at all; the hospital wouldn't give. What happened?"

"Got drunk. Went for a walk out the pike to sober up and got so woozy I had to lie down a minute, so I headed for the grassy strip the other side of the ditch alongside the road and—well, my foot slipped as I was stepping across the ditch and the ground, with a chunk of rock in its hand, reached up and slapped me in the face."

"Who found you, Carl?" I asked him.

He chuckled. "I don't even know. I woke up—or came to—in the sheriff's car on the way to the hospital. Tried to talk him out of taking me there, but he insisted. They checked me for a concussion and let me go."

"How do you feel now?"

"Do you really want to know?"

"Well," I said, "maybe not. Want a drink?"

He shuddered. I didn't insist. Instead, I asked him where he'd been since he'd left the hospital.

"Drinking black coffee at the Greasy Spoon. Think I'm able to make it home by now. In fact, I'm on my way. But I knew you'd have heard about it and thought you might as well have the—uh—facts straight in case—uh——"

"Don't be an ass, Carl," I told him. "You don't rate a stick of type, even if you wanted it. And, by the way, Smiley gave me the inside dope on Bonney's divorce, so I cut down the story to essentials and cut out the charges against Bonney."

"That's swell of you, Doc."

"Why didn't you tell me the truth about it yourself?" I asked him. "Afraid of interfering with the freedom of the press? Or of taking advantage of a friendship?"

"Well—somewhere in between, I guess. Anyway, thanks. Well, maybe I'll see you tomorrow. If I live that long."

He left and I wandered back to my desk. The Linotype was caught up to the typewriter by now, and I hoped Evans would show up soon—or Dr. Buchan from the asylum—so I could get ahead with at least one of the stories and not keep Pete working any later than necessary. For myself, I didn't give a damn. I was too keyed up to have been able to sleep anyway.

Well, there was one thing we could be doing to save time later. We went over to the stone and started pulling all the filler items out of the back pages so we could move back the least important stories on page one to make room for the two big stories we still had coming. We'd need at least two full page one columns—and more if we could manage it—for the capture of the bank robbers and the escape of the maniac.

We were just getting the pages unlocked, though, when Dr. Buchan came in. An elderly lady—she looked vaguely familiar to me, but I couldn't place her—was with him.

She smiled at me and said. "Do you remember me, Mr. Stoeger?" And the smile did it; I did remember her. She'd lived next door to me when I was a kid, forty-some years ago, and she'd given me cookies. And I remembered now that, while I was away at college, I'd heard that she had gone mildly, not dangerously, insane and had been taken to the asylum. That must have been—Good Lord—thirty-some years ago. She must be well over seventy by now. And her name was——

"Certainly, Mrs. Griswald," I told her. "I even remember the cookies and candy you used to give me."

And I smiled back at her. She looked so happy that one couldn't help smiling back at her.

She said, "I'm so glad you remember, Mr. Stoeger. I want you to do me a big favour—and I'm so glad you remember those days, because maybe you'll do it for me. Dr. Buchan—he's so wonderful—offered to bring me here so I could ask you. I—I really wasn't running away this evening. I was just confused. The door was open and I forgot. I was thinking that it was forty years ago and I wondered what I was doing there and why I wasn't home with Otto, and so I just started home, that's all. And by the time I remembered that Otto was dead for so long and that I was——"

The smile was tremulous now, and there were tears in her eyes. "Well, by that time I was lost and couldn't find my way back, until they found me. I even—*tried* to find my way back, once I remembered and knew where I was supposed to be."

I glanced over her head at tall Dr. Buchan and he nodded to me. But I still didn't know what it was all about. I didn't see, so I said, "I see, Mrs. Griswald."

Her smile was back. She nodded brightly. "Then you *won't* put it in the paper? About my wandering away, I mean? Because I didn't really mean to do it. And Clara, my daughter, lives in Springfield now, but she still subscribes to your paper for news from home, and if she reads in the *Clarion* that I—escaped—she'll think I'm not happy there and it'll worry her. And I *am* happy, Mr. Stoeger—Dr. Buchan is wonderful to me—and I don't want to make Clara unhappy or have her worry about me, and—you won't write it up, will you?"

I patted her shoulder gently. I said, "Of course not, Mrs. Griswald."

And then suddenly she was against my chest, crying, and I was embarrassed as hell. Until Dr. Buchan pulled her gently away and started her toward the door. He stepped back a second and said to me so quietly that she couldn't hear, "It's straight, Stoeger. I mean, it probably would worry her daughter a lot and she really wasn't escaping—she just wandered off. And her daughter really does read your paper."

"Don't worry," I said. "I won't mention it."

Past him, I could see the door open and Captain Evans of the state police was coming in. He left the door open and Mrs. Griswald was wandering through it.

Dr. Buchan shook hands quickly. He said, "Thanks a lot, then. And on my behalf as well as Mrs. Griswald's. It doesn't do an institution like ours any good to have publicity on escapes, of course. Not that I'd have asked you, myself, to suppress the story on that account. But since our patient had a really good, legitimate, reason to ask you not to——"

He happened to turn and see that his patient was already heading down the stairs. He hurried after her before she could again become confused and wander into limbo.

Another story gone, I thought, as I shook hands with Evans. Those cookies had been expensive—if worth it. I thought, suddenly, of all the stories I'd had to kill tonight. The bank burglary—for good and obvious reasons. Carl's accident—because it had been trivial after all, and writing it up would have hurt his reputation as a lawyer. The accident in the Roman candle department, because it might have lost Mrs. Carr's husband a needed job. Ralph Bonney's divorce—well, not killed, exactly, but played down from a long, important story to a short news item. Mrs. Griswald's escape from the asylum—because she'd given me cookies once and because it would have worried her daughter. Even the auction sale at the Baptist Church—for the most obvious reason of all, that it had been called off.

But what the hell did any of that matter as long as I had one really big story left, the biggest of them all? And there wasn't any conceivable reason why I couldn't print that one.

Captain Evans took the seat I pulled up for him by my desk and I sank back into the swivel chair and got a pencil ready for what he was going to tell me.

"Thanks a hell of a lot for coming here, Cap. Now what's the score about what you got out of Masters?"

He pushed his hat back on his head and frowned. He said, "I'm sorry, Doc. I'm going to have to ask you—on orders from the top—not to run the story at all."

CHAPTER EIGHT

He took his vorpal sword in hand;
Long time the manxome foe he sought—
So rested he by the Tumtum tree,
And stood a while in thought.

I DON'T know what my face looked like. I know I dropped the pencil and that I had to clear my throat when what I started to say wouldn't come out the first time.

The second time, it came out, if a bit querulously. "Cap, you're kidding me. You can't really mean it. The one big thing that's ever happened here—Is this a gag?"

He shook his head. "Nope, Doc. It's the McCoy. It comes right from the chief himself. I can't *make* you hold back the story, naturally. But I want to tell you the facts and I hope you'll decide to."

I breathed a little more freely when he said he couldn't make me hold it back. It wouldn't hurt me to listen, politely.

"Go ahead," I told him. "It had better be good."

He leaned forward. "It's this way, Doc. This Gene Kelley mob is nasty stuff. Real killers. I guess you found that out tonight about two of them. And, by the way, you did a damn good job."

"Smiley Wheeler did. I just went along for the ride."

It was a weak joke, but he laughed at it. Probably just to please me. He said, "If we can keep it quiet for about forty more hours—till Saturday afternoon—we can break up the gang completely. Including the big shot himself, Gene Kelley."

"Why Saturday afternoon?"

"Masters and Kramer had a date for Saturday afternoon with Kelley and the rest of the mob. At a hotel in Gary, Indiana. They've been separated since their last job, and they'd arranged that date to get together for the next one, see? When Kelley and the others show up for that date, well, we've got 'em.

"That is, uniess the news gets out that Masters and Kramer are already in the bag. Then Kelley and company won't show up."

"Why can't we twist one little thing in the story," I suggested. "Just say Masters and Kramer were both dead?"

He shook his head. "The other boys wouldn't take any chances. Nope, if they know our two boys were either caught or killed, they'll stay away from Gary in droves."

I sighed. I knew it wouldn't work, but I said hopefully, "Maybe none of the gang members reads the *Carmel City Clarion*."

"You know better than that, Doc. Other papers all over the country would pick it up. The Saturday morning papers would have it, even if the Friday evening editions didn't get it." He had a sudden thought and looked startled. "Say, Doc, who represents the news services here? Have they got the story yet?"

"I represent them," I said sadly. "But I hadn't wired either of them on this yet. I was going to wait till my own paper was out. They'd have fired me, sure, and it would have cost me a few bucks a year, but for once I was going to have a big story break in my own paper before I threw it to the wolves."

He said, "I'm sorry, Doc. I guess this is a big thing for you. But now, at least, you won't lose out with the news services. You can say you held the story at the request of the police—until, say, mid-afternoon Saturday. Then send it in to them and get credit for it."

"Cash, you mean. I want the credit of breaking it in the *Clarion*, damn it."

"But will you hold it up, Doc? Listen, those boys are *killers*. You'll be saving lives if you let us get them. Do you know anything about Gene Kelley?"

I nodded; I'd been reading about him in the magazine Smiley had lent me. He wasn't a very nice man. Evans was right in saying it would cost human lives to print that story if the story kept Kelley out of the trap he'd otherwise walk into.

I looked up and Pete was standing there listening. I tried to judge from his face what he thought about it, but he was keeping it carefully blank.

I scowled at him and said, "Shut off that God damn Linotype. I can't hear myself think."

He went and shut it off.

Evans looked relieved. He said, "Thanks, Doc." For no reason at all—the evening was moderately cool—he pulled out a handkerchief and wiped his forehead. "What a break it was that Masters hated the rest of the mob enough to turn them in for us when he figured he was done himself. And that you're willing to hold the story till we get 'em. Well, you can use it next week."

There wasn't any use telling him that I could also print a chapter or two of Cœsar's *Gallic Wars* next week; it was ancient history too.

So I didn't say anything and after a few more seconds he got up and left.

It seemed awfully quiet without the Linotype running. Pete came over. He said, "Well, Doc, we still got that nine-inch hole in the front page that you said you'd find some way of filling in the morning. Maybe while we're here anyway——"

I ran my fingers through what is left of my hair. "Run it as it is, Pete," I told him, "except with a black border around it."

"Look, Doc, I can pull forward that story on the Ladies' Aid election and if I reset it narrow measure to fit a box, it'll maybe run long enough."

I couldn't think of anything better. I said, "Sure, Pete," but when he started toward the Linotype to turn it back on, I said, "But not tonight, Pete. In the morning. It's half-past eleven. Get home to the wife and kiddies."

"But I'd just as soon——"

"Get the hell out of here," I said, "before I bust out blubbering. I don't want anybody to see me do it."

He grinned to show he knew I didn't really mean it and said, "Sure, Doc. I'll get down a little early, then. Seven-thirty. You going to stick around a while now?"

"A few minutes," I said, "'Night, Pete. Thanks for coming down, and everything."

I kept sitting at my desk for a minute after he'd left, and I didn't blubber, but I wanted to all right. It didn't seem possible that so much had happened and that I couldn't get even a stick of type out of any of it. For a few minutes I wished that I was a son-of-a-bitch instead of a sucker so I could go ahead and print it all. Even if it let the Kelley mob get away to do more killing, lost my housekeeper's husband her job, made a fool out of Carl Trenholm, worried Mrs. Griswald's daughter and ruined Harvey Andrew's reputation by telling how he'd been caught robbing his father's bank while running away from home. And while I was at it, I might as well smear Ralph Bonney by listing the untrue charges brought against him in the divorce case and write a humorous little item about the leader of the local antisaloon faction setting up a round for the boys at Smiley's. And even run the rummage sale story om the ground that the cancellation had been too late and let a few dozen citizens make a trip in vain. It would be wonderful to be a son-of-a-bitch instead of a sucker so I could do all that. Sons-of-bitches must have more fun than people. And definitely they get out bigger and better newspapers.

I wandered over and looked at the front page lying there on the stone, and for something to do I dropped the filler items back in page four. The ones we'd taken out to let us move back the present junk from page one to make room for all the big stories we were going to break. I locked up the page again.

It was quiet as hell.

I wondered why I didn't get out of there and have another

drink—or a hell of a lot of drinks—at Smiley's. I wondered why I didn't want to get stinking drunk. But I didn't.

I wandered over to the window and stood staring down at the quiet street. They hadn't rolled the sidewalks in yet—closing time for taverns is midnight in Carmel City—but nobody was walking on them.

A car went by and I recognized it as Ralph Bonney's car, heading probably, to pick up Miles Harrison and take him over to Neilsville to pick up the night side pay roll for the fireworks plant, including the Roman candle department. To which I had briefly——

I decided I'd smoke one more cigarette and then go home. I reached into my pocket and pulled out the cigarette package and something fluttered to the floor—a card.

I picked it up and stared at it. It read:

Yehudi Smith

Suddenly the dead night was alive again. I'd written off Yehudi Smith when I'd heard that the escaped lunatic had been captured. I'd written him off so completely that I'd forgotten to write him on again when Dr. Buchan had brought in Mrs. Griswald to talk to me.

Yehudi Smith *wasn't* the escaped lunatic.

Suddenly I wanted to jump into the air and click my heels together, I wanted to run, I wanted to tell.

Then I remembered how long I'd been gone and I almost ran to the telephone on my desk. I gave my own number and my heart sank as it rang once, twice, thrice—and then after the fourth ring Smith's voice answered with a sleepy-sounding hello.

I said, "This is Doc Stoeger, Mr. Smith. I'm starting home now. Want to apologize for having kept you waiting so long. Some things happened."

"Good. I mean, good that you're coming now. What time is it?"

"About half-past eleven. I'll be there in fifteen minutes. And thanks for waiting."

I hurried into my coat and grabbed my hat. I almost forgot to turn out the lights and lock the door.

Smiley's first, but not for a drink; I picked up a bottle to take along. The one at my house had been getting low when I left; only God knew what had happened to it since.

Leaving Smiley's with the bottle, I swore again at the fact that my car was laid up with those flat tyres. Not that it's a long walk or that I mind walking in the slightest when I'm not in a hurry, but again I was in a hurry. Last time it had been because I thought Carl Trenholm was dead or seriously injured—and to get away from Yehudi Smith. This time it was to get back to him.

Past the post office, now dark. The bank, this time with the night light on and no evidence of crime in sight. Past the spot where the Buick had pulled up and a voice had asked someone named Buster what town this was. There wasn't a car in sight now, friend or foe. Past everything that I'd passed so many thousand times, and off the main street into the friendly, pleasant side streets no longer infested with homicidal maniacs or other horrors. I didn't look behind me once, all the way home.

I felt so good I felt silly. Best of all I was cold-sobered by everything that had been happening, and I was ready and in the mood for a few more drinks and some more screwy conversation.

I still didn't completely believe he'd be there, but he was.

And he looked so familiar sitting there that I wondered why I'd doubted. I said "Hi", and shied my hat at the hat-rack and it hit a peg and stayed there. That was the first time that had happened in months so I knew from that that I was lucky tonight. As if I needed that to prove it.

I took the seat across from him, just as we'd been sitting before, and I poured us each a drink—still from the first bottle; apparently he hadn't drunk much while I'd been gone—and started to renew the apologies I'd made over the phone for having been away so long.

He waved the apologies away with a casual gesture. "It doesn't matter at all, as long as you got back." He smiled. "I had a nice nap."

We touched glasses and drank. He said, "Let's see; just where were we when you got that phone call—oh, which reminds me; you said it was about an accident to a friend. May I ask——?"

"He's all right," I told him. "Nothing serious. It was—well, other things kept coming up that kept me away so long."

"Good. Then—oh, yes, I remember. When the phone rang we were talking about the Roman candle department. We'd just drunk to it."

I remembered and nodded. "That's where I've been, ever since I left here."

"Seriously?"

"Quite," I said. "They fired me half an hour ago, but it was fun while it lasted. Wait; no, it wasn't. I won't lie to you. At the time it was happening, it was pretty horrible."

His eyebrows went up a little. "Then you're serious. Something did happen. You know, Doctor——"

"Doc," I said.

"You know, Doc, you're different. Changed, somehow."

I refilled our glasses, still from the first bottle, although that round killed it.

"It's temporary, I think. Yes, Mr. Smith, I had——"

"Smitty," he said.

"Yes, Smitty. I had a rather bad experience, while it lasted, and I'm still in reaction from it, but the reaction won't last. I'm still jittery from it and I may be even more jittery tomorrow when I realize what a narrow squeak I had, but I'm still the same guy. Doc. Stoeger, fifty-three, genial failure both as a hero and as an editor."

Silence for a few seconds and then he said, "Doc, I like you. I think you're a swell guy. I don't know what happened, and I don't suppose you want to tell me, but I'll bet you one thing."

"Thanks, Smitty," I said. "And it's not that I don't want to tell you what happened this evening; it's just that I don't want to talk about it at all, right now. Some other time I'll be glad to tell you, but right now I want to stop thinking about it—and start thinking about Lewis Carroll again. What's the one thing you want to bet me, though?"

"That you're not a failure as an editor. As a hero, maybe—damned few of us are heroes. But I'll bet you said you were a failure as an editor because you killed a story—for some good reason. And not a selfish one. Would I win that bet?"

"You would," I said. I didn't tell him he'd have won it five times over. "But I'm not proud of myself—the only thing is that I'd have been ashamed of myself otherwise. This way, I'm going to be ashamed of my paper. All newspapermen, Smitty, should be sons-of-bitches."

"Why?" And before I could answer he tossed off the drink I'd just poured him—tossed it off as before with that fascinating trick of the glass never really nearing his lips—and answered it himself with a more unanswerable question. "So that newspapers will be more entertaining?—at the expense of human lives they might wreck or even destroy?"

The mood was gone, or the mood was wrong. I shook myself a little. I said, "Let's get back to Jabberwocks. And—My God, every time I get to talking seriously it sobers me up. I had such a nice edge early in the evening. Let's have another—and to Lewis Carroll again. And then go back to the gobbledegook you were giving me, the stuff that sounded like Einstein on a binge."

He grinned. "Wonderful word, gobbledegook. Carroll might have originated it, except that there was less of it in his time. All right, Doc, to Carroll."

And again his glass was empty. It was a trick I'd *have* to learn, no matter how much time it took or how much whisky it wasted. But, the first time, in private.

I drank mine and it was the third since I'd come home, fifteen minutes ago; I was beginning to feel them. Not that I feel three drinks starting from scratch, but these didn't start from scratch. I'd had quite a few early in the evening, before the fresh air of my little ride with Bat and George had cleared my head, and several at Smiley's thereafter.

They were hitting me now. Not hard, but definitely.

There was a mistiness about the room. We were talking about Carroll and mathematics again, or Yehudi Smith was talking, anyway, and I was trying to concentrate on what he was saying. He seemed, for a moment, to blur a little and to advance and recede as I looked at him. And his voice was a blur, too, a blur of sines and cosines. I shook my head to clear it a bit and decided I'd better lay off the bottle for a while.

Then I realized that what he'd just said was a question and I begged his pardon.

"The clock on your mantel," he repeated, "is it correct?"

I managed to focus my eyes on it. Ten minutes to twelve, I said, "Yes, it's right. It's still early. You're not thinking of going, surely. I'm a little woozy at the moment, but——"

"How long will it take us to get there from here? I have directions how to reach it, of course, but you could probably estimate the time it will take us better than I can."

For a second I stared at him blankly, wondering what he was talking about.

Then I remembered.

We were going to a haunted house to hunt a Jabberwock—or something.

CHAPTER NINE

"First, the fish must be caught."
That is easy: a baby, I think, could have caught it.
"Next, the fish must be bought."
That is easy: a penny, I think would have bought it.

MAYBE you won't believe that I could have forgotten that, but I had. So much had happened between the time I'd left my house and the time I returned that it's a wonder, I suppose, that I still remembered my own name, and Yehudi's.

Ten minutes before twelve and we were due there, he'd said, at one o'clock.

"You have a car?" I asked him.

He nodded. "A few doors down. I got out at the wrong place to look for street numbers, but I was close enough that I didn't bother moving the car."

"Then somewhere between twenty and thirty minutes will get us there," I told him.

"Fine, Doctor. Then we've got forty minutes yet if we allow half an hour."

The woozy spell was passing fast, but I refilled his glass this time without refilling my own. I wanted to sober up a bit—not completely, because if I was sober, I might get sensible and decide not to go, and I didn't want to decide not to go.

Smith had settled back in his chair, not looking at me, so I looked at him, and wondered what I was doing even to listen to the absurd story he'd told me about Vorpal Blades and the old Wentworth house.

He wasn't the escaped lunatic, but that didn't mean he wasn't a screwball, and that I wasn't a worse one. What the hell *were* we going to do out there? Try to fish a Bandersnatch out of limbo? Or break through a looking-glass or dive down a rabbit hole to go hunting one in its native element?

Well, as long as I didn't get sober enough to spoil things, it was wonderful. Crazy or not, I was having a marvellous time. The best time I'd had since the Halloween almost forty years ago when we——But never mind that; it's a sign of old age to reminisce about the things you did when you were young, and I'm not old yet. Not very, anyway.

Yes, my eyes were focusing all right again now, but the mistiness in the room was still there and I realized that it wasn't mistiness but smoke. I looked across at the window and wondered if I wanted it open badly enough to get up and open it.

The window. A black square framing the night.

The midnight. *Where were you at midnight?* With Yehudi. *Who's Yehudi?* A little man who wasn't there. But I have the card. *Let's see it, Doc. Hmmm. What's your bug number?* My bug number?

And the black rook takes the white knight.

The smoke was definitely too thick, and so was I. I walked to the window and threw up the bottom sash. The lights behind me made it a mirror. There was my reflection. An insignificant little man with greying hair, and glasses, and a necktie badly askew.

He grinned at me and straightened his necktie. I remembered the verse from Carroll that Al Grainger had quoted at me early in the evening:

> *"You are old, Father William," the young man said.*
> *"And your hair has become very white.*
> *And yet you incessantly stand on your head.*
> *Do you think, at your age, it is right?"*

And that made me think of Al Grainger. I wondered if there was still any chance of his showing up. I'd told him to come around any time up to midnight and it was that now. I wished now that he would come. Not for chess. as we'd planned, but so he could go along on our expedition. Not that I was exactly afraid, but—well, I wished that Al Grainger would show up.

It occurred to me that he might have come or phoned and that Yehudi had failed to mention it. I asked him,

He shook his head. "No, Doc. Nobody came and the only phone call was the one you yourself made just before you came home."

So that was that, unless Al showed up in the next half hour or unless I phoned him. And I didn't want to do that. I'd been enough of a coward earlier in the evening.

Just the same I felt a little hollow——

My God, I *was* hollow. I'd had a sandwich late in the afternoon, but that had been eight hours ago and I hadn't eaten anything since. No wonder the last couple of drinks had hit me.

I suggested to Yehudi that we raid the icebox and he said it sounded like a wonderful idea to him. And it must have been, for it turned out that he was hungry as I. Between us we killed a pound of boiled ham, most of a loaf of rye and a medium-sized jar of pickles.

It was almost half-past twelve when we finished. There was just time for a stirrup cup, and we had one. With food in my stomach, it tasted much better and went down much more smoothly than the last one had. It tasted so good, in fact, that I decided to take the bottle—we'd started the second one by then—along with us. We might, after all, run into a blizzard.

"Ready to go?" Smith asked.

I decided I'd better put the window down. In its reflecting pane, over my shoulder I could see Yehudi Smith standing by the door waiting for me. The reflection was clear and sharp; it brought out the bland roundness of his face, the laughter-tracks around his mouth and eyes, the rotund absurdity of his body.

And an impulse made me walk over and hold out my hand to him and shake his hand when he put it into mine rather wonderingly. We hadn't shaken hands when we'd introduced ourselves on the porch and something made me want to do it now. I don't mean that I'm clairvoyant. I'm not, or I'd never have gone. No, I don't know why I shook hands with him.

Just an impulse, but one I'm very glad I followed. Just as I'm glad I'd given him food and drink instead of letting him go to his strange death sober or on an empty stomach.

And I'm even gladder that I said, "Smitty, I like you."

He looked pleased, but somehow embarrassed. He said, "Thanks, Doc," but for the first time his eyes didn't quite meet mine.

We went out and walked up the quiet street to where he'd left his car, and got in.

It's odd how clearly you remember some things and how vague others are. I recall that there was a push-button radio on the dashboard and that the button for WBBM was pushed in, and I recall that the gear shift knob was brightly polished onyx. But I don't recall whether the car was a coupé or a sedan, and haven't the vaguest idea what make or colour it was. I recall that the engine was quite noisy—my only clue as to whether it was an old car or a new one, that and the fact that the gear shift was on the floor and not on the steering-wheel post.

I remembered that he drove well and carefully and talked little, probably because of the noisiness of the motor.

I directed him, but I don't recall now, not that it matters, what route we took. I remember, though, that I didn't recognize the driveway of the old Wentworth place—the house itself was set quite far back from the road and you couldn't see it through the trees even in daylight—but a little farther on I recognized the farm that an aunt and uncle of mine had lived in many years ago and knew we'd passed our objective.

He turned back, then, and this time I spotted the driveway and we turned in and followed the drive back among the trees to the house itself. We parked alongside it.

"First ones here," Smith said in the hushed silence as he turned off the engine.

I got out of the car and—I don't know why; or do I?—I took the bottle with me. It was so dark outside that I couldn't see the bottle in front of my eyes as I tilted it upward.

Smith had turned out the headlights and was getting out of his side of the car. He had a flashlight in his hand and I could see again as he came around to my side of the car. I held out the bottle to him and said, "Want one?" and he said, "You read my mind, Doc," and took one. My eyes were getting a little used to the dark now and I could see the outlines of the house, and I thought about it.

God, but the place must be old, I realized. I knew it well from the weeks in summer when, as a kid, I'd visited my aunt and uncle just down the road for a taste of farm life—as against the big city of Carmel City, Illinois.

That had been over forty years ago and it had been old then, and untenanted. It had been lived in since, but for brief intervals. Why the few people who had tried to live there had left, I didn't know. They'd never complained—publicly, at least—of its being haunted. But none had ever stayed there for long. Perhaps it was merely the house itself; it really was a depressing place. A year or more ago the *Clarion* had carried an ad. for the rental of it—and at a very reasonable price—but no one had taken it.

I thought of Johnny Haskins, who lived on the farm between my uncle's place and this one. He and I had explored the place several times together, in daylight. Johnny was dead now. He'd been killed in France in 1918, near the end of the First World War. In daytime, I hope, for Johnny had always been afraid of the dark—just as I was afraid of heights and as Al Grainger was afraid of fire and as everyone is afraid of something or other.

Johnny had been afraid of the old Wentworth place, too—even more afraid than I was, although he was several years older than I. He'd believed in ghosts, a little; at least he'd been afraid of them, although not as afraid as he was of the dark. And I'd picked up a little of that fear from him and I'd kept it for quite a few years after I grew up.

But not any more. The older you get the less afraid of ghosts you are—whether you believe in them or not. By the time you pass the fifty mark you've known so many people who are now dead that ghosts, if there are any such, aren't all strangers. Some of your best friends are ghosts; why should you be afraid of them? And it's not too many years before you'll all be on the other side of the fence yourself.

No, I wasn't afraid of ghosts or the dark or of the haunted house, but I was afraid of something. I wasn't afraid of Yehudi Smith, I liked him too well to be afraid of him. Undoubtedly I was a fool to come here with him, knowing nothing at all about him. Yet I would have bet money at long odds that he wasn't dangerous. A crackpot, maybe, but not a dangerous one.

Smith opened the car door again and said, "I just remembered I brought candles; they told me the electricity wouldn't be on. And there's another flashlight in here, if you want one, Doc."

Sure I wanted one. I felt a little better, a little less afraid of whatever I was afraid of once I had a flashlight of my own and was in no sudden danger of being alone in darkness.

I ran the beam of the flashlight up on the porch, and the house was just as I remembered it. It had been lived in just often enough for it to have been kept in repair, or at least in fairly good shape.

Yehudi Smith said, "Come on, Doc. We might as well wait inside," and led the way up the porch steps. They creaked as we walked up them but they were solid.

The front door wasn't locked. Smith must have known that it wouldn't be, from the confident way he opened it.

We went in and he closed the door behind us. The beams of our flashlights danced ahead of us down the long dimness of the hallway. I noticed with surprise that the place was carpeted and furnished; it had been empty and bare at the time I'd explored it as a kid. The most recent tenant or owner who had lived here, for whatever reason he had moved away, had left the place furnished, possibly hoping to rent or sell it that way.

We turned into a huge living-room on the left of the hallway. There was furniture there, too, white-sheeted. Covered fairly recently, from the fact that the sheets were not too dirty nor was there a great amount of dust anywhere.

Something made the back of my neck prickle. Maybe the ghostly appearance of that sheeted furniture.

"Shall we wait here or go up in the attic?" Smith asked me.

"The attic? Why the attic?"

"Where the meeting is to be held."

I was getting to like this less and less. *Was* there going to be a meeting? Were others really coming here tonight?

It was five minutes of one o'clock already.

I looked around and wondered whether I'd rather stay here or go on up into the attic. Either alternative seemed crazy. Why didn't I go home? Why hadn't I stayed there?

I didn't like that spectral white-covered furniture. I said, "Let's go on up into the attic. Might as well, I guess."

Yes, I'd come this far. I might as well see it through the rest of the way. If there was a looking-glass up there in the attic and he wanted us to walk through it, I'd do that, too. Provided only that he went first.

But I wanted another short nip out of that bottle I was carrying. I offered it to Smith and he shook his head so I went ahead and took the nip and it slightly warmed the coldness that was beginning to develop in my stomach.

We went up the stairs to the second floor and we didn't meet any ghosts or any snarks. We opened the door that led to the steps to the attic.

We walked up them, Smith in the lead and I following, his plump posterior just ahead of me.

My mind kept reminding me how ridiculous this was. How utterly insane it was for me to have come here at all.

Where were you at one o'clock? In a haunted house. *Doing what?* Waiting for the Vorpal Blades to come. *What are these Vorpal Blades?* I don't know. *What were they going to do?* I don't know, I tell you. Maybe anything. Get with child a mandrake root. Hold court to see who stole the tarts or put the white knight back on his horse. Or maybe only read the minutes of the last meeting and the treasurer's report, by Benchley. *Who's Benchley?* WHO'S YEHUDI?

Who's your little whoozis?

Doc, I hate to say this, but——

I'm afraid that——

Very pitying, and oh, so sensibly true. *You were drunk, weren't you, Doc?* Well, not exactly, but——

Yehudi Smith's plump posterior ascending the attic stairs. A horse's posterior ascending after him.

We reached the top and Smith asked me to hold my flashlight aimed at the post of the stair railing until he got a candle lighted there. He took a short, thick candle from his pocket—one that would balance easily by itself without a holder—and got it lighted.

There were trunks and a few pieces of broken or wornout furniture scattered about the sides of the attic; the middle of it was clear. The only window was at the back and it was boarded up from the inside.

I looked around and, although the furniture here wasn't sheeted, I didn't like the place any better than I'd liked the big room downstairs. The light of one candle was far too dim to dispel the darkness, for one thing, in so large a space. And I didn't like the flickering shadows it cast. They might have been Jabberwocks or anything your imagination wanted to name them. There ought to be Rorschach tests with flickering shadows; what the mind would make out of them ought to be a lot more revealing than what the mind makes out of ink blots.

Yes, I could have used more light, a lot more light. But Smith had put his flashlight in his pocket and I did the same with the other one; it was his, too, and I didn't have any excuse to wear out the battery keeping it on. And besides it didn't do much good in so large a room.

"What do we do now?" I asked.

"Wait for the others. What time is it, Doc?"

I managed to read my watch by the light of the candle and told him that it was seven minutes after one.

He nodded. "We'll give them until a quarter after. There's something that I must do then, at the exact time, whether they're here or not. Listen, isn't that a car?"

I listened and I thought it was. Way up here in the attic, it wasn't clearly audible, but I thought I heard a car that could have been coming back from the main road to the house. I was pretty sure of it.

I uncorked the bottle again and offered it. This time Smith took a drink, too. Mine was a fairly long pull. I was getting sober, I thought, and this was no time or place to get sober. It was silly enough to be here, drunk.

I couldn't hear the car any more, and then suddenly—as though it had stopped and then started again—I could hear it, and louder than before. But the sound seemed to diminish as though the car had driven back from the road, stopped a minute, and then headed for the main road again. The sound died out.

The shadows flickered. There was no sound from downstairs.

I shivered a little.

Smith said, "Help me look for something, Doc. It's supposed to be here somewhere, ready. A small table."

"A table?"

"Yes, but don't touch if it you find it."

He had his flashlight out again and was working his way along one wall of the attic, and I went the other way, glad of a chance to use my flashlight on those damned shadows. I wondered what the hell kind of a table I was looking for. Thou preparest a table before me in the presence of mine enemies, I thought. But there weren't any of my enemies here, I hoped.

I found it first. It was in the back corner of the attic.

It was a small, three-legged, glass-topped table, and there were two small objects lying on it.

I started laughing. Ghosts and shadows or not, I laughed out loud. One of the objects on the table was a small key and the other was a small vial with a tag tied to it.

The glass-topped table Alice had found in the hall at the bottom of the rabbit hole—the table on which had been the key that opened the little door to the garden and the bottle with the paper label that said, "DRINK ME" tied around its neck.

I'd seen that table often—in the John Tenniel illustration of it in *Alice in Wonderland*.

Smith's footsteps coming up behind me made me stop laughing. After all, this ridiculous flummery might be something of a ritual to him. It was funny to me, but I liked him and I didn't want to hurt his feelings.

He wasn't even smiling. He said. "Yes, that's it. Is it one-fifteen yet?"

"Almost on the head."

"Good." He picked up the key with one hand and the bottle with the other. "The others must be delayed, but we shall take the first step. This, keep." He dropped the key into my pocket. "And this, I drink." He took the cork out of the bottle. "I apologize for not being able to share it with you—as you have so generously shared your drinks with me—but you understand, until you have been fully initiated——"

He seemed genuinely embarrassed, so I nodded understanding and forgiveness.

I wasn't afraid any more, now. It had become too ridiculous for fear. What was that "drink me" bottle supposed to do? Oh, yes, he'd shrink in size until he was only a few inches high—and then he'd have to find and use a little box labelled "EAT ME" and eat the cake inside and he'd suddenly grow so big that——

He lifted the bottle and said, "To Lewis Carroll."

Since that was the toast, I said, "Wait!" and got the cork quickly out of the bottle of whisky I was still carrying, and raised it, too. There wasn't any reason why I couldn't and shouldn't get in on that toast as long as my lips, as a neophyte's, didn't defile whatever sacred elixir the "drink me" bottle held.

He clinked the little bottle lightly against the big one I held, and tossed it off—I could see from the corner of my eye as I tilted my bottle—in that strange conjuring trick again, the bottle stopping inches away from his lips and the drink keeping on going without the loss of a drop.

I was putting the cork into the whisky bottle when Yehudi Smith died.

He dropped the bottle labelled "DRINK ME" and started to clutch at his throat, but he died, I think, even before the bottle hit the floor. His face was hideously contorted with pain, but the pain couldn't have lasted over a fraction of a second. His eyes, still open, went suddenly blank, utterly blank. And the thud of his fall shook the floor under my feet, seemed to shake the whole house.

CHAPTER TEN

And, as in uffish thought he stood,
The Jabberwock, with eyes of flame,
Came whiffling through the tulgey wood,
And burbled as it came!

I THINK I must have done nothing but stand there and jitter for seconds. Finally I was able to move.

I'd seen his face and I'd seen and heard him fall; I didn't have the slightest doubt that he was dead. But I had to be sure. I got down on my knees and groped my hand inside his coat and shirt, hunting for a heartbeat. There wasn't any.

I made even surer. The flashlight he'd given he had a round flat lens; I held it over his mouth and in front of his nostrils for a while and there was no slightest trace of moisture.

The small empty bottle from which he'd drunk was of fairly heavy glass. It hadn't broken when he'd dropped it, and the tag tied around its neck had kept it from rolling far. I didn't touch it, but I got on my hands and knees and sniffed at the open end. The smell was the smell of good whisky, nothing else that I could detect. No odour of bitter almonds, but if what had been in that whisky hadn't been prussic acid it had been some corrosive poison just about as strong. Or could it have been prussic, and would the smell of whisky have blanketed the bitter almond smell? I didn't know.

I stood up again and found that my knees were shaking. This was the second man I'd seen die tonight. But I hadn't so much minded about George. He'd had it coming, for one thing, and for another his body had been inside the crumpled-up car; I'd not actually seen him die. Nor had I been alone then; Smiley had been with me. I'd have given my whole bank account, all three hundred and twelve dollars of it, to have had Smiley with me there in the attic.

I wanted to get out of there, fast, and I was too scared to move. I thought I'd be less scared if I could figure out what it was all about, but it was sheerly mad. It didn't make sense that even a madman would have brought me out here under so weird a pretext so that I could be an audience of one to his suicide.

In fact, if I was sure of anything, I was sure that Smith hadn't killed himself. But who had, and why? The Vorpal Blades? *Was* there such a group?

Where were they? Why hadn't they come?

A sudden thought put shivers down my spine. *Maybe they had.* I'd thought I heard a car come and go, while we'd waited. Why couldn't it have dropped off passengers? Waiting for me downstairs—or even now creeping up the attic steps towards me.

I looked that way. The candle flickered and the shadows danced. I strained my ears, but there wasn't any sound. No sound anywhere.

I was afraid to move, and then gradually I found that I was afraid not to move. I had to get *out* of here before I went crazy. If anything was downstairs I'd rather go down and meet it than wait till it decided to come up here after me.

I wished to hell and back that I hadn't given Smiley that revolver, but wishing didn't get me the revolver back.

Well, the whisky bottle was a weapon of sorts. I shifted the flashlight to my left hand and picked up the whisky bottle, by its neck, in my right. It was still more than half-full and heavy enough for a bludgeon.

I tiptoed to the head of the steps. I don't know why I tiptoed unless it was to avoid scaring myself worse by making noise; we hadn't been quiet up here before and Smith's fall had shaken the whole house. If anyone was downstairs, he knew he wasn't alone in the building.

I looked at the square post at the top of the railing and the short, thick candle still burning on top of it. I didn't want to touch it; I wanted to be able to say that I hadn't touched anything at all, except to feel for a heartbeat that wasn't there. Yet I couldn't leave the candle burning, either; it might set the house afire if it fell over, as Smith hadn't anchored it down with molten wax but had merely stood it on its base.

I compromised by blowing it out but not touching it otherwise.

My flashlight showed me there was nothing or no one on the stairs leading down to the second floor and that the door at the bottom of them was still closed, as we had left it. Before I started down them I took one last look around the attic with my flash. The shadows jumped as the beam swept around the walls, and then, for some reason, I brought the circle of light to rest on Yehudi Smith's body lying sprawled there on the floor, eyes wide open and still staring unseeingly at the rafters overhead, his face still frozen in the grimace of that horrible, if brief, pain in which he'd died.

I hated to leave him alone there in the dark. Silly and sentimental as the thought was. I couldn't help feeling that way. He'd been such a nice little guy. Who the hell had killed him, and why, and why in such a bizarre manner, and what was it all about? And he'd said it was dangerous to come here tonight, and he was dead right, as far as he himself was concerned. And I——?

With that thought, I was afraid again. I wasn't out of here yet. Was someone or something waiting downstairs?

The attic stairs were uncarpeted and they squeaked so loudly that I gave up trying to walk quietly and hurried. The attic door creaked, too, but nothing was waiting for me on the other side of it. Or downstairs, I flashed my light into the big living room as I passed the doorway and got a momentary fright as I thought something white was coming toward me—but it was only the sheeted table and it had only seemed to move.

The porch and down the porch steps.

The car was still there on the driveway beside the house. It was a coupé, I noticed now, and the same make and model as mine. My feet crunched gravel as I walked to it; I was still scared but I didn't dare let myself run. I wondered if Smith had left the key in the car, and hoped frantically that he had. I should have thought of it while I was still in the attic and could have felt in his pockets. I wouldn't go back up there now, I realized, for anything in the world. I'd walk back to town first.

At least the car door wasn't locked. I slid in under the wheel, and flashed my light on the dashboard. Yes, the ignition key was in the lock. I slammed the door behind me and felt a little more secure inside the closed car.

I turned the key and stepped on the starter and the engine started the first try. I shifted into low gear and then, before I let out the clutch, I carefully shifted back into neutral again and sat there with the motor idling.

This wasn't the car in which Yehudi Smith had driven me here. The gear shift knob was hard rubber with a ridge around it, not the smooth onyx ball I'd noticed on the gear shift lever of his car. It was like the one on my car, which was back home in the garage with two flat tyres that I hadn't got around to fixing.

I turned on the dome light, although by then I didn't really have to. I knew already from the feel of the controls in starting and in shifting, from the sound of the engine, from a dozen little things.

This was *my car.*

It was so impossible that I forgot to be afraid, that I was in such a hurry to get away from the house. Oh, there was a little logic in my lack of fear, too; if anybody had been laying for me, the house would have been the place. He wouldn't have let me get this far and he wouldn't have left the ignition key in the car so I could get away in it.

I got out of the car and looked, with the flashlight, at the two tyres which had been flat this morning. They weren't flat now. Either someone had fixed them, or someone had simply let the air out of them last night and had subsequently pumped them up again with the hand pump I keep in my luggage compartment. The second idea seemed more likely; now that I thought of it, it was strange that two tyres—both in good shape and with good tubes in them—should have gone flat, completely flat, at the same time and while the car was standing in my garage.

I walked all the way around the car, looking at it, and there wasn't anything wrong with it that I could see. I got back in under the wheel and sat there a minute with the engine running, wondering if it was even remotely possible that Yehudi Smith had driven me here in my own car.

No, I decided, not remotely. I hadn't noticed his car at all except for three things, but those three things were plenty to make me sure. Beside the gear shift knob, I remembered that push-button radio with the button for WBBM pushed in—and my car has no radio at all—and there was the fact that his engine was noisy and mine is quiet. Right then, with it idling, I could barely hear it.

Unless I was crazy——

Could I have imagined that other car? For that matter, could I have imagined Yehudi Smith? Could I have driven out here by myself in my own car, gone up to the attic alone——?

It's a horrible thing to suspect yourself suddenly of complete insanity, equipped with hallucinations.

I realized I'd better quit thinking along those lines, here alone in a car, alone in the night, parked beside a haunted house. I might drive myself nutty, if I wasn't already.

I took a long drink out of the bottle that was now on the seat beside me, and then drove out to the highway and back to town. I didn't drive fast, partly because I was a little drunk—physically anyway. The horrible thing that had happened up in the attic, the fantastic, incredible death of Yehudi Smith, had shocked me sober, mentally.

I *couldn't* have imagined——

But at the edge of town the doubts came back, then the answer to them. I pulled to the side of the road and turned on the dome light. I had the card and the key and the flashlight, those three souvenirs of my experience. I took the flashlight out of my coat pocket and looked at it. Just a dime-store flashlight; it meant nothing except that it wasn't mine. The card was the thing. I hunted in several pockets, getting worried as hell, before I found it in the pocket of my shirt. Yes, I had it, and it still read *Yehudi Smith*. I felt a little better as I put it back in my pocket. While I was at it, I looked at the key, too. The key that had been with the "DRINK ME" bottle on the glass-topped table.

It was still there in the pocket Smith had dropped it into; I'd not touched it or looked at it closely. It was, of course, the wrong kind of key, but I'd noticed that at first glance when I'd seen it on the table in the attic; that had been part of my source of amusement when I'd laughed. It was a Yale key, and it should have been a small gold key, the one Alice used to open the fifteen-inch-high door into the lovely garden.

Come to think of it, all three of those props in the attic had been wrong, one way or another. The table had been a glass-topped one, but it should have been an all-glass table; the wooden legs were wrong. The key shouldn't have been a nickel-plated Yale, and the "DRINK ME" should not have contained poison. (*It had, in fact, a sort of mixed flavour of cherry-tart, custard, pine-apple, roast turkey, toffy, and hot buttered toast.*)—according to Alice. It couldn't have tasted anything like that to Smith.

I started driving again, slowly. Now that I was back in town I had to make up my mind whether I was going to the sheriff's office or going to call the state police. Reluctantly I decided I'd better go right to the sheriff. Definitely this case was in his department, unless he called on the state police for help. They'd dump it in his lap anyway, even if I called them. And he hated my guts enough as it was, without my making it any worse by by-passing him in reporting a major crime. Not that I didn't hate his guts just as much, but tonight he was in a better position to make trouble for me than I was for him.

So I parked my coupé across the street from the courthouse and took one more swig from the bottle to give me courage to tell Kates the story I was going to have to tell him. Then I marched myself across the street and up the courthouse stairs to the sheriff's office on the second floor. If I was lucky, I thought, Kates might be out and his deputy, Hank Ganzer, might be there.

I wasn't lucky. Hank wasn't there at all, and Kates was talking on the phone. He glared at me when I came in and then went back to his call.

"Hell, I could have done it on the phone from here. Go see the guy. Wake him up and be sure he's awake enough to remember any little thing that might have been said. Yeah, then call me again before you start back."

He put the receiver down and his swivel chair squeaked shrilly as he swung about to face me. He yelled, "There isn't any story on it yet." Rance Kates always yells; I've never heard him say anything in a quiet tone, or even a normal one. His voice matches his red face, which always looks angry. I've often wondered if he looks like that even when he's in bed. Wondered, but had no inclination to find out.

What he'd just yelled at me, though, made so little sense that I just looked at him.

I said, "I've come to report a murder, Kates."

"Huh?" He looked interested. "You mean you found either Miles or Bonney?"

For a minute neither name registered at all. I said, "The man's name is Smith." I thought I'd better sneak up on the Yehudi part gradually, maybe let Kates read it himself off the card. "The body is in the attic of the old Wentworth place out on the pike."

"Stoeger, are you drunk?"

"I've been drinking," I told him. "I'm not drunk." At least I hoped I wasn't. Maybe that last one I'd taken in the car just before I'd left it had been one too many. My voice sounded thick, even to me, and I had a hunch my eyes were looking a trifle bleary from the outside; they were beginning to feel that way from my side of them.

"What were you doing in the attic of the Wentworth place? You mean you were there tonight?"

I wished again that Hank Ganzer had been there instead of Kates. Hank would have taken my word for it and gone out for the body; then my story wouldn't have sounded so incredible when I'd have got around to telling it.

I said, "Yes, I just came from there. I went there with Smith, at his request."

"Who is this Smith? You know him?"

"I met him tonight for the first time. He came to see me."

"What for? What were you doing out there? A haunted house!"

I sighed. There wasn't anything I could do but answer his damn questions and they were getting tougher all the time. Let's see, how could I put it so it wouldn't sound *too* crazy?

I said, "We went there because it *is* supposed to be a haunted house, Kates. This Smith was interested in the occult—in psychic phenomena. He asked me to go out there with him to perform an experiment. I gathered that some other people were coming, but they didn't."

"What kind of an experiment?"

"I don't know. He was killed before we got around to it."

"You and him were there alone?"

"Yes," I said, but I saw where that was leading so I added, "But I didn't kill him. And I don't know who did. He was poisoned."

"Poisoned how?"

Part of my brain wanted to tell him, "Out of a little bottle labelled 'DRINK ME' on a glass table, as in *Alice in Wonderland*." The sensible part of my brain told me to let him find that out for himself. I said, "Out of a bottle that was planted there for him to drink. By whom, I don't know. But you sound like you don't believe me. Why don't you go out and see for yourself, Kates? Damn it, man, I'm reporting a *murder*." And then it occurred to me there wasn't really any proof of that, so I amended it a little: "Or at least a death of violence."

He stared at me and I think he was becoming convinced, a little.

His phone rang and his swivel chair screamed again as he swung around. He barked "Hello. Sheriff Kates," into it.

Then his voice tamed down a little. He said, "No, Mrs. Harrison, haven't heard a thing. Hank's over at Neilsville, checking up at that end, and he's going to watch the road again on his way back. I'll call you the minute I learn anything at all. But don't worry; it can't be anything serious."

He turned back. "Stoeger, if this is a *gag*, I'm going to take you apart." He meant it, and he could do it, too. Kates is only a medium-sized man, not too much bigger than I, but he's tough and hard as a rock physically. He can handle men weighing half again as much as he does. And he's got enough of a sadistic streak to enjoy doing it whenever he has a good excuse for it.

"It's no gag," I said. "What's this about Miles Harrison and Ralph Bonney?"

"Missing. They left Neilsville with the Bonney pay roll a little after half past eleven and should have been back here around midnight. It's almost two o'clock and nobody knows where they are. Look, if I thought you were sober and there *was* a stiff out on the pike, I'd call the state cops. I *got* to stay here till we find what happened to Miles and Bonney."

The state cops were fine, as far as I was concerned. I'd reported it where it should have been reported, and Kates would have no kickback if he himself called the state police. I was just opening my mouth to say that might be a good idea when the phone rang again.

Kates yelled into it, and then, "As far as the teller knew, they were heading right back, Hank? Nothing unusual happened at that end, huh? Okay, come back; and watch both sides of the road all the way in case they ran off it or something. . . . Yeah, the pike. That's the only way they could've come. Oh, and listen, stop at the Wentworth place on your way and take a look in the attic . . . Yeah, I said the attic. Doc Stoeger's here, drunk as a coot, and he says there's a stiff in the attic there. If there *is* one, I'll worry about it."

He slammed the receiver down and started shuffling papers on his desk, trying to look busy. Finally he thought of something to do and phoned the Bonney Fireworks Company to see if Bonney had showed up there yet, or called them. Apparently, from what I could hear of the conversation, he hadn't done either.

I realized that I was still standing up and that now, since Kates had given that order to his deputy, nothing was going to happen until Hank got back—at least half an hour if he drove slowly to watch both sides of the road. So I found myself a chair and sat down. Kates shuffled papers again and paid no attention to me.

I got to wondering about Bonney and Miles, and hoped they

hadn't had an accident. If they had had one, and were two hours overdue, it must have been a bad one. Unless both were seriously hurt, one of them would have reached a phone long before this. Of course they could have stopped somewhere for a drink, but it didn't seem likely, not for two hours at least. And, come to think of it, they couldn't have; the closing hour for taverns applied to the whole county, not just to Carmel City. Twelve o'clock had been almost two hours ago.

I wished that it wasn't. Not that I either needed or wanted a drink particularly at that moment, but it would have been much more pleasant to do my waiting at Smiley's instead of here in the sheriff's office.

Kates suddenly swivelled his chair at me, "*You* don't know anything about Bonney and Harrison, do you?"

"Not a thing," I told him.

"Where were you at midnight?"

With Yehudi, Who's Yehudi? *The little man who wasn't there.*

I said, "Home, talking to Smith. We stayed there until half past twelve."

"Anybody else there?"

I shook my head. Come to think of it, nobody but myself had, as far as I knew, even seen Yehudi Smith. If his body *wasn't* in the attic at the Wentworth place, I was going to have a hell of a time proving he'd ever existed. A card and a key and a flashlight.

"Where's this Smith guy come from?"

"I don't know. He didn't say."

"What was his first name?"

I stalled on that one. I said, "I don't remember. I've got his card somewhere. He gave me one." Let him think the card was probably out at the house. I wasn't ready to show it to him yet.

"How'd he happen to come to *you* to go to a haunted house with him if he didn't even know you?"

I said, "He knew *of* me, as a Lewis Carroll fan."

"A what?"

"Lewis Carroll. *Alice in Wonderland*, *Alice Through the Looking-Glass*." And a "DRINK ME" bottle on a glass table, and a key, and Bandersnatches and Jabberwocks. But let Kates find that out for himself, after he'd found a body and knew that I wasn't either drunk or crazy.

He said, "*Alice in Wonderland*!" and sniffed. He glared at me a full ten seconds and then decided, apparently, that he was wasting his time on me and swivelled back to his paper shuffling.

I felt in my pockets to make sure that the card and the key were still there. They were. The flashlight was still in the car, but the flashlight didn't mean anything anyway. Maybe the key didn't either. But the card was my contact with reality, in a sense. As long as it still said *Yehudi Smith*, I knew I wasn't stark raving mad. I knew that there'd really been such a person and that he wasn't a figment of my imagination.

I slipped it out of my pocket to look at it again. Yes, it still said, "*Yehudi Smith*", although my eyes had a bit of trouble focusing on it clearly. The printing looked fuzzy, which meant I needed either one more drink or several less.

Yehudi Smith, in fuzzy-edged type. Yehudi, the little man who wasn't there.

And suddenly—don't ask me how I knew, but I knew. I didn't see the pattern, but I saw that much of it. The little man who wasn't there.

Wouldn't be there.

Hank was going to come in and say, "What's this about a stiff in the Wentworth attic? *I* couldn't find one."

Yehudi. The little man who wasn't there. *I saw a man upon the stair, A little man who wasn't there. He wasn't there again today; Gee, I wish he'd go away.*

It was preordained; it *had* to be. That much of the pattern I saw. The name Yehudi hadn't been an accident. I think that *almost*, just then, I had a flash of insight that would have shown me most of the pattern, if not all of it. You know how it is sometimes when you're drunk, but not too drunk, you think you're trembling on the verge of understanding something important and cosmic that has eluded you all your life? And—just barely possibly—you really are. I think I was, at that moment.

Then I looked up from the card and the thread of my thought was lost because Kates was staring at me. He'd turned just his head this time instead of the squeaking swivel chair he was sitting on. He was looking at me speculatively, suspiciously.

I tried to ignore it; I was trying to recapture my thoughts and let them lead me. I was close to something. *I saw a man upon the stair*. Yehudi Smith's plump posterior ascending the attic stairs, just ahead of me.

No, the dead body with the contorted face—the poor piece of cold clay that had been a nice little guy with laughter lines around his eyes and the corners of his mouth—wouldn't be there in the attic when Hank Ganzer looked for it. It couldn't be there; its presence there wouldn't fit the pattern that I still couldn't see or understand.

Squeal of the swivel chair as Rance Kates turned his body to match the position of his head. "Is that the card that guy gave you?"

I nodded.

"What's his full name?"

The hell with Kates. "Yehudi," I said. "Yehudi Smith."

Of course it wasn't really; I knew at least that much now. I got up and walked to Kates' desk. Unfortunately for my dignity. I weaved a little. But I made it without falling. I put the card down in front of him and went back and sat down again, managing to walk straight this time.

He looked at the card and then at me and then at the card and then at me.

And then I knew I *must* be crazy.

"Doc,' he asked—and his voice was quieter than I'd ever heard it before—*"what's your bug number?"*

CHAPTER ELEVEN

"O Oysters," said the Carpenter,
"You've had a pleasant run!
Shall we be trotting home again?"
But answer came there none——

I JUST stared at him. Either he was crazy or I was——and several
times in the last hour I'd been wondering about myself. *What's
your bug number?* What a question to ask a man in the spot I was
in. What's yours?

Finally I managed to answer. "Huh?" I said.

"Your bug number. Your label number."

I got it then. I wasn't crazy after all. I knew what he meant.

I run a union shop, which means that I've signed a contract
with the International Typographical Union and pay Pete, my only
employee, union wages. In a town as small as Carmel City, you
can get by with a non-union shop, but I happen to believe in unions
and to think the Typographical Union is a good one. Being a union
shop, we put the union label on everything we print. It's a little
oval-shaped dingus, so small you can barely read the type if you've
got good eyesight. And alongside it is an equally tiny number which
is the number of my particular shop among the other union shops
in my area. By the combination of the place name which is part of
the label itself and the number of the shop beside it, you can tell
where any given piece of union printing has been done.

But that little oval logotype is known to non-union printers as
"the bug". It does, I'll admit, look rather like a tiny bug crawling
across the bottom corner of whatever it's put on. And non-union
printers call the shop number alongside the "bug" the "bug
number." Kates wasn't a printer, union or otherwise, but I
remember now that two of his brothers, both living in Neilsville,
were non-union printers, and naturally he'd have picked up the
language—and the implied prejudice back of it—from them.

I said, "My label number is seven."

He slapped the calling card down on the desk in front of him.
He snorted—quite literally; you often read about people snorting
but seldom hear them do it. He said, "Stoeger, you printed this
damn thing yourself. The whole thing is a gag. Damn you——"

He started to get up and then sat down again and looked at the
papers in front of him. He looked back at me and I think he was

going to tell me to get the hell out, and then apparently he decided he might as well wait till Hank got back.

He shuffled papers.

I sat there and tried to absorb the fact that—apparently, at any rate—that *Yehudi Smith* calling card had been printed in my own shop. I didn't get up to look at it. Somehow, I was perfectly willing to take Kates' word for it.

Why not? It was part of the pattern. I should have guessed it myself. Not from the typeface; almost every shop has eight-point Garamond. But from the fact that the "DRINK Me" bottle had contained poison and Yehudi wasn't going to be there when Hank looked for him. It followed the pattern, and I knew now what the pattern was. It was the pattern of madness.

Mine—or whose? I was getting scared. I'd been scared several times already that night, but this was a different variety of scaredness. I was getting scared of the night itself, of the *pattern* of the night.

I needed a drink, and I needed it bad. I stood up and started for the door. The swivel chair screamed and Kates said, "Where the hell you think you're going?"

"Down to my car. Going to get something. I'll be back." I didn't want to get into an argument with him.

"Sit down. You're not going out of here."

I did want to get into an argument with him. "Am I under arrest? And on what charge?"

"Material witness in a murder case, Stoeger. *If* there's a corpse where you say there's one. If there isn't, we can switch it to drunk and disorderly. Take your choice.

I took my choice. I sat down again.

He had me over a barrel and I could see that he loved it. I wished that I'd gone to my office and phoned the state police, regardless of repercussions.

I waited. That "bug number" angle of Kates' had thrown me off thinking about how it could be and why it would be that Yehudi Smith's calling card had been printed in my own print shop. Not that, come to think of it, the "how" had been difficult. I lock the door when I leave, but I lock it with a dime-store skeleton key. They come two on a card for a dime. Yes, Anybody could have got in. And Anybody whoever he was could have printed that card without knowing a damn thing about printing. You have to know the printer's case to set type in quantity, but anybody could pick out a dozen letters, more or less, to spell out Yehudi Smith simply by trial and error. The little hand press I print cards on is so simple that a child—well, anyway, a high school kid—could figure out how to operate it. True, he'd get lousy impressions and waste a lot of cards trying to get one good one. But Anybody, if he'd tried long enough, could have printed one good card that said *Yehudi Smith* and carried my union label in the bottom corner.

But why would Anybody have done something like that?

The more I thought about it the less sense it made, although one thing did emerge that made even less sense that the rest of it. It would have been easier to print that card without the union label than with it, so Anybody had gone to a little additional trouble to bring out the fact that the card *had* been printed at the *Clarion*. Except for the death of Yehudi Smith the whole thing might have been the pattern of a monstrous practical joke. But practical jokes don't include sudden death. Not even such a fantastic death as Yehudi Smith had met.

Why had Yehudi Smith died?

Somewhere there had to be a key.

And that reminded me of the key in my pocket and I took it out and stared at it, wondering what I could open with it. Somewhere there was a lock that it fitted.

It didn't look either familiar or unfamiliar. Yale keys don't. Could it be mine? I thought about all the keys I owned. The key to the front door of my house was a Yale type key, but not actually a Yale. Besides——

I took the keytainer from my pocket and opened it. My front door key is on the left and I compared it with the key I'd brought away from the attic. The notches didn't match; it wasn't a duplicate of that one. And it was still more different from my back door key, the one on the other side of the row. In between were two other keys but both were quite different types. One was the key to the door at the *Clarion* office and the other was for the garage behind my house. I never use the garage key; I keep nothing of value in the garage except the car itself and I always leave it locked.

It seemed to me that I'd had five keys instead of four, there on the keytainer, but I couldn't remember for sure and I couldn't figure out what the missing one was, if one really was missing.

Not the key to my car; I didn't keep that on the keytainer (I hate a keytainer dangling and swinging from my ignition lock, so I carry the car key loose in my vest pocket).

I put the keytainer back in my pocket and stared at the single key again. I wondered suddenly if it could be a duplicate of my car key. But I couldn't compare it to see because, this time, I'd left the key in the lock when I'd got out of the car, thinking I was going to be up here in the sheriff's office only a minute or two and that then he'd be heading out to the Wentworth place with me.

Kates must have turned his head—not his swivel chair, for it didn't squeak—and seen me staring at the key. He asked, "What's that?"

"A key," I said. "A key to unlock a riddle. A key to murder."

The chair did squeak then. "Stoeger, what the hell? Are you just drunk, or are you crazy?"

"I don't know," I said. "Which do you think?"

He snorted. "Let's see that key." I handed it to him.

"What's it open?"

"I don't know." I was getting mad again—not particularly at Kates this time; at everything. "I know what it's supposed to open."

"What?"

"A little door fifteen inches high off a room at the bottom of a rabbit hole. It leads to a beautiful garden."

He looked at me a long time. I looked back. I didn't give a damn.

I heard a car outside. That would be Hank Ganzer, probably. He wouldn't have found the body of Yehudi Smith in the attic out on the pike. I knew that, somehow.

And how Kates was going to react to that, I could guess. Even though, obviously, he didn't believe a damn word of it to begin with. I'd have given a lot, just then, to see inside Rance Kates' mind, or what he uses for one, to see just what he *was* thinking. I'd have given a lot more, though, to be inside the mind of Anybody, the person who'd printed Yehudi Smith's card on my hand press and who'd put the poison in the "DRINK ME" bottle.

Hank's steps coming up the stairs.

He came in the door and his eyes happened to be looking in my direction first. He said, "Hi, Doc," casually and then turned to Kates. "No sign of an accident, Rance. I drove slow, watched both sides of the road. No sign of a car going off. But look, maybe we should both do it. If one of us could keep moving the spotlight back and forth while the other drove, we could see back farther." He looked at his wrist watch. "It's only two-thirty. Won't get light until six, and in that long a time——"

Kates nodded. "Okay, Hank. But listen, I'm going to get the state boys in on this case—well, in case Bonney's car turns up somewhere else. We know when they left Neilsville, but we can't be positive they started for Carmel City."

"Why wouldn't they?"

"How would I know?" Kates said. "But if they did start here, they didn't get here."

I might as well not have been there at all.

I cut in. "Hank, did you go to the Wentworth place?"

He looked at me. "Sure, Doc. Listen, what kind of a gag was that?"

"Did you look in the attic?"

"Sure. Looked all around it with my flashlight."

I'd known it, but I closed my eyes.

Kates surprised me, after all. His voice was almost gentle. "Stoeger, get the hell out of here. Go home and sleep it off."

I opened my eyes again and looked at Hank. "All right," I said, "I'm drunk or crazy. But listen, Hank, was there a candle stub standing on top of the post at the top of the attic steps?"

He shook his head slowly.

"A glass-topped table, standing in one corner—it'd be the northwest corner of the attic?"

"I didn't see it, Doc. I wasn't looking for tables. But I'd have noticed a candle stub, if it had been on the stair post. I remember putting my hand on it when I started down."

"And you don't recall seeing a dead body on the floor?"

Hank didn't even answer me. He looked back at Kates. "Rance, maybe I'd better drive Doc home while you're making those calls. Where's your car, Doc?"

"Across the street."

"Okay, we won't give you a parking ticket. I'll drive you home in mine." He looked at Kates for corroboration.

Kates gave it. I hated Kates for it. He was grinning at me. He had me in such a nasty spot that, damn him, he could afford to be generous. If he threw me in the can overnight, I could fight back. If he sent me home to sleep it off—and even gave me a chauffeur to take me there——

Hank Ganzer said, "Come on, Doc." He was going through the door.

I got to my feet. I didn't *want* to go home. If I went home now, the murderer of Yehudi Smith would have the rest of the night to finish—to finish what? And what was it to me, except that I'd liked Yehudi Smith? And who the hell was Yehudi Smith?

I said, "Listen, Kates——"

Kates looked past me at the doorway. He said, "Go on, Hank. See if his car is parked straight and then I'll send him down. I think he can make it."

He probably hoped I'd break my neck going down the steps.

"Sure, Rance." Hank's footsteps going down the stairs. Diminuendo.

Kates looked up at me. I was standing in front of his desk, trying not to look like a boy caught cheating in an examination standing in front of his teacher's desk.

I caught his eyes, and almost took a step backward. I hated Kates and knew that he hated me, but I hated him as one hates a man in office whom one knows to be a stupid oaf and a crook. He hated me, I thought, as someone who, as an editor, had power—and used it—against men like him.

But the look in his eyes wasn't that. It was sheer *personal* hatred and malevolence. It was something I hadn't suspected, and it shocked me. I don't, after fifty-three years, shock easily.

And then that look was gone, as suddenly as when you turn out a light. He was looking at me impersonally. His voice was impersonal, almost flat, not nearly as loud as usual. He said, "Stoeger, you know what I could do to you on something like this, don't you?"

I didn't answer; he didn't expect me to. Yes, I knew some of the things. The can overnight on a drunk and disorderly charge was a starting point. And if, in the morning, I persisted in my illusions, he could call in Dr. Buchan for a psychiatric once-over.

He said, "I'm not doing it. But I want you out of my hair from now on. Understand?"

I didn't answer that, either. If he wanted to think silence was consent, all right. Apparently he did. He said, "Now get the hell out of here."

I got the hell out of there. I'd got off easy. Except for that look he'd given me.

No, I didn't feel like a conquering hero about it. I should have faced up to it, and I should have insisted that there *had* been a murder in that attic, whether there was a *corpus delicti* there now or not. But I was too mixed up myself. I wanted time to think things out, to figure what the hell had really happened.

I went down the stairs and out into the night again.

Hank Ganzer's car was parked right in front, but he was just getting out of my car, across the street. I walked over toward him.

He said, "You *were* a little far out from the kerb, Doc. I moved it in for you. Here's your key."

He handed me the key and I stuck it in my pocket and then reopened the door he'd just closed to get the bottle of whisky that was lying on the seat. No use leaving that, even if I had to leave the car here.

I stepped back, then, to the back of the car to take another look at those back tyres. I still couldn't believe them; this morning they'd been completely flat. That was part of the puzzle, too.

Hank came back and stood by me. "What's the matter, Doc?" he asked. "If you're looking at your tyres, they're okay." He kicked the one nearest him and then walked around and kicked the other. He started back, and stopped.

He said, "Say, Doc, something you got in your luggage compartment must've spilled over. Did you have a can of paint or something in there?"

I shook my head and came around to see what he was looking at. It did look as though something had run out from under the bottom edge of the luggage compartment door. Something thick and blackish.

Hank turned the handle and tried to lift.

"It's not locked," I said. "I never bother to lock it. Nothing in there but a worn-out tyre without a tube in it."

He tried again. "The hell it's not locked. Where's the key?"

Another piece of the pattern fell into place. I knew now what the fifth key, the middle one, on my keytainer should have been. I never lock the luggage compartment of my car except on the rare occasions when I take a trip and really have luggage in it. But I carry the key on my keytainer. And it was a Yale key and it hadn't been there when I'd looked a few minutes ago.

I said, "Kates has got it." It had to be. One Yale key looks like another, but the card, Yehudi Smith's card, had been printed in my own shop. The key would be mine, too.

Hank said, "Huh?"

I said again, "Kates has got it."

Hank looked at me strangely. He said. "Wait just a minute, Doc," and walked across to his own car. Twice, on the way, he looked back as though to be sure I wasn't going to get in and drive away.

He got a flashlight out of his glove compartment and came back. He bent down with it and took a close look at those streaks.

I stepped closer to look, too. Hank stepped back, as though he was suddenly afraid to have me behind him and peering over his shoulder.

So I didn't have to look. I knew what those streaks were, or what Hank thought they were.

He said, "Seriously, Doc, where's the key?"

"I'm serious," I told him. "I gave it to Rance Kates. I didn't know what key it was then. I'm pretty sure I do now.

I thought I knew what was in that luggage compartment now, too.

He looked at me uncertainly and then walked part way across the street, angling so he could watch me. He cupped his hands around his lips and called out. "Rance! Hey, Rance!" And then looked quickly back to see that I was neither sneaking up on him nor trying to get into the car to drive away.

Nothing happened and he did it again.

A window opened and Kates was silhouetted against the light back of it. He called back, "What the hell, Hank, if you want me come up here. Don't wake up the whole God damn town."

Hank looked back over his shoulder at me again. Then he called, "Did Doc give you a key?"

"Yes. Why? What kind of a yarn is he feeding *you*?"

"Bring down the key, Rance. Quick."

He looked back over his shoulder again, started toward me, and then hesitated. He compromised by staying where he was, but watching me.

The window slammed down.

I walked back around the car and I almost decided to light a match and look at those stains myself. And then I decided, what the hell.

Hank came a few steps closer. He said, "Where you going, Doc?"

I was at the kerb by then, I said, "Nowhere", and sat down.

To wait.

CHAPTER TWELVE

Then fill up the glasses as quick as you can,
And sprinkle the table with buttons and bran;
Put cats in the coffee, and mice in the tea—
And welcome Queen Alice with thirty-times three!

THE courthouse door opened and closed. Kates crossed the street. He looked at me and asked Hank, "What's wrong?"

"Don't know, Rance. Looks like blood has dripped from the luggage compartment of Doc's car. It's locked. He says he gave you the key. I didn't want to—uh—leave him to come up and get it. So I yelled for you."

Kates nodded. His face was toward me and Hank Ganzer couldn't see it. I could. It looked happy, very happy.

His hand went inside his coat and came out with a pistol. He asked, "Did you frisk him, Hank?"

"No."

"Go ahead."

Hank came around Kates and came up to me from the side. I stood up and held out my hands to make it easy for him. The bottle of whisky was in one of them. He found nothing more deadly than that.

"Clean," Hank siad,

Kates didn't put his pistol away. He reached into a pocket with his free hand and took out the key I'd given him. He tossed it to Hank. "Open the compartment," he said.

The key fitted. The handle turned. Hank lifted the door.

I heard the sudden intake of his breath and I turned and looked. Two bodies; I could see that much. I couldn't tell who they were from where I stood. Hank leaned farther in, using his flashlight.

He said, "Miles Harrison, Rance. And Ralph Bonney. Both dead."

"How'd he kill 'em?"

"Hit over the head with something. Hard. Must've been several blows apiece. There's lots of blood."

"Weapon there?"

"What looks like it. There's a revolver—an old one—with blood on the butt. Nickel-plated Iver-Johnson, rusty where the plating's off. Thirty-eight, I think."

"The money there? The pay roll?"

"There's what looks like a brief case under Miles." Hank turned around. His face was as pale as the starlight. "Do I got to—uh—move him, Rance?"

Kates thought a minute. "Maybe we better not. Maybe we better take a photo first. Listen, Hank, you go upstairs and get that camera and flash-gun. And while you're there, phone Dr. Heil to get here right away. Uh—you're sure they're both dead?"

"Christ yes, Rance. Their heads are beaten in. Shall I call Dorberg, too?" Dorberg is the local mortician who gets whatever business the sheriff's office can throw his way; he's Kates' brother-in-law, which may have a bearing on the fact.

Kates said, "Sure, tell him to bring the wagon. But tell him no hurry; we want the coroner to have a look before we move 'em. And we want the pix even before that."

Hank started for the courthouse door and then turned again. "Uh—Rance, how about calling Miles' wife and Bonney's factory?"

I sat down on the kerb again. I wanted a drink more badly than before, and the bottle was in my hand. But it didn't seem right, just at that moment, to take one. Miles' wife, I thought, and Bonney's factory. What a hell of a difference that was. But Bonney had been divorced that very day; he had no children, no relatives at all—at least in Carmel City—that I knew of. But then I didn't have either. If I was murdered, who'd be notified? The *Carmel City Clarion*, and maybe Carl Trenholm, if whoever did the notifying knew that Trenholm was my closest friend. Yes, maybe on the whole it was better that I'd never married. I thought of Bonney's divorce and the facts behind it that Carl—through Smiley—had told me. And I thought of how Miles Harrison's wife would be feeling tonight as soon as she got the news. But that was different; I didn't know whether it was good or bad that nobody would feel that way about me if I died suddenly.

Just the same I felt lonely as hell. Well, they'd arrest me now and that would mean I could call Carl as my attorney. I was going to be in a hell of a spot, but Carl would believe me—and believe that I was sane—if anybody would.

Kates had been thinking. He said, "Not yet—either of them, Hank. Milly especially; she might rush down here and get here before we got the bodies to Dorberg's. And we might as well be able to tell the factory whether the pay roll's there when we phone them. Maybe Stoeger hid it somewhere else and we won't get it back tonight."

Hank said, "That's right, about Milly. We wouldn't want her to see Miles—that way. Okay, so I'll call Heil and Dorberg and then come back with the camera."

"Quit talking. Get going."

Hank went on into the courthouse.

It wasn't any use, but I had to say it. I said. "Listen, Kates, I didn't do that. I didn't kill them."

Kates said, "You son of a bitch. Miles was a good guy."

"He was. I didn't kill him." I thought, I wish Miles had let me buy him that drink early in the evening. I wish I'd known; I'd have insisted and talked him into it. But that was silly, of course; you can't know things in advance. If you could, you could stop them happening. Except of course in the Looking-Glass country where people sometimes lived backwards, where the White Queen had screamed first and then later had stuck the needle into her finger. But even then—except, of course, that the Alice books were merely delightful nonsense—why hadn't she simply not picked up the needle she knew she was going to stick herself with?

Delightful nonsense, that is, until tonight. Tonight somebody was making gibbering horror out of Lewis Carroll's most amusing episodes. "Drink Me"—and die suddenly and horribly. That key—it had been supposed to open a fifteen-inch-high door into a beautiful garden. What it had opened the door to—well, I didn't care to look.

I sighed and thought, what the hell, it's over with now. I'm going to be arrested and Kates thinks I killed Miles and Bonney, but I can't blame him for thinking it. I've got to wait till Carl can get me out of this.

Kates said, "Stand up, Stoeger."

I didn't. Why should I? I'd just thought, why would Miles or Ralph mind if I took a drink out of this bottle in my hand? I started to unscrew the top.

"Stand up, Stoeger. Or I'll shoot you right there."

He *meant* it. I stood up. His face, as he stood then, was in the shadow, but I remembered that look of malevolence he'd given me in his office, the look that said, "I'd like to kill you."

He was going to shoot me. Here and now.

It was safe as houses for him to do so. He could claim—if I turned and ran and he shot me in the back—that he'd shot because I was trying to escape. And if from the front that I—a homicidal maniac who had already killed Miles and Bonney—was coming toward him to attack him.

That was why he'd sent Hank away and given him two phone calls to make so he wouldn't be back for minutes.

I said, "Kates, you're not serious. You wouldn't shoot a man down in cold blood."

"A man who'd killed a deputy of mine, yes. If I don't, Stoeger, you might beat the rap. You might get certified as a looney and get away with it. I'll make sure." That wasn't all of it, of course, but it gave him an excuse to help his own conscience. I'd killed a deputy of his, he'd thought. But he'd hated me enough to want to kill me even before he'd thought that. Hatred and sadism—given a perfect excuse.

What could I do? Yell? It wouldn't help. Probably nobody awake—it was well after three o'clock by now—would hear me in time to see what hapened. Hank would be phoning in the back office; he wouldn't get to the window in time.

And Kates would claim that I yelled as I jumped him; yelling would just trigger the gun.

He stepped closer; if he shot me in the front there'd have to be powder marks to show that he'd shot while I was coming at him. The gun muzzle centred on my chest, barely a foot away. I could live seconds longer if I turned and ran; he'd probably wait until I was a dozen steps away in that case.

His face was still in the shadow, but I could see that he was grinning. I couldn't see his eyes or most of the rest of his face, just the grin. A disembodied grin, like that of the Cheshire cat in Alice. But unlike the Cheshire cat, he wasn't going to fade away.

I was. Unless something unexpected happened. Like maybe a witness coming along, over there on the opposite sidewalk. He wouldn't shoot me in cold blood before a witness. Carl Trenholm, Al Grainger, anybody.

I looked over Kates' shoulder and called out, "Hi, Al!"

Kates turned. He had to; he couldn't take a chance on the possibility that there was really someone coming.

He turned his head just for a quick glance, to be sure.

I swung the whisky bottle. Maybe I should say my hand swung it; *I* hadn't even remembered that I still held it. It hit Kates alongside the head and like as not the brim of his hat saved his life. I think I swung hard enough to have killed him if he'd been bare headed.

Kates and the revolver he's been holding hit the street, separately. The whisky bottle slid out of my hand and hit the paving; it broke, The paving must have been harder than Kates' head—or maybe it would have broken on Kates' head if it hadn't been for the brim of his hat.

I didn't even stop to find out if he was dead. I ran like hell.

Afoot, of course. The ignition key of my car was still in my pocket, but driving off with two corpses was just about the last thing in the world I wanted to do.

I ran a block and winded myself before I realized I hadn't the faintest idea where I was going. I slowed down and got off Oak Street. I cut back into the first alley. I fell over a garbage can and then sat down on it to get my wind back and to think out what I was going to do. But I had to move on because a dog started barking.

I found myself behind the courthouse.

I wanted, of course, to know who had killed Ralph Bonney and Miles Harrison and put their bodies in my car, but there was something that seemed of even more immediate interest; I wanted to know if I'd killed Rance Kates or seriously injured him. If I had, I was in a hell of a jam because—in addition to everything else against me—it would be my word against his that I'd done it in self-defence, to save my own life. My word against his, that is, if he were only injured. My word against nothing at all if I'd killed him.

And my word wouldn't mean a damn thing to anybody until and unless I could account for two corpses in my car.

The first window I tried was unlocked. I guess they're careless about locking windows of the courthouse because, for one reason, there's nothing kept there that any ordinary burglar would want to steal, and for another reason because the sheriff's office is in the building, and somebody's on duty there all night long.

I slid the window up very slowly and it didn't make much noise, not enough, anyway, to have been heard in the sheriff's office, which is on the second floor and near the front. I put it down again, just as quietly, so it wouldn't be an open give-away if the search for me went through the alley.

I groped in the dark till I found a chair and sat down to collect what wits I had left and figure what to do next. I was fairly safe for the moment. The room I'd entered was one of the small ante-rooms off the court-room; nobody would look for me here, as long as I kept quiet.

They'd found the sheriff all right, or the sheriff had come around and found himself. There were footsteps on the front stairs, footsteps of more than one person. But back here I was too far away to hear what was being said, if any talking was going on.

But that could wait for a minute or two.

I wished to hell that I had a drink; I'd never wanted one worse in my life. I cussed myself for having dropped and broken that bottle—and after it had saved my life, at that. If I hadn't happened to have it in my hand, I'd have been dead.

I don't know how long I sat there, but it probably wasn't over a few minutes because I was still breathing a little hard when I decided I'd better move. If I'd had a bottle to keep me company, I'd have gladly sat there the rest of the night, I think.

But I had to find out what happened to Kates. If I'd killed him—or if he'd been taken to the hospital and was out of the picture—then I'd better give myself up and get it over with. If he was all right, and was still running things, that wouldn't be a very smart thing to do. If he'd wanted to kill me before I'd knocked him out with that bottle, he'd want to do it so badly now that he would do it, maybe without even bothering to find an excuse, right in front of Hank or any of the other deputies who were undoubtedly being woken up to join the manhunt, in front of the coroner or anybody else who happened to be around.

I bent down and took my shoes off before I got up. I put one in each of the side pockets of my coat and then tiptoed out through the court-room to the back stairs. I'd been in the building so many thousand times that I knew the layout almost as well as that of my own home or the *Clarion* office, and I didn't run into anything or fall over anything.

I guided myself up the dark back staircase with a hand on the banister and avoiding the middle of the steps, where they'd be most likely to creak.

Luckily there is an el in the upstairs hallway that runs from the front stairs to the back ones so there wasn't any danger of my being seen, when I'd reached the top of the stairs, by anyone entering or leaving the sheriff's office. And I had dim light now, from the light in the front hallway near the sheriff's office door.

I tiptoed along almost to the turn of the hall and then tried the door of the county surveyor's office, which is next to the sheriff's office and with only an ordinary door with a ground glass pane between them. The door was unlocked.

I got it open very quietly. It slipped out of my hand when I started to close it from the inside and almost slammed, but I caught it in time and eased it shut. I would have liked to lock it, but I didn't know whether the lock would click or not, so I didn't take a chance on that.

I had plenty of light, comparatively, in the surveyor's office; the ground glass pane of the door to the sheriff's office was a bright yellow rectangle through which came enough light to let me see the office furniture clearly. I avoided it carefully and tiptoed my way toward that yellow rectangle.

I could hear voices now and as I neared the door I could hear them even better, but I couldn't quite make out whose they were or what they were saying until I put my ear against the glass. I could hear perfectly well, then.

Hank Ganzer was saying, "It still throws me, Rance. A gentle little old guy like Doc. Two murders and——"

"Gentle, hell!" It was Kates' voice. "Maybe when he was sane he was, but he's crazier than a bedbug now. Ow! Go easy with that tape, will you?"

Dr. Heil's voice was soft, harder to understand. He seemed to be urging that Kates should let himself be taken to the hospital to be sure there wasn't any concussion.

"The hell with that," Kates said. "Not till we get Stoeger before he kills anybody else. Like he killed Miles and Bonney and damn near killed me. Hank, what's about the bodies?"

"I made a quick preliminary examination." Heil's voice was clearer now. "Cause of death is pretty obviously repeated blows on their heads with what seems to have been that rusty pistol on your desk. And with the stains on the pistol butt, I don't think there's any reason to doubt it."

"They still out front?"

Hank said, "No, they're at Dorberg's—or on their way there. He and one of his boys came around with his meat wagon."

"Doc." It was Kates' voice and it made me jump a little until I realized that he was talking to Dr. Heil and not to me. "You about through? With that God damn bandage, I mean. I got to get going on this. Hank, how many of the boys did you get on the phone? How many are coming down?"

"Three, Rance. I got Watkins, Ehlers and Bill Dean. They're all on their way down. Be here in a few minutes. That'll make five of us."

"Guess that fixes up things as well as I can here, Rance," Dr. Heil's voice said. "I still suggest you go around to the hospital for an X-ray and a check-up as soon as you can."

"Sure, Doc. Soon as I catch Stoeger. And he can't get out of town with the state police watching the roads for us, even if he steals a car. You go on around to Dorberg's and take care of things there, huh?"

Heil's voice, soft again, said something I couldn't hear, and there were footsteps toward the outer hall. I could hear other footsteps coming up the stairs. One or more of the day-shift deputies were arriving.

Kates said, "Hi, Bill, Walt. Ehlers with you?"

"Didn't see him. Probably be here in a minute." It sounded like Bill Dean's voice.

"That's all right. We'll leave him here, anyway. You both got your guns? Good. Listen, you two are going together and Hank and I are going together. We'll work in pairs. Don't worry about the roads leading out; the state boys are watching them for us. And there's no train or bus out till late tomorrow morning. We just comb the town."

"Divide it between us, Rance?"

"No. You, Walt and Bill cover the whole town. Drive through every street and alley. Hank and I will take places he might have holed in to hide. We'll search his house and the *Clarion* office, whether there are lights on or not, and we'll try any place else that's indoors where he might've holed in. He might pick an empty house, for instance. Anybody got any other suggestions where he might think of holing in?"

Bill Dean's voice said, "He's pretty thick with Carl Trenholm. He might go to Carl."

"Good idea, Bill. Anybody else?"

Hank said, "He looked pretty drunk to me. And he broke that bottle he had. Might get into his head he wants another drink and break into a tavern. Probably Smiley's; that's where he hangs out, mostly."

"Okay, Hank. We'll check—— That must be Dick coming. Any more ideas, anybody, before we split up?"

Ehlers was coming in now. Hank said, "Sometimes a guy doubles back where he figures nobody'll figure where he is. I mean, Rance, maybe he doubled back here and got in the back way or something, thinking the safest place to hide's right under our noses. Right here in the building."

Kates said, "You heard that, Dick. And you're staying here to watch the office, so that's your job. Search the building here first before you settle down."

"Right, Rance."

Kates said, "One more thing. He's dangerous. He's probably armed by now. So don't take any chances. When you see him, start shooting."

"At Doc Stoeger?" Someone's voice sounded surprised and a little shocked. I couldn't tell which of the deputies it was.

"At Doc Stoeger," Kates said. "Maybe you think of him as a harmless little guy—but that's the kind that generally makes homicidal maniacs. He's killed two men tonight and tried to kill me, probably thought he did kill me, or he'd have stayed and finished the job. And don't forget who one of the men he did kill was. Miles."

Somebody muttered something.

Bill Dean—I think it was Bill Dean—said, "I don't get it, though. A guy like Doc. He isn't broke; he's got a paper that makes money and he's not a crook. Why'd he suddenly want to kill two men for a couple of thousand lousy bucks?"

Kates swore. He said, "He's nuts, went off the beam. The money probably didn't have much to do with it, although he took it all right. It was in that brief case under Miles' body. Now listen, this is the last time I tell you; he's a homicidal maniac and you better remember Miles the minute you spot him and shoot quick. He's crazy as a bedbug. Came in here with a cock and bull story about a guy being croaked out at the Wentworth place—a guy named Yehudi Smith, of all names. And Doc had a card to prove it, only he printed the card himself. Crazy enough to put his own bug number—union label number—on it. Gives me a key that he says opens a fifteen-inch-high door to a beautiful garden. Well, that was the key to the luggage compartment of his own car, see? With Miles' and Bonney's bodies, and the pay roll money, in it. Parked right in front. He'd driven it here. Comes up and *gives me the key*. And tries to get me to go to a haunted house with him."

"Did anybody look there?" Dean asked.

Hank said, "Sure, Bill. On my way back from Neilsville. Went through the whole dump. Nothing. And listen, Rance is right about him being crazy. I heard some of the stuff he said, myself. And if you don't think he's dangerous, look at Rance. I'm sorry about it, I liked Doc. But damn it, I'm with Rance on shooting first and catching him afterwards."

Somebody: "God damn it, if he killed Miles——"

"If he's *that* crazy"—I think it was Dick Ehlers—"we'd be doing him a favour, the way I figure it. If *I* ever got that far off the beam, homicidal, damn if I wouldn't rather be shot than spend the rest of my life in a padded cell. But what *made* him go off that way? All of a sudden, I mean?"

"Alcohol. Softens the brain, and then all of a sudden, whang."

"Doc didn't drink that much. He'd get drunk, a little, a night or two a week; but he wasn't an alcoholic. And he was such a nice——'

A fist hit a desk. It would have been Kates' fist and Kates' desk. It was Kates' swivel chair that squealed and his voice that said, "What the hell are we having a sewing circle for. Come on, let's go out and get him. And about shooting first, that's *orders*. I've lost one deputy tonight already. Come on."

Footsteps, lots of them, toward the door.

Kates' voice calling back from it, "And don't forget to search this building, Dick. Cellar to roof, before you settle down here."

"Right, Rance."

Footsteps, lots of heavy footsteps, going down the steps. And one set of them turning back along the hallway.

Toward the County Surveyor's office.

Toward me.

CHAPTER THIRTEEN

And he was very proud and stiff;
He said, "I'd go and wake them, if——"
I took a corkscrew from the shelf;
I went to wake them up myself.

I HOPED he'd take Rance Kates' orders literally and search the place from cellar to attic, in that order. If he did, I could get out either the front or back way while he was in the basement. But he might start on this floor, with this room.

So I tiptoed to the door, pulling one of my shoes out of my pocket as I went. I stood flat against the wall by the door, gripping the shoe, ready to swing the heel of it if Ehler's head came in.

It didn't. The footsteps went on past and started down the back staircase. I breathed again.

I opened the door and stepped out into the hall as soon as the footsteps were at the bottom of the back steps. Out there in the hall, in the quiet of the night, I could hear him moving about down there. He didn't go to the basement; he was taking the main floor first. That wasn't good. With him on the first floor I couldn't risk either the front or the back stairs; I was stuck up here.

Outside I heard first one car start and then another. At least the front entrance was clear if I had to try to leave that way, if Ehlers started upstairs by the back staircase.

I took a spot in the middle of the hallway, equidistant from both flights of steps. I could still hear him walking around down on the floor below, but it was difficult to tell just where he was. I had to be ready to make a break in either direction.

I swore to myself at the thoroughness of Kates' plans for finding me. My house, my office, Carl's place, Smiley's or another tavern—every place I'd actually be likely to go. Even here, the courthouse, where I really was. But luckily, instead of all of them pitching in for a quick once-over here, he'd left only one man to do the job, and as long as I could hear him and he couldn't hear me—and probably didn't believe I was really here at all—I had an edge.

Only, damn it, why didn't Ehlers hurry? I wanted a drink, and if I could get out of here, I could get one somewhere somehow. I was shaking like a leaf, and my thoughts were, too. Even one drink would steady me enough to think straight.

Maybe Kates kept a bottle in the bottom drawer of his desk.

The way I felt just then, it was worth trying. I listened hard to the sounds below me and decided Ehlers was probably at the back of the building and I tiptoed to the front and into Kates' office.

I went back to his desk and pulled the drawer open very quietly and slowly. There was a whisky bottle there. It was empty.

I cussed Kates under my breath. It wasn't bad enough that he'd tried to kill me; on top of that, he'd had to finish off that bottle without leaving a single drink in it. And it had been a good brand, too.

I closed the draw again as carefully as I'd opened it, so there'd be no sign of my having been there.

Lying on the blotter on Kates' desk was a revolver. I looked at it, wondering whether I should take it along with me. For a second the fact that it was rusty didn't register and then I remembered Hank's description of the gun that had been used as a bludgeon to kill Miles and Bonney, and I bent closer. Yes, it was an Iver-Johnson, nickel-plated where the plating wasn't worn or knocked off. This was the death weapon, then.

Exhibit A.

I reached out to pick it up, and then jerked my hand back. Hadn't I been framed well enough without helping the framer by putting my fingerprints on that gun? That was all I needed, to have my fingerprints on the weapon that had done the killing. Or were they there already? Considering everything else, I wouldn't have been too surprised if they were.

Then I almost went through the ceiling. The phone rang.

I could hear, in the silence between the first ring and the second, Ehler's footsteps starting upstairs. But back here in the office, I couldn't tell whether he was coming up the front way or the back, and I might not have time to make it anyway, even if I knew.

I looked around frantically and saw a closet, the door ajar. I grabbed up the Iver-Johnson and ducked into the closet, behind the door. And I stood there, trying not to breathe, while Ehlers came in and picked up the phone.

He said, "Sheriff's office," and then, "Oh you, Rance," and then he listened a while.

"You're phoning from the *Clarion*? Not at Smiley's or there, huh? . . . No, no calls have come in. . . . Yeah, I'm almost through looking around here. Searched the first floor and the basement. Just got to go over this floor yet."

I swore at myself. He'd been down in the basement then, and I could have got away. But the building had been so quiet that his walking around down there had sounded to me as though it had been on the main floor.

'Don't worry, I'm not taking any chances, Rance. Gun in one hand and a flashlight in the other.''

There was a gun in my hand, too, and suddenly I realized what a damned foolish thing I'd done to pick it up off Kates' desk. Ehlers must have known it was there. If he missed it, if he happened to glance down at the desk while he was talking on the phone—

God must have loved me. He didn't. He said, "Okay, Rance," and then he put the phone down and walked out.

I heard him go back along the hallway and around the el and start opening doors back there. I had to get out quick, down the front steps, before he worked his way back here. As a matter of routine, he'd probably open this closet door too when he'd searched his way back to the office he'd started from.

I let myself out and tiptoed down the steps. Out into the night again, on to Oak Street. And I had to get off it quick, because either of the two cars looking for me might cruise by at any moment. Carmel City isn't large; a car can cruise all of its streets and alleys in pretty short order. Besides I still had my shoes in my pockets and—I realized now—I still had a gun in my hand.

Hoping Ehlers wouldn't happen to be looking out of any of the windows, I ran around the corner and into the mouth of the alley behind the courthouse. As soon as I was comparatively safe in the friendly darkness, I sat down on the alley kerbstone and put my shoes back on, and put the gun into my pocket. I hadn't meant to bring it along at all, but as long as I had I couldn't throw it away now.

Anyway, it was going to get Dick Ehlers in trouble with Kates. When Kates looked for that gun and found it missing, he'd know that I'd been in the courthouse and that Ehlers had missed me. He'd know that I'd been right in his own office while he'd been out searching for me.

And so there I was in the dark, in safety for a few minutes until a car full of deputies decided to cruise down that particular alley looking for me. And I had a gun in my pocket that might or might not shoot—I hadn't checked that—and I had my shoes on and my hands were shaking again.

I didn't even have to ask myself, *Little man, what now*. The little man not only wanted a drink; he really needed one.

And Kates had already been to Smiley's looking for me and had found that I wasn't there.

So I started down the alley toward Smiley's.

Funny, but I was getting over being scared. A little, anyway. You can get only just *so* scared, and then something happens to your adrenal glands or something. I can't remember offhand whether your adrenals make you frightened or whether they get going and operate against it, but mine were getting either into or out of action, as the case might be. I'd been scared so much that night that I—or my glands—was getting tired of it.

I was getting brave, almost. And it wasn't Dutch courage, either; it had been so long since I'd had a drink that I'd forgotten what one tasted like. I was cold damn sober. About three times during the course of the long evening and the long night I'd been on the borderline of intoxication, but always something had happened to keep me from drinking for a while and then something had sobered me up. Some foolish little thing like being taken for a ride by gangsters or watching a man die suddenly or horribly by quaffing a bottle labelled "DRINK ME" or finding murdered men in the back of my own car or discovering that a sheriff intended to shoot me down in cold grue. Little things like that.

So I kept going down the alley toward Smiley's. The dog that had barked at me before barked again. But I didn't waste time barking back. I kept on going down the alley toward Smiley's.

There was the street to cross. I took a quick look both ways but didn't worry about it beyond that. If the sheriff's car or the deputies' car suddenly turned the corner and started spraying me with head-lights and then bullets, well, then that was that. You can only get so worried; then you quit worrying. When things can't get any worse, outside of your getting killed, then either you get killed or things start getting better.

Things started to get better; the window into the back room of Smiley's was open. I didn't bother taking off my shoes this time. Smiley would be asleep upstairs, but alone, and Smiley's so sound a sleeper that a bazooka shell exploding in the next room wouldn't wake him. I remember times I've dropped into the tavern on a dull afternoon and found him asleep; it was almost hopeless to try to wake him, and I'd generally help myself and leave the money on the ledge of the register. And he dropped asleep so quickly and easily that even if Kates and Hank had wakened him when they'd look for me here, he'd be asleep again by now.

In fact—yes, I could hear a faint rumbling sound overhead, like very distant thunder. Smiley snoring.

I groped my way through the dark back room and opened the door to the tavern. There was a dim light in there that burned all night long, and the shades were left up. But Kates had already been here and the chances of anyone else happening to pass and look in at half-past three of a Friday morning were negligible.

I took a bottle of the best bonded Bourbon Smiley had from the back bar and because it looked as though there were still at least a fair chance that this might be the last drink I ever had, I took a bottle of seltzer from the case under the bar. I took them to the table around the el, the one that's out of sight of the windows, the table at which Bat and George had sat early this evening.

Bat and George seemed, now, to have sat there a long time ago, years maybe, and seemed not a tenth as frightening as they'd been at the time. Almost, they seemed a little funny, somehow.

I left the two bottles on the table and went back for a glass, a swizzle stick, and some ice cubes from the refrigerator. This drink I'd waited a long time for, and it was going to be a good one.

I'd even pay a good price for it, I decided, especially after I looked in my wallet and found I had several tens but nothing smaller. I put a ten-dollar bill on the ledge of the register, and I wondered if I'd ever get my change out of it.

I went back to the table and made myself a drink, a good one.

I lighted up a cigar, too. That was a bit risky because if Kates came by here again for another check, he might see cigar smoke in the dim light, even though I was out of his range of vision. But I decided the risk was worth it. You can, I was finding, get into such a Godawful jam that a little more risk doesn't seem to matter at all.

I took a long good swig of the drink and then a deep drag from the cigar, and I felt pretty good. I held out my hands and they weren't shaking. Very silly of them not to be, but they weren't.

Now, I thought, is my first chance to think for a long time. My first real chance since Yehudi Smith had died.

Little man, what now?

The pattern. Could I make any sense out of the pattern?

Yehudi Smith—only that undoubtedly wasn't his real name, else the card he gave me wouldn't have been printed in my own shop—had called to see me and had told me——

Skip what he told you, I told myself. That was gobbledegook, just the kind of gobbledegook that would entice you to go to such a crazy place at such a crazy time. He knew you—that is, I corrected myself—he knew a lot about you. Your hobby and your weaknesses and what you were and what would interest you.

His coming there was planned. Planned well in advance; the card proved that.

According to a plan, he called on you at a time when no one else would be there. Probably, sitting in his car, he'd watched you come home, knowing Mrs. Carr was there—in all probability he or someone had been watching the house all evening—and waiting until she'd left to present himself.

No one had seen him, no one besides yourself.

He'd led you on a wild-goose chase. There weren't any Vorpal Blades; that was gobbledegook, too.

Connect that with the fact that Miles Harrison and Ralph Bonney had been killed while Yehudi Smith was keeping you entertained and busy, and that their bodies had been put in the back compartment of your car.

Easy. Smith was an accomplice of the murderer, hired to keep you away from anybody else who might alibi you while the crime was going on. Also to give you such an incredible story to account for where you really were that your own mother, if she were still alive, would have a hard time believing it.

But connect that with the fact that Smith had been killed, too. And with the fact that the pay roll money had been left in your car along with the bodies.

It added up to gibberish.

I took another sip of my drink and it tasted weak. I looked at it and saw I'd been sitting there so long between sips that most of the ice had melted. I put more of the bonded Bourbon in it and it tasted all right again.

I remembered about the gun I'd grabbed up from Kates' desk, the rusty one with which the two murders had been committed. I took it out of my pocket and looked at it. I handled it so I wouldn't have to touch their dried stains on the butt.

I broke it to see if any shots had been fired from it and found there weren't any cartridges in it, empty or otherwise. I clicked it back into position and tried the trigger. It was rusted shut. It hadn't, then, been used as a gun at all. Just as a hammer to bash out the brains of two men.

And I'd certainly made a fool of myself by bringing it along. I'd played right into the killer's hands by doing that. I put it back into my pocket.

I wished that I had someone to talk to. I felt that I might figure out things aloud better than I could this way. I wished that Smiley was awake, and for a moment I was tempted to go upstairs to get him. No, I decided, once already tonight I'd put Smiley in danger—danger out of which he'd got both of us and without any help from me whatsoever.

And this was *my* problem. It wouldn't be fair to Smiley to tangle him in it.

Besides, this wasn't a matter for Smiley's brawn and guts. This was like playing chess, and Smiley didn't play chess. Carl might possibly be able to help me figure it out, but Smiley—never. And I didn't want to tangle Carl in this either.

But I wanted to *talk* to somebody.

All right, maybe I was a little crazy—not drunk, definitely not drunk—but a little crazy. I wanted to talk to somebody, so I did.

The little man who wasn't there.

I imagined him sitting across the table from me, sitting there with an imaginary drink in his hand. Gladly, right gladly, would I have poured him a real one if he'd been really there. He was looking at me strangely.

"Smitty," I said.

"Yes, Doc?"

"What's your real name, Smitty? I know it *isn't* Yehudi Smith. That was part of the gag. The card you gave me proves that."

It wasn't the right question to ask. He wavered a little, as though he was going to disappear on me. I shouldn't have asked him a question that I myself couldn't answer, because he was there only because my mind was putting him there. He couldn't tell me anything I didn't know myself or couldn't figure out.

He wavered a little, but he rallied. He said, "Doc, I can't tell you that. Any more than I can tell you whom I was working for. You know that."

Get it; he said "whom I was working for" not "who I was working for." I felt proud of him and of myself.

I said, "Sure, Smitty. I shouldn't have asked. And listen, I'm sorry—I'm sorry as hell that you died."

"That's all right, Doc. We all die sometime. And—well, it was a nice evening up to then."

"I'm glad I fed you," I said. "I'm glad I gave you all you wanted to drink. And listen, Smitty, I'm sorry I laughed out loud when I saw that bottle and key on the glass-topped table. I just couldn't help it. It *was* funny."

"Sure, Doc. But I had to play it straight. It was part of the act. But it was corny; I don't blame you for acting amused. And, Doc, I'm sorry I did it. I didn't know the whole score—you've got proof of that. If I had, I wouldn't have drunk what was in that bottle. I didn't look like a man who wanted to die, did I, Doc?"

I shook my head slowly, looking at the laughter-lines around his eyes and his mouth. He didn't look like a man who wanted to die.

But he had died, suddenly and horribly.

"I'm sorry, Smitty," I told him. "I'm sorry as hell. I'd give a hell of a lot to bring you back, to have you really sitting there."

He chuckled. "Don't get maudlin, Doc. It'll spoil your thinking. You're trying to think, you know."

"I know," I said. "But I had to get it out of my system. All right, Smitty. You're dead and I can't do anything about it. You're the little man who isn't there. And I can't ask you any questions I can't answer myself, so really you can't help me."

"Are you sure, Doc? Even if you ask the right questions?"

"What do you mean? That my subconscious mind might know the answers even if I don't?"

He laughed. "Let's not get Freudian. Let's stick to Lewis Carroll. I really *was* a Carroll enthusiast, you know. I was a fast study, but not that fast. I couldn't have memorized all that about him just for one occasion."

The phrase struck me, "a fast study." I repeated it and went on where it led me. "You were an actor, Smitty? Hell, don't answer it. You must have been. I should have guessed that. An actor hired to play a part."

He grinned a bit wryly. "Not too good an actor, then, or you wouldn't have guessed it. And pretty much of a sucker, Doc, to have accepted the role. I should have guessed that there was more in it than what he told me." He shrugged. "Well, I played you a dirty trick, but I played a worse one on myself. Didn't I?"

"I'm sorry you're dead, Smitty. God damn it, I *liked* you."

"I'm glad, Doc. I haven't liked myself too well these last few years. You've figured it out by now so I can tell you—I was pretty down and out to take a booking like that, and at the price he offered me for it. And, damn him, he didn't pay me in advance except my expenses, so what did I gain by it? I got killed. Wait, don't get maudlin about that again. Let's drink to it."

We drank to it. There are worse things than getting killed. And there are worse ways of dying than suddenly when you aren't expecting it, when you're slightly tight and——

But that subject wasn't getting us anywhere.

"You were a character actor," I said.

"Doc, you disappoint me by belabouring the obvious. And that doesn't help you to figure out who Anybody is."

"Anybody?"

"That's what you were calling him to yourself when you were thinking things out, in a half-witted sort of way, not so long ago. Remember thinking that Anybody could have got into your printing shop and Anybody could have set up one line of type and figured out how to print one good card on that little hand press, but why would Anybody——"

"Unfair," I said. "You can get inside my mind, because—because, hell, that's where you *are*. But I can't get into yours. You know who Anybody is. But I don't."

"Even I, Doc, might not know his real name. In case something went wrong, he wouldn't have told me that. Something like—well, suppose you'd grabbed that 'DRINK ME' bottle when you first found the table and tossed it off before I could tell you that it was my prerogative to do so. Yes, there were a lot of things that could have gone wrong in so complicated a deal as that one was."

I nodded. "Yes, suppose Al Grainger had come around for that game of chess and we'd taken him along. Suppose—suppose I hadn't lived to get home at all. I had a narrow squeak earlier in the evening, you know."

"In that case, Doc, it never would have happened. You ought to be able to figure that out without my telling you. If you'd been killed, you and Smiley, earlier in the evening, then—at least if Anybody had learned about it, as he probably would have—Ralph

Bonney and Miles Harrison wouldn't have been killed later. At least not tonight. A wheel would have come off the plans and I'd have gone back to—wherever I came from. And everything would have been off."

I said, "But suppose I'd stayed at the office far into the night working on one of those big stories I thought I had—and was so happy about. How would Anybody have known?"

"Can't tell you that, Doc. But you might guess. Suppose I had orders to keep Anybody posted on your movements, if they went off schedule. When you left the house, saying you'd be back shortly, I'd have used your phone and told him that. And when you phoned that you were on your way back I'd have let him know, while you were walking home, wouldn't I?"

"But that was pretty late."

"Not too late for him to have intercepted Miles Harrison and Ralph Bonney on their way back from Neilsville—under certain circumstances—if his plans had been held in abeyance until he was sure you'd be home and out of circulation before midnight."

I said, "Under certain circumstances," and wondered just what I meant by it.

Yehudi Smith smiled. He lifted his glass and looked at me mockingly over the rim of it before he drank. He said, "Go on, Doc. You're only in the second square, but your next move will be a good one. You go to the fourth square by train, you know."

"And the smoke alone is worth a thousand pounds a puff."

"And that's the answer, Doc," he said, quietly.

I stared at him. A prickle went down my back.

Outside, in the night, a clock struck four times.

"What do you mean, Smitty?" I asked him slowly.

The little man who wasn't there poured more whisky from an imaginary bottle into his imaginary glass. He said, "Doc, you've been letting the glass-topped table and the bottle and the key fool you. They're from *Alice in Wonderland*. Originally, of course, called *Alice's Adventures Underground*. Wonderful book. But you're in the second."

"The second square? You just said that."

"The second book. *Through the Looking-Glass, and What Alice Found There*. And, Doc, you know as well as I what Alice found there."

I poured myself another drink, a short one this time, to match his. I didn't bother with ice or seltzer.

He raised his glass. "You've got it now, Doc," he said. "Not all of it, but enough to start on. You might still see the dawn come up."

"Don't be so God damn dramatic," I said; "certainly I'm going to see the dawn come up."

"Even if Kates comes here again looking for you? Don't forget when he misses that rusty gun in your pocket, he'll know you were at the courthouse when he was looking for you here. He might recheck all his previous stops. And you're awfully damned careless in filling the place with cigar smoke, you know."

"You mean it's worth a thousand pounds a puff?"

He put back his head and laughed and then he quit laughing and he wasn't there any more, even in my imagination, because a sudden slight sound made me look toward the door that led upstairs, to Smiley's rooms. The door opened and Smiley was standing there.

In a nightshirt. I hadn't known anybody wore nightshirts any more, but Smiley wore one. His eyes looked sleepy and his hair—what was left of it—was tousled and he was barefoot. He had a gun in his hand, the little short-barrelled thirty-eight Banker's Special I'd given him some hours ago. In his huge hand it looked tiny, a toy. It didn't look like something that had knocked a Buick off the road, killing one man and badly injuring another, that very evening.

There wasn't any expression on his face, none at all.

I wonder what mine looked like. But through a looking-glass or not, I didn't have one to look into.

Had I been talking to myself aloud? Or had my conversation with Yehudi Smith been imaginary, within my own mind? I honestly didn't know.

If I'd really been talking to myself, it was going to be a hell of a thing to have to explain. Especially if Kates had, on his stop here, awakened Smiley and told him that I was crazy.

In any case, what the hell could I possibly say right now but "Hello, Smiley?"

I opened my mouth to say "Hello, Smiley," but I didn't.

Someone was pounding on the glass of the front door. Someone who yelled, "Hey, open up here!" in the voice of Sheriff Rance Kates.

I did the only reasonable thing to do. I poured myself another drink.

CHAPTER FOURTEEN

"You are old," said the youth," one would hardly suppose
That your eye was as steady as ever;
Yet you balanced an eel on the end of your nose——
What made you so awfully clever?"

KATES hammered again and tried the knob.

Smiley stared at me and I stared back at him. I couldn't say anything—even if I could have thought of anything to say—to him at that distance without the probability of Kates hearing my voice.

Kates hammered again. I heard him say something to Hank about breaking in the glass. Smiley bent down and placed the gun on the step behind him and then came out of the door into the tavern. Without looking at me he walked toward the front door and, at sight of him, Kates stopped the racket there.

Smiley didn't walk quite straight toward the door; he made a slight curve that took him past my table. As he passed, he reached out and jerked the cigar out of my hand. He stuck it in his mouth and then went to the door and opened it.

I couldn't see in that direction, of course, and I didn't stick my head around the corner of the el. I sat there and sweated.

"What you want? Why such a hell of a racket?" I heard Smiley demand.

Kates' voice: "Thought Stoeger was here. That smoke——"

"Left my cigar down here," Smiley said. "Remembered it when I got back up and came down to get it. Why all the racket?"

"It was damn near half an hour ago when I was here," Kates said belligerently. "Cigar doesn't burn that long."

Smiley said patiently, "I couldn't sleep after you were here. I came down and got myself a drink five minutes ago. I left my cigar down here." His voice got soft, very soft. "Now get the hell out of here. You've spoiled my night already. Didn't get to sleep till two and you wake me at half-past three and come around again at four. What's the big idea, Kates?"

"You're sure Stoeger isn't——"

"I told you I'd call you if I saw him. Now, you bastard, get out of here."

I could imagine Kates turning purple. I could imagine him looking at Smiley and realizing that Smiley was half again as strong as he was.

The door slammed so hard it must have come very near to breaking the glass.

Smiley came back. Without looking back at me he said quietly, "Don't move, Doc. He might look back in a minute or two." He went on around behind the bar, got himself a glass and poured a drink. He sat down on the stool he keeps for himself back there, facing slightly to the back so his lip movement wouldn't show to anyone looking in the front window. He took a sip of the drink and a puff of my cigar.

I kept my voice as low as he'd kept his. I said, "Smiley, you ought to have your mouth washed out with soap. You told a lie."

He grinned. "Not that I know of, Doc. I told him I'd call him if I saw you. I did call him. Didn't you hear *what* I called him?"

"Smiley," I said, "this is the screwiest night I've ever been through but the screwiest thing about it is that you're developing a sense of humour. I didn't think you had it in you."

"How bad trouble are you in, Doc? What can I do?"

I said, "Nothing. Except what you just did do, and thanks to hell and back for that. It's something I've got to think out, and work out for myself, Smiley. Nobody can help me."

"Kates said, when he was here the first time, you were a ho—homi—what the hell was it?"

"Homicidal maniac," I said. "He thinks I killed two men tonight. Miles Harrison and Ralph Bonney."

"Yeah. Don't bother telling me you didn't."

I said, "Thanks, Smiley." And then it occured to me that "Don't bother telling me you didn't" could be taken either one of two ways. And I wondered again if I *had* been talking to myself aloud or only in my imagination while Smiley had been walking down those stairs and opening the door. I asked him, "Smiley, do you think I'm crazy?"

"I've always thought you were crazy, Doc. But crazy in a nice way."

I thought how wonderful it is to have friends. Even if I *was* crazy, there were two people in Carmel City that I could count on to go to bat for me. There was Smiley and there was Carl.

But damn it, friendship should work both ways. This was my danger and my problem and I had no business dragging Smiley into it any farther than he'd already stuck his neck. If I told Smiley that Kates had tried to kill me and still intended to, then Smiley—who hated Kates' guts already—would go out looking for Kates and like as not kill him with his bare hands, or get shot trying it. I couldn't do that to Smiley.

I said, "Smiley, finish your drink and go up to bed again. I've got to think."

"Sure there's no way I can help you, Doc?"

"Positive."

He tossed off the rest of his drink and tamped out the cigar in an ash-tray. He said, "Okay, Doc, I know you're smarter than I am, and if it's brains you need for help, I'm just in the way. Good luck to you."

He walked back to the door of the staircase. He looked carefully at the front windows to be sure nobody was looking in and then he reached inside and picked up the revolver from the step on which he'd placed it.

He came walking over to my table. He said, "Doc, if you *are* a ho—homi—what you said, you might want to kill somebody else tonight. That's loaded. I even replaced the two bullets I shot out of it earlier."

He put it down on the table in front of me, turned his back to me and went back to the stairs. I watched him go, marvelling. I'd never yet seen a man in a nightshirt who hadn't looked ridiculous. Until then. What more can a man do to prove he doesn't think you're insane than give you a loaded gun and then turn his back and walk away. And when I thought of all the times I'd razzed Smiley and ridden him, all the cracks I'd made at him, I wanted——

Well, I couldn't answer when he said "Good night, Doc," just before he closed the door behind him. Something felt a little wrong with my throat, and if I'd tried to say anything, I might have bawled.

My hand shook a little as I poured myself another drink, a short one. I was beginning to feel them and this had better be my last one, I knew.

I had to think more clearly than I'd ever thought before. I couldn't get drunk, I didn't dare.

I tried to get my mind back to what I'd been thinking about—what I'd been talking about to the little man who wasn't there—before Smiley's coming downstairs and Kates' knocking had interrupted me.

I looked across the table where Yehudi Smith, in my mind, had been sitting. But he wasn't there. I couldn't bring him back. He was dead, and he wouldn't come back.

The quiet room in the quiet night. The dim light of the single twenty-watt bulb over the cash register. The creaking of my thoughts as I tried to turn them back into the groove. Connect facts.

Lewis Carroll and bloody murder.

Through the Looking-Glass and What Alice Found There.

What *had* Alice found there?

Chessman, and a game of chess. And Alice herself had been a pawn. That was why, of course, she'd crossed the third square by railroad. With the smoke alone worth a thousand pounds a puff—almost as expensive as the smoke from my cigar might have been had not Smiley taken it out of my hand and claimed it as his own.

Chessman, and a game of chess.

But who was the *player?*

And suddenly I knew. Illogically, because he didn't have a shadow of a motive. The Why I did not see, but Yehudi Smith had told me the How, and now I saw the Who.

The pattern. Whoever had arranged tonight's little chess problem played chess all right, and played it well. Looking-glass chess and real chess, both. And he knew me well—which meant I knew him, too. He knew my weaknesses, the things I'd fall for. He *knew* I'd go with Yehudi Smith on the strength of that mad, weird story Smith had told me.

But *why?* What had he to gain? He'd killed Miles Harrison, Ralph Bonney and Yehudi Smith. And he'd left the money Miles and Ralph had been carrying in that brief-case and put it in the back of my car, with the two bodies.

Then money hadn't been the motive. Either that, or the motive had been money in such large quantity that the couple of thousand dollars Bonney had been carrying didn't matter.

But wasn't a man concerned who was one of the richest men in Carmel City? Ralph Bonney. His fireworks factory, his other investments, his real estate must have added up to—well, maybe half a million dollars. A man shooting for half a million dollars can well abandon the proceeds of a two-thousand dollar holdup and leave them with the bodies of the men he has killed, to help pin the crime on the pawn he has selected, to divert suspicion from himself.

Connect facts.

Ralph Bonney was divorced today. He was murdered tonight.

Then Miles Harrison's death was incidental. Yehudi Smith had been another pawn.

A warped mind, but a brilliant mind. A cold, cruel mind. And yet, paradoxically, a mind that loved fantasy, as I did, that loved Lewis Carroll, as I did.

I started to pour myself another drink and then remembered that I still had only part of the answer, and that even if I had it all, I hadn't the slightest idea what I could do with it, without a shred of evidence, or an iota of proof.

Without even an idea, in my own mind, of the reason, the motive. But there must be one; the rest of it was too well planned, too logical.

There was one possibility that I could see.

I sat there listening a while to be sure there was no car

approaching; the night was so quiet that I could have heard one at least a block away.

I looked at the gun Smiley had given me back, hesitated, and finally put it in my pocket. Then I went into the back room and let myself out of the window into the dark alley.

Carl Trenholm's house was three blocks away. Luckily, it was on the street next to Oak Street and parallel to it. I could make all of the distance through the alley except for the streets I'd have to cross.

I heard a car coming as I approached the second street and I ducked down and hid behind a garbage can until it had gone by. It was going slowly and it was probably either Hank and the sheriff or the two deputies. I didn't look out to see for fear they might flash a spotlight down the alley.

I waited until the sound of it died away completely before I crossed the street.

I let myself in the back gate of Carl's place. With his wife away, I wasn't positive which bedroom he'd be sleeping in, but I found pebbles and tossed them at the most likely window and it was the right one.

It went up and Carl's head came out. I stepped close to the house so I wouldn't have to yell. I said, "It's Doc, Carl. Don't light a light anywhere in the house. But come down to the back door."

"Coming, Doc." He closed the window. I went up on the back porch and waited until the door opened and I went in. I closed the door behind me and the kitchen was as black as the inside of a tomb.

Carl said, "Damned if I know where a flashlight is, Doc. Can't we put on a light? I feel like hell."

"No, leave it off," I told him. I struck a match, though, to find my way to a chair and it showed me Carl in rumpled pyjamas, his hair mussed and looking like he was in for the grandfather of all hangovers.

He sat down, too, while the match flared. "What's it about, Doc? Kates and Ganzer were here looking for you. Waked me up a while ago, but they didn't tell me much. Are you in a jam, Doc? *Did* you kill somebody?"

"No," I said. "Listen, you're Ralph Bonney's lawyer, aren't you? I mean on everything, not just the divorce today."

"Yes."

"Who's his heir, now that he's divorced?"

"Doc, I'm afraid I can't tell you that. A lawyer isn't supposed to tell his clients' business. You know that as well as I do."

"Didn't Kates tell you Ralph Bonney is dead, Carl? And Miles

Harrison? They were murdered on their way back from Neilsville with the payroll, somewhere around midnight."

"My God," Carl said. "No, Kates didn't tell me."

I said, "I know you're still not supposed to tell his business until a will is probated, if there is one. But listen, let me make a guess and you can tell me if I'm wrong. If I guess right, you won't have to confirm it; just keep your mouth shut."

"Go ahead, Doc."

"Bonney had an illegitimate son about twenty-three years ago. But he supported the boy's mother all her life until she died recently; she worked, too, as a milliner but he gave her enough extra so that she lived better than she would have otherwise, and she sent the boy to college and gave him every break."

I stopped there and waited and Carl didn't say anything.

I went on, "Bonney still gave the boy an allowance. That's how he—hell, let's call him by name—that's how Al Grainger has been living without working. And unless he knows he's in Bonney's will, he's got proof of his parentage and can claim the bulk of the estate anyway. And it must be half a million."

Carl said, "I'll talk. It'll run about three hundred thousand. And you guessed right on Al Grainger, but how you guessed it, I don't know. Bonney's relations to Mrs. Grainger and to Al have been the best-kept secret I've ever known of. In fact, outside the parties concerned, I was the only person who ever knew—or even suspected. How did you guess?"

"By what happened to me tonight—and that's too complicated to explain right now. But Al plays chess and has the type of mind to do things the complicated way, and that's the way they happened. And he knows Lewis Carroll and——" I stopped because I was still after facts and I didn't want to start explaining.

The night was almost over. I saw a greenish gleam in the darkness that reminded me Carl wore a wrist watch with a luminous dial. "What time is it?" I asked him.

The gleam vanished as he turned the dial toward himself. "Almost five o'clock. About ten minutes off. Listen. Doc, you've got so much you might as well have the rest. Yes, Al has proof of his parentage. And, as an only child, illegitimate or not, he can claim the entire estate now that Bonney isn't married. He could have cut in for a fraction of it, of course, even before the divorce."

"Didn't he leave a will?"

"Ralph didn't ever make a will. Superstitious about it. I've often tried to talk him into making one, but he never would."

"And Al Grainger knew that?"

Carl said, "I imagine he would have."

"Is there any reason why Al would have been in such a hurry?" I asked. "I mean, would there have been any change in status if he'd waited a while instead of killing Bonney the night after the divorce?"

Carl thought a minute. "Bonney was planning to leave tomorrow for a long vacation. Al would have had to wait several months, and maybe he figured Bonney might re-marry—meet someone on the cruise he was going to take. It happens that way, sometimes, on the rebound after a divorce. And Bonney is—was only fifty-two."

I nodded—to myself, since Carl couldn't see me in the darkness. That last bit of information covered everything on the motive end.

I knew everything now, except the details and they didn't matter much. I knew why Al had done everything that he had done; he *had* to make an airtight frame on someone because once he claimed Bonney's estate, his own motive would be obvious. I could even guess some of the reasons why he'd picked me for the scapegoat.

He must have hated me, and kept it carefully under cover. I could see a reason for it, now that I knew more about him. I've got a loose tongue and often swear at people affectionately, if you know what I mean. How often, when Al had beaten me in a game of chess had I grinned at him and said, "All right, you bastard. But try to do it again."

Never dreaming, of course, that he *was* one, and knew it.

He must have hated me like hell. In some ways he could have picked an easier victim, someone more likely than I to have committed murder and robbery for money. Choosing me, his plan took more gobbledegook; he had to give me such a mad story to tell that nobody would believe a word of it and would think, instead, that I'd gone insane. Of course, too, he knew how much Kates hated me; he counted on that.

A sudden thought shook me; could Kates have been in on the deal with Al? That would account for his trying to kill me rather than lock me up. Maybe that was the deal—for a twenty or fifty thousand dollar cut of the estate, Kates had agreed to shoot me down under the pretence that I had attacked him or had tried to escape.

No, I decided on second thought, it hadn't been that way. I'd been alone with Kates in his office for almost half an hour while Hank Ganzer had been on his way back from Neilsville. It would have been too easy for Kates to have killed me then, planted a weapon on me and claimed that I'd come in and attacked him. And when the two bodies had been found in my car, the story would have been perfectly credible. It would even have pointed up the indication that I'd gone homicidally insane.

No, Kates' motives for wanting to kill me had been personal, sheer malice because of the things I'd written about him in editorials and the way I'd fought him in elections. He'd wanted to kill me and had seen a sudden opportunity when the bodies had been found in my car. He'd passed up a much better chance because, when I was alone with him for so long in his office, he hadn't known the bodies were there.

No, definitely this was a one-man job, except for Yehudi Smith. Al had hired Smith to keep me diverted, but when Smith's job was done, he was eliminated. Another pawn. Chess isn't a team game.

Carl said, "How are *you* mixed in this, Doc? What can I do?"

"Nothing," I said. It was my problem, not Carl's. I'd kept Smiley out of it; I'd keep Carl out of it, too. Except for the information and help he'd already given me. "Go up to bed, Carl. I've got a little more thinking to do."

"Hell with that. I can't sleep with you sitting down here thinking. But I'll sit here and shut up unless you talk to me. You can't tell whether I'm here or not anyway, if I shut up."

I said, "Shut up, then."

Proof, I thought. But what proof? Somewhere, but God knew where, was the dead body of the actor Al had hired to play the role of Yehudi. But this had been planned, and well planned. Suitable disposal of that body had been arranged for long before Al had taken it away from the Wentworth place. It wasn't going to turn up at random and one guess was as good as another as to where he'd hidden or buried it. He'd had hours to do it in and he'd known in advance every step he was going to take.

The car in which Yehudi Smith had driven me to the Wentworth house and which he'd switched for my own car after he'd used mine for the supposed holdup. No, I couldn't find that car as proof and it wouldn't mean anything if I did. It could have been—probably was—a stolen car, and now returned to wherever he'd stolen it from, never missed by its owner. And I didn't even remember what make or model it was. All I remember was that it had an onyx gear shift knob and a push-button radio. I didn't even know whether it was a Cadillac, convertible or a Ford business coupé.

Had Al arranged any kind of an alibi for himself?

Maybe, maybe not, but what did it matter unless I could find something against him besides motive? That, and my own certainty that he'd done it. I hadn't any alibi, none at all. I had an incredible story and two bodies and the stolen money in my car. And a sheriff and three deputies looking for me and ready to shoot on sight.

I had the murder weapon in my pocket. And another gun, too, a loaded one.

Could I go to Al Grainger and scare him into writing out and signing a confession?

He'd laugh at me. I'd laugh at myself for trying. A man with the warped brain that would work out something like Al's plan tonight wasn't going to tell me what time it was just because I pointed a gun at him.

A faint touch of light was showing at the windows. I could even make out Carl sitting there across the table from me.

"Carl," I said.

"Yes. Doc? Say, I was letting you think, but I'm glad you spoke. Just had an idea."

"An idea's what I need," I told him. "What is it?"

"Want a drink?"

I asked, "Is that the idea?"

"That's the idea. Look, I'm hung over to hell and back and I can't have one with you, but I just realized what a lousy host I was. Do you want one?"

"Thanks," I said, "but I had a drink. Listen, Carl, talk to me about Al Grainger. Don't ask me what to say. Just talk."

"Anything, at random?"

"Anything, at random."

"Well, he's always impressed me as being a little off the beam. Brilliant, but—well, twisted, somehow. Maybe his knowledge of who and what he was contributed to that. Smiley always felt that, too; he's mentioned it to me. Not that Smiley knows who or what Al is, but he just felt something was wrong."

I said, "My opinion of Smiley has changed a lot tonight. He's smarter, and a better guy, than both of us put together, Carl. But go on about Al."

"Touch of Oedipus, complicated by bastardy. Probably, in some obscure way, managed to blame Bonney for his mother's death. Not a real paranoiac, but near enough to do something like that. Sadism—most of us have a touch of it, but Al a little more than most."

I said, "Most of us have a touch of everything. Go on."

"Pyrophobia. But you know about that. Not that we haven't all got phobias. Your acrophobia and my being afraid of cats. But Al's is pretty bad. So afraid of fire that he doesn't smoke and I've noticed him wince when I've lighted a cig——"

"Shut up, Carl," I said.

I should have thought of it myself, sooner. A lot sooner.

I said, "I'll have that drink, Carl. Just one, but a good one."

I didn't need it physically, but I needed it mentally this time. I was scared stiff at the very thought of what I was going to do.

CHAPTER FIFTEEN

One, two! One, two! And through and through
The vorpal blade went snicker-snack!
He left it dead, and with its head
He went galumphing back.

THE windows were faint grey rectangles; now with my eyes accustomed to the decreasing darkness, I could see Carl almost clearly as he went to the cupboard and groped until he had the bottle he was looking for.

He said, "Doc, you sound happy enough that I'll have one with you. Hair of the dog, for me. Kill or cure."

He got two glasses, too, from over the sink, breaking only one glass by knocking it into the sink in the process. He said a nasty word and then brought the glasses to the table. I struck a match and held it while he poured whisky into them.

He said, "Damn you, Doc, if you're going to do this often, I'm going to get some luminous paint. I could paint bands around the glasses and the bottle. And say, know what else I could do? I could paint a chessboard and a set of chessmen with luminous paint, too. Then we could sit here and play chess in the dark."

"I'm playing, Carl, right now. I just reached the seventh square. Maybe somebody'll crown me on the next move, when I reach the king-row. Have you got any cleaning fluid?"

He started to reach for his glass, but he pulled his hand back and looked at me instead.

"Cleaning fluid? Isn't whisky good enough for you?"

"I don't want it to drink," I explained. "I want it not to burn."

He shook his head a trifle. "Again and slowly."

"I want some of the kind that isn't inflammable. You know what I mean."

"Wife's got some kind of cleaning fluid around. Whether it's that kind or not, I don't know. I'll look."

He looked, using my matches and examining the labels of a row of bottles in the compartment under the sink. He came up with one and looked at it closely. "Nope. This is marked 'Danger' in big letters and "Keep away from fire.' Guess we haven't got the non-inflammable kind."

I sighed. It would have been simple if Carl had had the right brand. I had some myself, at home, but I didn't want to go there. It meant a trip to the supermarket.

And I didn't ask Carl for a candle. I could get that at the supermarket, too, and I neither wanted Carl to think I was crazy or to have to explain to him what I was going to do.

We had our drink. Carl shuddered at his, but got it down. He said, "Doc, listen, isn't there *anything* I can do?"

I turned back at the door. "You've done plenty." I told him. "But if you want to do more, you might get dressed and ready. I might be phoning you soon if everything goes all right. I might need you then."

"Doc, wait. I'll get dressed now, and——"

"You'd be in the way, Carl," I told him.

And got out quickly before he could press me any farther. If he'd even guessed how bad a jam I was in or what a damn fool thing I was going to do, he'd have knocked me down and tied me up before he'd have let me out of there.

Dim grey light of early morning now, and I no longer had to grope my way. I'd forgotten to ask Carl the time again, but it must be about a quarter after five.

I was under greater risk, now, of being seen if Kates and the deputies were still cruising around looking for me, but I had a hunch that they'd have given up by now, convinced that I'd holed in somewhere. Probably now they were concentrating on the roads so I couldn't get out of town. And getting out of town was the farthest thing from my mind.

I stayed in the alleys, just the same. Back the way I'd come and ready to dive between garages or behind a garbage can at the first sound of a car. But there weren't any cars; five-fifteen is early even in Carmel City.

The supermarket wasn't open yet. I wrapped my handkerchief around the butt of one of my two revolvers—Two-Gun Stoeger, they call me—and broke a pane in one of the back windows. It made a hell of a racket, but there aren't any residences in that block and nobody heard me, or at least nobody did anything about it.

I let myself in and started my shopping.

Cleaning fluid. Two kinds; I needed some of the non-inflammable kind and, now that I thought of it, a bottle of the kind that was marked "Danger. Keep away from fire."

I opened both of them and they smelled about alike. I poured the inflammable kind down the drain of the sink at the back and replaced it with the kind that doesn't burn.

I even made sure that it wouldn't burn; I poured some on a rag and tried to light the rag. Maybe it would have been in keeping with everything else that had been happening if that rag *had* burned and I hadn't been able to put it out, if I'd burned the supermarket down and added arson to my other accomplishments of the night. But the rag wouldn't burn any more than if I'd soaked it with water instead of the gasoline-smelling cleaning fluid.

I thought out carefully what other items I'd need, and shopped for them; some rolls of one-inch adhesive tape, a candle, and a cake of soap. I'd heard that a cake of soap, inside a sock, made a good blackjack; the soap is soft enough to stun without killing. I took off one of my socks and made myself a blackjack.

My pockets were pretty well laden by the time I left the supermarket—by the same window through which I'd entered. I was pretty far gone in crime by them; it never occurred to me to leave money for my purchases.

It was almost daylight. A clear grey dawn that looked like the herald of a good day—for someone; whether for me or not I'd know soon.

I stuck to the alleys, back the way I'd come and three blocks on past Carl's house.

Al Grainger's. A one-storey, three-room house, about the size of mine.

It was almost six o'clock by then. He was asleep by now, if he was ever going to sleep. And somehow I thought he *would* be asleep by now. He'd have been through with everything he had to do by two o'clock, four hours ago. What he'd done might have kept him awake for a while, but not into the next day.

I cased the joint, and sighed with relief at one problem solved when I saw that the bedroom window wasn't closed. It opened on to the back porch and I could step into it easily.

I bent and stepped through it. I didn't make much noise and Al Grainger, sleeping soundly in the bed, didn't awaken. I had my gun—the loaded one—in my right hand and ready to use in case he did.

But I kept my right hand and the loaded gun out of sight. I got the rusty, unloaded Iver-Johnson, the gun that had been used as a bludgeon to kill Miles and Bonney, into my left hand. I had a test in mind which, if it worked, would be absolute proof to me that Al was guilty. If it didn't work, it wouldn't disprove it and I'd go ahead just the same, but it didn't cost anything to try.

It was still dim in the room and I reached out with my left hand and turned on the lamp that stood beside the bed. I wanted him to see that gun. He moved restlessly as the light went on, but he didn't awaken.

"Al," I said.

He wakened then, all right. He sat up in bed and stared at me. I said, "Put up your hands, Al," and held the gun in my left hand pointed at him, standing far enough back that he couldn't grab at me, but near enough that he could see the gun clearly in the pale glow of the lamp I'd lighted.

He looked from my face to the gun and back again. He threw back the sheet to get out of bed. He said, "Don't be a fool, Doc. That gun isn't loaded and it wouldn't shoot if it was."

If I needed any more proof, I had it.

He was starting to move his feet toward the edge of the bed when I brought my right hand, holding the other gun, around into sight. I said, "This one is loaded, and works."

He stopped moving his feet. I dropped the rusty gun into my coat pocket. I said, "Turn around Al."

He hesitated and I cocked the revolver. It was aimed at him from about five feet, too close to miss him if I pulled the trigger and just too far for him to risk grabbing at, especially from an awkward sitting-up-in-bed position. I could see him considering the odds, coldly, impartially.

He decided they weren't good. And he decided, probably, that if he let me take him, it wouldn't matter to his plans anyway. If I turned him over to the police along with my story, it wouldn't strengthen my story in the least.

"Turn around, Al," I repeated.

He still stared at me calculatingly. I could see what he was thinking; if he turned, I was probably going to slug him with the butt of the revolver and whatever my intentions, I might hit too hard. And if I killed him, even accidentally, it wouldn't help him any to know that they'd got me for one extra murder. I repeated, "Turn around, and put your hands out in back of you."

I could see some of the tenseness go out of him at that. If I was only going to tie him up——

He turned around. I quickly switched the revolver to my left hand and pulled out the improvised blackjack I'd made of a sock and a cake of soap. I made a silent prayer that I'd guess right on the swing and not hit too hard or not hard enough, and I swung.

The thud scared me. I thought I'd killed him, and I knew that he wasn't shamming when he dropped back flat on the bed because his head hit the head of the bed with a second thud that was almost as loud as the first.

And if he had been shamming he could have taken me easily, because I was so scared that I put the revolver down. I couldn't even put it in my pocket because it was cocked and I didn't know how to uncock it without shooting it off. So I put it on the night stand beside the bed and bent over him to feel his heart. It was still beating.

I got the rolls of adhesive tape out of my pocket and started to work. I taped around his mouth so he couldn't yell, and I taped his legs together at the ankles and at the knees. I taped his left wrist to his left thigh, and I used a whole roll of adhesive to tape his right arm against his side above the elbow. His right hand had to be free.

I found some clothes-line in the kitchen and tied him to the bed, managing as I did so to pull him up into an almost sitting position against the head of the bed.

I got a pad of paper, foolscap, from his desk and I put it and my ball-point pen within reach of his right hand.

There wasn't anything I could do but sit down and wait, then.

Ten minutes, maybe fifteen, and it was getting pretty light outside. I began to get impatient. Probably there wasn't any hurry; Al Grainger always slept late so no one would miss him for a long time yet, but the waiting was horrible.

I decided that I could take a drink again and that I needed one. I went out into his kitchen and hunted till I found a bottle. It was gin instead of whisky, but it would serve the purpose. It tasted horrible.

When I got back to the bedroom he was awake. So wide awake that I felt pretty sure that he'd been playing possum for a while, stalling for time. He was trying desperately with his free right hand to peel off the tape that held his left wrist to his thigh.

But with his right arm held tight against his side at the elbow he wasn't making much headway. When I picked up the gun off the night stand he stopped trying. He glared at me.

I said, "Hi, Al. We're in the seventh square."

I wasn't in any hurry now, none at all. I sat down comfortably before I went on.

"Listen, Al," I told him, "I left your right hand free so you can use that paper and the pen. I want you to do a little writing for me. I'll hold the pad for you so you can see what you're writing. Or don't you feel in the mood to write, Al?"

He merely lay back quietly and closed his eyes.

I said, "All I want you to write is that you killed Ralph Bonney and Miles Harrison last night. That you took my car out and intercepted them on the way back from Neilsville, probably on foot with my car out of sight. They knew you and would stop for you and let you in the car. So you got in the back seat and before Miles, who'd be driving, could start the car again you slugged him over the head and then slugged Bonney. Then you put their bodies in my car and left theirs somewhere off the road. And then you drove to the Wentworth place and left my car instead of whatever car I'd been driven there in. Or am I wrong on any little details, Al?"

He didn't answer, not that I'd expected him to.

I said, "There'll be quite a bit of writing, because I want you also to explain how you hired an actor to use the name of Yehudi

Smith and give me such an incredible story to tell that no one would ever believe me. I want you to tell how you had him entice me to the Wentworth place—and about that bottle you left there and what was in it. And that you'd instructed him that he was to drink it. And what his right name was and what you did with his body."

I said, "I guess that'll be enough for you to write, Al. You needn't write what the motive was; that'll be obvious after your relationship to Ralph Bonney comes to light, as it will. And you needn't write all the little details about how or when you let the air out of my tyres so I wouldn't be using my car nor how or when you used my shop to print that card with the name Yehudi Smith and my union label number. And you needn't write why you picked me to take the blame for the murders. In fact, I'm not proud of that part of it at all. It makes me a little ashamed of the thing I'm going to have to do in order to persuade you to do the writing I've been talking about."

I *was* a little ashamed, but not enough so to keep me from doing it.

I took the bottle of non-inflammable cleaning fluid that smelled like gasoline and opened it.

Al Grainger's eyes opened, too, as I began to sprinkle it over the sheets and his pyjamas. I managed to hold the bottle so he could read the "Danger" warning and, if his eyes were good enough for the smaller type, the "Keep away from fire" part.

I emptied the whole bottle, ending up with quite a big wet spot of it at a point at one side of his knees where he could see it clearly. The room reeked with the gasoline-like odour.

I got out the candle and my knife and cut a piece an inch long off the top of the candle. I smoothed out the wet spot on the sheet and put the candle top down carefully.

"I'm going to light this, Al, and you'd better not move much or you'll knock it over. And I'm sure a pyrophobiac wouldn't like what would happen to him then. And you're a pyrophobiac, Al."

His eyes were wide with horror as I lighted the match. If his mouth hadn't been taped, he'd have screamed in terror. Every muscle of his body was rigid.

He tried to play possum on me, again, probably figuring I wouldn't go through with it if he was unconscious, if I thought he'd fainted. He could do it with his eyes, but the muscles of the rest of his body gave him away. He couldn't relax them if it would have saved his life.

I lighted the candle, and sat down again.

"An inch of candle, Al," I said. "Maybe ten minutes if you stay as still as that. Sooner if you get reckless and wriggle a toe or finger. That candle isn't too stable standing there on a soft mattress."

His eyes were open again, staring at that candle burning down toward the soaked sheet, staring in utter horror. I hated myself for what I was doing to him, but I kept on doing it just the same. I thought of three men murdered tonight and steeled myself. And after all, Al's only danger was in his mind. That wet spot on the sheet was stuff that would keep the sheet itself from burning.

"Ready to write, Al?"

His horror-filled eyes shifted from the candle to my face, but he didn't nod; I thought for a moment that he was calling my bluff, and then I realized that the reason he didn't nod was because he was afraid to make even the slight muscular movement for fear of knocking over the short candle.

I said, "All right, Al. I'll see if you're ready. If you aren't, I'll put the candle back where it was, and I'll let it keep burning meanwhile so you won't have gained any time." I picked up the candle gently and put it down on the night stand.

I held the pad. He started to write and then stopped, and I reached for the candle. The pen started moving again.

After a while I said, "That's enough. Just sign it."

I sighed with relief and went over to the telephone. Carl Trenholm must have been sitting beside his own phone; he answered almost before it had finished ringing the first time.

"Dressed and ready?" I asked him.

"Right, Doc. What do I do?"

"I've got Al Grainger's confession. I want it turned over to the law to clear me, but it's not safe for me to do it direct. Kates would shoot before he'd read and some of the deputies might. You'll have to do it for me, Carl."

"Where are you? at Al's?"

"Yes."

"I'll be around. And I'll bring Ganzer to get Al. It's all right; Hank won't shoot. I've been talking reason to him and he admits somebody else could have put those bodies in your car. And when I tell him there's a confession from Grainger, he'll listen."

"How about Kates, though? And how come you were talking to Hank Ganzer?"

"He called up here, looking for Kates. Kates left him to go back to the office an hour or two ago and never got to the office and they don't know where he is. But don't worry, Kates won't take any shots at you if you're with Ganzer and me both. I'll be right around."

I phoned Pete and told him that all hell had been popping and that now we had a story we could use, one even bigger than the ones that had got away. He said he'd get right down to the shop and get the fire going under the Linotype's metal pot. "I was just leaving anyway, Doc," he said. "It's half-past seven."

It was. I looked out the window and saw that it was broad daylight. I sat down and jittered until Carl and Hank got there.

It was eight o'clock exactly when I got to the office. Once Hank had seen that confession he'd let Carl and me talk him into letting Grainger do any explaining that remained so I could get the paper out in time. It was going to take me a good two hours to get that story written and we'd probably go to press a little later than usual, anyway.

Pete got to work dismantling page one to make room for it—and plenty of room. I phoned the restaurant and talked them into sending up a big thermos jug of hot, black coffee and started pounding my typewriter.

The phone rang and I picked it up. "Doc Stoeger?" it said. "This is Dr. Buchan at the asylum. You were so kind last night about not running the story about Mrs. Griswald's escape and recapture that I decided it was only fair to tell you that you can run it after all, if there's still time."

"There's still time," I said. "We're going to be late going to press anyway. And thanks. But what came up? I thought Mrs. G. didn't want to worry her daughter in Springfield."

"Her daughter knows anyway. A friend of hers here—one whom we went to see while we were hunting our patient—phoned her to tell her about it. And she telephoned the asylum to be sure her mother was all right. So she already knows and you might as well have the story after all."

I said, "Fine, Dr. Buchan. Thanks a lot for calling."

Back to the typewriter. The black coffee came and I drank almost a full cup of it the first gulp and damn near scalded myself.

The asylum story was quick and easy to get out of the way so I wrote it up first. I'd just finished when the phone rang again.

"Mr. Stoeger?" it asked me. "This is Ward Howard, superintendent of the fireworks factory. We had a slight accident in the plant yesterday that I'd like you to run a short story on, if it's not too late."

"It's not too late," I said, "provided the accident was in the Roman candle department. Was it?"

"Oh, so you already knew. Do you have the details or shall I give them to you?"

I let him give them and took notes and then I asked him how come they *wanted* the story printed.

"Change of policy, Mr. Stoeger. You see there have been rumours going around town about accidents here that don't happen—but are supposed to have happened and to have been kept out of the paper. I'm afraid my grammar's a bit involved there. I mean that we've decided that if the truth is printed about accidents that really do happen, it will help prevent false rumours and wild stories."

I told him I understood and thanked him.

I drank more black coffee and worked a while on the Bonney-Harrison-Smith murder story and then sandwiched in the Roman candle department story and then went back to the big story.

All I needed now was——

Captain Evans of the state police came in. I glared up at him and he grinned down at me.

I said, "Don't tell me. You've come to tell me that I can, after all, run the story of Smiley's and my little ride with the two gangsters and how Smiley captured one and killed one. It's just what I need. I can spare a stick of type back in the want ads."

He grinned again and pulled up a chair. He sat down in it, but I paid no further attention; I went on typing.

Then he pushed his hat back on his head and said quietly, "That's right, Doc."

I made four typing errors in a three-letter word and then turned around and looked at him. "Huh?" I said. "I was kidding. Wasn't I?"

"Maybe you were, but I'm not. You can run the story, Doc. They got Gene Kelley in Chicago two hours ago."

I groaned happily. Then I glared at him again. I said, "Then get the hell out of here. I've got to work."

"Don't you want the rest of the story?"

"What rest of it? I don't need details of how they got Kelley, just so they got him. That's, from my point of view, a footnote on the local angle, and the local angle is what happened *here* in the county to George and Bat—and to Smiley and me. Now scram."

I typed another sentence. He said, "Doc," and the way he said it made me take my hands away from the typewriter and look at him.

He said, "Doc, relax. It *is* local. There was one thing I didn't tell you last night because it was *too* local and too hot. One other thing we got out of Bat Masters. They weren't heading for Chicago or Gary right away. They were going to hole up overnight at a hideout for crooks—it's a farm run by a man named George Dixon, up in the hills. An isolated place. We knew Dixon as an ex-crook but never guessed he was running a rest home for boys who were hiding out from the law. We raided it last night. We got four criminals wanted in Chicago who were staying there. And we found, among other things, some letters and papers that told us where Gene Kelley was staying. We phoned Chicago quick and they got him, so you can run the whole story—the other members of the gang won't keep that hotel date anyway. But we'll settle for having Kelley in the bag—and the rest of our haul at the Dixon farm. And that's local, Doc. Want names and such?"

I wanted names and such. I grabbed a pencil. Where I was going to *put* the story, I didn't know. Evans talked a while and I took notes until I had all I wanted and then I said again, "Now *please* don't give me any more. I'm going nuts already."

He laughed and got up. He said, "Okay, Doc." He strolled to the door and then turned around after he was half-way through it. "Then you don't want to know about Sheriff Kates being under arrest."

He went on through and was half-way down the stairs before I caught him and dragged him back.

Dixon, who ran the crook hideout, had been paying protection to Kates and had proof of it. When he'd been raided he'd thought Kates had double-crossed him, and he talked. The state police had headed for Kates' office and had picked him up as he was entering the courthouse at six o'clock.

I sent out for more black coffee.

There was only one more interruption and it came just before we were finally closing the forms at half-past eleven.

Clyde Andrews. He said, "Doc, I want to thank you again for what you did last night. And to tell you that the boy and I have had a long talk and everything is going to be all right."

"That's wonderful, Clyde."

"Another thing, Doc, and I hope this isn't bad news for you. I mean, I hope you were deciding not to sell the paper, because I got a telegram from my brother in Ohio; he's definitely taking that offer from out West, so the deal on the paper is off. I'm sorry if you were going to decide to sell."

I said, "That's wonderful, Clyde. But hold the line a second. I'm going to put an ad in the paper to sell it instead."

I yelled across the room to Pete, "Hey, Pete, kill something somewhere and set up an ad in sixty-point type. 'FOR SALE, THE CARMEL CITY CLARION, PRICE, ONE MILLION DOLLARS.' "

Back into the phone, "Hear that, Clyde?"

He chuckled. "I'm glad you feel that way about it, Doc. Listen there's one more thing. Mr. Rogers just called me. He says that we've discovered that the Scouts are going to use the church gym next Tuesday instead of this Tuesday. So we're going to have the rummage sale after all. If you haven't gone to press and if you haven't got enough news to fill out——"

I nearly choked, but I managed to tell him we'd run the story.

I got to Smiley's at half-past twelve with the first paper off the press in my hands. Held carefully.

I put it proudly on the bar. "Read," I told Smiley. "But first the bottle and a glass. I'm half dead and I haven't had a drink for almost six hours. I'm too keyed up to sleep. And I need three quick ones."

I had three quick ones while Smiley read the headlines.

The room began to waver a little and I realized I'd better get to bed and quickly. I said, "Good night, Smiley. 'Sbeen wonnerful knowing you. I gotta——"

I started for the door.

Smiley said, "Doc. Let me drive you home." His voice came from miles and miles away. I saw him start around the end of the bar.

"Doc," he was saying, "sit down and hang on till I get there before you fall down flat on your face."

But the nearest stool was miles away through the brillig, and slithy toves were gimbling at me from the wabe. Smiley's warning had been at least half a second too late.

The Screaming Mimi

CHAPTER ONE

You can never tell what a drunken Irishman will do. You can make a flying guess, you make make a lot of flying guesses.

You can list them in the order of their probability. The likely ones are easy: He might go after another drink, start a fight, make a speech, take a train. . . . You can work down the list of possibilities; he might buy some green paint, chop down a maple tree, do a fan dance, sing "God Save the King", steal an oboe. . . . You can work on down and down to things that get less and less likely, and eventually you might hit the rock bottom of improbability: he might make a resolution and stick to it.

I know that that's incredible, but it happened. A guy named Sweeney did it, once, in Chicago. He made a resolution, and he had to wade through blood and black coffee to keep it, but he kept it. Maybe, by most people's standards, it wasn't a good resolution, but that's aside from the point. The point is that it really happened.

Now we'll have to hedge a bit, for truth is an elusive thing. It never quite fits a pattern. Like—well, "a drunken Irishman named Sweeney"; that's a pattern, if anything is. But truth is seldom that simple.

His name really was Sweeney, but he was only five-eighths Irish and he was only three-quarters drunk. But that's about as near as truth ever approximates a pattern, and if you won't settle for that, you'd better quit reading. If you don't maybe you'll be sorry, for it isn't a nice story. It's got murder in it, and women and liquor and gambling and even prevarication. There's murder before the story proper starts, and murder after it ends; the actual story begins with a naked woman and ends with one, which is a good opening and a good ending, but everything between isn't nice. Don't say I didn't warn you. But if you're still with me, let's get back to Sweeney.

Sweeney sat on a park bench, that summer night, next to God. Sweeney rather liked God, although not many people did. God was a tallish, scrawny old man with a short but tangled beard, stained with nicotine. His full name was Godfrey! I say his full name advisedly, for no one, not even Sweeney, knew whether it was his first name or his last. He was a little cracked, but not much. No more, perhaps, than the average for his age of the bums who live on the near north side of Chicago and hang out, when the weather is good, in Bughouse Square. Bughouse Square has another name, but the other name is much less appropriate. It is between Clark and Dearborn Streets, just south of the Newberry Library; that's its horizontal location. Vertically speaking, it's quite a bit nearer hell than heaven. I mean, it's bright with lights but dark with the shadows of the defeated men who sit on the benches, all night long.

Two o'clock of a summer night, and Bughouse Square had quieted down. The soapbox speakers were gone, and the summer night crowds of strollers who were not habitués of the square were long in bed. On the grass and on the benches, men slept. Their shoelaces were tied in hard knots so their shoes would not be stolen in the night. The theft of money from their pockets was the least of their worries, there was no money there to steal. That was why they slept.

"God," said Sweeney, "I wish I had another drink." He shoved his disreputable hat an inch further back upon his disreputable head.

"And I," said God, "But not bad enough."

"*That* stuff again," Sweeney said.

God grinned a little. He said, "It's true, Sweeney. You know it is." He pulled a crumpled package of cigarettes from his pocket, gave one to Sweeney, and lighted one himself.

Sweeney dragged deeply at the fag. He stared at the sleeping figure on the bench across from him, then lifted his eyes a little to the lights of Clark Street beyond. His eyes were a bit blurry from the drink; the lights looked haloed, but he knew they weren't. There wasn't a breath of breeze. He felt hot and sweaty, like the park, like the city. He took his hat off and fanned himself with it. Then some three-quarter drunken impulse made him hold the hat still and stare at it. It had been a new hat three weeks ago; he'd bought it while he was still working at the *Blade*. Now it looked like nothing on earth; it had been run over by an auto, it had rolled in a muddy gutter, it had been sat on and stepped on. It looked like Sweeney felt.

He said, "God," and he wasn't talking to Godfrey. Neither, for that matter, was he talking to anyone else. He put the hat back on his head.

He said, "I wish I could sleep." He stood up. "Going to walk a few blocks. Come along?"

"And lose the bench?" God wanted to know. "Naw. I guess I'll go to sleep, Sweeney. See you around." God eased himself over sidewise on to the bench, resting his head in the curve of his arm.

Sweeney grunted and walked out the path to Clark Street. He swayed a little, but not much. He walked across the night, south on Clark Street, past Chicago Avenue. He passed taverns, and wished he had the price of a drink. A cop, coming toward him, said, "Hi, Sweeney," and Sweeney said, "Hi, Pete," but kept on walking. And he thought about one of Godfrey's pet theories and he thought, the old bastard's right; you can get anything you want if you want it badly enough. He could easily have hit Pete for half a check or even a buck—if he'd wanted a drink that bad. Maybe tomorrow he'd want one that bad.

Not yet, although he felt like a violin's E-string that was tuned too tight. Damn it, why *hadn't* he stopped Pete? He needed a drink; he needed about six more shots, or say half a pint, and that would put him over the hump and he could sleep. When had he slept last? He tried to think back, but things were foggy. It had been in an areaway on Huron over near the El, and it had been night, but had it been last night or the night before or the night before that? What had he done yesterday?

He walked across Ontario Street, across the night. He was swearing aloud as he walked, but didn't know he was doing it. He thought, The Great Sweeney Walking Across the Night, and tried to throw his thoughts out of perspective, but they wouldn't throw. Looking into the mirror had been bad. But, worse than that, now that he was thinking about himself, he could smell himself—the stale sweat of his body. He hadn't been out of the clothes he was wearing since—how long ago was it his landlady had refused to give him the key to his room? Ohio Street. Damn it, he'd better quit walking south or he would find himself in the Loop, so he turned east. Where *was* he going? What did it matter? Maybe if he walked long enough he'd get so damned tired he could sleep. Only he'd better stay within easy distance of the square so he'd have a place to flop if he felt ready.

Hell, he'd do anything for a drink—except, the way he looked and felt tonight, look up anybody he knew.

He turned north on State Street. Past Erie, Huron. He was feeling a little better now. Not much, but a little. Superior Street. Superior Sweeney, he thought. Sweeney Walking Across the Night, Across Time——

And then, quite suddenly, he was aware of the crowd standing around the entrance door of the apartment building a quarter of a block ahead of him.

It wasn't much of a crowd. Just a dozen or so queerly assorted people—the odd random dozen that would collect first on North State Street at two-thirty in the morning, standing there looking through the glass doors into the hallway of the building. And there seemed to be a funny noise that Sweeney couldn't quite place. It sounded almost like an animal growling.

Sweeney didn't hasten his steps. Probably, he realized, just a drunk that had had a fall or been sapped, lying unconscious—or dead—in there until the ambulance came and collected him.

He started out around the people standing there without ever turning to look over their shoulders. He almost got past, before three things stopped him, two of them were sounds and the third was a silence.

The silence was the silence of the crowd—if you can call a dozen people a crowd, and I guess you can if they've pressed two deep around a six-foot wide double doorway. One of the sounds was the siren of an approaching police car, less than a block away, just slowing down on Chicago Avenue to the north, getting ready to swing the corner into State Street. Maybe, Sweeney realized, what was in the hallway of the building was a corpus delicti. And if it was, with the cops coming, it wasn't smart to be seen heading *away* from the scene of a crime. The cops grabbed you to ask questions. If you were standing there gawking instead they'd shove you away and tell you to move on, and then you could move on. The other sound was a repetition of the one he'd heard first and he heard it clearly now, over the silence of the crowd and under the wail of the siren; it *was* the growling of an animal.

Add up all those reasons, and you can't blame him, can you? Not even after everything it led to. Sweeney turned and looked.

He couldn't see anything of course, except the backs of a dozen miscellaneous people. He couldn't hear anything except the growling of an animal in front of him and the wail of a police siren behind him. The car was swinging in to the curb.

Maybe it was the sound of the car, maybe it was the sound of the animal, but some of the people in the middle of the group started backing away from the glass double door of the apartment building. And Sweeney saw the glass doors, and—through them. Not very clearly, because there wasn't any light on inside the hallway. Just the light that came in from the street lamps illuminated the scene within.

He saw the dog first, because the dog was nearest the glass, looking out through it. Dog? It *must* be a dog, here in Chicago; if you'd seen it out in the woods, you'd have taken it for a wolf, and a particularly large and menacing wolf at that. It was standing stiff-legged about four feet back from the glass doors; the hairs on the back of its neck were raised and its lips were drawn back in a tight snarl that showed teeth that looked an inch long. Its eyes glowed yellow.

Sweeney shivered a little as his eyes met those yellow ones. And they *did* seem to meet Sweeney's; naked yellow savagery boring into red, bleary weariness.

It almost sobered him, and it made him look away, uneasily, at what lay on the floor of the hallway beside, and slightly beyond, the dog. It was the figure of a woman, lying face down on the carpeting.

The word *figure* is not lightly used. Her white shoulders gleamed, even in that dim light, above a strapless white silk evening gown that moulded every beautiful contour of her body—at least those contours visible when a woman is lying face downward—and Sweeney caught his alcoholic breath at the sight of her.

He couldn't see her face, for the top of her page-boy-bobbed blonde head was toward him, but he knew that her face would be beautiful. It would *have* to be; women don't come with bodies as beautiful as that without faces to match.

He thought she moved a little. The dog growled again, a low-pitched sound under the high-pitched squeal of brakes as the police car stopped at the curb. Without turning to look behind him. Sweeney heard the doors of the car open, and the heavy sound of footsteps. A hand on Sweeney's shoulder pushed him aside, not too gently, and a voice that meant business asked, "What's wrong? Who phoned?" But the voice wasn't talking to Sweeney particularly, and he didn't answer it, nor turn.

Nobody answered.

Sweeney teetered a little from the push, and then recovered his balance. He could still see into the hallway.

There was a flashlight in the hand of the blue-serged man beside him, and with a click it shot a beam of bright white light into the dim hallway beyond the glass doors. It caught the yellow glow of the dog's savage eyes and the yellow glow of the bobbed blonde hair of the woman; it caught the white gleam of her shoulders and the white gleam of her dress.

The man holding the flashlight pulled in his breath in a soft little whistle and didn't ask any more questions. He took a step forward and reached for the knob of the door.

The dog quit growling and crouched to spring. The silence was worse than the growl. The man in the blue serge took his hand off the knob as though he'd found it red hot.

"The hell," he said. He put a hand inside the left lapel of his coat, but didn't draw the gun. Instead he addressed the little knot of people again. "What goes on here? Who phoned? Is the dame in there sick or drunk or what?"

Nobody answered. He asked, "Is that *her* dog?"

Nobody answered. A man in a grey suit was beside the man in blue serge. He said, "Take it easy, Dave. We don't want to shoot the pooch if we don't have to."

"Okay," said Blue Serge. "So you open the door and pet the dog while I take care of the dame. That ain't no dog anyway; it's a wolf or a devil."

"Well——" Grey Suit reached a hand for the door, and pulled it back as the dog crouched again and bared its fangs.

Blue Serge snickered. He asked, "What *was* the call? You took it."

"Just said a woman lying passed out in the hallway. Didn't mention the dog. Guy put in the call from tavern on the corner north; gave his name."

"Gave *a* name," said Blue Serge, cynically. "Look, if I was sure the dame was just passed-out drunk, we could phone the humane society to pull off the pooch. They could handle it. I *like* dogs; but I don't want to shoot that one. Probably belong to the dame and thinks he's protecting her."

"Thinks hell," said Grey Suit. "He damn well is. I like dogs, too. But I wouldn't swear that thing's a dog. Well—— "

Grey Suit started peeling off his suit coat. He said. "So okay. I'll wrap this around my arm and you open the door and when the dog jumps me. I'll clip him with the butt of——"

"Lookit—the dame's moving!"

The dame *was* moving. She was lifting her head. She pushed up a little with her hands—Sweeney noticed now that she wore long white cloth gloves that came halfway to her elbows, and lifted her head so her eyes stared full into the bright spotlight of the flashlight's beam.

Her face *was* beautiful. Her eyes looked dazed, unseeing.

"Drunk as hell." Blue Serge said. "Look, Harry, you might kill the dog, even if you clip it with the butt of your gun, and somebody'd raise hell. The dame would raise hell when she sobers up. I'll wait here and keep watch and you get the station on the two-way and tell 'em to send the humane guys here with a net or whatever they use and——"

There was a gasp from several throats that shut Blue Serge up as suddenly as though a hand had been clapped across his mouth.

Somebody said "Blood," almost inaudibly.

Weakly, as in a daze, the woman was trying to get up. She got her knees under her body and had pushed herself up until her arms were straight. The dog beside her moved quickly, and Blue Serge swore and yanked at his shoulder-holstered gun as the dog's muzzle went toward the woman's face. But before the gun was out, the dog had licked the woman's face once with a long red tongue, whimpering.

And then, as both detectives made a quick move toward the door, the dog crouched again and growled.

But the woman was still getting up. Everyone could see the blood now, an oblong stain of it on the front of her white evening dress, over the abdomen. And—in the bright spotlight that made the thing seem like an act on a stage or something seen in the glass screen of a televised horror show—they could see the five-inch-long cut in the white cloth in the centre of the oblong stain.

Grey Suit said, *"Jesus, a shiv. The Ripper."*

Sweeney got shoved farther to one side as the two detectives pushed closer. He stepped around behind them, watching over their shoulders; he'd forgotten all about his idea of getting away as soon as he could. He could have walked away now and nobody would have noticed. But he didn't.

Grey Suit was standing with his coat half on and half off, frozen in the act of removing it. He jerked it back on now, and his shoulder jarred Sweeney's chin.

He barked, "Phone on the two-way for an ambulance and homicide, Dave. I'll try to crease the dog."

His shoulder hit Sweeney's chin again as he, too, pulled a gun from his shoulder holster. His voice got calm suddenly, as the gun was in his hand. He said, "Reach for the knob, Dave. The dog'll freeze to jump you and I'll have a clear shot. I think I can crease him."

But he didn't raise the gun, and Dave didn't move to reach for the knob. For the incredible thing was happening, the thing that Sweeney wasn't ever going to forget—and that, probably, no one of the fifteen or twenty people who, by now, were in front of the doorway was ever going to forget.

The woman in the hallway had one hand on the wall now, beside the row of mailboxes and buzzer buttons. She was struggling to a standing position now, her body erect, but still resting on one knee. The bright white light of the flash framed her like a spotlight on a stage, the whiteness of her dress and gloves and skin and the redness of that oblong patch of blood. Her eyes were still dazed. It must have been shock, Sweeney realized, for that knife wound couldn't have been deep or serious or it would have bled much, much more. She closed her eyes now as, swaying a little, she got up off the other knee and stood straight.

And the incredible thing happened.

The dog padded back and rearing up behind her, on his hind feet but without pushing his forepaws against her, his teeth went to the back of the white dress, the strapless evening gown, caught something, and pulled out and down. And the something—they found out later—was a white silk tab attached to a long zipper.

Gently the dress fell off and became a white silken circle around her feet. She had worn nothing under the dress, nothing at all.

For what seemed like minutes, but was probably about ten seconds, nobody moved, nothing moved. Nothing happened, except that the flashlight shook just a little in Blue Serge's hand.

Then the woman's knees began to bend under her and she went down slowly—not falling, just sinking down like someone who is too weary to stand any longer—on top of the white circle of silk in which she had stood.

Then a lot of things happened at once. Sweeney breathed again, for one thing. And Blue Serge sighted his gun very carefully toward the dog and pulled the trigger. The dog fell and lay in the hallway and Blue Serge went through the door and called back over his shoulder to Grey Suit. "Get the ambulance, Harry. Then tie that damn dog's legs; I don't think I killed him. I just creased him."

And Sweeney backed away and nobody paid any attention to him as he walked north to Delaware and then turned west to Bughouse Square.

Godfrey wasn't on the bench, but he couldn't have been gone long, for the bench was still empty and benches don't stay empty long on a summer night. Sweeney sat down and waited till the old man came back.

"Hi, Sweeney," God said. He sat down beside Sweeney. "Got a pint," he said. "Want a slug?"

It had been a silly question and Sweeney didn't bother to answer it: he held out his hand. And God hadn't expected an answer; he was holding out the bottle. Sweeney took a long pull.

"Thanks," he said. "Listen she was beautiful. God. She was the most beautiful dame——" He took another, shorter pull at the bottle and handed it back. He said, "I'd give my right arm."

"Who?" God asked.

"The dame. I was walking north on State Street and——" He stopped, realizing he couldn't tell about it. He said, "Skip it. How'd you get the likker?"

"Stemmed a couple blocks," God sighed. "I told you I could get a drink if I wanted it bad enough; I just didn't want it bad enough before. A guy can get anything he wants, if he wants it bad enough."

"Nuts," Sweeney said automatically. Then, suddenly, he laughed. "*Anything*?"

"Anything you want," said God, dogmatically. "It's the easiest thing in the world, Sweeney. Take rich men. Easiest thing in the world; anybody can get rich. All you got to do is want money so bad it means more to you than anything else. Concentrate on money, and you get it. If you want other things worse, you don't."

Sweeney chuckled. He was feeling swell now; that long drink had been just what he needed. He'd kid the old man by getting him to argue his favourite subject.

"How about women?" he said.

"What do you mean, how about women?" God's eyes looked a little foggy; he was getting drunker. And a touch of Bostonian broad *a* was coming back into his speech, as it always did when he was really drunk. "You mean could you get any particular woman you wanted?"

"Yeah," said Sweeney. "Suppose there's a particular dame, for instance, I'd like to spend a night with. Could I do that?"

"If you wanted to bad enough, of course you could, Sweeney. If you concentrated all your efforts, direct and indirect, to that one objective, sure. Why not?"

Sweeney laughed.

He leaned his head back, looking up into the dark green leaves of the trees. The laugh subsided to a chuckle and he took off his hat and fanned himself with it. Then he stared at the hat as though he had never seen it before, and began to dust it off carefully with the sleeve of his coat to reshape it so it looked more like a hat. He worked with the absorbed concentration of a child threading a needle.

God had to ask him a second time before he heard the question. Not that it hadn't been a foolish question to begin with; God hadn't expected an answer, verbally. He was holding out the bottle.

Sweeney didn't take it. He put his hat back on and stood up. He winked at God and said, "No, thanks, pal, I got a date."

CHAPTER TWO

DAWN was different. Dawn's always different.

Sweeney opened his eyes and it was dawn, a hot, grey, still dawn. Leaves hung listlessly on the trees over his head and the ground was hard under him. All his body ached.

Sweeney pushed the ground away from him and stood up. He legs worked. They carried him off the grass to the cement and along the walk to the bench where Godfrey lay still asleep and snoring gently. On the bench next to him lay the bottle, empty.

Sweeney pushed God's feet back and sat down gingerly on the edge of the bench. He put his rough chin in his filthy hands and rested his elbows on his knees, but he didn't close his eyes. He kept them open.

Had he finally gone over the edge, he wondered. The dame and the dog. He'd never hallucinated before.

The dame and the dog.

He didn't believe it. It was one of the few things that couldn't have happened. So it hadn't happened. That was logic.

He held his hand out in front of him and it was shaking, plenty, but no worse than it had before at times like this. He put it back down on the bench and used it and his other hand to push himself up. His legs still worked. They carried him across the square to Dearborn and south on Dearborn—a walking ache rather than a man—to Chicago Avenue. Brakes squealed as a taxi swerved to avoid hitting him as he crossed Chicago Avenue diagonally, without looking to either side. The taxi driver yelled something at him. Sweeney walked along the south side of Chicago Avenue to State Street and turned south.

He walked three-quarters of a block and there was the Door. He stopped and stared at it, and after a while he went close to it and looked through the glass. It was dim inside, but he could see through the hallway to the door at the back.

A newsboy came along, a bag of papers slung over his shoulder. He stopped beside Sweeney. He said, "Jeeze, that's where it happened, ain't it?"

"Yeah," said Sweeney.

"I *know* the broad," said the newsboy. "I leave her a paper." He reached past Sweeney for the knob of the door. "Gotta get in to leave some papers." Sweeney stepped aside to let him past.

When the newsboy came out, Sweeney went in. He walked back

a few steps beside the mailboxes. This, where he was standing, was where she'd fallen. He looked down, then stopped to look closer; there were a few little dark dots on the floor.

Sweeney stood up again and walked to the back. He opened the door there and looked through it. There was a cement walk that led back to the alley. That was all. He closed the door and flicked the light switch to the left of it, at the foot of the stairs leading upward. Two bulbs went on, one overhead at the foot of the stairs, the other overhead up front, by the mailboxes. The yellow light was sickly in the grey morning. He flicked it off again, then—as he noticed something on the wooden panel of the door—back on again. There were long closely-spaced vertical scratches on the wood. They looked fresh, and they looked like the claw-marks of a dog. They looked as though a dog had lunged against that door and then tried to claw his way through it.

Sweeney turned off the light again and went out, taking with him one of the papers the newsboy had left in clips under several of the mailboxes. He walked past the next corner before he sat down on a step and unfolded the paper.

It was a three-column splash, with two pictures, one of the girl and one of the dog. The heading was:

RIPPER ATTACKS DANCER; SAVED BY HER FAITHFUL DOG
Fiend Makes Escape: "Can't Identify," Victim Says.

Sweeney studied the two pictures, read the article through, and studied the pictures again. Both were posed, obviously publicity stills. "Devil" was the caption under the picture of the dog, and he looked it. In a newspaper picture, you couldn't see that yellow balefulness in his eyes, but he still didn't look like anything you'd want to meet in an alley. He still looked, Sweeney thought, more like a wolf than a dog, and a bad wolf at that.

But his eyes went back to the woman's picture. The caption, "Yolanda Lang," made Sweeney wonder what her real name was. But—looking at that picture of her—you wouldn't care what her name was. The picture, unfortunately, didn't show as much of her as Sweeney had seen last night. It was a waist-up shot, and Yolanda Lang wore a strapless evening gown moulded to show off her outstanding features—which Sweeney well knew to be genuine and not padding—and her soft blonde hair tumbled to her softer white shoulders. Her face was beautiful, too. Sweeney hadn't much noticed her face last night. You couldn't blame him for that.

But it was worth noticing, now that there was less distraction to keep his eyes away from it. It was a face that was sweetly grave and gravely sweet. Except something about the eyes. But on an eighty-line screen newsprint picture you couldn't be sure about that.

Sweeney carefully folded the newspaper and put it down on the step beside him. There was a crooked grin on his face.

He got up and trudged back to Bughouse Square.

He cut across the grass to Clark Street and stood there a minute. He had a dull headache now, and he wanted a drink damned bad. He held out his hand and watched it shake, and then put it in his pocket so he wouldn't have to think about it.

He started walking south on Clark. The sun was up now, slanting down the east-west streets. The traffic was getting heavy, and noisy.

He thought. Sweeney Walking Across the Day.

He was sweating, and it wasn't only from the heat. He smelled, too, and he knew it. His feet hurt. He was a hell of a mess, an aching mess, top and bottom and inside and out. Sweeney Walking Across the Day.

And across the Loop, and on south to Roosevelt Road. He didn't dare stop. He turned the corner east on Roosevelt Road, kept on going on a block and a half, and turned into the entrance of an apartment building.

He rang a buzzer and stood waiting till the latch on the door clicked. He opened it and trudged up stairs to the third floor. A door at the front was ajar and a bald head stuck through it. The face under the bald head looked at Sweeney, approaching, and a disgusted look came over it.

The door slammed.

Sweeney put a dirty hand on the wall to steady himself and kept on coming. He started to knock on the door, loudly. He knocked a full minute and then put a hand to his forehead to hold it a while, maybe half a minute. He leaned against the wall.

He straightened up and started knocking again, louder.

He heard footsteps shuffle to the door. "Get the hell away or I'll call copper."

Sweeney knocked again. He said, "Call copper then, pally. We'll both go down to the jug and explain."

"What the hell do you want?"

Sweeney said. "Open up." He started knocking again, louder. A door down the hall opened and a woman's frightened face looked out.

Sweeney knocked some more. The voice said, "All right, *all right*. Just a second." The footsteps shuffled away and back again and the key turned.

The door opened and the bald man stepped back from it. He wore a shapeless bathrobe and scuffed slippers, and apparently nothing else. He was a little smaller than Sweeney, but he had his right hand in the pocket of the bathrobe and the pocket bulged.

Sweeney walked on in and kicked the door shut beside him. He walked to the middle of the cluttered room. He turned around and said, "Hi, Goetz," mildly.

The bald man was still beside the door.

He said, "What the hell do you want?"

"A double saw," Sweeney said. "You know what for. Or shall I tell you in words of one syllable?"

"Like hell I'll give you a double saw. If you're still harping back to the goodam horse, I told you, I didn't shove the bet. I gave you your fin back. You took it."

"I took it on account," Sweeney said. "I didn't need the money bad enough then to get tough about it. Now I do. So okay, let's review the bidding. You touted me on that oat-burner. It was *your* idea. So I gave you a fin to bet, and the horse came in at five for one, and you tell me you didn't get the bet down for me."

"Good damn it, I didn't. The heat was on. Mike's was closed and——"

"You didn't even try Mike's. You just held the bet. If the horse had lost—like you expected—you'd have kept my fin. So whether you got the bet down or not you owe me twenty."

"The hell I do. Get out."

The bald man took his hand out of the bathrobe pocket and there was a little twenty-five calibre automatic in it.

Sweeney shook his head sadly. He said, "If it was twenty grand, I'd be afraid of that thing—maybe. For twenty bucks you wouldn't put a shooting on your record. For a lousy double saw you wouldn't have the cops up here snooping around. Anyway, I don't think you would. I'll gamble on it."

He looked around the room until he saw a pair of pants hanging over the back of the chair. He started for the pants.

The bald man snicked the safety off the little automatic. He said. "You son of a bitch——"

Sweeney picked up the pants by the cuffs and started shaking them. Keys and change hit the carpet and he kept on shaking. He said, "Someday, Goetz, you'll call a man a son of a bitch who *is* a son of a bitch, and he'll take you apart."

A wallet from the hip pocket of the trousers hit the carpet, and Sweeney picked it up. He flipped it open, and grunted. There was only a ten and a five in the wallet.

He took the ten out and put it in his own pocket and tossed the wallet toward the dresser. He said: "What's the matter with the pool ticket racket, Goetz? *That* bad?"

The bald man's face wasn't pretty. He said. "I told you; the heat's on. You got your money. Now get out."

"I got ten," Sweeney said. "I wouldn't take a man's last fin, pally. I'll take the other ten in trade. A bath and a shave and a shirt and socks."

Sweeney peeled off his coat and stepped out of his trousers. He sat down on the edge of the mussed-up bed and took off his shoes. He went into the bathroom and turned on the water to run in the tub.

He came out stark naked, holding a wadded-up ball that had been his shirt, socks and underwear and put it in the wastebasket.

The bald man was still standing by the door, but he'd put the little automatic back into the pocket of the bathrobe.

Sweeney grinned at him. Over the roar of water running into the tub, he said, "Don't call copper now, Goetz. With me dressed this way, they might get the wrong idea."

He went into the bathroom and shut the door.

He soaked a long time in the tub, and then shaved leisurely with Goetz's razor—providentially an electric one. Sweeney's hands were still shaking.

When he came out, the bald man was back in bed, his back to the room.

"Asleep, darling?" Sweeney asked.

There wasn't any answer.

Sweeney opened a drawer of the dresser and chose a white sports shirt and a soft collar. It was tight across the shoulders and the collar wouldn't button, but it was a shirt and it was clean and white. A pair of Goetz's socks proved a bit small, but they went on.

He eyed his own shoes and suit with disgust, but they'd have to do. Goetz's wouldn't fit. Sweeney did the best he could with a shoebrush and a clothes brush. He made sure the ten-dollar bill was still in the pocket of his trousers when he put them on.

He brushed his hat and put that on, and then stopped at the door.

He said, "Nighty-night, pally, and thanks for everything. We're even now." He closed the door quietly and went downstairs and outside into the hot sunlight. He walked north on Dearborn, past the Dearborn Station. In a little restaurant opposite the front of it, he had three cups of black coffee and managed to eat one doughnut of two he ordered. It tasted like library paste, but he got it down.

Under the shadow of the El, two blocks north, he got his shoes shined and then waited, shaking a little, in a tiny cubby-hole in the back of the shop while his suit was sponged and pressed. It needed more than sponging, but it didn't look too bad when he put it back on.

He took a look at himself in the long mirror and decided he looked fair enough by now. There were circles under his eyes and the eyes themselves—well, he wasn't a thing of beauty and a joy for ever, and he had to remember to keep his hands in his pockets until he got over the trembling, but he looked human.

He spread the collar of the white sports shirt on the outside of the collar of his coat, and that looked better, too.

He kept to the shady side of the street, walking north across the Loop. He was starting to sweat again, and felt dirty already. He had a hunch he'd feel dirty for a long time, no matter how many baths he took.

Sweeney Walking Across the Loop. At Lake Street, under the El again, he stopped in at a drugstore for a double bromo and another cup of coffee. He felt like a coiled spring that was tied down too tightly; he felt like a claustrophobiac locked in a tiny room; he felt lousy. The coffee seemed to be swishing around in his guts like bilgewater inside a leaky ship—tepid, brackish bilgewater filled with little green algae, if algae are green. Sweeney's were, and they wriggled, too.

He crossed Wacker Drive, hoping that a car would hit him, but none did; he walked across the bridge in the bright hot glare of sunshine and he lifted one foot and put it down and lifted the other and put that down, for six blocks to Erie Street; he walked east past Rush and then—not daring to stop—he put his clammy hands into his pockets and went into the areaway between two buildings and through an open doorway.

This was home, if it still was. This was the biggest hurdle, for today. He took his right hand out of a pocket and rapped gently on a door off the downstairs hallway. He put his hand back quickly.

Heavy footsteps came slowly, and the door opened.

Sweeney said. "Hello, Mrs. Randall. Uh——"

Her sniff cut off whatever he'd been going to say. She said, "No, Mr. Sweeney."

"Uh—you mean you've rented my room?"

"I mean—no, you can't get in it to get something to hock to keep on drinking. I told you that last week, twice."

"Did you!" asked Sweeney vaguely. He didn't remember, or did he? Now that she spoke of it, one of the two times came back to him dimly. "Guess I was pretty drunk." He took a deep breath. "But it's over now. I'm sober."

She sniffed again. "How about the three weeks you owe me? Thirty-six dollars."

Sweeney fumbled out the bills in his pockets, a five and three singles. "All I got," he said. "I can give you eight dollars on account."

The landlady looked from the bills up to Sweeney's face. "I guess you're on the level, Sweeney, about sobering up. If you've *got* money, you aren't after stuff to hock. You could do a lot of drinking on eight dollars."

"Yes," Sweeney said.

She stepped back from the door. "Come on in." And, after he had followed her in: "Sit down. Put your money back in your pocket. You'll need it worse than I do, till you get started again. How long'll that be?"

Sweeney sat down. "A few days," he said. "I can raise some money, when I'm okay again."

He put his hands, and the bills, back in his pocket. "Uh—I'm afraid I lost my key. Do you have——"

"You didn't lose it. I took it away from you a week ago Friday. You were trying to carry out your phonograph to hock it."

Sweeney dropped his head into his hands. "Lord, *did* I?"

"You didn't. I made you take it back. And I made you give me the key. Your clothes are all there, too, except your topcoat and overcoat. Your must have taken them before that. And your typewriter. And your watch—unless you got it on."

Sweeney shook his head slowly. "Nope. It's gone. But thanks for saving the other stuff."

"You look like hell. Want a cup of coffee? I got some on."

"It's running out of my ears," Sweeney told her. "But—yes, I'll have another cup. Black."

He studied her as she got up and waddled over to the stove. There ought to be more landladies like Mrs. Randall, he thought. Tough as nails on the outside (they had to be to run a room house) and soft as butter inside. Most of them were tough all the way through.

She came back with the coffee and he drank it. He got his key and went up the stairs. He got inside and got the door closed before he started to shake, and he stood there, leaning against the inside of the door until the worst of it was over. Then he made it to the washbasin and was sick at his stomach, and that helped, although the sound of the water running made his head hurt worse.

When that was over, he wanted to lie down and sleep, but instead he stripped off his clothes, put on a bathrobe, and went down the hall to the bathroom. He drew himself a hot tub and soaked in it for a long time before he went back to his room.

Before he dressed again, he rolled up the spotted and worn suit he'd been wearing and the too-small shirt and socks he'd taken from the man named Goetz and put them into the wastebasket. He put on all clean clothes, including his best summer-weight suit. He put on a silk tie that had cost him five bucks and his best pair of shoes.

He straightened up the room carefully, even meticulously. He turned on the radio side of his radio-phono combination until he got a time announcement between programmes and set the clock on his dresser and wound it. It was half-past eleven.

Then he got his Panama hat out of the closet and went out.

Mrs. Randall's door opened as he started down the stairs. She called out, "Mr. Sweeney?" and he leaned over the railing to look toward her. "Yes?"

"Forgot to tell you there was a phone call for you this morning, early, about eight o'clock. A Walter Krieg, from the paper you work for—or used to work for. Which is it?"

"Used to work for, I guess," Sweeney said. "What'd he say? What'd you say?"

"He asked for you and I said you weren't in. He said if you came back before nine to have you call him. You didn't—not that I was expecting you to—so I kinda forgot it. That's all that was said."

Sweeney thanked her and went on out. At the corner drugstore he bought a half pint of whisky and put it in his hip pocket. Then he went into the phone booth, dialled the *Blade*, and asked for the managing editor by name.

"Krieg?" he said. "This is Sweeney. Just got home. Got your message. Sober. What you want?"

"Nothing now. It's too late, Sweeney. Sorry."

"All right, it's too late and you're sorry. What *did* you want?"

"Eyewitness story, if you're sober enough to remember what you saw last night. A beat copper said you were around when the lid came off that Yolanda Lang business. Remember it?"

"More than the lid came off, and I damn well remember it. Why's it too late? You got one edition on the street but the main one coming up and two others. The home edition's not in, is it?"

"Going in in fifteen minutes. Take you longer'n that to—"

"Quit wasting time," Sweeney said. "Put a rewrite man on the phone now. I can give him half a column in five minutes. Gimme Joe Carey; he can take it fast."

"Okay, Sweeney. Hang on."

Sweeney hung on, getting his thoughts organized, until he heard Joe's voice. Then he started talking, fast.

When he was through, he put the receiver back on the hook and leaned weakly against the wall of the phone booth. He hadn't asked to have Walter Krieg put back on the line; that could wait. He'd do better going in and seeing Walter personally.

But not yet, not just yet.

He went back to his room and put the little half pint bottle of whisky on the arm of the comfortable Morris chair and a shot glass beside it. He hung up his suit coat and Panama, and loosened his collar and tie.

Then he went over to the phonograph and squatted down on his haunches in front of the shelf of albums. He studied the titles. Not that it mattered; he knew which one he was going to hear: the Mozart 40.

No, you wouldn't have thought it to look at him, maybe, but that was Sweeney's favourite—the *Symphony No. 40. in G Minor, K. 550.* He stacked the three records on the phonograph, flicked the switch to start the first one, and went over to the Morris chair to sit and listen.

The first movement, allegro molto.

Why should I tell you anything about Sweeney? If you know the Mozart 40, the dark restlessness of it, the macabre drive behind its graceful counterpoint, then you know Sweeney. And if the Mozart 40 sounds to you like a gay but slightly boring minuet, background for a conversation, then to you Sweeney is just another damn reporter who happens, too, to be a periodic drunk.

He was *out* of it now, off the binge, sober. Until the next time, which might be months, might be a couple of years. However long until enough hell accumulated inside him that he'd have to soak it out; until then he could be normal and drink normally. Yes, I know, alcoholics can't do that, but Sweeney wasn't an alcoholic; he could and did drink regularly and normally and only once in a while dive off into the deep end into a protracted drunk. There's that type of drinker, too, although of late the alcoholics have been getting most of the ink.

But Sweeney was out of it now, shaken but not shaking, sober. He could even get his job back, he felt sure, if he ate a little crow. He could climb out of debt in a few weeks and be back where he was, wherever *that* was.

CHAPTER THREE

SWEENEY headed for the *Blade*.

There's a nice pun in that, if you don't mind your puns obvious, *The Blade*. If you saw that pun yourself, forgive me for pointing it out. *You* got it, yes, but somebody else would have missed it. It takes all kinds of people to read a book.

Some people, for instance, see with their eyes; they want descriptions. So, if it interests you (it doesn't interest me) William Sweeney was five feet eleven inches tall and weighed a hundred and sixty-three pounds. He had sandy hair that was receding at the front and getting a little thin on top, but was mostly still there. He had a long thin face, vaguely horselike but not, on the whole, unpleasing to the uncritical eye. He looked to be about forty-three, which is not strange because that is how old he really was. He wore glasses with light-coloured shell rims for reading and working; he could see all right without them for any distance over four or five feet. For that matter, he could work without them if he had to, although he'd get headaches if he did it too long. But it was well that he *could* do without them for a while, because he was going to have to. They'd been in his pocket two weeks ago when he'd started his serious drinking and only God (I don't mean Godfrey) knew where they were now.

He threaded his way across the city room and into the office of the managing editor. He sat down on the arm of the chair across the desk from Krieg. He said, "Hi, Walter."

Krieg looked up and grunted, then finished the letter in his hand and put it down. He opened his mouth and closed it again.

Sweeney said, "I'll say it for you, Walter. First, I'm a son of a bitch to have let you down and gone on a binge without giving you notice. I'm through. You can't mess with guys like me. I'm an anachronism. The days of the drunken reporter are over and a modern newspaper is a business institution run on business lines and not a *Front Page* out of Hecht by MacArthur. You want men you can count on. Right?"

"Yes, you son of——"

"Hold it, Walter, I said it for you, all of it. And anyway, I wouldn't work on your damn paper unless you hired me to. How was the eyewitness story?"

"It was good, Sweeney, damn good. That was a break in a million, your being there."

"You say a cop mentioned I was there. I didn't see one I recognized. Who was it?"

"You'll have to ask Carey; he handled the story. Look, Sweeney, how often do you go on a bat like that? Or are you going to tell me that was the last one?"

"It probably wasn't. It'll happen again; I don't know when. Maybe not for a couple of years. Maybe in six months. So you wouldn't want me to work for you. All right. But since I'm *not* working for you, I got a little cheque coming for that eyewitness account. I'll let you do me one last favour, Walter. You can give me a voucher to get it now instead of putting it though the channels. That story was worth fifty bucks. If Carey wrote it like I told it to him. Will you settle for twenty-five?"

Krieg glared at him. "Not a damn cent, Sweeney."

"No? And why the hell not? Since when have you been *that* much of a lousy——"

"Shut up!" The managing editor almost roared it. "God damn it, Sweeney, you're the toughest guy to do a favour for I ever saw. You won't even give me the satisfaction of bawling you out, you take the words out of my mouth so I can't say 'em. Who told you you were fired? *You* did. The reason you don't get paid for that piddling little story you gave over the phone is that you're still on the payroll. You've lost two days' pay, that's all."

"I don't get it," Sweeney said. "Why two days? I been gone two weeks. What's two days got to do with it?"

"This is a Thursday, Sweeney. You started your drunk two weeks ago tonight and didn't come in Friday morning. Or Saturday. But you had two weeks' vacation coming. Maybe you forgot; you were on the list for September. I gave you a break by switching your dates so your started your vacation a week ago last Monday. You're still on your vacation right now and you're not due back for a few more days yet. Monday, to be exact. Here." Krieg yanked open a drawer of his desk and pulled out three cheques. He held them across to Sweeney. "You probably don't remember, but you came in to try to get your last cheque, only we didn't give it to you. It's there, two days short, and two full vacation week cheques.'

Sweeney took them wonderingly.

Krieg said, "Now get the hell out of here until Monday morning and report for work then."

"The hell," said Sweeney. "I don't believe it."

"Don't then. But—no bull, Sweeney—if it happens again before your *next* vacation, next year, you're through for good."

Sweeney nodded slowly. He stood up.

"Listen, Walter, I——"

"Shut up. Beat it."

Sweeney grinned weakly, and beat it.

He stopped at Joe Carey's desk and said, "Hi," and Joe looked up and said, "Hi, yourself. What gives?"

"Want to talk to you, Joe. Had lunch yet?"

"No. Going in——" He looked at his wrist watch. "——in twenty minutes. But listen, Sweeney, if it's a bite you've got in mind, I'm broke as well. Wife just had another kid last week and you know how that is."

"No," said Sweeney. "Thank God I don't know how that is. Congratulations, though. I presume it's a boy or a girl."

"Yeah."

"Good. Nope, it isn't a bite. Miraculously, I'm solvent. There is a God. In fact, do I owe you anything?"

"Five. Two weeks ago last Wednesday. Remember?"

"Vaguely, now that you mention it. So let's eat at Kirby's; I can cash a cheque there and pay you. I'll wander on down and meet you there."

Sweeney cashed the smallest of the three cheques at the bar in Kirby's and then went over to a table to wait for Joe Carey. The thought of food still nauseated him; eating anything at all was going to be so bad he'd rather get it over with before Joe came in. Watching Joe eat was going to be bad enough.

Sweeney ordered a bowl of soup as the least of evils. It tasted like hot dishwater to him, but he managed to get most of it down and shoved the bowl aside as Joe came in and sat down across the table.

He said, "Here's your five, Joe, and thanks. Say, before I forget, who was it saw me over on State Street last night? I thought I didn't know either of the coppers I saw there."

"Harness bull by the name of Fleming. Pete Fleming."

"Oh," Sweeney said. "I remember now; I met him on Clark Street before that. Let's see—I was walking south on Clark so be must have been going north. I walked south a few more blocks, cut over east and walked north on State. But I didn't see him."

"Probably got there as you were leaving. The car that answered the call—the cops in it were named Kravich and Guerney—cut in their siren on the way. Wherever Fleming was on his beat, he followed the siren and got there after they did. Thanks for the fin, Sweeney."

The waiter came up and Sweeney ordered coffee along with Carey's order.

Then he leaned across the table. He said, "Joe, what gives with this Ripper business? That's what I want to pump you about. I could dig up some of the dope from the morgue files, but you'll know more than they will. First, how long has it been going on?"

"You haven't read the papers for the last ten days?"

Sweeney shook his head. "Except for what was in one morning

paper today, about the Yolanda Lang business last night. There were references to other killings. How many?"

"Besides Yolanda Lang, two—or it could be three. I mean, there was a slashing on the south side two months ago that might or might not be the same guy. Broad by the name of Lola Brent. There were similarities between her case and the three recent ones that make the police think maybe it ties in, but they aren't sure. There are differences, too."

"She die?"

"Sure. So did the two other dames besides this Lang woman. She's the only one who didn't get killed. Pooch saved her. But you know about that."

"What's the last word on Yolanda Lang?" Sweeney asked. "She still in the hospital?"

"Supposed to be released this evening. She wasn't hurt much. Point of the shiv just barely went through the skin. She had a spot of shock; that's all."

"So did some other people," said Sweeney. "Including me."

Joe Carey licked his lips. "You didn't exaggerate that story any, Sweeney?"

Sweeney chuckled. "I underplayed it. You should have been there, Joe."

"I'm a married man. Anyway, the cops are going to keep a guard on the Lang femme."

"A *guard*? Why?"

"They figure the killer might be inclined to go back after her because he might think she could put the finger on him. Matter of fact, she can't, or says she can't. A man, tallish, in dark clothes is the best she can do."

"The light was off in the hallway," Sweeney said.

"The Ripper's waiting by the back door, at the foot of the stairs, probably standing outside it, holding it a little ajar. He hears her footsteps clicking along the hallway, steps inside and slashes. Only the pooch jumps past her after the guy and he jerks back through the door, almost missing the woman completely with the shiv and just barely gets away from the dog."

"It adds up," Sweeney said. "He'd be able to see her silhouetted against the light from outside through the front door, but he'd be just a shadow to her. The point is, was he after Yolanda Lang or was he just waiting for whoever came along?"

Carey shrugged. "Could be either way. I mean, she lived there and he could have been waiting for her because she was coming home after her last show. On the other hand, if he knew much about her, he knew the pooch would be along and it looks like he didn't figure on that. He *could* have, though. Known, I mean, the dog would walk behind her in the hallway and figure he could slash and get back out the door before the dog got him. But, if that was it, he missed his timing."

"She got home that time every night?"

"Every week night. She's on last at one-thirty week nights. They have shows later on Saturday and Sunday nights. She doesn't always go right home after the last show, though, she said. Sometimes stays around El Madhouse—that's the night club she's playing—know it?"

Sweeney nodded.

"—sometimes stays around for drinks or what not till they close at three. Or sometimes has dates and goes out after the show. A dame like that wouldn't be lonesome except when she wanted to be."

"Who's handling it—outside, I mean."

"Horlick, only he starts vacation Monday. I don't know who Wally will put on after that."

Sweeney grinned. "Listen, Joe, do me a hell of a big favour, will you? I *want* to work on it. *I* can't very well suggest it to Krieg, but you can, next time you talk to him. Suggest I got an inside start with that eyewitness businesa and since Horlick's leaving Monday and I'm coming back then, why not let me do the leg work. He'll fall for it if you suggest it. If *I* ask him—well, he might not let me, just to be cussed."

"Sure. I can do that, Sweeney. But—you'll have to bone up on the details on the other cases, and get in with the cops. They got a special Ripper detail, by the way, working on nothing else. Cap Bline of Homicide's running it and got men under him. And the crime lab's analyzing everything they can get their hands on, only there hasn't been much to analyze."

"I'll be up on it," Sweeney said. "Between now and Monday I'll study those files and get in with the cops."

"Why? On your own time, I mean. You got an angle, Sweeney?"

"Sure," Sweeney lied. "Got the assignment from a fact detective mag to write up the case, once it's solved. They don't handle unsolved cases, but it's promised to me once the case is cracked. Ought to get a few hundred out of it. Joe, if you talk Krieg into giving me the case, so I'll have all the facts ready to write once they get the guy, I'll cut you in for ten per cent. Ought to get you somewhere between twenty and fifty."

"What have I got to lose? Sure, I was going to do it for nothing."

"But now you'll be convincing," Sweeney said. "For a start, what are the names of the other dames who were slashed, the ones who died? You said the one on the south side a couple of months ago was Lola Brent?"

"Check. Ten days ago, Stella Gayford. Five days ago, Dorothy Lee."

"Any of the others strip teasers or show girls?"

"First one, this Lola Brent, was an ex-chorine. Living with a short-con man named Sammy Cole. Cops figured he killed her, but they couldn't prove it and they couldn't crack him. So they threw the book at him on some fraud charges that came out, and he's still in the clink. So if he *did* kill Lola, he didn't kill the others or make the try for Yolanda."

"What were the other two gals?"

"Stella Gaylord was a B-girl on West Madison Street. The Lee girl was a private secretary."

"How private? Kind that has to watch her periods as well as her commas?"

"I wouldn't know," Carey said. "That didn't come out. She worked for some executive with the Reiss Corporation. Don't remember his name. Anyway, he was in New York on a buying trip."

Joe Carey glanced up at the clock: he'd finished eating. He said. "Look, Sweeney, those are the main points. I haven't got time to give you any more; I got to get back."

"Okay," Sweeney said. "What hospital is the Lang dame in?"

"Michael Reese, but you can't get in to see her. They got cops six deep in that corridor. Horlick tried to get in and couldn't."

"You don't know when she'll be back at El Madhouse?"

"Nope. Her manager could tell you. Guy by the name of Doc Greene."

"What's the dope on him?"

"Listen, Sweeney, I got to get back. Ask *him* what the dope on him is."

Carey stood up. Sweeney reached for his check and got it. "I'm paying this. But tell me where I can locate this Greene character. What's his first name?"

"Dunno. Everybody calls him Doc. But wait—he's in the Goodman Block. Greene with a final *e*. You can find him from that. Or through the El Madhouse proprietor. He books all their acts, I think. So long."

Sweeney took a sip of his coffee, which he'd forgotten to drink, and it was cold. He shuddered with revulsion at the taste of it, and got out of Kirby's quick.

He stood in front a moment, hesitating which way to go, then headed back for the *Blade*. He didn't go to the editorial offices this time, though. He cashed his two other pay cheques at the cashier's window and then went to the stack room. He looked through papers of about two months before until he found the one that broke the story on the murder of Lola Brent. He bought that one and all the finals for a week following, and he bought finals for each of the past ten days.

It made quite a stack of papers, even when he'd thrown the stuffing out of the Sunday ones. He caught a cab to take them home.

On the way in, he knocked on Mrs. Randall's door; he paid her the thirty-six dollars he owed her, and paid for two weeks in advance.

Upstairs in his room, he put the pile of papers on his bed, and then, outside in the hall, he looked up Greenes until he found one in the Goodman Block. J. J. Greene, thtrcl. agt. He called the number and after brief argument with a secretary, got J. J. Greene.

"Sweeney, of the *Blade*," he said. "Could you tell me when your client is being released from Michael Reese?"

"Sorry, Mr. Sweeney, the police have asked me not to give out any information. You'll have to get it from them. Say, are you the reporter who wrote that eyewitness story in today's *Blade*?"

"Yes."

"Nice story. And swell publicity for Yolanda. Too bad she's on the dotted line for three more weeks at El Madhouse, or I could get her on for bigger dough."

"She'll be back dancing in less than three weeks, then?"

"Off the record, nearer three days. It was just a nick."

"Could I drop around and talk to you, Mr. Greene? At your office."

"What about? The police told me not to talk to reporters."

"Not even pass the time of day if you met one on the street? I never saw an agent yet that wouldn't talk to reporters. Maybe I even want to give some of your other clients publicity, and what could the cops find wrong with that? Or have they got something on you?"

Greene chuckled. "I wouldn't invite you here if the cops say not. But I'm leaving the office in about twenty minutes and I generally have a drink at one of the places I book. I have an idea that today I might stop in El Madhouse on my way north. In that case I'd be there in a little over half an hour. If you should happen to drop in——"

"I might just happen to," Sweeney said. "Thanks. Off the record, I take it Miss Lang still *is* at Michael Reese?"

"Yes. But you won't be able to see her there."

"Won't try it then," Sweeney said. "So long."

He hung up the receiver and wiped the sweat off his forehead with a handkerchief. He went back into his room and sat very quietly for five minutes or so. When he thought he could make it, he pushed himself up out of the chair and left.

The sun was very hot, and he walked slowly. On State Street, he stopped in a florist's shop and ordered two dozen American Beauties sent to Yolanda Lang at the hospital. After that, he kept plodding steadily through the bright heat until he reached El Madhouse, on Clark near Grand.

There wasn't a uniformed doorman, with a persuasive voice, in front at this hour of the the late afternoon; there wouldn't be until mid-evening, when the periodic floor shows were about to start. There were the posters though:

6 Acts 6
Yolanda Lang and Devil!
in
the Famous
Beauty and the Beast
Dance!

And, of course, there were photographs. Sweeney didn't stop to look at them. He walked from the blazing heat into the cool dimness of the outer bar, separated from the room with tables and the stage, where a cover charge topped higher prices.

He stopped inside, barely able at first to see, blinded by the transition from sunlight glare to neoned dimness. He blinked, and looked along the bar. Only three persons sat there. At the far end, a badly intoxicated man drooled over a too-sober blowzy blonde. Half a dozen stools away, a man sat alone, staring at his reflection in the dim blue mirror back of the bar, a bottle of beer and a glass in front of him. He sat there as though he was carved of stone. Sweeney felt pretty sure he wasn't Doc Greene.

Sweeney slid on to a stool at the end of the bar. The bartender came over.

"Greene been in?" Sweeney asked. "Doc Greene?"

"Not yet today." The bartender rubbed the clean bar with a dirty towel. "Sometimes comes in around this time, but today I dunno. With Yo in the hospital——"

"Yo," said Sweeney meditatively. "I like that. Gives everybody a southern accent. People turn to her at the bar and ask 'And what's Yo having to drink,' Huh?"

"A good question," said the bartender. "What *is* yo having to drink?"

"Well," said Sweeney, and thought it over. He had to get some nourishment into him somehow, a little at a time, until his appetite came back and he could look at a full meal without flinching. "Beer with an egg in it, I guess."

The bartender moved away to get it, and Sweeney heard the door behind him open. He looked around.

A moon-faced man stood just inside the doorway. A wide but meaningless smile was on his face as he looked along the bar, starting at the far end. His eyes, through round thick-lensed glasses, came to rest on Sweeney and the wide smile widened. His eyes, through the lenses, looked enormous.

Somehow, too, they managed to look both vacant and deadly. They looked like a reptile's eyes, magnified a hundredfold, and you expected a nictitating membrane to close across them.

Sweeney—the outside of Sweeney—didn't move, but something shuddered inside him. For almost the first time in his life he was hating a man at first sight. And fearing him a little, too. It was a strange combination of strange ingredients, for hatred—except in an abstract sort of way—was almost completely foreign to William Sweeney. Nor is fear a commonplace to one who seldom gives enough of a damn about anybody or anything to be afraid of him or it.

"Mr. Sweeney?" said the moon-faced man, more as a statement than a question.

Sweeney said, "Sit down, Doc.'

He put his hands in his pockets, quickly, because he had a hunch the shakes were going to come back.

CHAPTER FOUR

THE moon-faced man slid on to the stool around the turn of the bar from Sweeney, so the two of them faced one another. He said, "That was an excellent story you wrote about—what happened last night, Mr. Sweeney."

Sweeney said, "I'm glad you liked it."

"I didn't say that I liked it," Greene said. "I said it was an excellent story. That is something else again."

"But definitely," said Sweeney. "In this particular case, wherein lies the difference?"

Doc Greene leaned his elbows on the bar and laced pudgy fingers together. He said, judiciously, "A man, Mr. Sweeney, might enjoy a bit of voluptuous description of a woman; in other cases he might not enjoy reading it. For example, if the woman was his wife".

"Is Yolanda Lang your wife?"

"No," said the moon-faced man. "I was merely, you will recall, giving that as an example. You've ordered something?"

Sweeney nodded, and Greene looked at the bartender and held up one finger. The man came with Sweeney's beer-and-egg and put a shot glass in front of Greene.

While the shot glass was being filled. Sweeney cautiously took a hand out of his pocket and rested the tips of his fingers against the front of the bar. Carefully, so the shaking wouldn't show, he began to walk his fingers up the front of the bar, over the edge, and toward the glass in front of him.

His eyes watched the ones that looked so huge through the thick spectacles.

Greene's smile had gone away; now it came back, and he lifted his shot glass. "To your health, Mr. Sweeney."

Sweeney's fingers had closed around his own glass. He said, "To yours, Doc," and his hand was steady as he lifted the glass and took a sip. He put it back down and took his other hand out of his pockets. The shakes were gone.

He said carefully. "Perhaps you would like to cause my health to deteriorate, Doc. If you want to try, it would be a pleasure to oblige."

The moon-faced man's smile got wider. "Of course not. Mr. Sweeney. When I became a man, I put away childish things, as the great bard says."

"The Bible," said Sweeney. "Not Shakespeare."

"Thank you. Mr. Sweeney. You are, as I feared when I read that story under your by-line, an intelligent man. And, as I guessed from your name, a stubborn Irishman. If I told you to—let us descend to the vernacular—if I told you to lay off Yolanda, it would just make you that much more stubborn."

He held up a finger for a refill of the shot glass. He said, "A threat of any sort would be silly. It would be equally useful to point out to you the futility of your trying to make my—ah—client. As you may have—indeed as you *did*—notice, Yolanda is not unattractive. It has been tried by experts."

"You flatter yourself, Doc."

"Perhaps. Perhaps not. We aren't discussing my relations with Yolands."

Sweeney took another sip of his drink. He said, "You know, Doc, I hate you so damn much I'm beginning to like you."

"Thank you," said Greene. "I feel the same about you; each of us admires the other's capabilities, let us say. Or you will admire mine when you get to know me better."

"Already," said Sweeney. "I admire your line of patter. Immensely. The only thing I hate about you is your guts."

"And may the Ripper never expose them to the public gaze," Greene said. "Not that that seems likely, for thus far he has seemed to specialize in tenderer morsels." He smiled broadly. "Isn't civilization a marvellous thing. Mr. Sweeney? That two men can sit like this and insult one another, amicably but sincerely, and enjoy the conversation? If we followed the customs of a century or two ago, one of us would have struck the other across the face with the back of a hand before now, and one of us would be fated to die before the sun rises very far above tomorrow's horizon."

"A beautiful thought, Doc." Sweeney said. "I'd love it. But the authorities *are* fussy about such things. But back to Yolanda. Suppose you read correctly between the lines of my story. What are you going to do about it? Anything?"

"Of course. For one thing. I shall put every possible pitfall in your path. I shall warn Yolanda against you—not obviously, of course, but subtly. I'll make her think you're a fool. You are, you know."

"Yes," said Sweeney. "But she may discount the information, since it comes from a bastard. You are one, you know."

"Your intuition surprises me, Mr. Sweeney. As it happens, I really am, in the literal sense of the word. Quite possibly in the figurative sense also, but that is irrelevant. Or perhaps I should say that there is a strong probability that I was born of unwed parents; all I actually know is that I was brought up in an orphan asylum. I, myself, made me what I am today."

"Only you could have done it," Sweeney said.

"You gratify me. I didn't expect a compliment. But that was a digression. In addition to putting pitfalls in your path, I am going to help you."

Sweeney said, "Now you have me really worried."

The moon-faced man tented his fingers into a steeple. He said, "You intend to find the Ripper. It's natural that you'll try, first because you're a reporter, but second and more important—to you—you think it will give you an in with Yolanda. Trying will automatically bring you in contact with her—not as close a contact as you have in mind, maybe, but it will give you an excuse to meet her and talk to her. Also you think that if you *do* find the Ripper, you'll be a conquering hero and she'll fall into your arms in gratitude. Am I correct?"

"Keep talking." Sweeney said. "As if I need to suggest it."

"So. You've got two reasons for finding him. I've got two reasons for helping you. One—" He held up a fat finger. "—If you do find him, he might stick a knife in you. I think I'd like that. I hate *your* guts, too, Mr. Sweeney."

"Thank you kindly."

"Two—" Another finger joined the first. "—the police just might have something in thinking the killer will come back to finish the job on Yolanda. Despite the fact, and the newspapers' reporting of the fact, that Yo can't recognize him on a bet, he may decide to take a chance and play safe by killing her. That I would *not* like."

"That I can understand," Sweeney said. "Also I like it better than your first reason."

"And I don't think, Mr. Sweeney, that finding him will get you to first base with Yolanda. At least, I'll take a chance on that."

"Fine, Doc. One little thing, though. The police force of Chicago outnumbers me, considerably. Just out of curiosity, what makes you think that I, with my little slingshot, might do more than the whole blue army?"

"Because you're a crazy damn Irishman. Because you're a little *fey*; I suspected that from a sentence or two in your story, and I know it now. Because God loves fools and drunkards and you're both.

"Also because, under the sodden surface, you've got a hell of a keen brain, Mr. Sweeney; another thing I suspected before and know now. And you've got a crazy warped streak in you that might take you places where the police wouldn't think to go. Like the simpleton who found the horse by thinking he was a horse and going where he'd go if he really were a horse. Not that I would compare you to a horse, Mr. Sweeney. At least not to *all* of a horse."

"Thank you. I am a horse's ass with a hell of a keen brain. Tell me more," he said eagerly.

"I think I could. I really *am* a psychiatrist, Mr. Sweeney, although not a practising one. An unfortunate occurrence in what would have been my last year of internship got me kicked out on my ear. It occurred to me that satyriasis might be a logical prescription for nymphomania. We had a patient who was quite an advanced satyr, Mr. Sweeney, and I took the liberty of introducing him into the room of an enthusiastic nympholept and leaving them together for an extended period. My superiors were quite stuffy about it."

"I can understand that," Sweeney said.

"Ah, had they only known some of the other experiments I tried, which were *not* found out. But we digress."

"We do indeed," said Sweeney. "So you're going to help me find the Ripper. So go ahead and help."

Greene spread his hands. "It isn't much. I didn't mean that I have the killer's name and address in my notebook, ready to turn over to you. I merely meant that I'll gladly work with you, Mr. Sweeney; I'll give you such facts and data as I have. And, since you'll want to talk to Yolanda, I'll see that you do. You might have trouble doing even that, with the police on guard around her, as they will be."

He looked at his wrist watch. "Unfortunately, I haven't more time now. A business appointment. One must eat. Could you, Mr. Sweeney, meet me here tomorrow afternoon, about this same time?"

Sweeney frowned. He said, "I don't know. Maybe you're just wasting my time. Have you really got anything?"

"I've got Yolanda." Greene said. "She'll be released from the hospital by then. I'll bring her here with me. You'll be here, of course?"

"I'll be here, of course," said Sweeney.

"Good. We may be seeing quite a lot of one another. Let us, then, dispense with the amenities. Let us not say hypocritical good-byes. My two drinks were on you. Thank you for them, and the hell with you."

He walked out.

Sweeney took a deep breath. He let it out slowly.

The bartender strolled over. He said, "That'll be a dollar and a quarter. Don't you want your beer?"

"No. Pour it down the drain. But bring me a bromo and a shot."

"Sure. Mixed?"

"Not mixed."

He put two dollar bills on the bar. When the bartender came back, Sweeney said, "Quite a character, that Doc Greene."

"Yeah. Quite a character."

"What puzzles me about him is this," Sweeney said. "Those seemed to be his own teeth he was wearing, they weren't regular enough for false ones. How the hell could a guy like that keep his own teeth that long?"

The bartender chuckled. "Maybe it's them eyes of his. Like a hypnotist. I think a guy'd have to be pretty brave to take a poke at Doc. *I'd* rather not tangle with him. Funny, though, the way women go for him. You wouldn't think it."

"Including Yo?" Sweeney asked.

"I wouldn't know about Yo. She's a funny dame to figure out." He took Sweeney's bills and rang up a dollar eighty, putting two dimes on the bar.

Sweeney added a quarter to it and said, "Have one with me."

"Sure. Thanks."

"Skoal," said Sweeney. "Say, who's running El Madhouse now? Is it still Harry Yahn's?"

"Yahn owns it, or most of it, but he isn't running it. He's got another place over on Randolph."

"Sucker joint, like El Madhouse?"

The bartender smiled faintly. "Not this kind of sucker joint."

"Oh," said Sweeney. "It'd be a little bar with a big back room and if you know a guy named Joe at the door, you can leave your shirt in the back room."

The blowzy blonde at the far end of the bar was tapping the bottom of her glass on the wood impatiently. The bartender said, "This guy at the door is named Willie." He went down to mix a drink for the blonde.

Sweeney poured the bromo back and forth between the two glasses and drank it.

Then he got up and went into gathering dusk on Clark Street. He walked south, toward the Loop. He walked slowly, aimlessly, trying to think and not quite succeeding.

Along the street an empty taxi was coming. Sweeney hailed it, and gave his home address.

In his room, he slid the bottom newspaper out from under the stack on the bed and sat down in the Morris chair. He found the story of the first murder—the murder of the ex-chorine, Lola Brent. Six inches on page two, not much in the way of detail.

There hadn't been a Ripper, then. It was just a story of a woman—a not very important woman, at that—who had been found, dead, in the areaway between two buildings on Thirty-Eighth Street. A knife or a razor had been the weapon used. The crime had occurred in daylight between four and five o'clock in the afternoon. There had been no witnesses. A child returning home from a playground had discovered the body. Police were seeking a man with whom Lola Brent was alleged to have been living.

Sweeney took up the next paper. The story had a little better play in that one, and there were two pictures. One was of Lola Brent. She was blonde, and beautiful. She didn't look the thirty-five years the story said she was, you'd have taken her for early twenties.

The other picture was that of the man the police had arrested, Sammy Cole. He had black, curly hair and a face that was handsome in the ruggedly honest way that is a con-man's stock in trade. He denied killing Lola Brent, and was being held on an open charge.

The following day's story was a brief rehash; the only new angle was that Sammy Cole had confessed to several counts of operating a confidence game. The following several papers brought out nothing additional.

The Lola Brent crime had then, it appeared, faded into limbo, unsolved. There was nothing at all concerning it in the last two papers of the week's series starting two months before. There wouldn't, Sweeney knew, have been any mention of it—of importance—in the five and a half weeks' papers that he didn't have, the gap in between his first series and the series starting ten days ago.

He picked up the paper of ten days before and skimmed rapidly through the story of the murder of Stella Gaylord, the B-girl from Madison Street. He didn't try to memorize details here; he was going to concentrate on one crime at a time. He was looking, now, only for further mention of the killing of Lola Brent. He found it on the second day after the Stella Gaylord murder; it was then first suggested that the crime might be a psychopathic one, perpetrated by the same killer who had slashed Lola Brent six and a half weeks before.

The next day's lead was a build-up of that idea, with a comparative description of the wounds inflicted upon the two women. Each had been killed by a horizontal slash across the abdomen, but the weapon had not been the same one. The knife that had killed Lola Brent had been no sharper than average; but the blade that had slashed Stella Gaylord had been razor keen.

Sweeney skimmed through the rest of the papers, looking, this time, only for additional details about the Lola Brent case: one at a time was all his mind would handle and absorb in its currently fuzzy condition. Apparently, no further discoveries of importance had been made on the Brent case. The police were still not too sure that the killer of Lola Brent was the same homicidal maniac who had killed Stella Gaylord and five days later, Dorothy Lee.

But there wasn't any doubt about the latter two having been killed by the same hand.

Sweeney put down the last—the most recent—of the papers and tried to think. He now knew everything that had been given out to the papers on the Brent murder, but none of it seemed helpful. For that matter, what *could* be helpful—short of a lucky guess—when you were hunting a killer who killed without motive? Without motive, that is, applicable to the particular victim and not to any woman who was blonde and beautiful. Yes, there was that in common. The three who had been killed as well as Yolanda Lang, had all been blonde and beautiful.

Sweeney went to the phone in the hall and dialled a number. When he got the man he wanted, he asked, "Sammy Cole, the guy that Lola Brent was living with, still in the jug here in Chicago?"

"Yeah," said the man to whom Sweeney was talking. I won't mention his name because he's still holding down the same job and doing right well at it, and this would get him in trouble. Sweeney, you see, had something on him, and reporters aren't supposed to have anything on important public officials. They often do.

He said, "Yeah, we're still holding him. We could have salted him away before this, but returns are still coming in. Every once in a while we tie him in to a fraud charge and get it off the books."

"I'd like to talk to him," Sweeney said. "Tonight."

"Tonight? Look, Sweeney, can't you wait till regular hours tomorrow? It's after seven o'clock and——"

"You can fix it," Sweeney said. "I'll grab a taxi and be there quick."

That is how, within half an hour, Sweeney was sitting on the warden's desk and Sammy Cole sat on a straight chair a few feet away from him. They were alone in the office. Sammy Cole was recognizable from the newspaper picture of him Sweeney had seen shortly before, but barely recognizable. He still had black hair but it was cut too short to be curly. His face was ruggedly sullen instead of ruggedly honest.

"I told 'em," Sammy Cole said. "I told 'em every Goddam thing. I spilled my guts because *I'd* like to see whoever bumped Lola take the hot squat. There was the off chance it did tie in with something she'd been doing, see? So I spilled my guts and what does it get me? Enough raps so when I get out, *if* I get out, I'll be peddling pencils."

"Tough," Sweeney said. An envelope and a pencil came out of his pockets and he wrote "Want a drink?" on the back of the envelope and showed it to Sammy Cole.

"Jesus," said Sammy Cole, not at all irreverently. It would have been ambiguous to anyone listening in on a bug, but Sweeney took the half pint bottle, still two-thirds full, that he'd bought earlier at the drugstore out of his hip pocket and handed it to Sammy Cole. Sammy Cole handed it back empty and wiped his lips with the back of his hand. He said, "What you want to know?"

"I don't know," Sweeney told him. "That's the trouble. I don't know. But I got to start somewhere. When'd you see Lola last?"

"That morning—almost noon, I guess—when she went to work."

"To work? Were you that far down, Sammy?"

"Well—yeah and no. I was working on something that would have come through big. I was tired of hand-to-mouthing on the short-con stuff. What I was doing would have got us Florida for the winter, and a real stake. Laugh it off, but I was going to turn straight. For Lola. She didn't like the grifts. So she was keeping us eating while my deal came through.'

"Was she tied in on the big deal?"

"No. That was strictly me. But we worked out a little racket for her that brought in peanuts. A hundred or so a week for a few days' work. That's what she was on that day."

"Where? What was it?"

Sammy Cole wiped his lips again and bent sidewise to look questioningly in the direction of Sweeney's hip pocket. Sweeney shook his head and spread his hands.

Sammy Cole sighed. He said, "A gift shop on Division Street. Raoul's Gift Shop. That was her first day there, so I dunno much about it except what she told me, from applying for the job the day before, and what little I saw when I dropped in at six. That was part of the racket. This Raoul is a faggot."

"How would that tie in with a racket for Lola, Sammy? Unless you came in later?"

"Naw, nothing like that, I just mentioned it. All there was to the racket was Lola'd get a job selling stuff somewhere, preferably a place where she'd made a few big sales, not dime store stuff. Small store, usually, where she'd be alone when the boss went out to eat or something and left her alone a little. She'd drag down on some sales—ten bucks, fifty bucks, whatever the traffic would bear. We played extra safe because she wasn't on the blotter and I wanted to keep her off. I'd drop in later at a time we'd set and she'd slip me the moolah. She never had it on her for more'n a few minutes; she'd stash it somewhere after she dragged it down and get it just a minute before I was due to come in. It was safe as houses. Soon as she saw a mooch beginning to look suspicious at her, she'd do a fadeout; never worked anywhere longer'n a few days. Then she'd lay off a while and—well, you got the picture."

Sweeney nodded. "And she got the job at Raoul's the day before. How?"

"Newspaper ad. We had good references for her; that was my department. Job was in the morning papers. She got it in the afternoon and was to start at noon the next day. They're open till nine in the evening and she was to work noon to nine, lunch hour four to five."

"How come you didn't just arrange to meet her outside, during lunch hour?"

Sammy Cole looked at Sweeney contemptuously. "Lookit the angles," he said. "First, she'd have to walk out with the moolah *on* her, and that's taking a chance. Second, if he sends her out four to five, then the pansy's taking off at five, probably. Her best time to do a little business, on her own, would be from five to six, and I get there at six. If the pansy's still gone, good; if he's there, she can slip it to me. I buy something for two bits and she slips the dough in the paper bag with it. It's safe as houses."

"And you got there at six?"

"Sure. She wasn't there and I figured something was on the off beat. I phoned the flat and a cop answered so I hung up quick and stayed away. Not that I guessed what had happened—whatever the hell *did* happen. But I figured she'd got caught on a larceny rap and I'd be better off on the outside, to try to get her out of it. Hell, I was nuts about the dame. I'd have raised some moolah somehow to get her a shyster and bail her out. I'd've knocked a guy over if I had to, to get her out. And they still think maybe *I* killed her. Jesus."

"When'd you find out what really happened?"

"Morning papers. I'd holed in a hotel. I near went nuts. All I could think about was getting the son of a bitch that did it and chopping him up into hamburger, slow. But I didn't know how to go looking for him without walking into cops, and I wasn't going to be able to do a Goddam thing if I did that. So all I could figure was to keep under cover till the heat was off. But I guess I was too upset to be careful enough. They got me, and by the time I get outa here, the guy'll be dead of old age.

"So, Jesus. God how I hate a cop, but just the same I did all I could for 'em. I spilled my guts to 'em, just on the off chance something we'd been doing would give 'em a lead."

Sammy Cole slumped tiredly down in the chair and sighed. He looked up and asked, "Got a fag?"

Sweeney handed him a package of cigarettes and a book of matches and said, "Keep them. Look, Sammy, if you hadn't been picked up, what would you have done when the heat was off? Where'd you have started?"

"With the faggot, Raoul. Maybe he had something to do with it and maybe he didn't, but I'd have picked his petals off one at a time till I was sure."

"What happened at the gift shop? Did he catch her dragging

down on a sale, or what? He must have fired her if she went home, and she was found in the areaway outside your flat."

Sammy Cole said. "That I wouldn't know. The cops ask me questions; they don't tell me. All I know is what's in the papers and they don't give me any papers. You can get papers—and stuff—in stir, if you got money. But I'm broke flat."

Sweeney nodded and took a ten-dollar bill out of his wallet and handed it across. He said. "You get no dough out of me, pal, if you were hinting. Say, would Lola maybe have put the bite on some merchandise? Rings or something? Some gift shops have lots of small stuff that's valuable."

Sammy Cole shook his head definitely. He said. "That I'll guarantee; she didn't. I drummed that into her. Too many angles, too easy to get caught, too easy to have stuff traced back to you, and too hard to get more'n a twentieth of what the stuff's worth anyway. Not even a ring or a pair of earrings for herself; I drummed that into her."

"What was the long-con you were working on? Could that have tied in?"

"Nope, it couldn't. I didn't spill that because I was working *with* a guy, and I wouldn't rat on him. The cops couldn't rubber-hose it out of me because I'm no stoolie. And anyway, it *couldn't* have tied in with what happened *to* Lola because neither the guy I was working with or the guy we were working *on* knew her or knew she was alive. And she didn't know them or much about them. I mean, I'd told her what the game was, but not the details or the names. See?"

"Okay, Sammy. Thanks," Sweeney said. "I can't do you any good, I guess, but I'll keep you posted. So long."

He surprised the con-man by shaking hands with him and went out of the warden's office, nodding to the turnkey who'd been standing outside the door.

A clock in the outer corridor told him it was eight-fifteen, and he stood in front of the jail, watching both ways, until a cab came along and he hailed it.

"Division Street," he said, "We'll have to look up the address on the way north; I forgot to get it. It's a gift shop named Raoul's."

The taxi driver laughed. He said, "I know the joint. The guy tried to make me once. He's a queer. Say, you ain't——" he looked at Sweeney.

He said, "No, you ain't," and turned back to the wheel.

CHAPTER FIVE

SWEENEY stood looking into the window of Raoul's gift shop. Presumably he was staring at the array of merchandise in the display; mostly he was watching over the low partition at the back of the window. Two customers, both women, were within. With Raoul, the proprietor, that made the feminine complement of the shop one hundred per cent. No one would ever have to wonder about Raoul.

Sweeney studied the window and saw that it was not, in the fashion of many gift shops, cluttered with junky bric-a-brac and cheaply miscellany. The items displayed were few, and good. There were foo dogs from China, thunderbirds from Mexico, costume jewellery that was in good taste if a bit blatant, a pair of brass candlesticks of exquisitely simple design; there wasn't a single thing in the window that Sweeney could have taken exception to—except possibly the prices, and they weren't shown. His opinion of Raoul went up several notches.

One of the women inside made a purchase and came out. The other was obviously browsing and Raoul, after apparently offering to help her, relaxed gracefully against the counter.

Sweeney went inside. The proprietor, smiling a proprietary smile, came forward to meet him. The smile turned to a slight frown when Sweeney said, "From the *Blade*. Like to talk to you about Lola Brent," but he walked with Sweeney to the back of the shop, out of earshot of the remaining customer.

Sweeney asked, "She got the job when? The day before?"

"Yes. Several came in answer to an advertisement I put in the paper. Your paper, the *Blade*. She had excellent references from a gift shop in New York; I didn't guess they were fraudulent. She was well dressed, had a pleasing personality. And she was free, ready to start work at once. I told her to come in the next day."

"And she did, at noon?"

"Yes."

"And what happened? You caught her dragging down on a sale and fired her?"

"Not exactly. I explained it all to the police."

Sweeney said. "I could get it direct from them, but I'd rather not. If you don't mind too much."

Raoul sighed. He said, "From twelve until a little after three we were both in the store. There weren't many customers and I spent most of the time acquainting her with the stock, the prices, telling her things she should know about the business. At about a quarter after three I had to leave for a short while, on a personal matter. I was gone a little over half an hour. When I returned, I asked what business she'd done while I was gone and she told me that only one customer had been in the store and that he had bought a pair of six-dollar bookends. That was the only amount that had been rung on the register. But then I noticed that something else was missing."

"What was it?"

"A figurine, a statuette, which had been priced at twenty-four dollars. It had stood on the shelf over there." Raoul pointed. "It just happened that that particular statuette had been standing a bit askew and I had straightened it shortly before I had left on my errand. Shortly after my return, I chanced to notice that it was no longer there. There had been three figures on that shelf, and now there were only two, with the two moved closer together to avert leaving a conspicuous gap between them. So I asked Miss Brent if she had moved the statuette and she denied knowledge of it."

He sighed gently. "It was embarrassing, of course. I knew she could not be telling the truth, because—just as it happened—I was certain it had been there when I left."

"It couldn't have been shoplifted?"

"Hardly possible. The figure was ten inches high and, although slender, the arms of the figure were extended forward; it would have been a difficult object to conceal under a coat, and it would not have gone into a pocket at all. It was not the sort of object that is chosen by shop lifters, I assure you. Besides, Miss Brent had told me that only one person had been in the store. There was no doubt in my mind at all, Mr.—ah——"

"Sweeney. You accused her of having sold it and kept the dough."

"What else could I do? I told her that I had no desire to prosecute, and that if she would permit me to search her thoroughly back in the stock room, I would permit her to go, without calling the police."

"You found the money on her?"

"No. When she saw that I really meant to call the police unless she confessed and really meant to let her go if she did, she admitted the theft. She had the money, a twenty-dollar bill and four ones, in the top of her stocking. A woman's repository."

"Then you didn't have to search her. Or did you?"

"Of course I did. I had missed that particular item and she had confessed selling it, but—since she was admittedly dishonest—how did I know that that was the only item she had sold beside the bookends? I couldn't inventory the stock. She might also have made, let us say, a fifty-dollar sale of costume jewellery and concealed the money in her other stocking or in her brassiere or somewhere."

"Had she?"

"No. At least I found no money except a few dollars in her purse which I was willing to believe was her own property. She was—ah—a little sullen about being searched, but she was reasonable when she saw my reason for insisting. Also she was not sufficiently naïve to think that I wished to do so for any ulterior motive, if you understand what I mean."

"I understand what you mean," said Sweeney. "So it would have been about four o'clock when she left?"

"Yes. Not later than fifteen minutes after four. I did not notice the time exactly."

"She left alone?"

"Of course. And to anticipate your next question, I did not notice whether she met anyone outside. Naturally, knowing her to be dishonest, I kept my eyes on her as far as the door, but not beyond. I did not notice which direction she went. But of course she must have gone directly to her home, because I understand she was found dead in the areaway there at five o'clock. She would have had to transfer to get there, and go through the Loop; it would have taken at least half an hour from here, possibly longer."

"Unless she took a cab or someone gave her a lift."

"Of course. The taxi is not too likely, judging from the small amount of money she had in her purse."

Sweeney nodded. "Being picked up isn't too likely either. Her man was to meet her here in the store at six, but he'd hardly have been around the neighbourhood as early as four-fifteen."

Raoul's eyebrows rose a little. "He was to meet her here?"

"Yeah. To pick up whatever she'd dragged down by then."

"Indeed? The police didn't tell me that."

Sweeney grinned. "The police don't go out of their way to tell people things. That's why I wanted to talk to you about this instead of to them. Did Lola Brent, by the way, seem to recognize anybody who did come in that afternoon, while you were here?"

"No. I'm reasonably sure she didn't."

"What about the statuette? A woman's figure, I take it, but with or without clothes?"

"Without. Very definitely without, if you understand what I mean."

"I guess I do," Sweeney said. "Even some women, let alone statues, manage to be nakeder without clothes than others do. It's a gift."

Raoul raised his hands expressively. "I do not mean to imply. Mr. Sweeney, that the statuette was in any sense of the word pornographic or suggestive. It was, rather, quite virginal—in a very peculiar way."

"You intrigue me," said Sweeney. "How many ways of being virginal are there? I thought I knew everything, but—"

Raoul smiled. "There are many ways of expressing a single quality. Of, as it were, getting it across. Virginity, in this case, is expressed through fear, horror, loathing. Virginity—or perhaps I should say virginality——"

"What's the difference?" Sweeney asked, and then answered himself. "Wait. I think I get you. One is physical and the other is mental. Right?"

"Of course. They may or may not coincide. Many married women are virginal, although they are not virgins. They have never really been *touched*; the physical act alone—— And then again, a maiden who is *virgo intacta* may be far from virginal if her thoughts—ah—you see what I mean?"

"I do," Sweeney said. "But we wander from the statuette."

"Not far. Would you care to *see* the statuette? Not the one Miss Brent sold, of course, but a duplicate of it. I ordered two and liked them so well that I have one in my apartment in the next block. It's closing time now and—I assure you I have *no* ulterior motive, Mr. Sweeney.

"Thanks," said Sweeney "But I don't believe it's necessary. The statuette itself could hardly have anything to do with the crime."

"Of course not. I merely thought it would interest you abstractly." He smiled. "It is, incidentally, known as a Screaming Mimi."

"A what?"

"A Screaming Mimi. Girl's name—M-i-m-i. A rather obvious pun, of course, on the screaming meamies, if you know what they are."

"Intimately," said Sweeney. "And, if I may, I'm going to change my mind: I would like to meet this Mimi, Mr.——Is Raoul your last name?"

"Reynarde, Mr. Sweeney, Raoul Reynarde. If you'll pardon me just a moment——"

He walked over to the remaining customer to tell her it was closing time. Sweeney followed her to the door and waited there until Reynarde had turned out the lights. They walked a block and a half east on Division Street and up two flights of stairs to the apartment.

"I can't ask you to stay long, Mr. Sweeney," Reynarde said, as he flicked on the light inside the door. "I—ah—have a guest coming. But we'll have time for a drink. May I make you a highball?"

"Sure, thanks," said Sweeney. "But where is Mimi?'

"On the mantel yonder."

Sweeney's gaze, which had been roaming about the beautifully furnished—if a bit feminine—apartment, came to rest on a ten-inch-high statuette over the fireplace. He crossed the room and stood looking at it.

He saw now what Reynarde had meant. Definitely there was a virginal quality about the slim nude figure, but that you saw afterward. "Fear, horror, loathing," Reynarde had said, and all that was there, not only in the face but in the twisted rigidity of the body. The mouth was wide open in a soundless scream. The arms were thrust out, palms forward, to hold off some approaching horror.

"An exquisite thing," said Reynarde's voice from across the room, where he poured drinks at a little mahogany cabinet that was complete down to an ice-cube unit. "It is made of a new plastic that can't be told from ebony, unless you pick it up. The dull gloss is the same as ebony's, to the eye. If that figure were what it looks to be, hand-carved ebony, and original, it would be worth a lot of money." He waved a hand around the room. "Most things you see here *are* originals. I prefer them."

Sweeney grunted. "I don't agree with you there. I'd rather any day have a Renoir print than an art school original. But that's a matter of taste. Could you get me one of these?"

Reynarde's voice came from just behind Sweeney. "Your drink, Mr. Sweeney. Yes, I can get you a Screaming Mimi, or I think I can. The company that makes them—a small concern in Louisville, Kentucky, of all places—may possibly have some left. They generally make a few hundred of an item like that. But if you really want it, I may sell you that one. Although it has been on my mantel, it is still virginal."

He laughed. "Or I can, if you think that makes it second hand, return it to the store and sell it to you from there. One advantage of being a dealer, Mr. Sweeney; I need never grow tired of an art object or bit of bric-a-brac. Often I keep objects from the store here until I tire of them and then exchange them for others. I think that I am growing a little weary of the little lady by now. Your health, sir."

Sweeney drank absent-mindedly, without taking his eyes off the statuette, emptying the glass at a single draught. He said, "Before you change your mind, Mr. Reynarde—" He put his glass down on the mantel and counted twenty-four dollars out of his wallet.

"How," he asked "did it get named? Is that your name for it, or the company's?"

Reynard pursed his lips. "I don't believe I re—Oh, yes. The name came from the company that made it, but unofficially, as it were. The salesman told me that the catalogue code number for it is SM–1, and someone in their office with a sense of humour decided the SM stood for Screaming Mimi."

"Who did the statuette? The original, I mean."

"That I do not know. The company is the Ganslen Art Company. They make mostly bookends and chess sets, but they do some work in small statuary, often surprisingly good at the price. Shall I wrap the figure for you?"

Sweeney chuckled. "Put pants on Mimi? Never. I'll carry her naked through the streets."

"Another drink, Mr. Sweeney?"

"Thanks, no. I think Mimi and I must be going." He picked up the statuette gently.

Reynarde walked to the door with him and bowed slightly as they parted.

As the door closed behind him, Sweeney wondered why he *had* wanted the statuette. And why, in particular, he had resented Raoul Reynarde's probing into his reason for wanting it. He looked at the statuette in his hand, and shivered a little—mentally if not physically. It was neither pretty nor sensuous. Damn it, Reynarde was right; it would appeal only to a sadist, or to someone who had *some* abnormality in him. And yet he, Sweeney, had paid over twenty-four dollars of good money to take it home with him. Was he punch-drunk?

No, he wasn't. The fog inside his head was lifting, definitely. And through the fog, he almost had a glimpse of something that might have been the association Reynarde had suggested. Then the fog came down again.

Well, it would come back. Sweeney sighed and started for the stairway. Coming up the stairs was a plump, beautiful young man with blond curly hair. They passed in the hallway, and the young man looked curiously at the statuette Sweeney was carrying but made no comment. He rang the bell of Reynarde's apartment.

Sweeney went on down the stairs.

Outside, and the dark night was bright with lights, the air hot and humid. Sweeney walked west on Division Street and then south on Dearborn.

He wondered how long he could keep going like this; how long he would *have* to keep going before he could eat and then sleep. The nausea was back with him now. Food was a disgusting thought, but it was a hurdle to be taken, a hurdle that *had* to be taken.

Eventually.

At Chicago Avenue he turned half a block west and went into a small clean restaurant and sat down at the counter. A man in a white apron that made Sweeney think of a surgeon came up on the other side of the counter and stood there. He stood there staring at the black statuette Sweeney had placed on the counter in front of him.

"Mimi," Sweeney said, "meet Joe. Joe, meet Mimi. Or *is* your name Joe, Joe?"

The counterman grinned uncertainly. He said, "It's close, Jack. What's wrong with the little lady?"

"She is screaming," Sweeney said. He felt as though he wanted to, himself. "Jack, could you get me a very special dinner?"

"Such as what? If we got what it takes, we can make it."

"Bread," said Sweeney. "Two slices of white bread, plain, without butter. Not too fresh, but not really stale. With the crusts left on. On a white plate. I think maybe I could eat that. The bread, I mean, not the plate. Can you do it?"

"I'll ask the cook. Coffee, too?"

"Black," said Sweeney. "In a cup."

He closed his eyes and tried to concentrate on something to keep from thinking about the smells of the restaurant, but all he succeeded in doing was concentrating on the smells. When plate and cup rattled on the counter in front of him, he opened his eyes.

He took a sip of the scalding coffee and then began to nibble on one of the slices of bread. It was all right; it would go down and stay down.

He was almost through with the second slice when the waiter came back. He stood leaning against the ledge, looking at the statuette. He said, "That thing sort of *gets* you, when you look at it. It gives you the willies. Where'd you get it?"

"From a fairy," Sweeney said. "How much do I owe you?"

"About fifteen cents. Say, know what that statue makes me think of? The Ripper."

Sweeney almost dropped his cup of coffee; he put it down carefully.

The waiter hadn't noticed. He said, "I mean, a woman being attacked by the Ripper. No dame is *that* afraid of being raped or something. But a crazy guy with a knife in his hand coming after her—and she's back in a corner maybe——"

Sweeney got up slowly. He fumbled a five-dollar bill out of his wallet and put it down on the counter. He said, "Keep the change, Jack." He grabbed Mimi firmly about the waist and went out.

Again an automobile almost ran him down as he cut diagonally across Chicago Avenue.

The fog was gone. He knew now what his hunch had been and why he'd wanted the Screaming Mimi. He should have got it when Reynarde had said the figure would appeal to a sadist; he *would* have got it then if his mind had been clear.

But it was clear as gin now. An hour or two before she'd been killed, Lola Brent had sold a Screaming Mimi. The fact that she'd dragged down on the sale had nothing to do with her death, but the fact that she'd *made* that sale had. The purchaser had been an insane sadist who had waited outside and followed her home. It had been a break for him that she'd been fired and had gone straight home, where he could close up on her in the seclusion of the areaway. Would he have tried to kill her anyway, during her lunch hour, if she'd stayed on the job?

His mind was clear now, but his body felt like hell. He walked faster. He could sleep now, and he *had* to sleep. He had to get home before he fell down.

CHAPTER SIX

IN the morning, it was Friday. It was almost Friday noon. Sweeney woke and lay a while in bed, and then swung his feet out on to the floor and sat there a while. His head didn't ache. Outside of that he couldn't have found much to say for himself. The room seemed to be filled with an invisible fog. But he got his eyes focused on the clock and saw that it was eleven-forty. He'd slept about twelve hours.

On top of the radio-phono, on the half that didn't lift up, stood a little ten-inch high black statuette. It was the figure of a naked girl, her arms thrust out to ward off a ripper, her mouth open in a silent, eternal scream. Her body, which would have been beautiful relaxed, was subtly distorted, rigid with terror. Only a sadist could have liked it. Sweeney wasn't one; he shuddered a little and averted his eyes.

But it woke him up, seeing the Screaming Mimi. It woke him up to nightmare.

It made him want a drink; it made him think nostalgically of the sodden state of nonthinking in which he'd been only two days ago—a day and a half ago. It made him wish he was back there again.

And why not? He had plenty of money. Why not go out, right now, and have a drink and another?

Heat in waves came in at the open window. His body was wet with sweat. He was breathing hard.

He stood up, making an unconscious gesture of pushing back the heat and the fog, and got a bathrobe out of the closet. He went down the hall to the bathroom and sat on the edge of the tub while it filled with cold water. Almost cold water.

Getting into it woke him. He took a deep breath and sank down into it, clear to his neck, letting the coldness of it draw the heat from his body and feeling the mist clear from his mind.

Warmth, he thought, is what man wants, what he lives for, what he works for, until he gets too much of it—and then coldness is a wonderful and refreshing thing. The thought of lying there in an ever-cold grave, for instance, is a horrible thing in winter; in summer—

But that was maudlin. Like thinking of Lola Brent, the ex-chorine who had loved a con-man so much she'd taken to the grift herself, to help him. And she'd sold a small black statuette to a man who'd looked from it to her——

Sweeney swore. What did it matter to him, that a fading ex-pony was six feet under now? She'd have been there sooner or later anyway; five years from now, fifty years. Death is an incurable disease that men and women are born with; it gets them sooner or later. A murderer never really kills; he but anticipates. Always he kills one who is already dying, already doomed.

Actually, he never hurts the one he kills. The hurt is to whoever loved him or her, and has to keep on living. The man who'd killed Lola Brent had hurt Sammy Cole more than he'd hurt Lola.

If he, Sweeney, really came to hate Doc Greene and wanted to hurt him badly——

He sat up in the tub. What if——?

But no, that was silly. Sure, someone could have hated Doc Greene enough to want to get at him by killing Yolanda—but that left the other murders out of it; Lola Brent, Stella Gaylord, Dorothy Lee. A human being (a *sane* human being; but then, what is sanity?) couldn't conceivably hate four men enough to kill the women they loved.

And besides, it left out sadism and Mimi, and the Screaming Mimi was the key.

He didn't put his shoulders back down into the water, he got out of the tub instead and towelled himself off.

When he was dry he went back to his room and put on a pair of shorts and a pair of socks. That would be enough until he was ready to go out, in that heat.

What was next? Stella Gaylord, B-girl on Madison Street. He might as well take it chronologically. The murder of Lola Brent had been two months ago; the second murder, that of Stella Gaylord, had been ten days ago.

He put the stack of old newspapers on the chair, where he could reach it from the bed, and propped the pillow up against the footboard.

Why not music? he thought. It always helped him concentrate; he could, for some strange reason, better remember what he read if he read it against a background of music.

He put some records on and started the machine, then lay down on the bed and picked up the first paper, the one of ten days ago, that broke the Gaylord murder story.

It was on page one, but in the bottom right corner, six inches of type under a one-column head:

BODY OF GIRL
    SLAIN WITH KNIFE
        IS FOUND IN ALLEY

Sweeney read the six inches of type and decided that, as far as really important details were concerned, they might as well have let the headline stand alone.

Oh, there was the woman's name and address—on West Madison Street—and the place where the murder had occurred—the mouth of an alley off Huron Street between State and Dearborn. The body had been discovered at three-thirty in the morning and, according to the physician who had examined the body, the woman had been dead less than an hour.

Apparently there had been no robbery committed and—to Sweeney's amazed amusement—the story stated that the victim had not been attacked.

Police suspected that a homicidal maniac was at large, although the Lola Brent murder had apparently been forgotten; it was not mentioned.

The following day's paper had a picture of Stella Gaylord; it was a poor picture, apparently blown up from a snapshot, and you could tell that she was pretty but that was about all. There was more about Stella, too, including the address of the West Madison Street bar where she'd been working on percentage. She had been last seen alive when she'd left there, alone, at two o'clock, an hour and a half before the discovery of her body.

And for the first time, the murder of Stella Gaylord was tied in with the murder of Lola Brent, with the suggestion that possibly the same psychopathic killer had killed both of them.

The following day's paper had a few added details, but no new developments.

Sweeney got up to shut off the phonograph. The sight of the black statuette on top of it reminded him of something he had to do. He slipped on a bathrobe and went out into the hall, to the telephone.

He got a long distance operator and put a call to the Ganslen Art Company at Louisville. A few minutes later he had the general manager, a Ralph Burke, on the line.

"This is the Chicago *Blade*." Sweeney said. "Something about one of your statuettes has come up in connection with a murder investigation. It's an SM–1. Remember it, off-hand?"

"I'm afraid I'd have to look it up."

"Maybe this will help. It's a figure of a terrified girl; somebody at your place called it a Screaming Mimi."

"Oh, yes, certainly. I remember it now. What do you want to know about it?"

"Could you tell me how many of them you sold—and particularly how many of them you sold in Chicago?"

"We didn't sell many, I know. It didn't turn out to be a popular number at all. In fact, we never got around to listing it in our catalogue. We made a trial lot of one gross and we've got most of them left. We gave each salesman a sample six months ago and some of them sold a few. If you want to hold the line a minute I can look up how many were sold in Chicago. Or shall I call you back?"

"I'll hold the line," Sweeney said.

It was scarcely a minute before the manager's voice was back. He said, "I've got it all here—luckily we keep a separate record on each number. There were—uh—two sold in Chicago. Only two, and both to a place called Raoul's Gift Shop. Altogether we sold about forty of them—mostly on the East and West Coasts. Want the exact figures?"

"Thanks, no," Sweeney said. "What does the SM–1 designation mean, if anything?"

"The SM part doesn't; it's just our serial number, picked in rotation. Our number before that was SL and the one after it was SN. The figure one is the size and finish. If we'd put it out in other sizes and materials, they'd have been SM–2. SM–3, and so on. But we won't, in this case. Unless, the first time our salesmen carry it, they take orders for several gross, we drop the number from our line and don't even catalogue it. It wouldn't pay. And we make only the very popular things in various sizes and styles."

"What will you do with the hundred-odd Mimis you have left?"

"We'll get rid of them next year, in with mixed lots. If a customer orders, say, a dozen mixed figures, our choice, he gets them about half the usual list price; we get rid of our odd lot and remainders that way. At a loss, of course, to us—but it's better than throwing them away."

"Of course," Sweeney said. "Do you recall who nicknamed SM–1 the Screaming Mimi?"

"Our bookkeeper, it's a hobby of his to try to think up names that match the figures and the letter designations—says it helps him remember which is which." The manager chuckled. "He hits well once in a while. I remember our number SF. He called it Some Fanny, and it was."

"I'm tempted to order one," said Sweeney. "But back to Mimi. Who designed her, or sculptured her, or moulded her?"

"Fellow by the name of Chapman Wilson. Artist and sculptor, lives in Brampton. Wisconsin. He modelled it in clay."

"And sent it to you?"

"No, I bought it from him there, in Brampton. I do the buying myself, make trips several times a year. We've got quite a few artists we buy from and it's much more practical to go to their studios to look over what they have than to have a lot of stuff shipped here and have to ship most of it back. I bought SM–1 from him about a year ago, and two other numbers. I guessed right on the others; they're selling okay."

"This Chapman Wilson—did he model Mimi from life, or what?"

"Don't know; didn't ask him. The original was in clay, same size as our copies; about ten inches. I took a chance on it because it was unusual. Something unusual may go over really big, or it may not sell at all. That's a chance we take."

"Know anything about Chapman Wilson personally?"

"Not much. He's rather an eccentric, but then a lot of artists are."

"Married?"

"No. At least, I don't think so. Didn't ask him, but I didn't see a woman around, or any sign of one."

"You say he's eccentric. Could you go as far as psychopathic, maybe?"

"I don't think so. He's a little screwy, but that's all. Most of his stuff is pretty routine—and sells fairly well."

"Thanks a lot," Sweeney said. "Guess that's all I need to know. Good-bye."

He checked the charges on the call so he could settle with Mrs. Randall and went back to his room.

He sat down on the edge of the bed and stared at the black statuette. His luck had been better than he had hoped—only two Mimis had come to Chicago. He was looking at one of them. And the other——Maybe the Ripper was looking at it now.

The luck of the Irish, Sweeney thought. He'd been working on the case a day and had a lead the cops would give their eye teeth for.

And besides that, he felt pretty good for the shape he was in. He was even getting mildly hungry; he'd be able to put away a meal today.

He got up and hung his bathrobe on the hook, stretched luxuriously.

He felt swell. He grinned at Mimi. He thought, we're a jump ahead of the cops, Baby, you and I; all we got to do is find your sister.

The little black statuette screamed soundlessly, and Sweeney's grin faded. Somewhere in Chicago another Mimi was screaming like that—and with better cause. A madman with a knife owned her. Someone with a twisted mind and a straight razor.

Someone who wouldn't *want* to be found by Sweeney.

He shook himself a little, mentally, to get rid of that thought, and turned to the mirror over the washbowl. He rubbed a hand over his face. Yes, he'd better shave; he'd be meeting Yolanda later in the afternoon, if Doc Greene was as good as his word. And he had a hunch the agent would be.

He held out his hand and looked at it; yes, it was steady enough that he could use his straight razor without cutting himself. He picked up the shaving mug from the shelf above the washbowl and ran hot water into it, working up a lather with the brush. He lathered his face carefully and then looked, and reached, for the razor. It wasn't there, where it should have been lying.

His hand stayed that way, a few inches above the shelf, frozen like Mimi's scream, until he made a conscious effort to pull it back.

He bent forward and looked, very carefully and disbelieving, at the mark in the thin layer of dust, the mark that was just the shape of the razor.

Carefully he wiped the lather off his face with a wetted towel, and dressed.

He went downstairs. Mrs. Randall's door was ajar and she said, "Come on in, Mr. Sweeney."

He stood in the doorway. "When did you dust in my room last, Mrs. Randall?"

"Why—yesterday morning."

"Do you remember if——" He was going to ask if she remembered seeing the razor and realized he didn't have to ask that. Whether she remembered or not, that fresh spot in the dust was proof that the razor had been there after the dusting. He changed his question. "Was anybody in my room yesterday evening, or yesterday after I left?"

"Why, no. Not that I know of, anyway. I wasn't here yesterday evening; I went to a movie. Is something missing?"

"Not anything valuable." Mr. Sweeney said. "I guess, I must have taken it while I was drunk, the last time I was here. Uh—you haven't been in my room at all since yesterday morning?"

"No, I haven't. Are you going out this afternoon? I'll want to make your bed, and if you're going to be around anyway, I might as well do it now."

"I'll be leaving in a few minutes. Thanks."

He went back up to his room and closed the door. He struck a match and examined the mark in the dust minutely. Yes, there was some dust in the bare patch that was the shape of the closed razor, and half as much as in the surrounding area. Then the razor had been there for a while after the dusting. It must have been taken late yesterday afternoon or yesterday evening.

He sat down in the Morris chair and tried to remember whether he'd seen the razor at all, either last night when he'd come home with Mimi or earlier in the day when he'd been in his room to change clothes. He couldn't remember seeing it. He hadn't looked for it, of course; he'd shaved at Goetz's room, with Goetz's electric razor.

Was anything else missing? He went over to the dresser and opened the top drawer in which he kept small miscellaneous items.

The contents looked intact until he remembered that there'd been a two-bladed penknife in the drawer.

It wasn't there now.

Nothing else was missing. There was a pair of gold cufflinks in the drawer, in plain sight, that was worth three or four times what a penknife was worth. And a stickpin with a zircon in it that a thief or burglar could not have been sure wasn't a diamond. But only a knife had been taken from the drawer. And only a razor from elsewhere in the room.

He looked at Mimi, and he knew how she felt.

CHAPTER SEVEN

THE shining razor hovered above Sweeney's throat. It descended under his chin and scraped gently upward, taking away lather and stubble, leaving a clean, smooth swath. It rose again.

"Take this Ripper business," said the barber. He wiped the razor on a piece of tissue and poised it again. "It's got the whole down town jittery. It got me pinched last night."

Sweeney grunted interrogatively.

"Carrying a razor. I keep my good hone—I got a Swatty—at home because somebody'd walk off with it around this joint. So every once in a while I take a razor home, never thought anything of it. Put it in the breast pocket of my suit coat and the top of it shows and damn if a harness bull didn't stop me right on the street and get tough. I was lucky to be able to show identification I was a barber or he'd have run me in. Pretty near did anyway. Said for all anybody knew, the Ripper's a barber, too. But he ain't."

The razor scraped. "How do you know?" Sweeney asked.

"Throats. A barber that went nuts would cut throats with it. All day long people lay stretched out in front of him with their throats bare and their chins thrown back and he just can't help thinking how easy it'd be and how—uh—you know what I mean."

Sweeney said, "You got something there. You don't feel like cutting one today, I hope."

"Nope, not today." The barber grinned. "But once in a while—well, your mind does screwy things."

"So does yours," Sweeney said.

The razor scraped.

"One of the three dames he killed," said the barber, "used to work a block from here. Tavern down on the next corner."

"I know," Sweeney said. "I'm on my way there. Did you know the girl?"

"I seen her in there, enough to place her when I saw her picture in the paper. But I don't go in B-joints very often, not with the money I make. You get taken before you know it for five or ten bucks in percentage drinks, and what have you got? Not that I won't put out five or ten bucks if I get something for my money besides a little conversation. Me, I get enough conversation all day long. The whacks that sit in that chair!"

He put a steaming towel over Sweeney's face and patted it down. He said, "Anyway, I figure the Ripper uses a knife instead of a razor. You *could* use a razor like that, sure, but I figure it's be too awkward to hold for a long hard slash across the guts like he uses. You'd have to tape the handle to get a good grip on it, and then it'd be awkward to carry, taped open. And it'd be a dead giveaway if anybody saw it. I figure he'd use a pocketknife, one small enough he could carry it legally. A pre-war imported one with real steel in it, so he could have one of the blades honed down to a razor edge. Haircut?"

"No," said Sweeney.

"What do you figure he uses? A knife or a razor?"

"Yes," said Sweeney, getting up out of the chair, "What do I owe you?"

He paid, and went out into the hot August sunlight. He walked a block west to the address that had been given in the newspaper.

The place had a flashy front. Neon tubes, writhing red in the sun's glare, proclaimed that this was Susie's Cue. Hexagonal windows were curtained off to block the view within, but held chaste photographs of unchaste morsels of feminity. You could see in, if you tried, through a diamond-shaped glass in the door.

But Sweeney didn't try; he pushed the door open and went in.

It was cool and dim inside. It was empty of customers. A bartender lounged behind the bar and two girls, one in a bright red dress and the other in white with gold sequins, sat on stools together at the far end of the bar. There were no drinks in front of them. All three looked toward Sweeney as he entered.

He picked a stool in about the middle of the row and put a five-dollar bill on the mahogany. The bartender came over and one of the girls—the one in red—was getting off her stool. The bartender beat her there and Sweeney had time to ask for a rye and seltzer before the girl, now on the stool beside him, said "Hello."

"Hello," Sweeney said. "Lonesome?"

"That's my line; I'm supposed to ask that. You'll buy me a drink, won't you?"

Sweeney nodded. The bartender was already pouring it. He moved away to give them privacy. The girl in the red dress smiled brightly at Sweeney. She said, "I'm awfully glad you came in. It's been dead as a doornail in this joint ever since I got here an hour ago. Anyway you don't look like a jerk like most of the guys come in here. How'd you like to sit over in one of the booths? My name's Tess, so now we're introduced. Let's move over to one of the booths, huh, and Joe'll bring us—"

"Did you know Stella Gaylord?"

Stopped in mid-sentence, she stared at him. She asked, "You aren't another shamus, are you? This place was lousy with 'em, right after what happened to Stella."

"You did know her, then," said Sweeney. "Good. No, I'm not a shamus. I'm a newspaperman."

"Oh. One of those. May I have another drink, please?"

Sweeney nodded, and the bartender, who hadn't gone far, came up to pour it.

"Tell me about Stella."

"Tell you what?"

"Everything you know. Pretend I never heard of her. For all practical purposes, I haven't. I didn't work on the case. I was on vacation when it happened."

"Oh. But you're working on it now?"

Sweeney sighed. He'd have to satisfy her curiosity before he could satisfy his own. He said, "Not for the paper. I'm going to write it up for a fact detective magazine. Not just Stella Gaylord, but the whole Ripper business. As soon as the case is cracked, that is. The true detective mags don't buy unsolved cases. But I'll have to be ready to write it up quick, once the thing breaks."

"Oh. They pay pretty well for something like that, don't they? What's in it for me?"

"A drink," said Sweeney, motioning to the bartender. "Listen, sister. I'll be talking to about fifty people who knew Stella Gaylord and Dorothy Lee and Lola Brent, and to coppers who worked on it, and to other reporters. Wouldn't I be in a beautiful spot if I gave everybody a slice of it? Even if the case does break and I do sell the story, I'd come out behind, see?"

She grinned. "It never hurts to try."

"That it doesn't. And, incidentally, I *will* split with you if you can crack the case so I can sell it. You don't happen to know who killed her, do you?"

Her face hardened, "Mister, if I knew that, the cops would know it. Stella was a good kid."

"Tell me about her. Anything. How old she was, where she came from, what she wanted, what she looked like—anything."

"I don't know how old she was. Somewhere around thirty, I guess. She came from Des Moines, about five years ago, I think she told me once. I knew her only about a month."

"Was that when you started here, or when she did?"

"When I did. She'd been here a couple of months already. I was over on Halstead before that. It was a worse joint than this, for looks, but I made better dough. There was always trouble there, though, and God, how I hate trouble. *I* get along with people if they get along with me. I never start—"

"About Stella," said Sweeney. "What did she look like? I saw the newspaper picture, but it wasn't very good."

"I know. I saw it. Stella was kind of pretty. She had a beautiful figure, anyway; she tried to get into modelling once, but you got to have contacts. She was about thirty; her hair was kind of a darkish blonde. She ought to've hennaed it, but she wouldn't. Blue eyes. About five-five or so."

"What *was* she, inside?" Sweeney asked. "What was she trying to do?"

The red dress shrugged. "What are any of us trying to do? Get along, I guess. How'd I know what she was like inside? How'd anybody know? That's a funny question for you to ask. How's about another drink?"

"Okay," said Sweeney. "Were you working here with her the night she was killed?"

"Yeah. I told the cops what I knew about that."

"Tell me, too."

"She made an after-date. After two, that is; we closed at two. It was with a guy that was in around ten or eleven o'clock and talked to her for half an hour or so. I never saw him before, and he hasn't been in since."

"Did he pick her up at two?"

"She was going to meet him somewhere. His hotel, I guess." She turned and looked at Sweeney. "We don't do that with anybody. But sometimes, if we like a guy—well, why not?"

"Why not?" Sweeney said. "And you girls don't make much at this percentage racket, do you?"

"Not enough to dress the way we got to dress. And everything. This ain't a nice racket, but there are worse ones. At least we can pick which men we want to go out with, and we get ten or twenty propositions a day." She grinned at him impudently. "Not often this early, though. Yours will be the first today, when you get around to it."

"If I get around to it," Sweeney said. "What do you remember about the guy she was going to meet?"

"Practically nothing because I didn't notice him. After he went out, Stella came back to me—I was sitting alone just there for a few minutes—and mentioned she was meeting him after two and what did I think of the guy. Well, I'd just glanced at him sitting there with her before and all I remembered was that he was pretty ordinary looking. I think he had on a grey suit. He wasn't specially old or young, or tall or short or fat or anything or I'd probably have remembered. I don't think I'd know him again if I saw him."

"He didn't have a round face and wear thick glasses, did he?"

"Not that I remember. I wouldn't swear he didn't. And I'll save you one thing: nobody else around here noticed him or has any better idea. That's one thing the coppers dogged everybody about. No use asking George, behind the bar, or Emmy—that's the girl in the white dress. They were both here that night, but they didn't remember as much about it as I did."

"Did Stella have any enemies?"

"No. she was a nice kid. Even us girls who worked with her liked her, and mister, that's something. And to beat your next question, no, she didn't have any serious men friends and she didn't live with anybody. I don't mean she never packed an overnight bag, but I mean *living* with anybody, serious."

"She have a family, back in Des Moines?"

"Her parents were dead, she said once. If she had any other relatives anywhere she never talked about them. I don't guess she had any she was close to."

"The address on West Madison where she lived. That would be about three blocks from here, wouldn't it? What is it, a hotel or rooming house?"

"A hotel, the Claremore. It's a dive. Can I have another drink?"

Sweeney crooked a finger at the bartender. He said, "Mine, too, this time."

He shoved his Panama back on his head. "Look, Tess, you've told me what she looked like, what she did. But what was she? What made her tick? What did she *want*?"

The girl in the red dress picked up her glass and stared into it. She looked at Sweeney, then, squarely for the first time. She said, "You're a funny kind of guy. I think I could like you."

"That's swell," said Sweeney.

"I even like the way you said that. Sarcastic as hell, but—I don't know what I mean. You meet all kinds of guys in a business like this, and——" She laughed a little and emptied her glass. She said, "I suppose if *I* got myself killed by a ripper, you'd be interested in finding out what made *me* tick, what *I* really wanted. You'd—Oh, hell."

"You're a big girl now," Sweeney said, "Don't let it get you down. I *do* like you."

"Sure. Sure. *I* know what I am. So let's skip it. I'll tell you what Stella wanted. A beauty shop. In a little town somewhere, a long way from Chicago. Go ahead and laugh. But that's what she was saving up her money for. That's what she wanted. She saved her money, working as a waitress, and then got sick and it went. She didn't like this racket any more than the rest of us, but she'd been at it a year and in another year she'd've had enough saved up to make a break for herself."

"She had money saved up then. Who gets it?"

The girl shrugged. "Nobody, I guess, unless some relative shows up. Say, I just remembered something. Stella had a girl friend who's a waitress near where she was killed. An all night restaurant on State just north of Chicago Avenue. And she nearly always had something to eat after she got off at two. I told the cops maybe she went from here to that restaurant for a sandwich before she kept her date with the mooch. Or maybe she met him at the restaurant instead of at his hotel room or whatever."

"You don't know the waitress's name, do you?"

Tess shook her head. "But I know the restaurant. It's the third or fourth door north of Chicago Avenue, on the west side of State."

Sweeney said, "Thanks. Tess, I'd better push along." He glanced at the money on the bar, three singles and some change left out of the ten he'd put there. "Put it under the mattress. Be seeing you."

She put a hand on his arm. "Wait. Do you mean it? Will you come back?"

"Maybe."

Tess sighed, and dropped her hand. "All right, then, you won't. I know. The nice guys never do."

When Sweeney stepped out to the sidewalk, the impact of the heat was almost like a blow. He hesitated a moment and then walked west.

The Claremore Hotel, from the street, was just a sign and an uninviting stairway. Sweeney trudged up the steps to a tiny lobby on the second floor.

A swarthy, stocky man who hadn't shaved for at least two days was sorting mail behind a short counter. He glanced at Sweeney and said. "Filled up." He looked down at the mail again.

Sweeney leaned against the counter and waited.

Finally the stocky man looked up again.

"Stella Gaylord lived here," Sweeney said.

"Jesus God, another cop or a reporter. Yeah, she lived here. So what?"

"So nothing," said Sweeney.

He turned and looked down the dim corridor of doors with peeling paint, at the uncarpeted stairs leading to the floor above. He sniffed the musty air. Stella Gaylord, he thought, must have wanted that beauty shop pretty bad to have lived in a hole like this.

He looked back at the stocky man to ask a question and then decided, to hell with it.

He turned and walked down the stairs to the street.

The clock in the window of a cheap jewellery store next door told him he still had over an hour before his appointment with Greene and Yolanda Lang at El Madhouse.

It also reminded him that he still didn't have a watch, and he went in and bought one.

Putting change back in his wallet, he asked the jeweller, "Did you know Stella Gaylord?"

"Who?"

"Such is fame," Sweeney said. "Skip it."

Outside, he flagged a cab and rode to State and Chicago. The waitress who had been Stella's friend wouldn't be on duty now, but maybe he could get her address, and maybe he could learn something anyway.

The restaurant was called the Dinner Gong. Two waitresses were working behind the counter and a man in shirt sleeves, who looked as though he might be the proprietor, was behind the cash register on the cigar counter.

Sweeney bought cigarettes. He said, "I'm from the *Blade*. You have a waitress here who was a friend of Stella Gaylord. Is she still on the night shift?"

"You mean Thelma Smith. She quit over a week ago. Scared stiff to work in this neighbourhood, after what happened to the Gaylord girl."

"You have her address? Thelma's. I mean?"

"No. She was going out of town; that's all I know. She'd been talking about going to New York, so maybe that's where."

Sweeney said, "Stella was in here that night, wasn't she?"

"Sure. I wasn't on then, but I was here while the police were talking to Thelma. She said Stella came here a little after two o'clock and had a sandwich and coffee and then left."

"She didn't say anything to Thelma about where she was going?"

The proprietor shook his head. "But it was probably somewhere near here, or she wouldn't have come way up here from Madison for a sandwich. She was a chippie; the cops figure it she had a hotel-room date somewhere around here after she got through at the bar she worked at."

Sweeney thanked him and went out. He was pretty sure it wouldn't pay to try to trace Thelma Smith; the police had already talked to her. And if there'd been anything suspicious about her leaving town, they'd be doing the tracing.

While he was waiting for a chance to get across the traffic on Chicago Avenue, he remembered something he'd forgotten to ask Tess. When he got across the street he phoned Susie's Cue from the corner drugstore and asked for her.

"This is the guy you were talking to half an hour ago, Tess," he told her. "Just remembered something. Did Stella ever say anything about a statuette—a little black statuette of a woman, about ten inches high?"

"No. Where are you?"

"I'm lost in a fog," Sweeney said. "Were you ever up to Stella's room?"

"Yes, once just a few days before she—before she died."

"She didn't have a statuette like that?"

"No. She had a little white statuette on her dresser, though. A Madonna. She'd had it a long time, I remember her saying. Why? What gives about a statuette?"

"Probably nothing. Tess, does 'Screaming Mimi' mean anything to you?"

"I've had 'em. What is this, a gag?"

"No, but I can't tell you about it. Thanks, anyway. I'll be seeing you sometime."

"I'll bet."

When he left the drugstore he walked west to Clark Street and south to El Madhouse.

CHAPTER EIGHT

SHE looked just like the picture of her that had been in Sweeney's mind, except, of course, that she wore clothes. Sweeney smiled at her and she smiled back and Doc Greene said, "You'll remember her, Sweeney. You've been staring ever since you sat down."

Yolanda said, "Pay no attention to him, Mr. Sweeney. His bark is worse than his bite."

Greene chuckled. "Don't give Sweeney an opening like that, my sweet. He already suspects that I have canine ancestry." He stared at Sweeney through the thick glasses. He spoke softly: "I *do* bite."

"At least," said Sweeney to Yolanda, "he nips at my heels. I don't like him."

"Doc's all right, Mr. Sweeney. He grows on you."

"He'd better not to try to grow on *me*. Doc, do you shave with a straight-edge razor?"

"As it happens, yes."

"Your own, or do you borrow other people's?"

Behind the heavy lenses, Doc Greene's eyes narrowed slightly. "Someone has borrowed yours?"

Sweeney nodded. "Again your perspicacity mystifies me. Yes, someone has borrowed mine. And a small knife as well. The only two keen-edged tools in the place."

"Not counting your brain, Sweeney. He left you that. Or was it there at the time of the theft?"

"I doubt it seriously. It must have been in the evening while I was out rather than while I was sleeping. I deduce that from the fact that, when I looked in the mirror this morning, there was no fine red line across my throat."

Greene shook his head slowly. "You looked in the wrong place, Sweeney. Our friend the Ripper has a strong predilection for abdomens. Did you look there?"

"Not specifically, Doc. But I think I would have noticed when I took a shower."

Yolanda Lang shuddered a little and pushed her chair back, "I'm afraid I must run along, Mr. Sweeney. I've got to talk to the maestro about a new number. You'll come to see me dance tonight? The first number is at ten."

She held out her hand and smiled at him. Sweeney took the hand and returned the smile. He said, "Wild horses and so forth, Yo. Or may I call you Yolanda?"

She laughed. "I think I prefer it. You say it as though you meant it."

She walked toward the archway leading from the tavern to the night club at the rear. The dog, which had been lying beside her chair, followed her. So did the two detectives who had been sitting at the next table.

"Makes quite a parade." Doc Greene said.

Sweeney sat down again and made circles on the table with the bottom of his glass. After a minute he looked up. He said, "Hello, Doc. I didn't know you were here."

"Getting anywhere, Sweeney? Got a lead?"

"No."

Greene sighed deeply. "My bosom enemy, I'm afraid you don't trust me."

"Should I?"

"To an extent. And to what extent? To the extent that I tell you you can. That means as far as finding the Ripper is concerned." He leaned forward, elbows on the table. "As concerns Yolanda, no. As concerns yourself, no. As concerns Money, no—although that shall have no reason to rise between us. But as concerns the Ripper, yes. I shall worry about Yolanda until he is caught. I would even prefer that he is killed rather than caught, because he presumed to touch her."

"With a cold blade," said Sweeney. "Not with a hot hand."

"With anything. But that is past. It's the future that worries me. Right now there are two detectives guarding Yo all the time, three eight-hour shifts of them. But the police won't do that for ever. Find me the Ripper, Sweeney."

"And after that?"

"After that, the hell with you."

"Thank you, Doc. The only trouble is that you're so completely honest that I distrust you."

Greene sighed again, "Sweeney," he said. "I don't want you to waste time suspecting me. The police got that little idea yesterday because I couldn't account for where I was when the Ripper attacked Yolanda. I don't know where I was either, except that it was on the South Side. I was with a client—a singer at the Club Cairo—until midnight and I got pretty stinking. I got home, but I can't prove when, and I don't even know when.'"

"That happens," Sweeney said. "But why should I believe it?"

"For the same reason the police did, you should. Because it happens I have solid alibis on two of the other three attacks. I checked back, and the police checked back on what I told them.

"Not on the Lola Brent one, two months ago; that's too far back and I couldn't figure out where I was. But they told me the second one—What was her name?"

"Stella Gaylord."

"—was the night of July 27th, and I was in New York on business. I was there from the 25th through the 30th, and on the night of the 27th I was—luckily—with some damned respectable people from dinner time until three in the morning. Don't waste time or distract me by asking what I was doing with respectable people. That's irrelevant. The police have checked it. Ask Captain Bline.

"And on the first of August, last week, at the moment this secretary, Dorothy Lee, was killed, I was here in Chicago, but it just happens I was in court testifying on a breach of contract suit against a theatre manager. Judge Goerring and the bailiff and the court clerk and three lawyers—one of them mine and two of them the theatre's—are all the alibi I've got on that one.

"Now if you want to believe I'm half a ripper, working the first and fourth cases with a stand-in filling in for the second and third, you're welcome. But you aren't that much of a damn fool."

"You've got something there." Sweeney admitted. He took a folded piece of blank copy paper and a pencil from his pockets. "I'll even settle for *one* alibi, if it's the real McCoy. Judge Goerring's court, you say? When to when?"

"Case was called at three o'clock and ran till a little after four. Before it was called, I was in conference with all three lawyers for a good half-hour in an anteroom of the court. According to the newspapers, the Lee girl left her office alive at a quarter of three to go home. She was found dead in her apartment at five and they thought she'd been dead an hour. Hell, Sweeney. I couldn't have *planned* a better alibi. She was killed right while I was on the witness stand, two miles away. Will you buy it?"

"I'll buy it," Sweeney said. "What were the lawyers' names?"

"You're a hard man, Sweeney. Why suspect me, anyway, any more than Joe Blow up there at the bar, or the guy next to him?"

"Because my room was entered last night. Only a razor and a knife were taken, and razors and knives tie up with the Ripper. Up to last night damn few people knew I had any interest in the Ripper. You're one of them."

Greene laughed. "And how did I find out? By reading that eyewitness story you wrote for the *Blade*. What's the circulation of the *Blade*? Half a million?"

Sweeney said, "Excuse me for living. I'll buy you a drink on that, Doc."

"Bourbon straight. Now, have you got a lead to the Ripper yet?"

Sweeney signalled the waiter and ordered, then answered. "Not a lead," he said. "What were the names of the lawyers, Doc?" He poised the pencil over the copy paper.

"I thought you were mostly Airedale, Sweeney, but you're half bulldog. My lawyer's Hymie Fieman, in the Central Building. The opposition was Raenough. Dane and Howell. Dane—Carl Dane, I think it is—and a young neophyte named Brady, who works for them but isn't a member of the firm yet, were the two who were in conference and present at the hearing. And the judge was Goerring. G-o-e-r-r-i-n-g. He's a Republican, so he wouldn't alibi a Ripper."

Sweeney nodded moodily. He said, "Wish I could snap out of this hangover and think straight. I'm as nervous as a cat."

He unfolded the sheet of copy paper and smoothed it flat. Then he held out his right hand, back up and fingers spread wide, and put the piece of paper on it. The slight trembling, magnified, vibrated the edges of the paper.

"Not as bad as I thought," he said. "Bet you can't do any better." He looked at Greene. "In fact, five bucks you can't."

Greene said, "I should never bet a man at his own game, and I've never tried that, but you're on. You're a wreck, and I've got nerves like a rock."

Greene picked up the paper and balanced it flat on the back of his hand. The edges vibrated slightly, but noticeably less than they had on Sweeney's hand.

Sweeney watched the paper very closely. He asked, "Doc, did you ever hear of the Screaming Mimi?"

The rate of vibration of the edges of the paper didn't change at all. Watching them, Greene said, "Guess I win, Sweeney. Concede the bet?"

There'd been no reaction, but Sweeney cussed himself silently. The man who'd bought that statuette wouldn't have known the company's nickname for it; Lola Brent, as a new employee, wouldn't have known it to tell him.

Sweeney said, "A small black statuette of a woman screaming."

Doc Greene looked up from the paper, but the vibration of the edges—Sweeney's eyes stayed on the paper—didn't change.

Greene lowered his hand to the table. He said, "What is this? A gag?"

"It was, Doc. But you win the bet." Sweeney handed over the fin. "It's worth it. You answered my questions so I can believe you—for sure."

"You mean the Screaming Mimi and the black statuette? No, I never heard of either, Sweeney. A statuette of a woman screaming? One and the same thing? The statuette is called Screaming Mimi? M-i-m-i?"

"Right. And you never heard of either. I don't necessarily believe your saying so, Doc, but I do believe the edges of that piece of paper."

"Clever, Sweeney. A homemade lie detec——No, not that; a

reaction indicator. I'll keep your five, but I'll buy you a drink out of it. Same?"

Sweeney nodded. Doc signalled.

Doc put his elbows on the table. He said, "Then you were lying. You have got a lead. Tell Papa. Papa might help."

"Baby doesn't want help, from Papa. Papa is too anxious to get Baby cut up with a sharp shiv."

"You underrate me, Sweeney. I think I can get it without your help. And I'm curious, now. I will if I have to."

"Prove it."

"All right." Doc Greene's eyes looked enormous, hypnotic, through the lenses of his glasses. "A small black statuette called the Screaming Mimi. Most statuettes are sold in art and gift shops. One of the girls attacked worked, for one day—the day of her murder—in an art and gift shop. I forget where, but the newspapers would tell me. If I looked up the proprietor and ask him if he ever heard of Screaming Mimi, would it get me anywhere?"

Sweeney lifted his glass. "I did underrate you, Doc."

"And I you, Sweeney, when I almost believed you that you didn't have a lead. To your bad health."

"And yours."

They drank and then Greene asked. "So do I go to the proprietor of the art store and start from there, or do you break down and tell me?"

"I might as well. Lola Brent sold a small black statuette of a screaming, terrified nude just before she was killed. There's pretty good reason to believe the Ripper was her customer, followed her home and killed her. Likely the figure set him off; it's something that would appeal only to a psycho."

"Do you like it?"

"I dislike it, but I find it fascinating. It's rather well done, incidentally. And I followed up on it. Only two were sent to Chicago. I've got one. The Ripper's got the other."

"Do the police know that?"

"No. I'm pretty sure they don't."

"I told you, Sweeney. The luck of the Irish. By the way, are you crowding your luck too far, or are you going heeled?"

"Heeled?"

"Packing a rod, toting a gun. In a word, armed. If the Ripper—or anyone else—had called on me and removed my small armament of knife and razor, I'd bring up the artillery. If the Ripper knew where *my* room was, I'd sleep with a sawed-off shotgun across my chest. Or *does he know, Sweeney*?"

"You mean?"

"Yes."

Sweeney grinned. "You want my alibis? Well, I don't know

anything about two months ago. I doubt if I could check back. As for the next two murders, well, I was on a two-week drunk. Only God knows where I was and what I was doing, and I wasn't with God all the time. As for night before last, when Yolanda was attacked. I was at the scene of the crime at approximately the time of the crime. How's that for a set of alibis?"

Doc Greene grunted. He said, "I've heard better. I can't remember when I've heard worse, Sweeney, as a practical psychiatrist. I don't think you're the Ripper type, but I've been wrong. *Are* you?"

Sweeney stood up. He said, "I'm damned if I'll tell you, Doc. In the little duel of pleasantries between us, it's the one big edge I've got on you. I'm going to let you wonder. And if I am, thanks for warning me about the sawed-off shotgun."

He went outside and it was dusk. His headache was gone and he felt almost human again.

He walked south on Clark Street without thinking about where he was going. He let his mind alone and his mind let him alone, and they got along fine together. He heard himself humming and listening to himself long enough to find out what it was; it turned out to be the melody of a Brahms Hungarian dance, so he quit listening.

If only he could prove that Greene was the Ripper—

But there were two alibis. The police had accepted them. Anyway, Greene had *said* the police had become interested in him and then had accepted the alibis. But that was something he could check. That was something he *would* check.

Furthermore, he could at least start to check on it right now.

He was crossing Lake Street into the Loop and he kept on going to Randolph and turned west to the tavern, between Clark and LaSalle, where a lot of the boys from the *Blade* hung out.

None of them seemed to be hanging out there at the moment, so he ordered a shot and mixed it with soda so he could work on it a while to see if any of them were coming in.

He asked Burt Meaghan, who ran the place and who was alone behind the bar at the moment, "Think any of the boys will come around for pinochle after work this evening?"

"Be an unusual evening if they don't. Where you been keeping yourself, Sweeney?"

"Around and about. I've been on a bender, if you don't know. Doesn't anybody tell you these things, Burt?"

"Yeah. I'd heard. In fact, you were in here a few times the first week of it. Haven't seen you for over a week, though."

"You didn't miss much. Burt, do you know Harry Yahn?"

"Know of him. Not personally I don't know him. I don't move

in such high circles. He's got a place a couple blocks west of here that he runs himself. And an interest in a few others."

"I've been out of touch," Sweeney said. "What's the name of the place he runs himself?"

"Name on front of the tavern is the Tit-Tat-Toe; that's just the front, of course. Want an in?"

"Wouldn't need it. I know Harry from way back when. I just lost track of where he was operating."

"He ain't been there long. Month or so. 'Scuse me, Sweeney."

He went down to the other end of the bar to wait on another customer. Sweeney drew wet rings on the bar with the bottom of his glass and wondered if he'd have to see Harry Yahn. He hoped not, because monkeying with Harry Yahn was as healthy as trimming your fingernails on a buzz-saw. But he was going to need money from somewhere before this thing was over. He still had about a hundred and fifty dollars left out of the three cheques Wally had given him, but that wasn't going to go very far on all he had in mind.

There was a hand on his shoulder and he turned. It was Wayne Horlick. Sweeney said, "The very guy I wanted to see most. Talk about the luck of the Irish."

Horlick grinned at him. "Costs you ten bucks to be that lucky, Sweeney. I'm glad to see you too. Ten bucks' worth."

Sweeney sighed. "From when?"

"Ten days ago. In here. Don't you remember?"

"Sure," Sweeney lied. He paid up. "And a drink for interest?"

"Why not? Rye."

Sweeney downed the last sip of the drink he'd been working on and ordered two. He said, "Why I wanted to see you, if you're curious, is that you've been working on the Ripper case."

"Yeah. The recent parts of it, anyway. I don't know who did the Lola Brent part, couple of months ago. But I got put on the second one, the Stella Gaylord murder, and been at it ever since."

"Any leads?"

"Nary a lead, Sweeney. And if I did get one I'd turn it over to the cop quick-like and cheerful-like. The Ripper's one boy I wouldn't care to meet. Except through bars after Bline gets him. Did you know they've got a special Ripper detail working on nothing else, with Cap Bline in charge?"

"Carey told me. Think they'll get him?"

"Sure they'll get him—if he keeps on slicing dames. But not on any clues he's left with the ones he's already cut. Say, have you talked to this Yolanda Lang dame?"

"Yes, just an hour or so ago. Why?"

Horlick laughed. "Figured you'd try—after I read that eyewitness account of yours. Nice writing there, pal. Made everybody's mouth water. Mine included. Been trying for an interview with the dame ever since, but can't get it. I figured you would."

"Why?" Sweeney asked curiously. "I don't mean why would I try, but why did you figure I'd get one if you couldn't?"

"That *story* you wrote. Far be it from me to praise anybody else's writing, Sweeney, but that was a minor classic of journalism. And what's more to the point, it's ten thousand dollars' worth of free publicity for the dame—above and beyond the publicity from getting picked on by the Ripper, and being the first one to survive a Ripper attack. Doc Greene must love you like a brother."

Sweeney laughed. "Sure. Like Cain loved Abel. Say, Horlick, anything come out about any of the cases that didn't get in the papers? I've read up on—uh—Lola Brent and Stella Gaylord; haven't got around to the third dame yet. Dorothy Lee."

Horlick thought and then shook his head. "Nothing I can think of, nothing worth mentioning. Why? You really interested? Beyond getting that interview with the strip-teaser? You don't need to explain that."

Sweeney decided to stick to the lie he'd told Joe Carey. "Had in mind to write it up for a fact detective mag. Way to do that is have all the dope ready so the minute the case is cracked, I can beat the others to the punch."

"Good idea, if they ever crack the case. And they will, of course, if the guy keeps on ripping. He can't be lucky for ever. I hope Wally puts you on it instead of me, I don't like the job. Want me to put in a word for you?"

"Carey's going to, so you'd better not. Wally might get suspicious if we laid it on too thick. What do you know about Doc Greene?"

"Why? Going to try to pin it on him?"

"I'd love to. I love him like a brother, too. He tells me the cops got the same idea and that he has alibied on two of the jobs and they took his alibis. Know anything about it?"

Horlick shook his head. "That would have been since the Ripper tried for Yolanda, of course; in the last couple of days. No, Bline didn't tell me about investigating Greene. But then I guess they have investigated just about everyone who's ever been closely connected with any of the four dames."

"What's your impression of Greene, Horlick?"

"He gives me the creeps. Is that what you mean?"

"That," said Sweeney, "is *exactly* what I mean. For that, I'll buy you another drink. Rye?"

"Rye."

"Hey, Burt, a rye for Horlick. I'll pass this one."

And he really did pass it, and wouldn't let Horlick buy back. Half an hour later, he left and went home.

Mrs. Randall heard him come in and opened her door.

"Mr. Sweeney, there's a man to see you. He wanted to wait so I let him wait in my sitting room. Shall I tell him——"

A big man stepped around from behind her. He said, "William Sweeney? My name is Bline, Captain Bline."

CHAPTER NINE

SWEENEY stuck out a paw and the detective took it, but not enthusiastically. But Sweeney pretended not to notice. He said, "I've been wanting to meet you, Cap, since I heard you were on the case. Something I want to ask you. Come on up to my room."

Bline followed him up the stairs and into the room. He sat down in the chair Sweeney pointed out to him, the overstuffed one with the creaky springs; it groaned under his weight.

Sweeney sat on the edge of the bed. He glanced at the phonograph and said, "Want some music while we talk, Cap?"

"Hell, no. We're gonna talk, not sing duets. And it's me that's going to ask the questions, Sweeney."

"What about?"

"You're asking 'em already. Look. I don't suppose you remember where you were on the afternoon of June 8th, do you?"

"No, I don't. Unless I was working that afternoon. Even then, I wouldn't know offhand if I was in the office doing rewrite, or if I was out on a job. Unless—maybe if I checked the late edititons for that day and the early ones for the next, I could spot and remember which stories I worked on."

"You didn't work on any. You didn't work that day; you were off. I checked at the *Blade*."

"Then all I can tell you is what I probably did, which wouldn't mean much. I probably slept till about noon, spent most of the afternoon here reading or listening to music, probably went out in the evening to play some cards and have a few drinks. Or maybe a show or a concert. That part I might possibly be able to check on, but not the afternoon, and I judge that's what you're interested in."

"Right. And how about July 27th?"

"As hopeless as the next one you're going to ask about, Cap. August 1st, I mean. God knows where I was either time, except that I'm pretty sure it was in Chicago. Haven't been out of town in the last two weeks that I know of."

Bline grunted.

Sweeney grinned. He said, "Only I'm not the Ripper. Granted that I don't even know where I was or what I was doing when Stella Gaylord and Dorothy Lee were killed. I know I didn't kill Lola Brent—because I wasn't that drunk. I mean drunk enough not to remember something I did, any time in June. And I know

I didn't make the pass at Yolanda Lang because I do remember Wednesday night; I was beginning to come out of it then, and feeling like hell. Ask God."

"Huh?"

Sweeney opened his mouth and then closed it again. No use getting poor old Godfrey grilled at headquarters, and Godfrey couldn't alibi him anyway, not for the exact time the attack had been made on Yolanda. He said, "A manner of speaking, Cap. Only God could prove what I was doing Wednesday night. But cheer up, if the Ripper keeps on ripping, maybe I'll have an alibi for the next one."

"That will be a big help."

"Meanwhile, Cap, and seriously, what made you come here to ask me about alibis? Did a little bird tell you? A Greene one?"

"Sweeney, you know damn well why I'm here. Because you were there in front of that door on States Street Wednesday night. The Ripper was probably in front of that door. Way we figure it, he was standing at the back door of that hallway and reached in and slashed as the dame came toward him. Only he was a couple of inches short, and just nicked her, and the dog ran around her and jumped and he had to duck back and slam the door without having a chance for a second try. And then what would he do?"

"You asked it," Sweeney said. "You answer it."

"He might have got the hell out of there, of course. But if he followed the pattern of most psycho killers, he came out of the alley and walked around to the front and was in that knot of people looking through the door when the squad car came."

"Also maybe," Sweeney said, "having put in the call for the police from the tavern on the corner."

Bline shook his head. He said, "No, we found out who put in that call. Guy that had been standing at the bar there with two other guys, talking, for hours. He left there a little before two-thirty and he was back in a few minutes. Told the guys he'd been talking to and the bartender that there was something going on in a hallway down the street. That a dame was on the floor and a big dog wouldn't let anybody open the door and go in to see what was wrong with the dame, so maybe he better phone the cops. So he did, and then he and the other two guys—all three of them this time—went together to the place and were there when the squad car came. I've talked to all three of them—the bartender knew one and I found the others through him. They say there were about a dozen people in front of the doorway. That what you'd say?"

"Pretty close. Not over fifteen at the most."

"And the squad car coppers—even after they saw it was a Ripper job—didn't have sense enough to hold every one of them. We've located five out of the twelve or fifteen. If only we had *all* of 'em—"

"Who is the fifth?" Sweeney asked. "The three who were together and I made four; who else?"

"Guy who lived in the building. Guess he was the first one to see the woman and the dog. Came home and couldn't get in because the dog started to jump him every time he started to open the door. Other passers-by saw something was happening and stopped to look in too. When the guy from the tavern—the one who made the phone call—got there, there were six or eight people. When he got back with his two friends, there were nine or ten besides them."

"I was probably the next arrival," Sweeney said. "I got there just a minute before the squad car came. And to answer your next question, no, I didn't notice anybody else in the crowd. Couldn't identify any one of them. All I noticed was what was going on inside and what the squad car coppers did. Probably couldn't identify even them."

Bline said dryly, "We don't need them identified. I'd give a lot, though, to have every one of that crowd in front. Instead of five—and four of those five cleared."

"Not counting me?"

"Not counting you."

"What clears the man who lived in the building? The one who, according to his own story, was the first one there?"

"He's reasonably clear. Works a night shift on the *Journal of Commerce* on Grand Avenue; he's a printer. Didn't punch out on the time clock till one forty-five and it'd have taken him that long to get there, he wouldn't have had time to go in the alleyway, wait a while, and then go around to the front. Besides, he has solid alibis for all three other rippings; we checked them."

He frowned at Sweeney. "So of the five men we have located who were in that crowd in front of the door, you're the only one without an alibi for anything at all. By the way, here's your cutlery; the lab couldn't get anything on it."

He took an envelope from his pocket and handed it to Sweeney. Without opening it. Sweeney could feel that it contained his penknife and straight razor.

He said, "You might have asked me for them. Did you have a search warrant?"

Bline chuckled. "We didn't want you in our hair while we were casing the joint. As for a warrant, does it matter now?"

Sweeney opened his mouth and then closed it again. He was mad enough to start something; those things being gone had given him some bad moments. On the other hand, it was going to be helpful if not necessary to have Bline friendly to him; there were things the police could do that he couldn't.

So he said, mildly, "You might have left a note. When I missed those, I thought maybe the Ripper thought I was the Ripper. Say, Cap, what do you know about this guy Greene, Doc Greene?"

"Why?"

"I kind of like to think of him as the Ripper, that's all. He tells me he's got alibis and that you've checked them. That right?"

"More or less. No alibi for Lola Brent, and the one for Dorothy Lee isn't perfect."

"Not perfect? I thought that was the one where he was testifying in court under Judge Goerring."

"The times don't fit perfectly. His alibi takes him up to about ten minutes after four. Dorothy Lee wasn't found dead until about five o'clock—maybe a few minutes after. The coroner said she'd been dead at least an hour when he saw her at five-thirty, twenty minutes after Greene's alibi ends. He could have made it, in a taxi, from the court to her place in that time."

"Then it's no alibi at all."

Bline said, "Not an iron-clad one, no. But there are angles. She left work at two forty-five to go home because she was sick; ordinarily she worked till five. Even if Greene knew her—and there's no proof he did—he wouldn't have known he'd find her home if he rushed there right from court. Only someone who worked with her would have known that."

"Or anyone who dropped in her office or phoned for her."

"True, but Greene didn't drop in. He would barely have had time to phone, and still get to her place by four-thirty." Bline frowned. "You're stretching probabilities."

"Am I? Suppose Greene knew her—well. He could have had a date to pick her up at her apartment after five. But he gets through in court a little after four and goes there to wait for her. Maybe he even has a key, and lets himself in to wait, not knowing she came home sick and is already there."

"Oh, it's *possible*, Sweeney. I told you it wasn't a perfect alibi. But you've got to admit it isn't likely. The Ripper probably followed her home, seeing her on the street for the first time after she left work. Like he probably followed Lola Brent home from the gift shop. He couldn't have been waiting for Lola Brent at her place for two reasons—first, he couldn't have known she was going to be fired and come home early; second, she was living with a man, Sammy Cole; he couldn't have known Sammy wouldn't walk in on him."

"And anyway," Sweeney said, "Lola wasn't killed in her apartment but in the areaway outside the buildings. Sure, she was probably followed. And so was Stella Gaylord—followed as far as the mouth of the alley. But the Ripper doesn't always use the following technique. He didn't follow Yolanda Lang home; he was waiting for her outside that door at the back of the hallway in her building."

"You've really studied this case, haven't you, Sweeney?"

"Why not?" Sweeney asked. "It's my job."

"As I get it, you haven't been assigned to it yet. Or am I wrong?"

Sweeney considered whether to give Bline the song-and-dance about the fact detective magazine and decided not to; Bline might ask which magazine, and then check up on him.

He said, "Not exactly, Cap. But I was assigned on at least one angle of it when Wally Krieg told me to write that eyewitness account. And I figured because of that *in* I had on the case, he'd probably ask me to do more when I go back to work Monday, so I read up on the case, what's already been in the papers, and asked a few questions."

"On your own time?"

"Why not? I got interested in it. You'd still follow the case if you got taken off it, wouldn't you?"

"Guess I would," Bline admitted.

"How about Greene's other alibi, the New York one? How well did you check on that one?"

Bline grinned. "You're hell-bent to fit Greene into this, huh, Sweeney?"

"Have you met him, Cap?"

"Sure."

"That's why. I've known him a day and a half now, and I think the fact that he's still alive is pretty good proof I'm not the Ripper. If I was, he wouldn't be."

Bline laughed. "That ought to work both ways, Sweeney. He seems to like you almost as much as you like him. And you're still alive. But about the New York alibi; we gave it to the New York police and they checked the hotel he was staying at, the Algonquin. He was registered there from the 25th through the 30th."

Sweeney leaned forward. "That's as far as you checked? The Gaylord murder was on the 27th, and it's only four hours by plane from New York to Chicago. He could have left there in the evening and been back the next morning."

Bline shrugged. "We'd have checked further if there'd been any reason for it. Be honest, Sweeney; what have you got against him except that he rubs you the wrong way? And me too, I admit it. But aside from that, he knows *one* of the four dames who were attacked. To my mind, that's damn near an alibi in itself."

"How the hell do you figure that?"

Bline said, "When we get the Ripper, I'll bet you we find he knew *all* of the four women or none of them. Murderers—even psychopathic ones—follow that pattern, Sweeney. He wouldn't have picked three strangers and one friend; take my word for it."

"And you've checked——?"

"Hell, yes, we've checked. We've made up lists as complete as we could of everybody who knew each of the four women, and then we've compared the lists. There's been only one name that appeared on even two of the four lists, and that much is allowable to coincidence."

"Who is it?"

"Raoul Reynarde, the guy who runs the gift shop that Lola Brent got fired from the day she was killed. Turns out he also had a slight acquaintance with Stella Gaylord, the B-girl."

"Good God, what for?"

Bline grinned. "I see you've met him. But why not? Lots of faggots have friends who are women. You have male friends, don't you? Anyway it was just a slight acquaintance, both according to Reynarde and to the other friends of Stella Gaylord that we checked with."

"But he could have known the other two then. It's hard to prove he hadn't met——"

"In one case, no; we can't ask Dorothy Lee. We could only ask her other friends and none of them knew Reynarde. But we could and did ask the strip-tease dame. And Yolanda Lang doesn't know him from either name or photograph."

"You checked him for alibis?"

"Fairly good ones on two of the cases. Especially on the Lola Brent one. He couldn't have followed her home after he fired her without closing the store and there's fairly good evidence—negative evidence, anyway—that he didn't close it."

Sweeney sighed. "Wash him out, then. I still like Doc Greene."

"Sweeney, you're nuts. All you mean is that you *don't* like him. Not a thing to point to him otherwise. We've got a hell of a lot better suspect than Greene."

"You mean me?"

"You're damn right I mean you. Look, not even a shadow of an alibi for *any* murder. Your extreme interest in the case. The fact that you are psychically unbalanced—or you wouldn't be an alcoholic. And that, in one case out of the four, we can put you right at the scene of the crime at the time of the crime. I'm not saying that's enough evidence to hang a dog on, but it is more than we've got on anybody else. If you weren't——"

"If I weren't what?"

"Skip it."

Sweeney said, "Wait, I get it. You mean if I wasn't a reporter, you'd probably drag me in and sweat me down a bit on the off chance. But you figure I'll be writing on the case and that you couldn't hold me long and once I got out the *Blade*'s stories would play merry hell with the captain in charge of the Ripper detail."

Bline's laugh was a little embarrassed. He said, "I guess that isn't too far off, Sweeney. But damn it, man, can't you give me something that'll let me write you off, so I won't have to waste so much time on you? There ought to be some way you could check where you were at the time of at least one of the murders."

Sweeney shook his head. "I wish there was, Cap." He glanced at his wrist watch. "Tell you what, though, I'll do the next best thing; I'll buy you a drink. At El Madhouse. First show goes on at ten; that's in a few minutes now. You know she's dancing again tonight already."

"I know everything. Except who the Ripper is. Sure, Sweeney, I was thinking of dropping in there tonight anyway. Let's go."

At the door, before he reached back to turn out the light, Sweeney looked at the black statuette on the radio, the slim, naked girl, arms outraised to ward off ineffable evil, a silent scream eternally frozen on her lips. He grinned at her and tossed her a kiss before he flicked off the light and followed Bline down the stairs.

They hailed a cab at Rush Street. Sweeney said, "El Madhouse" to the driver and then leaned back and lighted a cigarette. He looked at Bline, sitting back, relaxed, his eyes closed. He said, "You don't really think I might be the Ripper, Cap. Or you wouldn't relax like that."

"Like what?" Bline's voice was soft. "I was watching your hands and letting you think my eyes were all the way closed. And there's a gun in my right coat pocket, the side away from you, with my hand on it. I could use it quicker than you could pull a knife, if you started to."

Sweeney laughed.

And then he wondered what was funny about it.

CHAPTER TEN

EL MADHOUSE was crowded. It seemed strange to Sweeney that he hadn't thought of that. With all the publicity Yolanda Lang had received—the best of it at Sweeney's own hands—he realized that he should have realized that the joint would be jammed. As they went in the door, he could see the husky waiter stationed at the inner doorway turning people away. Over the waiter's shoulder he could see that more tables than usual had been crowded into the big back room, and that every table was crowded.

A three-piece orchestra—not good but not bad—was playing back there now, and a woman with gravel in her throat was singing a torch song, probably the first number of the floor show. But from the outer room, the barroom, you couldn't see the stage—or floor or platform, whichever it would be.

He grunted disgustedly, but Bline took him by the arm and started with him toward a table from which a couple was just rising. They got the seats and Bline said, "We don't want to go back there yet. Show's just starting, and Yolanda won't come on for forty minutes or so."

"We'll play hell getting back there at all. Unless—Yolanda told me to come around and catch the show; maybe she had more sense than I did and made a reservation for me. I'll check; you hold this seat for——" He started to get up again.

"Sit down and relax," Bline told him. "You got a police escort. Any time we want, we'll go back there, if they have to put chairs on top of tables for us. Don't think they'll have to, though; I told one of the boys to save me a place at his table, and we can crowd an extra chair in if there's room for one."

He caught a rushing waiter by the arm and said, "Send Nick over right away, will you?"

The waiter tried to pull loose. "Nick's busy. We're all going nuts tonight. You'll have to wait your——"

Bline's free hand pulled back his lapel for a brief flash of silver plate. He said, "Send Nick over."

"Who's Nick?" Sweeney asked, when the waiter had vanished into the crowd.

"Nick runs the place, nights, for Harry Yahn." He grinned. "I don't really want to see him, but it's the only way we'll get drinks right away. What you having?"

"Whisky highball. Maybe I'll have to buy one of those badges. It's a system, if it works."

"It works," Bline said. He looked up as a dapper, stocky man came up to the table. "Hi, Nick. Everything under control?"

The stocky man grunted. "If there weren't so many deadheads in the house, we'd be doing better. Four coppers back there already taking up room, and now you come."

"And Sweeney, Nick. This is Sweeney, of the *Blade*. He comes, too. You can crowd in an extra chair for him, can't you?"

"Cash customer?"

"Cash customer," Sweeney said.

Nick smiled, and from the smile Sweeney expected him to rub his hands together, too. But instead he stuck one out to Sweeney. "I was kidding, Mr. Sweeney. It's on the house for you. I read that story you wrote. But it cost us money, too."

"The hell," said Sweeney. "How?"

"Greene. He's holding us up, and we got to pay it to cash in." He turned around and grabbed a flying waiter, the same one Bline had grabbed. "What you gentlemen having?"

"Whisky and soda for both of us," Bline told him.

"Make it three, Charlie, and make it next," Nick told the waiter. Then he said. "Just a minute; I get a chair." He brought one from somewhere and sat down at the table with them just as the drinks came.

"Bumps," Sweeney said. "And how come Greene could hold you up; isn't Yolanda under contract?"

"Sure she is. For four more weeks. But——"

Sweeney cut in: "Doc Greene told me for three."

"Greene wouldn't tell the truth on a bet, even where it don't matter, Mr. Sweeney. If it'd been three weeks, he'd've told you four. Sure, she's under contract through September 5th, but the contract's got a clause."

"Most contracts have," Sweeney said.

"Yeah. Well, this clause says she don't have to work if she's sick or hurt. And Greene got one of the docs at the hospital to write a paper that says that because of shock she shouldn't ought to work for a week or even two weeks."

"But would she get paid for that time if she didn't?"

"Sure she wouldn't. But look what we can cash in on her if she does. Lookit the crowd tonight, and they're spending money, too. But because Doc had us by the nuts we had to offer a one-grand bonus if she'd forget she was shocked. A bonus—that's what Doc calls a bribe."

"But *is* she okay to dance this soon?" Sweeney asked. "She really was suffering from shock. I saw her face when she stood up in that hallway."

"You didn't mention her face."

"Sure I did. Before the dog pulled the zipper. Say, Nick, how come she wasn't wearing her bra and a G-string under that dress? I never thought to ask, but unless the police rules here have changed, she'd have been wearing them for the show."

"Wasn't she? They don't show much. I thought you was just exaggerating to make it a better story."

"So help me God," said Sweeney.

"Well, it could be. We got a pretty good dressing room with a shower here, and Wednesday was a hot night. Probably she took a shower after the last show and didn't bother to put on anything under a dress to run home in if she expected to go right to sleep. Or something."

"If it had been something, she wouldn't have been alone." Sweeney pointed out. "But we got off the track. Isn't it a bit soon for her to start dancing again?"

"Naw. If she got shocked, she was over it by the time she had a night's sleep. And the scratch was just a scratch. She'll be wearing a strip of adhesive tape six inches long, but that's what the customers are paying to see. Well, not all they're paying to see." He pushed back his chair and stood up. "Well, I got to do things. Want to go back now? Yo won't be on for half an hour yet, but the rest of the show don't stink too much."

The voice of an M.C. telling jokes came from the back room and both Sweeney and Bline shook their heads, Bline said, "We'll look you up when we want to move back."

"Sure. I'll send you two more drinks here, then."

He went away, taking his chair back to wherever it had come from.

Sweeney asked Bline, "Yolanda just do one number?"

"Right now, yes. Before the excitement, she was on twice. A straight strip tease for the third number on the show, and then the specialty with the dog for the last number. But Nick told me this afternoon that to get her to go back on right away, they agreed to let her do just the one number, the specialty, on each show. Not that that matters, they'll get as big crowds here to see her do one number a show as two."

Their drinks came. Bline looked down into his for a moment and then squarely at Sweeney. He said, "Maybe I was a little rough on you tonight, Sweeney. In the cab, I mean."

Sweeney said, "I'm glad you were."

"Why? So you can pan me in the *Blade* with a clear conscience?"

"Not that. As far as I know to date, you don't deserve any panning. Not for the way you've handled the case. But now I can hold out on you with a clear conscience."

Bline frowned. "You can't hold back any evidence, Sweeney.

Not and get away with it. What is it you're holding back?" He leaned forward suddenly intent. "Did you notice anything there on State Street Wednesday night that you didn't tell about in the write-up? Recognize anybody, maybe or notice anybody acting suspiciously? If you did——"

"I didn't. You've got the whole truth and nothing but the truth on that. I mean, if in playing around with the case and doing my own investigating and question-asking, I come on anything that you missed, it's my own business. I mean, until I get enough of it to beat you out on cracking the case."

Bline said, "Let's take it as of now. Right here and now. Will you give me your word of honour on the answer to one question?"

"If I answer it at all, I'll answer it straight. It isn't, by any chance, whether I'm the Ripper, is it?"

"No, if you *are*, I wouldn't expect a straight answer. So I'm asking this on the assumption that you're not. But by God, Sweeney, if you won't answer this, *Blade* or no *Blade*, I'm going to take you in and work on you. And the same goes if you do answer it and I ever find out it wasn't straight.

"Do you know or even think you might know, who the Ripper is? Either by sight or by name, do you even suspect anybody?"

"No, definitely not. Unless it's Doc Greene, and I haven't a damn bit of reason for that except that I'd *like* him to be."

Bline sat back. He said, "Okay, then, I've got a lot of men under me on this, and besides that we've got the whole police force keeping an eye out. If you, all by yourself, get anything we miss, it's your baby. It'd probably get you a knife in the belly, but that's your business."

Sweeney said, "Fair enough, Cap. And for those kind words—especially about the knife. I'll even forgive you for taking my razor and penknife without telling me and scaring the pants off me when I found them gone. Why didn't you leave a note?"

"Wanted to see how you'd react. If you'd been the Ripper, and found them gone, you'd have probably been even worse scared; you'd like as not have taken it on the lam and we'd have picked you up. You know, Sweeney, I've just about decided you're not the Ripper."

"Awfully sweet of you, Cap. But I'll bet you tell that to all the boys. By the way, have I been tailed while you thought I was it?"

"Today, yes. Hadn't got around to you yet yesterday. But I'll pull the guy off of you now, I guess. Especially now that you know about it."

"I might suggest you put him on Doc Greene. Say, was it Doc's salesmanship that made you suspect me to begin with?"

Bline grinned. "You two really do love one another. Is that

enough of an answer to your question? Well, what do you say we go in out of the rain? She'll be on in ten minutes."

They found Nick and he took them past the big waiter who guarded the portal. The gravel-voiced torch singer was at it again as they threaded their way through barely navigable aisles among the close-packed, crowded tables. No tête-à-tête tables tonight, Sweeney noticed; at least four people were at every table and five or even six were at some of them. Two hundred people, more or less, were jammed in a room whose normal complement wasn't much over half that number.

They had barely started across the room when Sweeney felt his arm gripped from behind and turned. Bline was leaning his head close. He had to yell to make himself heard above the music and the noise but pitched his voice so it wouldn't carry past Sweeney. "Forgot to tell you, Sweeney. Keep your eyes open in here. Watch the faces and see if you see anybody you remember being by that door on State Street. Get me?"

Sweeney nodded. He turned and started following Nick again, but this time kept watching as many faces along the route as he could. He didn't think he'd remember anybody who'd shared Wednesday night's spectacle with him; all he'd really seen outside the door had been the backs of heads. But it didn't hurt to try, and Bline's idea that the Ripper might have come around to the front and joined the crowd seemed quite reasonable. Also, he agreed with the thought that the Ripper might have come here tonight.

Nick led them to a table where three men sat; one chair was empty, tilted against the table's edge. He said. "I'll send over a waiter with another chair, they can crowd you in here. Same to drink, both of you?"

Bline nodded, then said. "Sit down, Sweeney. Want to talk to an outpost or two before I squat."

Sweeney took the chair and glanced at his three companions, all of whom were watching the singer and paying no attention to him. One of them looked familiar, the others were strangers to him. He watched the singer. She wasn't bad to watch, but he wished he didn't have to listen to her, too.

The chair arrived, as did the drinks, before Bline came back. Sweeney moved over to make more room, and Bline said, "Sweeney—Ross, Guerney, Swann. Anything doing boys?"

The one called Swann said, "Guy over at the corner table acts a little screwy; I been keeping an eye on him. The one with the carnation in his buttonhole. Maybe he's just a little drunk."

Bline watched that way a while. He said, "Don't think so. The Ripper wouldn't call attention to himself dressing up like that and wearing a flower, would he? And I don't think the Ripper'd get drunk."

"Thanks for that last thought," Sweeney said.

Bline turned to him. "See anybody might have been there that night?"

"Only the guy across from me there, the one you introduced as Guerney. Isn't he one of the boys from the squad car?"

Guerney had turned back at the sound of his name. He said, "Yeah. It was me that creased the dog."

"Nice shooting."

Bline said, "Guerney's one of the best shots in the department. His partner's here, too, Kravich. He's at the bar out there, watching 'em as they come and go."

"Didn't notice him."

"He noticed you. I saw him start toward you when you came in the door; then he saw I was with you and turned back. Sure you haven't seen anybody else that——"

"No," said Sweeney. "Shhhh."

The M.C. was on stage—it had turned out to be actually a stage, although a small one, about eight feet deep and twelve feet wide—and was building up an introduction to Yolanda Lang and her world-famous Beauty and the Beast dance.

The lights dimmed, and the room was quiet. As miraculously quiet as though two hundred people were holding their breath. You could hear the click of the switch as a spotlight went on, from somewhere in the back of the room, throwing a bright circle of yellow light on the left side of the stage. Everyone watched the yellow circle of light. A drum began to throb and the tone and pitch of it pulled Sweeney's eyes away from the stage and toward the three-piece orchestra; the three-piece orchestra wasn't there. Rather, two-thirds of it weren't there; the pianist and the sax-player had left the platform. The trap-drummer had left his traps and sat before a single kettledrum, a big one, turned low. His only weapons were two drumsticks with big well-padded heads.

Smart, thought Sweeney, and he wondered if Yolanda or her manager deserved the credit for that idea. Resonant rhythm without music. And not even the lousiest drummer can corn up a kettledrum with padded sticks, set out of reach of his cymbals, blocks and bells.

The drum throbbed a slow crescendo and the spotlight dimmed; you caught a flash of movement in the dimness, then as the yellow circle blazed bright again, she stood there full in its centre, stood poised, unmoving.

And she *was* beautiful; there was no doubt of that. The picture Sweeney had been carrying in his mind had not been exaggeration, not in the slightest. He thought, now, that she was the most beautiful woman he had ever seen. And by the collective catch of breath of the audience, he knew that he was not alone in thinking so. What, he wondered was she doing in a dive like this, on Clark Street in Chicago? Even if she couldn't dance——

She wore a gown exactly like the one she had worn for the scene in the hallway, except this one was black and that had been white. This one was better, Sweeney thought. Contrast of black and white. It was strapless, moulded to every curve of her body.

She was barefoot; the black gown her only visible garment. No ribbon, no gloves, no bolero; this wasn't to be a gradual strip tease like other strip teases; it would be one blinding flash from black to white, from cloth to flesh.

The drum throbbed.

You thought she was a statue there, and then—so gradually that you weren't sure at first—she moved. Merely to turn her head.

And when it was turned your eyes followed hers. You saw, as she saw, what crouched in semi-darkness on the other side of the stage. It was Devil, the dog; only he wasn't a dog at all now. He was all devil. He crouched there, his jaws slightly parted in a silent snarl of bared white teeth, his yellow eyes luminous in the dimness.

The drumbeat died down to almost-inaudibility. And in the almost-silence, the dog snarled loudly. It was the same sound, exactly the same sound, that Sweeney had heard before, two nights ago. It had put a cold chill down his spine then, and it put a cold chill down his spine now.

Still half-crouched, the dog took a stiff-legged step toward the woman. He snarled again and crouched to spring.

There was a sudden quick movement across the table from him that pulled Sweeney's eyes from the tense drama on the stage. And at the same instant that Sweeney saw the movement, Bline's big hand reached across the table and grabbed Guerney's arm.

There was a gun in Guerney's hand.

Bline whispered hoarsely, "You Goddamn fool, it's part of the act. He's trained to do that; he's not going to hurt her."

Guerney whispered back. "Just in case. In case he *does* jump her. I could get him before he got her throat."

"Put back that gun, you Goddamn sap, or I'll break you."

The gun went slowly back into the shoulder holster, but Sweeney saw, out of the corner of his eye, that Guerney's hand stayed on the butt of the gun.

Bline said, "Don't get trigger-happy. The dog jumps her; it's part of the act, Goddamn it."

Guerney's hand came out from under his coat, but stayed near his lapel. Sweeney's eyes jerked back to the stage as a sudden intake of breath from the audience backgrounded a yip from a woman at a table near the stage, a yip like a suddenly stopped scream.

The dog was leaping.

But the woman moved, too, one step aside and the dog flew past her and down, alighted and turned in a flash of brownness, crouched again, and now she was in the middle of the stage as he leaped. Again she was not there when he landed.

And Sweeney wondered if that was going to go on indefinitely, but it didn't. That was the last time. The dog—as though convinced that leaping was futile—crouched now in the centre of the stage, turning as she danced around him.

And she could dance; well, if not superlatively; gracefully, if not significantly. The dog, now no longer snarling, pivoted, his yellow eyes following every move she made.

Then, alongside the now-tamed dog, the Beast, Beauty sank to her knees and put her hand upon the dog's head, and he snarled but tolerated the caress.

The drum throbbed, the beat accelerated.

And then, as Yolanda gracefully rose to her feet, facing the audience from the centre of the yellow circle of light that already, but very gradually, was starting to fade, the dog padded behind her. It reared up, as tall as she, and then as it started downward its teeth caught the tab sewed to the tag of the zipper and pulled.

And the black dress as had the white one, fell suddenly into a circle about her feet.

She was incredibly beautiful despite—Sweeney thought—the fact that she was overdressed. Overdressed in a narrow, transparent bra of wide-mesh net, diaphanous as dew and confining as air, that seemed to accentuate rather than conceal the beauty of her voluptuous breasts; and in a G-string which, in the slowly fading light, might not have been there at all, which needed to be taken on faith in the integrity of Chicago's vice squad; and one more garment: a six-inch strip of black adhesive tape, slightly slanting, across her white belly just below the navel. And somehow the contrast of that black on white made her seem even more naked than she had seemed when—two nights ago—Sweeney had seen her actually so.

The drumbeat faded slowly. Yolanda raised her arms—her breasts lifting with them—and spread her bare feet apart; the dog, from behind her, walked between her legs, halfway and stood there with her astride him; his head raised to look out over the audience as though daring any man to approach that which he now guarded.

"Cerberus guarding the portals of Heaven," Sweeney whispered to Bline.

Bline said, "Huh?"

The drumbeat faded, and the light faded and then went out and the stage was dark. When the lights went on, the stage was empty.

And the lights went on brightly all over the room, and the floor show was over. People applauded madly, but Yolanda Lang did not return, even to take a single bow.

Over the noise, Bline asked Sweeney, "How'd you like it?"

"It, or her?"

"It. The dance."

"Probably symbolic as hell, but symbolic of what, I don't know. I don't think the choreographer did either. If there *was* a choreographer. My idea is that Doc Greene figured it out. It's just crazy enough—and just smart enough—for his fine Italian hand."

Bline said, "Greene's not Italian. I think he's mostly German."

Sweeney was spared answering because Guerney had turned around and Bline was looking at him balefully. He said. "You Goddamn fool, for a plugged nickel I'd make you turn in your gun and go without one."

Guerney flushed and looked foolish. "I wasn't gonna shoot, Captain, unless——"

"Unless the dog jumped at her. And he did, twice. Good God, but that would have been a stink for the department."

Sweeney felt sorry for the squad-car copper. He said. "If you *had* shot that dog, Guerney, I'd have stuck up for you."

Bline said. "And a lot of good that would have done him, unless you could have got him a paper route carrying the *Blade*".

Nick saved Guerney further embarrassment by appearing at their table. He said. "Another round of drinks is coming, gentlemen. How'd you like the show? Sure is a well-trained pooch, she's got, ain't it?"

Sweeney said, "He showed more self-control, under the circumstances, than I would have."

"Me either," Guerney said. He started to grin, but caught Bline's eye and found he was still in disgrace. He said, "Gotta see a man about a—I mean, I gotta go to the can. Excuse me."

He threaded his way off between the tables. Nick slid into the vacated chair and said, "I'll stay a minute till he gets back. Did you notice anything during the show, Captain?"

Sweeney said, "Everything the G-string didn't cover. You know, sometime I'd like to see her without *anything* on."

Nick stared at him. "Huh? I thought, according to your story in the paper——"

Sweeney shook his head gloomily, "Gloves," he said. "She wore long, white gloves."

Bline snorted. He said. "This guy has a one-track mind, Nick. What did you mean, did I notice anything during the show?"

Nick leaned forward. "Only this; that part where she's posed there, still, facing the audience and front-stage-centre, with the light fading out. Look, I shouldn't take a chance changing my own show—not that it matters; we could get a crowd here to listen to her sing Annie Laurie in a diving suit—but I been worried about that. I don't want her killed either, and if the Ripper should show here, that'd be his chance."

"Maybe, but how?"

"The audience is in the dark, almost dark anyway. And if he decided to throw that shiv of his, it'd be hard to tell just where it come from."

Bline looked thoughtful and then shook his head. "Sounds pretty remote. Nick. Unless he's already a knife-thrower, and it's a million to one against, it'd take him months of practice to learn. And I don't think he'd use a gun—guys like that stick to one weapon and one style of using it—and I don't think he'd try to kill her in a crowd anyway. I think the big danger point is on her way to and from here, or at her place at night. And we're taking care of that."

"For how long?"

"Until the Ripper's caught, Nick. At least as long as she'll be playing here, so *you* don't need to worry."

"You have someone go through her flat before she goes in when she goes home?"

Bline frowned. "Look, Nick, I'm not telling anybody *exactly* what precautions we're taking or not taking. Especially with a reporter sitting here who'd put it in the paper so the Ripper would be sure to know."

"Thanks," said Sweeney, "for demoting me from suspect to reporter. But that suggestion of going through her flat before she goes into it is good, if you aren't already doing it. If I were the Ripper and wanted to get her, I wouldn't try it on the street again; I'd be under her bed waiting for her. Say, does Devil sleep in the same room with her?"

Bline looked at him sharply. "That's not for publication. But yes."

"About that knife-throwing," Nick said. "What about if he can throw them?"

Sweeney said, "Here he comes. Ask him if he can."

CHAPTER ELEVEN

Doc Greene was coming toward them, worming his way through the people who were leaving after the first floor show, a wide, satisfied grin on his bland, round face that Sweeney would have loved to slug.

Bline looked to see who was coming and then looked at Sweeney disgustedly. He said, "You and that damn hunch."

Nick stood up and said, "Hi, Doc. Well, I got to go. So long."

Doc nodded to him, and asked Bline how he liked the show.

Bline said, "Great. Sit down, Greene."

Guerney, coming back, hesitated as he saw his chair being taken. Bline motioned to him and then told him to take a break and get some fresh air outside. Guerney left.

Doc Greene grinned at Sweeney. Not a nice grin. He said, "Do I have to ask how you like it?"

"No," Sweeney told him. "I hear you held Nick—or rather, Harry Yahn—up. For a thousand bucks."

"I wouldn't call it a hold-up. Yolanda shouldn't be dancing so soon after what happened. It's taking a chance with her health. Naturally, she deserves something extra for that, if she does."

"Does she get it?"

"Naturally. Of course, as her manager, I get my cut."

"What per cent is that?"

"That's my business."

"And business is good," Sweeney said. "You know, Doc, there's something I'd like to ask you."

"I might even answer it."

"How come Yolanda is playing a place like this? It's peanuts to the bookings you could get her."

"You're telling me. But we're under contract here; I told you that. Yahn won't let us break the contract. Know what we're getting here? A lousy two hundred a week. I could get her a thousand a week damn easy, and we have to be tied down here for another month. And by that time——"

"You don't get me," Sweeney said. "What I mean is why *was* she working for a lousy two hundred a week? Even without the publicity, she ought to be nearer to the big time than Clarke Street."

Greene spread his hands. "Maybe you could do better for her.

It's easy to say, Sweeney. Only you won't get a chance to try; I got her signed up under contract."

"For how long?"

"Again, my business."

Sweeney said, "I suggest you haven't wanted to get her better bookings, for reasons of your own."

"You're very suggestive. Would you like me to make a suggestion?"

"I could guess it in advance. But I can make another one." Sweeney glanced quickly to see that Bline was listening. He said, "How's this for a suggestion? Maybe the Ripper never attacked Yolanda at all. Maybe it was a publicity stunt. Nobody *saw* the Ripper slash at her. Maybe you cooked it up; she could have given herself that little cut with, say, a safety razor blade, and then she could have laid down on the floor till someone saw her through the glass."

"Having swallowed the razor blade?"

"Having possibly, dropped it in her mailbox slot. She was standing right by the mailboxes."

Bline said, "No, Sweeney. The hallway was searched including the mailboxes. No weapon. And it wasn't in a shoe or in her dress, either. She was searched at the hospital. Don't think we didn't think of the possibility of it being a hoax."

Sweeney said stubbornly, "Doc could have been been there and gone off with the blade, as easily as the Ripper could have been there and gone off with his weapon."

Greene bowed ironically. "Thank you, Sweeney. For implying for the first time that I'm not the Ripper."

"Don't mention it. And then, Cap, there's still another possibility. Maybe you've already thought of it. But that wound was pretty slight; not enough to incapacitate her. How do you know she got it in the hallway at all?

"I mean, she could have come home, gone up to her apartment, made that slit with a razor and washed the razor or whatever and put it away, then she could go back downstairs and lie in the hallway till somebody saw her."

Bline said, "We thought of that. Several little things against it, and one big one. Little things like the scratch marks on the back door. They could have been put there, sure, for the purpose of being found. And the fact that it would take a lot of nerve to give yourself a cut like that. *Could* be done, sure. Another little thing, it couldn't have been sure—unless you were in on it, Sweeney—that you'd be there to give it that write-up. Were you in on it?"

Sweeney grinned. "Sure. That's why I'm suggesting it now. Doc won't give me my cut, so I'm turning him in. But what's the one big thing that proves it wasn't a put-up job?"

"The shock. Sweeney. She got over it within twelve hours, yes, but she was really suffering from shock when she got to the hospital. Bad. And genuine. I talked to the doctors who treated her, and they're positive it couldn't have been acting—nor drugs, either, for that matter. It was bona fide shock and you can't fake it."

Sweeney said. "Okay. It was an idea while it lasted. I'm glad it was wrong. It would have made a prize sucker out of me for the story I wrote."

Greene said blandly, "I'll tell Yo what you thought and that you suggested it to the police. She'll like you better for it, no doubt."

Sweeney glared at him.

Greene smiled and leaned across the table. He said, "The thing I like about you, Sweeney, is that your reactions are so completely predictable, so primitive, so utterly lacking in subtlety. You should know that I would do no such foolish thing as to inform Yolanda of your base insinuation."

"Any why not?"

"Because I *am* subtle, and civilized. The last thing I would do is to make Yolanda angry at you, lest anger react. Women are subtle, too, whether civilized or not. But you wouldn't understand that. Even you, however, should have realized that if I were actually going to snitch to Yolanda, the last thing I would have done is to forewarn you that I would."

Bline was grinning at Sweeney. He said, "I'm liking this. It's your turn."

Sweeney said, "I'd rather discuss this outside."

"The animal plane," Greene said. "The three things for which the Irish are famous: drinking, fighting, and—well, the third, in Sweeney's case, is reduced to *voyeurism*." He leaned still farther across the table and he no longer smiled. "And even for that, Sweeney, I hate your very guts."

"The mask slipped then," Sweeney said. "You really are a psychiatrist, Doc?"

"I really am."

"And you honestly do not recognize that you yourself are not sane? Look, I don't know your relations with Yolanda—and don't bother trying to tell me, because I wouldn't be able to believe you, either way. But, whichever, your attitude toward her is not sane and normal. As her manager, you let her get up in front of a crowd of creeps in a honky-tonk, strip for them, and get their tongues hanging out, and you tolerate it. Maybe you even like it; maybe you've got a case of inverted voyeurism. Or something. I wouldn't know what, but you ought to, if you're a psychiatrist."

Bline was looking from one to the other of them, chuckling. He said. "At it, boys; I'll referee. The first one to lose his temper to the extent of taking a poke at the other loses—and maybe goes to the hoosegow."

Neither Greene nor Sweeney even glanced at him.

Sweeney said, "Thousands of men must have wanted her and tried to get her. You couldn't have reacted to all of them as you've reacted to me; your adrenals wouldn't have stood the strain. So there's something different in my case. Know what it is, Doc?"

Greene was wary, his eyes hooded. You could have counted to ten, slowly, before he answered, and then it was only to say, "No, I don't." He sounded honestly puzzled.

"Then I'll tell you. It's because these other guys have only wanted, and tried. You know I'm going to succeed."

Bline must have been watching Greene's face, because he was on his feet and leaning over the table even as Greene started across it. Greene's chair went over backward, but he stopped as Bline caught his arms, although he paid no attention to Bline. He said softly, "I'm going to kill you, Sweeney."

Then he jerked loose from Bline's grip, turned and walked away.

Nick was suddenly there. "Anything wrong, gentlemen?" he asked.

"Everything is lovely," Sweeney told him.

Nick looked uncertainly from one to the other of them. He said. "Shall I send another drink?" Sweeney said, "Thanks, no, not for me," and Bline said, "I'll pass this one, too, Nick."

"There's not going to be any trouble?"

"No, Nick," Bline said. "But—yeah, I'll have a drink at that, if I can."

Nick nodded and left them. Bline relaxed in the chair and turned to Sweeney. "Just wanted to get rid of him. Sweeney, you'd better be careful."

"I guess maybe you're right, Cap. I honestly don't think he's completely sane. That's why I goaded him; I wanted to show you."

"Of course he didn't mean what he said about killing you; he wouldn't have said that in front of me if he really meant it. He was just trying to throw a scare into you; that's all."

Sweeney said, "I wish I was sure of that. If he's sane, yes. But—Ripper or no Ripper—I wouldn't bet on his being sane."

"How about yourself?"

Sweeney grinned. "I may be crazy, but I'm not insane." He stood up. "Maybe that's enough excitement for one evening. Guess I'll hit for home."

"Your door got a good lock?"

Sweeney frowned at him. "You should know," he said. "Unless I left it unlocked the other night when you borrowed my razor."

Bline stood up too. He said, "I'll walk with you a block or two, I can use some fresh air."

When they were outside, walking north on Clark, he said, "If your razor being missing really scared you, Sweeney, I'm sorry about it. Happened this way; I sent two of the boys around to bring you in for questioning Thursday night and told 'em to bring your arsenal too. I didn't tell them to bring the arsenal if you *weren't* there, and they overstepped a little. One of them—I won't say who—is pretty good on locks and loves a chance to show off he can open them."

"I know who that would be. You needn't tell me."

"Don't be foolish. Sweeney. Lots of guys on the force are good at locks."

"But only one of them has been to my room before, and anybody else would have had to ask Mrs. Randall instead of going straight up. And with her there they couldn't have gone on it. So that makes it the guy I'm thinking about. And I thought he was a friend of mine."

"Forget it, Sweeney. God damn it, man, friendship doesn't count when you're looking for a killer. And I'd told him you were under strong suspicion. Sweeney, we've *got* to get that guy before he butchers any more dames."

"For the dames' sake, or so you don't lose your job?"

"Both, I guess, but it's not all on account of my job. I wasn't on the Lola Brent one two months ago, but they dumped it in my lap after the second case, when it began to look like there was a psycho loose. I looked at the B-girl, Gaylord, at the morgue for a starter, and I saw the steno, Dorothy Lee, before they moved her. They weren't nice to look at. Christ."

He turned to look at Sweeney. "You saw a job of his work—a botched one. It wouldn't be so funny to you if you'd seen the real McCoy."

"I don't think it's funny."

"Then I wish you and Doc Greene would lay off that Punch-and-Judy show of yours and quit messing things up trying to make each other out to be the Ripper. Yeah, he fooled me, Sweeney. It was after a talk with him Thursday evening that I sent the boys around for you and your cutlery. I didn't know then that he was using me as a cat's-paw because he hated you for personal reasons.

"And if I try to get you to suspect him, I guess you think it's for personal reasons, too."

"Isn't it? Mostly?"

Sweeney sighed. "That and a hunch."

"Well, play your hunch if you want to. But don't expect me to. Greene's couple of alibis may not be perfect, but they're good enough for me—especially because, like I told you, I figure that the killer either knew *all* the dames or none of them. One kind of nut might kill the woman he's crazy about, but it's another kind that follows strangers home and kills them. For my money—not that I'm a psychiatrist—the same kind of nut doesn't do both."

They were nearing the corner of Erie and Bline slowed down. He said, "You turn east here. Guess I'll go back to the madhouse. And look, stay away from Greene. I don't want to have to jug you both for mayhem, and it's going to be that or worse if you keep tangling."

He stuck out a hand. "Friends, Sweeney?"

"I'm not the Ripper? You're sure?"

"Reasonably sure."

Sweeney took his hand, and grinned. "And I'm getting to be reasonably sure you're not a son of a bitch, Cap. I sure had you pegged as one for a while."

'Can't say I blame you. Well, so long."

Sweeney stood for a moment on the corner. He saw Bline look around and then cut diagonally across the street, which took him out of his way if he was returning to El Madhouse. He understood when, a hundred yards down, Bline stopped to talk to a man who had been looking into the window of a hockshop, and then Bline and the man walked south together.

That meant—unless there'd been two of them, which he doubted—that Bline had pulled Sweeney's tail off the job. To make sure, he pretended to turn south at Erie and State and then waited in the doorway of a store next to the corner one to see of anyone would turn into State Street after him. No one did.

He whistled a little as he went back to Erie and on east to his room. There was no Ripper waiting for him. But there was Mimi.

Number SM–1 of the Ganslen Art Company of Louisville, Kentucky, Screaming Mimi.

He picked her up and held her gently, and she screamed at him, pushing towards him with tiny, fending hands; again that little chill went down his spine.

Somewhere in Chicago there was another Mimi just like this one, and *she* had something to scream about. The Ripper had her.

Call her Mimi number one. What if the Ripper knew that he, Sweeney, had Mimi number two?

But the Ripper couldn't know that. At least, not unless the Ripper was Raoul Reynarde, who'd sold him Mimi number two, after Lola Brent had sold Mimi number one to the Ripper and had tried to drag down the money on the sale. And if Raoul was the Ripper, then Raoul wouldn't have had any reason to tell him about Mimi and—Hell, if Raoul was the Ripper then the whole story about Lola having sold a Mimi might have been out of the whole cloth, to distract attention from himself. But then Raoul would have told the police about it. Well, of course. Raoul had told the police the same story, but the police hadn't happened to follow through by looking at a duplicate of the statuette on which Lola had dragged down, and so they'd missed the point—the point that the man who'd bought the statuette had been the Ripper. Raoul himself had missed it. He, Sweeney, might have missed it except for the hunch that made him buy Mimi from Raoul—and then the remark of the counterman in the lunchroom.

He put Mimi down, very gently. He wished she'd stop screaming, but she never would. A silent scream can never be silenced.

No, definitely the police didn't know about Mimi; otherwise Bline would never have sat here in the same room with her without noticing or mentioning her. He'd looked right at her at least once.

And, of course, he'd mentioned Mimi to Doc Greene and Doc hadn't reacted. But—although he couldn't believe it—Doc might have been able to control his nerves enough not to let that sheet of paper move when "small black statuette" had been sprung on him. No, if Greene really was—despite alibis, despite everything—the Ripper, then maybe the whole Mimi lead was a blind alley; maybe the Ripper hadn't made that purchase from Lola Brent at the gift shop.

Sweeney, he told himself, you can't have your cake and eat it too; if Mimi is a legitimate lead to the Ripper, then Greene can't be the Ripper—as you damn well would like to have him be.

He sighed.

Then he sat down on the bed and started the job he'd come home to do—reading up on the third murder, the Dorothy Lee one. He felt that he knew Stella Gaylord and Lola Brent pretty well by now.

He picked up the *Blade* of August 1st.

That story, of course, he didn't have to look for; it was the third Ripper job, and it splashed page one banners the day it broke, in the biggest type size the *Blade* used short of a declaration of war or an armistice.

RIPPER SLAYS ANOTHER WOMAN

There was a three-column picture of Dorothy Lee, and Sweeney studied it. She was blonde—like Lola, like Stella, like Yolanda—and definitely pretty, if not beautiful. It was a good portrait photograph and—if it was taken recently—she was probably in her early twenties. Details were not too clear, as though it had been blown up from a small picture or—more likely, since it was a portrait—they'd had to make the halftone from a toned sepia print instead of a glossy. At any rate Dorothy Lee had been at least attractive; she might have been beautiful.

The story said she was beautiful, but the story would have said that in any case, provided only that she was under forty and didn't have buck teeth or crossed eyes.

The story said that she was Dorothy Lee, 25, beautiful blonde private secretary of J. P. Andrews, sales manager of the Reiss Corporation at an address on Division Street that Sweeney recognized as being near Dearborn. Her home address, he noticed with surprise, was on East Erie Street, only a block from his own. Only a block from where he sat right now reading about it. Good Lord, he thought, why hadn't Bline mentioned that? Of course—Bline thought he already knew it, since he was working on the case.

And maybe that was another reason why Bline had suspected him.

Before reading on, he pictured mentally a map of Chicago and mentally marked the scene of the four forays of the Ripper. Three had been quite near, on the Near North Side. One, the attempt on Yolanda, five blocks away, another, the murder of the B-girl in the mouth of the alley off Huron between State and Dearborn, had been about four blocks; Dorothy Lee's murder, one block.

True, the very first murder, that of Lola Brent, had been on the South Side, miles away, but it had probably started on the Near North Side—when the killer had trailed her home from the gift shop on Division Street, only a dozen blocks north. As he might possibly have trailed Dorothy Lee home from the Reiss Corporation on that same street.

He fixed those imaginary x's on the imaginary map in the mind and then went back to the newspaper.

The body had been found a few minutes after five o'clock by Mrs. Rae Haley, divorcée, who lived in the apartment next to Miss Lee's. Returning home after an afternoon at the movies, Mrs. Haley noticed what seemed to be a stream of blood—and which, it later turned out, really was blood—coming from under the doorway of Dorothy Lee's apartment.

Of course it might have been that Dorothy—with whom Mrs. Haley was acquainted—had dropped and broken a jar of tomato juice or a bottle of ketchup. Nevertheless, this was the third Ripper case, and Mrs. Haley, along with most of the rest of Chicago, was Ripper-conscious. She had *not* knocked on Dorothy's door, perhaps to have it opened by someone she had no desire to meet. She had dashed into her own apartment and locked and chained the door; then she had phoned down to the janitor, telling him what she had seen.

David Sheeler, the janitor, had put an old service revolver in his pocket and climbed from the basement to the third floor—which contained five small apartments, including those of Miss Lee and Mrs. Haley. With the gun ready in his hand he had tried the doorbell first and then the door, which was locked. He then bent down to examine the little red rivulet and decided that it was quite probably blood; David Wheeler had once been a hospital orderly and knew what blood looked like.

He had rung the bell of Mrs. Haley's apartment and, when she opened it on the chain, told her that the police had better be sent for. Mrs. Haley had phoned them herself, being too frightened by that time to open her door wider than the length of the chain, even to admit Wheeler. Wheeler had stood guard in the hallway until the police arrived. They had broken down the door of the apartment and had found Dorothy Lee on the floor about three feet back from the locked door.

They had found that the chain of the door had not been fastened and that the lock was a snap type which would have locked automatically after the killer when he had closed the door after him. There seemed little reason to doubt that he had left by the door. Both of the windows of Dorothy Lee's apartment were open, but neither led to a fire escape and there was no way, short of dropping twenty feet to a concrete areaway, that he could have left by a window.

The police believed, from the position of the body, that the killer had barely entered the apartment. Miss Lee still wore her hat (it had been a hot day and she had worn no coat) and had obviously just returned to her room. Police believed the killer had followed her home and had rung the doorbell almost as soon as Miss Lee had closed the door.

When she had opened the door, he had stepped through and used his knife. Perhaps she had not had time to scream; if she had, no one had heard her. Police were still canvassing tenants of the building to see which, if any, had been in their apartments at the time.

Having made the fatal cut, police reasoned, the Ripper had immediately backed out of the door, closing it and letting it lock after him. Aside from the body, there was no sign of his presence in the apartment, which was neat and in perfect order. Miss Lee's purse was on a small table near the door; it contained about fourteen dollars in bills and change. Neither her wrist watch nor an opal ring had been taken from the body.

She had left work at two forty-five, complaining of a toothache, the office manager had suggested that she visit a dentist and take the rest of the afternoon off. Her movements from that time on, until her death, had not yet been traced, but police were canvassing dentists on the New North Side and in the Loop to ascertain which one she had seen and when. The coroner's physician who had examined the body found evidence that she had really visited a dentist; there was a temporary packing in a tooth that appeared to be abscessed.

If the temporary packing hadn't stopped her toothache, the

Ripper had. According to the physician who had examined the body at five-thirty she had at that time been dead between one and two hours—between half-past three and half-past four. She had, then, probably been dead at least a half hour when Mrs. Haley at five o'clock had seen the blood which led to the discovery of the crime.

The story ended with statements by the Chief of Police and by Captain Bline, in charge of the special detail attempting to find the Ripper.

Sweeney took up the next paper and looked for further details.

The dentist had been found, a Dr. Krimmer, who had his office on Dearborn Street, a little over three blocks south of Division Street. Recognizing her picture in the *Blade*, he had come forward before the police canvass reached him.

Dorothy Lee had come to him at about three o'clock, suffering from a toothache. She had no appointment and was a new patient, but because she was obviously in distress, he had taken her out of turn, as soon as he finished work on the patient then in his chair. That would have been, he estimated, about ten minutes after three.

She had been in his chair only ten or fifteen minutes; he had been able to give her only a temporary treatment to relieve the pain. He had suggested an appointment for further work the next morning. She had asked if he could take her in the afternoon instead, explaining that she worked Saturday morning but was off in the afternoon and, with an afternoon appointment, she would not have to lose more time from work.

He had given her an appointment at four o'clock, his first free time after noon, but told her that if the tooth became seriously painful earlier in the day she should come to him then and he would manage to take her out of turn to relieve the pain.

He had no record of the exact time she had left his office, but he thought it would hardly have been earlier than twenty minutes after three nor later than half-past.

Sweeney thought that through and saw that it did not change the situation concerning the time of the crime. She could have reached home as early as three-thirty if she had taken a taxi. Sweeney looked at his mental map again and estimated distances. If she had walked over to State from Dearborn and taken a State Street car south to Erie, then walked from State and Erie, she would have reached home about a quarter of four. Had she walked all the way—a total distance of about a dozen blocks—she would have reached home by four o'clock or a few minutes sooner. Assuming, of course, that she had not stopped over anywhere en route.

He skimmed through the few succeeding issues of the paper and found no new developments of importance.

He went back to the first one and studied the picture of Dorothy

Lee again. It looked vaguely familiar—which wasn't strange if she lived only a block away. Damn it, he'd probably passed her on the street half a dozen times. He looked at the picture again and wished that he had known her. Of course, if he had known her, he'd have found her just another uninteresting stenographer, stupid, vain and self-centred, who preferred Berlin to Bach and *Romantic Confessions* to Aldous Huxley. But now violent death had transfigured her and those things didn't seem to matter. Maybe, really, they didn't matter.

He jerked his mind back from the edge of maudlinness to the problem at hand.

The Ripper.

Bline had been right, then, about Doc Greene's alibi, it wasn't perfect, but it was good. If his alibi covered him—with the word of attorneys and a judge—until ten minutes after four, miles away, he *could* have taxied to the Near North Side in time to pick up the trail of Dorothy Lee if, and only if, she had stopped over somewhere between the dentist's office and her home. But it didn't seem likely. To rush from court—

Damn Greene, he thought. If only he could positively eliminate Greene, maybe he could get some constructive thoughts in other directions.

He got up and began to pace back and forth, trying to think.

He glanced at this watch and saw that it wasn't yet quite midnight and the evening was a pup.

Maybe he could eliminate Greene, tonight. Maybe—better, if possible—he could implicate him, tonight.

A spot of burglary, suitably chaperoned, might accomplish either.

He grabbed for his suit coat and Panama.

CHAPTER TWELVE

He locked the door on Mimi, leaving her alone and screaming in the dark. He stopped at the phone in the hallway and dialled the number of an inexpensive hotel on downtown Clark Street. He gave a room number; it was rung, and an annoyed voice answered.

Sweeney said, "Ehlers? This is Sweeney."

"The hell, Bill; I was just going to turn in. Tired. But since when you call me Ehlers instead of Jay?"

"Since last night."

"Huh?"

Sweeney said, very distinctively, "Since yesterday evening when you entered my room without a warrant."

"Huh? Listen, Sweeney, it was orders. And what was Bline's idea in telling you it was me?"

"Bline didn't tell me. And it wasn't orders."

Ehlers said, "Oh—hell. All right, what you want me to do, get down on my knees and say I'm sorry?"

"No," Sweeney said, "Something harder than that—and more practical. Keep you clothes on till I get there. In about ten minutes; I'll take a cab."

He put the receiver back on the hook. Fifteen minutes later he knocked on the door of Jay Ehlers' room.

Ehlers opened it and said, "Come in, Sweeney." He looked faintly embarrassed and faintly belligerent. His coat and tie were off, but he hadn't undressed any farther than that.

Sweeney sat down on the bed, lighted a cigarette, and looked at Ehlers.

He said, "So you thought I might be the Ripper."

"That wasn't *my* idea, Sweeney. It was the captain's."

"Sure, and it was all right for him. Bline didn't know me: he hadn't been a friend of mine for ten years or more. And he sent you and your pal around to bring *me* in—and any cutlery you found around. I wasn't home and it was your bright idea to show how smart you are with locks and burgle my room. You didn't follow orders, you exceeded them. And how many drinks have we had together in ten or twelve years, how many games of cards, how much money have we borrowed from one another—And how about the time I—Hell, I won't remind you of that."

Ehler's face was reddening. He said, "I remember the time you saved my job; you don't have to remind me. All right, so I should have thought twice. But is this leading to something or did you just come up here to get a bawling-out off your chest?"

"It's leading to something. I'm going to give you a chance to wash it out. I'm going to let you open a door for me, a door to a man's office."

"You crazy, Sweeney? Whose?"

"Doc Greene's."

"Can't do it, Sweeney. You're crazy."

"Were you crazy when you opened the door of my place? You did that on your own hook, without a warrant and without orders."

"That's different, Sweeney. At least I had orders to exceed. I was told to get your razor and any knives you had, for the lab. What are you looking for in Greene's office?"

"The same thing. Only I won't bother them unless they're blood-stained, and if we get anything on him you can have the credit."

"You don't think Greene really *is* the Ripper, do you?"

"I hope to find out, one way or the other."

"What if we get caught?"

"Then we get caught. We try to talk our way out of it."

Ehlers stared at Sweeney and then shook his head. He said. "I can't, Sweeney. I'd lose my job no matter how much talking we did. And I got a chance to put in for lieutenant within a few months."

"To put in for it, but not to make it."

"What do you mean?"

Sweeney said, "It means we're not friends any more, Ehlers. It means you start off on the *Blade*'s s.o.b. list, and go on from there. It means I'm going to spread the good word about you to every reporter I know. It means you wouldn't get your name in ink if you stopped a bank robbery single-handed but we'll drown you in ink if you spit on the sidewalk. It means this is your chance to make up for the dirty trick you pulled on me and if you don't take it, by God, I'll pull every string I can get hold of—in the department itself as well as in print—to break you."

"Yeah? Goddam it, you can't—"

"I can try. I start off tomorrow morning by bringing suit against the police department for entering my room without a warrant, through a locked door, and for petty larceny.'

Ehlers tried to laugh. "You couldn't make it stick."

"Of course I couldn't. But don't you think the commissioners would start their own little investigation to see what it was really all about? They'd jump on Bline and Bline would tell them the truth. And they'd back you to save the department from paying damages, and let you lie out of it, and no, I couldn't prove my point and collect. But you'd sure rate highly with the commissioners after that. Lieutenancy hell; you'll be back in harness, pounding pavement so far out there wouldn't be any pavement."

"You wouldn't do that, Sweeney."

Sweeney said. "I thought you wouldn't burgle my room, and I was wrong. You think I wouldn't do that, and you're wrong."

"Where is Greene's office?" Ehlers was perspiring slightly; it may have been the heat.

"Goodman Block, not far from here. A few blocks, in fact. And I know the building and there won't be any trouble or any danger. I won't take over fifteen minutes inside."

He saw he'd won his point, and grinned. He said, "And I'll buy you a drink first. Dutch courage, if you're more afraid of Greene than you were of me."

"That was different, Sweeney."

"Sure it was different: I was a friend of yours. Greene isn't. Come on."

They caught a cab on Clark Street after Ehlers had turned down the Dutch courage in favour of a drink afterwards, and that was okay by Sweeney. They took the taxi only to within half a block.

The Goodman Block was an old ten-storey office building, tenanted mostly by not-too-prosperous lawyers, agents, brokers and (Sweeney happened to know) headquarters of several bookies and at least one small numbers ring.

Sweeney had figured it would be the type of building that would be open twenty-four hours a day for those of its tenants who wanted to burn midnight oil, and saw that he was right. He and Ehlers walked past on the opposite side of the street and saw that lights still burned in several of the offices. And, through the entrance, they could see that an elevator man was on duty, reading a newspaper while he sat on a chair beside the open elevator door.

They kept on walking and Ehlers asked, "Going to take a chance on having him take us up? We can give him a song-and-dance, but even so, he'll remember us."

They crossed over. Sweeney said, "We'll try not to use him. We'll wait—a little while, anyway—outside the entrance and out of his sight, we'll be able to hear the bell ring and the elevator start if he gets a call from upstairs, and we can get through the lobby without his seeing us."

Ehlers nodded agreement, and they waited quietly outside until, luckily only ten minutes later, they heard the buzzer of the elevator and the clang of its door closing.

Sweeney picked Greene's room number 411, off the building directory as they went through the outer hall; they were on the stairway between the second and third floors when the elevator passed on its way down from whatever upper floor it had serviced.

They tiptoed quietly the rest of the way to the fourth floor and found 411. Fortunately no other office on that floor seemed to be occupied; Ehlers did not have to use particular caution in applying his picklocks. He got the door open in seven minutes.

Inside, they turned on the lights and closed the door. It was a little cubbyhole of an office. One desk, one cabinet, one file, one table, three chairs.

Sweeney shoved his hat back on his head as he looked around. He said, "This won't take long, Jay. Sit down and relax; you've done your share, unless I run across a locked drawer; there isn't any lock on that file."

The bottom drawer of the three-drawer file contained a pair of overshoes, a half-full bottle of whisky and two dusty glasses. The middle drawer was empty.

The top drawer contained correspondence—all incoming correspondence; apparently Greene didn't make carbons of his own letters. It disgusted Sweeney to find that the correspondence was filed only in approximately chronological order; that there was no separate section or folder for Yolanda; he'd hoped for some clue to what he thought was Doc's rather unusual way of handling her. But he didn't want to spend too much time on the file and glanced only at sample letters pulled out at random and put back when he'd looked at them. All he learned was that Greene really did business as a booking agent and did have other clients and get bookings for them. Not, as far as he could tell, on any big-time circuits or top clubs.

He left the file and tried the cabinet. Stationery supplies on the shelf, an old raincoat hanging on one of the hooks, and a portable typewriter case standing on the bottom. He looked in the raincoat's pockets and found nothing but a dirty handkerchief and a pair of month-old theatre stubs. He opened the portable typewriter case to make sure that it contained a typewriter, and it did.

It looked pretty much like the one he himself had owned—up to the point on his recent bender when he'd taken it out to sell. It was the same make and model but when he looked at it closely he saw it wasn't the same typewriter, which would have been a fascinating discovery.

The drawer of the table contained nothing more fascinating than an old hectograph, two of the three chairs were empty and the third chair contained only Jay Ehlers, who was staring at him with a saturnine expression.

Jay asked, "Well, find anything?"

Sweeney grunted an answerless answer and turned to the desk. On top of it was a blotter pad, a pen set and a telephone. He looked under the blotter pad; there was nothing there. He tried the drawers. Only the left-hand top one was locked. He said, "Hey, pal. Your department."

That was the drawer that interested him. He went through the others hastily while Jay opened the locked one. There wasn't anything in any of the other drawers of particular interest to Sweeney, except, possibly, one full bottle of whisky. And right now he wasn't interested in that.

Jay opened the drawer and glanced at his watch. He said, "Snap it up, Bill. You said fifteen minutes and we've been here twenty-three already."

Inside the locked drawer was a ledger and a thick brown envelope marked: "Current Contracts."

Sweeney looked at the ledger first, but it turned out to be a journal rather than a ledger, not indexed, and listing receipts and expenditures in chronological order. He thumbed through it rapidly but saw that he wasn't going to get anything from it—aside from the fact, which he didn't doubt anyway, that Greene had a legitimate business as a booking agent. Probably the figures wouldn't be too straight anyway, but were kept for income tax purposes.

He took up and opened the envelope marked "Current Contracts."

There were a dozen of them there, but only one interested Sweeney, that was the contract between El Madhouse, Nick Helmos signing, and Yolanda Lang. The contract called for two hundred dollars a week for the joint services of Yolanda Lang and Devil. But neither Yolanda nor the dog had signed it; the signature was Richard M. Greene.

Sweeney upped an eyebrow. He asked, "Can't she write?"

"Can't who write?"

Sweeney said, "I can understand why the dog didn't sign it."

"Look, I thought you were looking for a razor or a shiv."

Sweeney sighed. What he'd really been looking for most was a small black statuette. But if Doc had that, it was at his flat or hotel or wherever he lived, not at his office. And—even if he could find out, at this late hour, where Doc lived—he couldn't crowd his luck by burglarizing it tonight.

And, anyway, why couldn't he get Doc Greene off his mind so he could concentrate on other angles? A trip to Brampton, Wisconsin, for instance, to talk to the sculptor—what was his name? Chapman Wilson—who had made Mimi. There was a chance, an off chance, that might lead somewhere. He didn't see where or how. And maybe, getting back to Greene, damn him, a trip to New York to see whether Greene's alibi—his only solid one—was really one hundred per cent solid. The police there might or might not have dug under the surface face that he was registered at a hotel. Sweeney doubted that they had.

Or, if he had a lot of money, he might save himself that trip by having a New York private detective to do the job for him. But that would have to be on Sweeney; the *Blade* would never cover it.

Damn money! He still had a hundred dollars or so out of the cheques Wally Krieg had given him, but at the rate it was vanishing, he'd barely get by for the ten days before another cheque would be coming from the *Blade*, let alone spending any money on the Ripper or on Yolanda.

He heard Jay Ehlers move, restlessly, and looked back at the contract in his hand. He said. "Just a minute, Jay."

He read the contract through and frowned. He read one paragraph again to make sure it really said what he thought it said, and it did. He put the contract back in the envelope with the others, got the envelope in the drawer, and told Jay to relock it.

Jay said, "Well, find what you were looking for?"

"No. Yes. I don't know what I was looking for, but I found something."

"What?"

"I'm damned if I know," Sweeney said. But he thought he did; he'd found some money if he was willing to take a chance.

Jay grunted as the lock clicked. He said, "Come on, then. Let's clear out of here. We'll argue about it over a drink."

Sweeney turned out the lights and waited in the hallway while Jay relocked the door of Room 411.

They walked very quietly down to the second floor and there Sweeney put his finger to his lips and then pressed the button on the elevator signal. As soon as they heard the door clang shut a floor below them, they started down the stairs and were on the first floor by the time the operator opened the door on the second. They were out of the building and two doors away by the time the elevator got back down to the first floor.

Ehlers said, "He'll know somebody pulled a fast one to get out of the building without being seen."

Sweeney said, "Sure he will, but he didn't see us. And he won't chase us.'

He didn't.

They waited until they were out of sight around the corner before they flagged a cab. Sweeney asked Jay where he wanted the drink and Jay suggested Burt Meaghan's; it was only two blocks from his hotel and he could walk back from there.

In Burt's place, Sweeney started toward the bar but Ehlers took Sweeney's arm and pulled him toward a table instead. He said, "We got a minute's talking, Bill, in private."

At the table he glowered at Sweeney until their drinks had come and the water had gone. Then he said. "Okay, Bill. I burgled your room and I shouldn't have. But I burgled another place for you to make up, so we're even. Right?"

"Right."

"We're friends?"

"Friends. All is forgiven."

Jay said, "All right, then, we start from there. We're friends now, but we're not going to keep on being friends if you hold out on me. I want the pitch; I want to know why you wanted into Greene's office and what you got there, and didn't get. I'm a cop, Sweeney, and I'm working on the Ripper case. Just as a flunky under Bline, sure, but I'm still working on it. I want to know what the score is. I can't *make* you tell me, because you got me by the short hairs. I can't tell Bline or anyone else you were in Greene's office because I'd lose my job for my part in it. You're safe as hell, but by God, I write *you* off *my* books if you don't tell me."

Sweeney nodded. "Fair enough, Jay. So okay, I've had a strong suspicion that Greene is the Ripper. No reason for it at all; just a dumb hunch, because I hate the guy so much. Well, a little more than that: I think he fits the role. Psychiatrist or not, I think he's psychopathic. A couple of hours ago at El Madhouse, I got through his guard and he threatened to kill me. Out loud in front of the police. To be specific, in front of Cap Bline. And another copper—hell, two coppers, guys named Ross and Swann, sitting right at the table. I got his goat on purpose to try him out."

"The hell. But what's that got to do with his office?"

Sweeney said. "I hoped I could find something there that would help me make up my mind, pro or con, about Greene. But—word of honour, Jay, I didn't. I didn't find a damn thing to indicate Greene might be the Ripper. I didn't find a damn thing to indicate he isn't, except the proof that he really is what he says he is, an agent and manager for night club talent."

"Keep on. What did you find?"

"Something that interested me personally, Jay. I found the contract for Yolanda and Devil versus El Madhouse. And there's something in it, I think I can use. But illegally; you wouldn't want to know about it."

"Illegally how?"

"To pick up a piece of change that I need."

"Who from?"

"The guy who owns El Madhouse."

"You mean Nick Helmos or Harry Yahn?"

"Yahn, Nick's just a figurehead."

Jay Ehlers pursed his lips and stared into his glass for a moment. He said, "Careful, Bill. Harry Yahn's a tough mug."

"I know it. But I'm going to bite him. I'm going to make the bite small enough that it won't pay him to use his torpedoes on me. He's tough, but he's smart. He won't take a chance for peanuts."

"Me, I'd rather buck the Ripper, Bill."

Sweeney grinned. "Me, too. But I'm going to buck Yahn for the dough to buck the Ripper with."

"You're crazy, Bill."

"I know it. Another drink?"

Ehlers said he'd better turn in, and left. Sweeney wandered over to the pinochle game and watched the play for a few minutes, then went to the bar for one more drink.

The few he'd had at El Madhouse had worn off completely and the one he'd had just now wasn't enough to feel. One more drink, even two, wouldn't hurt him.

He had two, and they didn't hurt him.

CHAPTER THIRTEEN

THE two drinks didn't hurt him, but they didn't do him any good, either. He was cold sober when he went out of Meaghan's Bar into the night. The lonely, teeming night. The warm, chilling night. The bright, dark night.

He was afraid, and it annoyed him that he should be afraid. He didn't mind being afraid of the Ripper; that was the Unknown, the Mysterious. But he didn't like being afraid of Harry Yahn. Harry Yahn was a mug. There wasn't anything mysterious about Harry Yahn; and the things that were unknown about him were strongly suspected by the police, whether they could be proved or not.

Harry Yahn was a plenty tough mug, but still just a mug. Sweeney told himself that and told himself that he wasn't afraid, because the bite he was going to put on Yahn wasn't big enough to bother a man with an income like Yahn's.

The funny thing was that he'd had Yahn in mind as a possible source of revenue even before the trip to Greene's office tonight; there were some things that Sweeney knew about some things that Yahn had done, several years ago, that would have been worth money—to anyone desperate enough to try to collect it. But this new angle was better, and safer—a little safer, but a lot better.

It wasn't blackmail, exactly.

The neon sign said redly. "Tit-Tat-Toe Club." Sweeney took a deep breath and went in. It was an ordinary bar, only moderately swank, and not as large as Meaghan's place. It was populated at the moment by one bartender and half a dozen customers. It looked like the type of bar that might be a front for something else. It was.

Sweeney went to the bar and decorated it with a bill. The bartender lumbered over and Sweeney said. "Shot. Water chaser." And then before the bartender could turn away, "Is Harry here?"

"Harry who?"

"The name is Sweeney. Bill Sweeney. He knows me."

The bartender turned to the backbar for glass and bottle. As he poured the shot he said. "Knock on the back door there, around the corner from the john. If Willie knows you, you get in."

"Willie doesn't. But Harry does."

"Tell that to Willie. He can talk; he can ask Harry. If Harry's here."

"Okay," Sweeney said. "Have one with me."

"Sure."

"And wish me luck."

"Sure," said the bartender. "Luck."

"Thanks."

"For what?"

Sweeney laughed, and felt better. He went back around the corner from the john and knocked on a heavy door. It opened a few inches and a face looked out, the eyes—and they weren't nice eyes—well above the level of Sweeney's head.

Under the eyes was a broken nose, and under the nose was a pair of thick lips that said "Yeah?" and showed broken teeth between them.

Sweeney said, "Willie Harris. I didn't know the Willie on the door was Willie Harris."

"Yeah. What you want?"

"The hell, Willie. Don't you remember me? I covered three of your fights when I was doing Sports. Bill Sweeney. I was on the *Trib* then."

The door opened wider, eight inches instead of six. Willie said, "Yeah?"

Punchy, Sweeney thought. He said, "Okay, you don't remember all the reporters ever talked to you. Listen, Willie. I want to talk to Harry Yahn. On business. Not the games. He knew me. Tell him Bill Sweeney wants to talk to him. Bill Sweeney."

Short sentences like that, Willie would get. He said, "Sweeney. I'll see."

"Bill Sweeney. Hang on to it, Willie. Bill Sweeney."

The door closed.

Sweeney leaned against the wall and lighted a cigarette. When an inch was gone from the length of the cigarette, the door opened again, wider.

Willie looked out to be sure nobody but Sweeney was there and said. "Okay, He'll talk to yah."

He led Sweeney along a short stretch of hallway and pointed to a door. "In there. Go ahead."

Sweeney went in. He said, "Hello, Harry," and Yahn said, "Hi, Sweeney. Sit down."

Harry Yahn, seated at a battered desk that looked as though it had been bought second hand for about ten dollars, looked like Santa Claus without his whiskers. He was fat and smiling, he looked both complacent and complaisant. Sweeney wasn't fooled. But he was glad, at least, that they were alone.

"Haven't seen you for a long time, Sweeney. Still on the *Blade*?"

Sweeney nodded. "Read that story about Yolanda?"

"Which one?"

"The eyewitness one, the scene in the hallway. In the *Blade*."

"The hell, did you write that? I skimmed it, but I didn't happen to notice the by-line."

Sweeney didn't call him a liar. He merely said, "Yeah, I wrote it. And a damn fine job, if I say so myself—and why shouldn't I, since everybody else does?"

"Y'know, Sweeney, that story hasn't hurt business at El Madhouse a bit. Where you staying? I'm going to tell the boys to send a case of whisky over for you."

"Thanks," Sweeney said, "but I'm on the wagon. Almost. And I've got a better idea, Harry. How about letting me handle the publicity for you for the next four weeks—while Yolanda's playing there?"

Yahn pursed his lips and stared at Sweeney. He said, "That would have been a better idea before all this happened. We don't need it now, El Madhouse is turning them away, Nick tells me, and what'd we do with more suckers? Hang 'em from the rafters? And we've got Yolanda under contract for only four more weeks, like you say, and it'll hold up that long."

He laughed. "You gave it away, Sweeney. Sure, I'd have paid you to get that story you wrote into print, but it *was* in print; it's a dead horse now. And look—there was plenty publicity outside of that. Just getting jumped by the Ripper, that's enough to pull them into see Yolanda. Your eyewitness story just tied it up in cellophane. Nope, Sweeney, we got all the publicity we can make use of."

Sweeney shrugged. He said, "It was just an idea. I'll work on it from the other end, then."

"The other end?"

"Doc's end. A little more publicity—and I think I could swing it—and he could book Yolanda for real money in any one of several places with twenty times the take of El Madhouse. He could get two, maybe three thousand a week instead of two hundred. Or instead of four hundred and fifty if you prorate over four weeks the thousand buck bonus she's getting for going back to work right away."

Harry Yahn's eyes were half closed, as though he was bored. He said, "It's an idea. If she can keep the publicity hot for four weeks more, she might still pull down that kind of money, or almost that kind."

Sweeney said, "She's worth it right now. I caught your first show at El Madhouse tonight, Harry, and did a little figuring. You ought to have capacity crowds for four weeks. Capacity's two hundred each show, three shows, six hundred a night. Let's be conservative as hell and say each mooch pays five bucks and that one buck out of that is clear profit. Six hundred bucks a night profit for a week is four thousand two hundred: times four weeks, sixteen thousand, eight hundred dollars."

Yahn said dryly, "We did some business before we had Yolanda."

"Sure, about half as much as you'll be doing for the next four weeks. And with half as much, the overhead is higher. Let's say having Yolanda for the next four weeks will bring in about ten thousand dollars profit that you wouldn't have otherwise. Fair enough?"

"Too high. But what are you leading up to?"

"All right, it's too high. Let's say it's worth seven thousand dollars. Is seven thousand conservative enough?"

Yahn's eyes were almost closed and he was smiling faintly; he looked now more like a sleeping Buddha than like Santa Claus. Sweeney wasn't fooled: Harry Yahn was neither sleeping nor contemplating nirvana. Not when money, in the thousands, was the subject of conversation.

Yahn said, "I hope you're leading somewhere."

Sweeney stalled deliberately by taking out a cigarette and lighting it. Then he said, "If I do publicity for Greene and Yolanda instead of the El Madhouse, I would advise my friend Doc to book Yolanda elsewhere right away instead of waiting four weeks. But that would cost you seven thousand dollars, Harry, and I wouldn't like to do that, because I've always considered you a friend of mine."

"Yolanda is under contract for four more weeks."

Sweeney smiled. He asked. "Have you read the contract?"

Yahn's eyes opened fully halfway and he looked at Sweeney.

He asked. "Are you representing Greene on this? Did he send you to shake me down?"

"No. And nobody is trying to shake you down, Harry."

Harry Yahn said a nasty word. He said, "It doesn't wash, Sweeney. If there was a hole in that contract that would let Greene book Yolanda elsewhere, he'd be in there pitching. For himself. Why would he tell you about it?"

Sweeney leaned back comfortably in his chair. He said, "He didn't tell me about it. He doesn't know about it, yet. He and I had a little bet about how much Yolanda and Devil were getting at El Madhouse and he showed me his copy of the contract—with Nick's signature—to win his bet. And he won the bet. But while I had the contract in my hand I happened to read it. Have you?"

"What's the gimmick?"

"Sweet and simple. It must have been an El Madhouse contract, a standard one you give your talent there, because it's full of escape clauses for the party of the first part, which is El Madhouse. But there's also an escape clause for the party of the second part, only it's one that wouldn't be worth a damn in any ordinary case. But this isn't an ordinary case."

"And what is the clause?"

"One that wouldn't be worth the paper it's written on to anybody else, Harry. It provides that the contract may be cancelled by the party of the second part by payment of the face amount of the contract—by refunding all moneys received under the contract and paying an amount equal to the balance still to be received under the contract.

"Yolanda's contract is for seven weeks, three down and four to go, at two hundred a week. Doc could buy her out of that for seven times two hundred—fourteen hundred dollars. And if he could book her elsewhere for two thousand a week for the next four weeks, he and Yolanda would be ahead six and a half thousand dollars. Maybe more, I think right now he could get more than two grand a week from her current publicity, even if I don't add to it."

Sweeney leaned forward and stubbed out his cigarette in the ash tray on Yahn's desk, he said. "The only bad thing about it is that Greene's gain would be your loss."

"Greene doesn't know that's in the contract?"

"Obviously not. He probably read the contract when it was signed, but a clause like that wouldn't have meant anything then. Only in case a performer's value suddenly increases ten times overnight would a clause like that really be an escape clause. And the odds are a thousand to one against his happening to read the contract. He thinks he knows what's in it."

Sweeney stood up. He said, "Well, so long, Harry. Sorry we couldn't see eye to eye on my doing a little publicity for your club."

"Sit down, Sweeney."

Yahn jabbed a button on his desk and it seemed he had hardly lifted his finger off it before Willie Harris was in the doorway. He said, "Yeah, Boss?"

"Come in and close the door, Willie. And just stick around."

"Want me to take this guy apart for you?"

Yahn said, "Not yet. Willie. Not if he sits down."

Sweeney sat down. Willie stood, ready. If you looked at Willie's face you might have got the idea that Willie hadn't taken anybody apart for a long time and had been missing it badly. Anyway, that's the idea Sweeney got. He quit looking at Willie's face, and got out another cigarette and lighted it, moving very slowly and carefully so as not to startle Willie. He wished that he felt as casual as he hoped he was acting.

Yahn picked up the phone on his desk and dialled a number. He asked for Nick. He said, "Harry, Nick. You got the contract from Yolanda Lang in the safe there. Get it out and put it in your pocket and then call me back. Right away, and privately. Use that phone in the back office and be sure nobody's in hearing distance, see? And don't let anybody notice what you're taking out of the safe. . . . Okay."

He put the phone back on the hook and looked at Sweeney. Sweeney didn't say anything. Nobody said anything. In three minutes the phone rang.

Sweeney said, "Tell him the sixth paragraph, Harry. That'll save time."

Yahn talked briefly and then listened. He said, "Okay, Nick. Put it back. And don't mention this . . . Yeah, that's why I had you read it to me. We'll talk it over tomorrow. How's business?" He listened a moment and then said, "Okay," and hung up.

Sweeney asked. "How *is* business?"

Yahn didn't look at him for a moment. Then he did look at him. He said, "Well, what do you want?"

Sweeney said, "I figure handling publicity for you for the month in question ought to be worth nine hundred bucks."

Harry Yahn didn't look like either Santa Clause or Buddha. He asked, "And if Greene finds out anyway? Happens to reread that contract?"

Sweeney shrugged. "It could happen. There won't be any reason why he would."

Harry Yahn laced his fingers over his stomach and stared a moment at his knuckles. Without looking up, he said, "Willie, go tell Haywood to give you nine hundred. Bring it here." Willie went.

Harry Yahn asked. "How come nine hundred? How'd you hit on that odd amount?"

Sweeney grinned. Inside, the grin was a little shaky and he hoped the outside of it looked better. He said, "I figure you for a four-figure man. Harry. I cut just under. If I'd asked for a thousand—I might have got something else."

Harry laughed, he looked like Santa Claus again. He said, "You're a smart son of a bitch, Sweeney." He got up and slapped Sweeney on the back. Willie came in with money in his hand. He handed it to Yahn and Yahn handed it to Sweeney without counting it. Sweeney didn't count it either; he put it in his pocket.

Yahn said, "Show him out, Willie. And let him in again any times he comes." Willie opened the door and Sweeney went out to the hall; Willie started after and Yahn called him back for a moment. Then Willie came out and opened the door to the outer hallway.

As Sweeney started through it, Willie's hand, as big as both of Sweeney's put together would have been, grabbed his shoulder and spun him around. Willie's other hand, doubled into a fist the size of a football but harder and heavier, slammed into Sweeney's stomach. Willie let go of his shoulder and Sweeney fell, doubled up. He wasn't out, but he couldn't get his breath and he was sick at his stomach. And the pain was so great that he wished the blow *had* knocked him out, especially if there was more coming.

There wasn't.

Willie stepped back. He said, "Harry said to give you that, too." He added, as though explaining why Sweeney had got by so luckily, "He said just one, and easy." It was very obvious that Willie Harris would have preferred it to be more and harder.

He closed the door.

Within a minute Sweeney was able to get to his feet and, a bit doubled over, make it as far as the john. He was sick and after that he was able to stand almost straight. He bent over the wash bowl and rubbed cold water into his face, which the mirror showed him to be almost as white as the porcelain bowl.

But he was breathing almost regularly by now. His abdomen was almost too sore to touch and, very gingerly, he let his belt out two notches to take pressure off it.

He leaned back against the wall and took the money out of his pocket and counted it. It was nine hundred all right, and it was real. He'd got all he'd asked for, and only one thing more. He'd been lucky, plenty lucky.

He put the money into his wallet and walking as though on eggs, he went out through the bar of the Tit-Tat-Toe Club. He didn't look at the bartender or at anyone else on his way through.

He stood outside breathing the cool night air. Not in deep breaths; that would have been unbearably painful. He didn't look around to see if anyone came out after him; he knew no one would.

He'd been unbelievably lucky. Even that poke in the stomach was a good sign, in a way. Harry wouldn't have told Willie to do that if he'd intended to send some of the boys to work him over seriously, or to shoot him. He hadn't really thought there was much danger of being shot—not for nine hundred dollars. But a working-over had been a real possibility, a working-over that might have put him in the hospital for a week or a month and would have played hell with all his plans. Now he felt reasonably confident that he'd been paid in full, both ways. He was going to be plenty sore for a few days, and he was going to have to sleep on his back—and very gingerly at that. But there wasn't any permanent harm done. Worse things had happened to him—and for less.

A cab came cruising by and he hailed it. He walked to it as an old man walks and it hurt him to pull the door open.

He said, "Drive over to the lake and north along it for a while. I'm a little sick; I can use some fresh air."

He got in. Closing the door jarred him.

The cabby peered back at him. He asked, "How sick, Mac? Not going to mess up my cab, are you?"

"Not sick that way. And I'm sober."

"Want me to take you to a sawbones?"

Sweeney said. "I had a poke in the guts, that's all."

The cabby said, "Oh," and started the cab. He drove east to Michigan Boulevard and north until they were on Lake Shore Drive. Sweeney leaned back in the cab and began to feel better, especially after they were on the Drive and a cool breeze off the lake came in the open windows.

The cab didn't jar him; the gentle motion seemed to help.

He felt pretty good with nine hundred bucks in his pocket and no worse price for it than this. A prizefighter took a hell of a lot worse and, except for the top few, for a hell of a lot less.

He wasn't angry at Willie. Willie was punchy to begin with, and had been carrying out orders—even though he'd enjoyed doing it and would have enjoyed doing more. But too many punches had addled Willie's brains, what few he had ever had.

He didn't blame Harry Yahn either. After all, it *had* been black-mail. Harry had let him off easy.

He saw they were passing Diversey Parkway and said, "Guess that is far enough, you can head back now."

"Okay, Mac. Feeling better?"

"Practically okay."

"Should I have seen the other guy?"

Sweeney said, "Yeah, you should have seen the other guy. He's about six feet three and weighs about two-twenty."

"The hell you say. Must have been Willie Harris. I picked you up in front of the Tit-Tat-Toe."

"Forget I said it," Sweeney told him. "I was kidding you."

"Okay, Mac. Where'll I drop you off?"

"Bughouse Square."

"Bughouse Square at this hour? What the hell you want to do there?"

Sweeney said, "I wish to commune with God."

The cabby didn't answer that. In fact, he didn't say another word until he announced the fare at Sweeney's destination.

CHAPTER FOURTEEN

BUGHOUSE SQUARE stirred restlessly in the warm night as Sweeney walked into it. The benches were lined with human cargo; there were men sleeping on the grass, too. Shut off from the lake breeze by the buildings on Dearborn, the leaves of the trees hung dead still, the blades of grass did not ripple; the stirring was the restless moving of men who slept or tried to sleep because they had nothing else to do.

The fourth bench on the right on the northeast diagonal walk, that's where God would be if he was there. He was there, looking older and more disreputable than when Sweeney had last seen him. But maybe that was partly contrast; Sweeney's own looks and dress were different tonight from what they were when he had last seen Godfrey. Unconsciously, one judges others by comparison with oneself; and two people both of whom have eaten onions cannot smell each other's breath.

But Sweeney didn't try to smell God's breath; he shook God's shoulder, gently and then harder, and God blinked and looked up. He said, "Whattahell?"

Sweeney grinned at him. He said, "Don't you know me?"

"No, I don't know you. Beat it before I call a cop."

"Want a drink, God? Badly enough?"

"Badly enough to what?"

Sweeney said, "To reach in your right-hand coat pocket."

Godfrey's hand reached into his pocket, clutched something, and stayed there. His voice was a little hoarse. He said, "Thanks, Sweeney. Haven't had a drink since afternoon; it'd have been a hell of a morning. What time is it?"

"About half-past three."

God swung his feet off the bench. He said, "Good. How's it coming with you, Sweeney?"

"Good."

God pushed himself up off the bench. Sweeney said, "Look at the figure on the corner of that bill before you hand it over."

God pulled his fist out of his pocket and looked at a corner of the crumpled bill. He glared at Sweeney. He said, "A Goddam capitalist. Showing off."

He thrust his fist back into his pocket and got up off the bench. He walked away without looking back.

Sweeney, grinning, watched him until he'd reached the

street—mostly to be sure that nobody had heard or seen and would follow. No one followed.

Sweeney went the opposite direction and caught a cab on Chicago Avenue. It was almost four o'clock when he got home, and he was tired. But before he went to his room he called the Northwestern Station from the phone in the hall.

Yes, they told him, Brampton, Wisconsin, was on the Northwestern Road; the next train that would take him there left at six o'clock, in a little over two hours. The train after that? None that went through Brampton before evening. What time did the 6.00 a.m. train get in? One-fifteen in the afternoon.

Sweeney said thanks and put the receiver back on the hook.

In his room he looked longingly at his bed, but he knew that if he lay down to try to get an hour's sleep before he started for the train, he'd never be able to get up when the alarm clock went off.

And if he waited until the evening train, he'd be losing a day's time right when it mattered most. This was Saturday already and Monday morning he had to be back at the *Blade* ready for work and—even if Wally came through and assigned him to the Ripper case—Wally would never sanction a trip to Brampton on the paper's time. Let alone sanction a trip to New York to check on Greene's alibi there. Well, unless something came up that would save him from having to do that, he could fly there and back next weekend on his own time. And his own money; that was no longer a worry.

An hour ago, with his own hundred, he'd had a thousand dollars. Now, after tithing with God, he still had nine hundred.

If he had any sense, he realized, he'd do something with part of it; he wouldn't carry that much money with him.

But he didn't have that much sense.

He looked again at the clock and sighed. He looked at Mimi and swore at her for being so important that he was losing sleep to trace down her origin and talk to her creator, little as that was likely to get him.

He went over and turned her around on top of the radio so her back was toward him and he couldn't hear her scream. But, even from the back, every line of her body showed terror.

He felt for her so strongly that, for a moment, he contemplated enthanasia. But even if he did break her there would be a gross minus one of her still screaming somewhere.

Wearily—and very gingerly because of his tender abdomen—he undressed. He bathed, shaved and put on clean clothes, decided he wouldn't have to take anything with him, and left for the station. He would be too early but he wanted to allow time for a couple of drinks. Not *as* drinks, but because with them he ought to be able to sleep on the train; otherwise he'd probably be too tired, after six, to sleep in a coach or chair car. He'd have paid double price for a Pullman but knew he couldn't get one; railroads have the strange idea that people should ride horizontally only at night.

He had to walk to State Street, through the grey still dawn, before he caught a cab. He took it to a place on West Madison within a block of the station which he knew would be open even at the late or early hour of five. He had his two drinks—and a third for the road. He considered, before he remembered that he was on the wagon, buying a bottle to take along on the train; but he remembered in time and didn't buy it. Besides, too much to drink would get him wide awake again.

He got to the station at a quarter to six, hoping that the train would be loading by then, and it was. Luckily there was a chair car on the train and the ticket agent sold him a ticket for it and said that he wouldn't need a reservation, that the chair car wouldn't be crowded.

It wasn't. He picked the most comfortable-looking seat in the car, sat down carefully, and put his ticket in the band of his hat so the conductor wouldn't have to wake him. He sprawled out his legs and put his hat, ticket side up, over the bruised portion of his anatomy. It was a lightweight Panama so it didn't hurt too much.

Or if it did, he didn't know it; he was asleep almost the minute he closed his eyes. He opened them briefly a couple of hours later and found the train pulling out of a station. It was Milwaukee, and it was raining. When he opened his eyes again it was a few minutes after noon, the train was in Rhinelander, and the sun was shining. And he was as hungry as a horse.

He found the diner and ate the biggest meal he'd eaten in weeks. And finished his second cup of coffee just in time to get off at Brampton.

He went into the station and looked in the phone book; no Chapman Wilson was listed. Sweeney frowned and walked over to the ticket window. He asked. "You happen to know where in town Chapman Wilson lives?"

"Chapman Wilson?"

"Yes."

"Never heard of him."

"Thanks."

Sweeney left the station on the side opposite the tracks and took a look at Brampton. About five thousand population, he estimated. In a town that size, it shouldn't be too hard to locate someone, even if they didn't have a phone.

He was already, he found, on the main street; the business district about four blocks long, started immediately to his left. He went into the first store he came to and asked about Chapman

Wilson. He drew a blank. And in the second, the third, and the fourth. Not to mention the fifth and sixth.

The seventh place was a tavern and he ordered a drink before he asked his question. When the drink came, he asked. The drink was good but the answer wasn't.

Sweeney swore to himself as the bartender moved off. Could he have misunderstood the man he'd talked to at the Ganslen Art Company? No, he'd said it clearly enough: "Fellow by the name of Chapman Wilson, lives in Brampton, Wisconsin. He modelled it in clay."

At least he was sure of the Chapman Wilson. Could he have misunderstood the Brampton part?

He motioned the bartender over. He asked. "Is there any other town in Wisconsin that has a name that sounds like Brampton?"

"Huh? Oh, I see what you mean. Let's see. There's Boylston, up near Duluth."

"Not close enough."

"Stoughton? Burlington? Appleton? And there's a Milton, but the full name is Milton Junction."

Sweeney shook his head sadly. He said, "You forgot Wisconsin Rapids and Stevens Point."

"They don't sound like Brampton."

"That's what I mean," Sweeney said. "Have a drink."

"Sure, thanks."

"But you've never heard of a Chapman Wilson?"

"No."

Sweeney took a meditative sip from his glass. He wondered if he could raise anyone by phone at the Ganslen Art Company in Louisville. Probably not, on a Saturday afternoon. He might possibly manage to locate the man he'd talked to there—Burke? Yes, Burke was the name. But it wasn't too good a chance.

Sweeney, the rest of his life, was never proud of it, but it was the bartender who saved the day. He asked, "What's this Chapman Wilson do?"

"Sculptor. Artist and sculptor."

For seconds nothing happened. Then the bartender said, "I'll be damned. You must mean *Charlie* Wilson."

Sweeney stared at him. He said, "Don't stop there, Esmeralda. Go on."

"Go on where?"

"To pour us another drink. And then tell me about Charlie Wilson. Does he model little statuettes?"

The bartender laughed. "That's the guy. Crazy Charlie."

Sweeney gripped the edge of the bar. He said, "What do you mean, Crazy Charlie? Crazy, as in *razor*?"

"Huh? Razor? Oh, you mean what *started* him. It was a knife, not a razor."

"A blonde," said Sweeney. "A beautiful blonde?"

"You mean the dame? Yeah, mister, she was both of those. Purtiest thing in town. Until she got attacked with that knife."

Sweeney closed his eyes and counted up to two slowly. It was too good to be true, and he had been about to leave town and go back to Chicago.

It had to be too good to be true, things didn't happen like this. He said, "You mean *attacked*, as in Ripper?"

"Yeah. Like that Chicago business on the radio."

"You are not referring, by any chance, to a small black statuette? You mean a real woman was attacked up here?"

"Sure. A blonde, like the radio said all the dames in Chicago were."

"When?"

"Three years ago. While I was sheriff."

"While you were sheriff?"

"Yeah. I was sheriff up to two years ago. Bought this place then and couldn't keep up both, so two years ago I didn't run."

"And you handled the Ripper case?"

"Yeah."

Sweeney said. "I am proud to meet you. My name is Bill Sweeney."

The bartender stuck a big paw across the bar. "Glad to know you. My name's Henderson."

Sweeney shook his hand. "Sweeney," he said, "of the Chicago *Blade*. You're just the man I was looking for, Sheriff."

"Ex-Sheriff."

"Look, Sheriff, is there any way we can talk privately for a little while without you having to interrupt yourself?"

"Well—I don't know. Saturday afternoon and all that."

"I'll buy a bottle of the most expensive champagne you got, and we'll split it while we talk."

"Well—I guess I can get the frau to take over for ten or fifteen minutes. We live upstairs. Only let's split a pint of Haig and Haig instead; the champagne I got isn't very good and anyway it'd take time to ice it."

"Haig and Haig it is," Sweeney put a bill on the bar.

Henderson rang up money and gave Sweeney a little back. He took a bottle from the backbar, put it in his hip pocket, and said, "Come on; I'll get Ma."

He led the way to a door at the back that opened to a flight of stairs. He called up them. "Hey, Ma! Can you come down a few minutes?"

A voice called out, "Okay, Jake," and a few seconds later a tall, thin woman came down the stairs. Henderson said, "This is Mr. Sweeney, Ma, from Chicago. We want to talk a while upstairs. Can you take over?"

"All right, Jake. But don't you get started drinking. This is Saturday, with Saturday night coming up."

"Won't touch a drop, Ma."

He led Sweeney up the stairs and into a kitchen. He said, "Guess we can talk best here, and glasses and everything are handy. Want anything to mix it with?"

"Haig and Haig? Don't be silly. Sheriff."

Henderson grinned. "Sit down. I'll get glasses and open this."

He came back with glasses and the opened bottle and poured a generous shot for each of them. Sweeney lifted his, "To crime."

"To crime," Henderson said. "How're things in Chicago?"

"Ripping," Sweeney said. "But let's get to Brampton. First, let's make sure this Chapman Wilson I'm talking about and your Crazy Charlie are one and the same person. Tell me something about him."

"His name is Charlie Wilson. He's an artist and a sculptor; guess what money he makes out of it is mostly from the stuff he models. He sells them to some companies that make statuettes and stuff. Arty little things. Guess he doesn't sell many paintings."

"That's the guy," Sweeney said. "Probably uses Chapman as a professional first name; Chapman Wilson sounds better than Charlie Wilson. But how crazy is he?"

"Not really. When he's sober, he's just—what you call it?—eccentric. He's pretty much of a lush, though, and when he gets tanked up—well, I've had to kick him out of my place half a dozen times. Mostly for trying to pick fights." Henderson grinned. "And he's about five feet two and weighs about a hundred and ten pounds soaking wet. Anybody take a real poke at him, they'd probably kill him, and yet he's always wanting to start a fight when he gets tanked. A real screwball."

"Does he make a good thing out of his work?"

"Hell, no. Doubt if he makes five hundred bucks in a year. He lives in a little shack out at the edge of town that nobody else'd live in; gets it for a few bucks a month. And proud as hell; thinks he's a great artist."

"Maybe he is."

"Then why doesn't he make some money out of it?"

Sweeney opened his mouth to mention Van Gogh and Modigliani and a few others who'd been great artists and had made less than five hundred bucks a year out of it; then he remembered his audience and that time was flying.

He asked, instead, "And Charlie Wilson is now running around loose? In Brampton?"

"Sure. Why not? He's harmless."

"Well, this Ripper business. How does Charlie Wilson tie in with that?"

"He shot him."

"You mean Charlie shot the Ripper or the Ripper shot Charlie?"

"Charlie shot the Ripper."

Sweeney took a deep breath. "But the Ripper got away?"

"Hell, no. Killed him dead as hell. Charlie got him with a shotgun from about two yards away. Blew a hole through him you could stick your head through. Only good thing Charlie ever did in his life. He was kind of a hero around town for a while."

"Oh," said Sweeney. He felt disappointed. A dead ripper wasn't going to be much help to him. He took another sip of the Scotch. "Let's start it from the other end. Who was the Ripper?"

"His name was Pell, Howard Pell. A homicidal maniac who broke out of the county insane asylum—that's about twenty miles from here. Let's see, it was four years ago; I told you wrong when I said three because it was in the first year of my second two-year term and that would've been at least four years ago, maybe a few months more than that even. Yeah, a few months more because it was in spring, I remember, and it's August now. Think it was in May."

"And what happened?"

"Well, this Pell broke out of the asylum. Killed two guards with his bare hands; he was a big guy, built like an ox. Bigger than I am. Outside, the siren hadn't gone off yet and he flagged a car and the damn fool driver stopped to pick him up. Guy named Rogers. Pell got in the car and killed Rogers. Strangled him."

"Didn't he use a knife at all?"

"Didn't have one yet. But he got one all right, then and there. This Rogers was a canvasser selling a line of aluminium kitchen ware. But he had some sidelines and one of them was a carving set. The knife in it was a beauty, ten inches long and an inch wide, sharp as hell. Don't know exactly what he was searching the car for, but he found that. And liked it. He tried it out on Rogers, even though Rogers was already dead. Want the details on that?"

"Not right now." Sweeney said. "But I could use another drink. A short one."

"Sorry." Henderson poured it. "Well, he operated on Rogers and threw his body out of the car into the ditch. Not all at once, y'understand."

Sweeney shuddered slightly and took a quick sip of the Scotch. He said, "I'd just as soon not understand too thoroughly. Go on."

"Well, this was about eight o'clock in the evening, just after dark. Anyway, that's when they found the two guards dead and Pell gone from the asylum. They called me quick—along with sheriffs of other counties around, and local police officers and everybody and meanwhile what guards they could spare fanned outward from the asylum in cars to start the search.

"Well, right off they found what was left of this guy Rogers, and the car tracks showed 'em what'd happened so they knew Pell had a car. They cut back to the asylum and phoned me and everybody that Pell would be in a car and to set up roadblocks and get him.

"We got roadblocks up quick, but he fooled us. He did head toward Brampton all right, but a little outside of town he turned the car into a side road and left it there. And he came in across the fields on foot so he got through us. Even though between us, me and the police chief here in Brampton, we had every road guarded by that time. Within fifteen minutes of the time we got the call from the asylum."

"Fast work," Sweeney said, approvingly.

"Goddam tooting it was fast work, but it didn't do any good, because he got through us on foot. The next day we could trace back exactly the way he went from the car because he had so much blood on him. Y'see he cut up Rogers right in the driver's seat of the car and then had to get there himself to drive the car, and he was kind of covered with blood all over. God, he even had it in his hair and on his face and his shoes were soaked with it. And looking like that, with the bloody knife in his hand, was how he come across Bessie taking a shower."

"Who is Bessie?"

"Who *was* Bessie. Bessie Wilson, Charlie's younger sister. She was about eighteen, then, maybe nineteen. She was staying with him then because she was sick. She didn't live in Brampton, she had a job in St. Louis, hatcheck girl in a night club or something, but she got sick and broke and came back to stay with Charlie; their parents had been dead ten years or so.

"Guess she didn't know, when she came back, how broke he was or she wouldn't've come, but she probably, through the letters he'd written her, thought he was doing pretty good. Anyway she was sick and needed help, and what happened to her here in Brampton didn't help her any, I guess. Maybe it'd been better if she'd been killed right out."

"This Pell attacked her?"

"Well, yeah and no. He didn't actually lay a hand on her, but it drove her nuts and she died later. It was this way. That shack of Charlie's is just one fair-sized room that he uses to live in and work in both and that's where they lived. But there's another little shack, sort of like a tool shed, out in back of it on the lot. The can's in there, and Charlie fixed up a shower in there, too. In one corner, just a makeshift kind of shower.

"Anyway, this would've been about half-past eight, the kid sister,

Bessie, decides to take a shower and goes out of the shack and along the path to the shed, in a bathrobe and slippers, see? And that must've been just about the time Pell is coming to their yard, cutting into town and keeping off the streets and the road, so he sees her go into the shed.

"And with the carving knife in his hand, he goes up and yanks the shed door open."

"Wouldn't there be a catch on it?"

"I told you he was big as an ox; he just yanks it open so hard the hook pulls off. And Bessie is standing there naked under the shower getting ready to reach up and turn it on. And he takes a step inside, toward her, waving the knife. How's about another drink?"

"An inspiration," said Sweeney.

Henderson poured two.

He said, "You can't blame her for going nuts, can you? Sick to begin with, and seeing *that*. Guy over six feet, two-twenty pounds, in a nuthouse uniform that started out being grey but that ended up being red, with blood in his hair and on his face, and coming at her with a ten-inch carving knife. God."

Sweeney could picture it. He'd seen Mimi.

He took a sip of Scotch. He asked, "What happened?"

CHAPTER FIFTEEN

HENDERSON said, "Well, I was two blocks away and I heard her scream and keep on screaming. It was maybe five minutes before I got there—and of course it was all over long before that—but she was still screaming then.

"What happened was that the first scream she let out, Charlie grabbed for his shotgun—he's got one because he does a lot of hunting, not so much for fun like most of us but because he gets some of his eating that way. And he ran out the back door of the shack and saw the guy with the knife in the doorway of the shed and past him he could see Bessie back in the corner under the shower that wasn't turned on yet, screaming her head off.

"So he runs toward the door, it's only about ten feet from the shack to the shed and runs a little to one side so he can shoot Pell without shooting Bessie too, and from right outside the door he lets go with the shotgun and, like I said, puts a hole through Pell that you could stick your head through."

"But *must* I?" Sweeney asked. At the blank look on the ex-sheriff's face, he changed his question. "And Bessie Wilson went crazy?"

"Yeah, and died about six-seven months later. Crazy as a bedbug. No, not in the asylum near here; that's for incurables. And for a while they thought they could cure Bessie. It was in some little private sanatorium downstate near Beloit. There was a lot of publicity on the case and one of the doctors down there got interested. He had a new treatment and thought he could cure Bessie and took her on as a charity case. But it didn't work; she died six-seven months later."

Sweeney asked, "And Charlie? Did he go off the beam then, or was he crazy before that?"

"Like I told you, he isn't really crazy. But he was off the beam before that, and I guess that didn't make him any worse. He's an artist. That's crazy to begin with, isn't it?"

Sweeney said, "I guess it is. Where is this shack of his?"

"On Cuyahoga Street; that's eight blocks west of here, almost at the edge of town in that direction. I dunno the number if there's a number on it, but it's a block and a half north of Main Street—that's the street you're on now—and there are only a few houses in that block and his is the only one-room shack and it's painted green; you can't miss it. Another drink? There's still a couple left in here."

Sweeney said, "Why not?"

There didn't seem to be any reason why not, so Henderson poured them and they killed the bottle.

Sweeney stared moodily into his. This had looked so good, less than half an hour ago. He'd found a Ripper. Only the Ripper was dead, four and a quarter years dead, with a hole in him that Sweeney could stick his head through if he wanted to, only he didn't want to, especially with the Ripper four and a quarter years dead.

Sweeney took a sip of his drink and glared at Henderson as though it was Henderson's fault.

Then he thought of a new angle. It didn't seem likely. He asked. "This Charlie Wilson. He ever out of town?"

"Charlie? Not that I know of. Why?"

"Just wondering if he ever got to Chicago."

"Naw, he couldn't afford train fare to Chicago. And besides he didn't."

"Didn't what?"

"Didn't commit your three Ripper murders. Our new sheriff—Lanny Pedersen—was talking about them the other night downstairs. Naturally, we thought of the coincidence of our having had a Ripper here, even if he was dead, and I asked Lanny what about Charlie, if maybe Charlie could have—uh—sort of got the idea from what he saw, or something, and he said he'd thought of that and that he hadn't thought so or anything but that he'd checked with Charlie's next door neighbours out on Cuyahoga Street, and Charlie hadn't been out of town at all. They see him every day and most of the day because he does most of his painting or sculpting outdoors in his yard."

Sweeney took another sip. "And this Pell," he asked. "There's no doubt but that it was Pell that Charlie shot? I mean, the shotgun didn't mess him up so he couldn't be recognized or anything?"

"Nope, didn't touch his face. No doubt about identification at all, even if he didn't have the bloody uniform on and everything. Shotgun blast hit him in the chest; guess he must have heard Charlie at the door and turned around. Blew a hole in his chest that you could put your head through."

Sweeney said, "Thanks just the same," and stood up. "I guess it was a bust, Sheriff. I had an idea I could tie your Ripper case up with ours, but it doesn't look like it can be done with Charlie alibied and everybody else concerned dead. And anyway, you thought of it before I did. Well, thanks anyway."

He waited while Henderson washed out the glasses they'd used and hid the empty bottle at the bottom of the garbage pail, and then went downstairs with him and Henderson relieved his wife at the bar. She glared at him before she went back upstairs and he had a feeling that Henderson's precautions with the glasses and the bottle had been futile. Even if she didn't find the bottle, she'd know that there had been one.

There were only four customers in the bar and Sweeney unhappily set up a drink around for them before he went out. He had only a short beer for himself.

He trudged back to the railroad station and asked what time the next train left for Chicago.

"Eleven-fifteen," the agent told him.

Sweeney glanced up at the clock and saw it was only half past four. He asked. "Is there an airport around where I can get a plane to Chi?"

"A plane for Chicago? Guess the nearest place is Rhinelander. You can get one there."

"How do I get to Rhinelander?"

"By train," the agent said. "The eleven-fifteen. That's the next train headed that way."

Sweeney swore. He bought a ticket for Chicago on the eleven-fifteen and had the agent wire to reserve him a lower berth. Anyway, he'd get to Chicago early Sunday morning with a good night's sleep under his belt.

He sat down on a bench in the station and wondered how he'd ever manage to kill over seven and a half hours without drinking too damn much if he drank at all. And if he did that, he'd probably miss the eleven-fifteen and that would ruin tomorrow, which was his last day on his own before he had to go back to the *Blade*.

Well, he'd still talk to this Chapman Wilson. And if Wilson was a lush, a bottle would be the best way to get him to talk. He bought a bottle, a fifth this time, at a liquor store on his way down Main Street to Cuyahoga. He found Cuyahoga and the small green shack with a shed behind it. But there wasn't any answer to his knock at the door.

He tried the door of the shed, but there wasn't any answer there either. The door of the shed was unlocked; it was fixed to lock only from the inside. Sweeney pushed it open and looked in. Inside, one corner had been partitioned off with beaverboard and was obviously a toilet. In the opposite back corner, sans curtains or partition, was the crude shower the ex-sheriff had described.

A string hanging beside the door operated to turn on the light, a bare bulb in the middle of the ceiling. Sweeney turned it on, and he could see the far wall, between the shower and the toilet, the place where the charge of the shotgun must have hit, and gone through; there was a square of beaverboard nailed over it now.

Sweeney went back to the front of the shack. It was five o'clock and already beginning to be dusk; he might just as well wait here as do anything else he could think of.

He sat down on the wooden step and put his package—the bottle—down on the grass beside the step, resisting an impulse to open it before Charlie came home.

It was six o'clock, and twilight, when he saw Charlie coming. He recognized him easily from Henderson's description—five foot two, a hundred ten pounds dripping wet. He looked even lighter than that, possibly because he wasn't dripping wet, not on the outside, anyway. From the way he walked he was not suffering from an internal drought.

He could have been, Sweeney decided as he turned in the gate and came closer, anywhere between twenty-five and forty-five. He had straw-coloured, uncombed hair and wore no hat; his clothes were rumpled and he hadn't shaved for at least two days. He eyes were glassy.

Sweeney stood up. "Mr. Wilson?"

"Yeah." The top of his head was just level with Sweeney's chin.

Sweeney stuck out a hand. He said. "Sweeney. Like to talk to you about a certain statuette you made. Ganslen's number SM–1, a girl screaming——"

Charlie Wilson's hand came out, too, but it passed Sweeney's instead of shaking it. And the hand was doubled up into a fist that landed in Sweeney's sore stomach. Sweeney's stomach screamed silently and tried to crawl through his backbone.

Sweeney himself said something inarticulate and bent almost double, which put his chin in handy reach for an opponent Charlie Wilson's height. Charlie's fist hit his chin and knocked him off balance, but didn't straighten him up. Nothing would have persuaded Sweeney to straighten up, just then. Nothing at all. He didn't really feel the poke on his chin at all because the pain in his stomach was too intense. You don't feel a mosquito bite when you've got your leg in a beartrap.

Sweeney staggered back, still doubled up, and sat down on the doorstep again, his hands protectively clasped over his stomach. He didn't care if Charlie Wilson kicked him in the face, as long as he didn't touch his stomach again. He didn't care about anything in the world except protecting his stomach. Still with his hands over it, he leaned sideways and started to retch.

When he recovered sufficient interest to look up, Charlie Wilson, arms akimbo, was staring down at him with an utterly amazed expression on his face. His voice matched his expression. He said. "I'll be damned. I licked you."

Sweeney groaned. "Thanks," he said.

"Didn't really hurt you, did I?"

Sweeney said, "It feels lovely. Everything's lovely. Everything's wonderful." He retched again.

"Didn't mean to hurt you, really. But hell, I always get licked whenever I take a poke at anybody, so I try to take as good a poke or two as I can get in before it happens. Hey, want a drink? I've got some gin inside. Inside the hovel, I mean; not inside me. That's whisky."

"What's whisky?"

"Inside me. Want a shot of gin?"

Sweeney picked up the wrapped fifth of whisky beside the step. "If you open that——"

Wilson got it open by using the rough edge of a key on the celluloid and turning the cap with his teeth. He handed the bottle to Sweeney and Sweeney took a long drink. Sweeney handed back the bottle. "You might as well have one too. To the start of a beautiful friendship. And just what *did* start it?"

"I hate reporters."

"Oh," said Sweeney. He thought back. "And just what gave you the idea I'm a reporter?"

"You're the third in a week. And who else would——?" He broke off, a puzzled look coming into his eyes.

Sweeney said, "Who else indeed? But let's start over again and differently. You're Chapman Wilson?"

"Yes."

"My name is Sweeney. Mortimer Sweeney. I'm with the Ganslen Art Company Of Louisville."

Charlie Wilson put a hand to his forehead. He said, "Oh, my God."

"You may well say it."

"I'm sorry as hell. Look, can you stand up yet? So I can get the door open. Don't; I've got a better idea. I'll go around back and open it from inside and then I can help you in."

He went around the side of the shack, looking considerably more sober than when he'd first come up the walk. Sweeney heard a back door being opened and then the front door. It nudged his back.

Wilson's voice said, "Sorry, I forgot it opens out. You'll have to stand up anyway to let me get it open. Can you?"

Sweeney stood up. Not all the way up, but far enough for him to move to one side and then go in when the door opened. He made it to the nearest seat, which was a camp stool without a back; that didn't matter because he didn't feel inclined to lean back anyway.

Wilson poured a generous slug from Sweeney's bottle into each of the glasses and came over with one of them for Sweeney.

Sweeney took a sip and looked around him. The walls, every

available inch of them, were hung with unframed canvasses. There were landscapes vaguely in the manner of Cezanne that Sweeney rather liked, and there were abstractions that looked interesting. Sweeney wasn't enough of an expert to know how good they were, but he could tell that they weren't bad. There didn't seem to be any portraits or figure work.

At one side of the room a sculptor's stand held a partially finished twelve-inch statuette of what appeared to be a gladiator.

Wilson had followed Sweeney's gaze. He said. "Don't look at that. It isn't finished, and it's horrible anyway." He walked across the room and threw a cloth across the clay figure, then sat down on the edge of the cot across from Sweeney.

Sweeney had begun to feel better. He said. "It's not bad—the gladiator, I mean. But I'd say oil is your real medium and that the statuettes are pot-boilers. Right?"

"Not exactly, Mr. Sweeney. Of course if you weren't from Ganslen I'd say you were exactly right. By the way, what is your job there?"

Sweeney had been thinking about that. He didn't know anything about the set-up of the Louisville art firm and, more important, he didn't know how much Wilson knew; Wilson might even have visited there and be pretty familiar with the officers. Besides, he didn't want to do any buying or rejecting. He said. "I'm just a salesman for them. But when the boss heard I was passing through Brampton on this trip, he told me to stop off and see you."

"I'm sorry as hell, Mr. Sweeney, but I—uh——"

"That's all right," Sweeney lied. "But first, what's this business about two other reporters—I mean, two reporters having been here to see you? From what papers, and why?"

"From St. Paul papers. Or maybe one was from Minneapolis. It was about that statuette you mentioned, your SM–1. That's why I thought you were another reporter, I guess. What was it *you* wanted to ask about that?"

Sweeney said. "Let's get it straight first about what these oth—these reporters wanted to know about SM–1."

Wilson frowned. "On account of these Ripper murders in Chicago they wanted to do a rehash of my shooting of the maniac I had to shoot here about four or five years ago. Both of them knew about the statuette I made of Bessie, so I guess they must have talked to Sheriff Pederson before they came out here."

Sweeney took a thoughtful sip of whisky. "Had either of them seen it, or a photo of it?"

"I guess not. What they wanted to know mostly was what company I'd sold it to. If they'd seen one, they could have found what company made it. They stamp their name under the base."

"Then the sheriff here knew you'd made such a statuette but didn't know what company you sold it to?"

"That's right. And he never saw it. I got a crying jag about it one night when he jugged me for disorderly conduct."

Sweeney nodded and felt relieved. Then the St. Paul-Minneapolis papers didn't have the important part of the story about Screaming Mimi. They had the inconsequential part—the part he'd learned today from the ex-sheriff—but they didn't know the important, the *all*-important, fact that Chicago's Ripper had a copy. And they didn't have even a photo of the statuette. All they had was a rehash of an old local story; it would make their own papers but wouldn't go out on the AP and UP wires to spoil Sweeney's angle.

Wilson leaned back against the wall behind the cot he was sitting on and crossed his legs. He said, "But what is it Ganslen sent you to talk to me about, Mr. Sweeney?"

"Something that I'm afraid won't work, if you don't like the idea of publicity for the statuette and how it originated. You see, we're taking a loss on that particular number, as things stand. We made a gross of them to try them out—and we'd have lost money if the whole gross had sold, but it sold too slowly to justify our making it in quantity. But it's even worse than that. We're stuck with about a hundred out of the original gross; it just turned out not to have any general appeal at all."

Wilson nodded. "I told Mr. Burke that when he took it. It's one of those things; you like it a lot or else you don't like it at all."

"How did you feel about it, as an artist? How did it strike you?"

"I—I don't know, Mr. Sweeney. I should never have done it, and I should never have sold it. It's too—personal, Jesus God, the way Bessie looked standing there screaming, the way I saw her through the doorway past that——Well, the picture just stuck in my mind until I finally had to do it to get it *off* my mind. It was haunting me up to last year. I had to either paint it or model it and I'm not good at figure work with the brush so I modelled it. And once I did that, I should have destroyed it."

"But I'd just finished it when Mr. Burke stopped in on one of his buying trips, and he liked it. I didn't want to sell it to him, but he insisted, and I needed the money so badly I couldn't turn it down. Hell, it was like selling my own sister, it *was*, in a way. I felt so lousy about it I stayed drunk a week, so the money didn't do me any good anyway."

Sweeney said. "I can see how you must have felt about it."

"But I told Mr. Burke then I didn't want any publicity about it and he promised he wouldn't give the story of it to anybody to try to sell more of them. So why does he send you now to open the subject again?"

Sweeney cleared his throat. "Well—he thought that, under new circumstances, you might change your mind. But I can see you still feel pretty strongly about it, so I won't even try to persuade you."

"Thanks, Mr. Sweeney. But what new circumstances do you mean?"

"The same thing those St. Paul reporters meant. You see, right now, there's Ripper activity operating in Chicago, and it's a big story—not just local, but a coast-to-coast big crime story, about the biggest thing since Dillinger. Right now, while the iron's hot, we could sell a flock of them if we could cash in on *that* publicity, advertising them—and honestly—as a statuette of a woman being attacked by a Ripper, and from life. From the memory of a sculptor who'd actually seen the attack—and prevented it. But we'd have to release the whole story to do that."

"I see what you mean. And it would mean a little extra, I guess, in royalties to me. But—no, I guess not. As I said, I'm sorry I sold it at all and to drag poor Bessie before the public again—— How's about another drink? It's your whisky."

"Ours," said Sweeney. "You know, Charlie, I like you. Not that I thought I would after the way you greeted me."

Wilson poured refills. He said, "I'm really sorry as hell about that. Honestly, I thought you were another of those Goddam reporters like the first two, and I'd made up my mind I wasn't going to *take* another one of them."

He sat down again, glass in hand. "What I like about you best is your not trying to talk me into letting Ganslen release publicity on it. I might weaken if you did. God knows I need money—and God knows it wouldn't do me any good if I got it that way.

"Even with the God-awful prices you get for your statuettes, you might sell thousands of them with a story like that back of them. And with that much money——"

Sweeney asked curiously. "How much money? I mean, Burke didn't happen to mention exactly what the arrangements with you were on the deal."

"The usual. Usual for me, anyway; I don't know what kind of a contract they gave their other sculptors, but on all the statuettes they buy from me, it's a hundred bucks down and that covers all they sell up to a thousand copies—that's the point, Burke says, where they start to break even on a number and over that they show a profit. Is that right?"

"Close enough," Sweeney said.

"So if they would sell two or three thousand copies, I'd have one or two thousand coming in royalties—and that hasn't happened yet. And God help me if it did—in this case. I told you I stayed drunk for a week on the hundred bucks I got out of selling that figure of Bessie the first time. Well, if I cashed in a thousand or two out of the story of it getting dragged through the papers again—after she's dead, at that—well, I'd go on such a *God*-damn drunk I probably wouldn't live through it. Even if I did, the money wouldn't. I'd be broke and broken, and hate myself the rest of my life."

Sweeney found he could stand up, not too certainly. He stuck his hand across the space between them. He said, "Shake, Charlie. I like you."

"Thanks. I like you, Sweeney. Another drink? Of your whisky?"

"*Our* whisky. Sure, Charlie. Say, which *is* your first name. Charlie or Chapman?"

"Charlie. Chapman Wilson was Bessie's idea. Thought it sounded more like an artist. She was a swell gal, Sweeney. A little screwy sometimes."

"Aren't we all?"

"I guess I am. They call me Crazy Charlie around here."

"Around Chicago they probably call me Crazy Sweeney." He picked up his glass. "Shall we drink to craziness?"

Charlie looked at him sombrely for a moment. He said, "Make it to our kind of craziness, Sweeney."

"What oth——Oh. To our kind of craziness, Charlie."

They touched glasses and drank, and Sweeney sat back down.

Charlie stared into his empty glass. He said. "*Real* craziness is something horrible, Sweeney. That homicidal maniac, covered with blood and the carving knife in his hand. I still get nightmares about his face as he turned away from Bessie and looked at me as he heard me coming.

"And Bessie—she was such a swell girl. And to see her go to pieces—well, you can hardly call it going to pieces; that implies something gradual. And she went wild-crazy all at once from that horrible experience. Why, we had to hold her down to get clothes on her; she was stark naked when——But you know that, of course, you've seen that statuette. I—I think it's a good thing that she died, Sweeney. *I'd* rather be dead than insane, really insane. Like she was."

He dropped his head into his hands.

Sweeney said. "Tough. And she was only nineteen."

"Twenty, then. She was twenty-one when she died in the asylum almost four years ago. And she was swell. Oh, she wasn't any angel. She was kind of wild. Our parents died ten years ago when I was twenty-four and Bessie was fifteen. An aunt of ours tried to take her but she ran off to St. Louis. But she kept in touch with me.

"And when she got in trouble five years later, it was me that she came to. She was——Well, that business with the maniac gave her a miscarriage and took care of that." He looked up. "Well, maybe she's better off—— Life can be a hell of a mess."

Sweeney got up and patted Charlie on the shoulder. He said, "Quit thinking about it, kid." He poured them each a drink and put Charlie's glass into Charlie's hand.

Sweeney had sense enough to keep an eye on his watch while they were talking. When it was ten-fifteen, an hour before his train time, he told Charlie he'd better leave.

"Driving?"

"No. Got a reservation on the eleven-fifteen. But it's quite a hike to the station. I've had a swell evening."

"You won't have to hike. There's a bus runs back and forth the length of Main Street. You can catch it on the corner a block and a half down. I'll walk down with you."

The cool night air felt good and began to sober him up.

He liked Charlie and wanted to do something for him. More than that, he suddenly saw *how* he could do something for him. He said, "Charlie, I got an idea how I can get you those royalties on the Scream—on SM–1, without that publicity you don't want. It'll be publicity for the statuette itself, but it won't have to bring either you or your sister into the picture at all."

"Well, if you can do that——"

They were at the corner and Charlie was waiting with him until the bus came along.

"Sure, I can do it. Just on the Chicago angle. Look, Charlie, I know something nobody else knows—and it'll give you a flock of publicity for that statuette in its own right, apart from the way it was conceived and executed. Your name or your sister's won't have to come in it at all."

"If you can keep Bessie out of it——"

"Sure, easy. That isn't even the real story, as far as the story I'm going to break is concerned. It's frosting, but we can leave it off the cake. And for your sake I'll send Ganslen a telegram and tell them to start making more SM–1's right away to cash in on the boom. And listen, Charlie, do you ever get to Chicago?"

"Haven't for a couple of years. Why?"

"Well, look, when you get some of these royalties, drop down and we'll have an evening together; I'll show you the town. We'll hang one on. If you get in town in the daytime, phone me at the *Blade*, city room. If you get in after dark, phone——"

"City room? *Blade*? You a reporter?"

Sweeney said despairingly. "Oh, Lord." He shouldn't have; he should have put his hand over his stomach right away, quick. But he didn't.

Charlie's fist went in it, up to Charlie's wrist, and Sweeney folded like a jackknife, just in time for Charlie's other fist to meet his chin coming down. But, as before, he didn't even feel the punch on his chin.

He heard Charlie say, "You lousy, double-crossing son of a bitch. I wish you'd get up and fight."

Nothing was farther from Sweeney's mind, or rather, from what was left of Sweeney's mind. He couldn't even talk. If he'd opened his mouth something might have come out, but it wouldn't have been words.

He heard Charlie walk away.

CHAPTER SIXTEEN

THERE'S no need to describe how Sweeney felt; that was the third time he'd been hit in the stomach and it didn't feel any different, except in degree, from the first two times. To go into detail would be sadistic, not to say redundant. And it's bad enough that *he* had to go through it a third time; you and I do not.

After a few minutes he managed to get to the curb and sit there doubled up until, after about ten more minutes, he heard and saw the bus coming and and managed to get to his feet, if not quite erect, and boarded it.

He sat doubled up in the bus, he sat doubled up in the station, and then on the train he lay doubled up in his lower berth. He didn't get to sleep, soundly, until early dawn, just as the train got into Chicago.

By the time he got to his room, though, the worst was over, and he slept. It was well into the afternoon—thirteen minutes after two, if you wish exactitude—when he awoke. But by then the worst was over and he could walk without being bent over.

And it was Sunday and the last day of his vacation, and three o'clock by the time he was bathed and dressed.

He went outside and looked east and west along Erie Street with a jaundiced eye and finally made up his mind to go east and see if he could find any angle on the Dorothy Lee murder that the police had missed. He didn't think he would. He didn't.

Luck was with him in finding both the janitor and Mrs. Rae Haley, the woman who had phoned the police, in. But luck was against him in finding out from either of them anything significant that he didn't already know. He ran out of questions to ask after fifteen minutes with the janitor, who had not known Miss Lee personally at all. It took him an hour and a half to listen to everything Mrs. Haley thought of to tell him, and at the end of that hour and half he knew a lot more than he had known about Dorothy Lee—nearly all of it favourable—but none of it in the slightest degree helpful, unless negatively.

Rae Haley, a buxom wench with hennaed hair and just a touch too much make-up for a Sunday afternoon at home, turned out to be an ad-taker for a rival newspaper, but seemed nonetheless eager to talk to the *Blade*—or to Sweeney.

She had known Dorothy Lee fairly well and had liked her; Dorothy was "nice and quiet." Yes, she'd been in Dorothy's apartment often. They had eaten together frequently, taking turns, each in her own apartment, in doing the cooking, and that way avoiding each having to cook a separate meal. Not all the time, of course, but several times a week. So she knew Dorothy's apartment pretty thoroughly and, as he had suspected, Sweeney found that "small black statuette" drew a blank. The apartment was rented furnished and Dorothy hadn't gone in for buying pictures or bric-a-brac of her own. She did, though, have a nice table-top phonograph and some nice records, mostly "Sweet swing." Sweeney concealed a shudder.

Yes, Dorothy had had boy friends; at one time or another she'd gone out with four or five of them, but none had been "serious." Mrs. Haley had met each of them and knew their names, she'd given the names of all of them to the police. Not because there was any possibility that any of them had been concerned in the horrible thing that had happened to Dorothy, but because the police had asked for the names and had insisted. But apparently the police had found all of them to be all right, because if they had arrested one of them it would have been in the papers, wouldn't it? Sweeney assured her that it would have been. She said that they were all nice boys, very nice boys, and when one of them had brought her home he'd always said goodnight at the door and hadn't come in. Dorothy had been a nice girl.

The walls of these apartments were almost paper-thin and she, Mrs. Haley, would have known if. She carried the sentence only that far and stopped delicately.

Sweeney was thinking of his promise to Charlie to send that telegram to the general manager of Ganslen. He was planning how to word it when he remembered where he was and realized that Mrs. Haley was still talking and that he hadn't been listening at all. He listened for long enough to find out that he hadn't been missing a thing, and made his getaway, turning down an invitation to stay for dinner.

He walked downtown to the Loop and found a Western Union office open. He sat down with a pencil and pad of blanks and tore up two tries before he evolved a telegram that even came close. Then he read that one over again, saw several things missing in it, and gave up. He tore that one up too and walked to a telephone exchange where he asked to see, and was given, a Louisville telephone directory. Luckily Sweeney had a good memory for names and he recalled from his previous call to Ganslen Art Company, the first name as well as the last name of the general manager. He found a home telephone listed.

He got a handful of change and went into a booth. A few minutes later he was talking to the general manager and buyer of Ganslen.

He said, "This is Sweeney of the Chicago *Blade*, Mr. Burke. I talked to you a few days ago about one of your statuettes, the SM–1. You were kind enough to tell me who modelled it."

"Yes, I remember."

"To return the favour, I want to tip you off to something that will make some money for you and for Chapman Wilson. Only I'm going to ask you to keep this confidential until the *Blade* breaks the story tomorrow. You'll agree to that?"

"Uh—exactly what am I agreeing to, Mr. Sweeney?"

"Merely that you don't tell anyone at all what I'm going to tell you now until after tomorrow noon. You can go ahead meanwhile and act on the information; you can start getting ready to cash in."

"That sounds fair enough."

"Okay, here's the dope. You sold two SM–1's in Chicago. Well, I've got one of them and the Ripper's got the other one. You've heard of our Ripper murders, haven't you?"

"Of course. Good Lord! You mean——"

"Yeah. Tomorrow the *Blade* will print a picture of Screaming Mimi—about four columns wide on page one, if I judge right—and break the story. Probably the Ripper will be caught. A friend of his landlady or someone will have seen it in his room and phone the police. He can hardly have had it for two months without *someone* having seen it.

"But whether he's caught through it or not, it's a nationwide big story. You're likely to be swamped for weeks with orders for Mimi. I'd suggest you put her in production immediately—work a night shift tonight if you can get anybody down to your factory or workshop or whatever it is. And if I were you I wouldn't sell those hundred-odd copies you have; I'd get them to dealers quickly to use as samples to take orders. Get them to Chicago dealers, in particular; as fast as you can. Start one of your salesmen up this way tonight with a trunk full of them."

"Thank you, Mr. Sweeney. I can't say how much I appreciate your giving me this much notice on——"

"Wait," said Sweeney. "I'm not through yet. One thing I want you to do. Put a special mark somewhere on each one you sell from now on, so it can be told from the one the Ripper's got. Keep the mark secret so he can't duplicate it, and let the police know what the mark is when they come to you—as they will after that story breaks. Otherwise, they'll be on my neck for tipping you off to flood the Chicago market with them, see? But they'll see that, in the long run, we're doing them a favour. If there are more Mimis coming, the Ripper may keep his, whereas if he knows his is going to keep on being the only other one in Chicago, he'll get rid of it quick. And he won't know about the secret mark all the others will have. Listen, make the secret mark a tiny chip out of the bottom of the base in the right front corner—so it'll look accidental if anyone looks at just *one* of them."

"Fine. That will be simple."

"I'll do it on mine. And you've got a record, I hope, of just where the forty or so that you actually sold throughout the country went, haven't you?"

"Our books would show that."

"Good, then if an unmarked Mimi shows up, it can be traced back to prove it's not the one the Ripper bought. And one more thing——"

"Yes?"

"I'm not going to drag in the origin of Mimi. Charlie—Chapman Wilson's pretty sensitive about what happened to his sister, and this is a big enough story without using that. After all, that's past history and our Ripper is very much current. He said you promised not to use that for publicity—to stick to your promise to him."

"Of course, Mr. Sweeney. And thanks again, tremendously."

After he hung up, Sweeney dropped another nickel but Yolanda's phone wasn't answered so he got it back. It was too early for her to be at the night club; she was probably out eating somewhere. Well, maybe he'd better skip trying to talk to her until after tomorrow when he'd broken the Screaming Mimi story in the *Blade*. And maybe by then the Ripper would be caught and she wouldn't have an escort of cops everywhere she moved.

He went back for another handful of change, an even bigger handful this time. A nickel of it got him the long distance operator again. He let the New York operator do the looking up this time for he felt pretty sure Ray Land would have a home telephone in his own name. Ray Land had been a Chicago homicide cop once; now he was running a small agency of his own in New York.

Ray was home.

Sweeney said. "This is Sweeney. Remember me?"

"Sure. So?"

"Want you to investigate an alibi for me. In New York." He gave the details. Greene's name and hotel and the exact date. "I know he was registered at the hotel on that day and the day before and the day after. The police checked that. What I want to find out—for sure, not a probability—is whether he was really there that night, the 27th.

"Can try. It's almost two weeks ago. How far do you want me to go?"

"As far as you can. Talk to everybody at the hotel who might have seen him come in or go out, the maid who'd have made up his room in the morning, everything like that. Listen, the crucial time is 3 o'clock in the morning. If you can definitely locate him six hours or less either side of that, I'll settle."

"Twelve hours isn't so bad. Maybe I can do it. How much you want me to spend?"

"Spend all you want provided you do it right away. Within reason, that is. I'll wire you a hundred cash for a retainer. If you go a little over it, even double it, okay."

"That ought to cover it, Sweeney. It'll cover two days' time and since it's right on Manhattan there won't be any expenses to speak of. If I can't get anything in two days, I probably can't at all. Why the six hour leeway?"

"I want to convince myself that he wasn't in Chicago at 3 a.m. Counting time to and from airports on either end, getting a plane and everything, that's the least he could have done it in. Maybe five hours would be safer. If you can prove he was at the hotel as late as ten in the evening or as early as eight the next morning, I'll be convinced. And, just in case it could have been a ringer, someone else there using his name, here's a description." Sweeney gave it. He added, "If you can't alibi him, you might try that description at the airport. Or if it comes down to that, I'll try to get you a photo. Check with me after you've got everything you can get at the hotel. Good enough?"

"Good enough. I'll get around there this evening. It'll be the night shift I'll mostly want to talk to."

Outside the telephone exchange, Sweeney found that it was getting dark and that he was getting hungry. He remembered he hadn't seen a Sunday paper and might have missed something; he found copies of two of them still left on a news-stand and very early editions, still sticky with ink, of two Monday morning papers. He bought all four and took them into a restaurant with him.

Reading while he ate he found out that nothing new had happened or transpired. All the papers were keeping the story alive—it was too big a story to let an issue pass without *something*—but the something added up or cancelled out to nothing.

He stretched the eating and the reading until it was almost ten o'clock and then left. He remembered the retainer and stopped in at the Western Union office again to send it to Ray Land.

That still left him over seven hundred dollars and he wished there was some way he could spend some of it on Yolanda. Well, there'd be time for that after the cops quit watching her. Meanwhile, there *was* one sighting shot he could take. He found a flower shop in a hotel still open and ordered two dozen red roses sent to her at El Madhouse as soon as they could get a messenger to take them there. He tried writing on, and tore up, three cards. On the fourth, he wrote "Sweeney" and let it go at that.

He caught a taxi and directed it to El Madhouse; it would get him there just in time for Yo's first performance of the evening.

It did, and Nick soon found a place for him.

After the floor show (you wouldn't want me to describe it again, would you?) he wandered out to the bar and managed to get a place at it. But it was ten minutes before he could get a drink.

He sipped it and brooded.

Unless breaking the story that the Ripper had bought and now presumably still owned a copy of Ganslen's SM–1 brought results, it looked as though he was stymied. That was the only real lead he'd found: the fact that the killer of Lola Brent, two months ago, had undoubtedly been the same person who had purchased from her the statuette whose purchase price she had dragged down. Sweeney didn't doubt that for a second; it fitted too perfectly to be a coincidence. It *had* to be.

But for the rest he had nothing. The trip to Brampton had been completely a blind alley—an alley populated with little men who kept pounding on his sore stomach, before and after getting drunk with him. And almost worse than those punches had been the anticlimax of learning—after he'd heard first of a Ripper, a blonde, and a crazy artist—that the Ripper and the blonde were dead long since and the crazy artist was well alibied. And even if Charlie Wilson hadn't been alibied, Sweeney couldn't picture him as the Ripper. He had a hair-trigger temper, but he wasn't the type that ran to carving knives.

Well, tomorrow would tell the tale. If a four-column picture of SM–1 splashed on the front page of the *Blade* didn't make something happen——

He sighed and took another sip of his drink.

Someone tapped him on the shoulder.

CHAPTER SEVENTEEN

SWEENEY turned and found himself staring full into the thick glasses that magnified Greene's eyes and made them so frightening.

Sweeney grinned and said, "Hi, Doc. What'll you have?"

"I've got a drink, over at a table. And Nick's holding my chair and another. Come on over."

Sweeney picked up his drink and followed Greene to a corner table. Nick, standing beside it, said, "Hi, Mr. Sweeney," and then hurried off about his business. Sweeney and Green sat down.

"Getting anywhere?" Greene asked.

"Maybe. I don't know. I'm breaking a big story tomorrow; the biggest one to date."

"Outside of the actual murders."

"Maybe bigger," Sweeney said.

"It would be useless for me to ask what it is, I suppose."

"You've got something there, Doc. But cheer up; it'll be on the streets in twelve hours."

"I'll watch for it. I'm still worried about something happening to Yo. So I hope you have really got something." He took off his glasses and polished them. Sweeney, studying him, saw that he looked quite different without them. He looked tired, genuinely worried. Stranger, though, he looked human. Sweeney almost wished he had back the hundred dollars he'd just wired to New York. Almost, not quite.

Doc Greene put the glasses back on and looked at Sweeney through them, and his eyes were enormous again. Sweeney thought the hundred dollars was well spent.

Greene said, "Meanwhile, Sweeney, take good care of yourself."

"I will. Any special reason?"

Green chuckled. "Yes, for *my* sake. Since I lost my temper the other night and shot off my mouth, Captain Bline has had me on the carpet. Everything but a rubber hose. It seems he took my little threat seriously."

"And was he right?"

"Well—yes and no. You did, that one time, get under my skin and I think I meant it when I said it. Of course, after cool deliberation I realized I'd been silly. By saying that, I did the one thing that made you completely safe—from me. If you ever want to kill a man, Sweeney, don't make the announcement before the police and hope to get away with it."

"As I said, for *my* sake. Bline told me—*promised* me—that if anything happens to you after my threat, my silly threat, he'd arrest me and rubber-hose me to hell and back. Even if I had an alibi, he'd figure that I hired the job done. I'm going to be a dead duck, Sweeney, if anything happens to you."

Sweeney smiled. "Doc, you almost tempt me to commit suicide, without leaving a note."

"Don't, please. Not that I think you would, but you worry me talking about breaking a big story tomorrow. You might say that to someone who wouldn't want a big story to break for fear of what it might be. You see what I mean."

"I see what you mean. But you're the first person in Chicago whom I've told. The only other one is hundreds of miles from here. Of course, you could pass it on."

"Perish the thought, Sweeney. Your safety has become a matter of importance to me. I've told you why." He shook his head slowly. "I am amazed at myself for having said such a foolish thing—in such company. I, trained psychiatrist—Have you had any psychiatric training, Sweeney? From the skilful way you manœuvred me into loss of control——Well, there's no harm done if nothing happens to you. But until this mess is over, I'll chip in half the cost if you want to hire a bodyguard. Willie, maybe? Have you met Willie Harris?"

"Willie is wonderful," Sweeney said. "But I doubt if Harry Yahn would care to part with him. No, thanks, Doc, whether you're serious or not I'll take my chances without a bodyguard. Or if I should hire one, I won't tell you about it."

Greene sighed. "You still don't trust me, Sweeney. Well, I've got to run along. To see a client in another club. Take care of yourself."

Sweeney went back to the bar and had his drink replenished. He drank it very slowly and thought about how he was going to write the story for tomorrow's *Blade*.

He didn't wait for the second show. Tomorrow might turn out to be a big day, and it was after midnight already. He went home and to bed, read a while and got to sleep by two o'clock. His alarm woke him at half-past seven, and it was Monday.

It was Monday, and it was a bright, cheerful day; the sun was bright but not unduly hot for August the eleventh. No clouds in the sky, but a cooling breeze off the lake. Not bad at all.

He had a good breakfast and got to the *Blade* promptly at nine.

He hung up his coat and hat and then, before the city editor could catch him, he headed right for Wally Krieg's office. The package containing SM–1 was under his arm.

Wally looked up as he came in. He said, "Hi, Sweeney. Reported to Crawley yet?"

"Nope. Want to show you something first." He started to unwrap the package.

"All right, but after that report to Crawley. Somebody took a jewellery salesman for his samples last night and we want to get on it quick. Over at——"

"Hush," said Sweeney. He got the package unwrapped and set Mimi on the desk, facing the managing editor. "Mimi, meet Wally Krieg. Wally, meet Mimi. Screaming Mimi."

"Charmed. Now take that thing out of here and——"

"Hush," said Sweeney. "She's got a sister. *One* sister, in all of Chicago."

"Sweeney, what are you getting at?"

"The Ripper," said Sweeney. "He's got Mimi's sister. We got Mimi—and don't think she doesn't go on the expense account for the full purchase price. That is, if you want to send her up to the photo department and run a pic of her on page one today."

"You say the Ripper's got one like her? Are you sure?"

"Reasonably sure. There were two in Chicago; the Ripper bought the other one from Lola Brent just before he followed her home and killed her. It's probably what set him off. Look at it!"

"And his is the only other one in Chicago?"

"Yes," said Sweeney. "Well, if you're not interested I'll go stick it in my desk drawer and then look up Crawley." He picked up Mimi and started out the door. Wally said "Hey!" and he waited.

"Wally," he said. "I'm getting fed up on this Ripper business. Maybe you'd better keep me off it. Of course I could get the whole thing for the first edition today, but you can have Mimi anyway, if you want her, and one of the other boys can check her pedigree—with Raoul Reynarde—and trace her back like I did, and give you the story for tomorrow or part of it for a late edition today. But I'd just as soon not——"

"Sweeney, quit blithering. Shut the door."

"Sure, Wally. From which side?"

Wally just glared at him and Sweeney decided that enough was enough and shut it from the inside. Wally was getting the city ed. on the phone. He barked that someone else should go on the jewellery case and that Sweeney was on special assignment. He jiggled the receiver and got the photo department and apparently was satisfied with whoever answered the phone, for he told him to come down right away.

Then he swung on Sweeney. He said, "Put that thing down, carefully, before you drop it and break it."

Sweeney put Mimi back down on the desk. Wally stared at her. Then up at Sweeney.

He said, "What the hell are you waiting for? A kiss? Go ahead and write the story. Wait a minute, don't start yet. Lots of time before first edition; sit down and tell me about it first. Maybe there are angles somebody else can be doing while you're batting it out."

Sweeney sat down and told most of it. As much, at least, as he intended to put into the story itself. There was an interruption while a photographer came in and Wally gave him Mimi with instructions—and with threats of almost unbelievable things that would happen to him if Mimi were dropped and broken before the photograph had been taken. The photographer left, walking carefully and holding Mimi as though she were made of eggshell. Sweeney resumed, and finished.

Wally said, "Good. Go ahead and write it. Only you didn't do the story any good phoning Ganslen and telling them to cash in while it's hot. The police aren't going to like that. They'll want there to be only *one* Mimi in Chicago for as long a time as possible. And I mean *one*; I'm going to order this one broken to pieces as soon as I see a good photo of it. Put that in the story. It narrows things down. Plenty. What the hell did you want to phone that art company for; to tip them off?"

Sweeney felt uncomfortable. It *had* been a boner, and he didn't want to explain about Charlie Wilson and his real reason for the call. He said, weakly, "Thought I ought to pay 'em back for the favour they did me on the first call, Wally. Telling me only two had been sold in Chicago. Without that—"

Wally said, "Well, I'll phone them and head them off while you write the story. Look, mention that the statuette was made by Ganslen Art Company, Louisville, and they won't *have* to send any salesmen or samples to Chicago or anywhere in this area. They'll be swamped with orders by telephone, just from that information and the photo in the paper. Every dealer in the area will be calling them.

"I'll phone and tell them that. Who'd you talk to?"

"General manager. Burke."

"Okay, I'll talk to Burke and tell him to go ahead and take all the orders he wants from this area but to stall as long as he can on shipping and not to send any samples right away. And I'll make sure he's taking your suggestion on putting a special mark on each of them. Don't mention *that*, though, in the story. And bring it here when you've finished; I want to pass on it personally."

Sweeney nodded and stood up. Wally said, "And one other thing I'm going to do and that's phone Bline. If we break this story without tipping him off first, we'll be number one on the department's s.o.b. list. I'm going to give him the story first and tell him we're breaking it today but we're giving him advance notice."

"What if he crosses you by giving it to the other papers?"

"I don't think he will. If he does, they still won't have Mimi or a pic of her. The story itself isn't worth much without the pic and

I'm going to splash that smack in the middle of the front page. Four columns by about fifteen inches."

"Shall I mention that we're running the pic in full colour—black?"

"Get the hell out of here."

Sweeney got the hell out and sat down at his desk. He realized as he pulled paper into the ancient Underwood, that both of Wally's ideas had been good; it wouldn't hurt the story to give the cops a couple of hours' notice, and it wouldn't hurt Ganslen's sales (or Charlie's royalties) if they didn't fill orders from Chicago for a week or so. The story would stay good—and would turn better if it actually led to the capture of the Ripper.

He looked at his wrist watch, saw that he had an hour to go, and started typing. His phone rang and it was Wally. Wally asked, "Going to have plenty of time? Or would you rather dictate it to a fast rewrite man?"

"I can do it."

"Okay. Send it to me as it comes out of the mill, a page at a time. I'll have a boy waiting at your desk. Slug it MIMI."

Sweeney slugged it MIMI and kept typing. A minute later a copy boy was breathing down his neck, but Sweeney was used to that and it didn't bother him. He sent the last page in ten minutes before the first edition deadline.

After that he lighted a cigarette and pretended to be busy so Crawley wouldn't think of anything else for him to do right away, until deadline was past and he figured Wally would be free again, and then he wandered into Wally's office again.

"How's Mimi?" he asked.

"A broken woman. Look in my wastebasket if you don't believe me."

"I'd rather not," Sweeney said.

A boy came in with papers fresh off the press and put three of them on Wally's desk. Sweeney picked one up and glanced at the page one layout. There was Mimi, all right, slightly larger than actual size. She had the banner head, two columns of story, four columns of picture. And Wally had by-lined the story for him.

Sweeney said, "Nice layout," and Wally grunted, reading.

Sweeney said. "Nice story, too. Thanks for telling me so." Wally grunted again.

Sweeney said, "How about the rest of the day off?"

This time Wally didn't grunt; he put down the paper and got ready to explode. "Are you *crazy*? You've been off two weeks, come back to work for two hours and——"

"Relax, Wally. Don't break a blood vessel. Where do you think that story came from? Out of the air? I've been working twenty hours a day on it, more or less, for three days. On my own time.

I came in with that story ready to write up. And brought Mimi with me for company. And why? Because I worked till four o'clock this morning and got two hours sleep, that's why. Dragged myself out of bed half-awake to come in and write the biggest story of the year for you and then you——"

"Shut up. All right, get the hell out of here. Of all the Goddam goldbricks——"

"Thank you. Seriously, Wally, I *am* going home. I'll be in my room to rest, but I won't get undressed—and if anything breaks on this story call me quick. I'll be on it just as fast as I would if I were waiting around here. Okay?"

"Okay, Sweeney. If anything breaks you're on it. And listen, Sweeney—win, lose or draw, it's a swell story."

"Thanks," Sweeney said. "And thanks to hell and back for carrying me while I was—gone."

"This makes up for it. You know, Sweeney, there are damn few real reporters left. And you're——"

"Hold it," said Sweeney. "Pretty soon we'll be crying into our beer, and we haven't got any beer to cry into. I'm going to beat it."

He beat it.

He took one of Wally's papers with him so he wouldn't have to hunt one up elsewhere or wait for one on the street, and went home. He took a cab, partly because he still had more money than he knew what to do with, and partly because—temporarily—he really did feel tired as hell. It was partly the letdown, but mostly the fact that, for a while now, there was nothing intelligent to do but to wait.

Either the story of Mimi would lead to a big break in the story of the Ripper or it wouldn't. If it did, it would probably happen this afternoon or this evening. Or possibly tonight.

If it didn't—well, then it didn't. He'd be back at work at nine o'clock tomorrow morning and he didn't think, now, that Wally would keep him off the Ripper case. He'd just have to forget Mimi and try to dig up another angle, somewhere. Probably going over again, and more thoroughly, a lot of the ground he had already covered.

At home, he made himself comfortable and read the story through, leisurely and carefully. Wally had added to it, splicing in some recapitulation on the stories of the other three women who had been attacked (for the Mimi story had concerned directly only Lola Brent, who had sold Mimi to the Ripper), but he had changed hardly a word of what Sweeney had written.

This time he even read the continuation on an inside paper, then he folded the paper together and put it with the others that covered the various Ripper murders.

He sat down and tried to relax, but couldn't. He went over to the phonograph—it seemed naked now without the naked statuette atop it—and played the Brahms Fourth. That helped a little, although he couldn't really concentrate on it.

The phone rang. He got there in nothing flat, slamming the door of his own room to shut off part of the sound of the phonograph—which was about one second quicker than stopping to shut off the phonograph itself would have been.

It was Wally. He said, "Okay, Sweeney. Get over to State Street. You know the address."

"What's up?"

"They got the Ripper. Now listen, we got a headline and a bulletin going in the Final—it's going to press now—and we're not holding it for details. We got the main facts, and the full story will have to go in tomorrow. It's an even break; we'll beat the morning papers on the bulletin and the main facts, but they'll beat us on getting a detailed story.

"So there's no rush. Get over there and get the full dope, but you can write it up when you get in tomorrow."

"Wally, what happened? Did he make another try at Yolanda Lang? Is she all right?"

"I guess so. Yeah, he made another try and this time the dog got him, like it almost did last time except that last time he slammed the door on the dog——"

"I *know* what happened last time. What happened *this* time?"

"I told you, dammit. They *got* him. He's still alive but probably won't be long. Took him to a hospital, but don't waste time; they won't let you talk to him. He went out a window. At the dame's place. I mean. Good work, Sweeney; that Mimi story of yours broke it. He not only had the statuette, but had it *with* him."

"Who? I mean, have they got his name?"

"Name? Sure, we got his name. It's Greene, James J. Greene. Captain Bline says he's suspected him all along. Now quit pumping *me*; get over there and get the story."

The receiver banged in Sweeney's ear, but he stared into the black mouthpiece of the wall phone for seconds before he put his own receiver back on the hook.

CHAPTER EIGHTEEN

It wasn't quite believable somehow. He'd thought it all along, and yet the reality was hard to swallow. For one thing, one simple thing, he couldn't think of Doc Greene as being dead. But Horlick—who was already there when Sweeney got there—was saying that he was.

"Yeah," he said, "Bline got a call from the hospital; he sent two of the boys with Greene to try to get a detailed confession and get it signed, but I guess they didn't make it, and that he couldn't have signed it anyway what with both arms broken, among other things. And he wasn't very coherent, what I heard of him. I got here before they took him away."

"How come so quick, Wayne?"

"Bull luck. I was already on my way here. For part of the follow-up tomorrow on that Mimi story you broke today, Wally sent me to interview Yolanda Lang, to ask her if she'd ever seen such a statuette. And if not, and it probably would have been not, I was to get a story anyway by asking her what her reaction was to a picture of it—whether it looked like she felt when the Ripper was coming at her in the hallway. That kind of crap. And I got here about the time the police ambulance did."

"And, Yolanda isn't up there?"

"Nope, she ran out with the dog, just after it happened. Shock again, or fright. She's probably having the meamies somewhere but she'll show up. I'm going in with what I got; you go on upstairs and see if you can get more if you want to. Bline's up there."

He went his way, south on State Street, and Sweeney pushed his way through the knot of people who were standing around the doorway of the apartment building on State just south of Chicago Avenue, the same doorway through which Sweeney had started only a few nights ago and had seen a woman and a dog. This time the crowd was bigger, although there was nothing to be seen through the glass. Sweeney pushed through to a policeman guarding the door. His press card got him inside and he ran up the stairs to the third floor.

Yolanda Lang's apartment was the rear north one of four on the third floor. There wasn't any need checking the number on the door because the door was open and the place was full of cops. At least it looked full of cops; when Sweeney got in, he saw there were only two besides Bline.

Bline came over to him, "Sweeney, if I wasn't so happy, I'd break your neck. How long did you have that Goddam statuette?"

"Don't remember exactly, Cap."

"That's what I mean. But—well, we got the Ripper, and without another ripping, although that must've been a pretty close thing. And I'll settle for that. I'm even ready to buy you a drink. Guess I'm through here; I'll leave one of the boys to wait for the Lang dame to be sure she's all right when she comes back."

"Is there any doubt that she isn't?"

"Physically, sure. He didn't touch her with the knife at all this time, the pooch got in ahead. But she's probably in a mental tizzy, worse than last time. Hell, not that I blame her."

"Did Devil kill Greene?"

"Well, he chewed him up a bit but didn't kill him; Doc must've managed to keep an arm over his throat. But he went out that window and that killed him all right. Must've backed up against it and a lunge of the dog knocked him out backwards."

Bline had gestured to a wide-open window and Sweeney went over to it and looked out. Two stories below was a small cement courtyard. It was pretty well littered with junk people had thrown out of windows.

Sweeney asked, "Where's the statuette?"

"Down there in the courtyard, most of it. We found enough pieces of it to identify it. Doc must still have had hold of it when he went out the window. Probably trying to club off the dog with it. The knife was there, too; he must've had the statuette in one hand and the knife in the other—it's a wonder the dog managed not to get hurt. But I guess Doc had to keep one arm to cover his throat and wasn't fast enough with the other. A dog like that is hell on wheels in a fight."

Sweeney looked down into the courtyard and shivered a little.

He said, "I'll take that drink, Cap. And I'll buy back. Let's get out of here."

They went to the corner of State and Chicago, the tavern from which the phone call had been made the night of the first attack on Yolanda. Bline bought.

Sweeney said, "I know everything except what happened. Can you put it in order for me?"

"The whole thing? Or just this afternoon?"

"Just this afternoon."

Bline said, "Yolanda was alone in her apartment—as of a few minutes after three o'clock. We know that because I had a guy stationed to watch the place, from across the hall. We'd sublet the flat across from hers for that purpose, and there was a man stationed there at all times, except of course when she was working at the club. He had a peephole rigged so he could watch the door to her place.

"He saw Doc Greene come up with a shoebox under his arm and knock on the door, see? Well, that was all right; Doc had called there before and I'd said it was okay to let him in. If it had been a stranger, Garry—that's the guy who was on duty—would have had his door open and a gun ready."

Sweeney asked, "Did Doc call on business? I mean, when he'd been there before?"

Bline shrugged. "Don't know and didn't care. We're not the vice squad; we were just hunting the Ripper. And I'd thought, from Greene's alibis, that he was in the clear. Well, I was wrong. Did you really suspect him, Sweeney, or did you keep needling him just because you didn't like him?"

"I don't really know, Cap. But what happened?"

"Well, Yolanda answered the door and let him in. He was in there about five minutes when things started to happen. Garry heard Yolanda scream and the dog growl and Greene yell, almost at once, and he yanked his own door open and started across the hallway. He yanked at Yolanda's door, but it was locked—a snap lock—and he was just about to put a bullet through the lock when the door opened.

"He says Yolanda had opened it and she pushed past him into the hallway, her face as white as a sheet and looking like something pretty horrible had happened. But there wasn't any blood on her; she wasn't hurt. Garry tried to grab her with his free hand—he had his gun in the other—but the dog jumped at him and he had to let go to cover his throat. The dog took a piece out of his sleeve but didn't happen to get hold of his arm.

"By that time Yolanda was past him and starting down the stairs and the dog wheeled and followed her. So he didn't have to shoot the dog. And as long as Yolanda seemed all right, he ran into Yolanda's apartment to see what went on there. There didn't seem to be anyone in there and he wondered what happened to Greene; then he heard a groan from the courtyard and looked out the open window—it's a pretty big one, the kind that swings out instead of raising—and there was Doc Greene lying in the courtyard.

"So he phones for me and the ambulance and we get here. Greene was still alive, but dying and not very coherent. He could just say a few words but they were enough."

Sweeney asked, "What do you figure sent Greene around there?"

"How do you figure how a homicidal maniac reasons, Sweeney? How the hell do I know? But I think it was your story about that statuette that set him off. He had it, and maybe Yolanda knew that he had it and the jig would be up as soon as she happened to see your front pages. Why he took it along in a shoebox when he went to kill her, I don't know.

"But he had it out of the box, in one hand, and the knife in the other hand—when the dog saved her by getting him. Chewed him up pretty bad, maybe he even jumped out of the window to get away from the dog, but I think it's more likely he got backed up against it and went out accidentally when the dog jumped for him again."

"What do you figure happened to Yolanda?"

"Shock again, of course. She's probably wandering around in a daze, but she's well protected. She'll snap out of it by herself, probably, and come back. If not, she can't be hard to find—a dame like that with a dog like that. Well, I got to get in and report. So long, Sweeney."

Bline left and Sweeney ordered another drink. And another and then one more. It was getting dark when he left the tavern and went back to Yolanda's flat. There was still a policeman at the door. Sweeney asked him if Yolanda had come back, she hadn't.

He strolled over to Clark Street, stopped in at Ireland's and ordered a lobster. While it was cooking he went to the phone booth and called Ray Land, the private detective he'd hired in New York.

He said. "This is Sweeney, Ray. You can call it off."

"That's what I figured, Sweeney. Heard on the radio while I was eating dinner that your Chicago Ripper was caught and his name was familiar. So I figured you wouldn't want me to keep on. Well, I put in a day on it, so you got fifty bucks coming back. I'll send you a cheque."

"Get anywhere on it?"

"Hadn't yet. It was tough going, what with it being two weeks ago. Best bet I had was a maid who managed to remember that one morning his bed hadn't been slept in, but she couldn't remember which morning it was. I was going to see her again after she'd had time to think it over. Shall I send you that cheque care of the *Blade*?"

"Sure. And thanks, Ray."

He called Captain Bline at headquarters and asked, "Any reports on Yolanda yet?"

"Yeah, Sweeney. A funny one." Bline's voice sounded puzzled. "She turned up at El Madhouse some time ago. Just half an hour after Greene had tried to attack her. She got some money from Nick and left again. And no report on her since."

"The hell," said Sweeney. "How did she act?"

"A little funny, Nick said, but not too bad. He said she was pale and a little jittery, but he didn't think anything of it; he hadn't heard about what happened to Doc yet, and she didn't say anything about it. Just wanted some money—gave him a song-and-dance about being able to buy something she wanted for a hell of a bargain if she did it right away for cash. Nick said he figured somebody had offered her a stolen mink coat or something for a few hundred bucks and she wanted it but was a little afraid of the deal and that was why she was nervous."

"How much did he give her?"

"A week's salary. She had it coming as of tomorrow night anyway, so he figured he might as well give it to her a day sooner."

"That's funny."

"Yeah, but I think I can figure it. I'd guess it that she just wanted to hide out for a day or two. It was shock, but temporary, that sent her chasing out of the building after Greene tried to attack her a second time; but she must've got over the worst of it quick if she could talk normally to Nick within a half hour. Only I'll guess she just didn't feel up to facing us and all the reporters and everything. But she'll show up in a few days when she gets her balance back. She won't miss cashing in on her contract and all that publicity and everything."

"Could be. You hunting for her?"

Bline said, "No. Why should we? We could find her easily enough, just checking hotels. But from what Nick says, she's all right, so it isn't our business. If I thought she was wandering around in a daze from shock or something——"

"She didn't go back home to get any clothes or anything?"

"No, our man's still there and he's to phone me if she shows back there. Guess that's partly what she wanted money for, so she wouldn't have to go back there and face the music."

"Okay, Cap," Sweeney said. "Thanks a lot."

He got back to his table just as the lobster arrived.

He ate it thoughtfully. He didn't know exactly what he was being thoughtful about until the lobster had been reduced to a shell.

And then, suddenly, he knew what he had been thinking and it scared hell out of him.

CHAPTER NINETEEN

HE didn't hurry. His coffee came and he drank it slowly, still horrifying himself by what he was thinking. And then it got worse, for he found he wasn't thinking it any more; he *knew* it. A lot of it was guess work, but each guess dropped into place like a piece of jigsaw puzzle that will fit nowhere else and at no other angle.

He paid the check and walked south to El Madhouse. Nick saw him the moment he went in and came to meet him. He said, "Hi, Sweeney. I'm worried; know anything about where Yo is, or if she's coming tonight?"

Sweeney said, "I'm worried, too. Listen, Nick, did you happen to notice when Yolanda left here whether she took a taxi?"

"No. She walked north."

"How was she dressed?"

"In green, what they call a daytime dress. No coat or hat. And the dog was along, but not on a leash. Sometimes she has him on a leash, sometimes not. Say, it's hell about Doc, isn't it?"

"Yeah," said Sweeney.

He went outside and wondered how lucky he was going to be. It had been about five hours ago that Yolanda had left here. It was a break that she'd walked north, away from the Loop. In the Loop, it would have been impossible to trace her.

He was lucky. A block north, and thirty questions later, he found a newsboy who'd been at his stand all afternoon, and he'd seen Yolanda Lang; sure, he knew her. By sight, he explained. She'd passed him and turned west on Ohio Street.

Sweeney turned west on Ohio Street.

It wasn't too difficult. A gorgeous blonde in bright green, with a dog that looked like a fugitive from a James Oliver Curwood story. Within two blocks he found two people who had seen them.

In the third block, without turning off Ohio Street, he hit the jackpot. A tobacconist had not only seen girl and dog, he had seen them enter a building across the street—"the one right there, with the sign, 'Furnished Rooms'."

Sweeney entered the building with the sign that said. "Furnished Rooms."

Just inside the door was a bell and a sign that said "Ring for Landlady." Sweeney rang for landlady.

She was big and slovenly; she had a mean eye. Sweet reasonableness wasn't going to work, and she didn't look as though she'd scare. Sweeney pulled out his wallet.

He took a twenty-dollar bill out of it, she could see the figure in the corner. He said, "I'd like to talk to the girl who took a room late this afternoon. The one with the dog."

She didn't even hesitate in reaching for the bill. It disappeared into the neckline of her dress, into a bosom so redundant that Sweeney wondered if she'd be able to find a bill without searching. She said. "She took a room on the second floor—the door right opposite the head of the stairs."

Sweeney said, "Thanks." He took another bill, of the same denomination, from his wallet. She reached for that one, too, but he didn't give it to her, he said, "I'm rather curious to know the circumstances; what she told you and what she's done since she came here."

"What do you want with her? Who are you?"

Sweeney said. "Okay, it doesn't matter. I'll just go up and talk to her." He started to put the second twenty back into his wallet.

She said, very quickly. "She came here late this afternoon and wanted a room. I said we didn't take dogs and she said she'd pay extra if I did and that the dog was well behaved, so I gave her the room. She didn't have any baggage. Not even a coat or hat."

"How long did she say she'd be staying?"

"She didn't know. But she said she'd pay for a full week no matter how short a time she stayed."

"How much *did* she pay you?"

She hesitated. "Twenty dollars."

Sweeney looked at her. He thought, *you bitch. And you sell her out for another twenty*. Aloud, he asked, "And since then?"

"She went out and left the dog in her room. She came back with a lot of packages. Then she took the dog down for a walk on a leash; she hadn't had one on him before. And she was disguised; she had on a black wig and shell-rimmed glasses and a different dress. You'd have hardly knowed her."

"Was it a wig or a dye job?"

"A dye job couldn't have dried that quick."

"Anything else you can tell me about her?"

She thought for a moment, but shook her head. Sweeney held out the second bill, holding it carefully so his hand wouldn't be touched by hers. He watched its course into her capacious bosom and thought that for forty dollars he wouldn't reach down there to take his two twenties back.

Something in his expression made her take a step backwards.

And that was fine, Sweeney didn't want to have to brush against her as he went by and up the stairs. Halfway up, he heard her door slam. For forty dollars, she didn't care what he wanted with her new guest. Sweeney wished he hadn't given her any money; he could have got most of that information out of her anyway. He felt ashamed of himself for having taken the easy way.

And then he stood in front of the door on the second floor at the head of the stairs, and he quit thinking about the landlady who'd directed him there.

He tapped gently at the door.

There was a rustle of movement within, and it opened a few inches. Wide eyes stared back at him through shell-rimmed glasses, under black hair. But the eyes themselves he'd seen before, and often. They'd stared at him blankly through the glass of a door on State Street on a night that seemed many years ago. They'd looked at him across a table at El Madhouse. They'd looked at him from the El Madhouse stage.

And they'd looked at him from the face of a small black statuette that screamed as silently as its model had screamed noisily.

Sweeney said, "Hello, Bessie Wilson."

Her eyes widened and she gasped. But she stepped back and Sweeney walked in.

It was a small room, and dingy. It contained a bed. A dresser and a chair, but Sweeney didn't notice them. To Sweeney, the room seemed full of dog. Even though the landlady had talked about the dog, even though he himself had been thinking about it and had traced Yolanda through it, he had somehow managed to overlook the fact that Devil would be here.

But Devil was. He crouched, ready to spring at Sweeney's throat. The sound that came from deep in Devil's chest was that ominous buzzsaw sound that Sweeney had heard once before.

Yolanda said, "Quiet, Devil. Guard him." She had closed the door.

Sweeney felt something wet on his forehead. He felt something cold crawling down his neck. It came to him now that he had been so interested in solving the problem that he had completely forgotten the personal danger its solution would place him in.

He stared at Yolanda Lang—at Bessie Wilson.

Even with the black wig, with the glasses, she was incredibly beautiful. Her only visible garment was a house-coat; under it, her feet were bare. The house-coat had a long zipper down the front.

Sweeney wondered if—and then realized he didn't have time to wonder. He'd better say something, anything.

He said, "I finally figured it out, Bessie, except a few details. The doctor or psychiatrist from the sanatorium near Beloit, the one who took an interest in your case after—after what happened to you at Brampton. That must have been Doc Greene—wasn't it?"

He'd have felt better if she'd answered—even to say, uselessly, that she didn't know what he was talking about—but she didn't speak.

She took off the glasses and the wig and put them on the dresser beside the door. She shook her head and her blonde hair fell again into the page-boy bob. She regarded him gravely—but silently.

Sweeney's throat felt dry. He had to clear it before he could talk. He said. "It *must* have been Greene, whether he was using that name then or not. And he fell madly in love with you. Literally madly—so insanely that he ran out on his career to be with you. Or did he get into some trouble that made him have to leave his profession anyway?

"Did you know that he sent your brother a letter, telling him that you had died? He did; Charlie thinks you're dead. But Greene must have signed papers to get you out, and then quit his job to bring you to Chicago.

"He must have thought he'd cured you as nearly as you could be cured. He must have known that you'd never be fully sane, but figured that, as a psychiatrist, he could handle you and control you. And he could and did. I guess—until something that he didn't know about you set you off. He was a pretty brilliant guy, Yolanda. I'll bet he did the choreography for that dance you and the dog do. And it's good, damned good. I wondered for a while why he didn't get you better bookings—but it must have been because he didn't dare risk letting you become really famous, under the circumstances. He kept you in the small time deliberately—as deliberately as he covered his real relationship to you, as doctor and patient, by becoming a bona fide agent and getting other clients."

Sweeney cleared his throat again, hoping she'd say something.

She didn't. She just looked at him. And the dog looked at him yellowly, ready to spring at the slightest word or signal from its mistress—or at the slightest move from Sweeney.

He said, "And you were all right until that day, two months ago, when you happened to go into Raoul's gift shop and bought that statuette from Lola Brent. Did you recognize that statuette, Yolanda?"

He thought she might answer that. She didn't.

He took a deep breath and the dog began to growl because his shoulders had moved. Sweeney stood very still and the dog quit growling.

He said, "Your brother Charlie made that statuette, Bessie. You were the model for it. It expressed, pretty perfectly, what you felt when—when the thing that drove you insane happened. Whether you recognized yourself in the statuette and knew that it was Charlie's work I don't know. But seeing that statuette undid everything Doc Greene had done for you.

"Only there was a *transference*. Seeing yourself—in the

statuette—as the *victim*, seeing yourself in that state from the outside, you became, in your mind, the attacker. The killer with the knife.

"And the woman from whom you bought the statuette was a beautiful blonde, and your mania fixed on her. You went out and bought a knife and waited, with it in your purse, until she left to go home. And because she was fired, it wasn't a long wait. You followed her home and killed her—as the ripper in Brampton would have killed you if Charlie hadn't shot him. So——"

There wasn't anywhere to go from the "So——" and it hung there. When it got tired of hanging there, Sweeney said. "You took the statuette home and—did you make a fetish of it, Yolanda? It must have been something like that. Did you worship it, with a ritual that involved a knife? Or what?"

No answer yet, and he thought her eyes were starting to glaze a little, staring at him. He went on talking because he was afraid of what would happen when he stopped.

"And you killed twice more. Each time, a beautiful blonde. Each had passed your place on State Street just before she was killed. I'd guess that each time was just after some mystical ritual with the statuette after which you went down to the street and followed—and killed—the first woman who went by and who was blonde and beautiful, who fitted your fixation.

"And it wasn't until after that third killing that Doc Greene suddenly found out, or suddenly realized, that it was *you* who'd been doing them. He didn't know about the statuette then, but somehow he learned or realized who the Ripper was. And it scared him stiff. He would have been in a beautiful mess if the truth came out. They'd merely put you in an institution again, but Doc—I don't know exactly what grounds they'd get him on, but they'd get him plenty; they'd throw the book at him. So he tried something pretty desperate. Did you know it was he who attacked you that night, Yolanda?"

If she'd only answer—

He said, "Doc tried a really heroic cure. Shock treatment. he thought being attacked again might reverse your fixation—at least put you back into the type of insanity you had before. And *anything* would be better than having you homicidal. He probably figured he could handle anything short of homicidal insanity.

"So he attacked you that night in the hallway. Of course he wouldn't have used an ordinary knife or razor—because he didn't want to hurt you physically. What he used would have been a piece of wood say, with a razor blade projecting out only an eighth of an inch or less, so it would make just a surface cut. And unorthodox as his psychiatry was, it worked—up to a point. If he'd known, then, about the statuette and had hunted it up in your apartment while you were in the hospital, you might not have gone haywire again.

"But he didn't know about the statuette until after I broke the story in today's paper. He must have had a hunch all along that I was going to crack this thing, though, because he kept in touch with me, pretending he was interested in getting the Ripper caught so *you'd* be safe from another attack. We had a lot of fun, Doc and I. I'm sorry he's——"

Sweeney took a deep breath. He said, "But when Doc read today's paper, he learned about the statuette and saw that it was what had set you off. So he decided to get it away from you right away. He went up to your flat this afternoon with an *empty* box, that would hold it. He didn't want to be seen carrying a package *out* that he hadn't brought *in*; he didn't want anyone who might be watching your place to wonder what was in the package. He was still gambling his life to save you, and this time he lost.

"He found the statuette—in your dresser or closet or wherever you kept it—and the knife with it. He had both of them in his hands, and the sight of him touching your fetish threw you into—well, you sicked Devil on him, and Devil killed him."

Sweeney glanced down at Devil, and wished he hadn't.

He looked back at Bessie Wilson. He said, "You didn't know for sure whether he was dead or not, down there in the courtyard, and didn't know what he'd tell the police if he wasn't, so you ran. But he didn't tell on you, Yolanda. Instead—because he knew he was dying—the damn fool took the rap for you; he said *he* was the Ripper. He must have thought, or at least hoped, that once the statuette was broken and you didn't have it any more, you'd be all right again, even without him."

He stared at her and opened his mouth to ask the sixty-five dollar question—*Are you? Are you all right now?*

But he didn't have to ask it, because the answer was there, in her eyes.

Madness.

Her right hand fumbled for the tab of the zipper of her housecoat, found it, zipped downward. It fell down in a circle about her bare feet. Sweeney caught his breath a little, just as he had that night when he had looked through the glass into the hallway.

Reaching behind her, she opened the top left drawer of the dresser, felt inside it. Her hand came out holding a knife, a brand-new eight-inch carving knife.

A nude high priestess holding the sacrificial knife.

Sweeney sweated. He started to raise his hands and the dog growled and crouched before he'd moved them an inch. He quit moving them.

He made his voice quiet and steady. "Don't, Yolanda. I'm not the one you want to kill. I'm not blonde or beautiful. I'm not a prototype of Bessie Wilson who was attacked by a maniac——"

He was watching her eyes and it came to him that she didn't understand a word he was saying by now, that the connection had broken, just when he did not know. Yet she had started a step forward when he had stopped speaking and had stood still, the knife in her hand and ready—but words, the sound of his voice, had arrested her in midstep. Words, not what he said, but the fact that he was talking——

Her foot was moving again, the knife coming up. Again Sweeney took the mere ghost of a backward step, and again the dog growled and crouched to spring at his throat.

"Four score and seven years ago," Sweeney said, "our fathers brought forth on this confinement a new nation, conceived in liberty and dedicated to the proposition that all men are created equal . . ."

Yolanda stood still again, an almost cataleptic stillness.

Sweat was running down Sweeney's sides, from his armpits. He said. "Now we are engaged in a great civil war, testing whether—uh—that nation——That's all I remember. Mary had a little lamb, its fleece was white as snow . . ."

He finished Mary and the lamb, hit high spots of the *Rubaiyat*, Hamlet's soliloquy. After a while he remembered that he could repeat himself, and after another while he found that—if he did it a sixteenth of an inch at a time—he could ease his way back toward the wall behind him and finally, lean against it.

But he couldn't move, even a sixteenth of an inch, towards the door or toward Yolanda. He couldn't raise his hands.

And after a time—a long time—his voice was so tired he couldn't talk any more. But he kept on talking anyway. If he stopped talking for as much as ten seconds he was going to die.

Sweeney could tell from the one small window of the room, on the side opposite from the wall he leaned against that it was dark outside. Years later a clock somewhere tolled midnight. Centuries after that, the window began to get light again.

". . . Beneath a spreading chestnut tree," said Sweeney hoarsely, "the village smithy stands. The smith, a mighty man is he, beneath the spreading chestnut tree. A rose by any other name would waste its fragrance on the desert air, and all our yesterdays have lighted fools the way to dusty death. And when the pie was opened, they all began to sing . . ."

Every muscle of his body ached. He marvelled, with what was left of his mind, at how Yolanda could stand there—incredibly beautiful, incredibly naked—and not move at all. Catalepsy, of course, hypnosis, whatever you called it, it was hard to believe——

". . . Alas, poor Yorick!" said Sweeney. "I knew him, Horatio:

a fellow of infinite jest, of most excellent—uh—The owl and the pussycat went to sea, in a beautiful pea green boat . . .''

It got lighter, slowly. It was nine o'clock in the morning before there was a knock at the door. An authoritative knock.

Sweeney raised his voice, with as much effort as it would have taken him to raise a piano. It was a hoarse croak. "Bline? Come in with your gun ready. The dog will jump one of us.''

The dog, growling, had moved to a position where he could watch both Sweeney and the knocked-on door. But the door moved and Sweeney didn't, and the dog jumped at Bline, in the doorway. But Bline had been warned; his coat was wrapped around his forearm, and as the dog leaped and closed its jaws on the coat, the barrel of Bline's pistol tapped the dog's skull.

"The mouse ran up the clock," Sweeney was saying in a voice that wasn't much above a hoarse whisper, "the clock struck one——Thank Heaven you finally came, Cap. I knew you'd see holes in Doc's story when you had time to think it out and that you'd come looking for Yolanda and get to her the same way I did. Listen, Cap. I have to keep on talking and I can't stop. She isn't even looking at you and doesn't know what's going on except that if I stop talking——Walk up on her from that side and get the knife——"

Bline got the knife. Sweeney, still mumbling hoarsely, slid slowly down the wall.

And then it was late evening. Godfrey was there on the park bench and Sweeney sat down beside him. "Thought you were working," God said.

"I was. But I broke such a big story Wally let me talk him into getting off a while without pay. A week, two weeks, or whenever I get back."

"You sound hoarse, Sweeney. Did you spend a night with that dame you were raving about?"

"That's why I'm hoarse," said Sweeney. "Listen, God, this time I left money, quite a bit of money, with my landlady. But I held out three hundred. Do you think we can get drunk on three hundred bucks?"

God turned his shaggy head to look at Sweeney. "If we want to badly enough. If you want something badly enough, you can get anything you want, Sweeney. Like spending a night with that dame. I told you you could."

Sweeney shuddered. He pulled two flat pint bottles out of the side pockets of his coat and handed one of them to God . . .

Knock Three-One-Two

5:00 P.M.

HE had a name, but it doesn't matter; call him *the psycho*.

That's what the newspapers and everyone who read them called him now, since his second murder two months ago. At first he'd been called by various designations: insane rapist-killer, homicidal maniac, sexual psychopath, and others. For convenience, for short-hand, it had boiled down to the psycho. The police called him that too, although they had been moving heaven and earth to find a better name for him, a name like Peter Jones or Robert Smith, a name that would let them find and apprehend him before he killed again. And again.

And now tonight the Need was on him again. The need to rape and kill a woman.

He stood in the hallway of an apartment building, before a door. Nervous tension was making him flex and unflex his hands—his tremendously strong, strangler's hands that had already killed twice and, if everything went well, were about to kill again. He forced himself to hold them still. Not that it mattered here and now, with no one watching him, but it was a habit that had been growing on him and one that he had to break, lest he forget sometime and do it when people were watching him and make them wonder about him, about why he did it. And maybe go on wondering from there; in this city right now just about everybody was watching his neighbor suspiciously, watching for just such little signs as that.

He took a deep breath and then raised a hand and knocked on the door. A light, almost diffident knock, not a peremptory one.

He heard the click of high heels coming to the door. And her voice called out, "Yes? Who is it?"

He made his voice as soft as his knock had been, and as unfrightening, just loud enough to carry to her. "Western Union, ma'am. Collect telegram, from Pittsburgh." Collect, of course, so she couldn't ask him to slide it under the door. And the "from Pittsburgh" should allay any suspicion she might have, since that's where her husband had gone yesterday, on a business trip. She might wonder why he'd wire her collect—but there could be reasons for that.

He heard the knob turn and tensed himself, ready. Then the door opened—a few inches, on a chain—and knew that he had failed. He threw himself back flat against the wall alongside the door so she wouldn't get a glimpse of him.

And ran, down the flight of stairs and out to the street. Thank God her apartment was a back one and didn't have a window on the street from which she could still get a look at him. Once out the door he forced himself to walk slowly to his car. He got in and drove away, being careful not to drive too fast or too slow.

What a hell of a lousy break. He'd checked that apartment three days ago and there hadn't been a chain bolt on the door then. Her husband must have put it on for her just before he left on his business trip.

Well, at least he had got away safely.

He was five blocks off and had just turned into a main traffic artery when he heard the sound of squad car sirens converging on the building he had just left.

5:02 P.M.

After his wife had left, Ray Fleck paced the flat in rage and despair. With rage, at first, predominating. Damn her, damn her, he thought. What kind of wife would flatly refuse to help her husband when he was in a jam, a real jam? The bitch, she could give him the money so easily, and never feel it. All she had to do was cash in that accursed insurance policy. What did she need it for? A policy on *herself*. And it had a cash surrender value of over three thousand dollars—maybe almost four thousand by now; several payments had been made since they'd last argued about it.

Or she could at least borrow against it, and all he needed was five hundred bucks. Four hundred and eighty, to be exact, but he'd made a round figure. But no, that damned policy of hers was sacrosanct; she wouldn't even borrow against it. Sacrosanct for what, for God's sake? Sure it was her savings, her stake, and she'd taken it out herself, had started saving that way, before they were married. But now that she *was* married and had a husband to support her, why should she feel she needed a stake? Unless she was planning to leave him, or thinking that she might decide to do so—that was possible. They had had some pretty bitter quarrels, the past two years out of the three they'd been married. But she'd fought to keep that policy even during the first year, and they'd been pretty happy at first. He'd been in a lucky streak, riding high, and they'd both been in love. Women love you when you're in the chips. When it comes to money, women are a one-way street. You can spend it on them, but try to get some of it back. Just try.

Besides, some of the money in that policy was his, rightfully his. Hadn't he, for most of that first year, given her money to pay the premiums on it? Under protest, of course; he'd tried to talk her out of wanting to keep on carrying it. "Honey," he'd said, "what do we want a policy on *you* for? I don't want you to die, but if you should die I don't want ten grand out of it." But she'd had an answer for that. Women always have an answer.

"Ray, darling," she'd said, "I'd agree with you if this were just an insurance policy—but it isn't. It's a ten-year endowment policy, and that's a way of saving. A good way. I've carried it for over four years now and in less than another six years we'll have ten thousand dollars in cash. Won't that be nice?"

"Yeah, but it's a long time away—and those are damn high

premiums. Why short ourselves now to have money when we're old? What good will ten thousand do us then?"

She laughed. "We won't exactly be old in six years. I'll be twenty-nine and you'll be thirty-five. As to what we can use it for—a house, if we haven't already bought one by then. It doesn't have to be big or expensive, but I want us to have a home by then, maybe it would be enough to let you start in business for yourself; you've said you would like to, if you had capital."

That made sense to him. Not the part about "a home of our own"; he was a city dweller and wouldn't live in a house in the suburbs if somebody gave him one, but he could talk her out of that idea when the time came.

But with ten thousand capital, all at once, he *could* do himself a lot of good. He was a liquor salesman and seldom made less than a hundred a week in commissions: he averaged considerably higher than that. He worked for J. & B. Liquor Distributors, and he had a good following among taverns and liquor stores all over the city. And he had at least some contacts with salesmen for wholesalers and distillers; they knew he was a good salesman. If he could set himself up as an independent distributor, make a profit on what he sold instead of just a commission, he'd be on his way toward making big money instead of peanuts. But it would be a long, slow pull. He'd need capital, all right.

He'd made only one more effort. "But wouldn't it be better to put that much money in the bank instead? Then if there was an emergency, we could get at it easier."

But Ruth had shaken her head firmly. "We *could* put money in the bank, but you know you wouldn't most weeks. Having regular premiums to meet will *make* us save. And if an emergency comes up we can borrow against the policy—and get the money the same day, since the company has an office here. But, Ray, I'd do it only for a real emergency—an accident or serious illness, an operation, something like that. Not to let you bet heavily on a horse race because you've got a hot tip, or to let you pay off a gambling debt if you run in the hole." Well, she'd warned him.

But he'd given in, and had given her money to keep up the premiums for a while, ten or eleven monthly premiums. Then he'd run into a streak of bad luck instead of good and had told her he couldn't give her the money; he just didn't have it.

She'd taken it calmly. "All right, Ray. But I'm *not* going to cash in that policy. I'll take a job, part time anyway, and make enough to pay the premiums myself. More than that, I hope."

And she had taken a job, and had worked ever since. He hadn't objected. Why should he? If the damn policy meant that much to her, why shouldn't she earn the money to keep it up? And, for that matter, to kick in on household expenses or at least to buy her own clothes? Why should he have to earn everything for both of them and let her do nothing?

She'd held several jobs. Checker at a supermarket, ticket seller at a movie. Currently, and for the past eight or nine months, she was working an evening shift as a waitress in a Greek restaurant. Thirty hours a week, from five-thirty to eleven-thirty five nights a week. Usually when he was home at this time he drove her to work—and sometimes when he was doing nothing important around eleven-thirty, picked her up after her work. But this afternoon he'd had to leave his car at a garage to have some work done on it (that would be another damn bill on top of everything else) so the question hadn't arisen. Just as well, since they'd quarreled so bitterly. They'd probably have kept on quarreling in the car, and it would have done him no good. He recognized by now that he'd lost the argument; she was adamant and she'd stay that way. She hadn't believed him when he'd told her he was in physical danger.

Well, he didn't really believe that himself. Joe Amico was tough but he wasn't a gangster, and he wasn't going to risk having anybody killed for four hundred and eighty bucks.

True, he might go to the length of having someone beat up a little if he thought the guy was welshing on him, didn't even *intend* to pay off. But Joe knew him better than that. He'd owed Joe before and had always paid off—although never anything like almost five hundred bucks; *how* had it ever run that high? Joe knew he had a good job and was good for the money eventually.

All he needed was a lucky streak, and he was due for one. Overdue for one. At poker, maybe if the horses kept running badly for him. Sometimes when the horses ran badly the cards ran well for him. And vice versa.

There was a poker game tonight that might do the trick, if he had or could raise enough of a stake to sit in on it. Yes, this was Thursday night, and Harry Brambaugh always had a Thursday night poker game at his place. From eleven o'clock on, sometimes well into the next day. But—

Although he knew approximately how much money he had, he took out his wallet and counted it. Twenty-eight bucks, twenty-eight lousy bucks. Not enough to sit in on a game at Harry's. He ought to have a hundred to start with to buck that game, not a stake that could go in the first pot he got into beyond the ante. But if he could raise a hundred—well, a lucky streak could easily run it to enough to let him pay off Joe Amico and maybe some left over.

Raising a hundred didn't sound nearly as impossible as raising four hundred and eighty. Even if he had to borrow ten bucks apiece from ten guys. With all evening to do it in.

The phone rang. He picked it up and said "Ray Fleck."

And then recognized the voice that said "Hi, Ray," and wished he'd let the phone ring. It was Joe Amico.

He said, "Listen, Joe, I haven't been able to do anything yet—but I'm working on it. I'll raise it somehow, pretty soon. I'm sorry, but you know I'm good for it."

"I know you're good for it. You'd better be. But I want you to drop in and see me this evening."

"Sure, Joe, if you want me to. I'm coming downtown anyway. But it won't do any good. I'm flat."

"Flat or not, you come in. I'll be here till ten. Any time between now and then. Got me?"

"Okay, Joe. I'll see you."

He sighed as he put down the phone. Well, he was going downtown anyway; that had been the truth. And probably Joe was going to give him an ultimatum, a time limit. And it would be an unpleasant interview but at least he'd know the worst. He'd know how long he had to raise the money. Or whether Joe would take it in weekly payments if he simply couldn't raise it any other way. He'd hate that; he'd hate it like hell. Because, for a hell of a long time, it would leave him no surplus to do any betting with. And his luck was due to change; it *had* to change.

He strolled to the front window and stood looking down at the street, wondering whether he should go downtown now and eat whenever he got hungry, or save himself money by rustling something to eat here before he left. Since Ruth had to leave for work at five he had to fend for himself or eat out the five evenings she worked, but he didn't mind that; sometimes he enjoyed cooking simple things for himself, and of course she did the cleaning up and dishwashing the next morning.

Aside from that he was glad she worked an evening shift; in fact, he'd talked her into doing it. He was out almost every evening himself; he'd explained to her that it was his best time for selling. And that was partly true. Some of his bar owner customers delegated the duller daytime hours to a bartender who wasn't authorized to do any buying and themselves took over the bar, with or without the help of a bartender or two, during the evening hours. Even tonight he should probably make a business call or two, although he didn't feel in the mood to do it. Just downtown bars, of course, since he wouldn't have his car till tomorrow. Yes, he could see Harry Webber and Chuck Connolly; they were both due to be called on.

Brakes squeaked on the street below and his eyes swiveled toward the source of the sound, the nearby corner. It was a near accident. A kid, a boy about ten, had run across the street right in front of an oncoming car and the driver had slammed on his brakes and skidded, had managed to stop with only inches to spare. A close thing, a very close thing. But the kid ran on and the driver must have been the more shaken up of the two; he sat there almost a minute before starting up the car again.

Accidents can happen, even though this one didn't. And unbidden a thought rose in Ray Fleck's mind. What if an accident should happen to Ruth, on her way to work right now or on her way home tonight? Not that she'd run in front of a car like that crazy kid had, but pedestrians can be hit even when they're not at fault. By a drunken driver or a driver who loses control of his car. Sometimes cars even ran up onto a sidewalk and—

Oh, the chances of anything like that happening, of Ruth being killed, were a million to one against. Pretty poor odds—but good God, wouldn't it be a perfect answer to his problem, to all his problems, if it *should* happen? As beneficiary of her policy he'd have ten thousand dollars, ten whole grand, all at once. What he owed Amico would be peanuts; he'd still have nine and a half grand. It would be enough; he could make the break right away. He'd no longer be Ray Fleck, liquor salesman, but Ray Fleck, Distributor. And on the way to a real income.

Funny he'd never thought seriously about the possibility of his ever collecting that ten grand as a beneficiary. Maybe because Ruth was such a healthy girl; she hadn't been sick a day in the three years of their marriage. But even a healthy person can have an accident.

Or— He pushed that thought aside. He was no angel and he'd done a lot of dishonest things in his life, but he wasn't a murderer. Even if he was he'd never get away with it. If a woman is killed her husband is always the prime suspect, even if he hasn't any insurance on her.

Forget it, he told himself, and forgot it. Abruptly he made up his mind not to stick around the flat until he got hungry enough to eat here, to save a buck. What was a buck in the jam he was in? And the sooner he got downtown the more chances he'd have to raise a stake to get in that poker game with, at eleven. The game that was the only chance he knew of to win any real money tonight. The game he *had* to get into.

He left the flat, walked down the two flights of stairs and out to the street. He was lucky; a taxi was going by and he flagged it and got in. Downtown was only a short cab ride, half a buck plus tip, and he hated waiting for buses. "Main and Willis," he told the driver. "Drop me off at the northwest corner."

That was the corner where Benny had his newsstand and his first stop would be to pick up a Racing Form. Not that he'd be placing any bets tonight—or tomorrow unless he won really big at poker, but he always liked to study the Form anyway and do his handicapping. Besides Benny always—when he remembered; Benny's memory wasn't too good—held out a Form for him and if Benny had, he didn't want to leave him stuck with it. Poor Benny. Crazy Benny, some people called him; but Ray didn't think he was really crazy, just a little lacking upstairs, prone to forgetting things. And sometimes (Ray had heard, although he'd never run into this himself) to remembering things that hadn't really happened. But he ran the newsstand all right and never made a mistake in making change.

He paid off the taxi and strolled to the wooden enclosure from which Benny sold his papers. "Hi, Benny," he said. "Remember to hold a Form for me?"

"Sure, Mr. Fleck, I *always* remember to." And this time Benny really had remembered. He reached behind him and took a copy of the Racing Form down from a shelf at the back of the stand. Ray put down the coins to pay for it and picked it up, started to fold it as he turned, then had a sudden thought and turned back. Since he was going to have to raise his poker stake by borrowing a little each from as many friends as he could put the bite on, why not start here and now by seeing if Benny was good for a sawbuck? He'd never borrowed anything from Benny before, but what was to lose trying.

"Benny," he said. "I'm a little short on dough, wonder if you could lend me ten bucks. Just till Saturday, day after tomorrow, when I get my commission check."

Benny's big moon face didn't show any surprise. He said, "Why—why, I guess I can, Mr. Fleck." He took from under the counter the cigar box in which he kept bills—coins he kept in a change dispenser on his belt—and opened it. There were quite a few bills in it and for a second Ray considered whether he should ask if Benny could make it twenty instead; then he saw that all of the bills he could see were singles and maybe all of them were. In fact apparently all of them were because Benny didn't fish through them to look for a ten or two fives; he started counting out ten singles, one at a time, with the slow carefulness with which he always counted money or made change. He handed the ten bills over and Ray stuffed them into his wallet. "Thanks, Benny."

"Mr. Fleck. I just thought uh somethin'. You'll have to mail that money to me. I won't be here Saturday."

"Sure. Taking a vacation, huh? You better give me an address."

"You won't need no address, Mr. Fleck. I mean, you'll know from the papers. I been thinkin' it over all day and made up my mind. I'm goin' to give myself up to the p'lice, before I do anything more. Soon as I close up the stand tonight."

"What are you talking about Benny? Before you do any more what?"

"You been readin' in the papers about this sex psycho—" He pronounced the *ch* as in checkers. "Psycho— whatever it is?"

"Psychopath. What about him?"

"I'm him, Mr. Fleck. I killed them two women."

Ray Fleck put his head back and laughed heartily. "Benny, you're cr— I mean, get that idea out of your head. You didn't kill those women. *I know.* You wouldn't hurt a rabbit, Benny."

He started chuckling as he turned and walked away.

Feeling a little ashamed of himself, too, for having laughed in Benny's face. But he hadn't really been laughing *at* Benny at all, although he'd never be able to explain that to poor Benny. He'd been laughing at the crazy fact, the ridiculous fact, that Benny had chosen to make his confession to the one and only person in the entire city—outside of the psychopathic killer himself—who could know and did know, immediately and certainly, that Benny, no matter how crazy he might be, was *not* the killer.

5:20 P.M.

GEORGE MIKOS surveyed his domain, his restaurant, and found it good. Everything was set up and ready for the dinner hour. No customers at the moment, except for one man having coffee at the counter, but they'd start coming in soon. Only one waitress on duty at the moment, but Ruth Fleck would be coming in ten minutes, and he knew he could count on her getting there; Ruth was dependable.

He turned and went through the swinging door back to the kitchen, ducking his head a little as he did so. He was a big man, six feet two inches tall, and that doorway was an inch or so too short for him. When he'd first bought the restaurant he'd intended to have the doorway made higher but he hadn't got around to it and by now he was so used to ducking that it was completely automatic; he didn't even know he did it.

The cook was scraping the top of the range, but looked around as he heard George come through the door. "Everything under control?" George asked him. "Sure, George," the cook said.

"Fine. I'll be in my office a while. Give a yell for me if and when I might be needed, either back here or up front."

He went into the room, a fair-sized room, off the kitchen that served him as an office. He left the door ajar. The kitchen and restaurant noises, the banging of pots and the clatter of dishes and such, wouldn't bother him; he was conditioned to hear them and evaluate them subconsciously. To know, especially from the frequency with which waitresses called back orders, when things were getting busy enough so his help might be needed, even if the cook did not, as he suggested, give a yell for him.

He sat down at the oak typewriter desk. The typewriter was already raised into typing position. There was a sheet of paper in it, blank except for a numeral 3 at the top; it was to be the third page of a letter he'd started early in the afternoon.

Before resuming the letter he picked up the two pages of it he'd already written and reread them rapidly.

Dear Perry:

It was wonderful to hear from you again after lo, these many years (almost ten of them, isn't it?) since we roomed together at college. I'm so glad you happened to run into Walt, that he was able to give you my address.

Congratulations on having gone to a Ps.D. And on having opened your own office as a consulting psychologist—in New York and on Park Avenue, no less; it must be really a happy hunting ground and if you're not coining money already you will be soon.

No, I have not continued my formal education. Nor do I intend to, any more. By now I yam what I yam, a Goddam Greek who runs a restaurant. But I read a lot, study some; I'm not letting my mind stagnate completely. I try to keep up with things. For instance I subscribe to and read the *Journal of Psychology*, even though—I realize now—I'll never be more than a layman in that field. And although about half of my reading is escape reading, the other half isn't; I read classics too. My knowledge of and taste in literature is far ahead of what it used to be in our college days.

As for keeping in shape, I go to a gym two, sometimes three, mornings a week. I still go in for Graeco-Roman wrestling, when I can find an opponent, and I haven't found one here who can take me at it.

You want a description of my restaurant, what it's called, everything about it. *Everything* about it would be a large order and wouldn't interest you unless you think you might start one of your own, and I doubt if you have that in mind. But I'll give you a rough idea.

First, it's called *Mikos'*; I don't go in for fancy names and have no intention of trying to hide the fact that a Greek runs it. It's small—but not tiny. Between counter and tables it will seat thirty people, and during rush hours, usually does seat that many or almost that many.

It'll never make a Duncan Hine's rating, but neither will anyone ever call it a Greasy Spoon; it's clean. Our forte is good food at reasonable prices.

I employ an average of ten people. Not that many all at once, of course; they work varying shifts, since we're open from 7 A.M. till 11:30 P.M.

I myself come in at about 11 A.M., before the lunch hour, and stay until closing time. That sounds a long working day—twelve and a half hours—but don't let it fool you because I actually work only about half of the time. There's a fair-sized room off the kitchen which I've converted into a combination office and den. I do my bookkeeping here, write checks for bills and salaries, type menus, all that sort of thing—but that doesn't take over an average of four hours a day.

Another two or three hours a day I spend in the kitchen or up front, helping out wherever needed. Some days more than that if someone fails to show up and we're short handed. But other days things go smoothly and I'm not needed at all. Call it an average of two hours a day.

So you see my actual working day is about six hours; the rest of the time I'm around, in case of emergency or to solve problems if any arise, but in general my time is my own. I read or study or think. If for any reason I'm short on sleep I take naps. Or I write letters, as I'm doing now.

And so much for the restaurant, except for the most important thing about it: it makes money. More than I, as a bachelor with relatively simple tastes, can spend. I've been investing in land just outside the city limits to the west, and as the city is growing in that direction, and rapidly, the land is equally rapidly appreciating in value. So, within another five years—but I'm beginning to sound as though I'm bragging and I'll stop. Suffice it to say there is no wolf at my door.

You ask me how my love life is doing. Probably your question was facetious, but I'm going to give it an honest answer.

That was where the second page of the letter had ended. George Mikos turned to the typewriter to go on and then decided, before starting page 3 to take a look to make sure Ruth Fleck had shown up; it was just five-thirty, her starting time.

He went to the door and opened it wider, and had to look no farther. She was just about to pass it, coming from the closet where the employees hung their coats.

"Hello, Ruth," he said. And then, "Ruth, you've been crying. Is something wrong? Is there anything I can do? Can you come in and talk a moment?"

She hesitated. "I— There *is* something I'd like to ask you about, George. But please not now. Later, after the dinner rush, I'll be calmer and much more sensible."

She went on, without giving him a chance to say anything more, through the swinging door into the restaurant. George watched until it had swung shut behind her. Then he pushed his own door partly shut again and went back to the desk. This time he started typing.

Now, and for the first time in my life, at least since late adolescence, I am in love, deeply in love, and with a woman with whom I have not had an affair and with whom I don't want to intend to have an affair, even if I could. At least I have found the right woman for me and I want everything or nothing. I want to marry the girl.

There is a fly in the ointment; the fly is the husband she already has. I am trying to convince her to divorce him and to marry me. Offhand, this may sound reprehensible, but I do not think that it is, really. Her husband is, if I may change my entomological metaphor, a louse.

He is a liquor salesman; that's nothing against him, but there is plenty else that is. He is a compulsive, congenital gambler, mostly on the horses; he's a type of horse player who does his own handicapping and thinks he can beat the game, which of course he can't. He probably earns at least a hundred a week but spends, or rather loses, at least half of that gambling, for which reason his wife has to work—and works for me as a waitress. Most of the time he's broke and in debt, living on his next week's commission check.

I don't think he's brutal to Ruth (that's her name; his is Ray Fleck) physically. I almost wish he were, because I think that if he ever struck her she would leave him, which, of course, is what I want to happen.

I know quite a bit about him, including the fact that he is at least occasionally unfaithful to her—which in itself justifies to me my breaking up their marriage if I can.

No, I didn't tell Ruth anything about what I heard. I was afraid that, whether or not those reports would decide her to divorce Fleck, she'd be angry at me for having had the presumption to tell her. Besides for all I know she may already know or at least suspect that Fleck cheats on her. Wives, I am told, can usually tell. What's the opinion of a consulting psychologist on that?

But that's not what I really want to ask you about. It's something that doesn't concern me personally.

We have among us here a rapist-killer, obviously a psychotic, who has already raped and killed two women. Raped and killed in that sequence; he is not a necrophile. His first rape-killing was about four months ago, his second two months ago. The interval between two crimes is hardly sufficient to establish a time interval. But if it does, if it takes him about two months to build up pressure to make him kill again, then he is about due to strike a third time. His method—

But wait. Before I give the details, such as they are, I'll tell you where I come in, and where you come in. The captain in charge of our homicide department is a friend of mine. He is understandably a very worried guy. He's been under pressure from the chief of the police, the police commissioner, the newspapers and the public to get friend psychopath. He may get demoted if he doesn't. And he hasn't a single clue or lead.

He knows, of course, that I majored in psychology and every time we see one another he heckles me to make deductions about the killer. Or even guesses. I've made a few, but I'm afraid that, whether they are correct or not, they're not very helpful on the practical level of police work.

Maybe you can do better. You've studied a lot more abnormal psychology than I have. Anyway, I'm going to toss you the few known facts about our psycho and ask if you can make any suggestions that I haven't already made. I'll pass them on to the captain. If you can come up with anything at all helpful, it may save a life, or several lives. Here goes:

Both victims were young housewives. Both were attractive. Each was home alone (home was a house in one case, an apartment in the other) at the time of the attack. In one case the husband was out of town on business, in the other working a swing shift at an airplane parts factory.

In neither case was there any sign of forcible entry; the woman herself must have admitted him or at least opened the door for him.

Both women were knocked unconscious with a blow to the chin, then carried to a bed; their clothes were torn off them and they were raped, then strangled to death. Still, from the lack of anything indicating a struggle, unconscious from knockout. (Don't ask me how the autopsies could prove or even indicate that the rape preceded the strangling but my friend tells me that the medical examiner is absolutely certain, so I'm willing to take his word for it.)

Both crimes occurred in the evening. We happen to know the exact time of one of them, ten o'clock. This was the one who lived in an apartment. The couple who lived in the apartment under hers heard a thud at that hour; they're certain of the time because the husband was just switching channels on the television to get their favorite ten o'clock program. Knowing that their upstairs neighbor was home alone they looked at one another, each wondering whether she might have had a fall and need help. But before either spoke to the other they heard footsteps moving around and decided she was all right, that she'd either dropped something fairly heavy or had a fall that hadn't hurt her.

That was the first of the two murders. We don't know the time of the second one so accurately. The woman's body wasn't found until early the next afternoon when her husband returned from his business trip. After so many hours the M.E. could only say that death had occurred late the previous evening, probably between nine o'clock and midnight.

We know him to be a man of considerable strength, not only from the steam behind the knockout blows he struck but from the way in which he ripped the clothes from his victims after carrying them to a bed. One of the women was wearing a quilted house coat that zipped open about halfway down the front; he tore it the rest of the way, and quilted material does not tear easily.

From the speed and accuracy with which he struck the police theorize that he may be or may have been a boxer. Also, from his strength, they believe he is more likely to be a laborer than a white collar worker. I'll go along with both of these deductions as possibilities or probabilities and not as certainties. A man with no boxing experience but with good coordination and a little luck could have struck those blows. And if he has a good mind (except for its warp) and/or a good education he'd certainly be doing something better than manual labour.

So much for the physical side, and to the mental. First, I do not believe he is a moron. He must have cased those jobs and known that the woman would be alone at the time he came. Otherwise he had incredible luck—and I refuse to credit the incredible. Also, he left no fingerprints at the scene of either crime; he either wore gloves or avoided touching any surface that would take them. A moron wouldn't think of fingerprints.

But to a more important point, the nature of his psychosis. I have a theory; I hope you'll be able to expand on it if you agree or to offer a better one if you disagree.

I believe that he fears women to a psychotic degree, and hates them because he fears them. Call him a womanophobe. And because of his fear of women he is self-conscious in the presence of one to the point of complete impotence, even if the woman is willing; only with an unconscious woman can he find an outlet for his sex drive. His reason for killing women after he has used them can be sheer psychopathic hatred, flaring to highest pitch with or immediately after the orgasm. Or it can be caution; a dead woman can't describe him or identify him. My guess is that his reason for killing is a mixture of both those reasons.

If this description of his psychosis is correct it is almost certain that he is a bachelor. I use the "almost" because he may have been married once; an early very bad marriage might have been the starting point of his psychosis. But, whether once married or not I'd say it's certain that he is not currently living with a woman.

And I'd say that it's probable that, if he has any choice of occupations, he's working at a job that brings him into as little contact with women as possible. And living at a Y.M.C.A., a men-only hotel or—if he makes enough money—in a bachelor apartment.

Those are only probabilities, though. He may be smart enough, and actor enough, to have perfectly normal business and social contacts with women. If that's true he's going to be a lot harder to catch.

Speaking of how smart he is, we'll have a strong indication of that if and when he attempts a third crime. If he tries the same *modus operandi* he used the first two times he'll show himself to be much more stupid than I think he is. Because that method simply won't work a third time.

The women of this city are scared, have been scared ever since the second crime. Women alone in a house or flat simply don't open the door, even by day, until and unless they're damned sure who's on the other side of it. Chain bolts have been selling so fast that the hardware stores keep reordering by air express and still can't quite keep up with the demand. And from the number of speakeasy-type peepholes that have been made in doors you'd think we were back in the days of Prohibition again.

The scare has had an odd incidental effect on our economy. Normally, in a city this size, there are several hundred house-to-house salesmen and canvassers working. Here and now there are none. For the past two months, since the second rape-killing, they have been able to gain entry into such a small percentage of homes that they simply can't make a living. They've all had to move on elsewhere to greener pastures or switch to some other occupation. Even big outfits like Fuller and Watkins have closed their local offices—temporarily, they hope. And not only salesmen are affected, but mailmen—if they have a C.O.D. or a registered letter that must be signed for—bill collectors, deliverymen, meter readers, collectors for charity drives, what have you.

It's amazing what strange effect two crimes by a . . .

George Mikos paused to think out the rest of the sentence and in the pause heard his cook's voice. "Hey, George, better come out and give a hand."

"Coming," he called back. And came.

6:15 P.M.

He wasn't hungry, but Ray Fleck decided that he'd better eat. He'd slept late and had only coffee for breakfast, and only a light lunch. And this evening he'd had two drinks already in his quest for money to get him into the poker game; like as not he'd have to take at least a dozen more in the course of the evening, and if he wanted to be able to play good poker he'd damn well better lay a foundation of food under that dozen drinks.

The bad thing about the two drinks he'd already had was that he'd taken them in vain. Worse than in vain because instead of helping him raise money they'd cost him the ten bucks he'd borrowed from Benny and had put his slender capital back where it had been before. He'd seen through the window of the Palace Bar that Dick Johnson was there; Dick was usually a soft touch and he went inside and bellied up the bar beside Dick. He tried to buy him a drink, but Dick beat him to it by signalling the bartender with two upraised fingers, so Ray waited until he'd had a chance to buy back before he put on the bite, for twenty. And, because he'd genuinely forgotten, he was startled when Dick reminded him that he already owed him ten dollars from three weeks before. "My God," Ray said, "I clean forgot. Why the hell didn't you remind me sooner?" And then, because it was the only way out, he laughed and made a joke of it, pulled a ten out of his wallet and handed it to Dick. "Now we're all even; let's start over. Can you lend me twenty, just till Saturday?" He'd still come out ten ahead, he thought. But Dick Johnson had shaken his head. "Sorry, Ray boy, I'm short this week myself. Need all I've got, and this ten comes in handy too." And there went the ten he'd just got from Benny.

He stopped at the corner of Fourth and Main, the middle of downtown, to make up his mind where to eat. Feratti's seemed like a good bet; they put out good dinners for two-fifty—unless you ordered steak or lobster or something fancy—and he wouldn't be tempted, as he might be in some of the other good restaurants, to waste some of his drinking capacity on a cocktail or two before dining; Feratti's didn't have a liquor license. He turned on Fourth and headed for Feratti's.

And, as he walked, found himself thinking about Benny again. He never should have laughed like that at Benny. Especially now that he'd learned Benny was good for a sawbuck in an emergency once in a while. Of course maybe he was worrying about nothing; maybe Benny's feelings hadn't been hurt at all. But if he passed Benny's stand again this evening he ought to stop, buy a paper as an excuse, and see how Benny acted. If Benny was mad or had been hurt, he'd know easily and now, the same evening, would be the time to square things. And he wasn't a salesman for nothing; he could convince Benny that he hadn't been laughing at *him* but at a joke he'd just thought of, and tell Benny a joke. Some simple joke that even a moron couldn't help getting.

And then, if he could figure out a way to do it, try to talk Benny out of going to the cops to give himself up as the psychopathic killer. Not that the cops would really believe Benny, but they might keep him out of circulation for a while and maybe work him over a bit for details, until they were sure.

Because the cops couldn't eliminate Benny as readily and surely as he, Ray Fleck, could. The cops didn't know what the psycho looked like, and he did. At least enough to be positive that he didn't look even remotely like Benny.

It had been about two months ago, the night of the second murder—although he hadn't known that until the next day. It had been somewhere around ten o'clock in the evening. And it had happened in the nineteen hundred block on Eastgate. Howie Borden lived at 1912 Eastgate and Ray had agreed to pick him up around ten that evening; Howie was going to take him to a stag party at Howie's lodge, and Ray was to provide the transportation since Howie had a badly sprained right wrist and couldn't drive.

He'd got there just about ten and had parked in front of Howie's house and beeped the horn. Howie had raised a window and called out, "Be about five minutes yet. Come on in." But he'd called back that he'd wait in the car. He didn't want to go in because Howie's wife might be around, and she always made him feel uncomfortable.

Since he knew that five minutes might easily mean fifteen or twenty, he turned out his car lights for the wait. He was sitting there staring at nothing through the windshield a few minutes later when he saw the man.

The man came through the gate in the fence in front of a house on the other side of the street and three or four houses away. Ray noticed the man at all for only two reasons. One was the fact that in an otherwise completely static vista the eye is drawn to the only moving object. The other was the fact that as the man stood there just outside the gate he looked both ways and while he did so his hands at his sides were flexing and unflexing, as though they were cramped from gripping something very tightly and for quite a while. The gesture an oarsman might make when he unclamps his hand from the oars after rowing a mile or so, or a lumberjack when he lets go his axe to rest his hands after a bout of chopping. Or that a strangler might make— But Ray Fleck didn't think of that at the time. The man went the other way and was out of sight and out of mind by the time Howie came out and got in the car.

It wasn't until late the following afternoon, when he read the mid-afternoon edition of the evening paper, that he knew he had seen the murderer leaving the scene of his second crime. The address was 1917 Eastgate, on the opposite side of the street from Howie Borden's, and about three houses away in the direction in which Fleck's car had been facing. If the address had left any doubt in his mind that the house was the one he'd seen the man leaving, the doubt was dispelled by a picture of the house's exterior that was published with the story. It showed a three-foot iron fence in front; the house the man had left had been the only house on that side of the short block that had been fenced in. And that flexing and unflexing of the hands. . . .

Give him credit. He considered going to the police to tell them what he had seen, considered it seriously. He was home and alone at the time, as Ruth had just left for work, so he had all the time to think that he wanted. He paced the apartment for all of twenty minutes before coming to a decision. The decision was negative on three counts.

First, he couldn't give them a description that would really mean anything and he couldn't—or he was fairly sure he couldn't—identify the man if he ever saw him again. He'd seen him at a distance of about a hundred feet and in pretty dim light; the nearest street light had been behind Fleck's car, farther from the man than Fleck had been. His impression had been of a man of average height and average build—or maybe a little heavier than that. It could have been his own description, except— Except what? Thinking back, he decided that, although their weight was probably about the same, the man had been a bit narrower in the waist, a bit broader in the shoulders. But he could have been wrong even about that, the nearest to a positive point he could think of; after all he was trying to describe a vague and elusive memory, something he'd hardly noticed at the time. He thought the man had worn a dark suit and a dark hat, but he wasn't sure of those things either. The face had been a white blur in the instant it was turned toward him, before the man had turned and walked the other way.

What good could a description like that do the cops? It could fit a hundred thousand guys. It could eliminate a few, sure—teenage kids, skinny guys or fat ones, runts or six-footers. Yes, it would eliminate a few who might otherwise be suspects. Benny, for instance; Benny was well over six feet, well over two hundred pounds.

But would the cops *believe* that his impression, his memory, was as vague as all that? He doubted it. Having nothing to lose they'd operate on the theory that he might have got a better look than he remembered, that if he saw the man again his memory might come back and let him make a positive identification.

And he knew what that meant—line-ups. They'd expect him to attend the line-up every morning for God knows how long. Could they force him to? Maybe not, but they could be damned unpleasant about it, maybe make trouble for him, if he tried to refuse. Maybe they could even hold him, for a while anyway until a lawyer could get him out of it, as a material witness.

But even that wasn't the worst thing against taking his story, such as it was, to the police. Even if the police tried to keep it under wraps there was always a chance some damn reporter would get hold of the story and print it. Complete with his name and address. And how'd you like to have a crazy killer know who you were and think, however wrongly, that you knew him by sight and could put the finger on him the first time you saw him?

The cops would try to protect him, sure. But what if the killer was smarter than the cops? He had been, so far. And how *long* would the cops be able to keep up a twenty-four-hour guard duty on him, and wouldn't it mess his personal and private life to hell and back while they did?

So Ray Fleck had sensibly kept his mouth shut about what he'd seen that night. He'd even almost forgotten about it himself; he was thinking about it this evening only because of that ridiculous would-be confession of Benny's. Crazy Benny might be, but the sex killer, no.

At Feratti's he took his favourite table. It was a small one against one side of the room but a light fixture in the wall right above it made it the best lighted table, and he needed good light to read the fine print and hieroglyphics of a Racing Form. He took his out of his pocket and unfolded it, turning first to the Aqueduct results for yesterday. He swore under his breath when he saw that Black Fox had won in the fifth and had paid ten to one for a win ticket. Black Fox was a horse he'd been following and had figured was due to win. If he'd had twenty-five bucks on the nag it would have made him more than half what he owed Amico and would have taken the pressure off. Damn Joe for having cut off his credit; otherwise he'd probably have made that bet, phoned it in. He glanced over results of the other races but with less interest; none of them were races he'd have bet anyway. He'd handicapped some of them but he'd have to play the favorite in each if he played at all, and he almost never played favorites. You didn't win enough money to matter if they came in and they could always fool you and run out of the money. Really long shots weren't good either. The way to cash in on handicapping is to find a horse that pays better than the real odds against it, say a horse quoted at five or six to one but with one chance out of three or four of coming in. Then was the time to get the bank roll down, when the odds were in your favor.

He heard the deferential clearing of a throat and looked up; Sam, the waiter who always served this table, was standing there with a menu in his hand. "'Scuse me, Mist' Fleck. You wanna order now? Or shall I come back when you've had more time to figger them ponies?"

"I'll order now, Sam. Won't need a menu. Bring me the Special Sirloin."

"Yes, suh, Mist' Fleck. Medjum rare, like allus. An' Ah'll tell th' chef to pick out a nice big one."

Ray Fleck frowned as the waiter ambled off. He hadn't really intended to order a steak. But it didn't matter much. He'd be able to eat it; he was always able to eat. And it was probably better at that to get a good meal under his belt while he was at it.

He killed time with his Racing Form—not that he was going to do any betting tonight and probably not tomorrow, but a horse player has to stay in touch whether he's betting or not—until Sam brought his dinner. Then he gladly put the Form back in his pocket and dived in. Just ordering a steak and waiting for it had made him hungry, and he ate heartily. And rapidly, wolfing the steak as fast as he could cut it into bites. Ruth always kidded him about how fast he ate, but he could never see any use in dawdling over food.

And them, replete, he took a cigar from his pocket, unwrapped and lighted it. He sighed with satisfaction as he inhaled the rich smoke.

The evening stretched ahead of him, a pleasant evening now, an exciting evening. True, he had to see Joe Amico, and that would be unpleasant, and a bit embarrassing. But he could handle Joe all right, no sweat at all.

And, true, he had to spend part of the evening raising money for a poker stake, but that ought to be easy; he knew hundreds of people; he'd run into dozens of them during the course of the evening. And once he had a stake, he was going to be lucky in the game. He had more than a hunch. He felt sure of it.

He caught Sam's eye and lifted a finger, a signal for Sam to bring over the check. Sam brought it over and put it face down in front of him. But he didn't have to turn it over; he knew a sirloin steak was four bucks and this one had been well worth it. He counted our four singles from his wallet and then, the fifth one in his hand, hesitated. Sam liked to gamble. "Double or nothing on the tip, Sam?"

Sam's teeth flashed, white and black. "Sho', Mist' Fleck. How? You want flip a coin and me call it?"

Suddenly Ray Fleck had a better idea. He didn't mind Sam winning, but if he did win it would be two bucks cash tonight. And cash tonight was more important than something he could pay off the next time he ate in Feratti's. He said, "Got a better idea, Sam, I'll give you *two* tips. One of 'em's on a beetle named Birthday Boy in the fourth at Aqueduct tomorrow. Oughta pay about six to one, but I dope it he's got a better chance than that of winning. Want me to make book on him for you for a buck?"

Sam laughed. "Birthday Boy! Man, that's a real hunch bet, fo' me. Tomorra's my birthday, Mist' Fleck. Sho. An' I'm goin' to try to put some more dough down on him aftah wuk tonight. You said fourth race, Aqueduct?"

"That's it. Say, I'm seeing my bookie tonight. Want me to put down your bet for you? Might as well save you the trouble."

"That'd be fine, suh. Ah might miss the man Ah mostly bet with." Sam pulled wadded bills out of his pocket. Straightened out they proved to be a five and a half dozen ones. He handed the five to Ray Fleck. "Sho 'preciate yo puttin' this down fo' me, Mist' Fleck. Thanks muchly."

"Don't mention, it, Sam. Glad to." And of course he was glad, because it put him five bucks ahead. Unless, of course, Birthday Boy won, but that was something he wouldn't have to worry about until tomorrow. Not even tomorrow, come to think of it; if the nag did come in he'd owe Sam about thirty bucks but he wouldn't have to drop into Feratti's right away to pay off. He could wait till next week, after his next pay check. Sam wouldn't come looking for him.

After Sam had left he put the money in his wallet and, while he had it open, counted what was there. He was a little surprised to find out it was exactly what he'd left home with no more and no less, twenty-eight bucks.

Then he figured, and that was right. He'd got ten from Benny but had had to give the same amount to Dick Johnson. The five he'd just got from Sam covered his taxi fare and his dinner. He'd bought the Racing Form and had paid for a couple of drinks, but he must have had enough change to cover those things.

Well, he was still even. But damn it, he'd have to keep his mind on raising more, and damn fast. By rights he should have at least a hundred to sit in on that poker game. Fifty was rock bottom; he could hardly go around with less than that. Even with fifty, he'd have to count on winning some early pots or he'd go broke before he hit his stride and got really started.

Good God, wasn't there *someone* who could and would lend him a sizable chunk of cash, say a hundred, in one chunk without his having to try to chisel it out five or ten bucks at a time?

There *had* to be. With all the friends he had. . . .

Ruth now. She was not only being selfish as hell, but she was being penny wise and pound foolish. If she'd only cash in that ridiculous, horribly expensive endowment policy and turn over the money to him so he'd be on his feet again, she wouldn't have to work. He could and would support her. If she'd only borrow five hundred against it, she'd take him off the spot. And damn it, wasn't anything she had half his anyway? Sure, it was. This was a community property state.

Damn her, if he divorced her everything they owned would be split down the line and he'd get half of it. But he didn't have any grounds for divorce. He sometimes suspected that damned Greek she worked for of being soft on her—but he doubted that Ruth had ever encouraged him or had anything to do with him. And even if she had, how could he prove it? He couldn't afford to put private detectives on her, not now. Someday maybe. And even if he tried now and succeeded, a divorce took time. And cost money; it might even cost more than he'd get out of any property settlement.

Damn the stubborn bitch, he thought; when she gets an idea in her head. . . .

But there must be someone besides Ruth who could help him. And who would.

Suddenly he remembered a short story he'd read once, a long time ago. He wasn't much of a reader, outside of newspapers and the Racing Form, but once—before he had met Ruth—a girl he'd been going with had given him as a present a book called *Great Short Stories of the World*. And not long after that he'd been home sick for a week with a case of bronchitis and had read most of the stories in the book and had even enjoyed some of them. One of them—he couldn't remember the title—had been by a Frenchman, Maupassant or somebody. It had been about a man who'd been in a bad financial jam. He'd needed money in a hurry and had gone to his wife, in whose name he'd put a lot of his property, and had asked her for money; she'd turned him down flat. In despair he'd gone to his mistress for help—and she'd given him back all the jewelry he'd given her, and he'd been saved.

Why not? Dolly wasn't exactly his mistress but she was the next thing to one. And while he hadn't given her, any jewelry to speak of, except a wrist watch once, he'd given her, times when he'd been flush, plenty of other valuable presents. Hundreds of dollars' worth over the year and a half he'd known her. Of course she didn't love him; he knew that. But she liked him a lot and she was understanding. Wouldn't she lend him a hundred bucks if he asked her? Suddenly he felt sure that she would. Especially if he gave her a profit motive by telling her that if she lent him a hundred now he'd give her back a hundred and twenty-five in a week or two. And a hundred bucks tonight would sure be worth more than that some other time, when he was solvent again.

Sure, Dolly would do it. If not because of Cupid, then out of cupidity. Ray Fleck grinned to himself. Maybe there was something to reading great literature after all. If he hadn't read that story he might never have thought of Dolly Mason as a source of money. If only she was home, and alone, so he could see her this evening. . . .

Well, he could find out right away. He got up and got his hat first so he could leave right after the call, and then went to the phone booth. He dialed Eastgate 6-6606, Dolly's number—and a very easy one to remember. When the phone rang a dozen times or so he frowned, realizing that it wasn't going to be answered.

Then he thought to look at his wrist watch and realized why. Dolly was out somewhere eating dinner at this time. Her apartment had a kitchen but she never kept food in it; she always ate out. Alone, if there wasn't anyone to take her out. She never cooked, either for herself or for company.

He hung up and got his dime back, then left the booth. On his way out he passed Sam turning in some money at the cashier's desk and said, "Happy birthday, Sam. Hope your hunch hits."

Sam said, "Thanks muchly, Mist' Fleck. Ah hopes we both hits."

7:25 P.M.

It was dark outside now, and the blackness pressed against the windowpanes of the restaurant. Funny, Ruth Fleck thought, how black that blackness looked, because if you went outside through the door the sidewalk wasn't really dark at all. It was lighted by a street lamp not far away and by the lights of the restaurant itself shining through the big front windows. But from inside it looked like a solid wall of darkness.

Things were quiet now; the early dinner rush was over. There were four people still eating at one of the tables, a couple had just come in and were studying the menu at another, but both tables were in Margie's territory. At this time of evening, with two waitresses on, Ruth had only the counter—there were three people eating at it but they had all been served—and the two tables nearest the back end of the counter. In a few minutes there'd be only one waitress on; Ruth took off from seven-thirty to eight, to eat and rest. When she came back on Margie left for the day and Ruth took care of things quite easily alone. Mikos' Restaurant was a family type restaurant on the main street of a suburb; its customers were people of the type who ate their dinners relatively early and business after eight wasn't too heavy. Sometimes there was a flurry between ten and eleven—people dropping in on their way home from movies—and George came on and helped her.

She looked at her customers at the counter. One was just finishing and she walked down the counter to him. "Dessert, sir?" He was a clean-looking, well-dressed young man with blue eyes and dark curly hair. He looked up at her. "Thanks, no. I'd like some more coffee, though."

And, while she was pouring it, "I beg your pardon, hope you won't think I'm being fresh, but I heard the other waitress call you Ruth. May I ask the rest of your name? Mine's Will Brubaker."

Here comes a pass, Ruth thought. But she didn't really mind; it happened about once an evening and she'd probably have wondered if it hadn't happened—have wondered whether she was losing her appeal and attractiveness. Of course there was always George Mikos to convince her that she wasn't. George was a rock.

And this young man was nice, shy; he'd had to work up his courage to take the first step of asking her name. She smiled at him. "Ruth Fleck", she said. "Mrs Ruth Fleck." She didn't embarrass him by emphasizing the *Mrs.* but it was clear enough.

"Oh," he said. "I'm sorry."

"For what? It's my fault, not yours. I keep my rings in my purse while on duty because I don't like to work with them on. So you couldn't have known I was married." She took out her pad of checks and a pencil. "I'm going back into the kitchen now to eat my own dinner. I'd better give you your check."

"Sure. Uh—shall I pay it now?"

"Oh, no. The other waitress will take care of you at the register." She smiled again, a little mischievously this time. "Her name is Margie Weber and she's single."

He grinned and said "Thanks." He should have, Ruth thought. Margie was a very cute little redhead, much prettier, Ruth thought, than she herself was. And occasionally Margie did let customers make dates with her if they were nice enough; she might well think this one was nice enough.

The clock on the wall now said seven-thirty. Ruth caught Margie's eye and pointed toward the back of the restaurant to show that she was taking off. Margie nodded.

Ruth went back into the kitchen and through it to the closet-dressing room where the waitresses put their coats and those who didn't wear their uniforms to and from work (Ruth did) changed into them. She looked into the full-length mirror on one wall and liked what she saw there. She was tall for a woman; in high heels she was only an inch shorter than Ray, who was five feet ten. But she was slender and had a nice figure. The tiny waitress cap enhanced rather than hid her golden hair. Her eyes were deep blue. The only fault she could find was in her face; it was a square, honest face, attractive but not beautiful, with high cheekbones almost like an Indian's. The mouth was perhaps a trifle too wide, but the better for that when she smiled.

Right now, though, she wasn't smiling and her face looked tired. Well, it had a right to be, she'd cleaned the house thoroughly today, quite a bit of work to undertake before coming on for an evening shift that kept her on her feet almost all the time. That and the quarrel with Ray; quarrels always left her physically as well as emotionally exhausted.

But her eyes no longer showed that she'd been crying; two hours of work had taken care of that. Her nose was a little shiny though and she powdered it lightly, turned and looked over her shoulder to make sure her slip didn't show, and then went out into the kitchen again.

Tex, the cook, was taking advantage of a hiatus in order to scrape the big range. He nodded to her. "Some nice little club steaks, Ruth. Shall I fry one for you?" She shook her head. "Thanks no, Tex. I'll just help myself to something." She took a plate and went with it to the steam table, helped herself to a stuffed bell pepper, a small helping each of beets and peas, and took it to the table in the corner. It felt good to sit down and get off her feet.

She heard George Mikos come out of his office and walk up behind her. He said, "That isn't much of a meal for a healthy wench, Ruth."

She looked up at him over her shoulder. "I'm just not hungry. I'm going to have to make myself eat this much. I guess I don't feel very well."

"Want to take the rest of the evening off? I can handle things easily. Or maybe Margie would want to get in a little overtime."

"Oh, no, George. I'm not sick. Just a little tired." She smiled up at him. "I'll get my second wind soon." She wasn't exaggerating; it happened every evening when she'd done quite a bit of housework. She'd be tired for the first few hours of the evening and then get second wind and feel fine the rest of the time.

"All right," he said. "When you're through eating don't forget you wanted to talk to me about something."

He walked away and she could tell by the sound of his footsteps that he went through the swinging doors to the front of the restaurant. She noticed for the hundredth time how lightly he walked for so big a man. She wondered if he was a good dancer and decided he probably was; most men who are light on their feet are. Ray hated dancing and she'd danced only a few times since she'd been married.

Ray took her out about once a month, on one of her evenings off, never to a show and never to dance. Even if they went to a night club where there was dancing between floor shows. Ray's idea of an evening out with her was to sit at a booth in a tavern or, if he was flush, at a table in a night club, to drink and talk. To talk, that is, if he ran into friends of his whom he could get to sit in the booth or at the table with them, as generally happened. If they were alone he was generally quiet and moody as though taking her out was a duty and he resented the loss of an evening that it entailed. And in either case they generally got home earlier than he himself would have come home had he been without her.

She supposed she might as well admit it—to herself; her marriage with Ray had been, thus far at least, a failure. But she also had to admit that it was partly her fault; she should have known him longer—and got to know him better. She had known, of course, that he enjoyed gambling, but she had no objection in principle to gambling, as long as it was in moderation. Her father, whom she had loved deeply, had gambled all his life and had been a wonderful man. She just hadn't known Ray well enough to know that with him gambling wasn't a mild vice, as it had been with her father, but was an obsession, the most important thing in his life. He was addicted to it as some even more unfortunate people become addicted to morphine or heroin. He had neither the will nor the will power to stop, and she felt sorry for him.

She wondered sometimes if Ray realized by now that their marriage had been a worse mistake for him, in all probability, than it had been for her. His mistake had been not in marrying her in particular; she was probably as tolerant a wife as he could have found. It had been in marrying at all. He had been made to be a bachelor. (Spoiled by a doting mother? He never talked about his early life and all she knew about his parents was that they were dead, as were her own.) He wasn't made for married life, for domesticity. He didn't want a home of his own; he'd have been happier living in a hotel, as he had lived before marriage, even than living in a rented flat. She wondered if he'd ever thought of their getting a divorce; he'd never mentioned one, not even late this afternoon when they'd had their worst quarrel to date. Or had that been because he still hoped that she might relent and either cash in or borrow against that policy to give him the money he wanted?

She'd finished eating and got up and put her plate, knife and fork with the dirty dishes. The kitchen clock showed her that only ten minutes of her lunch period had gone by, and George was still up front.

It was uncomfortably hot in the kitchen. The door to the alley was open and the light outside was on. She went through it and a step to one side to stand there for a breath of cool, fresh, air. Well, cool air, anyway; the row of garbage cans to the other side of the door kept it from being too fresh.

There were quiet footsteps again, and then George stood beside her. He said, "You shouldn't be out here in the alley alone."

"It's safe, George. It's right under a light and right outside the door. I'd have plenty of time to get back inside if I saw or heard anyone coming from either direction."

"I suppose so," he said. "I guess I worry too much. But did you read the editorials in both of yesterday's papers?"

"No, I didn't. Something about the—the psycho?"

"Yes, and it was something that needed to be written. In fact, the police suggested to the editors of both papers that it *be* written, and my friend, the captain in charge of homicide, talked it over with me before he made the suggestion to them. I've got a copy of one of the editorials—and the other says approximately the same thing—in my office if you'd care to read it. Or I can tell you what it says, if you'd prefer."

Ruth said, "I think I'd as soon you tell me, if you don't mind. I suppose it warns women to stay out of dark alleys."

"Among other things, yes. You see, Ruth, a criminal—whether

sane or psychotic—does tend to repeat the pattern of a crime. The *modus operandi*. But unless he's a moron he'll vary the pattern if and when his *modus operandi* becomes impossible, for any reason, for him to repeat.

"And that's exactly what our psychotic killer is going to find himself up against if and when he decides to commit another crime. We don't know what kind of a gimmick he used to get his first two victims to open their doors to him, but whatever it was it's not likely to work for him again. Every woman in the city is scared and has been since the second crime, since it's looked as though he may be starting a series of such crimes."

"I see," Ruth said. "And the police think he'll try a different—uh—*modus operandi* the next time?"

"They do. He'll almost have to, to succeed. Just what he'll try, they don't know, of course. He might slug a woman on the street and drag or carry her into an alley or an areaway. He might break into her place while she's away and be there waiting for her when she comes home and lets herself in. Those are the two main possibilities, but there are others. The point is, a woman can't consider herself safe just because she keeps the door bolted whenever her husband is out. Not that she should neglect that precaution, either. He may try his former method several times, and vary it only if he finds out that it doesn't work. You *do* have a chain bolt, don't you?"

"Not a chain bolt, just an ordinary one. I've been using it since the scare started. Ray doesn't like it much, having to wake me up to let him in when he gets home after I do, but he goes along with it."

"I hope you make sure it's Ray before you unbolt the door."

"Oh yes. And not just by recognizing his voice. We have a code. It's—"

"Don't tell me." He interrupted almost sharply. "I mean if you have a recognition code that's good, but you shouldn't tell *anybody* what it is. Ruth, you said at five-thirty there was something you wanted to talk to me about. Shall we talk here, or go into my office?"

"I guess we can go inside. I'm cooled off now."

He followed her through the kitchen and into his sanctum, leaving, as always, the door a little ajar. He motioned her to the comfortable reading chair, then turned the chair at the desk around to face her and sat down. He said, "I hope it's not bad news, Ruth. That you're thinking about leaving or anything like that."

"No, nothing like that, George. Do you know a man named Joe Amico? He's a bookie."

George frowned. "I know him slightly. And know a little about him. He's not small time but not quite big time either, somewhere in between. He operates from an apartment on Willis. I don't know whether or not he lives there too. What do you want to know about him?"

"Ray has gone in debt to him, betting, and can't pay off. About five hundred dollars, he says. He wants me to cash in or at least borrow against my insurance policy—the one I told you about—and give him the money to pay off Amico. He says if he doesn't pay Amico will have him beaten up badly, maybe even killed. I–I didn't quite believe him and I said no. But what if I'm wrong? I'd never forgive myself if something *did* happen to Ray, something bad, because I wouldn't give him the money. What do you think?"

George Mikos shook his head slowly. "It's a bluff. I don't know whether Ray was trying to bluff you or Amico was trying to bluff him, but Amico isn't going to risk everything he's got by going in for violence, over an amount like five hundred dollars.

"He's a fairly slimy character, I'd say—a half-pint who wouldn't weigh over a hundred pounds soaking wet who has an inferiority complex over his size and tries to act like a Little Caesar to make up for it—but he's also a smart operator who has a good thing and knows it. He pays protection, and gets it, but the police aren't going to let him get away with beating up people, let alone rubbing them out. Besides, he's more interested in getting his five hundred dollars than in fixing things so he can't get it."

Ruth sighed audibly with relief. But she couldn't quite believe it. "You mean Ray could just not pay him and nothing would happen?"

"Not quite that. He'd make trouble, I imagine. But not in the way of physical violence. He could get Ray marked lousy with all the other gamblers so they wouldn't have anything to do with him. He might even manage to make him lose his job; Amico has connections. But he'd do that only as a last resort—he'd much rather get his money even if he had to take it so much every week, and he couldn't very well do that if he lost Ray's job for him. No, Ruth, I don't think you have anything to worry about. Nor has your husband, except that he's going to have to get along with less spending money—or gambling money—for a while."

Ruth Fleck stood up. "Thanks, George, thanks an awful lot. I–I was horribly worried that I'd done the wrong thing, but what you told me is exactly what I hoped you'd say. Thanks a million."

"Sit down again, Ruth. It isn't eight o'clock yet, is it?"

"I'm afraid it is—almost. And I don't want to make Margie have to stay overtime. Maybe we can talk again later."

When Ruth got back up front the first thing she noticed was that the shy young man had left. Either he hadn't had a chance to talk to Margie or she had turned him down, otherwise—since she'd be getting off work so soon—he'd have waited around. There was one customer at the counter but Margie had served him and he was just starting to eat. There were parties in one of the booths and at two of the tables, but they'd been served too.

Margie came over and talked a minute and then, cold on the stroke of eight, went back to change into her street clothes. Since she was so often picked up at eight for a date Margie never wore her uniform to and from work, as Ruth did.

Ruth checked the big chromium coffee urn to make sure there was plenty in it and then went up to the cash register; there was a stool behind it where she could sit down when there was nothing for her to do. She sat down and looked out through the window, at nothing.

She did, as she had told George, feel better now, much better. Her conscience didn't bother her as to whether or not she had done the right thing in turning Ray down on the money. She'd hated the nagging thought that she might be getting him into serious trouble, sent to the hospital or even killed.

But if losing his job was the worst thing that could happen to him—well, that might be for the better. He was a good salesman and could easily get another job—selling hardware or groceries or something safe. With his weaknesses the job he had, making him spend most of his working time in taverns, was the worst job possible for him. In another job he might make less money for a while but that would be all right. Or even if he kept his present job, having gone into debt over his head from gambling might be a good thing to have happened to him. If he had to pay Joe Amico off a little at a time out of his earnings he wouldn't have much left to gamble with and might, during however long it took him, get out of the habit of gambling so heavily. That was all she asked. She didn't mind if he kept on betting on the horses if he made small bets, ones he could afford to lose.

At any rate he was past the limit of his credit now; he'd *have* to behave himself for a while. And if, after he'd worked himself out of the hole this time, he didn't straighten out—

She didn't carry through with the thought consciously, because she still did love him, at least a little, and she hated the thought of divorce. But down deep she knew it was something that would have to happen eventually, unless Ray changed—and down deep she knew that he would never change. And her insurance policy was an ace in the hole there; if he should want to contest a divorce she'd have to go to Nevada to get one—but her policy would cover even that.

George Mikos would be more than glad to finance one for her, but she'd never let him do that. Nor would she let her growing feeling for George, her knowledge of how *secure* it would be to be married to him, affect her decision. Whether or not she would stay with Ray depended solely, in all fairness, on Ray himself, whether he overcame his weakness or let it overcome him.

She wondered what he was doing now, out there in the darkness. . . .

8:03 P.M.

Out there in the darkness—but downtown, where it wasn't dark at all—Ray Fleck was passing a tavern. It was called Chuck's Chuckhouse, although it was basically a tavern and served only cold sandwiches in the way of food, and was run by Chuck Connolly. It was the one business stop Ray really *should* make this evening: he was overdue to make a call there and Chuck always gave him a good order, including half a dozen to a dozen cases of Ten High, which he used as his bar whisky. Ray had been distracted by his financial troubles and hadn't worked very hard that afternoon. He had only a few small orders to turn in and seeing Chuck tonight would make the difference between having a good batch of orders to turn in at the office tomorrow or a poor one. Besides, if he waited too long to call Chuck might possibly change his bar whisky and order from another outfit. Losing Connolly as a customer would cut into his income appreciably.

Just the same, tonight, he wanted to be sure the place wasn't crowded before he went in. It's customary for a liquor salesman to stand a round of drinks for the house when he walks in to get an order and Ray Fleck didn't want to get stuck for ten bucks or so for that round. True, he'd put it on the swindle sheet—and make it a little higher than it actually was—and get his money back eventually. But that wouldn't help tonight; he'd spent three bucks since his steak dinner and hadn't been able to borrow anything so he was down to twenty-five already and getting seriously worried about that stake. This seemed to be a hell of a bad night for running into people he could borrow from, and a ten-buck round would put him down to fifteen dollars.

So he walked past first, turning his head to glance in the window, but staying on the outside of the sidewalk so Chuck would be unlikely to see him.

But he was lucky; Chuck was behind the bar and there were only three men in front of it, so he turned and came back and this time went in. He could see now that there was also a couple sitting in a booth. That meant seven drinks, counting one for himself and one for Chuck, but it still wasn't too bad.

Chuck said, "Hi, stranger. Wondered if you'd deserted me." Ray said, "Hi, Chuck. Set 'em up, huh? I'm going to use your telephone a minute." He went on past and to the phone booth at the back and dialled Dolly Mason's number for the third time this evening. There still wasn't any answer.

He came back and sat down at the bar, watched while Chuck made drinks. He made two for the people in the booth first and took them over. He said, "Compliments of Mr. Fleck there." The couple looked over and thanked him and Ray nodded to them. He didn't know any of the customers so he didn't have to talk to them; he was just as glad because he didn't feel like talking.

Damn Dolly Mason, he thought. Was she going to be out all evening, just when he needed to see her? The more he thought about it the surer he felt that Dolly was his only good chance to borrow money in any sizable chunk this evening. And also that she'd give it to him if he could connect with her. He'd ask for a hundred; surely she'd have at least half that much on hand. It made sense, that short story he'd read once; the Frenchman knew what he was talking about. A wife will turn you down when a mistress won't. A wife has got you hooked, and knows it; a mistress is more understanding. Well, he'd keep phoning every fifteen or twenty minutes until he got her.

Oh, he wasn't the only man in Dolly's life, not by a long shot. He knew that. But she liked him a lot; he didn't think it was *only* because of the presents he gave her that she was so nice to him. If it was only that, then she was really a wonderful actress; she should be in Hollywood instead of here.

Dolly was tiny, not over five feet tall, and very slightly on the plump side, a brunette with olive skin. Just the opposite of Ruth on all counts; that was probably what had attracted him to her in the first place. A man likes a change. And she was vivacious while Ruth was quiet. She liked to drink; Ruth didn't, much. She was frankly passionate whereas Ruth—well, Ruth hadn't been cold at all when they were first married but she was tending more and more to become that way. Of course she said that was his fault, but he had a hunch that wives always said that.

Connolly was making drinks for the bar now, one screwdriver and two highballs for the strangers and a highball for Ray; he'd pour his own drink last, the short straight shot he always took when someone bought him a drink.

Ray watched him, thinking how easy it would be to borrow ten or twenty bucks from Connolly, once he'd got his order. But it was the one principle he'd always stuck to—never borrow money from a customer. His one virtue, he thought sourly; let them carve it on his tombstone when he was dead: "He never borrowed money from a customer." Besides, if he ever did and J. & B. Distributors ever found out about it he'd lose his job like a shot. A salesman always had to appear prosperous whether he was or not.

Connolly passed around the drinks. There were thanks and skoals and everybody took a sip except Connolly who downed his short straight shot at a gulp and then looked quizzically at Ray. "Well, I guess you want an order, huh?"

"Could use one." Ray grinned at him. "And you could use some liquor by now, I'd guess. Here, let me pay for this round before I forget." He put a five on the bar and Connolly rang up three-seventy and put a dollar, a quarter and a nickel on the bar in front of Ray. Ray jittered; the bar owner didn't sound too friendly. Was he going to say he'd already given an order to someone else?

"Yep," Connolly said. "I can use some liquor. Don't stay away so long next time. I'll give you an order, but you better mark it rush so it'll be delivered tomorrow. I'm damn near out of a few things. Come on down to the other end of the bar."

He moved that way and Ray picked up his drink—but left his change where it was—and followed, walking around the three men he'd bought drinks for. On the way, now that his mind was relieved about the order, he had a sudden thought. Maybe he could leave here with more money than he'd come in with at that. Connolly played the ponies, not regularly but frequently, and they often talked about the races and traded tips or hunches. If he could talk Connolly into making up his mind about something for tomorrow, he could say he was going to see Joe Amico later, which he was, and offer to place the bet. And, of course, keep it to cover himself, as he'd done with Sam the waiter. It could be a nasty wallop if it hit, worse than Sam's bet would be, but tomorrow was another day and it was tonight he was worried about.

But he'd better get business over with first so the other matter would look casual, so when he sat down across from Connolly at the front end of the bar he took out an order blank and spread it open on the bar in front of him, took out his ball point. "Okay, Chuck," he said. "How many Ten Highs?"

He got a good order, better than expected. Ten cases of the bar whisky, a case each of gin and vodka, the equivalent of a couple of mixed cases of Scotch, rye and other brands of bourbon, and some wine. A mixed case of vermouth, half dry and half sweet, and a few odd bottles of cordials and liqueurs. It didn't take long; Connolly always knew exactly what he wanted and the exact quantities and talked almost as fast as Ray could write it down. And Ray had learned long since not to try to increase any of the orders Connolly gave him or to try to sell him anything he didn't ask for.

Connolly was just saying "That's it, Ray," when two more men walked into the bar. Again strangers to Ray; his friends seemed to be staying home in droves this evening. Connolly excused himself to serve them and Ray called after him, "On me, Chuck." That would just about kill the change out of his five and he hoped no other customers would walk in till he could get away.

He took the Racing Form from his pocket, spread it open on the bar in front of him and pretended to be studying it; that would automatically bring conversation into the right channel when Connolly came back.

It did. He was actually studying, not pretending at all, when he heard Connolly's voice. "See anything that looks good?"

He looked up. "Sure, Chuck. Blue Belle in the fifth. That's a filly you've been following, ain't it?"

"Yeah, but she's cost me money doing it, damn her. Hasn't run in the money last five times out. Used to be a good horse, especially on a fast track, but I'm beginning to think she's had her day."

"Hell, Chuck, ten to one they've been holding her back. She was running too well for a while and it shot the hell out of the odds. Now the odds are good again and I figure she's due. Now's the time to win back, and maybe get even more than she owes you."

"Maybe you got something there. I ain't seen a Form today. Lemme see who she's running against."

Ray handed him the Form and pointed out the race so he'd not have to look for it. He said, "And Aqueduct'll be a fast track tomorrow. No rain there for two weeks and none in sight."

"Yeah." Connolly said after a minute. "I guess I'll put something down on her."

"I'll be seeing Amico soon as I leave here," Rax said casually. "Got a date with him. If you want me to save you calling him I'll put your bet down for you when I put mine."

"Might as well," Connolly said; he took his wallet out of his hip pocket and then hesitated. "Wonder whether to put ten on the nose or fifteen across the board."

An across-the-board bet, Ray thought, would get him five bucks more—and would cost him less if the horse did win. "I'm playing her across myself," he said. "Thirty bucks, ten each way. So if she even runs third I'll break even."

One thing he'd learned long ago: if you give a man a tip on a horse let him think you're betting at least as much as he is and preferably more. That way if the horse loses he blames you less, because you've lost too; you're a fellow sufferer.

This time it paid off even better than he'd expected. Connolly hesitated only a second and then took a twenty and a ten out of his wallet, handed them over. "Make mine the same way," he said. "If you can go thirty I guess I can."

"Good," Ray said. He put the bills into his wallet, holding it with the open edge toward himself so Connolly wouldn't be able to see how little had been in it before—a ten and two fives.

He looked at his wrist watch and pretended to be surprised by what he saw there. "Good God," he said. "A quarter after—and

I told Amico I'd seen him at eight. I'd better run. Maybe see you later in the evening, Chuck. So long."

Outside he took a deep breath of the cool evening air and decided that he felt swell, and that his luck had turned. Thirty bucks in one crack, even if he'd had to spend five to get it. And he now had fifty—enough, if a bare minimum, to get into the big game that would *really* change his luck.

And since his luck had changed maybe he'd find Dolly home now if he called again.

He went into the drugstore on the next corner and dialed her number in the phone booth. And this time, after seven rings—a lucky number?—Dolly's voice answered, a bit breathlessly.

8:17 P.M.

Dolly Mason heard the first ring of the phone when she was in the hallway outside her apartment, returning from dinner with Mack Irby. Mack was with her and she thought she had a free evening to spend with him. She ran to the door, fished the key out of her handbag and stuck it in the lock. It jammed there for several rings of the telephone inside, till Mack said, "Let me, Doll." He reached around her and turned the key. Dolly got to the phone just as it finished the seventh ring. "Hello," she said, a bit breathlessly.

"Hi, Dolly," the phone said to her. "This is Ray. Ray Fletcher."

"Oh. Hi, Ray honey. Long time no see."

"Too long. Can I see you a while tonight? Just for a few minutes?"

"Well—maybe just for a little while. But not right away. 'Bout an hour from now, huh?"

"An hour? Can't you make it a little earlier than that, Dolly?"

"Well, maybe a little earlier." She looked at her wrist watch. "Nine o'clock? That's a little over forty minutes."

"Swell. See you at nine. 'Bye now, till then."

The phone clicked before Dolly could say anything more, so she cradled it.

Mack Irby, who had made himself comfortable in an overstuffed chair, looked at her with amusement. "You wouldn't of had to stall the guy, Doll," he said. "He could of come right away. Me, I chase easy. I'm on the free list."

"Damn you, Mack honey. You're not *on* the free list. You *are* the free list. And the reason I didn't tell him to come right away is I didn't want him to come right away."

Dolly didn't mind Mack kidding her about the free list, but that was because Mack was special; if anyone else had ever said anything like that, she'd have bawled the hell out of him—and meant it.

Dolly Mason was not a prostitute. She'd never taken money from a man and never would. She earned her own living, as a beauty operator. And it was a fairly good living because she owned a one-third interest in the beauty shop and shared in the profits. Her two-room apartment—living room and bedroom, with a kitchenette off the first and a bath off the second—was in a good building in a good neighborhood. Despite the fact that it was fairly expensive as were her clothes and her standards of living in other directions, she had a modest balance in the bank. Her living standards would not, of course, have been quite so high if she did not accept presents—some of which she used and some of which she converted into money—from a score of men, but she would still have lived comfortably. And why shouldn't she accept presents from men—for doing something she thoroughly enjoyed and would have done for free if it were not for the fact that there were men, more men than she could possibly take care of, who would gladly bring her presents for doing what she most enjoyed.

Dolly Mason had been graduated five years ago from high school in a small town a hundred miles downstate with a reputation that made it quite inadvisable for her to stay in that town. If she hadn't had sex relations with every boy in her class it hadn't been her fault, and she'd made up the deficit by having slept with quite a number of older men.

Fortunately for Dolly her father had died just a week after her graduation, leaving Dolly—since her mother had died years before—the sole beneficiary of a few thousand dollars in insurance. She had left town and had come to the city immediately after the funeral. She had kept her capital mostly intact by working part time while she took a beauty course, had worked two years as an operator for someone else to gain experience, and then had used what was left of her capital to buy her way into a small but profitable suburban beauty shop.

She liked any and all men, but since she had a wide choice of them she limited her friendships (as she thought of them) to ones who were reasonably young, reasonably attractive, and reasonably prosperous. They had to be reasonably generous in giving her presents from time to time. And no matter how generous they were, they had to be reasonably good in bed.

Of all men she liked Mack Irby the best. She'd met him when she'd been working about a year as a beauty operator and about a year before she'd bought into the shop. She'd thought at first that she was in love with him and for a few weeks had actually eschewed promiscuity and given herself only to him. But love, to Dolly, meant only that she enjoyed sex with Mack more than with anyone else. She'd probably have married Mack during the first week or so that she'd known him if he'd asked her, but fortunately he hadn't, for she soon found out that no one man could possibly keep her happy. Not even Mack, who was more virile than most men.

So she'd gone back to promiscuity, but since Mack wasn't jealous she'd kept him as a paramour. It was about this time that she began to get the idea that, while she was going to keep her amateur standing by never accepting money, there was no reason why men—other men, not Mack, that is—shouldn't give her presents in appreciation of her favors. In fact, Mack had suggested it.

By now, only Mack was on what he called her free list. She expected presents from him only at Christmas and on her birthday. Not that she didn't get anything else at all from him. He took her to dinner several nights a week; most of her other male friends were married and afraid to take the risk of being seen with her in public. And, because of his line of work, Mack was able to do her other valuable favors. He was "in" with the cops and able to fix traffic tickets. Once he'd even managed to square a drunken driving rap which, since it was a second offense, would otherwise have carried a mandatory jail sentence. He had connections through which he could sell for her at a fair price, certainly more than she herself could have got for them, presents which were given to her and which she didn't want to keep for herself. And a few times when a man whom, for one reason or another, she had dropped from her friendship roster had become troublesome in his efforts to see her again, Mack had talked to him and Dolly had been bothered no longer.

Mack had been a policeman once, on the vice squad. Now he was a private detective, a lone operator who, if he was a bit on the shyster side and did mostly divorce work, stayed nearly enough honest to be on good terms with the police. Which made him a very valuable friend and protector for a girl like Dolly, who, although she did nothing seriously illegal, frequently skated on somewhat thin ice.

"Ray," Mack was saying to her. "That's the guy who's a liquor salesman, no? The one who brings you a case of whisky once in a while?"

Dolly nodded. "He said he just wanted to stay a little while, Mack honey. If he means that and doesn't change his mind maybe I can phone you after he goes and you can come back. Where'll you be?"

"At the office, I guess. I've got some skip-trace reports I might as well write up. I'll be there a couple of hours. I'll go home after that if I haven't heard from you. Should hit the pad early tonight anyway."

"Swell," Dolly said. "Mack honey, you make us a couple drinks while I take a quick shower. I won't be three minutes."

She walked quickly into the bedroom. She undressed quickly, putting away the clothes she took off since she wouldn't have to dress again this evening; she could just put on a robe when Mack left.

She wondered if Ray would bring a case of whisky with him tonight; that was something she was always glad to get. She thought back and decided that he wouldn't. He'd brought a case the last time he'd come. Dolly didn't expect her friends to bring her a present *every* time they came to see her, if they'd brought something fairly valuable the previous trip. Something like a dozen pair of nylons, dollar forty-nine variety, anything that cost no more than twenty or twenty-five dollars (and it had better not cost much less than twenty) was good only for the time it was brought. Something worth fifty was worth a couple of visits and so on up the line. Dolly didn't keep books on the presents brought her but she had a good memory and always knew who was due to bring something and who wasn't. She didn't have her rules printed and posted on the inside of her door, as rules and prices are posted inside hotel room doors, but the men who came to see her soon got the idea and could figure it the same way Dolly did. No, Ray probably wouldn't bring anything tonight and she didn't expect him to. A case of whisky, the brand he'd brought, was worth at least fifty dollars. He would have paid less, of course, since he'd have been able to get it wholesale, but Dolly didn't care about that; it was still worth at least fifty to her.

She was in the bathroom almost exactly the three minutes she'd predicted. Two minutes under the shower and one with the bath towel; she didn't dry herself too thoroughly because Mack liked her with her skin a trifle moist. And during the minute of toweling she had time to admire her body in the full length mirror on the inside of the bathroom door.

Her breasts were especially beautiful, she thought, and why shouldn't she think so when she knew they drove men crazy. Already their shell-pink, tip-tilted nipples were hardening in anticipation.

Naked and glowing she walked through the bedroom and into the living room. Mack was sitting on the sofa; two freshly made highballs, strong ones, were on the coffee table in front of it.

Naked she ran lightly across the room and sat in his lap, kissed him. His arms went around her, one of his hands cupping one of her breasts, a perfect fit.

He pulled back to break the kiss, groaned softly.

"Little bitch," he said. "How can a man enjoy a drink with you like this. The drinks will have to wait."

He picked her up and carried her into the bedroom. She laughed; this was what she'd wanted, to have to wait for her drink until afterward.

8:24 P.M.

He stood outside a living room window of the little three-room cottage looking in, watching her. By moving from one side of the window to the other he could see almost all of the room, and she, even if she looked toward the window, would not be able to see him. There was a net curtain inside the window. From the outer darkness he could see through it clearly into the lighted room, but from where she sat the curtain would be opaque. He could—except for his Need and his desperate impatience—stand here as long as he wished to make his plans and calculate his chances.

He thought they were good. The cottage was on the outskirts of town, in a neighbourhood not very built up as yet. There were only a few houses in the block.

There was one almost directly across the street but it was dark and there was no car in the carport alongside it. Obviously either no one lived there or no one was home.

The nearest house on the right was vacant and had a "For Rent" sign on it. People were home and lights were on in the nearest house to the left—but it was well over a hundred yards away and besides either a radio or television set was turned on quite loudly. He could hear it from here. Over the volume of sound so close to them would they be able to hear the sound of a scream? He didn't think so. But it was a risk he would have to decide to take—or not to take. He'd never be able to get through the window and get to her to knock her out without her having time to scream once.

The window at which he stood was at the side of the house and he could see the inside of the front door—and the chain bolt on it. Probably just about every house or apartment in town had one now. Well, the method he'd tried three times had succeeded twice but now he might as well forget about it.

The danger that was greater than a scream being overheard was in plain sight on a stand right beside the door. The telephone. Would he be able to get through the window and to her before she could get to the phone and finish dialing a number? If she got a call through—even managed to get an operator and call *help*—he wouldn't have time to have his way with her. But if by then he was in the room with her, if she'd seen him, he could still take a few seconds to kill her quickly, so she'd never describe or identify him, and still, he hoped, be out of the neighborhood before the police came.

It would all depend on how quickly he could pry that window up and get into the room.

He weighed the other chances against him. He'd checked the garage behind the house; the door was open and the car was gone. That meant that her husband, if she had one, was out and not in the bedroom or the kitchen. Of course the husband might return too soon, but that would be too bad for the husband unless he was a heavyweight champion boxer. He'd hate to have to interrupt himself to do it, but he could handle any ordinary unarmed man. The only difference would be that he'd be leaving two corpses behind him this time instead of one. Or three or more corpses if by any chance a child or children were asleep in the bedroom. He wouldn't mind killing them at all; he hated children almost as much as he hated women.

His eyes went back to the woman. She was sitting on the sofa, her feet curled under her, reading a magazine. Well—what was he waiting for?

He took the heavy chisel out of his pocket and put its edge between the bottom of the window and the sill, then put both hands on the handle and leaned his full weight against it. It made no appreciable sound; she hadn't looked up from her magazine. But it was in as far as he could push it, and was it in far enough?

There was only one way to find out. He threw all his strength into pushing down on the handle of the chisel, and this time there was noise—but it was a noise of splintering wood and not the snapping of the window catch above. He had failed.

She looked up now, and there was fright in her face, but not panic. She didn't scream. But she ran for the telephone and started dialling.

And there was no chance of getting to her in time now, with a second try at the window. He ran to the car he had parked a quarter of a block away. Stupid, he thought; he should have found the telephone wire outside the house and snapped it. Then he'd have had time to get in while she struggled with a dead phone. Next time, if he tried this method again, he'd do that. And he'd have a hammer to use with the chisel, to drive it far enough in so the catch would snap instead of the wood splintering.

This time he was six blocks away when he heard the approaching sirens. But would one of them by any chance stop and investigate a car driving away from the address to which they'd been called? There wasn't much traffic out here, and the cops just might get that bright idea. They weren't in sight yet so he quickly parked at the curb in front of a house, turned off his lights and lay down across the front seat out of sight. They wouldn't investigate an apparently empty parked car this far from their destination.

They didn't. Two of them screamed past him. No more seemed

to be coming, so he started his car and drove back into town, thinking despairingly that he wouldn't dare make a third attempt tonight after two unsuccessful ones. He'd have to case and plan his next kill carefully.

For tonight, he thought, the Need would have to go unsatisfied. He'd have to settle for the poor consolation of a few drinks to calm his nerves, and then sleep.

That's what he thought. But then, he had not yet met Ray Fleck.

8:26 P.M.

Ray Fleck's reluctant footsteps stopped on the sidewalk of an apartment building on Willis Street, just on the edge of the downtown business district and he hesitated before entering it, as a man hesitates before stepping under a cold shower.

This talk with Joe Amico was bound to be an unpleasant one. But Joe had told him to come, and before ten o'clock, and Joe was mad at him already and would be madder if he didn't show up. So he'd better get it over with.

In a way, he thought, it was lucky Dolly Mason had told him not to come before nine; that gave him time to come here—Joe's apartment was only three blocks from the drugstore from which he'd phoned Dolly—and still get to Dolly's in plenty of time. Surely Joe wouldn't want to keep him more than a few minutes. What was there to say to Joe except to reassure him that he'd pay the money as soon as he could possibly raise it?

Yes, it was far better to get the interview with Joe over with now. That way, if Dolly lent him money, even fifty dollars, he could stay with her a while, almost two hours, until time to head for the game. That way he'd at least be sure of keeping his capital intact. And he knew that if she was free she'd let him stay. For that matter, it might be just as well for him to stay with Dolly even if she couldn't or wouldn't lend him money. If he spent the time elsewhere he was at least as likely to diminish his fifty dollars as to augment it.

He entered the building and saw that the self-service elevator door was closed and that the indicator above it showed that it was at the fourth floor and going up. So he didn't wait for it but went to the door that led to the staircase instead; Joe's apartment was on the third floor and he'd rather walk two flights than wait.

Going up the stairs his mind went back to Joe. Damn him, he thought, it was as much Joe's fault as his that he was in this jam; Joe should have told him how deep in the hole he was getting. He hadn't kept track and had thought he was in only for maybe a couple of hundred. Until yesterday when he'd tried to phone in a fifty dollar bet. Big Bill Monahan, who worked for Joe and who usually answered the phone at the apartment, had said, "Just a minute, Ray. Joe said he wanted to talk to you the next time you phoned." And Joe had come on. "Ray-boy, don't you realize you're in the soup for four-eighty? You'd better pay that off before you do any more betting." He'd told Joe that he'd stop in, thinking at first to ask Joe to show him the slips on the bets; from the names of the horses and the amounts he'd know whether all the bets were his or not. Maybe Joe or Big Bill had made a mistake. But after the call he'd tried to remember all the bets he could and had added them. They'd come to four hundred and ten dollars and since he was sure that he hadn't remembered all of the bets, he was willing to take Joe's word on the total.

But why hadn't Joe called him on it sooner? Twice before Joe had called him on running into debt, both times when the amount involved was a couple of hundred. Both times, he'd been able to raise the money within a few days. The first time he'd done it on a signature loan, but that wouldn't work again because he'd got behind on his payments and had had a fight with the loan outfit. He'd paid it off eventually but the damn company had marked him as a poor credit risk. And loan companies keep one another posted on things like that. He'd found out when he'd applied for a second loan from another outfit and had been turned down. He'd raised the money that time by putting up his car for security but that wouldn't work again either right now. He'd had his present car only six months and had made only five payments on it. It was financed over a two-year period and he still owed too much on it for him to borrow anything against it. He could probably sell it for a few hundred more than he owed on it but he needed a car to hold down his job.

He pressed the door buzzer and after a moment Big Bill opened the door a few inches on the chain and looked out through the opening. He said, "Hi, Ray," and then closed the door momentarily so he could take the chain off and open it wide. It was a silly system; Ray had kidded Bill about it once and he'd shrugged and said, "Boss's orders." It was still silly. Were they afraid of a raid? Amico paid for protection and got it. He had to take a raid once in a while but he was always tipped off in advance exactly when one was coming—usually just before a local election. When a raid came, Amico wouldn't be there nor would there be any clients. The cops would serve the warrant on Bill Monahan or whoever was working for Amico at the time, and find and confiscate some betting slips—phony ones with fake names on them; Amico would have the real ones. Monahan would appear in court and pay a fine or, if the police wanted to make a better showing than usual, sit out a short jail sentence. Amico wouldn't even get his name in the papers, and would meanwhile be opening up in a new location, already rented in advance, and spreading the word on his new address and phone number. No raid was expected tonight or Big Bill wouldn't have let him in; clients never get caught in one.

Big Bill closed the door behind Ray and said, "Joe's laying down. Had a headache and took some aspirins."

"Maybe he's asleep," Ray said, "Maybe I better come back some other—"

"No, he wants to see you. Said if he was asleep when you came to wake him up. Just a minute."

Big Bill crossed the room—a living room furnished like any living room except for the addition of a desk with two telephones on it—opened the door of the next room and looked in. He turned back and said, "He's awake. Go on in."

Ray Fleck went in and, in case he was going to have to take a bawling out, closed the door behind him. The room was a bedroom and Joe Amico was lying on the bed but on top of the covers and fully dressed. Ray had never seen him otherwise; like many small men Joe prided himself on being dapper. Even on the hottest days of summer he always wore a suit coat over a white shirt and a necktie and the shirt was always so fresh and clean that Ray thought he must change shirts at least twice a day and possible oftener. The bed was a big one and Joe was so small that he looked almost like a doll lying there on it.

"Hi, Ray-boy," he said. "Pull a chair around where I can see you from here. I'm gonna stay flat. This damn headache—"

It was going to be all right, Ray thought; Joe wasn't angry and wasn't going to get tough about the dough. He pulled a chair around to the side of the bed and sat down. He remembered that Joe had once mentioned sinus trouble and asked, "Sinus headache?"

"Yeah. Get 'em every once in a while, in streaks, in series like. One at the same time every day for about two weeks. They get worse each day for the first week and taper off during the second. I'm over the hump this time; this is about the tenth day."

"Can't a doctor do anything for them?"

"Naw, I been to a dozen of 'em. The pills they give me don't help any more than plain aspirin. And it ain't bad enough for an operation; I get a streak of headaches only about once a year and I'd rather stand 'em than have a—what do they call it?—sinusotomy. What are you doing about that money, Ray-boy?"

"Trying to raise it, Joe," Ray said. And then, to give himself some leeway: "Might take a few days or even a week, but I'll get it."

"What if you can't?"

"Hell, I can—somehow. I've always paid you before, haven't I?"

"Yeah. But what if you can't scare it up this time, in one chunk? I know how much you make—about how much anyway—and that's quite a piece of cash for you. Close to a month's income. I shouldn't of let it get that big but I wasn't keeping track and didn't realize how far into me you were till Bill called my attention to it yesterday."

"Sure, Joe, it's quite a piece of cash. But don't worry; I'll get it. And this damn losing streak can't last forever."

"Maybe not, but one can last a hell of a lot longer than yours has. That's what I wanted to talk to you about. I think you'd better lay off any kind of gambling till you're back even again—and that'll give your luck time to turn maybe. I don't run an installment business but I'm willing, in your case, to let you pay it off by the week. Say fifty a week; that'd take you a little less than ten weeks."

Ray winced. "My God Joe! I can't pay fifty a week—I wouldn't have enough left to live on. How about twenty-five—if I can't raise the whole thing, that is."

"Fifty might be rough on you, yeah. How about thirty-five?"

"Okay," Ray said. "Give me a week to see if I can raise the four-eighty. Then if I can't pay you at least most of it I'll start forking over thirty-five every payday. A deal?"

"A deal. All right, that's settled. Isn't anything else you wanted to tell me, is there?"

A little puzzled—what was Joe getting at?—Ray said, "Nothing I can think of. Except thanks, and I'll do my best to raise the dough without having to make it in installments. Well, so long.

Crossing the living room on his way out he walked almost jauntily. It was over with, and it hadn't been half as bad as he'd expected. He had a full week to raise or win the money and even if he didn't succeed things wouldn't be too bad. At thirty-five a week it would take a hell of a long time to pay off four-eighty but it would still leave him money for small bets and as soon as he started winning he could pyramid.

Monahan went to the door with him and opened it; they said so longs and then the door closed behind him. But it opened again when he was halfway to the stairs and Monahan stepped out into the hall and said, "Come back, Ray. You forgot something."

Forgot something? He hadn't forgotten anything. As he walked back he was thinking of Joe's "Isn't anything else you wanted to tell me, is there?" That had been puzzling too. What went on?

He went back. Big Bill held the door open from outside, then following him in and closed it. This time there was the sound of the chain.

Joe Amico had come out of the bedroom, and in a hurry, because for the first time Ray saw him less than completely immaculate; his straight black hair was mussed from having lain on the bed and he hadn't taken time to comb it. He was sitting on a corner of the desk, legs dangling, and he no longer looked like a doll. You could have taken him, though, for a malevolent little marionette with eyes as cold and hard as marbles.

He didn't raise his voice but it was as cold and hard as his eyes. "How long you been making book yourself, Ray-boy." This time the "Ray-boy" didn't sound like an affectionate nickname; it sounded like a swear word.

"Wha—" Suddenly in the middle of a word Ray Fleck realized what had happened, what *must* have happened. "My God, Joe," he said. "That bet I took to place with you for Chuck Connolly—he must've phoned you to change it or something and said I had the money for you. I have, but *honest*, Joe, I forgot, completely forgot."

"How many other times have you made book yourself on dough somebody gave you to give me?"

"Never, Joe, honest to God, never." And, in fact, he'd never before done it, to speak of. A few times, not over half a dozen, he'd taken a small bet, never over two or five, to give Joe, thinking that he'd be seeing him or phoning in some bet of his own; then had decided against laying anything that day himself and hadn't bothered to phone in the peanut bet. Once one of the horses had won and he'd paid off on it, twelve-forty on a two-dollar win bet. But never until tonight had he deliberately held out a bet to raise money.

He was taking his wallet out of his pocket with a hand that he tried to keep from trembling, opening the wallet to take out the three tens Connolly had given him. But Joe was saying. "The whole thing, Ray-boy. The wallet."

His eyes had been looking down at the bills in the wallet, trying to focus on it to pick out the three bills. He looked up in surprise and that made it too late. Big Bill jerked the wallet out of his hand and tossed it to Amico, who held it in his hand, tapping a corner of it on his knee, not as yet opening it.

He said, "How many bets in here besides Connolly's?"

"None, Joe. Honest to God. I've *never*—"

"Shut up. You stink, Ray-boy. Chuck Connolly didn't call me up to change his bet; I wouldn't of even known about it if you hadn't told me. Sam Washburn called me, Sam the waiter at Feratti's. I eat there often and know him; he almost always takes a buck bet instead of a tip, and sometimes adds cash of his own.

"So he called just before you came here, said he'd got worried about his bet on Birthday Boy and wanted to change it a little. Said he gave you five besides a one tip, all on the horse's nose. Got a little doubtful about the hunch and wanted to play the six across the board. And I had a hunch about *you*, Ray-boy—that you've dragged down on me before by playing bookie on your own. I decided to see if you'd give me that six bucks. I gave you every break, even asked you, God damn it, if you had anything else to tell me. Waited till you were clear out the door before I sent Bill to get you back. And what happens when I get you back? You know I've got something on you and you pop off on a deal I wouldn't of known about otherwise. And then stand there with your bare face hanging down and swear Connolly's is the *only* bet you ever dragged down." He held up the wallet. "How many other bets from today and tonight you still got in here?"

"None, Joe. Honest to God, I——"

"Shut up," Joe Amico opened the wallet and, without taking them out, checked the bills in it. "Fifty bucks. How much was Connolly's bet, and on what? Don't bother lying because I'll check with Connolly on it."

"Thirty," Ray said miserably. "Thirty across, on Blue Belle; Fifth, Aqueduct."

Amico put the wallet down on the desk beside him. "Bill," he said, "take thirty-six out of that. Make slips on both bets—you heard 'em. Then give him his wallet and his lousy fourteen bucks change back."

Monahan went around behind the desk.

Ray said, "My God, Joe, I know this looks like I was dragging down on you on purpose, but—"

"Shut up. From now on don't say a God damn word, till I finish and ask you if you understand, and then you damn well better say yes. Just yes and nothing else."

"Somebody else taking bets in my name, dragging down on me, that's one thing—*the* one thing I won't stand. Don't matter if it's six bucks—that's all I knew about for sure at first—or thirty-six or a million. Or six cents, for that matter.

"We're through, Ray-boy, finished. You come around here with a grand in cash and want to lay it, I don't take it. I don't deal with chiselers.

"I made you a nice easy deal—four months I'd of took to get all that four-eighty at thirty-five bucks a week. I meant it and you could of had the deal, but at the same time I was testing you, to see if you were going to give me that lousy six bucks. I knew if you ever dragged down on me you would tonight, on account of you're behind the eight-ball."

Monahan came around from behind the desk and held out Ray's wallet to him. Ray took it and put it back into his pocket with a hand that was shaking badly.

Joe Amico was saying, "Do I have to tell you that deal's off now? You got a new deal and here it is. I want that money, *all* of it, by this time tomorrow night. You got twenty-four hours to raise it. I don't care how you raise it. Sell your car. Sell your wife. Rob a bank."

"Joe, I *can't*—"

"I said shut up. Bill, if he opens that yakker of his again put a fist in it. Ray-boy, I almost *hope* you can't. Because I'll get a four-eighty kick outa what I'm going to do if you don't.''

He looked at his wrist watch. "Just twenty-four hours from right now I start putting out the word that you're marked lousy, that you're a cheap crook and a welsher besides. I start with all the tavern and liquor store owners I know—and I know plenty. Chuck Connolly will be on top of the list. I tell 'em if they're friends of mine they won't deal with a rat like you. I'll ask 'em to pass the word to the other guys in their racket, the ones I don't know. And some of the boys, the ones I know best and do business with, are going to phone in your boss and complain about you, about the way you treat 'em, the way you act in their joints.

"It'll take a little while for the word to get all the way around, but you'll be lucky, Ray-boy, to make fifty bucks in commission next week or to hold your job for two weeks."

"Oh, and you'll never lay another bet, even if you ever get any money to lay. I do know every other bookie in town and they come right after the bar owners. And I know who at least some of your friends are, too, and I spread the word there. By a couple weeks from now you won't be able to sit in even a penny-ante stud game in a private house."

"Okay, that's it. Now you can talk—one word and it better be yes, and no more than that. Do you understand?"

"Yes," Ray said. Hopelessly he turned to go; nothing he could possibly say would help right now, even if he dared to say it.

"Not quite yet," Amico said. "Bill, touch him up a little. Take it easy and don't mark him. Just something to help him remember."

Ray had sense enough to know that it wouldn't do any good to fight back; he'd get hurt worse if he did. He stood still and tried to make himself limp when Big Bill left's hand grabbed a handful of the front of his coat and shirt, thinking that if he went down from whatever came first maybe they'd let it go at that.

But what came first was a pair of flat-handed slaps to the face—back of the hand to one side, palm to the other. Slaps that rocked his head, stung like hell, and made his ears ring.

Then Big Bill, still holding with his left, pulled his right hand back and drove a fist like the business end of a battering ram into the pit of Ray's stomach. Tha pain was so great that, as his hands went to his stomach, he tried to double over and would have except for the big hand still holding his clothes bunched in front of his chest. From somewhere miles away and through a haze of redness he heard Monahan's voice say, "Enough, Joe?" and Amico's voice say, "Yeah. Put him in a chair. Don't put him out in the hall till he can walk. We don't want him laying on our doorstep."

He was in a chair and nothing was holding him now; he could double over forward in the chair and he did. He was retching.

From somewhere not quite so far away he heard Amico's voice again. "And don't let him out till you're sure he won't puke on the hall carpet, either. If he pukes in here keep him till he's able to clean it up."

He heard the door open and close; Amico had gone back into the bedroom. He heard a phone ring and then Big Bill's voice answering it and then saying, "Ten to win on Rawhide in the fourth, twenty to show on Dark Angel in the seventh. Right, Perry."

He could straighten up now, and he wasn't going to puke. His stomach still hurt like hell and his cheeks stung and his ears rang, but he thought he could stand up now. He *had* to stand up and get out of here fast. For a moment he couldn't remember why, and then it came to him. His date with Dolly. She was his only chance now, or the only one he could think of. Joe Amico had meant every word he'd said.

He raised his arm to look at his wrist watch. Yes, he could still make it in time if he was lucky in catching a taxi quickly outside. Lucky that this was Willis Street and taxis were fairly frequent; He put his hands on the arms of his chair and stood up. Not quite straight; the pain in his stomach made him bend forward a little at the waist.

"You okay?" Big Bill asked him. His voice was impersonal, neither friendly nor unfriendly.

"Sure. I got to get out of here. I'm going to be late for a date if I don't leave now."

"Walk back and forth a few times. When I see you can navigate, okay."

He was a little tottery walking across the room the first time, better coming back. After a few trips he was walking almost normally, as much as it hurt him to do so.

Big Bill got up and went to the door and opened it. "Okay, Ray. No hard feelings?"

"No," Ray said.

As he walked through Big Bill said, "Believe it or not, I pulled my punch on that poke in the gut." And then, before Ray could answer, not that there was anything *to* answer, the door closed behind him and he heard the chain slide into the slot.

No stairs this time. He went to the shaft of the self-service elevator and pushed the button. The indicator showed that it was on the top floor, but it started down. He leaned against the wall opposite the elevator door to wait for it.

Suddenly he remembered something and reached for his wallet. Amico had told Monahan to take thirty-six out, but what if Monahan hadn't put back the change? But Monahan had; the wallet held a ten and some singles. Fourteen lousy bucks.

He *had* to get money from Dolly now. And he might as well try for five hundred while he was at it—what was to lose trying? If he got that much—and he'd offer *any* kind of interest to get it—he'd stay out of the poker session and not risk losing any of it. He'd keep it intact to be *sure* of being able to pay Joe tomorrow.

But fifty or a hundred wouldn't do him any good with Joe, so if that was all he could get, running it up would be his only chance.

Dolly, Dolly he thought; *please, Dolly. Be like the mistress of the man in the French short story.*

The elevator came and the door slid open automatically. He stepped inside.

A minute later he was at the curb, looking frantically both ways for a taxi. None was in sight and he ran, doubled over a bit because his stomach hurt, to the corner, where he'd have a better chance of flagging one.

8:47 P.M.

See now as through a defective windowpane that lets in light but distorts the images that the light bears. See now into Benny Knox as he himself sees out. See a twisted cosmos peopled by phantoms who buy newspapers as they pass and then are seen no more, except for a few who come regularly enough to become real for a while and to be remembered most of the time. Through this pane Benny sees a frightening but basically simple universe run by a good God of Vengeance when sin is done.

But first let us see him from the outside, as others see him. Benny Knox was born thirty-five years ago to a mother who died in bearing him, her firstborn. His father was a Baptist minister, a fiery fundamentalist to whom Heaven and Hell were fully as real as Earth. His father, who never remarried, raised him.

During infancy he seemed perfectly normal and not only seemed but was perfectly healthy and he was always big for his age. If during the next years, those of his preschool childhood, signs of retardation began first to show and then to multiply, his father, who after all had no standard of comparison, failed to recognize them.

The fact that he was retarded wasn't known until he was entered in the first grade of school (his father hadn't 'believed in' kindergarten; all they did there was let children play and Benjamin already knew how to play). Within a month he had been examined by a school psychologist and the Reverend Matthew Knox had been called in for conference and advised to send his son to a special school for subnormal children.

Benny had attended that school for eight years, until he was fourteen. Then the school's principal had told Benny's father: "I'm afraid we've done all we can for Benjamin. He has approximately the equivalent of a third-grade education. Perhaps a little better than that in some subjects—such as reading and arithmetic. Not so good in some others, subjects that require memorizing, such as geography or spelling.

"Socially, the picture is neither too good nor too bad. He gets along reasonably well with people, especially his contemporaries, but only when circumstances force him to. He greatly prefers solitary occupations and activities. He seems to daydream; whether or not that will decrease or increase as he grows older, only time will tell.

"Morally—well, he's almost too good. It's obvious that he had very strong religious training at home and is—well, almost too literally convinced of everything he was taught."

The Reverend Matthew Knox had frowned slightly. "What he was taught at home *was* literally true," he had said.

"Of course. But, unless tempered with reason, some of the teachings of Christianity are—ah—hardly survival characteristics in our society. Or in any society for that matter. Generosity is a virtue, for example, but it must be practiced with moderation. Recently I happened to learn of a boy having come to school without his lunch. Not, mind you, because his parents are poor; they aren't. Just because he forgot it. Benjamin gave the boy his lunch and went hungry that day. When I learned of it I talked to him and explained that while it would have been a good thing for him to share his lunch with the boy he should not simply have given it away and gone hungry himself. There have been other such instances but that's the most recent one."

Benny's father had nodded thoughtfully. "I'll talk to him about it," he said. As a matter of fact, he already had, a great many times. Benny simply couldn't keep such things as baseball gloves, roller skates or kite reels, and when something was gone it was always because he had given it to a poor boy who didn't have one. Several times, when Benny knew the name of the poor boy and where he lived, the Reverend Knox had gone and got the article back; never had he encountered any poverty more real than his own. He had finally solved the problem—and without crossing Benny's desire to give to the poor—by issuing and occasionally repeating a flat order to the effect that before he gave anything of his to a poor boy he should bring the boy home with him; he would then talk to the boy and decide whether or not the boy was really poor and needed the article in question worse than Benny did. With rare exceptions, when Benny had forgotten, this had worked. Apparently none of the boys who had been taking advantage of Benny had wanted to face an inquisition at Benny's home first. But apparently Benny had not known that this edict had extended to school.

"And there is one other thing," the principal was saying "that troubles me about Benjamin. I must say that it troubles me *much* more than his indiscriminate generosity—for I believe you can train him out of that without too much difficulty. He has a tendency to confess to having done things he did not do. His teacher tells me that several times when some prank or bit of minor vandalism has been committed she has talked to the class about it and then asked whoever was guilty of it to raise his hand; each time Benjamin's hand went up. And each time some minor punishment was meted out to him for what she believed he had done. Then one day the prank in question happened to be one she knew positively Benny could not have done, and he still raised his hand. It was a caricature of the teacher drawn on the backboard during lunch hour and it was rather well done for a child's drawing; Benny is very poor at drawing. The teacher sent Benjamin to me to have a talk.

"His answers to me were vague and confusing. I honestly don't know whether he knew he was innocent and had some compulsive reason for offering himself as a scapegoat—perhaps guilt feelings about something else—or whether he really thought, once the question was put to him, that he had really done it."

The Reverend Knox was troubled; this was something new to him. True, whenever he had asked Benny whether or not he had committed some certain dereliction, the answer had almost always been affirmative, but he had never questioned the boy unless he was already reasonably sure Benny was guilty, so the affirmation had never been a surprise. He asked, "Could Benjamin have been with the boy who made the drawing—aided and abetted him, as it were—and thus felt that he shared the guilt and have raised his hand for that reason?"

"No. Once the teacher seriously considered drawing styles, the identity of the culprit became obvious; only one boy in the class could have done it. Once the question was put to him directly he confessed—as a matter of fact he was justifiably a little proud of the drawing—and admitted that another boy had been with him but it wasn't Benjamin. Benjamin hadn't even known of the drawing."

"I'll have a talk with him," Benny's father had said.

And he'd had a number of talks with him during the first year or two Benny was out of school. He'd made a number of tests, too. For example, if he himself should accidentally break a drinking glass in the kitchen, later he'd show Benny the broken glass and ask if he had done it. All too often, for a while, Benny would admit guilt. This always led to another and longer talk, and finally he felt sure that he had cured Benny of this fault—and he had, for a long time. Like the principal, he had never been able to decide whether Benny had deliberately made a false confession to court punishment or whether he really thought, when asked, that he had committed the offense in question.

He had given thought, too, to Benny's being able to make a living for himself in the world. At first, since Benny was too young for a full-time job, he had bought him a newspaper route. After a few mistakes, Benny had done all right on it. It was teaching Benny responsibility, he thought, and the five or six dollars a week it brought in helped out immeasurably. After a while the only help he needed was to be reminded once a month when it was time to make his collections.

When Benny was sixteen and already bigger than most men his

father decided that it was time to help him find a niche in the world in the way of a full-time job. The good minister was himself in failing health and beginning to realize that by the time of his own death Benny needs must have not only a means of earning a full livelihood but a way of living alone without constant parental care and advice. The only alternative would be, after his own death, for Benny to be institutionalized and become a public charge. This was to be avoided if at all possible. Over the course of the next two years he found Benny a variety of jobs—in vain. Benny could handle almost any of them, with constant supervision, but no employer could afford an employee whom he had to watch all the time. Even at manual labor jobs, although he was plenty husky enough to handle them, Benny managed to get into trouble. Set him to digging a ditch and he would dig it into the next county unless you were there to stop him.

When Benny was eighteen and had never held a full-time job longer than a few weeks, and few that long, the Reverend Knox learned that he only had about six months to live. Fortunately, at about the same time, he chanced to learn that an elderly man who for many years made a living running a newspaper stand on a busy downtown street corner was about to retire and wanted to sell his business. Newspapers were the only thing Benny had ever got along with; if he could run a newspaper route maybe he could sell newspapers over a counter. In some ways the latter was even simpler. Every transaction was a simple cash deal instead of a more complicated monthly collection. Knox had a long talk with the retiring vendor, and bought the concession. The seller stayed on for a few days to show Benny what ropes there were. Knox saw the circulation managers of the two newspapers Benny would handle and the manager of the distribution agency that supplied him with the items he would sell; with each of them he arranged to have Benny's bills sent to the parsonage. There was nothing to it, and Benny got along fine from the start. Each evening he brought home his receipts for the day and turned them over to his father, who took care of paying his bills and managed his money for him, starting him out each day with the amount and variety of change he'd need to start business at the stand.

There remained only one problem to solve before he could die, and Knox had had its solution in mind for a long time; he had waited only until he was sure his son could earn a living. A Mrs. Saddler, a widow and a good woman, was a member of his congregation and she ran a boarding house within walking distance of downtown. He went to see her and made arrangements for Benny to room and board with her, and for her, for a small but adequate percentage of Benny's earnings, to take over the management of his affairs.

That, too, had worked out. Each night he brought his money home to her, as he had to his father. She managed it for him, took out what she had coming for room and board, gave him an allowance of spending money—which went for candy and ice cream sodas, his only dissipation—bought clothes for him when he needed any, and put the surplus in the bank, part of it in a special checking account against which she drew for his business expenses, the rest in a savings account in his name—but which she reminded him of only when some extra expense or minor emergency necessitated his help in drawing some of it out.

This accomplished, the Reverend Knox had quit fighting the Reaper. He had given up his ministry and his parsonage, had gone to a hospital and died.

And all had gone well for fifteen years, until Benny Knox was thirty-three. On the surface anyway; Mrs. Saddler sometimes wasn't sure what went on down inside of Benny when occasionally he had dark, unhappy, brooding spells; she wasn't able to get him to talk about them although ordinarily he prattled to her freely about anything and everything. And nothing had ever come of the spells; they'd always worn off.

Until suddenly at the height of one of them Benny, she subsequently learned, had gone to the police station one morning and had confessed to having committed a murder that had been much in the newspapers for two weeks. It had been, according to how one might look at it, a bad time or a good time for him to have confessed to that particular crime; the police had just apprehended the real killer only an hour before; the news had not yet hit the papers or Benny would have read about it. Benny did read the newspapers during dull periods at the newsstand—the parts of them that he was able to understand and make sense of, which included crime stories and the comic page and not much else.

The police knew who Benny was and what he was; after fifteen years his downtown newsstand was a landmark and just about everyone in town knew him by sight. Many policemen knew him well enough to stop and talk a moment when they were passing his stand. So they brushed Benny off gently. They asked for his wallet and looked at the identification in it to see if it had an "in case of accident or illness notify" card with a name and address and it did. They phoned Mrs. Saddler and, after talking to her long enough to establish her relationship with Benny, they explained to her what had happened and asked her to come in and talk with them, after which she could take Benny back home with her. Which she did. And she talked to him until he was finally convinced that he had just imagined what he had tried to tell the police. Or perhaps he was not completely convinced until he read an afternoon paper with the story of the capture and confession of the real killer.

Along with many people with higher I.Q.'s than his, Benny believed implicitly everything he read in print.

The next time Benny Knox confessed to a crime he did not commit, again a murder, was two years later—a year ago, when Benny was thirty-four. That time he did not get off so lightly, for several good reasons. The crime was not yet solved, and it had been a wanton, purposeless killing that bore all the earmarks of having been committed by a mentally deranged person. A few days later it turned out to have been committed by a pair of teenage heroin addicts, but until then Benny had rather a rough time of it. His story was hard to disprove; it made sense insofar as it covered all the facts that had appeared in the papers. Only one thing saved him from being actually charged with the crime and getting his name and picture in the papers as a murderer—which would have been very bad for business at the newsstand, even though he would subsequently have been cleared. Some people would still have been afraid of him. The thing that had saved Benny had been his choice of a weapon. The news stories had said only that the man had been beaten to death with a blunt, heavy weapon. After the autopsy the police knew that the weapon had been a section of rusty pipe; not only did some of the wounds clearly indicate its diameter but tiny fragments of rust had been found embedded in the victim's skull. But they had not given this particular bit of information to the newspapers, and Benny's imagination had supplied him with a baseball bat as the blunt heavy weapon he had used. Moreover, he was unable to remember where he had obtained it or what he had done with it afterward.

The police, that time, were not so ready and willing to release Benny Knox. He'd given them a hard time and caused them a lot of work. For a while they'd seriously considered charging him despite the one discrepancy in his story. The rest of it made sense and could have been true. Further, they were convinced that he was, or at least had been, sincere in thinking he had committed the crime. That made him a psychopath, and it could be that he was a potentially dangerous one. If he could imagine himself to have committed a crime possibly someday he might really commit one.

They held him while Dr. Kranz, an alienist who was a friend of the police commissioner's and who usually advised the police on borderline cases like Benny's, talked to him twice and also had a long talk with Mrs. Saddler, who knew more about Benny's background and history than anyone else. Dr. Kranz saved Benny.

"Benny Knox," he wrote in his informal report to the commissioner, "seems to have a mental age of about eight. While it is true that many adults with that mental age find themselves unable to adjust to the world and to earn their own way in it, thereby requiring institutionalization, others do make the adjustment, especially ones who still have parents or other mentors to guide and help them.

"Mrs. Saddler stands *in loco parentis* to Knox, and she is a very sane and sensible woman. With her help, he does all right. Of course she is about twenty years older than he (that is my guess; I did not ask her age) and it is statistically probable that she will predecease him, but even this may not lead to his becoming a public charge. Mrs. Saddler is aware of the problem and has in mind solving it when the time comes, in other words, if and when she finds herself getting too old to run her boarding house any longer. She knows other rooming and boarding house keepers, some younger than herself, and believes she will have no difficulty in finding one willing to take over Benny. She says he is pleasant, tractable and easy to get along with, and his earnings are sufficient and he will represent a profit and not a burden to whoever takes care of him. The biggest problem, in fact, will be to find someone sufficiently honest not to make too much of a profit on him.

"So much of his adjustment to society despite his subnormality and now to what you've been waiting for me to discuss, his abnormality, his fantasy of believing that he has committed crimes of which he is innocent and wishing to be punished for them. From what I can learn he seems to have been a wonderfully 'good' boy and probably did nothing that, even in his own mind, merited the punishment he now seeks. I would say that his guilt feelings were given to him by his father. His father—who raised Benny alone after his mother died in childbirth—was a fiery fundamentalist minister. He taught his son what he himself believed—a good but vengeful God, original sin, a very literal brimstone Hell, eternal damnation for the sinner. These are very heady and frightening doctrines even for a person of normal mentality.

"He feels himself guilty of unnameable sins and since he cannot name them—and thereby obtain punishment and through punishment forgiveness—he builds the fantasy of having committed a real sin, one of which he *can* be punished. A nameable real sin becomes surrogate for an unnameable one.

"The prognosis? Incurable. He may 'grow out of it' or its symptoms may become worse or at any rate more frequent.

"Does this mean he should be put in an institution? I personally do not think so. He will probably again—and possibly again and again—become a mild thorn in your side by confessing to other crimes. As a matter of police routine you'll have to check his story out, and thereby run into a little extra work and expense. But—at his present rate of two years having elapsed between his last confession and his current one—the cost of this slight amount of police work once in a while will be a minute fraction of the cost to society of institutionalizing him and supporting him for the rest of his life. So my recommendation is that you give society a break by letting Benny support himself as long as he can.

"I don't think there's any chance of his becoming dangerously insane. I can't guarantee that, of course—but neither can I guarantee it in your case or mine. And I can say for him what I can say for you or me: at present none of the three of us shows signs or inclinations toward any dangerous aberration.

"I do suggest one precaution, however. Any time he again comes in with a confession, whether or not it's one you can immediately rule out without investigation, hold him until I can talk to him again and determine whether his degree and kind of mental disturbance is at that time such that I might want to change my recommendation."

That had been a year ago. Now Benny Knox was disturbed again. Not suddenly, not just tonight; his realization that he was the man who had murdered the two women, the man the police were looking for, had come to him gradually over the past week. At first he hadn't been sure, he couldn't really remember. But that wasn't surprising; from time to time there were so many things that he couldn't remember. Even now he couldn't remember *why* he had killed them—it must have been just because he was bad, evil. People were born evil and only through God and Jesus could they become good and even then before they could get into Heaven they must confess to the evil things they had done and be punished before they could be forgiven.

He closed his eyes and had a mental picture of his father and his father was holding out a hand to him and saying, "You've done wrong, Benjamin. Confess and let them punish you so you can be forgiven, or I'll never see you again. You'll go to hell and burn forever." His father's face was really his father's face, for there was a picture of his father's face on Benny's bureau and he saw it every day and couldn't forget what his father had looked like. But his father's body was clad in shimmering robes and seated on a throne. Benny often got his father in Heaven and his Heavenly Father mixed up and was as likely to pray to one as to the other.

He said, "Yes, Father, I will," aloud and opened his eyes. They fell upon his hands lying in front of him on a pile of newspapers. Big, strong hands. Strangler's hands. Hands that could kill easily, and had killed.

Footsteps approached and stopped, and he looked up. Officer Hoff stood there, grinning down at him. "Hi, Benny. Will you take your big paws off that pile of papers so I can take one?"

Benny lifted his hands and dropped them in his lap, out of sight, and Officer Hoff took one of the papers and put it under his arm. He didn't put down a dime, but Benny hadn't expected him to; policemen didn't have to pay for papers. He didn't know why not, but the man from whom his father had bought the newsstand had explained to him that policemen didn't have to pay for little things like newspapers. It was part of the cost of doing business, he'd explained, whatever that meant. You didn't charge policemen for their papers and then they liked you and helped you if you needed help. Well, he needed help now. Maybe Officer Hoff would want to arrest him right now. Officer Hoff was a nice man.

He said, "Mr. Hoff, I killed them two women. You want to arrest me? Or should I walk around to the station myself?"

Officer Hoff had quit grinning. He shook his head sadly. "Not again, Benny. You didn't—"

"I really did, Mr. Hoff. I—choked them to death." Benny held up his hands, the evidence.

Officer Hoff shook his head again. "Well—I'll radio in from the car. Maybe they'll want me to bring you in. I'll see. We're pretty busy tonight."

He walked downstreet to the curb where the squad car was waiting, another officer at the wheel. He got into the squad car. Benny was afraid at first that they'd drive off, and then he saw that the squad car wasn't moving. And after a couple of minutes Officer Hoff got out of it and came back.

He said, "No, they don't want us to bring you in. Lieutenant Burton—you know him? Red hair?"

Benny hadn't known the name but when Officer Hoff said, "Red hair," he remembered he'd talked a lot with a policeman with red hair, down at the station. He couldn't remember what they'd talked about, but he remembered the hair. He nodded.

"Well, he wants to see you. But there isn't any hurry. You can go ahead and sell the rest of your papers, no use their going to waste. Then you go to the station and he'll see you."

Benny nodded again. "All right, I'll go round."

"Be sure you do, and don't forget." He shook his head a third time. "Benny, you didn't kill them dames—we checked you out on it, long ago. You and a lot of other people. But just the same don't you forget to go to the station. If you don't go there after you quit we'll have to come to the rooming house to get you."

"I won't forget, Mr. Hoff. I'll go there."

Benny sadly watched Officer Hoff get back into the squad car and watched the squad car drive off.

Officer Hoff hadn't believed him either. But the policeman with the red hair would believe him, when Benny told him all about it.

9:00 P.M.

A clock somewhere was striking nine as Ray Fleck got out of the taxi in front of Dolly Mason's apartment, and he knew that he was on time. He'd had trouble finding a cab and had thought he was going to be late—not that a few minutes late would have mattered but if he was very late Dolly would be annoyed; Dolly got annoyed easily if you were late for a date with her. Then just at the right moment a cab had pulled in to the curb right near him to discharge passengers, and he'd caught it.

A turn in his luck? God, he hoped so. *Everything* had been going wrong today and tonight, up till then. What had got into him to pop off about Connolly's thirty-dollar bet when it had been Sam's that Amico had been talking about! A lousy six bucks, and he *had* forgotten it by then. Connolly's thirty had been the one on his mind. Hell, he thought disgustedly, he really couldn't blame Amico for not believing that he'd not been covering bets and dragging down right along, when he'd come up with a boner like that.

But Jesus, did Joe have to get so tough about it? Twenty-four hours to raise four hundred and eighty bucks, or else. His face was still sore from the two flat-handed slaps Monahan had given him and his stomach still ached from the blow there. But those things would pass, the pain of them and the humiliation of them. But if he lost his job he was sunk, really sunk. If he lost his job the way Joe would make him lose it, under a cloud with the J. & B. Distributors and on the outs with most of his customers to boot, he'd never get a reference and never get another job, here or anywhere else, selling liquor.

Many people thought Ray Fleck was a good all-round salesman who could do well selling almost anything to almost anybody, but Ray knew better; he'd tried. His first foray into selling had been just after he'd quit high school about three-fourths of the way through his senior-year—he was failing in several subjects and wasn't going to be graduated anyway—and it had been a try at selling brushes door to door. He'd hated it, especially the long hours the company had expected him to work, and he'd stuck it out less than a week, during which time he'd earned seven dollars and some odd cents. He'd tried to stay home and loaf around for a while but finally became fed up with his father calling him a no-good and with not having any spending money, and he started to look for work again. During the next seven years he held a lot of jobs but none of them for very long. All in all he worked about half of the time, but he got by because his father, a certified public accountant, had a fairly good income and after a while gave up trying to collect anything from his son in the way of room and board, so all the money Ray did make went for clothes and entertainment.

The jobs he held were many and varied. Soda jerk, counterman, assistant shipping clerk, driver of a delivery truck, what have you. He never held any job longer than a few months; half of them he quit because the work was too hard or too boring; he was fired from the rest for a variety of reasons, usually for goofing off. Once, in a bad period, he was fired for dipping into a till but luckily the employer didn't prosecute so he didn't have a police record because of it. The job he had held longest, and had most hated, during that period had been with the army when he had been drafted at twenty. And he had held that job only five months instead of the usual period. He had suddenly developed a violent allergy to wool, and since the army wasn't geared to provide special uniforms and bedding for him, it had the choice of discharging him or letting him ride out his hitch in the infirmary. It discharged him. The allergy had gradually diminished; by now he could wear wool suits except in very hot weather, but in cold weather he still used quilts or comforters instead of blankets.

Several of his jobs during that period had been selling jobs; he'd tried insurance, automobiles, hardware, and a few other things. But he hadn't lasted at those jobs as long as at others. He could turn on a pleasing personality and could make people like him, but he lacked the perseverance and determination necessary to succeed at selling, which is a lot tougher job than most people think.

Until at the end of the seven years he found himself and found the one job he both liked and could do well at. It was time that he found it, for his parents had just died, his mother, only a month before his father, and free food and board were out; he *had* to keep a job if he wanted to eat regularly.

And the job he had finally found was a natural for him. He liked hanging out in taverns. He liked to be able to buy rounds of drinks and being able, within reason, to put them on an expense account. He liked the hours. The only part of the job that he considered work was the calls he had to make at liquor stores and he was willing to do that chore for the sake of the rest of the job. He liked drinking and he had an excellent capacity for holding his drinks. The job brought him into contact with others who, like himself, loved gambling and enjoyed talking horse racing, dog racing, the odds on a pennant race or matching coins for drinks. Best of all, the job let him make money—and make it doing what came naturally.

And now he was going to lose that wonderful job, unless he could raise four hundred and eighty bucks in twenty-four hours. Joe Amico had meant every word of what he'd said, and Joe could make his threats good, too. He wouldn't last a week in his job if Joe started spreading the word around. He *had* to raise that money now; it was a matter of desperate necessity.

He paid off the taxi, and that left him thirteen dollars, thirteen lousy dollars.

Dolly, he thought, don't fail me now! He'd already decided, in the taxi, not to start off by asking for any special amount; he'd just tell her he was in a desperate jam and needed every cent he could possibly get. Maybe she'd come up with five hundred and take him off the hook completely. If that happened, he wouldn't risk the poker game at all; he'd make sure of having the dough for Amico, to save his job. That came ahead of everything else, now.

Of course she probably wouldn't have five hundred in cash at the apartment, that would be too much to hope for, but a check would be all right; he'd have all day tomorrow to cash it. How much could he offer her for five hundred? To pay her back six hundred within two weeks? That ought to be enough to tempt her, but hell, he could go even higher if he had to. After all, he hadn't given her his right name so she couldn't locate him to heckle him. Not that he wouldn't pay her back as soon as he could—if she was reasonable, like wanting six for five. If he had to promise her anything extortionate, like a thousand for five hundred, then she could whistle for it and it would serve her right for being greedy.

He hurried up the two flights of stairs and along the corridor, knocked on Dolly's door.

She opened it, first on the chain, and then when she saw who it was she said, "Hi, Ray honey. Just a sec," and closed the door a moment to slide off the chain and open it wide.

He went in and she stepped aside and then closed the door behind him. The chain went on again. Few women were taking chances these days, even if a man was with them.

Dolly Mason, he saw, was practically ready for action. Her otherwise bare little feet were in mules and she wore a thin silk kimono, brilliant red, with obviously nothing at all—except Dolly—underneath it. But he was too desperately worried to be interested. Business came first, right now. Of course if he got enough money from her to end his worries for tonight, then he could relax and romp.

"Dolly," he blurted. "I'm in a jam, a hell of a jam. Life or death, almost. I need to borrow some money—just for a week or so. Have you got any?"

She took a short step back from him; she'd been going toward him to put her arms around him as she always did when he came in. "Honey, *I* haven't got any money. Where did you get a wild idea like that?" She looked toward a handbag lying on an end table by the sofa. "I've got just eight dollars—and I can't spare any of that because it's got to last me till payday, three days. Look, I'll show you if you don't believe me."

She started toward the handbag but he said, "Never mind, I believe you. I didn't mean that kind of money anyway. And cash doesn't matter. A check will do because I can cash it tomorrow and that'll be in time, because tomorrow night's my deadline. And you'll make money on it—not lose. If you can lend me five hundred I'll give you back six, in two weeks. That's how God damn important it—"

Suddenly she was laughing. Not a cruel laugh, but an amused one. "Ray honey, I haven't *got* a bank account, not even a savings account, let alone a checking one. I'm sorry if you're in trouble, but what made you think *I* had any money? Honest, I haven't."

Ray Fleck took a step backward and dropped onto the sofa, put his elbows on his knees and his face into his hands. He was beat. He hadn't realized until this moment how much he'd been counting on Dolly—and how ridiculous it had been for him to have done so. He didn't know whether or not Dolly was lying about not having a bank account, but he knew, and for sure, that even if she had she wasn't going to lend him any money. Not even fifty bucks that he might manage to run up in the poker game, let alone the five hundred that it would take to bail him out of trouble. She didn't trust him that much and it wouldn't do any good to plead, to offer her a thousand back instead of six hundred. Even if she had a checking account, she'd never admit now that she'd been lying and write him a check against it.

"Ray honey, I'm sorry. Honest."

He took his hands away from his face, stared at her dully. "It's all right, Dolly. I shouldn't have—" He shook his head slowly. He'd started to say that he'd been a damn fool to expect anything but this, but there wasn't any point in finishing the sentence. The only thing to do now was to get going, go some place where he could think, and try to figure something out. He knew there wasn't an earthly chance that he could raise the four eighty tonight, but if he didn't waste time he might still build back his stake enough to let him sit in tonight's game. His luck *had* to change sometime.

"Ray, you do look beat," Dolly said. "Would a drink help? Let me make you a drink."

He started to say no, and then nodded instead. He really did need a drink now, and it seemed like ages since he'd had one. It had been at Connolly's, before that horrible scene at Amico's. "Sure," he said. "Make it a strong one, huh?"

"One strong drink coming up," Dolly said. She went around the screen that hid the kitchenette. He heard her taking down glasses from the little cupboard over the sink.

What an ass he'd been to remember that short story about the mistress who had given her—

Jewelry? Dolly had jewelry. He didn't know how much of it or how valuable it was, but it could be worth plenty. Not that she'd give or lend it to him, of course, but he knew where she'd kept it, or some of it. It was in a little hand-tooled leather box on top of the dresser in the bedroom. He'd never seen down inside it but he'd seen her open it and put jewelry into it. The last time he'd been here she'd been wearing long dangling earrings with green stones—emeralds?—and she'd taken them off the last thing and put them into the box before she'd thrown herself face down on the bed and rolled over into his waiting arms.

The jewelry in that little box might be worth plenty. Did he dare? There wouldn't be time now, even though the bedroom door stood ajar; it was clear across the living room from him and she'd surely hear him moving if he tried to go there. He'd have to go to bed with her to get a chance at the box, but it would be easy then; she always went to the bathroom for a minute or two immediately after.

Did he dare? Why not? He'd taken chances before, although never quite in this way, but then he'd never been in this bad a fix before either. Besides, it wouldn't really be stealing; it would be borrowing without telling Dolly about it. He'd make it up to her someday, when he was solvent again. If he couldn't get her back the same jewelry he could get her other stuff like it.

Thank *God* he hadn't given her his right name. Fletcher instead of Fleck was a little close for comfort, but all she knew about him outside of his right first name was that he was a liquor salesman. But there were a lot of liquor salesmen in the city—and the police wouldn't *know* that he'd given her his right first name, since they could find out quickly enough that he hadn't given a right last one.

Dolly came back with two drinks, both dark enough to show that she'd really made them strong.

He took the drink she held out to him and downed half of it at a gulp. It was strong enough to burn on the way down and it did help, it did make him feel better.

Dolly sat down on the sofa beside him, not pulling the kimono closed, and snuggled up against him. "Ray, honey," she said, "there's something might make you feel even better than a drink."

"A sure cure for everything?" he asked; "Maybe, Dolly. Maybe it would help. But I got to think a minute first, get something clear in my mind.

He put his free arm around her, but made no move otherwise. He didn't want to take her to bed unless he was going to take the gamble of emptying that jewel box, and if he made a pass or even kissed her he'd be committing himself. Besides, he knew that if he could get aroused, and let himself, he wouldn't have the will power not to follow through, no matter what he decided about the jewels.

But he had to decide quickly. Was the risk too great? Hell, he couldn't deny there *was* a risk—why had he told Dolly what his job was? If he'd kept that under his hat too, it would be safe as houses. But that would be pretty much of a lead, if the police really worked on it, and there was no reason why Dolly shouldn't and wouldn't report it to the police. Of course if she didn't miss it for several days she couldn't be sure who had taken it, but that was too much to hope for. Probably she wouldn't miss it tonight but probably when she dressed for work in the morning she'd go to the box for some piece of jewelry, costume or real, and that would be it. But it would still take the cops a while to get to him and if he could get rid of the stuff first—and he thought he knew where and how to do that—there'd be no proof. It would be just his word against hers and his reputation was at least as good as hers—hell, he had friends on the force who would vouch for him. Maybe his reputation was better; he'd never been in cop trouble, and maybe Dolly had. And—

He thought of the trouble he'd be in if he didn't raise the money for Amico, and suddenly made up his mind. He'd take the gamble. That is, if he *could*.

He took another slug of his drink and then put it down on the end table, and leaned over and kissed Dolly. Her lips parted moistly, but nothing happened—to him, that is. Then his hand found one of her breasts and squeezed gently before he bent down and kissed the firm erect nipple of the other one and ran his tongue around it. He felt something stir in his loins and knew that everything was going to be all right. He wasn't worried or scared enough to disgrace himself in bed.

As a matter of fact, everything was better than all right. He found that the excitement of the risk he was going to take added to rather than took from his sexual excitement. It didn't last long but while it lasted it was wonderful; Dolly seemed to think so too.

And when she scampered into the bathroom afterward he walked quickly to the dresser and emptied the tooled leather box into his hand, walked back to the bed and put pieces of jewelry into the left pocket of his trousers. He'd hardly glanced at it, except to see that there were about a dozen pieces and that they included earrings with the green stones that might be emeralds and that there was also a diamond ring and a wedding ring.

He was pulling the trousers on when Dolly came out of the bathroon. He didn't have to pretend to be in a hurry; he was. He told her he had an important business appointment and was late for it already and left the moment he'd finished dressing.

When the chain slid home behind him he breathed a deep sigh of relief. He'd got away with it, thus far. And just maybe the whole answer to his problem was in his left trouser pocket. He'd soon know.

9:32 P.M.

MACK IRBY stopped his two-finger typing and leaned back in the creaky swivel chair to light himself a cigarette. This was the only part of his job that he really hated, making reports. He'd rather tail a wife for her husband or a husband twelve hours straight than spend the half hour writing up a report on the activities of the suspected spouse. Whenever possible he talked a client into settling for verbal reports, but it wasn't always possible to get a client to agree to that. Some of them insisted on having words on paper for their money.

His dream was to have enough men under him so he could afford a stenographer-bookkeeper to take down the reports as dictation—he wouldn't mind talking them—and to take care of sending out and paying bills and the rest of the paper work. He wouldn't even insist that his office help be young and pretty—God, he had all the sex he wanted or needed with Dolly. He'd settle for anybody who could type.

But it seemed as though even this modest dream was a long way from coming true. He did all right for himself, one way or another (some of them not too honest) but strictly as a lone wolf operator. True, he had connections with other detective outfits that let him farm out work at times when he had more than he could handle alone, but he'd never had even one operative working under him full time. He'd never get rich, but most of the time he thought it was best that way; when you work alone you can cut corners you wouldn't take the risk of telling someone else to cut for you. So in all probability the nearest he'd ever have to office help was what he had already, a telephone answering service. That was an absolute must, since he spent so little of his working time actually in the office; he couldn't have operated without it.

He took a deep drag of his cigarette, put it down on the edge of his desk, already scarred by a hundred cigarette burns, and went back to his typing. "Subject entered Crillon Bar at 3:15, looked around first, then went to the bar and ordered a drink. Talked, apparently casually, to the bartender while he drank it, but kept an eye on the door as though waiting for someone. At 3:25 the woman already described in previous report entered. She nodded to him and went to a booth. He joined her there and ordered drinks for both of them. At 3:34 he—"

The phone rang and he picked it up and said, "Mack Irby speaking."

"Mack." It was Dolly's voice. "Fletcher just left and—"

"All right," he said, interrupting her to save time. "I'll be around, but I'm going to finish this one report first. I'll be there in about—"

"Wait, Mack. It's not just that. He stole my jewelry, the few things I had in that leather box on my dresser. Not worth much, but— Do you think I should call the police and report it? And if I do, maybe you shouldn't come, maybe you shouldn't be here when they get here. What do you think?"

"Don't call the cops," he said flatly.

"But why not? Like I said, the stuff isn't worth much, but they might get it back for me."

"They might, Doll. But I might be able to do even better than that. Sit tight. This report can wait till tomorrow. I'll be there in five minutes."

He hung up the phone, got his hat and turned out the lights, locked the office, and left. Downstairs he got in his car. It was, as any car used for shadowing should be, inconspicuous—a five-year-old Studebaker Commander painted gray—but there was a bit of souping-up under the hood and it was kept in perfect condition; it could go over a hundred if it had to. He drove the dozen blocks to Dolly's in three minutes flat. He let himself into the building with the key he carried and it was exactly the five minutes he had predicted when he rapped lightly on Dolly's door. He heard her coming and called out, "It's me, Doll, Mack," to save her the business with the chain.

She let him in. She was still—or again—wearing the red kimono she'd put on when he'd left at nine, and he wondered if she'd have had sense enough to have dressed before she called the police, if he had let her call them. He kissed her, and then firmly disentangled her.

"This is business," he said. "So no monkey-business. I'll sit here and you sit over there and don't distract me."

"All right, Mack honey. But can't I make us each a drink?"

"No, no— Well, all right. I can be asking questions while you make 'em." He sat down on the sofa and tossed his hat onto the end table. Dolly went behind the kitchenette's screen and he raised his voice a little so she could still hear him easily.

"So the family jewels are gone. Point one. Can you be absolutely positive this Fletcher took them? Obviously you missed them right after he left, but how long ago do you know for sure they were still in the box?"

"While you were here, Mack, just before he came. Remember I had on those costume earrings—the ones with the green stones—and I took them off when I undressed. I hate earrings in bed, especially dangly ones. And I put them in the box on the dresser. The other things were there then too, or I'd have noticed."

"That makes it sure, all right. How come you missed the stuff so soon after he left? You weren't starting to get dressed again, were you?"

Dolly came around the screen, again with a glass in each hand and again the red kimono gaped open all the way down the front. Mack Irby took his drink from her and then resolutely averted his eyes. "Pull that damn kimono shut and sit down—over there. Now answer my last question."

Dolly sat down across from him and obediently pulled the top of the kimono closed. But she crossed her legs and it fell away from them; quite a lot of Dolly still showed. She said, "No, I wasn't going to get dressed again. I just—well, I just had a sudden hunch, right after he left and just before I called you, and I looked around to see if anything was gone. I looked in my purse first; there wasn't much money in it but it was still there, and then I looked in the jewelry box and it was empty and I knew my hunch had been right.

"You see, Mack, he was in an awful hurry and kind of—well, furtive is the word, I guess, when he left. Almost like he was scared. And besides that, he's in some kind of jam over money. What he really came here for was to try to borrow some from me."

Mack Irby laughed shortly. "He sure didn't know you, Doll. What kind of money did he want? Did he mention an amount?"

"Five hundred. He offered to pay six back in a week or two. That would have been fair enough, if I knew him. But I probably don't even know his right name—and if Ray Fletcher *is* his right name he could be planning to blow town for all I know."

"You played it smart, I'd say. Offering that much interest is suspicious, and besides, the fact that he swiped your jewelry shows he ain't very honest. If you'd of lent him the money you'd never of got it back. Now you said the jewelry wasn't worth much. How much is not much?"

"Well, it was mostly costume stuff. Some of the things maybe cost up to twenty bucks apiece, but they wouldn't have any resale value. The wedding ring, worth ten or fifteen—I mean, that's what it would have cost new, not what he could get for it. And that diamond ring, the one with the flaw. You remember it."

Mack Irby remembered the ring. One of Dolly's "friends" had given it to her about a year ago. She'd turned it over to Mack to have appraised and maybe to sell it for her. It had *looked* like a good stone and as though it might weigh almost a carat; they'd thought it might be worth several hundred dollars. But the appraisal had been disappointing. Mack's jeweler friend had told him its diameter was deceptive; it was too shallow, cut too thin. And it had a bad flaw, one you could see with the naked eye if you looked at just the right angle. Seventy-five was all he offered for it. And at that price, since it looked to be worth much more, Dolly had decided to keep it.

Dolly seldom wore rings, but once in a while someone wanted to take her out of town for a weekend, and if the someone was a free enough spender she sometimes went. Since they'd be registering as man and wife she kept a plain wedding ring to wear on such occasions. And she thought that a diamond ring worn with it would look good and add verisimilitude.

Mack said, "If that's the lot, he won't get more than fifty bucks from a fence—if a fence would be willing to bother with the stuff at all. If he needs five hundred, he's in for a disappointment. All right, so much for the stuff. And now about Fletcher. I think we can take it for granted the name's a phony, or he wouldn't of risked robbing you."

He thought a moment. "But there's still a possibility. If the jam he's in is so bad he's figuring on blowing town anyway, the name business might not worry him. Let's check something."

He walked over to the telephone table and picked up the directory and opened it. After a minute he said, "There's only one Ray Fletcher listed, a Ray W. Fletcher, seventy-one sixteen South Kramer. How long ago did your Ray Fletcher leave here?"

Dolly looked at her wrist watch—and was suddenly glad she'd kept it on instead of taking it off as she sometimes did. It was a good watch, worth more than all the items she'd lost put together. She said, "About fifteen minutes ago."

Mack said, "That address is to hell and gone on the south side. Take him at least half an hour to get there, so if that Ray Fletcher is home now we can eliminate him."

He picked up the phone and dialed. A man's voice answered, "Ray Fletcher speaking," and Mack said, "Sorry, wrong number," and put the phone down.

He went back to the sofa. "Not our boy, he's home. All right, what do we know about our boy? He told you he's a liquor salesman and I'd say that's probably true, account of his bringing you a case of whisky most of the times he brought you anything. Did he ever mention what outfit he works for?"

Dolly shook her head.

"The cartons the whisky came in. Were they stamped with the name of the distributor?"

"I didn't notice if they were. And the last carton got thrown out at least a month ago. But listen, the whisky was always Belle of Tennessee brand. Would that help? I mean, do all distributors handle all brands?"

"That might help. It'll pretty well pinpoint him if it's a brand his outfit has exclusive franchise for. But damn it, I won't be able to work that angle till tomorrow—and I want to get to him tonight if I possibly can, while he's still got the stuff on him. We won't be in such a strong position if he's got rid of it, or even stashed it somewhere."

He took another sip of his drink. "All right, Doll. Start at the beginning. Where and how did you meet the guy?"

"He called up one evening and said John Evans—that's a guy I was seeing once in a while then—had given him my name and phone number and suggested he give me a ring sometime. Wanted to know if he could drop up and meet me, and bring some liquor. I wasn't doing anything that evening and he sounded nice over the phone so I said sure."

"Know how to get in touch with this John Evans?"

"No. I don't know what happened but I haven't seen him in over a year."

"And John Evans was probably a phony name too. Damn it, Doll, this is a digression but you ought to know the right names of the men you see. Not for blackmail or anything—I know you don't go in for anything like that—but just for your own protection. Like tonight. You can do it. Sooner or later a guy gets in the can and leaves his pants outside and all you got to do is take a quick gander in his wallet for his right name and address. And from then on you'll know who he really is."

"But okay, let's get back to Ray Fletcher. Do you think he's married?"

"I'm almost sure. He never took me out anywhere, for one thing, just came to the apartment. Single guys—I know a few of them—like to show me around; I'm decorative. And another thing; he never stayed all night, usually left around twelve or one. And other little things—yeah, I'm sure he's married."

"Know what kind of a car he drives?"

She shook her head again. "He must drive one, but he never brought it upstairs with him."

"You sure don't know much about him. All right, physical description. Don't see how that'll help tonight, but we might as well get it over with."

"Well, he's about your build, maybe an inch taller."

"Go on."

She giggled. "He's about an inch taller, but you're about an inch longer, Mack."

He looked at her disgustedly. "A lot of help that is, unless I find him in a Turkish bath."

Suddenly he snapped his fingers. "Doll, was he wearing tonight a gray suit, white shirt, blue tie. Sandy hair, no hat?"

"How—? Oh, sure you must have passed him on your way out. He got here just a minute after you left."

"Good. Then skip the rest of the description; I'll know him if I see him again. We passed in the doorway. But damn it, Doll, you haven't come up with anything yet that will let me find him tonight, and you gotta. Put down that drink and think hard. As many times as he was up here he must have said or done *something* that'd give me a lead. Think hard."

Dolly Mason closed her eyes and thought hard. After a minute she said, "He's a horse player. Usually had a racing form with him, in his pocket. At first, until I convinced him I don't bet, he used to give me tips on horses—and offered to place bets for me if I wanted to take the tips."

"Keep going."

Dolly's eyes opened wide. "Mack honey, I got something, I think Ray is his right *first* name."

"That helps. How do you know?"

"One evening, maybe six months ago, he must of made up his mind suddenly to make a bet. He used my phone to call some bookie to phone in the bet. Twenty bucks to win—I don't remember the horse or the track. He started out by saying 'This is Ray'; no last name but the bookie must have known him from that."

"Doll, we're getting somewhere. Think hard. Did he call the bookie by any name?"

"I think he did, but— Yeah, I remember. He said 'This is Ray, Joe,' and then went on and gave the bet."

Mack said, "I know two bookies named Joe. It couldn't be Joe Renfield; he takes only cash bets, no phone business. Runs a cigar store and books on the side. So it's Joe Amico. I'll know in a minute."

He crossed to the telephone table, looked up a number and dialed it. When a voice answered he said, "This is Bill? Mack Irby. Is Joe there? Can I talk to him?"

Bill said sure and a minute later Joe's voice said, "Hi, Mack. What can I do for you?"

"Joe, you got a customer named Ray. He's a liquor salesman. Can you give me the rest of his name?"

"What do you want with him, Mack? Listen, he owes me dough and if you're going to get him in trouble I'll never collect."

"It's the other way around," Mack said. "He's in trouble all right, but he'll be in worse trouble if I don't find him right away, tonight. He stole some jewelry from a client of mine. If I can get to him before he sells it, there'll be no beef; my client'll settle for getting the stuff back. If he fences it before I get to him, it'll be too late for that, see? I can find him tomorrow easy enough—how many liquor salesmen are there in town named Ray? But that might be too late to keep him out of jail."

Joe Amico grunted. "Guess you got a point. And I guess I pushed him too hard. All right, his last name's Fleck. F-l-e-c-k. I don't remember his address offhand, but it's in the phone book."

"Attaboy, Joe. You wouldn't make a guess which fence he might head for?"

"No, I wouldn't. I know some fences, and so do you, but I don't know which of 'em, if any, Ray might know or know about."

"Okay, one more thing, Got any idea where I might find him tonight? If he didn't head home, that is. I'll give his number a ring first."

"Best I could guess is some downtown tavern, almost any of them. He makes the rounds. Your best bet would be to make 'em too. Will you know him if you see him, Mack?"

"Yeah. Thanks to hell and back, Joe. So long."

He put down the phone and quickly looked up Ray Fleck in the phone book. He looked at the address first. Yes, it was close enough. If Fleck had headed straight for home he'd be there by now. And just maybe that's what he's done, if he was scared.

He dialed the number and while it rang a dozen times he held his hand over the mouthpiece and spoke to Dolly. "Your boy friend is Ray Fleck. Three-one-two Covington Place. But I guess he didn't head for home." He cradled the telephone. "So I go looking for him."

Dolly ran over to him, put her arms around his neck and pressed her body against his.

"Mack honey, do you have to start *right* away? Would fifteen or twenty minutes matter?"

Mack Irby laughed. "All right, I don't guess fifteen or twenty minutes will matter."

The red kimono fell almost completely away as he picked her up and carried her into the bedroom.

9:59 P.M.

RAY FLECK reached the edge of downtown afoot. He had walked in from Dolly's, not to save the price of a taxi—what would one lousy buck have mattered out of the thirteen that was all the cash he had left?—but simply because he hadn't seen a cruising cab. And by the time he reached the first place from which he could have phoned for one he was so near town that he knew he'd get there sooner if he kept on walking than if he phoned and waited for a cab.

He was still a bit scared at what he had done, but he was also excited. He didn't know what he had, and it might be anything. Maybe a thousand dollars' worth of stuff, for all he knew. At least a couple of hundred dollars worth, he thought; the diamond ring alone, from the quick glimpse he got of it, ought to be worth at least that much, even at a fence's price. And he felt certain that, at least, was genuine; people just don't put a glass or a rhinestone into that kind of mounting, like an engagement ring. Or if they do, they use a chunk of glass or rhinestone that's bigger and flashier, one that looks like a three-carat diamond instead of a one-carat one. But the other stuff could be anything. Oh, probably some of it was costume jewelry, but if even a few pieces were real, he'd settle happily. And if the greenstones in those earrings were emeralds they'd be worth at least twice what the diamond was worth. Maybe more. Each of the two stones was at least twice the size of the diamond, and he thought he remembered having heard that good emeralds cost just about as much per carat as diamonds.

Several times he'd been tempted, after he was out of the immediate neighborhood of the scene of his crime and over the worst of his initial panic, to stop under a street light and take a look at what he had, but he resisted the impulse. He didn't know a thing about jewelry and not even a close examination under a bright light would really tell him anything. If some of the pieces were marked *14K* and others *gold filled* it would give him a clue but it would tell him nothing about the stones and the stones were what counted.

He might as well hunt Fats Davis right away and let Fats make the appraisal. He'd thought of Fats before he'd lifted Dolly's jewelry, while he was still making up his mind whether to or not.

He was reasonably sure Fats was a fence. Several people had told him so and he had no reason not to believe them. He didn't know Fats very well but he thought Fats knew him well enough to trust him and do business with him if he did buy and sell hot ice. At any rate, Fats would be able to make an appraisal for him; Fats, whatever his business was now, had been a jeweler once. Everybody knew that much about him.

He might have trouble finding Fats because he didn't know his right first name. He wouldn't be listed in the phone book under *Davis, Fats* and there'd probably be a hundred or more Davises in the book, too many to try phoning down the line.

But Fats hung out around the downtown joints and there was an even chance he'd run into him if he made the rounds. And if he didn't find Fats he'd be sure sooner or later to run into someone who knew him well enough to tell him how to make contact, or who at least would know Fat's first name.

Jick Walters' place would be the best bet; he'd run into Fats oftener there than in any other tavern. And Jick at least knew Fats, although Ray didn't know how well.

He headed for Jick's, but since there were two other taverns he had to pass on the way, he made a quick stop in each of them. Business was slow in both; there were only a few customers and none of them people he knew. But he knew both bartenders and asked them about Fats. One of them didn't know him at all; the other knew him, but no better than Ray did and didn't come up with anything helpful, even a first name.

Business was slow at Jick's, too, but at least Jick himself was behind the bar. He waited till he'd ordered a drink and Jick had made it for him before he broached the subject.

"Jick, I'm looking for Fats Davis. But I don't know his first name so I can't find him in the phone book. You know how I can get in touch with him? It's important."

"Yeah, I know," Jack said.

"How?"

Jick grinned. "Turn right and walk a dozen steps. He's in the end booth down there."

Ray looked that way. He'd thought the booth was empty, but he realized now that Fat's head wouldn't show over the top of the partition. Fats was almost literally a five-by-five. He wasn't more than two inches over five feet and couldn't have been more than a few inches under five feet around the waist.

"Swell," Ray said. "What's he drinking? I'll take one over to him."

"Straight shots. But go ahead, Ray. I'll bring his drink over."

"Thanks, Jick." Ray picked up his own drink and strolled back. "Hi, Fats," he said. "Can I talk to you a minute?"

Fat's little eyes weren't especially cordial when he looked up, but he nodded, and Ray slid into the other side of the booth, facing the front of the tavern.

"Want to ask you how much some stuff is worth," Ray said. "And if by any chance you want to buy it, that'll be swell."

"Got it with you?"

Ray nodded. "But I ordered you a drink when Jick told me you were here. Let's wait till he's—"

But Jick was already there with a shot and a chaser and put them down on the table. When Ray had paid him and he'd gone back behind the bar, Fats asked, "More than one piece?"

"Yeah," Ray said, and reached for his pocket.

But Fats said, "Wait a minute," and took a clean handkerchief from his pocket, unfolded it and spread it in front of him. "Put it on this," he said, "so one of us can pick it up in one grab if anybody starts back this way. You're facing front; slide over to the outer edge of your seat so you can watch that way."

Ray took the crumpled handkerchief out of his pocket first and then managed to get hold of all the jewelry at once. He put it in the middle of Fat's spread handkerchief and then, as Fats had suggested, slid over to where he could watch toward the front of the tavern. He didn't think anybody would head back—there were only four other customers in the place—but it was best to play safe.

But he watched Fats out of a corner of his eye. Fats stirred through the stuff with a stubby index finger. He picked up one of the earrings with the green stones first, looked at it closely and then put it down again. He felt glad things had worked out this way, that Fats hadn't made him tell what he thought he had to sell. If the earrings were glass it would have made things embarrassing if he'd told Fats they were emeralds. And the other way around would have been worse. If he'd told Fats it was all costume jewelry except the diamond, then Fats could cheat him all too easily if the stones really were emeralds.

Fats picked up the diamond ring and took a jeweler's loupe from his pocket. He screwed the loupe into his right eye and studied the diamond through it. Briefly. Then he put the ring back with the other pieces and the loupe back in his pocket. He wadded up the handerchief and pushed it across to Ray Fleck.

"Put it in your pocket," he said. "It's all junk. What did you think *I* could do with it? Keep the handkerchief. Fair trade for the drink."

He picked up his shot and tossed it down, took a short sip from the water chaser and then wiped the thick lips with the back of his hand.

"My God, Fats," Ray said. "You trying to tell me that isn't even a diamond in that ring? I know the other stuff is costume jewelry, but—" He did know it now.

"Sure, it's a diamond. *What* a diamond. Got a flaw in it you could crawl inside, and it's a cheater cut, thin like a poker chip."

"You mean it's not worth *anything*?"

Fats Davis shrugged. "Maybe fifty bucks, mounting and all. It's not too bad a mounting."

Ray Fleck was stunned, but he didn't doubt that Fats was telling the truth. Of course Dolly, smart little bitch that she was, wouldn't keep anything valuable right on top of her dresser where any man who visited her could swipe it—as easily as he had. If she owned anything valuable in the way of jewelry she'd at least keep it out of sight and probably locked up at that.

Well, anyway, fifty bucks would again put him in shape to sit in on the poker. He sighed. "Okay, Fats. I'll settle for fifty bucks."

Fats shook his head. "Huh-uh. I don't want it. I said the ring might be worth that—but I don't mess with peanut stuff. You take as much risk and don't make anything."

"What risk?" Ray asked. "Damn it, Fats, I didn't steal this stuff. It's mine." He realized that sounded silly. "My wife's, I mean, but this is a community property state and that makes it mine too."

"I'll buy that," Fats said. "But does she know you're selling it? There could still be a beef. She misses it and calls copper, and you got to go along with her, or confess up. And tell what you did with the stuff—and that gets my name on the blotter even if they can't hang a rap on me. Huh-uh, Fleck." He shook his head again. "If the stuff was worth a couple of grand, I'd take a chance maybe, but not for junk jewelry."

"Fats, she knows about it, gave it to me to see if I could get anything out of it when I told her I was in a jam. Listen, the costume pieces are stuff she was tired of. And she was married before, and the engagement and wedding rings are from her first marriage—and that's how come neither of us knew the diamond wasn't as good as it looked. We never had it appraised or anything."

"Take it to a hock shop if it's a clean deal. They'll give you as much as I offered on the diamond, and maybe even a little something on the other junk. Like the wedding band; you'll get old gold value for that, if nothing more."

"But damn it, Fats. I need the money tonight. The hock shops are closed."

Fats sighed. "All right, get your wife on the phone and let me talk to her. If she says she gave you that ring to sell I'll buy it. Otherwise no dice."

"She's out with friends, damn it. I can't reach her on the phone. But I'm telling you the truth, Fats."

Fats slid out of the booth and stood up. "Sorry, pal. No dice." He turned to the front and said, "Oh-oh. Fuzz. Better get that back in your pocket. I'm getting out of here."

Looking past Fats as he walked to the front, Ray saw that two uniformed policemen had just come in. One of them he knew,

Hoff. The other he knew by sight as Hoff's partner. A momentary chill went down his spine, but then he realized they couldn't possibly be looking for him. Not possibly. Just the same he was relieved when Hoff caught his eye and waved a hand casually, then stopped at the bar with his partner.

He quickly stuffed the handerchief with the junk jewelry back in his pocket and stood up. He wanted to get out of here too, although he didn't know yet where he was going.

He intended to walk past the two policemen but Hoff stopped him by turning as he approached and saying, "Hi, Ray. Have a drink." And it would have looked funny if he'd turned it down.

"Thanks, sure," he said. "How goes it?"

Hoff nodded to Jick and then turned back. "Hell of a night. The psycho's out. Every squad car we've got is out and they're ordering us around like crazy. We dropped in for a quickie."

He had to pretend to be interested. "You mean he's killed another dame."

"No, not yet, but he's on the prowl. Made a try late this afternoon. Dame alone in a flat on Koenig. Knocked on the door and called out 'Western Union,' and she opened up—but on a chain. When he saw or heard the chain he ran fast; she didn't get a look at him. She phoned in, but he was out of the neighborhood by the time we got there."

"Sounds like it was him all right," Ray said. Jick had put a drink in front of him and he said, "Thanks," and lifted his glass to Hoff.

Hoff said, "And he made another try just a little while ago—or we think it was him, anyway. Must of decided women weren't opening doors for him any more. Dame in a cottage out on Autremont heard someone trying to break in a window and phoned in. Nobody when we got there—but there were chisel marks on a window, so she wasn't imagining things."

"That could have been a burglar, couldn't it?"

"Burglars don't break in lighted places with someone inside. He could of seen her from the window he tried. And the phone too. Quit trying the window and ran when he saw her dialling."

Hoff's partner leaned around him. "Well, we know now he drives a car, anyway. She heard it start up while he was still talking over the phone." He clunked down his glass. "Hoffy, we gotta go. This was a quickie, remember?"

"Can't I buy you boys one?" Ray Fleck asked.

Hoff said, "Thanks, Ray, but no. We're taking a chance being outa the squad car this long. If the radio operator calls our number and we don't answer, we're on the carpet plenty. So long."

They went out. Ray looked at his glass and was surprised to find that it was empty. Morosely, for lack of a better idea, for lack of any place to go or anything else to do, he put money on the bar and said, "One more, Jick."

Jick picked up the glass. "Anything wrong, Ray? You look kind of—well, not so good."

"Everything's wonderful," Ray said. "It's a great, wide wonderful world."

Except, where was he going to get four hundred and eighty bucks by tomorrow night?

10:25 P.M.

BENNY KNOX had left his newsstand early; usually he didn't leave until eleven o'clock or when he'd sold out on papers, whichever came first. But tonight at a quarter after ten there'd been only a few papers left and he'd decided not to wait any longer; he'd waited that long only because Mr. Hoff had told him to finish out the evening and then go to the police station to turn himself in. That had disappointed him; he had hoped that Mr. Hoff and his partner would take him in themselves in the squad car, with the siren going and the red light flashing. He had had rides in automobiles only a few times in his life and never one in a squad car.

Now inside the police station he stood in front of the tall receiving desk, at which a gray-haired man was busily writing. The man hadn't looked up yet. That is, he'd looked up when Benny had come in but then had looked down and started writing again. Benny stood there waiting and feeling awkward, but he didn't want to interrupt the man. Under Benny's arm was clutched the cigar box, now with a rubber band around it, that held his receipts for the day. One thing about the money in it puzzled him. He'd counted it before he left the stand, because he always did, and there were about ten dollars less in it than there should have been. He couldn't figure out what could have happened to ten dollars—except for a vague recollection of someone laughing at him; he remembered feeling angry about that but he couldn't remember who the someone had been or how it connected with the ten dollars.

The gray-haired man at the desk put down his pen but he still didn't look toward Benny. He picked up the telephone and said into it, "Get me Burton." And then a few seconds later, "Lieutenant, Benny Knox is here. Shall I send him on upstairs, or—" And then, "Okay."

He put down the phone and looked at Benny. "The lieutenant wants to talk to you, in his office." He jerked a thumb. "Down that corridor, second door on your right."

Benny found the door and knocked on it lightly. He opened it and went in when a voice called out for him to do so. The lieutenant with the red hair was back of a desk.

He said, "Sit down, Benny. Officer Hoff radioed in earlier that you want to confess to two murders. Is that right?"

Benny sat down. "Yes, sir, Lieutenant. I did kill them women, both of them. I choked 'em to death." He held up the evidence—his hands.

The red-haired lieutenant nodded gravely. "Benny, we'll have to hold you overnight and Doc Kranz will talk to you tomorrow. What happens after that depends on what he says. Do you understand?"

Benny nodded. Although he didn't see where a doctor came in, that didn't matter as long as they were going to put him in jail and punish him. Then God and his father would forgive him and everything would be all right.

The lieutenant said, "One thing, Benny. That woman who takes care—that you stay with. Does she know you were coming here? If not, I'll phone her to save her worrying when you don't come home tonight."

Benny shook his head, feeling ashamed of not having thought about Mrs. Saddler. She *would* worry about him. And wait up. She never went to bed until he got home.

"Let's see," the lieutenant said, reaching to pull the phone book over in front of him. "Her name's Saddler, isn't it? And on Fergus Street?"

"I got her number here, sir," Benny said, glad of a chance to be helpful. He took a card from his pocket and handed it across the desk. It was an "in case of accident or illness, notify" card with Mrs. Saddler's name, address and phone number on it. She'd asked him to carry it always and once in a while asked him to show it to her so she'd be sure he hadn't lost it.

"Thanks Benny." The lieutenant took the card and gave the number on it to the switchboard operator over the phone. And then he was saying, "Mrs. Saddler? I'm phoning you about Benny—this is Lieutenant Burton speaking—so you won't worry when he doesn't get home tonight.

"Yes, he's here and he's just confessed to two murders—the two recent sex killings—and . . . Yes, I know he didn't do them. We're not charging him with them. But you remember what I explained to you about a year ago—that if Benny ever confessed to anything again we'd have to hold him until Dr. Kranz has a chance to talk to . . . No, I wouldn't dare call the doctor tonight; the chief would have my ears if I did. . . . Sometime tomorrow, and we'll try to get him to make it early enough so Benny won't lose the whole day if Doc says so . . . Oh no, Mrs. Saddler, it wouldn't do any good at all for you to come down. We wouldn't be able to let you see him anyway, tonight. But we'll take good care of him, and we'll phone you again tomorrow as soon as there's anything to report. I won't be on duty then, but I'll leave a memo . . . All right, I'll tell him. Goodnight, Mrs. Saddler."

He put the phone down and smiled at Benny. "She said to tell you good night for her, and for *you* not to worry. You've got a fine friend there, Benny."

Benny nodded. He did feel sorry about Mrs. Saddler and that she'd never see him again unless she visited him in jail. She was like a mother to him, or the nearest to a mother he'd ever known. Then he remembered something the lieutenant said to her.

"But, Lieutenant, sir, you told her I didn't do it. I *did*, honestly, I remember, I choked them. You got to believe me."

"Just a minute, Benny," the lieutenant said. He picked up the phone again. "Give me the jail—Wait, don't. Just call them yourself and tell them to send down a couple of boys to pick up a customer, in my office. Thanks."

He looked back at Benny. "Now Benny listen. Maybe you're not yet in the mood to believe *me*, but I'm going to tell you this anyway. I like you and I hope you get by Doc Kranz again, and I think you'll have a better chance of doing that if I can get you started thinking straight tonight. Then maybe tomorrow you'll realize how wrong you were thinking.

"Listen, Benny, we *know* you didn't commit those murders, and I'll tell you how we know. After each one of them we checked a hell of a lot of suspects. Every man who had a record of sex offenses, any kind. Every known psychopath, everyone known to us to be seriously abnormal or subnormal mentally. You—uh—"

"I know I'm not very bright, Lieutenant. I don't mind your saying so as long as you don't laugh at me. I don't like people to laugh at me."

"I'm not laughing, Benny. Listen to me, listen hard. We checked you on both of them. On one you've got an absolutely solid alibi; you *couldn't* have done it. We know just when that one happened, ten o'clock in the evening. We could rule you out without even leaving the station, because Hoff remembered it was ten o'clock, within a few minutes, when he picked up a paper from you at your stand, three miles or so from where the woman was being killed. Your alibi on the other murder isn't quite so solid, because we don't know exactly what time it happened. But we know you were at your stand all evening till eleven and you got home about twenty after, just the time it takes you to walk that far. We can't prove you didn't sneak out later, of course—but you *didn't*, Benny. Whoever killed either one of those women killed both of them. That's for sure if anything is."

Benny looked and felt miserable. The lieutenant didn't believe him, and neither had Mr. Hoff. That much at least of the lieutenant's speech had registered.

He said unhappily. "But I *did* kill them, both of them. I remember, Lieutenant. I'm sure."

"You just think you're sure, Benny. Now before you go to sleep tonight and in the morning after you wake up you think over what I said and make yourself a little less sure. I—"

The door opened and two men in the uniforms of turnkeys from the city jail on the upper floors of the building came in. One of them, the tall one, said, "Package for us, Lieutenant? You through with him?"

The lieutenant sighed. "Yeah, I guess I'm through with him. This is Benny Knox, boys. He'll be your guest tonight. A disposition order will come up sometime tomorrow."

"Sure. Just in the tank?"

"Hell, no. Benny never took a drink in his life; don't put him in with the drunks. You've got cell space, haven't you?"

"Yeah. What's with the cigar box he's got? A time bomb, maybe?"

"It's got money in it," the lieutenant said, "And be sure there's the same amount when you turn it in."

The tall turnkey grinned. "Why, Lieutenant! Have you frisked him otherwise?"

"No, Benny wouldn't be carrying a— Oh, I suppose we might as well protect ourselves by following the routine. He just might get a funny idea, at that. You take care of it."

"All right, chum," the turnkey said to Benny. "Come on; we'll take care of you. We'll give you the bridal suite, and you can be making up your mind whether you want a blonde or a brunette to go with it."

Benny realized that was a joke so he didn't try to answer. He went with them along two corridors and up several flights in an elevator, then along another corridor and through a door into an office in which there was a desk with a young male clerk behind it.

At the desk they asked him for the cigar box; they opened it and the clerk counted it. When he called out and wrote down the total, it was the same amount Benny himself had counted it to be just before he'd left the newsstand. Meanwhile the turnkeys had asked him to empty his pockets onto the desk and he had. They patted him a few places and then gave him back what he'd taken out of his pockets except for one thing, a small penknife he used for cutting the rope around bundles of papers and for cleaning his fingernails. They asked him to take off his belt and he did. He wasn't wearing a necktie; he never wore one except to church. And they didn't take his shoelaces because he was wearing moccasins. Hard shoes hurt his feet and he always wore moccasins except on Sunday.

Then they took him down another corridor, through a steel door, past the barred doors of cells. Then they opened a cell door and the tall turnkey said, "All right, chum, this is it. Home, sweet home."

Benny went in and they closed the door behind him. The closing door made a loud bang and someone somewhere yelled out, "Quiet, you bastards!" And then they went away and left him alone.

The cell was long and narrow, about six feet by fifteen. Enough light came in from the corridor through the bars so he could see his way around. There was a double-decker bunk bed—with no one in either the upper nor the lower—two chairs and, back in the far corner, a commode. That was all, or it was all that he could see now, in the dimness.

He sighed and took off his suit coat, hung it over the back of one of the chairs and put his moccasins under the chair.

He started to get into the lower bunk and then remembered that he's never slept in a high bed, an upper bunk, in his life and he wondered if it would feel any different, so he climbed into the upper and stretched himself out.

The lieutenant had told him there was something he should think about tonight and he tried to remember what it was. But within seconds, and before he could remember, he was asleep.

10:45 P.M.

RAY FLECK still stood at the bar in Jick's, where Hoff and his partner had left him, nursing a drink and moodily making wet circles on the bar with the bottom of his glass. Twice Jick, who wasn't very busy, had said something to him but he'd answered briefly and without looking up so Jick knew he hadn't wanted to talk and had moved along the bar to someone else.

He was thinking about the poker game that would be starting soon now and he was blowing hot and cold on the idea of trying to get into it. There was still one chance that he could; the diamond ring. It was a strictly cash game, no checks cashed and no borrowing. But he might be able to make an exception to the borrowing rule if he had security like that to offer. Sure, he could. He remembered now one night when Luke Evarts had gone broke and had managed to keep going a while by borrowing thirty-five bucks from Doc Corwin, putting up as security an almost new and quite expensive wrist watch. And the diamond ring, damn it, *looked* good, looked like it ought to be worth several hundred dollars, and none of the boys was a jeweler or carried a magnifying glass. One of them might be willing to lend him a hundred on it, or at least fifty.

Of course it would be embarrassing as hell to have to go up there to Harry Brambaugh's flat with no money at all and have to try to raise money, on whatever security, to get into the game. Much more embarrassing than going there with a reasonable amount of money and raising more, as Luke had done with the wrist watch, after losing it. It would really be embarrassing if he went there and was unable to play at all, if no one would lend him even fifty on the damn ring.

But that wasn't the important reason why he was beginning to blow cold on the poker. In as bad a jam as he was in a little embarrassment, losing a little face, was something he could put up with. If he didn't raise Amico's money he was going to lose worse than face. He was beginning to worry about his luck, as far as tonight was concerned. Everything, but everything, had gone sour on him (he thought: he didn't know that his real troubles hadn't started yet). Bad luck runs in streaks and he didn't have the slightest indication that his was going to change tonight.

And a better idea had come to him, standing there at the bar.

He could go home soon, even now, and be there, sober when

Ruth got home around midnight. She'd be surprised to see him, after their quarrel, and maybe even pleased, if she was over her mad.

But whether she was still mad or not he wouldn't let it develop into a quarrel again. He'd be calm and patient with her, and he'd be able to explain this time what he'd not been able to explain this afternoon—exactly what Joe Amico's ultimatum had been, exactly what Joe's deadline was and what he'd do if the money wasn't given him by then. She'd listen; he'd *make* her listen. She was a stubborn bitch all right and that damned policy was the thing she was most stubborn about, but she *did* have common sense. If he could explain to her and convince her, and he thought he could, that his keeping his job depended completely on his having five hundred dollars tomorrow, she'd at least see that her own selfish interests were in this case identical with his.

Jick Walters was across the bar from him again. He didn't say anything but he glanced interrogatively at Ray's glass, and Ray saw it was empty. Ray nodded, and put money on the bar while Jick made him another drink.

He could do it, he thought. He could talk Ruth into it—if he could avoid losing his temper and stay calm and reasonable, keep her that way. And thank God the home office of her insurance company was right here; they could go to it together any time tomorrow and she'd be able to get a check while they waited. No sweat at all about Amico's deadline; he wouldn't wait till evening to get the money to him.

It would work. He wondered why he hadn't thought of it sooner, right after Amico had read the riot act to him, instead of wasting time trying first to borrow money from Dolly, and then stealing her junk jewelry. He'd get rid of that tomorrow, too, if Ruth was reasonable about the insurance business. He'd mail it back to Dolly—and then call her up and tell her he'd done so, apologize, and explain. And if she was reasonable about it and not too mad, he'd even be able to see her again sometime, when he was solvent again.

But handling Ruth came first. He found himself planning what he'd say to her, as he'd plan a sales talk. He'd have to eat a little crow, and make some promises. Not to quit gambling; she'd never believe him if he promised that, and disbelief would antagonise her. But he would promise—and sincerely, because he never wanted to get into a jam like this again—never again to gamble on credit and go in over his head. He could promise too to pay back the loan against the policy, at, say, twenty-five a week, so the full ten thousand would be coming when the endowment was due. And even make the payments for a few weeks until things were on an even keel again. He could tell her——

"Beg your pardon, Mr. Fleck. Like to talk to you."

He'd been aware, while thinking, of someone coming up alongside him at the bar and ordering and getting a drink, and now he turned to see who it was. He didn't know the guy. Medium height, stocky and husky-looking, reddish face, and eyes like pale blue marbles.

"You don't know me," the man said. "My name's Mack Irby."

Ray Fleck nodded, not too cordially. "Glad to know you, Mr. Kirby," he said. "Got to leave in a minute but—what's it about?"

"Irby, not Kirby. Mack Irby—does sound like Kirby when you say both names together. Look, it's kind of private. End booth back there's empty, and so's the one next it. Let's go back to the end booth."

Ray frowned. "I said I got just a minute. You can tell me what it's about right here." The guy might be a damn insurance salesman, for all he knew. Or more likely a bill collector.

Irby said, "Let's say I want to talk about a friend of yours, Mr. Fleck. His name's something like yours. It's Ray Fletcher."

Ray Fleck winced. He knew that the wince was visible, even obvious, but he couldn't help it; the shock had been too great. Here was trouble, new trouble, just when he'd thought he had figured a safe answer to the problem of his debt to the bookie. Now this. He had no doubt what it concerned. At various times in his life and for various reasons he'd used a name other than his own, but not always the same one; to no one but Dolly Mason had he ever given his name as Fletcher.

But how had he been found so quickly? The only thing he could think of was that Dolly must have known all along, or for a long time, what his real identity was. There'd been times—not tonight—when she'd been briefly alone with his clothes while he'd gone into the bathroom; on any of those occasions she could have taken a quick look at identification in his wallet or papers in his pocket. Just what a girl like Dolly would do. Why hadn't he thought of . . .

"Well, Fleck?" There was an edge of impatience in Irby's voice now. "Want to talk in the back booth, or down at headquarters?"

"The booth," Ray said. His voice didn't come out quite right. But he picked up his glass and started toward the rear of the tavern. And a sudden thought came and with it a sudden hope that this wasn't as bad a jam as he had feared. It wasn't a pinch—at least not yet. The cop—he *must* he a cop; he looked and acted like one—hadn't pinched him; he wanted to talk, and in private.

That meant Dolly hadn't simply called the police, given his name and description and reported the theft. She hadn't wanted the publicity, for obvious reasons. This Irby must be a friend of hers on the force—either a plain-clothes cop or a regular cop who was off duty when she called him. And she'd have told him she didn't want to make a complaint if she could get her stuff back without making one. Thank God, he thought, Fats Davis hadn't bought any of the stuff after all, and he still had it intact, ready to hand back. If he'd sold the ring for fifty they'd claim it was worth more and there'd still be trouble.

But, he thought as he slid into the booth, he'd let Irby talk first. He wouldn't make the mistake he'd made with Amico earlier by talking out of turn, admitting to having dragged down Connolly's thirty-buck bet when Sam-the-waiter's smaller bet was the only one Amico had known about. Just conceivably, although he didn't see how, this current deal didn't even concern the jewelry at all.

Irby slid in across from him, where Fats had sat only half an hour ago.

Irby said, "Keep your hands on top of the table, Fleck. The stuff's in your left pants pocket—you unconsciously put your hand over it while we were walking back to make sure it was still there. And I wouldn't want you to try to get any idea of ditching it here in the booth. I'd have to take you in right away if you tried that."

It was the jewelry then, all right. And there wasn't any use in his denying it—or of volunteering any information either. Ray Fleck just nodded. And kept his hands in sight.

Irby said, "All right, I'll put my cards on the table. Or my card." He took a card from the breast pocket of his coat and put it down in front of Ray. *Mack Irby, Private Investigator*. And an address and a phone number. "Put it in your pocket. You might want to use me sometime to get you out of a jam. But not *this* jam; I've already got a client. And you can guess who it is, without straining yourself."

Ray Fleck nodded again. And to avoid discussion and keep things moving he put the card into his own breast pocket.

"Meanwhile," Irby said, "don't let the fact that I'm a private detective and not a cop dazzle you into thinking I can't arrest you, or that I won't if I have to. I carry a deputy's badge, for one thing. And if I didn't I can still make a citizen's arrest if I find someone in the act of committing a crime. And you are; you're in possession of stolen property. And if you think I can't handle you—" He pulled back his coat far enough so Ray could see the butt of a flat automatic in a shoulder holster. "Just don't try to make a run for it."

"I'm not running," Ray said. "But you wouldn't shoot a man for—"

"In the leg I would. Try me and see."

"Look, Irby," Ray said. "You don't want to arrest me or you would have right away. Dolly just wants her junk back, and I'm willing to give it back. I've still got it all. So why don't I just give it to you and call it square. And you can give her my apologies too."

"It's not that simple, Fleck. My client will settle for restitution—but full restitution, and the way she wants it. You know how women are. They get tired of clothes and of jewelry and would rather have new things than old ones. She'd much rather have the cash value of that jewelry than the stuff itself back, so she could buy new to replace it. And there's the matter of the fee I'll have to charge her. I think she should be reimbursed for that, don't you?"

Ray Fleck licked his suddenly dry lips. "Is this a shakedown, blackmail? If it is, it won't work. I'm broke, flat broke and in debt already."

"Let's take those points one at a time, Fleck. First, blackmail. Blackmail is a crime. If you think I'm trying to blackmail you, you can arrest me. Citizen's arrest. And I'll arrest you for grand larceny and we'll handcuff ourselves together—I've got cuffs, right in my hip pocket—and go in to headquarters and accuse each other. I can make my charge stick, especially if I don't let you get rid of what's in your pocket, and I assure you I won't let you. Your charge would be your word against mine, and my word's damned good down there. They'd laugh at you. Shall we do it that way?"

Ray Fleck put out a hand for his glass but the hand trembled and he put it down on the table again. "All right, you've got me. But damn it, you can't get blood out of a turnip. I *am* broke. I—"

Irby put up a hand to stop him.

"I know quite a bit more about you, Fleck, than I did when I started looking for you a little less than an hour ago. You weren't in the first five bars I tried, but the bartender or owner knew you in every one of them. I know you're married. And I know which outfit you sell for—J. and B. and that you've been with them for quite a while. Nobody guessed your income at less than a hundred a week and most thought more. So, broke at the moment or not, I figure you can raise the money somehow—and I don't care how you do it—to make adequate restitution to Miss Mason. And I figure the amount should be a nice even thousand dollars."

At the expression on Ray's face, Irby raised a hand. "I don't know whether you've tried to fence the stuff as yet. If you have, you're aware it won't bring anything like that sum. But don't forget there's a terrific difference between a fence's price, and a retail jeweler's. And Miss Mason will be replacing those items at retail; I'd say it will cost her five hundred dollars, or almost that. Say that half of the other five hundred is my fee—and I'm sure you'll agree that under the circumstances that shouldn't come out of Miss Mason's pocket. Call the other half punitive damages, or payment for the mental anguish Miss Mason suffered in learning that a friend whom she'd trusted turned out to be a sneak thief. Break it down any way you like, but that's the amount it's going to add up to."

Ray Fleck said bitterly, "It *is* blackmail then. Damn you, Irby, I'm tempted—"

"To spend six months in jail—and lose your job, your friends, and probably your wife if she's worth anything to you? Just to save a lousy grand?"

Irby leaned forward to reach into his left hip pocket and brought out a pair of handcuffs. "I tried to give you a break," he said, "but if you'd rather go to jail, let's get it over with."

Ray said miserably, "You win. But—how long will I have to raise it? It may take me—"

"We'll worry about that later. For tonight, if you want to walk out of here free, two painless steps are all you got to do. First, write a check for a thousand dollars made out to Miss Dolly Mason, date it today." He held up a hand to stop Ray's protest. "Don't tell me you haven't got a thousand dollars in your account. I'll concede that, or you wouldn't be broke. I'll tell my client when to cash it. Let me worry about that."

Ray said sullenly, "I've got a dollar and some cents in the account, just enough to hold it open. All right. But I've got to get my wallet out of my hip pocket to get a check." Irby nodded, and he took out his wallet and took from it one of several blank checks he kept folded in one of the compartments. Irby offered him a pen, but he shook his head and took his own from his inside coat pocket, and wrote the check.

"Don't put the pen away," Irby told him. "One more step." He read the check carefully and put it into his own wallet. Then he took from his coat pocket a folded sheet of blank paper. He unfolded it and put it in front of Ray Fleck. "Now a confession. Put the date down and I'll dictate the rest."

"Confession! My God, you've got the check. Why do you want a confession too?"

"Think, Fleck. We might have to prove what that check was given for. Maybe you haven't thought of this yet, but you will: if I let you walk out of here free what's to prevent you from ditching the stolen property down the nearest sewer right away—and then, first thing tomorrow morning, stopping payment on the check? And if she tried to make trouble your story—you'd think of it—would be you'd given her the check on a drunken generous impulse and had reconsidered, especially when you sobered up and realized you didn't have money in the bank to cover it. Be embarrassing for you to have to tell a story like that, but how could Dolly disprove it?"

Ray Fleck understood and nodded miserably; his mind *had* been playing around with some such idea, although he hadn't worked out the details yet. He wrote down the date. And what Irby dictated to him after that. It wasn't long, but it sewed him up completely and left no loopholes. It even accounted for the fact that restitution was being made by check instead of return of the jewelry by stating that he had already disposed of several items of the stolen property. It didn't incriminate Dolly in any way by implying that he had ever been intimate with her.

He signed it and pushed it across. Irby folded the paper and put it in his pocket. He said, "Okay, you can have this back when my client has cashed the check."

Ray Fleck stared miserably down into his glass, not wanting to look at his tormentor. It was going to take him months, he was thinking, to get himself out of this, even if Ruth came through and took him off the hook on his gambling debt.

He heard Irby slide out the booth. And then, standing outside, Irby bent over the end of the booth table. "By the way, Fleck," he said, "you owe Joe Amico some money too. That's only a gambling debt and this is a larceny rap. This comes first. Understand?"

Startled, Ray looked up, into those light blue marble-like eyes. He said, "Good God, man, I've got only till tomorrow evening on that. I can't possibly raise a thousand in a day. It'll take me weeks."

"It better not," Irby said. "This comes ahead of a gambling debt, and I'm not kidding. If you're paying off Amico tomorrow evening, you're paying this off sooner. Tomorrow's Friday, and it's not going to wait over the weekend. Your bank closes at three tomorrow, and Miss Mason will be there just before then with the check. If it's 'insufficient funds' the confession and the check both go to the police."

"God, Irby, I can't possibly—"

"You better, and I don't care how. See a loan shark, sell your house, your car or your wife, anything. Rob a bank for all I care. But this check will be presented for cashing at your bank at three tomorrow."

He turned and walked away, as casually as though he hadn't left a desperate man behind him. Ray Fleck reached for his drink. His hand shook badly but there was so little left in the glass that he didn't spill any. He drank it at a gulp.

He wanted to get out, away from everybody, to walk the night alone and try to think, *to think*. But he wanted Irby to have time to get clear first. He strode to the front of the tavern and stood looking out of the window. He saw Irby get into a car parked across the street and drive away.

Then he himself left, and walked. Not even a car to drive in tonight, he thought, feeling sorry for himself, and as though thinking about that one little trouble would help him forget his *real* troubles. But he didn't dare try to forget them, he realized; he had to find an answer. If there was an answer.

He saw an open sewer grating at the first corner and for a moment he was tempted to push the damned jewelry, handkerchief and all, through it. But the thought came to him that that would be a useless gesture now. With the written confession in Irby's hands, soon in Dolly's, having the stuff on him was no additional danger to him now. Besides, it was worth *something*. If a fence had considered giving him fifty for the ring, probably a hock shop proprietor would give him at least that and maybe more tomorrow. And since the police didn't have a list for checking there'd be no danger selling the ring openly now. No use throwing fifty bucks or more down the sewer. Maybe *Uncle* would give him a few bucks, say five for all of it, for the costume stuff.

He thought again of the ring in connection with the poker game. The game would be starting by now. But—oh, hell it was hopeless. He needed fifteen hundred now, fourteen hundred and eighty to be exact, and he'd never seen money like that change hands in the game. A few hundred, never more than five or six, was as much as he'd ever seen anybody win or lose, and not that much very often. It would have been a miracle if he'd have got in the game and won enough to pay off Amico.

His only chance, his *only* chance, now was Ruth and her insurance policy. (What if she'd get killed by a car on the way home from work tonight? He'd have the whole ten thousand coming, as her beneficiary, and his troubles would be gone. Eight and a half thousand left after paying off one and a half thousand. But things like that never happened, not when you desperately needed to have them happen.) But what remotely credible story could he make up when he'd needed only five hundred late this afternoon? Not that he'd lost another thousand gambling—if she did believe that, it would make her so mad she'd be more likely to walk out on him than meekly agree to borrow that much on the policy for him. And she probably wouldn't believe him to begin with, and he couldn't blame her; he'd never gambled for stakes like that before, a grand in one evening. The four-eighty to Amico had been lost in his bad-luck run over several weeks.

But there had to be *some* way out. There *had* to be.

He'd walked two blocks before he decided that walking wasn't doing him any good. His mind was going in circles, getting nowhere. He could think better sitting down. And besides, the shock of Mack Irby had knocked off his slight edge, had knocked all the alcohol out of him. And he could think better with a slight edge, just a slight one, than cold sober. He needed a drink and needed it badly.

The Palace Bar was coming up. It was a place he ordinarily

didn't like and seldom drank at, especially since he'd never been able to get the place on his customer list. It was mostly a working-man's bar, doing a beer trade. But they did sell whisky, and any port in a storm. Maybe it would be a better place right now than most because he'd almost certainly not run into anybody he knew there. And he didn't want to see anybody he knew.

He played safe by looking into the window first. There were a few men in the place, mostly down at the far end of the bar, but they were all strangers. Still better, he didn't even know the bartender. Kowalsky, who ran the place, wasn't there himself and the bartender must be a new man he'd put on recently.

Ray Fleck went in and took a stool at the corner of the bar, facing the back. The bartender came over and he ordered a double, a highball. It came and he paid for it.

He sipped at it and tried to think, but nothing came, nothing constructive. He thought, damn Amico; if Amico hadn't put the heat on him, if Amico hadn't been so tough, he'd still be all right; he'd have got Amico paid off sooner or later and he wouldn't have been tempted to steal Dolly's stuff. And damn Dolly and double damn Irby; he hadn't had time to get to her place yet, but soon they'd be celebrating his check and confession and laughing at him. And then going to bed together to celebrate some more. Irby hadn't fooled him by calling his client *Miss Mason*; he was one of her men all right, and probably her steady. He wondered how many other shakedown rackets they'd worked together.

Most of all, damn Ruth. It all had started by her being selfish and unreasonable this afternoon, refusing him the five hundred he'd needed then. If she'd been reasonable and sensible then, none of the rest would have happened, none of it.

Irby had said facetiously "sell your wife." God, if only he *could* sell her. What a mistake it had been for him ever to have married in the first place. A sudden thought came to him: that damn Greek she worked for was soft on her. Maybe— No, it wouldn't work; Mikos wouldn't lend him money, soft on Ruth or not. Mikos would want him to get into trouble, bad enough trouble so Ruth would leave him and give Mikos a free field with her.

But there *had* to be an answer.

He stared down into his highball, looking for one.

11:16 P.M.

THIS is the transcript of a conversation that might possibly have happened. If you believe in such things you'll come to see that it could have happened. If you do not believe, it doesn't matter.

"He is set up, Sire. Everything is ready when you say the word."

"You're sure he is sufficiently frightened, sufficiently desperate?"

"Yes, Sire."

"Ready for murder? Remember, he has committed every other sin, but he has not ever thought of murder. Not seriously, that is."

"Only because, Sire, he has known that he could not get away with it. Now we present him with the perfect opportunity. A chance to kill his wife in such a way that it cannot possibly be pinned on him. A method by which, if he alibis himself as he will, will not even cause him to be suspected."

"We can make sure by adding a little touch or two to what he thinks is his string of bad back."

"It is unnecessary, Sire. And it would disturb the timing, which is very delicate. We would have to rearrange much."

"Very well. We shall follow the original plan. Check time and start the count-down."

"Four seconds, Sire. Three. Two. One. Now."

"Let him look up from his drink."

In Pete Kowalsky's Palace Bar, Ray Fleck looked up from his drink. And saw the psychopath.

11:17 P.M.

Avaunt, ye demons, and away with imaginary conversations. Let us to a very real, if suddenly conceived, plot for murder.

In Pete Kowalsky's Palace Bar, Ray Fleck looked up from his drink, in which he had found no answer to his problem, and saw the answer walking toward him.

That is, he saw a man walking toward him from the back end of the tavern, undoubtedly coming from the john; he must have been in it when Ray had come in the place a minute or so ago. Ray didn't know the man, but still he looked vaguely familiar. He was medium in height and stocky, probably about Ray's own weight except that he had broad shoulders and a narrow waist, just the opposite of Ray's distribution of weight. He had a somewhat coarse, brutal face—anyway a face that looked as though it could look brutal. And dark intense eyes that looked—well, haunted was probably the best word. For some reason he couldn't name a cold chill went down Ray Fleck's spine. He'd seen that man *somewhere* before. Where?

The man hadn't noticed Ray and obviously didn't know he was being watched and wondered about. He stopped behind the bar stool that was the second one down from Ray's and stood there a moment. There was an almost finished drink on the bar in front of that stool and apparently he was deciding whether to sit down again and finish it or to go on out of the tavern.

And in that moment he stood there Ray knew why the chill had gone down his spine. For a moment the man's hands, *big* hands, flexed and unflexed—and then went rigid as though he'd suddenly realized what he was doing and had forced himself to stop. Then he slid onto the stool in front of the drink.

Now Ray knew, suddenly but beyond all doubt, where, when and under what circumstances he'd seen the man. He knew he was sitting two stools away from the psychopathic killer who was terrorizing the city. And who, according to what the squad car cops had told him in Jick's only half an hour or so ago, was on the prowl again and had already tried to get at two women.

His first thought was to get out of there fast and phone the police from the drugstore that was still open directly across the street. And hope the man would still be here when they came. Then he saw the dangers of that. For tonight—until they'd had time to dig into the background and find evidence—it would be his word against the psycho's. And the cops would keep him for hours, questioning him—and bawling the hell out of him for not having reported what he'd seen when he'd seen it two months ago. They'd make him sound like more of a heel than a hero for reporting it now. And suppose he phoned in and the cops didn't get here in time to catch their man they'd be even tougher with him. And if the deal got in the newspapers the psycho would know there was someone around who could identify him, and he'd know who. That would be a hell of a spot to be in. And what did he have to gain? He had troubles of his own.

And then the second thought came to him, full blown and foolproof. And he knew he had to do it right away before he lost his nerve. Or before the man finished his drink and left.

He took the rest of his own drink at a draught and called out, "Hey, bartender," to the bartender he didn't know. "One more double." And then casually to the man who sat almost beside him, "Have one with me, pal?"

The man shook his head. "Thanks. Gotta go."

Ray made his voice sound just a trifle thick and slurred; to play this convincingly he shouldn't seem cold sober. He said, "One for the road, then. Look, I won't want you to buy back, won't let you. I'm a liquor salesman, see, so any drink I buy anybody goes on the 'spense account. Besides, I hate to drink alone. Hey, bartender, make it two up this way."

"Okay," the man said. "Guess one more won't hurt me."

Ray pretended to look at his wrist watch. "One's about all I'll have time for myself. Got to get in an all-night poker game and it's starting about now. Say, my name's Ray Fleck—don't tell me yours 'cause I'm lousy on names and won't remember it anyway. I'll call you Bill. You married, Bill?"

The man shook his head. And the bartender came with their drinks. Ray paid him and left his wallet on top of the bar; he was going to need it in a minute.

"Well, I am," he said. "Married, I mean. Got the prettiest, sweetest little wife in town. And you know it worries me—with what's been happening—to leave her all alone, in a building all by herself, while I play all-night poker. But hell, a man's got to get out once in a while, and I think this is my lucky night."

He was thinking: it could be; it could be, if this works.

The man picked up his glass. "Thanks," he said. "Here's how."

"Bumps," Ray said. He took a pull from his own glass.

"Yeah," he said. "All alone in the building, the whole damn building, that's what worries me a little. We live in a third floor, top floor, flat over a store, see. And the second floor flat is vacant right now; people moving in on the first of the month but that's a week yet. And she's the prettiest—Say, let me show you."

He opened a compartment of his wallet and took out two snapshots of his wife. He always carried them. Not out of sentiment but because so many other men carried pictures of their wives or kids or both and he didn't want to be left out if it came to a photo showing match. Besides, Ruth *was* damned pretty. One of the photos was a close-up and made her look sweet and tender. The other had been snapped at the beach, Ruth in a bathing suit. She'd probably have been annoyed that he carried that one and showed it to other men, who usually whistled when they saw it, but what she didn't know didn't hurt her.

He pushed the pictures over to the man and used the motion as an excuse to slide over one stool and sit next to him. "That's Ruth," he said. "Ruth Fleck, if you forgot my name. Ain't she a honey?"

"Sure is."

The man was bent over the photographs on the bar, studying them as closely as though he were nearsighted. Ray Fleck couldn't see his eyes, which was perhaps just as well; they might have unnerved him and he needed every bit of nerve and every bit of acting ability he had, to put this over.

He asked casually, "Ever eat at a restaurant called Mikos'? Out on North Broadmoor?"

The man still didn't look up. "Know where it is; I've driven past. But I never ate there. Why?"

"Just that if you had you might have seen Ruth. She's working there, just temporarily. Waitress on the evening shift till eleven thirty, gets home about midnight."

The man pushed the pictures back. He still didn't look at Ray; now he was looking at his drink, and put a hand around it, moving the glass in slow circles. "Good looking, all right. But what you worrying about? You got a chain bolt on the door, ain't you? Everybody has, somebody told me."

Suddenly Ray's mouth felt dry, and he knew he was winning. He had to wait a second to get saliva in his mouth so he could talk naturally. "Ordinary bolt, not a chain bolt. But she has to open up when I come—" He broke off and laughed suddenly.

"What the hell, I clean forgot. We got a system, Ruth and me. A code knock so she knows it's me if I get home after she does. She don't open the door otherwise. But I haven't had to use if for a few weeks and I clean forgot about it for the minute."

He took a sip of his drink and put the glass down again. "Imagine me forgetting, when we picked a code I couldn't forget. Same as our address. We live at three one two Covington Place, see, three knocks, then one, and then two. That way I don't have to yell out my name or anything and anyway somebody else could say 'It's

Ray,' so that wouldn't mean anything. Say, who do you think will be playing in the series this year?"

The man shrugged. "I don't follow baseball."

"I don't either, much," Ray said. "But I'd sure like to see the Yankees lose a pennant for once. Spoils baseball, same team winning every year in one league."

"Yeah," the man said. "I go along on that." He finished his drink and slid off the stool. "Well, I gotta go. Unless you'll let me buy back."

"Nope. This better be my last, if I'm gonna play poker."

"Okay, then. Thanks."

Ray didn't turn as the man walked behind and past him to the door. But after the man was outside he turned just slightly and managed to watch out of the corner of his eye, through the window, without appearing to be watching. The man crossed the street and went into the drugstore. He headed for the phone booth and started stumbling through the phone book that hung on a chain beside it.

Checking up on what Ray had told him by verifying the address in the phone book? It could be. But then the man looked up another number, thumbing to another part of the directory, and then entered the phone booth and closed the door behind him.

What call would he be making, Ray wondered. To Ray's own phone number, just to verify that no one answered there? That wouldn't prove much. Calling someone to tell them that he wouldn't be home till later? That didn't seem too likely; he probably lived alone, and besides he'd had to look up a number. He'd certainly know the number wherever he lived.

Then Ray realized what call the man would be making. He was checking Ray's story down the line. First he'd looked up Ray's listing to make sure of the address, then he'd looked up Mikos' restaurant and was now calling it. He'd ask for Ruth Fleck and be told—Ray glanced at his wrist watch and saw that it was eleven thirty-four—that yes, Ruth Fleck worked there and had just left to go home. Mikos would still be there to answer the phone; he knew enough about restaurant routine to know that Mikos always stayed at least a little while after Ruth left, to check the cash register, maybe put chairs on tables, do whatever else had to be done to shut up shop for the night.

He reached out a hand for his drink, and saw that the hand was shaking so badly from reaction that he put it quickly down on the bar instead. He had to get himself under control now, and stay that way. He didn't dare let himself think about what was going to happen to Ruth.

The die was cast now, and there was no way he could call back what he had done. All that remained was to sit there until he was calm again, and think things out. He needed an alibi.

Ruth would die any time after midnight. And so, from midnight on, he had to have a solid, airtight, unbreakable alibi. One with lots of witnesses. With a ten-thousand-dollar motive for killing his wife, the police would be utter fools if they didn't at least slightly suspect him of having done the murder himself, using the psycho's *modus operandi*—knockout, rape, strangling, in that order—and so his alibi had to be above suspicion. Already he knew approximately how he was going to work it, but there were still a few details to think out.

And his nerves. But they'd be all right; they were probably all right now. He lifted his hand from the bar and reached for his drink. It still trembled a little, but not so badly. In a few more minutes he'd be completely okay.

If he could keep himself from thinking about Ruth.

11:34 P.M.

RUTH FLECK had not yet left the restaurant. George had told her to go at eleven thirty, but the last customer, at the counter, had obviously been within a minute or two of finishing and she'd decided to wait. It had paid off, too, with a two-bit tip that he probably wouldn't have left if he'd seen her leave; he wouldn't have known that George would hold the tip for her and give it to her tomorrow evening.

She'd carried his dishes back and was putting on the light summer coat over her uniform dress when she heard the phone ring up front. She didn't hurry because George was up there starting to check the cash register, and anyway the call was unlikely to be for her. Nobody she knew would be calling her at this hour except possibly Ray—and if he looked at his watch before calling he'd think that she'd already left.

But George's voice called out "Ruth. For you." And she called back "Coming" and hurried a bit.

George was back at the register when she came through the swinging doors, and the wall phone was off the hook, dangling on its cord. She went to it and said, "Hello." But no voice answered and after a second she realized that the faint buzz she heard was a dial tone.

She hung up the phone and looked toward George. "That's funny," she said. "Nobody on the line. It must have been Ray, but he must have been cut off. Maybe I should wait around a few more minutes to see if he tries again."

There was suddenly a peculiar expression on George Mikos' face. He left the register and came around the counter.

"That wasn't your husband," he said. "He's called often enough for me to know his voice. This voice was deeper. But I think you better wait a minute anyway. Sit down."

Ruth was puzzled but she pulled a chair out from under the nearest table and sat. George sat on one of the counter stools and stared at her. "Ruth, outside of Ray, do you know anyone at all who might have any reason at all for calling you at this time?"

Ruth thought, and shook her head slowly. "No," she admitted. "No man, anyway. Just what did he say? Could he have got the wrong number and you misunderstood the name he asked for?"

"No. And the conversation was so short I can give it to you verbatim. He said, "Is Ruth Fleck there?" Incidentally, that's proof, besides the voice, that it wasn't your husband. The several times he's called when I've answered he's always said, 'Hi, George. Can I talk to Ruth?' Knows my voice and calls me by name, and never bothers adding the Fleck to yours.

"But back to this call. I said. 'She's just about to leave, but she's still here. Just a minute.' And then I called out to you, and went back to the register. And that's all."

"He couldn't have misunderstood you and thought you said I'd just left?"

"Pretty unlikely, Ruth. My diction is at least passable, and it was a good connection. Besides, although my mouth was away from the mouthpiece when I called you I called loudly enough and was still close enough that he'd surely have heard that."

He frowned. "Have you had any other mysterious phone calls recently? Such as answering the phone and having someone hang up when he hears your voice?" Ruth shook her head. "Or such as wrong numbers? Or a call from a stranger who could be a phony for all you know, asking what television program you're watching, or anything like that?"

Ruth shook her head more slowly this time. "No, George. Oh, wrong numbers once in a while, things like that. But not recently. Not that I remember right now, anyway. Most calls we get are for Ray, and the caller always leaves a name or a number or both. Or if they're for me, they're from someone I know."

"And you've never been followed that you know of? Never had anything happen to indicate that someone has been checking up on you or asking questions about you?"

"No. George, you're taking this awfully seriously. I can guess what you're thinking—but why would the psychopath pick on *me*?"

"For the same reason," George said, "that he picked on those other women. Doubled in spades, because you're prettier than they were. And you've got a husband who— What time does Ray usually come home at night?"

"Usually about ten or fifteen minutes after the taverns close at one o'clock. I always stay up that long to wait for him. If he isn't home by—oh, about one twenty—I figure he probably got into a poker game or something and go to sleep. Then he has to knock loud enough to wake me—but that's not too hard; I'm a light sleeper."

"That would give the psycho a full hour, from midnight till one, most nights. Some nights longer, if he's been casing your husband too and happens to know he's going to be later. Ruth, I don't like that phone call at all. To be honest about it, it worries the bejesus out of me."

"You're scaring me too, George. I guess you want to, so I'll be careful. And I will. I told you about the special knock Ray uses when he gets home late. I wouldn't open the door except to that knock. But isn't it enough of a precaution?"

"I suppose so, unless Ray's told someone about it. Suppose he got talking to a friend in a tavern—but with the psycho in hearing distance—and told him about it. There's plenty of·talk about the psycho, including in taverns. If the subject came up naturally, mightn't he tell what precaution you and he are using, if he knew and thought he could trust whoever he was talking to."

"Well—he might mention that we use a code knock. But he surely wouldn't tell just what the code knock *is*. There'd be no reason for him to tell that—unless he deliberately wanted to get me murdered. And he's not that bad, George."

George Mikos sighed. "I suppose you're right there. But don't you see that, code knock or no, you can be in danger? That you *are* in danger if friend psycho is checking up on you and has you on his little list, even as a possibility?"

"I realize that—but still, if I don't open the door—"

"Wait, I hadn't finished. If he's even intelligent enough to read the newspapers he knows by now that women alone just aren't opening doors these days, not unless they have chain bolts on them anyway. He knows he's going to have to vary his procedure if he's going to succeed again. And what simpler variation would there be than for him to find a woman who went home alone, late, and be waiting for her *inside* her house or flat when she gets there?

"Let me make a hypothetical case to show you that could be. Let's say he picked you out a week ago. Maybe he eats here; maybe you've talked to him and he got to know your name. Let's say the first night he followed you home and knows where you live.

"Let's say he's been checking up on you ever since. It wouldn't be hard for him to learn that you're married, but only you and your husband live in that flat."

"Only Ray and I live in the whole building right now, George. It's a small, narrow building, two flats over a hardware store. And the flat on the second floor, under us, is vacant. I understand it's been rented for the first, and we'll have neighbours soon, but—"

"That makes it a perfect setup for him, Ruth. Better than he could have hoped for. He wouldn't have to come in the restaurant here again, or follow you home again. Let's say he's just been keeping an eye on your building late evenings and nights since. He's seen you get home about midnight every night. And he's seen Ray— How long has it been since Ray has got home early, before a few minutes after one?"

"Not for over a week."

"All right. Then he knows you get home at midnight, and Ray doesn't get home until after one. Since there are only two of you in the whole building he wouldn't have to know Ray even by sight to know that the man who came in an hour or more after you got home is your husband. He wouldn't have to know a thing about Ray except that he gets home after one. He probably figures Ray holds a night job somewhere and that's when he gets off, so he's even surer than he should be that Ray isn't going to get home earlier. Are you following me, Ruth?"

"I'm getting plenty scared, if that's what you mean."

"So he knows he's got an hour with you there alone, and that's probably a lot more time than he needs. His attacks are probably as quick as they are sudden and brutal.

"So all he has to do is break into your flat any time before midnight and wait for you. Break in or let himself in with a skeleton key or something. How good is your lock?"

"Just an ordinary one. And of course the bolt isn't thrown inside the door when no one's there. I guess a skeleton key would get him in."

"He could be there right now waiting for you. And that call for you here—he could have made it right from your phone, just to assure himself that you were getting off on time and not working late. He must have expected me to say that you'd just left, and when I said you were still here he couldn't think quickly enough of anything unsuspicious to say to you so he hung up before you got to the phone. And he did learn that you'll be there soon; I gave him that information gratuitously when I told him you were still here but just about to leave."

"George, this is—horrible. It's an awful lot to build on one unexplained phone call but—but it could be. Do you think we should go to the police?"

He shook his head slowly. "Not tonight. I'm afraid they'd think, as you suggested, that it's an awful lot to build on one unexplained phone call. They might think it worth investigating and they might not. In any case, they'd want to talk to us first, maybe have us come in, and that would waste a lot of time. And don't forget that if he *is* there waiting for you, he isn't going to wait forever. If you're not home by—oh, say, half past twelve, he'll figure something's gone wrong and beat it."

"No, I'm going to handle it myself, tonight. I'm going to drive you home. You're going to give me your key and then wait in the car till I go up and check your flat. Thoroughly. You go up only when I tell you it's safe as houses. And then lock yourself in and don't open the door till your husband uses his trick knock. And bolt the door again after him. That way you'll be safe tonight.

"And we'll worry about the police tomorrow—unless by then we've found some explanation of that phone call—I'll go right to my homicide captain friend and lay it in his lap. If he takes this as seriously as I do you'll be under police protection from then on.

I'd call him tonight but I happen to know he's out of town till tomorrow morning. And I don't want to mess with any lesser lights. Come on."

He stood up and went to the front door to double check that it was locked. "My car's out back. We'll go that way."

Ruth had stood but she said, "George—I don't like this. Your going up there alone, I mean. If he's *there*, he's dangerous. You don't know how big and strong he may be."

He grinned. "I know how big and strong *I* am. And clothed in armour of righteousness at that. Believe me, nothing would make me happier than finding him."

"But—he might be armed. Do you have a gun?"

"He probably isn't. People who kill with their hands seldom carry other weapons. But yes, I've got a gun, back in the sanctum. I'll take it along if only to make you feel easier. And a flashlight to help me find wall switches and look under beds. Come on."

This time she followed him and waited in the kitchen while he went briefly into his office. They turned out the rest of the lights and left.

In the car, which was parked on a vacant lot across the alley, she gave him the address and directions, since he'd never been there before. It was only five minutes by car, she thought; she'd be getting home earlier than usual instead of later. The bus took half an hour because it was roundabout and she had to transfer once.

She had a thought, as he started. "George, what if Ray came home early and is there? What are you going to tell him?"

"The truth, what else? And he'll have no cause for suspicion, if that's what you're worrying about. If I were taking you there for an assignation I'd hardly leave you in the car and go up alone, would I? Besides, next to the psycho I'd *like* to find him there. I'd feel safer about leaving you. And there's a possibility, just a possibility, that he could tell us something about that mysterious phone call. For some reason or another he might have asked or told someone to call you. And the hanging up *could* have been a misunderstanding or an accidental disconnection. Why did you ask? He isn't jealous of me, is he?"

"I've never given him any cause to be. I mean, I haven't talked about you too much or anything like that. He knows I think you're nice, and generous, and a good employer."

"Uh-huh. Do you have any reason for thinking he might come home earlier than usual tonight? Or, for that matter, later?"

"Well, there could be—either way. I told you about our quarrel this afternoon because I wouldn't borrow money against the policy for him. It was pretty bitter. He might deliberately stay out later because of that, if he's still mad. Or he might come home early or be there already for the opposite reason, I mean if he's repentant or wants to apologize. But I doubt that. If he *is* home early it's more likely to reopen the argument and have another try at convincing me. Or— This is Thursday, isn't it?"

"Yes. What's that got to do with it?"

"Only that quite frequently he plays poker Thursday nights, all night or quite late. But he probably won't play tonight—he didn't have too much money and I guess it's a pretty steep game, one he wouldn't try to get into with a few dollars."

"He might have borrowed some. But skip Ray. Tell me something about the flat I'll be casing in a minute. Has it got a fire escape, could it be broken into from the outside?"

"No fire escape. There's a front and back door. The back door leads to stairs that go down to the alley. But it's kept bolted and I never use it except to take down garbage or trash. I won't do that tonight."

"Nor tomorrow either. You're going to be extra careful in all directions at least until I've had a talk with my friend in homicide and see what we can work out with him. How many windows?"

"Five—no, six. Two at the front that look on the street, three along one side and one kitchen window at the back. But he couldn't get at any of them without using a long ladder, and I can't picture him taking the risk of carrying one around."

George said, "Just the same I'm going to see that all windows are closed and locked when I go up there. It's a coolish night and you can survive without ventilation for that long. How about access to or from the roof?"

"There's a trap door, but it's outside the kitchen door; if he came through it he still wouldn't be inside the flat. Besides, it's kept fastened on the inside."

"This the right block?"

"Yes. Third building from the next corner, on your right."

She started fishing in her handbag for her key and had it ready for him by the time the car stopped directly in front.

He got out and closed the door, spoke through the open window. "Don't leave the car. If he's by any chance watching from somewhere and approaches the car—if *anyone* approaches the car—start yelling like hell, loud enough for me to hear you up there. Not that your yelling wouldn't make him run in any case."

He left her and Ruth Fleck lighted a cigarette and waited till he came back. This time he came to her side of the car and opened the door for her. "False alarm," he said cheerfully. "Not a psycho in sight—and I checked carefully. Closets, under the bed, anywhere a man could hide."

She got out of the car. "Thanks, George. I can't tell you how much I—"

"Don't try then. And I'm not leaving you this second anyway. Escort service right to your door, and I want to hear the bolt slide when you've closed it after you. Here's your key."

He stopped at the door of the flat and didn't try to enter after her. She turned to face him. "Good night, George. And thanks again, a million."

"Forget it. But listen a moment. My guess that he might be waiting here for you was wrong, but I'm still worried and I guess you are too. Would you feel safer spending the night in a hotel room? You could write a note for Ray—I'd have had to bring you here to do that in any case—and then I could drive you on downtown. It might be the safest thing."

She shook her head. "No, I'll be all right here."

"Okay. But one final instruction—and I don't mean not to open the door except for your husband; you know that. It's this; if you hear anyone trying to get in either door or at a window, if you even *think* you hear anything suspicious, don't waste time phoning the police—you could be dead by the time they get here. Just open a front window, lean out and start screaming bloody murder at the top of your lungs, loud enough to carry six blocks away. He wouldn't follow through on trying to get in while you're doing that. Okay, good night—and let me hear the bolt slide."

"Good night, George."

She closed the door and slid the bolt, stood there a moment listening to his footsteps going down the stairs and thinking how wonderful he'd been to her and how concerned he'd been about her. And how brave to have come up here alone when he'd really thought that a dangerous criminal, a murderer, might be waiting.

When she turned she saw by the clock that it still lacked six minutes of midnight. Because of the lift, she was home earlier than usual despite all the talking they'd done and the time George had taken to search the flat.

She went into the bathroom and started drawing water in the tub. She was tired, if not sleepy, and a hot bath would be just the thing to relax her body and her nerves.

11:55 P.M.

RAY FLECK looked at his watch again and saw that it was just time for him to leave. He'd sat there nursing his drink ever since the psycho had left—thinking. There couldn't be any possible slip-ups on his alibi and he'd thought it out and covered every contingency.

The all-night poker game at Harry Brambaugh's was, of course, the basis of it. But he'd worked things out so that game would alibi him for all night no matter what happened. Someone in the game might or might not buy the diamond ring to let him play. And if someone did buy it, he might still go broke within the first hour, and that would be no good at all. His alibi had to be for *all* night, clear up to dawn.

He'd told the psycho, in effect, that an attack on Ruth would be safe any time after midnight; he couldn't possibly pinpoint it by suggesting a specific time or even a deadline. And for all Ray knew the guy might as easily make his call at two or three in the morning as at half past twelve. Besides, even if he had any way of timing it, he didn't dare get home too soon after the psycho had left. The minute he got home and found Ruth dead he'd have to call the police—and if she were freshly dead they'd still suspect him of having killed her and having done it in such a way as to throw suspicion on the psycho. He didn't dare find her until she'd been dead at least a couple of hours, and with him having a solid alibi for the time at which she'd died.

To be safe he didn't dare get home before five in the morning, and six would be better.

So, since the psycho had left, he'd been planning carefully; he was going to have an all-night alibi from Harry and whoever else was in the game, whether or not he could sell the ring and whether or not he went broke quickly if he did sell it. All it took was the right build-up.

Harry had a downtown apartment, only a block and a half from here. Five minutes walk and if he left at five of twelve he could establish the time of his arrival by saying "Cold on the stroke of midnight," when he walked into the room. That wouldn't sound suspicious or as though he was trying to establish an alibi because it was a phrase he often used anyway. So did some of the other boys. It was a quotation from a poem or something, and it was a cliché that fitted in any time the question of time came up at or within a minute of midnight.

Second step: The minute he got in he'd tell Harry he felt lousy, had an upset stomach and a headache. He'd say it would probably wear off, but did Harry have a Bromo-Seltzer or an Alka-Seltzer around, and maybe a couple of aspirin tablets too. And Harry would have; Harry had a bad stomach and headaches himself and was always well stocked with patent medicines. Harry would give him something and he'd take it. Point made.

Then, at the poker table but before sitting down, he'd explain apologetically that he was short on cash but had a hell of a bargain in a diamond ring, if anyone might be interested in buying it, and he'd pass it around. He'd try to get a hundred, but settle for fifty if someone wanted it but quibbled about price. Either someone would buy it or no one would buy it.

If no one bought, well he'd laid his groundwork, by convincing Harry he was sick. He'd say he didn't feel up to going home right away, and would Harry mind if he lay down on the sofa a while first. Harry had a comfortable sofa right in the living room, the room in which they played cards. Lying there he'd be in sight of everyone in the game. And Harry was a nice guy; he certainly wouldn't mind. That sofa had been used before for similar purposes; once in a while someone got tired in the middle of a game and wanted to rest a while and then get back in.

So he'd pretend to go to sleep on the sofa—or really go to sleep if he could. And stay there till the game broke up, which was never before five o'clock.

Same deal with a minor variation if he sold the ring but lost the money too soon. His upset stomach and headache would have come back by then; he'd take more Alka-Seltzer and aspirin and then lie down a while to give them a chance to work.

It would work. Parts of the story might sound mildly strange to the police when they questioned him, but there'd be too many witnesses for them to have any serious doubts. Especially if Milt Corbett was there as one of the witnesses, as he probably would be; Milt was a prominent member of the city council and the strength of his word would be as the strength of ten, to the police.

He left a dollar tip on the bar, to make the bartender remember him; it wouldn't hurt to be able to extend his alibi backward a bit in case Ruth died very shortly after midnight, and left.

He'd timed it right; it was midnight on the head when he rang the bell of Harry Brambaugh's apartment.

Stella, Brambaugh's wife, opened the door. On a chain, of course, but she opened it the rest of the way when she recognized Ray. He was a little surprised to see that she was wearing a robe and had her iron gray hair in pin curlers; usually she stayed dressed and made coffee and sandwiches about one o'clock, and then went to bed.

"Cold on the stroke of midnight," Ray said. "Game been going on long?"

"Ray, I tried to call you but you weren't home. There isn't any game. Harry got a telegram while we were eating tonight; his brother is seriously hurt in a car accident and he had to leave right away, the first plane. He gave me a list of six men to call up and I got all of them except you."

Ray frowned, thinking frantically. "Mrs. Brambaugh, I wonder if you could give me that list. I know all the boys on it, but not all their phone numbers. And maybe we can still get a game going, especially if you'd let me use your phone so I can call them right away."

She shook her head. "I might find the list in the wastebasket, but it wouldn't work anyway, Ray. Three of them said they wouldn't have been able to make it tonight anyway. I don't know whether Harry would have played four-handed or not; he'd probably have postponed it. But that leaves only two besides yourself, and they've probably got doing something else by now. Or gone to bed."

His mind went in frantic circles as he walked down the stairs and out into the night. What now? He could alibi himself by going to any tavern where he was well known, between now and one o'clock when the tavern would close. God, oh God, what could he do? He could go to a hotel, but what good would that be as an alibi? The clerk could testify when he checked in and when he checked out, but could he give positive testimony that he had not sneaked out and back in again sometime during the night?

Of course if he picked up a woman and took her to a hotel, or to her own place— He considered that and abandoned it reluctantly. The testimony of a woman like that would be of only slight value, for one thing. For another, the chances of his finding such a woman were slight, especially since he had less than an hour to do it in. There'd been a recent crackdown and available pickups in bars were currently few and far between. Outside of bars, he didn't have the faintest idea where to start looking. He didn't have a little black book of addresses; for the last few years, his only extramarital adventures had been those with Dolly, and Dolly—well, he could forget Dolly tonight, if not forever.

Besides, he was broke. He couldn't have over a few dollars left after all the drinks, many of them doubles, that he'd been buying.

For a moment he entertained the wild idea of walking in front of a car, getting himself injured and taken to the hospital. But that was too risky; he could be killed—or permanently crippled, which would be almost as bad. Or if for safety he picked a slowly moving car and just let it knock him down his injuries would probably be so superficial that a hospital would simply check him over and discharge him immediately. Could he feign a heart attack? No, it would take the admitting physician only half a minute with a stethoscope to learn that his heart was as sound as a preinflation dollar. Acute appendicitis? Hardly, with his appendix already out and a scar to prove it. Or—no, damn it, he knew too little about illnesses to be able to get away with feigning anything. He'd never had a sick day in his life, except for that attack of appendicitis and the time he'd been in the army infirmary on account of his allergy to wool.

The hospital idea wouldn't work. But what else would be open all night after the taverns closed?

The answer was so simple that he wondered why he'd sweated thinking about hotels and hospitals. The jail was open all night. It wouldn't hurt him to spend a night in the drunk tank, to save his life, and to pay a ten-buck fine in the morning. Maybe even no fine, just a warning, for first offense; and, what alibi could possibly be better than being in jail? He wondered why he hadn't thought of it the moment he'd learned that the poker game was called off.

But he'd better make it good and *really* get drunk, roaring drunk, not depend on acting. He looked at his watch. It was only five minutes after twelve. Fifty-five minutes to go and that was plenty of time, if he drank straight shots, doubles. He had a hell of a good capacity for liquor if he took it in highballs and reasonably spaced his drinks—as he had thus far tonight—but straight whisky always hit him hard and fast. With the slight edge he already had, five or six straight doubles would be plenty, if he took them no more than five minutes apart.

Money wouldn't be a problem, even though he had only two buck's, enough for two doubles, left. Since he'd never done so before, he could borrow five or ten from almost any bar owner or bartender in town. And even five, with what he had, would get him seven doubles, more than enough. He'd been walking without thinking where he was going, but now he looked to see where he was. Half a block from the Log Cabin, run by Jerry Dean. It would be as good a place as any. He was known there at least as well as at any other tavern, and Jerry was at least as likely to lend him money as anyone else; he'd spent hundreds of dollars in Jerry's.

Jerry was behind the bar and, Ray was glad to see, so was his son Shorty Dean, whom Jerry was teaching to be a bartender. Two witnesses would be better than one—and he might as well establish the time right away. He put a dollar on the bar and asked for a straight double. Then while Jerry was pouring it he glanced up at the wall clock. "Hey, your clock's half an hour off."

Jerry looked up at the clock and then at his own watch. "Seven after twelve. That's what I got. How about you, Shorty?"

Shorty had five after, but said his watch had been running a minute or two slow a day.

"Then seven after must be right," Ray said. He held his own watch to his ear. "Hell, mine's stopped. Must have forgot to wind it." He wound it and pretended to set it. "Say, Jerry, I ran short of cash tonight. Can you spare a sawbuck, just till tomorrow night?"

"Sure, Ray." Jerry pulled out a wallet. "Can even make it a double-saw, if you want."

"Swell," Ray said. He left the bill on the bar and tossed off his double. It tasted like hell to him; he didn't like the taste of raw whisky. But he ordered another.

Twenty minutes and four drinks later he was feeling high, definitely high. His tongue was thick and if he stared fixedly at anything or anybody he found himself seeing double; to keep his eyes focused he had to move them frequently. And he knew that the full force of the drinks hadn't hit him yet; fifteen minutes or half an hour more and he'd feel them a lot worse.

"One more," he said.

"Listen, Ray, you've had plenty. Don't you think you'd better call it off for tonight?" Jerry sounded genuinely concerned. "Uh—are you driving?"

"Nope. Car's being worked on. So one more, then I'll call it off. Okay?"

But he sat staring at the one more, and he was realizing that maybe getting arrested for being drunk wasn't as easy as getting drunk was. How do you get arrested if there isn't a cop around? Was he going to have to start trouble or a fight so Jerry would have to call the cops? He hated trouble, and he hated fights worse, but—

And then the answer came through the door. Officer Hoff and his squad car partner, the pair he'd talked to earlier in Jick's place, came in. Hoff said, "Hi, Jerry. Two damn quick quickies. Hi, Ray. How goes it?"

This was his chance. With drunken dignity Ray got off the stool and started back toward the juke box. He tried to stagger—and found that he didn't have to try. He almost fell, caught himself with a hand against the wall, and apparently forgot where he'd been going and came back to his stool, but stood there behind it, swaying. He reached for his drink and spilled half of it, got the rest down and dropped the glass. He swayed back onto the stool—he was exaggerating, acting, but not much—and sat there glowering at Hoff. "Goddam cop," he said thickly. "God, how I hate cops."

"Look, Hoffie," Jerry said conciliatingly, "he's drunk, so don't get' mad. And don't blame him. This hit him sudden like, or I'd of cut him off sooner. He's been in here only twenty minutes or so, and he acted cold sober till just now. I'd hate to see him get jugged—Ray's a nice guy. Could you guys spare time to run him home and get him out of trouble?"

Hoff said, "Sure, Jerry. Ray's all right. It can happen to any of us." He downed his shot quickly and then came back and put his hand on Ray's arm. "Come on, Ray. Time for beddy-bye. Where do you live?"

Ray slid off the stool and jerked away. If only violence was going to get him arrested, then he might as well get it over with. "Keep your goddam hands off me. Mind your own damn business." And he started a roundhouse swing. He didn't really know whether or not he was trying to make it connect—but it didn't. And then he saw Hoff's fist coming up in a short sharp uppercut for his own chin—saw it, but not in time to duck. The lights went out.

He came to, to the sound and motion of a car. Thank God it had worked; they were taking him in. He shook his head to clear it a little and saw that Hoff was sitting beside him in the back seat, the partner was driving.

Hoff said, "Take it easy, Ray, I can handle you but I don't want to have to hurt you. And you're not pinched—this time. I got your address from your wallet—and put your money that was on the bar in it. We're taking you home to the little wifie."

Oh, God, Oh God, he thought; *this can't be happening. They can't take me home now. It's only half past twelve or a few minutes later. It's too early, it's hours too early.*

Under an alcoholic haze, part of his mind worked; it scuttled like a rat trying to get out of a trap. And it found a hole—a dangerous hole, but still a hole.

He reached into his left pants pocket and pulled out a handkerchief, unfolded it. As they passed a street light, jewels flashed. "Lookit, Hoffie," Ray said. "Why I was getting drunk. Stole this. Conscience. Give m'self up."

Hoff called out, "Hey, Willie. Pull in to the curb and give me the dome light on."

On the way back downtown, the way toward the police station, Hoff kept questioning him and he kept ducking. Yeah, he'd stolen the jewels. Didn't remember who from. Drunk. Needed sleep, let him tell 'em everything tomorrow when he'd sobered up.

He played drunker than he was and he was thinking that he hadn't really given anything away. Tomorrow he could deny everything. He could say he'd found the jewelry, in a handkerchief just as it was, and how could they prove he hadn't. They'd doubt him, but they couldn't prove a thing. Dolly and Irby weren't reporting the robbery, now that they had the check and confession, so there'd be no theft report to match the stuff. Why then had he told Hoff he'd stolen it? How did he know why? He was drunk, didn't remember anything after taking a swing at Hoff in Jerry's place. Some drunken impulse must have made him tell Hoff that, but he couldn't remember what it was, couldn't even remember having been in a squad car.

He was safe. They might doubt him, but they couldn't prove a thing, except the drunk and disorderly charge—and they certainly wouldn't press even that after they had to tell him that his wife had been killed during the night, by the psycho. And on that angle, he was even safer; his alibi was solid from seven minutes after twelve on. From midnight on, really; Stella Brambaugh could testify she'd talked to him cold on the stroke of midnight, and just seven minutes away from Jerry's Log Cabin. Even farther back than that if the dollar tip had made the bartender at the Palace Bar remember him, and remember what times he'd been there. But even midnight was safe enough; Ruth didn't even get home until then.

Hoff said, "Ray, we've got to take you in. Want me to phone your wife so she'll know where you are?"

"God no," Ray said, and then made his voice calmer. "She won't worry about me—thinks I'm in an all-night poker game so won't 'spect me home anyhow."

"Okay. We're going to have to book you on suspicion of theft. Want a lawyer? He might get you out on bail right away."

"Hell, no Hoffie. Too drunk to do any good if I did get out. Too drunk, too sleepy. Just book me and jug me, and let me get some sleep."

"If that's the way you want it," Hoff said. The squad car pulled up in front of the station.

1:01 A.M.

BARE feet tucked under her, Ruth Fleck sat on the sofa in the living room. After her leisurely bath she'd put on pyjamas and a quilted housecoat, but no slippers; she liked to go barefoot around the house. The reading lamp was on and she had a magazine in her lap, opened to the beginning of a story. But she hadn't started it yet; she was still thinking about her coming conversation with Ray.

Not about what she was going to say; she'd already decided that, but about how she was going to say it. She was going to give him an ultimatum, but to spare his pride as well as to avoid another argument, she wanted to figure how to word it so it wouldn't sound like an ultimatum.

She'd thought about it all evening at work and had finally, if a bit reluctantly, decided to give him the five hundred he needed to pay off his bookie. George was probably right in saying that Joe Amico wouldn't have him beaten up, let alone taken for a ride. But still, Ray *was* in trouble, with that big a debt hanging over him and she should help him out, this once. She'd agree to go downtown with him tomorrow and arrange the loan against the policy.

But she was going to attach a condition to it, and she thought she had every right to do so. He'd have to promise, and mean the promise and stick to it, to quit gambling on credit—or for heavy stakes, whether on credit or not. Gambling was in his blood, and she knew it would be meaningless for her to demand his promise never to gamble again. He might make such a promise—for the sake of getting the money from her—but he wouldn't mean it in the slightest and wouldn't keep it for a single day. She might as well make a clean break with him right now as to demand a promise like that.

Would she be better off in any case to make a clean break? She pushed that thought away. She should give him one more chance before she decided anything like that. And maybe the sweating he was doing right now about that five-hundred-dollar debt had taught him the lesson he needed. She'd see.

She'd give him the money—and the ultimatum. Henceforth his gambling had to be moderate and for cash only, when he could afford it. If he wanted to make two-dollar bets or even an occasional five- or ten-dollar bet, for cash, that was all right. But no more going in over his head, on credit. Certainly that was a reasonable thing for a wife to expect.

But if he ever got into trouble like this again—well, again she'd borrow five hundred against the policy (that would still leave nine thousand coming, a nice nest egg, when the policy matured in another five years or so) but she wouldn't give it to Ray to pay off gambling debts. She'd use it herself for a trip to Reno. That was just about what such a trip, and a divorce, would cost her. Less than that, of course, if she could find work there during her waiting period, but she wouldn't count on that. A lot of women who go there for divorces must look for work to help out and to occupy their time during the six weeks—she thought it was six weeks—they had to wait for their divorces. The labor market might be glutted.

She hoped he wouldn't be late tonight—but no matter how late he might be, she was going to wait up for him. Morning was a bad time to talk with him, especially about anything serious. He was always irritable and grumpy in the morning, likely to fly off the handle over even the most innocent remark she might make.

She heard footsteps coming up the stairs and thought *Good, he's even a little earlier than usual.* It was only a few minutes after one; he couldn't have waited even till the bars closed to start home. Maybe that was a good sign.

She got off the sofa and went to the door. But, remembering the phone call and George's warning, she didn't reach for the bolt or the knob until he knocked.

He knocked. Three knocks, a short pause; one knock, a short pause, then two knocks.

She threw back the bolt and opened the door.

1:05 A.M.

SILENTLY screaming, Benny Knox awakened from the nightmare. Occasionally, not too often, he had nightmares but this one was the worst ever.

It was a hell of a nightmare, quite literally. He'd been in hell, the very literal hell that his father had talked about so often, either to him alone or in sermons that Benny had heard. He was stark naked and standing knee deep in a lake of boiling, bubbling pitch. His feet and legs hurt horribly.

At the edge of the lake, a few feet away, stood three devils. Bright red devils with tails and horns and hoofs. Two of them had long pitchforks and they were jabbing them into Benny's chest and stomach, to drive him farther and deeper into the boiling lake. His arms were stuck; he couldn't use them to try to ward off the pitchforks. The pitchforks hurt badly and he was forced to take a step backward and was suddenly in the boiling pitch up almost to his waist. The slope was steep, and with another step or two he'd be completely in the lake.

The other devil, the one in the middle, didn't have a pitchfork. He was just standing there laughing. And even through his dream Benny knew that he had heard that exact laugh before, and that he'd seen that devil's face before—but he couldn't remember where or when.

Over the laughter and from somewhere overhead, came a Voice. The voice of God or the voice of his father; he didn't know which.

"Hell forever, my son, for you have done evil. You can be forgiven only if you can make *them* believe you, and be punished on Earth for the evil you have done."

He tried to scream and answer but his voice was stuck too, like his arms. Then one of the pitchforks jabbed at his eyes and he had to take another step backward. He lost his balance and fell. As the boiling pitch closed over his head, he awoke.

Or had it been just a dream? Might not it have been a vision sent him by God or by his father in Heaven, to warn him, to instruct him?

He lay there sweating in the upper bunk, and then he remembered what Mrs. Saddler had told him to do whenever he awakened from a nightmare: get up and walk, walk till you're wide awake again and the nightmare goes away.

He climbed down from the upper bunk and walked—as far as

he could in the cell, three paces one way and three back and three paces one way and three paces back— But the dream, if it had been a dream, stayed with him, more vivid than any of his memories of anything else that had happened to him that day or recently.

A sound made him pause in his pacing and look into the lower bunk. The sound was a snore. He saw that he was no longer alone in the cell; while he'd slept they'd put someone else there and he was now lying in the lower bunk. Fully dressed, as Benny was, except for shoes and coat. Even in the dim light of the cell, the man looked familiar to him.

Benny bent over him.

It was Mister Fleck. That surprised him, but what surprised him a thousand times more was that it was also the devil in his nightmare or vision, the devil without a pitchfork, the one who had laughed at him. The face of Mr. Fleck and of that devil were the same. And he remembered now why the laugh of that devil had sounded as though he'd heard it before. It was Mister Fleck's laugh, as Mister Fleck had laughed at him early in the evening, when he'd told Mister Fleck that he'd killed those women. The police hadn't *believed* him, but they hadn't laughed at him.

And suddenly he knew what he had to do to make the police really believe him, to make them believe that he'd done evil and must be punished.

He put his hands on Mister Fleck's shoulders and pulled him up to a sitting position. "Mister Fleck!" he said.

Mister Fleck's eyes opened and blinked. "Huh?" he said.

Benny was very earnest because this was very serious. "Listen, Mister Fleck," he said. "I'm sorry, but I got to kill you. I got to kill you like I killed them women so the police will believe I killed them."

"Huh? Benny—"

"I want you to know, Mister Fleck, I ain't mad at you. Even if you laughed at me. It's bad to kill because you're mad and I want you to know I ain't mad. I just got to kill you. And besides, it won't be evil for me to kill you to make them believe me. It won't be evil, Mister Fleck, because you're a devil."

Mister Fleck opened his mouth to say something, or to scream, but nothing came out because Benny's hands were tight around his throat and getting tighter. A minute later they let go, and something limp and dead fell back on the lower bunk.

Benny Knox went to the door of the cell and grabbed his bars, rattling the door loudly. Even more loudly he yelled, "Policemen! Policemen! Come here and see. *Now* do you believe me? *Now* will you try to tell me I never killed nobody?"

This time they believed him.

2:45 A.M.

In his office off the kitchen of the restaurant, George Mikos paced a while, too keyed up to sit down and type, which was what he'd come here to do. Finally he sat down at the desk, took the cover off the typewriter and put fresh paper into it, He began to type:

Dear Perry:

This has been the damnedest night. If you'll forgive the cliché, hell has been popping right and left.

Yes, this is a new letter and not a continuation of the one I started to you earlier. Everything has changed so completely that it would seem silly to go on with that one. But I'll enclose it, uncompleted, with this, so you'll have the background to understand what this one is about.

It started a few minutes after eleven thirty, when I'd just closed up and was starting to check the register. There was a phone call and a man's voice—not her husband's—asked for Ruth Fleck. She was still here, getting ready to leave. I called her to the phone but there was no one on the line when she got there.

You can deduce what I guessed from that, when she admitted she could think of no possible reason why any man except her husband should be calling her at that time of night.

I insisted on driving her home, and I also had her wait in the car while I went up and searched her flat to make sure there wasn't a reception committee waiting for her there. (I told her I was bringing a gun so she wouldn't worry about me doing this; actually I don't even own one). Then I escorted her upstairs; made sure she bolted herself in, and left.

But I didn't go very far. I was more worried than I let her think (luckily) and I drove off only in case she'd be watching from a front window or listening for the sound of my car starting. I U-turned at the corner and drove back the way I'd come, parked on the opposite side of the street and a quarter of a block away. I'd decided to watch the doorway of that building until I saw her husband come home, no matter how late it might be.

She had a code of some kind worked out with her husband so she'd know it was he when he came home and I'd impressed on her not to throw the bolt otherwise. But I was still worried about her for two reasons. First, she was confident Ray wouldn't have done any talking in bars about that code knock, but I wasn't. Secondly, while neither the door to her flat nor the bolt on it were flimsy, neither were they so strong that a husky, heavy man might not be able to break in with one good hard lunge. And it turned out I was right on both of those counts.

At about one o'clock I saw, or thought I saw, Ray Fleck come around the corner and go into the entrance of the building. But he'd hardly disappeared and I hadn't yet turned the ignition key in the car when I did the god-damndest double take and realized that the man I'd seen had *not* been Ray Fleck. He'd been about the same height and weight but not the same build; his bulk had been across the shoulders and he had a narrow waist, whereas Fleck's weight distribution is just the opposite.

And I was out of the car and running. If my second impression had been wrong, if it had really been Fleck I'd seen, I was about to make an awful ass of myself, but I was willing to chance that rather than to take the opposite chance. When I got to the third floor I saw the door was closed and not broken down—so I must have been right about Fleck talking; she'd never have opened the door except to that special knock. I didn't waste time trying the knob, which was just as well since the door had been bolted again from the inside; I threw my weight against the door, so hard that I still have a sore right shoulder, and the door burst open and I almost fell into the living room.

He'd heard, of course; he was in the doorway of the bedroom and rushed me before I got my balance. I managed to turn my head in time to take a vicious blow on the ear (it's still ringing) instead of the jaw. I took a couple of steps back to get on balance and then started to move in on him. I'm a wrestler; I wanted to grapple instead of trying to slug it out. He cooperated, in away; he rushed me, head down for a solar plexus butt, both fists cocked low to start pumping into my stomach or groin as soon as he connected with the butt.

He couldn't have pleased me more. I moved just enough aside at the last split second to let his head graze past my right side and then I clamped down my arm and had a solid headlock on him. I twisted my body around and twisted his neck with it. Until there was a quite audible snap as his neck broke, and the fight was over. It had probably lasted all of three seconds.

I didn't even bother to check whether or not he was dead; if by any chance he wasn't, he wasn't going to be dangerous for a long time. I just dropped him and ran into the bedroom.

Ruth was lying on the bed, unconscious, where he'd no doubt carried her after knocking her out with a single blow as he came through the doorway.

But otherwise, I'd got there in time. She hadn't been raped, let alone strangled. Her jaw was beginning to swell but it didn't look as though it was broken—and I learned later at the hospital that it wasn't. She was breathing normally, and her heartbeat was okay.

He'd ripped open the housecoat that she was wearing, and torn the tops of her pajamas. I put a cover over her partial (and very beautiful) nakedness and then went to the living room again. I checked the psychopath to see if he was dead; he was. And then I used the phone to call for a police ambulance. The guy I got on the phone annoyingly wanted details, but I told him a woman had been injured by the psycho and I wanted the ambulance fast and I'd do all the talking they wanted after she was hospitalized. I told him they didn't have to worry about the psycho any more; they could send a meat wagon for him at their leisure. He wasn't going anywhere. Then I hung up.

And then went back to wait by Ruth, in case she should recover consciousness before the ambulance came.

But I'd sat there only a few minutes, and hadn't heard any sirens yet, when the phone rang. I answered it and—

Now hold on to your hat, Perry. Here comes the incredible part. It was the city jail, wanting Ruth Fleck. When I'd convinced them that she couldn't come to the phone but I'd take any message, I was told that I should tell her that her husband was dead. He had been killed—strangled, mind you—by a man in the same double cell with him. Fleck had given himself up and was being held on suspicion of theft. His killer was (or had been) a harmless moron who was being held overnight because he'd made a false confession of murder. He was unable to give any coherent account of why he'd killed Fleck; he talked about laughter, and devils, and the police not believing him. Although they'd known the man was slightly unbalanced mentally, he'd always been completely harmless, and they'd thought nothing of putting another prisoner in the same cell with him.

That was all I could learn; tomorrow I'll see what more I can learn, and I hope it's something that will make things make sense. I hate coincidences, and it takes a lot to make me believe in one. Especially one as extravagant as a man getting himself strangled to death on the same night his wife would, except for my intervention, have been strangled to death—and not by the same strangler.

The man at the jail said Ray'd *given himself up*. I can't see him doing that, on any charge, unless he had some damned good reason for *wanting* to be in jail.

Maybe the story will come out somehow, or maybe we'll never know. Ray Fleck can't tell us his end of it. Nor the psychopath his end.

For that reason only, I'm sorry I killed him. That is, I guess I am. I might have been able to subdue him without killing him, but it would have taken time. And besides there was the risk of my losing the fight. What if he'd been able to get in a lucky punch and knock me out? He'd have strangled me while I was unconscious—and then he'd have gone back to Ruth. Neither of us would have been alive right now. No, I couldn't have taken that chance.

Ruth was still unconscious when we got her to the hospital, and they gave her a sedative so she'd stay that way a while, or rather so the unconsciousness would blend into normal sleep.

So I haven't talked to her yet. They told me she should have at least a few hours of normal sleep, and kicked me out. I can go back at five A.M.

So I have a couple of hours to kill and that's what I'm doing now, writing this.

Perry, how'd you like to be my best man? Maybe I'm overconfident, but I don't think so. I'm almost certain that Ruth will marry me, now that she's free. I don't know how soon; there'll have to be what people call a decent interval. And it'll be up to Ruth how long that is. As far as I'm concerned, I'd marry her tomorrow and start out our honeymoon by attending Ray Fleck's funeral. She'd hardly go along with that, but she didn't really love him any more and I'm hoping she'll think that not over a few months will be long enough.

And I'm serious about the best man business. And if Ruth will accept my plans, you wouldn't even have to come here to do the job. I've been thinking for a long time of taking a vacation and a trip to Europe; I'd probably have done it before now if I hadn't fallen in love with Ruth and wanted to stick around for that reason. And combining a European tour with a honeymoon would be combining pleasure with pleasure. We could be married in New York en route, so you could stand up for us there, stay a week for a look at New York if Ruth wants to (and I imagine she will; she's never been there) and then hop off for Europe.

I feel as though I'm dreaming, and I suppose I am—but it's a dream that will come true, I know it will.

Your old friend,
George Mikos.

The Fabulous Clipjoint

CHAPTER ONE

IN MY DREAM I was reaching right through the glass of the window of a hockshop. It was the hockshop on North Clark Street, the west side of the street, half a block north of Grand Avenue. I was reaching out a hand through the glass to touch a silver trombone. The other things in the window were blurred and hazy.

The singing made me turn around instead of touching the silver trombone. It was Gardie's voice.

She was singing and skipping rope along the sidewalk. Like she used to before she started high school last year and got boy-crazy, with lipstick and powder all over her face. She was not quite fifteen, three and a half years younger than I. She had make-up on now, in this dream of mine, thick as ever, but she was skipping rope, too, and singing like a kid, "One, two, three, O'Leary; four, five, six, O'Leary; seven, eight. . . ."

But through the dream I was waking up. It's confusing when you're like that, half one way and half the other. The sound of the elevated roaring by is almost part of the dream, and there's somebody walking in the hallway outside the flat, and—when the elevated has gone by—there's the ticking of the alarm clock on the floor by the bed and the extra little click it gives when the alarm is ready to explode.

I shut it off and rolled back, but I kept my eyes open so I wouldn't go back to sleep. The dream faded. I thought, I wish I had a trombone; that's why I dreamed that. Why did Gardie have to come along and wake me up?

I thought, I'll have to get up right away. Pop was out drinking last night and still wasn't home when I went to sleep. He'll be hard to wake up this morning.

I thought, I wish I didn't have to go to work. I wish I could take the train to Janesville to see my Uncle Ambrose, with the carnival. I hadn't seen him for ten years, since I was a kid of eight. But I thought about him because Pop had mentioned him yesterday. He'd told Mom that his brother Ambrose was with the J. C. Hobart carney that was playing Janesville this week and that was the nearest they'd get to Chicago, and he wished he could take a day off and go to Janesville.

And Mom (who isn't really my mom, but my step-mother) had got that looking-for-trouble look on her face and asked. "What do you want to see that no-good bastard for?" and Pop had let it go.

Mom didn't like my Uncle Ambrose; that was why we hadn't seen him for ten years.

I could afford to go, I thought, but it would make trouble if I did. I figured like Pop did; it isn't worth it.

I got to get up, I thought. I swung out of bed and went into the bathroom and spattered water into my face to get wide awake. I always used the bathroom and dressed first, and then I woke Pop and got us some breakfast while he got ready. We went to work together. Pop was a linotype operator and he'd got me on as an apprentice printer at the same shop, the Elwood Press.

It was a gosh-awful hot day, for seven in the morning. The window curtain hung as still as a board. It was almost hard to breathe. Going to be another scorcher, I thought, as I finished dressing.

I tiptoed along the hall toward the room where Pop and Mom slept. The door to Gardie's room was open and I looked in without meaning to. She was sleeping on her back with her arms thrown out and her face without any make-up on it looked like a kid's face. A kind of dumb kid.

Her face, looking like that, didn't match the rest of her. I mean, maybe because it had been such a hot night she'd taken off her pyjama tops and she had nice, round, firm breasts. Maybe they'd be a little too big when she got older but now they were beautiful and she knew it and was proud of them. You could tell that by the way she wore tight sweaters so they would show.

She really is growing up fast, I thought; and I hope she's smart because otherwise she'll be coming home knocked up one of these days, even if she isn't fifteen yet.

She'd probably left her door wide open on purpose so I'd look in and see her that way, too. She wasn't my sister, really, see; not even a half sister. She was Mom's daughter. I'd been eight and Gardie a snot-nosed brat of four when Pop had remarried. My real mom was dead.

No, Gardie wouldn't miss a chance to tease me. She'd like nothing better than to tempt me into making a pass at her—so she could raise hell about it.

I went on past her open door thinking, damn her, damn her. There wasn't anything else I could think or do about it.

I stopped in the kitchen long enough to light a fire under the kettle so it would start to boil for coffee, and then I went back and rapped softly on the door of their bedroom and waited to see if I'd hear Pop move.

He didn't, and that meant I'd have to go in and wake him. I hated to go into their bedroom, somehow. But I knocked again and nothing happened, so I had to open the door.

Pop wasn't there.

Mom was on the bed alone, asleep, and she was dressed all but her shoes. She had on her best dress, the black velvety one. It was awful mussed now and she must have been pretty tight to go to sleep with it on. It was her best dress. Her hair was a mess, too, and she hadn't taken her make-up off and it was smeared and there was lipstick on the pillow. The room smelled of liquor. There was a bottle of it on the dresser, almost empty and with no cork in it.

I looked around to be sure Pop wasn't anywhere at all in the room; and he wasn't. Mom's shoes lay in the opposite corner from the bed, quite a ways apart as though she'd thrown them there from the bed.

Pop had never come home at all.

I closed the door even more quietly than I'd opened it. I stood there for a minute wondering what to do, and then—like they tell you a drowning man will grab at a straw—I started to look for him. Maybe he came home drunk, I told myself, and went to sleep somewhere in a chair or on the floor.

I looked all over the flat. Under the beds, in the closets, everywhere. I knew it was silly, but I looked, I had to be sure he wasn't anywhere there; and he wasn't.

The water for coffee was boiling away now, spouting out steam. I turned off the fire under it, and then I had to stop and think. I guess I'd stalled by hunting, so I wouldn't have to think.

I thought, he could have been with somebody, one of the other printers, maybe. He might have spent the night at somebody's place because he got too drunk to get home. I knew I was kidding myself; Pop knew how to hold liquor. He never got that drunk.

But I told myself, maybe that's what happened. Maybe Bunny Wilson? Last night was Bunny's night off; he worked the night shift. Pop often drank with Bunny. A couple of times Bunny had stayed at our place; I'd found him asleep on the sofa in the morning.

Should I phone Bunny Wilson's rooming house? I started for the phone, and then stopped. Once I started phoning, I'd have to go on. I'd have to phone the hospitals and the police and carry through with all of it.

And if I used the phone here, Mom or Gardie might wake up and—well, I don't know why that would have mattered, but it would have.

Or maybe I just wanted to get out of there. I tiptoed out and down one flight, and then I ran down the other two flights, I got across the street and stopped. I was afraid to phone. And it was almost eight, so I'd have to do something quick or be late to work. Then I realized that didn't matter; I wasn't going to work today anyway. I didn't know what I was going to do. I leaned against a telephone pole and felt sort of hollow and light-headed as though I weren't quite all there, not all of me.

I wanted it over with. I wanted to *know* and get it over with, but I didn't want to go to the police and ask. Or was it the hospitals you called first?

Only I was afraid to call anybody. I wanted to know and I didn't want to know.

Across the street, a car was slowing down. There were two men in it, and the one on the outside was leaning and looking at street numbers. It stopped right in front of our place, and the two men got out, one on each side. They were coppers; it was written all over them, even if they didn't wear uniforms.

This is it, I thought.

Now I'm going to know.

I went across and followed them into the building. I didn't try to catch up; I didn't want to talk to them. I just wanted to listen when they started talking.

I followed them up the stairs, half a flight behind. On the third floor one of them waited while the other walked down the hall and looked at numbers on doors. "Must be next floor," he said.

The one at the head of the stairs turned and looked at me. I had to keep on coming. He said, "Hey kid, what floor's fifteen on?"

"Next one," I said. "Fourth floor."

They kept on going, and now I was only a few steps behind them. Like that we went from the third floor to the fourth. The one just ahead of me had a fat behind and his trousers were shiny in the seat. They stretched tight every time he took a step up. It's funny; that's all I remember about how they looked, either of them, except that they were big men and coppers. I never saw their faces. I looked at them, but I never saw them.

They stopped in front of fifteen and knocked, and I kept on going right past them and up the flight to the fifth, the top, floor. I kept on going until I reached the top and took a few steps, and then I reached down and pulled off my shoes and went back halfway down the stairs, keeping out of sight back against the wall. I could hear and they couldn't see me.

I could hear everything; I could hear the shuffle of slippers as Mom came to the door; I could hear the door creak just a little as it opened; and in the second of silence that followed, I could hear the ticking of the clock in the kitchen through the opened door. I could hear soft, barefoot steps that would be Gardie coming out of her room to the turn in the hall by the bathroom where, without being seen, she could hear who was at the door.

"Wallace Hunter," said one of the coppers. His voice was rumbly like an el car a long way off. "Wallace Hunter live here?"

I could hear Mom start breathing faster; I guess that was enough of an answer, and I guess the look on her face must have answered his. "You—uh—Mrs. Wallace Hunter?" because he went right on. "'Fraid it's bad news, ma'am. He was—uh—"

"An accident? He's hurt—or—"

"He's dead, ma'am. He was dead when we found him. That is—we think it's your husband. We want you to come and identi—that is, as soon as you're able. There's no hurry, ma'am. We can come in and wait till you're over the shock of—"

"How?" Mom's voice wasn't hysterical. It was flat, dead. "How?"

"Well—uh—"

The other copper's voice spoke. The voice that had asked me what floor fifteen was on.

"Robbery, ma'am," he said. "Slugged and rolled in an alley. About two o'clock last night, but his wallet was gone so it wasn't till this morning we found out who—*Catch her, Hank!*"

Hank must not have been fast enough. There was a hell of a loud thud. I heard Gardie's voice, excited, then, and the coppers going on in. I don't know why, but I started for the door, my shoes still in my hand.

It closed in my face.

I went back to the stairs and sat down again. I put my shoes on, and then I just sat there. After a while someone started down the stairs from the floor above. It was Mr. Fink, the upholsterer, who lived in the flat directly over ours. I moved close against the wall to give him plenty of room to pass me.

At the bottom of the flight, he stopped, one hand on the banister post and looked back at me. I didn't look at him; I watched his hand. It was a flabby hand, with dirty nails.

He said, "Something wrong, Ed?"

"No," I told him.

He took his hand off the post and then put it on again. "Why you sitting there, huh? Lost your job or something?"

"No," I said, "Nothing's wrong."

"Hell, there ain't. You wouldn't be sitting there. Your old man get drunk and kick you out or—"

"Let me alone," I said. "Beat it. Let me alone."

"Okay, if you want to get snotty about it. I was just trying to be nice to you. You could be a good kid, Ed. You oughta break away from that drunken bum of a father of yours—"

I got up and started down the steps toward him. I think I was going to kill him; I don't know. He took a look at my face and his face changed. I never saw a guy get so scared so quick. He turned around and walked off fast. I stayed standing there until I heard him going down the next flight.

Then I sat down again and put my head in my hands.

After a while I heard the door of the flat open. I didn't move or look around through the banister, but I could tell by voices and footsteps that all four of them were leaving.

After all the sound had died away downstairs, I let myself in with my key. I turned on the fire under the kettle again. This time I put coffee in the dripolator and got everything ready. Then I went over to the window and stood looking out across the cement courtyard.

I thought about Pop, and I wished I'd known him better. Oh, we'd got along all right, we'd got along swell, but it came to me now that it was too late, how little I really knew him.

But it was as though I was standing a long way off looking at him, the little I really knew of him, and it seemed now that I'd been wrong about a lot of things.

His drinking, mostly. I could see now that that didn't matter. I didn't know why he drank, but there must have been a reason. Maybe I was beginning to see the reason, looking out the window there. And he was a quiet drinker and a quiet man, I'd seen him angry only a few times, and every one of those times he'd been sober.

I thought, you sit at a linotype all day and set type for A & P handbills and a magazine on asphalt road surfacing and tabular matter for a church council report on finances, and then you come home to a wife who's a bitch and who's been drinking most of the afternoon and wants to quarrel, and a stepdaughter who's an apprentice bitch.

And a son who thinks he's a little bit better than you are because he's a smart aleck young punk who got honour grades in school and thinks he knows more than you do, and that he's better.

And you're too decent to walk out on a mess like that, and so what do you do? You go down for a few beers and you don't intend to get drunk, but you do. Or maybe you did intend to, and so what?

I remembered that there was a picture of Pop in their bedroom, and I went in and stood looking at it. It was taken about ten years ago, about the time they were married.

I stood looking at it. I didn't know him. He was a stranger to me. And now he was dead and I'd never really known him at all.

When it was half-past ten and Mom and Gardie hadn't come back yet, I left. The flat had been an oven by then, and the streets, with the sun coming almost straight down, were baking hot too. It was a scorcher all right.

I walked west on Grand Avenue, under the el.

I passed a drugstore and I thought, I ought to go in and phone the Elwood Press and tell them I wasn't going to be in today. And that Pop wouldn't be there either. And then I thought the hell with it; I should have phoned at eight o'clock and they know by now we're not coming.

And I didn't know yet what to tell them about when I'd be back. But mostly I just didn't want to talk to anybody yet. It wasn't completely real, like it would begin to be when I'd have to start telling people, "Pop's dead."

It was the same with the police and thinking and talking about the funeral there'd have to be, and everything. I'd waited for Mom and Gardie to come back, but I was glad they hadn't. I didn't want to see them, either.

I'd left a note for Mom telling her I was going to Janesville to tell Uncle Ambrose. Now that Pop was dead she couldn't say anything about my telling his only brother.

It wasn't so much that I wanted Uncle Ambrose; going to Janesville was mostly an excuse for getting away, I guess.

On Orleans Street I cut down to Kinzie and across the bridge, and down Canal to the C&NW Madison Street Station. The next St. Paul train that went through Janesville was at eleven-twenty. I bought a ticket and sat down in the station and waited.

I bought early afternoon editions of a couple of papers and looked through them. There wasn't any mention of Pop, not even a few lines on an inside page.

Things like that must happen a dozen times a day in Chicago, I thought. They don't rate ink unless it's a big-shot gangster or somebody important. A drunk rolled in an alley, and the guy who slugged him was muggled up and hit too hard or didn't care how hard he hit.

It didn't rate ink. No gang angle. No love nest.

The morgue gets them by the hundred. Not all murders, of course. Bums who go to sleep on a bench in Bughouse Square and don't wake up. Guys who take ten-cent beds or two-bit partitioned rooms in flophouses and in the morning somebody shakes them to wake them up, and the guy's stiff, and the clerk quickly goes through his pockets to see if he's got two bits or four bits or a dollar left, and then he phones for the city to come and get him out. That's Chicago.

And there's the jig found carved with a shiv in an areaway on South Halstead Street and the girl who took laundanum in a cheap hotel room. And the printer who had too much to drink and had probably been followed out of the tavern because there'd been green in his wallet and yesterday was payday.

If they put things like that in the paper, people would get a bad impression of Chicago, but that wasn't the reason they didn't put them in. They left them out because there were too many of them. Unless it was somebody important or somebody died in a spectacular way or there was a sex angle.

Like the percentage girl who probably took the laudanum some-where last night—or maybe it was iodine or an overdose of morphine or, if she was desperate enough, even rat poison—she could have had a day of glory in the press. She could have jumped out of a high window into a busy street, waiting on a ledge until she got an audience gathered, and the cops trying to get her back in, and until the newspapers had time to get cameramen there. Then she could have jumped and landed in a bloody mess but with her skirts up around her waist as she lay dead on the sidewalk for a good pic for the photographers.

I left the newspapers on the bench and walked out the front door and stood there watching the people walk by on Madison Street.

It isn't the fault of the newspapers, I thought. The papers just give these people what they want. It's the whole goddam town, I thought; I hate it.

I watched the people go by, and I hated them. When they looked smug or cheerful, like some of them did, I hated them worse. They don't give a damn, I thought, what happens to anybody else, and that's why this is a town in which a man can't walk home with a few drinks under his belt without getting killed for a few lousy bucks.

Maybe it isn't the town, even, I thought. Maybe most people are like that, everywhere. Maybe this town is worse just because it's bigger.

I was watching a jeweller's clock across the street and when it got to be seven minutes after eleven, I went back through the station. The St. Paul train was loading and I got on and got a seat.

It was as hot as hell in the train. The car filled quickly and a fat woman sat beside me and crowded me against the window. People were standing in the aisles. It wasn't going to be a good trip. Funny, no matter how far down you are mentally, physical discomforts can make you feel worse.

I wondered, what am I doing this for anyway? I should get off, go home, and face the music. I'm just running away. I can send Uncle Ambrose a telegram.

I started to get up, but the train began to move.

CHAPTER TWO

THE CARNIVAL LOT was mechanized noise. The merry-go-round's calliope fought with the loudspeakers on the freak show platform, with the thunder of an amplified bass drum booming out a call to bally for the jig show. Under the bingo top a voice called numbers into a microphone and could be heard all over the lot.

I stood in the middle of it all, still stalling, wondering if I could find Uncle Ambrose without having to ask for him. I remembered only vaguely what he looked like. And all I knew about what he did with the carney was that he was a concessionaire. Pop had never talked about him much.

I'd better ask, I decided. I looked around for somebody who wasn't busy or wasn't yelling, and saw that the man at the floss-candy pitch was leaning against an upright, staring at nothing. I walked over and asked where I could find Ambrose Hunter.

He jerked a thumb down the midway. "Ball game. Milk bottle one."

I looked that way. I could see a fat little man with a moustache reaching over the counter, holding out three baseballs at some people who were walking by. It wasn't Uncle Ambrose.

But I walked over anyway. Maybe my uncle hired him, and he could tell me where my uncle was. I got closer.

My God, I thought, it *is* Uncle Ambrose. His face was familiar now. But he'd been so much taller and—well, to a kid of eight, all grown ups seem tall, I suppose. And he'd put on weight, although I could see now that he wasn't really fat, like I'd thought at a first look. His eyes, though, were the same; that was how I knew him. I remembered his eyes. They sort of twinkled at you, like he knew something about you that was a secret, and was funny as hell.

Now I was taller than he was.

He was holding the baseballs out to me now saying, "Three throws for a dime, son. Knock 'em down and win a—"

Of course he couldn't know me; you change so much from eight to eighteen nobody could possibly know you. Just the same, I guess I was a little disappointed that he didn't know me.

I said, "You—you wouldn't recognize me, Uncle Ambrose, I'm Ed. Ed Hunter. I just came from Chicago to tell you—Pop was killed last night."

His face had lighted up like he was really glad to see me when I'd started, but it sure changed when I finished. It went slack for a second, and then it tightened up again, but in a different shape, if you know what I mean. There wasn't any twinkle in his eyes, and he looked like a different guy entirely. He looked, just then, even less like I'd remembered him to be.

"Killed how, Ed? You mean—"

I nodded. "They found him in an alley, dead. Rolled. Payday night and he went out for some drinks and—" I thought there wasn't any use going on. It was obvious from there.

He nodded slowly, and put down the three baseballs in one of the square frames on top of the low counter. He said, "Come on, step over. I'll let down the front."

He did, and then said, "Come on, my quarters are back here." He led the way back past the two boxes on which the dummy milk bottles which you were supposed to knock off with the baseballs were stacked, and lifted the sidewall at the back.

I followed him to a tent pitched about a dozen yards back of his concession. He opened up the flat and I went in first. It was a tent about six by ten feet at the base, with walls that came up straight for three feet and then tapered to the ridge. In the middle you could stand up comfortably. There was a cot and a big trunk at one end and a couple of canvas folding chairs.

But the first thing I'd noticed was the girl asleep on the cot. She was small and slender and very blonde. She looked about twenty or twenty-five, and even asleep her face was pretty. She was dressed except that she'd kicked off her shoes and she didn't seem to be wearing much if anything under the cotton print dress.

My uncle put his hand on her shoulder and shook her awake. He said, when her eyes opened. "You got to beat it, Toots. This is Ed, my nephew. We got to talk here, and I got to pack. You go get Hoagy and tell him I got to see him right away and it's important, huh?"

She was pulling on her shoes already, wide awake. She'd waked up quickly and completely in a second, and she didn't even look sleepy. She stood up and smoothed down her dress, looking at me.

She said, "Hi, Ed. Your name Hunter, too?" I nodded.

"Get going," my uncle said. "Get Hoagy for me."

She made a face at him, and went out.

"Gal with the posing show," my uncle said. "They don't work till evening, so she came in here for a nap. Last week I found a kangaroo in my bed. Yeah, no kidding, John L., the boxing kangaroo—in the pit show. With a carney, you can find *anything* in your bed."

I was sitting in one of the canvas chairs. He'd opened the trunk and was putting stuff from it into a battered suitcase he'd pulled out from under the cot.

"Y'in there, Am?" a deep voice yelled from outside.

"Come on in, Hoagy," my uncle said.

The flap lifted again, and a big man came in. He seemed to fill the front end of the tent as he stood there, his head almost touching the ridgepole. He had a flat, completely expressionless face.

He said, "Yeah?"

"Look, Hoagy," my uncle said. He stopped packing and sat down beside the suitcase. "I got to go to Chicago. Don't know when I'll get back. You want to take over the ball game while I'm gone?"

"Hell, yes. I'm sloughed here and ten to one I'll be sloughed in Springfield. And if Jake gets a chance to use the blow after that, let him get a cooch. What cut you want?"

"No cut," said my uncle. "You'll have to give Maury the same slice I give him, but the rest is yours. All I want is, you keep my stuff together till I get back. Keep track of my trunk. If I don't get back before the season ends, store it."

"Sure, swell. How'll I keep in touch with you?"

"General Delivery, Chicago. But you don't need to. Nobody's sure of the route past Springfield, but I can follow you in *Billboard*, and when I get back I get back. Okay?"

"Hell, yes. Have a drink on it." The big man slid a flat pint bottle out of his hip pocket and handed it to my uncle. He said. "This is your nephew Ed? Toots is gonna be disappointed; she wanted to know if he was gonna be with us. Maybe he's missing something, huh?"

"I wouldn't know," Uncle Ambrose said.

The big man laughed.

My uncle said, "Look, Hoagy, will you run along? I got to talk to Ed. His dad—my brother Wally—died last night."

"Jeez," said the big man. "I'm sorry, Am."

"That's all right. Leave me this bottle, will you, Hoagy? Say, you can run up the front right now if you want. The crowd's fair; I was getting a play."

"Sure, Am. Say, I'm goddam sorry about—Aw hell, you know what I mean."

The big man went out.

My uncle sat looking at me. I didn't say·anything and neither did he for a minute or two. Then he said, "What's wrong, kid? What's eating you?"

"I don't know," I told him.

"Don't give me that," he said. "Look, Ed, I'm not as dumb as I look. I can tell you one thing. You haven't let your hair down. You haven't cried, have you? You're stiff as a board, and you can't take it that way; it'll do things to you. You're bitter."

"I'll be all right."

"No. What's eating you?"

He was still holding the flat pint bottle Hoagy had given him. He hadn't taken the cap off. I looked at it and said, "Give me a drink, Uncle Ambrose."

He shook his head slowly. "That isn't the answer. If you drink, it ought to be because you want to. Not to run away from something. You've been running away ever since you found out, haven't you? Wally tried—Hell, Ed, you don't—"

"Listen," I said. "I don't want to get drunk. I just want one drink. It's something I got to do."

"Why?"

It was hard to say. I said, "I didn't know Pop. I found that out this morning. I thought I was too good for him. I thought he was a rumdum. He must have felt that. He must have felt I thought he was no good, and we never got to know each other, see?"

My uncle didn't say anything. He nodded slowly.

I went on. "I still hate the stuff. The taste of it, I mean. I like beer a little, but I hate the taste of whisky. But I want to take a drink—to him. To make up, just a little bit somehow. I know he'll never know, but I want to—to take a drink *to him*, like you do, sort of to—Oh, hell, I can't explain it any better than that."

My uncle said, "I'll be damned." He put the bottle down on the cot and went over to the trunk. He said, "I got some tin cups in here somewhere. For a cups-and-ball routine. It's almost illegal for a carney to drink out of anything but a bottle, but hell, kid, we got to drink that one together. I want to drink to Wally, too."

He came up with a set of three nested aluminium cups. He poured drinks—good generous ones, a third of a tumblerful—into two of them, and handed me one.

He said, "To Wally." I said, "To Pop," and we touched the rims of the aluminium cups and downed it. It burned like the devil, but I managed not to choke on it.

Neither of us said anything for a minute, and then my uncle said, "I got to see Maury, the carney owner. Let him know I'm going."

He went out quick.

I sat there, with the awful taste of the raw whisky in my mouth, but I wasn't thinking about that. I thought about Pop, and that Pop was dead and I'd never see him again. And suddenly I was bawling like hell. It wasn't the whisky, because outside of the taste and the burn there isn't any effect for a while after you take a first drink. It was just that something let go inside me. I suppose my uncle knew it was coming, that way, and that's why he left me alone. He knew a guy my age wouldn't want to bawl in front of anyone.

By the time I was over crying, though, I began to feel the liquor. My head felt light, and I began to feel sick at my stomach.

Uncle Ambrose came back. He must have noticed my eyes were

red, because he said, "You'll feel better now, Ed. You had that coming. You were tight like a drumhead. Now you look human."

I managed a grin. I said, "I guess I'm a bush-leaguer on drinking, though. I'm going to be sick, I think. Where's the can?"

"With a carney, it's a doniker. Other side of the lot. But hell, this is just a dirt lot. Go ahead and be sick. Or go outside, if you'd rather."

I went outside, around back of the tent, and got it over with.

When I came back, my uncle was through packing the suitcase. He said, "One drink oughtn't to have made you sick, kid, even if you aren't used to it. You been eating?"

"Gosh," I said, "not since supper last night. I never thought about it."

He laughed. "No wonder. Come on. We go to the chow top first; you put yourself outside a meal. I'll take the suitcase, and we hit for the station from there."

Uncle Ambrose ordered me a meal and waited until he saw me really start to eat it, then he said he'd be gone a little while again, and left me eating.

He came back just as I was finishing. He slid into the seat across the table and told me, "I just phoned the station. We can make the train that gets in Chi at six-thirty this evening. And I called Madge"—Madge is Mom's name—"and got the lowdown. Nothing new's come up, and the inquest's tomorrow afternoon. It's at Heiden's funeral parlours, on Wells Street. That's where—where he is now."

"Wouldn't—I thought he'd be taken to the morgue," I said.

My uncle shook his head. "Not in Chicago, Ed. The system's to take a body—unless it's somebody or something special—to the nearest private mortuary. City stands the bill, of course, unless relatives turn up and arrange for the mortician to handle things. A funeral, I mean."

"What if they don't turn up?"

"Potter's Field. Point is, they open an inquest right away to get down testimony while it's fresh. Then they adjourn it if they have to."

I nodded. I asked, "Was Mom mad because I sort of—well—ran off?"

"I don't think so. But she said the detective in charge of the case had wanted to talk to you, and was annoyed. She said she'd let him know you were on the way back."

"The hell with him," I said. "I can't tell him anything."

"Don't be like that, kid. We want him on our side."

"Our side?"

He looked at me strangely. "Why, sure, Ed," he said, "on our side. You're with me, aren't you?"

"You mean you're going to—to—"

"Hell, yes. That's why I had to fix things with Hoagy and Maury—he bought the carney this season but kept Hobart's name on it—so I could stay away as long as I had to. Hell, yes, kid. You don't think we're going to let some son of a bitch get away with killing your dad, do you?"

I said, "Can we do anything the cops can't?"

"They can put only limited time on it, unless they get hot leads. We got all the time in the world. That's one point. We got something they haven't got. We're the Hunters."

I got a tingling sensation when he said that, like a shock.

I thought, *we are the Hunters*. The name fits. We're going hunting in the dark alleys for a killer. The man who killed Pop.

Maybe it was screwy, but I believed him. We've got something the cops haven't got. We're Hunters. I was glad now I hadn't sent a telegram.

I said, "Okay. And we'll *get* the son of a bitch."

The twinkle was back in his eyes. But back of it was something—something deadly. In spite of that twinkle, he didn't look like a funny little fat man with a big black moustache any more. He looked like somebody you wanted on your side when there was trouble.

When we got off the train in Chicago. Uncle Ambrose said, "We'll separate here for a while, kid. You go back home, make your peace with Madge and wait for the detective, if she says he's coming around. I'll phone you where I am."

"And after that?" I asked.

"If it's not too late, and you're not ready to turn in, maybe we can get together again. We might even figure something to do—I mean getting a start. You find out what you can from that detective. And from Madge."

"Okay," I said. "But why don't you come home with me now?"

He shook his head slowly. "The less Madge and I see of each other, in general, the better we'll get along. She was okay over the phone when I called from Janesville, but I don't want to crowd it, see?"

"Look," I said. "I don't want to stay there. Why can't I get a room, too? Near yours or maybe even a double. If we're going to be working together—"

"No, Ed. Not right away, anyway. I don't know how things are between you and Madge, but you got to live at home—at the very least till after the funeral. It wouldn't look right or be right if you left now. See?"

"I guess so. I guess you're right."

"And if you left, and Madge didn't like it, she'd blame me and we'd both be in her doghouse and well—look, if we're going to work on the case we got to stay friendly with everyone connected with it. Get what I mean?"

I said, "Mom didn't do it, if that's what you mean. They scrapped once in a while, but she wouldn't have killed him."

"That isn't what I mean, no. I don't think she would have, either. But we got to have you staying at home, for a while. That's where your dad lived, see? We got to be able to trace this thing every way from the middle. Not just from the outside. You keep in with Madge, just like I want you to keep in with the detective, so you can ask 'em questions any time we find any questions need asking. We'll need every break we can get. Understand?"

Mom was there alone when I got home. Gardie was out somewhere; I didn't ask where she was. Mom was wearing a black dress that I didn't recognize. Her eyes were red, like she'd been crying plenty, and she didn't have on any make-up except a little lipstick that was a bit smeared at one corner of her mouth.

Her voice didn't sound like her at all. It was flat, sort of half-dead, without much inflection in it.

We were like strangers, somehow.

She said, "Hello, Ed," and I said, "Hello, Mom," and I went on in the living room and sat down and she came in and sat down too. I sat by the radio and fiddled with the dials without turning it on.

I said, "Mom, I'm sorry I—well, kind of ran out on you this morning. I should have stayed around." I was sorry, too, although I was glad I'd got Uncle Ambrose.

"That's all right, Ed," she told me. "I—I guess I understand why you wanted to get out. But how did you know about it? I mean, you weren't here when the cops came and—"

"I was on the stairs," I said. "I heard it. I—I didn't want to come in. Did you call the Elwood Press and tell them?"

She nodded. "We called from the undertaker's. I thought you'd gone to work alone, and we called to tell you. The foreman was nice about it. Said for you to take off as long as you wanted. To come back whenever you're ready. You—you are going back, aren't you, Ed?"

"I guess so," I said.

"It's a good trade. And W-Wally said you were getting along swell learning it. You ought to stick to it."

"I guess I will."

"Have you eaten, Ed? Can I get something for you?"

She was sure different. She'd never given much of a damn before whether I ate or not.

"I ate at Janesville," I said. "Uncle Ambrose went to a hotel. He said he'd phone and let us know where he took a room."

"He could have come here."

I didn't know what to say to that. I went back to fiddling with the radio dials, not looking at her. She looked so miserable I didn't want to look at her.

After a while she said, "Listen, Ed—"

"Yes, Mom."

"I know you don't like me, much. Or Gardie. I know you'll want to go out on your own now. You're eighteen, and we're just step-relatives to you and—I don't blame you. But will you stay here awhile, first?

"After a while, we'll work it out. Gardie and I will find a smaller place, and I'll get a job. I want her to finish high school, like you did. But the rent's paid till the first of September, and we'll have to give a month's notice then and pay another month, and this place is too big for just us and—you see what I mean. If you can stay here that long—"

"All right," I said.

"It'll help out. We can get along till then, can't we, Ed?"

"Sure."

"Right after the funeral, I'll get a job. A waitress again, I guess. We can sell the furniture before we leave here. It's all paid for. Not worth much, but maybe we can get enough to almost cover the funeral cost."

I said, "You can sell it, but you don't need to worry about the funeral. The union mortuary benefit ought to cover that."

She looked puzzled, and I explained about it. Pop had been out of the trade for a few years, a bit back, and didn't have continuous membership long enough to draw the maximum, but there ought to be about five hundred coming from the international and the local together. I didn't know exactly, but it would be close to that.

She asked, "You're sure, Ed? That there *is* a benefit, I mean?"

"Positive," I said. "The I.T.U.'s a good union, all right. You can count on it. Maybe something from Elwood, too."

"Then I'm going down to Heiden's right now."

"What for, Mom?"

"I want Wally to have a good funeral, Ed. The best we can give him. I thought we'd have to go in debt for it, and maybe square off part of it with the furniture. I told him I thought about two hundred was all we could afford. I'm going to tell them to double that."

I said, "Pop wouldn't want you to spend it all on that. You should have some to start on. To get you and Gardie set up. And there'll be rent and expenses besides the funeral, and—well, I don't think you ought to do it."

She stood up. "I'm going to. A skimpy little funeral—"

I said, "It's day after tomorrow. You can change it tomorrow, after we know how much the mortuary benefit is. Wait till tomorrow morning, Mom."

She hesitated and then said, "Well, all right. Tomorrow morning won't be too late. I'm going to make some coffee, Ed. We'll have a cup; even if you're not hungry you can drink coffee."

"Sure," I said. "Thanks. Can I help?"

"You sit right here." She glanced at the clock. "The man from homicide that wants to talk to you—his name's Bassett—will be here at eight o'clock."

She turned in the doorway. She said, "And thanks, Ed, for—for deciding to stay, and everything. I thought maybe—"

There were tears running down her face.

I felt almost like crying myself. I felt like a damn fool sitting there not saying anything. But I couldn't think of what to say.

I saw, "Aw, Mom—"

I wished I could put my arms around her and try to comfort her, but you can't do something like that all of a sudden when you never have. Not in ten years.

She went on out into the kitchen and I heard the click of the light switch. I felt all mixed up again inside.

CHAPTER THREE

BASSETT CAME AT EIGHT O'CLOCK. I was drinking coffee with Mom and she put out another cup, and he sat across the table from me. He didn't look like a police detective. He wasn't big; just average height, my height, and no heavier than I am, either. He had faded reddish hair and faded freckles. His eyes looked tired behind shell-rimmed glasses.

But he was nice, and he was friendly. He wasn't like a copper at all.

Instead of asking a flock of questions, he just asked, 'Well, what happened to you, kid?" and then listened while I told him all about it from the time I'd knocked on the door of their room and Pop hadn't answered. Only thing I didn't mention was Mom's being dressed all but her shoes. That couldn't have anything to do with it, and wasn't any of his business. Wherever she'd gone, it didn't matter any now.

When I'd finished, he sat there, not saying anything at all, just sipping at his coffee. I didn't say anything, and neither did Mom. The phone rang, and I said it was probably for me, and went into the living room to answer it.

It was Uncle Ambrose. He had a room at the Wacker on North Clark Street, only a few blocks away.

"Swell," I said. "Why don't you come on around, right now? Mr. Bassett—the detective—is here."

"Like to," he said. "Is it okay with Madge, you think?"

"Sure. It's okay. Make it right away."

I went back to the kitchen and told them he was coming.

"You say he's a carney?" Bassett asked.

I nodded. "He's a swell guy," I said. "Look, Mr. Bassett, mind if I ask you something, straight?"

"Shoot, kid."

"What are the chances of the pol—of you finding the guy who did it? Kind of slim, aren't they?"

"Kind of," he said. "There's almost nothing to go on, see? A guy who pulls a job like that takes a plenty big chance of getting caught—at the time he does it. He's got to worry a squad car might go by—and they flash their spots down alleys in that district. He's got to watch out for the beat cop. The guy he tackles just might show fight and get the best of him.

"But once he's done it, see, and got away in the clear, he's pretty safe. If he keeps his lip buttoned–well, there's a chance in a thousand, ten thousand maybe, that he's not got away with it."

I said, "On a case like this"—somehow I wanted to keep it general; I didn't want to talk about Pop: "just what would that one chance be?"

"Could be a lot of things. Maybe he takes a watch off the man he kills. We turn over the number to the pawnshop detail and maybe later it turns up in a pawnshop and we can trace it back."

"Pop wouldn't have had his watch," I said, "He left it to be repaired a few days ago."

"Yeah. Well, another way. He might have been followed. I mean, he may have flashed money in a tavern, so when he leaves somebody leaves just after him. Somebody in the tavern might remember that and might give us a description, or even know the guy. See?"

I nodded. "You know where he was last night?"

"On Clark Street, first. Stopped in at least two taverns there; could be more. Had only a couple of beers in each. He was alone. Then we picked up the last place he was; we're fairly sure it was the last place. Out west on Chicago Avenue, other side of Orleans. He was alone there, too, and nobody left just after he did."

I asked, "How do you know that was the last place?"

"He bought some bottle beer there to take home. Besides, that was around one o'clock, and he was found at about two. And then where he was found was between here and there, like he'd started home. Then there aren't any taverns to speak of between here and there, along that route. The couple there are, we checked damn thoroughly. He could've stopped in one of them, but—well, what with the bottle beer and the time and everything, it's odds he didn't."

"Where—where *was* he found?"

"Alley between Orleans and Franklin, two and a half blocks south of Chicago Avenue."

"Between Huron and Erie?"

He nodded.

I said, "Then he must have walked south on Orleans and cut through the alley toward Franklin. But—gosh, in *that* neighbourhood, why'd he want to go through an alley?"

Bassett said, "Two answers to that. One is—he'd been drinking a lot of beer. Far as we know, he hadn't drunk much else, and he'd been out and around from nine o'clock to one. A guy starting home with a skinful of beer might easy want to cut through an alley, although like you say, it's no neighbourhood to do it in."

"What's the other answer?"

"That he didn't cut through the alley at all. He was near the Franklin end. So he could have walked over Chicago to Franklin and south on Franklin. He's stuck up at the mouth of the alley, and the stick-up man, or men, take him into the alley, roll him there and then slug him. Those streets are pretty deserted that time in the morning. There've been plenty of holdups there under the el on Franklin.''

I nodded thoughtfully. This Bassett didn't look like a detective, but he wasn't a dumb cluck at all. Either of the things he'd said could have happened. It had to have been one way or the other, and the odds looked about even.

And they looked pretty slim for getting the guy who did it. Like he said, about a thousand to one against.

Could be, I thought, he's smarter than Uncle Ambrose on things like this. He was smart enough to have traced Pop pretty well, and that was no cinch in a district like this. On Clark Street and on Chicago Avenue they don't like coppers. Even the most of them who are inside the law.

When Uncle Ambrose came, Mom let him in. They talked a few minutes out in the hall and I could hear their voices but I couldn't tell what they were saying. When they came in the kitchen they were friendly. Mom poured another cup of coffee.

Bassett shook hands with him and they seemed to take to one another right away. Bassett started asking him questions, just a few. He didn't ask him whether I'd been in Janesville; he asked, quite casually, what train I'd come on and how service was coming back and some things like that. And little points he could check with the story I'd told him so he'd know if I'd been telling him the truth.

A smart duck, I thought again.

But I didn't know the half of it until Uncle Ambrose started asking a few questions about the investigation. Bassett answered the first couple and then one corner of his mouth went up a little.

He said, "Ask the kid here. I gave him the whole story, such as it is. You two are going at it together. I wish you luck.''

My uncle looked at me, his eyebrows up just a trifle. Bassett wasn't watching me, so I shook my head a little to let him know I hadn't blabbed to the detective. A smart duck. I don't know how he figured that angle so quickly.

Gardie came in and got reintroduced to Uncle Ambrose. Mom had sent her out to a movie, and I guess she'd really gone to one or she wouldn't have been home so early.

I got a kick out of the way Uncle Ambrose patted her on the head and treated her like a kid. Gardie didn't like it; I could tell that. Five minutes of old-home-week and she went off to her room.

Uncle Ambrose grinned at me.

The coffee was cold and Mom started to get some fresh but

Uncle Ambrose said, "Let's go down and have a drink instead. What say, Bassett?"

The detective shrugged. "Okay by me. I'm off duty now."

Mom shook her head. "You two go," she told them.

I dealt myself in, said I was thirsty and wanted some Seven-Up or a coke. Uncle Ambrose said, "Sure," and Mom didn't squawk, so I went downstairs with them.

We went to a place on Grand Avenue. Bassett said it was a quiet place where we could talk. It was quiet all right; we were almost the only ones in there.

We took a booth and ordered two beers and a Coca-Cola. Bassett said he had to phone somebody and went back to the phone booth.

I said, "He's a nice guy. I kind of like him."

My uncle nodded slowly. He said, "He's not dumb and he's not honest, and he's not a louse. He's just what the doctor ordered "

"Huh? How do you know he's not honest?" I wasn't being naïve; I know plenty of coppers aren't; I just wondered how Uncle Ambrose could be so sure so quick—or if he was just talking through his hat.

"Just look at him," he said. "I don't know how, but I know. I used to run a mitt-camp with the carney, Ed. It's a racket, sure, but you get so you can size people up."

I remembered something I'd read. "Lombroso has been dis—"

"Nuts to Lombroso. It isn't the shapes of their faces. It's something you feel. You can do it with your eyes shut. I don't know how. But this red-headed copper—we're going to buy him."

He took out his wallet, and holding it under the table so the couple of men at the bar, up front, couldn't see what he was doing, he took a bill out of it and then put it back in his hip pocket. I got a look at the bill, though, as he folded it twice and palmed it. It was a hundred bucks.

I felt a little scared. I couldn't see why he would need to bribe Bassett at all, and I was afraid he was wrong, and offering it would start trouble.

Bassett came back and sat down.

My uncle said, "Look, Bassett, I know what you're up against on a case like this. But Wally was my brother, see, and I want to see the guy who killed him sent up. I want to see him fry."

Bassett said, "We'll do our best."

"I know you will. But they won't allow you too much time on it, and you know that. I want to help any way I can. There's one way I know of. I mean, there's times putting out a few bucks here and there will get a song out of somebody who won't sing otherwise. You know what I mean."

"I know what you mean. Yeah, sometimes it helps."

My uncle held out his hand, palm down. He said, "Put this in your pocket, in case you get a chance to use it where it might get us something. It's off the record."

Bassett took the bill. I saw him glance at the corner of it under the table, and then he put it in his pocket. His face didn't change. He didn't say anything.

We ordered another round of drinks, or they did. I still had half my coke left.

Bassett's eyes, behind the shell-rimmed glasses, looked a little more tired, a little more veiled. He said, "What I gave the kid was straight. We don't know a damn thing more. Two stops on Clark Street; stayed maybe half an hour in each. That one last stop on Grand Avenue; where he bought the beer. Ten gets you one that was the last stop he made. If we could get anything it ought to be there. But there wasn't anything to get.'

"What about the rest of the time?" my uncle asked.

Bassett shrugged. "There are two kinds of drinkers. One holes in someplace and stays put to do his drinking. The other kind ambles. Wallace Hunter was the ambling kind, that evening anyway. He was out four hours and stuck around about half an hour—long enough to drink two-three beers in each of the three places we've put him. If that's the average, he probably stopped in six or seven places—you got to allow some time for the walking."

"He drank only beer?"

"Mostly, anyway. One place, the bartender wasn't sure what he drank. And on Chicago Avenue, he had one shot with his last beer, then bought the bottle to go. Kaufman's place. Kaufman was behind the bar. Said he seemed a little tight, quiet drunk, but not staggering or anything. In control."

"Who's Kaufman? I mean, outside of being a tavern owner."

"Nobody much. I don't know how straight he is, but we haven't got anything on him if he isn't. I checked with the boys at the Chicago Avenue station on that. As far as they know, his nose is clean."

"You talked to him. Is it?"

Bassett said. "He could do with a handkerchief. But I think he's clean on this. He came up with identifying your brother's picture after I'd jogged him a little. Used the same line on him as the others; I mean, told 'em we knew he was there and was only interested in getting the time he left. First he said he never saw him. I said we had proof he'd been in there, just wanted to know when, and it wouldn't get him in any trouble. So he got some glasses out of a drawer and looked again, and then kicked in."

"All the way?"

"I think so," Bassett said. "You'll get a look at him and a listen to him tomorrow, at the inquest."

"Swell," my uncle told me. "Look, you don't know me at the

inquest. Nobody does. I just sit at the back, and nobody knows who I am. They won't want me to testify anyway."

Bassett's eyes unveiled a little, just a little. He asked, "You think you might want to run one?"

"I think maybe," my uncle said.

They seemed to understand one another. They knew what they were talking about. I didn't.

Like when Hoagy, the big man, had been talking to my uncle about the blow being sloughed. Only that was carney talk; at least I knew why I didn't understand it. This was different; they were talking words I knew, but it still didn't make sense.

I didn't care.

Bassett said, "One angle's out. No insurance."

That did make sense to me. I said, "Mom didn't do it."

Bassett looked at me, and I wondered if I liked him as much as I'd thought.

Uncle Ambrose said. "The kid's right. Madge is—" He stopped himself. "She wouldn't have killed Wally."

"You can't tell with women. My God, I've known cases—"

"Sure, a million cases. But Madge didn't kill him. Look, she might have waited till he got home and gone for him with a butcher's knife or something. But this wasn't like that. She wouldn't have followed him into an alley and blackj—Say, *was* it a blackjack?"

"Nope. Something harder."

"Such as?"

"Almost anything heavy enough to swing and without a point or sharp edge on the side that hit. A club, a piece of pipe, an empty bottle, a—almost anything."

A blunt instrument, I thought. That's the way the papers would describe it, if the papers would print it.

I watched a cockroach that was crawling across the floor away from the bar. It was one of the big black kind, and it moved in hitches, scurrying a little and then stopping still. It would run for about ten inches, stop a second, then another ten inches.

One of the men at the bar was watching it. He walked toward it, and it scurried out from under his foot just in time.

The second time it wasn't so lucky. There was a crunching sound.

"Look," Bassett was saying. "I got to get home. I just phoned there and my wife is kind of sick. Nothing serious, but she wanted me to bring some medicine. See you at the inquest tomorrow."

"Okay," said my uncle. "We can't talk there, though, like I said. How about meeting afterwards here?"

"Fine. So long, kid."

He left.

I thought, a hundred bucks is a lot of money. I was glad I hadn't a job where people might offer me a hundred bucks for doing something I shouldn't do.

Not that, come to think of it, he was being paid for doing anything really wrong. Just for being on our side, for levelling with us. For giving us the straight dope on everything. That was all right; it was only the taking money for it that was wrong. But he had a sick wife.

And then I thought, my uncle didn't know he had a sick wife. But my uncle knew he'd take the hundred.

My uncle said, "It's a good investment."

"Maybe," I said. "But if he's dishonest, how do you know he'll play straight with you? He can give you nothing for that hundred dollars. And that's a lot of money."

He said, "Sometimes a dime is a lot of money. Sometimes a hundred isn't. I think we'll get our money's worth. Look, kid, how about making the rounds? I mean, looking over the places he stopped. One thing I want to know. You feel up to it?"

"Sure," I said. "I can't sleep anyway. And it's only eleven."

He looked me over. He said, "You can pass for twenty-one, I think. If anyone asks, I'm your father and they ought to take my word for it. We can both show identification with the same name. Only we don't want to."

"You mean we don't want them to know who we are?"

"That's it. Any place we go in, we order a beer apiece. I drink mine fast and you just sip yours. Then we get the glasses mixed see? That way—"

"A little beer won't hurt me," I said. "I'm eighteen, damn it."

"A little beer won't hurt you. That's all you're going to get. We change glasses. See?"

I nodded. No use arguing, especially when he was right.

We walked over Grand to Clark and started north. We stopped on the corner of Ontario.

"This is sort of where he started," I said. "I mean, he would have come over on Ontario from Wells, and started north."

I stood there looking down Ontario, feeling almost that I would see him coming.

It was very silly, I thought, he's lying on a slab at Heiden's. They've taken out his blood and filled him up with embalming fluid. They'd have done that quick because the weather is so hot.

He isn't Pop any more. Pop has never minded hot weather. Cold got him down; he hated to go out in cold weather, even for a block or two. But hot weather he didn't mind.

Uncle Ambrose said, "The Beer Barrel and the Cold Spot, those are the two places, weren't they?"

I said, "I guess Bassett said that when I wasn't listening. I don't know."

"Wasn't listening?"

"I was watching a cockroach," I said.

He didn't say anything. We started walking, watching the names of the places we went past. The taverns averaged three or four to a block on North Clark Street from the Loop north to Bughouse Square. The poor man's Broadway.

We came to the Cold Spot just north of Huron. We went in and stood at the bar. The Greek behind the bar hardly looked at me.

There were only a few men along the bar, and no women. A drunk was asleep at a table near the back. We stayed only for the one beer apiece, Uncle Ambrose drinking most of mine.

We did the same at the Beer Barrel, which turned up on the other side of the street, near Chicago. It was the same kind of place, a little bigger, a few more people, two bartenders instead of one and three drunks asleep at tables instead of one.

There was no one near us at the bar, so we could talk freely.

I said, "Aren't you going to try to pump them? To find out what he was doing or something?"

He shook his head.

I wanted to know, "What *were* we trying to find out?"

"What he was doing. What he was looking for."

I thought it over. It didn't make any sense that we could find that out without asking any questions.

My uncle said, "Come on, I'll show you."

We went out and walked back half a block the way we had come and went in another place.

"I get it," I told him. "I see what you mean."

I'd been kind of dumb. This was different. There was music, if you could call it that. And almost as many women as men. Faded women mostly. A few of them were young. Most of them were drunk.

They weren't percentage girls. Maybe a few of them, I decided, were prostitutes, but not many. They were just women.

We had our one beer apiece again.

I thought, I'm glad Pop didn't come here, places like this, instead of the Beer Barrel and the Cold Spot. He'd been out drinking. Just drinking.

We went north again and crossed back to the west side of the street and turned the corner at Chicago Avenue.

We passed the police station. We crossed LaSalle and then Wells. He could have turned south here, I thought. It would have been about half-past twelve when he came this way.

Last night, I thought. Only last night, he came this way. Probably walking on the same side of the street we were on. Only last night and about at this time. It must be almost twelve-thirty right now, I thought.

We walked under the el at Franklin.

A train roared by overhead and it shook the night. Funny that the el trains are so loud at night. In our flat on Wells, a block from the el, I can hear every one at night, if I'm awake. Or early in the morning, when I first get up or am still lying in bed. The rest of the time you can't hear them.

We walked on, as far as the corner of Orleans Street. We stopped there. Across the way was a Topaz Beer sign. It was on the north side of Chicago Avenue, two doors past the corner. It would be Kaufman's place. It would have to be because it was the only tavern in the block.

Pop's last stop.

I asked, "Aren't we going over there?"

My uncle shook his head slowly.

We stood there maybe five minutes, doing nothing, not even talking. I didn't ask him why we weren't going over to Kaufman's.

Then he said, "Well, kid—?"

I said, "Sure."

We turned around and started walking south on Orleans.

We were going there now. We were going to the alley.

CHAPTER FOUR

THE ALLEY was just an alley. At the Orleans end there was a parking lot at one side and a candy factory at the other. There was a big loading platform alongside the candy factory.

The alley was paved with rough red brick and there were no curbs.

There was a street light, one of the smaller size they use in the middle of a block, opposite the Orleans end.

Down at the Franklin end, under the elevated, there was another such light, right at the left of the mouth of the alley. It wasn't particularly dark. You could stand at the Orleans end and look through it.

It was dim down in the middle of the alley, but you could see through it, and if anyone was in there you could see him silhouetted against the Franklin end.

There wasn't anyone in there now.

Down in the middle of the alley were the backs of flat buildings, ramshackle old ones, that fronted on Huron and on Erie. The ones on the Erie side had wooden back porches with railings, and wooden steps that led up to the back doors of the flats. The ones on the Huron side were flat and flush with the alley.

Uncle Ambrose said, "If he came this way, it must have been somebody following him. He could have seen anyone waiting in the alley."

I pointed up at the porches. I said, "Somebody up on one of them. A man staggers through the alley below them. They go down the steps, getting down just after he passes, catch up with him near the other end of the alley, and—"

"Could be, kid. Not likely. If they were on the porch, then they live there. A guy doesn't do something like that in his own back alley. Not that close to home. And I doubt if he was staggering drunk. Course you got to discount how sober a bartender says a guy is when he leaves the place. They don't want to get themselves in trouble."

"It could have been that way," I said, "Not likely, but it could have been."

"Sure. We'll look into it. We'll talk to everybody lives in those flats. We're not passing up off chances; I didn't mean that when I said it wasn't likely."

We were talking softly, like you do in an alley at night. We were past the middle of the alley, past the flats. We were at the back of the buildings that fronted on Franklin Street. On both sides they were three-story bricks, with stores on the bottom floor and flats above.

My uncle stopped and bent down. He said, "Beer-bottle glass. This is where it happened."

I got a funny feeling, almost a dizziness. This is where it happened. Right where I'm standing now. This is where it happened.

I didn't want to think about it, that way, so I bent down and started looking, too. It was amber glass, all right, and over an area of a few yards there was enough of it to have come from two or three bottles.

It wouldn't be just like it fell, of course. It would have been kicked around by people walking through the alley, trucks driving through. It was broken finer now, and scattered more. But right around here, the centre of the area where the glass was, would be where the bottles were dropped.

My uncle said, "Here's a piece with part of a label. We can see if it's the brand Kaufman sells."

I took it and walked out under the street light at the end of the alley. I said, "It's part of a Topaz label. I've seen thousand's of 'em on beer Pop's brought home. Kaufman has a Topaz sign, but it's an awful common beer around here. It wouldn't prove it for sure."

He came over and we stood looking both ways on Franklin Street. An el train went by almost right over our heads. A long one, it must have been a North Shore train. It sounded as loud as the end of the world.

A noise loud enough, I thought, to cover revolver shots—let alone the noise a man would make falling, even with beer bottles. That might have been why it happened here, near this end of the alley, instead of back in the middle where it was darker. Noise counted, too, along with darkness. When they got here, the killer closing up behind Pop, the el had come by. Even if Pop had yelled for help, the noise of the el would have made it a whimper.

I looked at the store fronts on either side of the alley. One was a plumbing supplies shop. The other was vacant. It seemed to have been vacant a long time; the glass was too dirty to see through.

My uncle said, "Well, Ed."

"Sure. I guess this is—is all we can do tonight."

We walked down Franklin to Erie and across to Wells.

My uncle said, "I just figured what's wrong with me. I'm hungry as hell. I haven't eaten since noon and you haven't eaten since about two o'clock. Let's go over to Clark for some grub."

We went to an all-night barbecue place.

I wasn't hungry until I took a bite out of a pork barbecue sandwich, and then I gobbled it down, the French fries and the slaw too. We each ordered a second one.

My uncle asked, while we waited, "Ed, what are you heading for?"

"What do you mean?"

He said, "I mean what are you going to do with yourself? During the next fifty-odd years."

The answer was so obvious I had to think it over. I said, "Nothing much, I guess. I'm an apprentice printer. I can take up linotype when I'm a little farther on my apprenticeship. Or I can be a hand-man. Printing's a good trade."

"I suppose it is. Going to stay in Chicago?"

"I haven't thought about it," I told him. "I'm not going to leave right away. After I finish my apprenticeship, I'm a journeyman. I can work anywhere."

He said, "A trade's a good thing. But get the trade. Don't let it get you. The same with—Oh, hell, I'm not Dutch. I'm talking like a Dutch uncle."

He grinned. He'd been going to say, the same with women. He knew that I knew it and so he didn't have to say it. I was glad he gave me credit for that much sense.

He asked instead, "What do you dream, Ed?"

I looked at him; he was serious. I asked, "Is this the mittcamp lay? Or are you psychoanalyzing me?"

"It's the same difference."

I said, "This morning I dreamed I was reaching through a hock-shop window to pick up a trombone. Gardie came skipping rope along the sidewalk and I woke up before I got the trombone. Now I suppose you know all about me, huh?"

He chuckled. "That would be shooting a sitting duck, Ed. Two ducks with one bullet. Watch out for one of those ducks. You know which one I mean."

"I guess I do."

"She's poison, kid, for a guy like you. Just like Madge was—Skip it. What's about the tram? Ever play one?"

"Not to speak of. In sophomore year at high I borrowed one of the school board's. I was going to learn so I could get in the band. But some of the neighbours squawked, and I guess it did make a hell of a noise. When you live in a flat—Mom didn't like, it, either."

The guy behind the counter brought our second sandwiches. I wasn't so hungry now. With the stuff on the side, it looked awfully big. I ate a few of the French fries first.

Then I lifted the lid of the barbecue sandwich and tilted the ketchup bottle and let it gurgle on thick.

It looked like—

I smacked down the lid of the sandwich and tried to think away from what it looked like. But I was back in the alley. I didn't even know if there'd been blood; maybe there hadn't. You can hit to kill without drawing blood.

But I thought of Pop's head matted with blood and a blot of blood on the rough brick of the alley last night—now soaked in, worn off or washed away. Would they have washed it away? Hell, there probably hadn't been any blood.

But the thought of that sandwich was making me sick. Unless I could get my mind off it. I closed my eyes and was repeating the first nonsense that came into my mind to keep from thinking. It was *one, two, three, O'Leary: four, five, six, O'Leary—*

After a few seconds I knew I'd won and I wasn't going to be sick. But I looked around at Uncle Ambrose and kept my eyes off the counter.

I said, "Say, maybe Mom's waiting up for me. We never thought to tell her we'd be late. It's after one."

He said, "My God. I forgot it too. Golly, I hope she isn't. You better get home fast."

I told him I didn't want the rest of my second barbecue anyway, and he'd almost finished his. We parted right outside; he went north to the Wacker and I hurried home to Wells Street.

Mom had left a light on for me in the inner hall, but she hadn't waited up. The door of her room was dark. I was glad. I didn't want to have to explain and apologize, and if she'd been waiting up, worried, she might have blamed Uncle Ambrose.

I got to bed quickly and quietly. I must have gone to sleep the first instant I closed my eyes.

When I woke up, something was funny in the room. Different. It was morning as usual and again the room was hot and close. It took me a minute or two, lying there, to realize that the difference was that my alarm clock wasn't ticking. I hadn't wound or set it.

I don't know why it mattered much what time it was, but I wanted to know. I got up and walked out to look at the kitchen clock. It was one minute after seven.

Funny, I thought; I woke up at the usual time. Without even a clock running in my room.

Nobody else was awake. Gardie's door was open and her pyjama tops were off again. I hurried past.

I set and wound my alarm clock and lay down again. I might as well sleep another hour or two, I thought, if I can. But I couldn't go back to sleep; I couldn't even get sleepy.

The flat was awfully quiet. There didn't seem to be much noise even outside this morning, except when an el car went by on Franklin every few minutes.

The ticking of the clock got louder and louder.

This morning I don't have to wake Pop, I thought. I'll never wake him again. Nobody will.

I got up and dressed.

On my way through to the kitchen I stopped in the doorway of Gardie's room and looked in. I thought, she wants me to look; I want to look, so why shouldn't I? I knew the answer damn well.

Maybe I was looking for a counter-irritant for the cold feeling about not having to wake up Pop. Maybe a cold feeling and a hot one ought to cancel out. They didn't, exactly, but after half a minute I got disgusted with myself and went on out to the kitchen.

I made coffee and sat drinking it. I wondered what I was going to do to fill in the morning. Uncle Ambrose would sleep late; being with a carney he'd be used to sleeping late. Anyway there wasn't much to do about the investigation until after the inquest. And then, until after the funeral.

Besides, in the light of morning now, it seemed a bit silly. A fat little man with a moustache and a wet-behind-the-ears kid thinking they could find, out of all Chicago, the heister who had got away with a job.

I thought about the homicide man with the faded red hair and the tired eyes. We'd bought him for a hundred dollars, or Uncle Ambrose thought we had. He'd been partly right anyhow; Bassett had taken the money.

I heard bare feet padding, and Gardie came out into the kitchen in her pyjamas. The tops, too. The toenails of her bare feet were painted.

She said, "Morning, Eddie. Cup coffee?"

She yawned and then stretched like a sleek kitten. Her claws were in.

I got another cup and poured, and she sat down across the table.

She said, "Gee, the inquest's today." She sounded excited about it. Like she would say, "Gee, the football game's today."

I said, "I wonder if they'll want me to testify. I don't know to what."

"No, Eddie, I don't think so. Just Mom and me, they said."

"Why you?"

"Identification. I was the one really identified him first. Mom almost fainted again at the parlours, at Heiden's. They didn't want her to faint, so I said I'd look. Later when she was a little calmer, after the detective, Mr. Bassett, had talked to her, she wanted to look too, and they let her."

I asked, "How did they find out who he was? I mean, he couldn't have had identification left on him, or they'd have been up here in the middle of the night, after they found him."

"Bobby knew him. Bobby Reinhart."

"Who's Bobby Reinhart?"

"He works for Mr. Heiden. He's learning the undertaking business. I've gone out with him a few times. He knew Pop by sight. He came to work at seven, and told them right away who it was, as soon as he went in the—the morgue room."

"Oh," I said. I placed the guy now. A slick-looking little punk, about sixteen or seventeen. He greased his hair and had always worn his best clothes to school. He thought he was a woman-killer and pretty hot stuff.

It made me a little sick to think of him maybe helping work on Pop's body.

We finished the coffee, and Gardie rinsed out the cups and then went back to her room to dress. I heard Mom getting up.

I went in the living room and picked up a magazine. It was starting to rain outside, a slow steady drizzle.

It was a detective magazine. I started a story and it was about a rich man who was found dead in his hotel suite, with a noose of yellow silk rope around his neck, but he'd been poisoned. There were lots of suspects, all with motives. His secretary at whom he'd been making passes, a nephew who inherited, a racketeer who owed him money, the secretary's fiancé. In the third chapter they'd just about pinned it on the racketeer and then *he's* murdered. There's a yellow silk cord around his neck and he's been strangled, but not with the silk cord.

I put down the book. Nuts, I thought, murder isn't like that.

Murder is like this.

For some reason, I got to remembering the time Pop took me to the aquarium. I don't know how I remembered that; I was only about six years old then, or maybe five. My mother had been alive then, but she hadn't gone with us. I remember Pop and I laughing a lot together at the expressions on the faces of some of the fishes, the surprised astonished look on the faces of some of them that had round open mouths.

Now that I thought about it, Pop had laughed a lot in those days.

Gardie told Mom she was going to a girl friend's house and would be back by noon.

It rained all morning.

At the inquest, it seemed you mostly sat around and waited for it to start. It was in the main hall at Heiden's mortuary. There hadn't been any sign out "Inquest Today" but word must have got around, because there were quite a few people there. There were seats for about forty and they were all taken.

Uncle Ambrose was there, in the back row on one side. He'd tipped me a wink and then pretended not to know me. I let myself get separated from Mom and Gardie and took a seat near the back on the other side of the room.

A little man with gold-rimmed glasses was fussing around, up front. He was the deputy coroner in charge. I found out later his name was Wheeler. He looked hot and fussy and annoyed, and in a hurry to get things started and get them over with.

Bassett was there, and other cops, one in uniform, the others not. There was a man with a long thin nose who looked like a professional gambler.

There were six men in chairs lined up along one side of the front of the hall.

Finally, whatever was holding up things must have been settled. The deputy coroner rapped with a gavel and things quieted down. He wanted to know if there was any objection to any of the six men who had been chosen as jurors. There wasn't. He wanted to know, of them, whether they had known a man named Wallace Hunter, whether they knew the circumstances of his death or had discussed the case with anyone, whether there was any reason why they couldn't render a fair and impartial verdict on the evidence they would hear. He got negatives and headshakes on all counts.

Then he took the six of them into the morgue to view the body of the deceased, and then to be sworn.

It was very formal, in an informal sort of way.

It was corny. It was like a bad movie.

When that was all out of the way, he wanted to know if there was a member of the family of the deceased present. Mom got up and went forward. She held up her right hand and mumbled something back when something was mumbled at her.

Her name, her address, her occupation, her relation to the deceased. She had seen the body and identified it as that of her husband.

A lot of questions about Pop; his occupation, place of employment, residence, how long he'd lived there and all that sort of thing.

"When did you last see your husband alive, Mrs. Hunter?"

"Thursday night, somewhere about nine o'clock. When he went out."

"Did he say where he was going?"

"N-no. He just said he was going down for a glass of beer. I figured Clark Street."

"Did he go out like that often, alone?"

"Well—yes."

"How often?"

"Once or twice a week."

"And usually stayed out—how late?"

"Around midnight usually. Sometimes later. One or two o'clock."

"How much money did he have with him Thursday night?"

"I don't know exactly. Twenty or thirty dollars. Wednesday was payday."

"You can't say any closer than that?"

"No. He gave me twenty-five dollars Wednesday night. That was for groceries and—and household expenses. He always kept the rest. He paid rent and gas and light bills and things like that."

"He had no enemies that you know of, Mrs. Hunter?"

"No, none at all."

"Think carefully. You know of no one who would—would have cause to hate him?"

Mom said. "No. Nobody at all."

"Nor anyone who would benefit financially from his death?"

"How do you mean?"

"I mean, did he have any money, did he have an interest in any business or venture?"

"No."

"Did he carry any insurance? Or was any insurance carried on him?"

"No. He suggested it once. I said no, that we ought to put the money that would go for premiums in the bank instead. Only we didn't."

"Thursday night, Mrs. Hunter, did you wait up for him?"

"I did, yes, for a while. Then I decided he was going to be late and I went to sleep."

"When your husband had been drinking, Mrs. Hunter, would you say he was—well, careless about taking chances such as walking down alleys or in dangerous neighbourhoods, things like that?"

"I'm afraid he was, yes. He was held up before, twice. The last time a year ago."

"But he wasn't injured? He didn't attempt to defend himself?"

"No. He was just held up."

I listened closely now. That was news to me. Nobody had told me Pop had been held up before, not even once. Then something fitted. A year ago he'd said he'd lost his wallet; he'd had to get a new social security card and union card. Probably he'd just figured it was none of my business how he'd lost it.

The deputy coroner was asking if any of the police present wanted to ask any further questions. Nobody did, and he told Mom she could go back to her seat.

He said, "I understand we have a further identification. Miss Hildergarde Hunter has also identified the deceased. Is she present?"

Gardie got up and went through the rigmarole. She sat down in the chair and crossed her legs. She didn't have to adjust her skirt; it was short enough already.

They didn't ask her anything except about having identified Pop. You could tell she was disappointed when she went back to her seat beside Mom.

They put one of the plain-clothes men on the stand next. He was a squad-car cop. He and his partner had found the body.

They'd been driving south, just cruising slowly, on Franklin Street under the el at two o'clock and the alley was dark there and they'd flashed their spotlight in it and seen him lying there.

"He was dead when you reached him?"

"Yes. Been dead about an hour maybe."

"You looked for identification?"

"Yes. He didn't have any wallet or watch or anything. He'd been cleaned. There was some change in his pocket. Sixty-five cents."

"It was dark enough back where he lay that anyone walking by would not have seen him?"

"I guess not. There's a street light on Franklin at that end of the alley, but it was out. We reported that too, afterward, and they put in a new bulb. Or said they were going to."

"Was there any indication of a struggle?"

"Well, his face was scratched, but that could have been from falling. He fell face forward when he was hit."

"You don't know that," said the coroner, sharply. "You mean, he was lying on his face when you found him?"

"Yeah. And there was broken glass from several beer bottles and the spot smelled of beer. The alley and his clothes were wet with it. He must have been carrying—Oh, all right, that's a deduction again. There was beer and beer-bottle glass around."

"Was the deceased wearing a hat?"

"There was one lying by him. A hard straw hat. What they call a sailor straw. It wasn't crushed; it couldn't have been on him when he was hit. That, and the way he was lying, makes me think he was slugged from behind. The heister came up on him, knocked off his hat with one hand and swung the billy with the other, like. You can't take off a guy's hat to slug him from the front without him knowing it and he'd put up a—"

"Please confine yourself to facts, Mr. Horvath."

"Okay—what *was* the question, now?"

"Was the deceased wearing a hat? That was the question."

"No, he wasn't wearing one. There was one lying by him."

"Thank you, Mr. Horvath. That will be all."

The cop got down from the witness chair. I thought, we were figuring things wrong last night, because we figured on the street light. It was off at the time. It would have been plenty dark at the Franklin end of the alley.

The deputy coroner was looking at his notes again. He said, "Is there a Mr. Kaufman present?"

A short, heavy man shuffled forward. He wore glasses with thick lenses and behind them his eyes looked hooded.

His name, he testified, was George Kaufman. He owned and ran the tavern on Chicago Avenue known as Kaufman's Place.

Yes, Wallace Hunter, the deceased, had been in his tavern Thursday night. He'd been there half an hour—not much longer than that anyhow—and then had left, saying he was going home. In Kaufman's place he'd had one shot and two-three beers. In answer to a question, Mr. Kaufman admitted it might have been three or four beers, but not more than that. He was sure about it being only one shot.

"He came in alone?"

"Yeah. He came in alone. And left alone."

"Did he say he was going home when he left?"

"Yeah. He was standing at the bar. He said something about going home. I don't remember the words. And he bought four bottles to take out. Paid for 'em and left."

"You knew him? He'd been in before?"

"A few times. I knew him by sight. I didn't know his name until they showed me his picture and told me."

"How many others were in your tavern at the time?"

"Two guys together were there, when he came in. They were getting ready to leave then, and they left. Nobody else came in."

"You mean he was the only customer?"

"Most of the time he was there, yeah. It was a dull evening. I closed early. A little after he left."

"How long after?"

"I started to clean up the place for closing then. It was about twenty minutes before I got it closed. Maybe thirty."

"Did you see how much money he had?"

"He broke a five. He took it out of his wallet, but I didn't see inside his wallet when he took it out or put the singles back. I don't know how much more he had."

"The two men who left when he came. Do you know them?"

"A little. One of 'em runs a delicatessen on Wells Street. He's Jewish; I don't know his name. The other guy comes in with him."

"Was the deceased in an intoxicated condition, would you say?"

"He'd been drinking. He showed it, but I wouldn't say he was drunk."

"He could walk straight?"

"Sure. His voice was a little thick and he talked kind of funny. But he wasn't really drunk."

"That's all, Mr. Kaufman. Thank you."

They swore in the coroner's physician. He turned out to be the tall guy with the long thin nose, the one I'd thought looked like a faro dealer in a movie.

His name was Dr. William Haertel. His office was on Wabash

and he lived on Division Street. Yes, he'd examined the body of the deceased.

What he said was technical. It boiled down to death from a blow on the head with a hard, blunt object. Apparently it had been struck by someone standing behind the deceased.

"At what time did you examine the body?"

"Two forty-five."

"How long would you say he had been dead at that time?"

"One to two hours. Probably closer to two."

A hand touched my shoulder, timidly, as I was leaving Heiden's. I looked around and said, "Hello, Bunny."

He looked more like a scared little rabbit than usual. We stepped to one side of the doorway and let the others go past us. He said, "Gee, Ed, I'm—You know what I mean. Is there anything I can do?"

I said, "Thanks, Bunny, but I guess not. Not a thing."

"How's Madge?' How's she taking it?"

"Not too good. But—"

"Look, Ed, if there's anything at all I can do, call on me. I mean, I've got a little money in the bank—"

I said, "Thanks, Bunny, but we'll get by okay."

I was glad he'd asked me instead of Mom. Mom might have borrowed from him, and probably I'd have had to pay it back. If we didn't have it, we'd get by without it.

And Bunny didn't have money to lend out and not get back, because I knew what he was saving for. A little printing shop of his own was Bunny Wilson's dream, but it costs plenty to start one. It's a tough game to get started in, and it takes capital.

He said, "Should I drop around, Ed? To talk to you and Madge? Would she want me to?"

"Sure," I told him. "Mom likes you a lot. I guess you're about the only one of Pop's friends she really likes. Come around any time.

"I will, Ed. Maybe next week, my evening off. Wednesday. Your dad was a swell guy, Ed."

I liked Bunny, but I didn't want any more of that. I got away from him and went on home.

CHAPTER FIVE

OVER THE PHONE, Uncle Ambrose said, "Kid, how would you like to be a gun punk?"

I said,"Huh?"

"Hang on to your hat. You're going to be."

"I haven't got a gun and I'm not a punk."

He said, "You're half right. But you won't need a gun. All you're going to do is scare a guy half out of his wits."

"Sure it won't be me that's scared?"

"Go ahead and be scared. It'll stiffen you up and help the act. I'll give you some tips."

I asked, "Are you really serious?"

He said, "Yes," flatly, just like that, and I knew he was.

"When?" I asked him.

"We'll wait till day after tomorrow, after the funeral."

"Sure," I said.

After I'd hung up, I wondered what the hell I was letting myself in for. I wandered into the living room and turned on the radio. It was a gangster programme and I turned it off again.

I thought, I'd make a hell of a gun punk.

Now that I'd had time to think it over, I had an idea what he meant. I was really a little scared.

It was Friday evening, after the inquest. Mom was down at the undertaker's, making final arrangements. I don't know where Gardie was. Probably a movie.

I went to the window and looked out. It was still raining.

In the morning it had stopped.

It was still damp and misty, and it was a hot muggy dampness. I put on my best clothes, of course, for the funeral, and they stuck to me like they were lined with glue.

I'd put my suit coat on, just to be all dressed, but I took it off and hung it up again until nearer time.

I thought, a gun punk. Maybe my uncle is a little nuts. All right, maybe I'm a little nuts too. I'll try it, whatever he wants.

I heard Mom getting up. I went out.

I stood looking at the outside of Heiden's.

After a while, I went in. Mr. Heiden was in his office, in his shirt sleeves, working with some papers. He put down a cigar and said, "Hello. You're Ed Hunter, aren't you?"

"Yes," I said. "I wondered—I just wanted to know if there's anything I can do?"

He shook his head. "Everything's set, kid. Not a thing."

I said, "I didn't ask Mom. Have you got pallbearers and everything?"

"Fellows from the shop where he worked, yes. Here's the list."

He handed me a slip of paper and I read the names. The foreman at the shop, Jake Lancey, was at the top of the list, and three other linotype operators and two hand-men. I hadn't thought about the shop at all. It made me feel a little funny to find they were coming.

He said, "The funeral's at two. Everything's set. We're having an organist."

I nodded. "He liked organ music."

He said, "Sometimes, kid, members of the family would rather—well, take a last look and kind of say good-bye in private. Like now, and not file past the bier at the funeral. Maybe that's why you came in, kid?"

I guess it was. I nodded.

He took me into a room just off one of the halls, not the one where the inquest had been, but one the same size off the other side of the main corridor, and there was a coffin on a bier. It was a beautiful coffin. It was grey plush with chromium trimmings.

He lifted the part of the lid that uncovered the upper part of the body, and then he went out quietly, without saying anything.

I stood looking down at Pop.

After a while, I put the lid down gently, and went out. I closed the door of the little room behind me. I got out of the place without seeing Mr. Heiden again, or anybody.

I started walking east, then south. I walked through the Loop and quite a way out on South State Street.

Then I slowed down and stopped and started back again.

There were a lot of florists' shops in the Loop, and I remembered I hadn't done anything about flowers. I still had money from my pay cheque. I went in one and asked if they could send out some red roses right away for a funeral that would be in a few hours. They said they could.

After that, I stopped for a cup of coffee and then went home. I got there at about eleven.

The minute I opened the door I knew something was wrong.

I knew by the smell. The hot close air was full of whiskey. It smelled like West Madison Street on Saturday night.

My God, I thought. Three hours till the funeral.

I closed the door behind me, and for some reason I locked it. I went to the door of Mom's bedroom and I didn't knock. I opened it and looked in.

She was dressed, wearing the new black dress she must have

bought yesterday. She was sitting on the edge of the bed, and there was a whisky bottle in her hand. Her eyes looked dazed, stupid. They tried to focus on me.

She'd put her hair up, but it had come down again on one side. Her face muscles had gone lax and she looked old. She was drunk as hell.

She swayed a little back and forth.

I was across the room and had the whisky bottle before she knew what was happening. But after I had it, she made a grab at it. She got up to come after it and nearly fell. I pushed her and she fell back on the bed. She started to curse me, and to get up again.

I got to the door, took out the key and put it in on the outside. I locked the door on the outside before she got hold of the knob.

I hoped Gardie was home; she *had* to be home to help me. She could handle Mom better than I could. I had to have help.

I ran into the kitchen first and held the whisky bottle upside down over the sink and let it gurgle out. It seemed to me that the first thing I had to do was to get rid of the whisky.

Mom's voice came from behind the locked door. She was cursing and crying and trying the knob. But she didn't yell and she didn't hammer; thank God she wasn't loud.

The doorknob quit rattling as I put down the empty bottle on the sink.

I started for Gardie's room and then there was another sound that stopped me cold.

It was a window going up. The window from Mom's bedroom into the airshaft.

She was going to jump.

I ran back and got hold of the key to unlock the door. It stuck a little, but the window was sticking too. That window had always stuck, had always been hard to open. I could hear her struggling with it. She was just sobbing, not cursing or crying.

I got the door open and got there just as she was trying to go through. She'd got the window open only a little over a foot and it had stuck there, but she was trying to crawl through.

I yanked her back and she reached for my face to scratch me.

There was only one thing. I hit her on the chin, hard. I managed to catch her before she fell too hard. She was out cold.

I stood there a minute, trying to get my breath back, and trembling, cold clammy wet with sweat in that hot and stinking room.

Then I went for Gardie.

She'd slept through it. Somehow she'd slept through it. It was eleven o'clock and she was still sound asleep.

I shook her and she opened her eyes and then sat up. Her arms folded across her breasts in sudden modesty because she wasn't awake enough yet to be immodest and her eyes went wide.

I said, "Mom's drunk. Three hours to the funeral. Hurry up."

I handed her a wrapper or robe or whatever it was off the back of a chair and hurried out. Her footsteps came right behind me.

I said, "In her bedroom. I'll get the water going." I went into the bathroom and turned on the cold water in the tub. I turned it on all the way; it would splash out for a while while the tube was empty, but to hell with that.

Back in the bedroom, Gardie had gone right to work. She was taking off Mom's shoes and stockings.

She asked, "How did she do it? Where were you?"

I said, "I was out from eight till just now. She must have got up about the time I left and gone right down and bought the bottle. She's had a full three-hour start."

I took Mom's shoulders and Gardie took her knees and we got her on the bed and started working her dress off over her head.

I got worried about something. I said, "She's got another slip she can wear, hasn't she?"

"Sure. Think we can get her around in time?"

"We got to. Leave her slip on then. The hell with it. Come on; we'll walk her to the bathroom."

She was a dead weight. We couldn't walk her. We had to half-carry half-drag her, finally, but we got her there.

The tub was full by then. Getting her into it was the hardest part. Gardie and I both got pretty wet, too. But we got her in.

I told Gardie, "Keep her head out. I'll start some coffee and make it thick as soup."

Gardie said, "Open a window in her room and let that smell out."

I said, "I did. I opened a window to air it out."

I turned on the fire under the kettle and put coffee in the pot ready to pour water through. I put in as much as it would hold, way up to the top.

I ran back to the bathroom. Gardie had tied a towel around Mom's hair and was splashing cold water in her face. She was waking up. She was moaning a little and trying to move her head to get away from the splashing water. She was shivering, and her arms and shoulders were covered with goose flesh from the cold water.

Gardie said, "She's coming around. But I don't know—My God, Eddie, three hours—"

"A little less," I said. "Listen, when she comes to, you can help her out of the tub and help her dry off. I'm going down to the drugstore. There's some stuff. I don't know what you call it."

I went in my room and quickly put on a dry shirt and pair of pants. I'd have to wear my everyday suit to the funeral, but that couldn't be helped.

When I went by the bathroom the door was closed and I could hear Gardie's voice and Mom's. It was thick and fuzzy, but it wasn't hysterical and she wasn't cursing or anything. Maybe we can do it in time, I thought.

The coffee water was boiling. I poured it in the dripolator top and put a low head of fire under the dripolator to keep it hot.

I went down to Klassen's drugstore. I figured I'd do better to level with him, because I knew him and I knew he wouldn't talk about it. So I told him enough of the truth.

"We got proprietary stuff," he said. "It's not so hot. I'll fix you something."

"Her breath, too," I said. "She'll have to be close to people at the funeral. You got to give me something for that."

We did it. We got her straightened out.

The funeral was beautiful.

I didn't mind it, really. It wasn't exactly Pop's funeral to me. When I'd been alone with him, there in the little room, well, that was it, as far as I was concerned. I'd said good-bye to him, sort of, then.

This was just something you had to go through with, on account of other people and out of respect for Pop.

I sat on one side of Mom, and Gardie on the other. Uncle Ambrose sat next to me on the other side.

After the funeral, Jake, the foreman from the shop, came up to me. He said, "You're coming back, aren't you, Ed?"

"Sure," I said. "I'm coming back."

"Take as long as you want. Things are slow right now."

I said, "I've got something I want to do, Jake. Would a week or two weeks be all right?"

"As long as you want. Like I said, we're slack now. But don't change your mind about coming back. It won't be the same, working there, without your dad. But you're getting a good start at a good trade. We want you back."

"Sure," I said. "I'm coming back."

He said, "There's some stuff in your dad's locker. Shall we send it over to your place, or do you want to drop in and get it?"

"I'll drop in and get it." I said. "I want to pick up the cheque I've got coming for three days, too. Dad's got one too; Monday through Wednesday."

"I'll tell the office to have 'em both made out and ready for you, Ed," Jake said.

After the cemetery, after they'd thrown dirt on the coffin, Uncle Ambrose came home with us.

We sat around and there wasn't much to say. Uncle Ambrose

suggested we play some cards, and he and Mom and I played for a little while. We played rummy.

When he left, I walked out in the hall with him. He said, "Take it easy this evening, kid. Rest up and get set for action. And look me up at the hotel tomorrow afternoon."

"Okay," I told him. "But isn't there anything I can do this evening?"

"Nope," he said. "I'm seeing Bassett, but no reason for you to go along. I'm going to put a bug in his ear about investigating who lives in those apartments, with their back porches on the alley. He can do the spade work better than we can, and if there's a lead, we'll dig in there, too."

"Too? You mean, Kaufman?"

"Yeah. He was lying about something at the inquest. You saw that, did you?"

"I wasn't sure," I said.

"I was. That's where Bassett missed the boat. But we'll take care of it. Look me up about the middle of the afternoon. I'll wait in my room."

At about seven o'clock, Mom thought it might be a good idea if I took Gardie to a movie, down in the loop maybe.

I thought, why not?

Maybe Mom wanted to be alone. I studied her, without seeming to watch her, while Gardie was looking over the movie ads in the paper. Mom didn't look or act like she was getting ready to drink again.

She sure shouldn't want to, I thought, after this morning. That had been bad, but she'd snapped out of it beautifully. At the funeral she'd talked to people and everything and none of them could have guessed. I didn't think even Uncle Ambrose had guessed what had happened. Nobody but me and Gardie and Klassen, the druggist.

Her eyes had been red and her face puffy, but then they'd have been that way anyway from crying.

She really loved Pop, I thought.

Gardie wanted to go to a show that sounded like a mess of mush to me, but there was a good swing orchestra on the stage, so I didn't argue.

I was right; the picture smelled. But the ork had a brass section that was out of the world. Way out. They had two trombones that knew what it was all about. One of them, the one that took solos, was as good as Teagarden, I thought. Maybe not on the fast stuff, but he had a tone that went down inside you.

I thought, I'd give a million bucks to do that, if I had a million bucks.

The finale was a jump number and Gardie's feet got restless.

She wanted to go somewhere and dance, but I said nix. Going to a show was bad enough, the night of the day of the funeral.

When we got home, Mom wasn't there.

I read a magazine awhile, and then turned in.

I woke up in the middle of the night. There were voices. Mom's, pretty drunk. Another voice that sounded familiar but that I couldn't place.

It was none of my business but I was curious whose voice that was. I finally got out of bed and went to the door where I was closer. But the male voice quit talking and the door closed.

I hadn't heard a word of it, just the voices.

I heard Mom go into her room and close the door. From the way she walked she'd been drinking plenty, but she was under better control than this morning. She hadn't sounded hysterical or anything; the voices had been friendly.

I decided not to worry about the window.

Back in bed, I lay there for a long time thinking, trying to place that voice.

Then I got it. It was Bassett, the homicide dick, with the faded red hair and the faded eyes.

I wonder, I thought. Maybe he thinks she did it, and got her drunk to pump her. I didn't like that.

Maybe that wasn't the reason at all, and I don't know that I liked that any better. If Bassett was on the make, I mean. I remembered he'd said he had a sick wife.

I didn't like either one. And if he was combining business with pleasure, well—that made him more of a Grade A bastard than either one would alone. And I'd liked the guy. Even after he'd taken a bribe from Uncle Ambrose, I'd liked him.

I couldn't get to sleep for a while. I didn't like anything I thought of.

I woke up in the morning with a bad taste in my mouth.

There was still that muggy dampness in the air. I thought, am I going to wake up every morning at seven whether I set that damn alarm or not?

It wasn't until I was up and getting dressed that it occurred to me Bassett might be okay after all. I mean, I could have been wrong on both counts. Mom could have gone out to make the rounds of Clark Street and he could have run into her accidentally and brought her home. For her own good, I mean.

I got dressed and I didn't know what to do.

While I was drinking coffee, Gardie came out into the kitchen.

"Hi, Eddie," she said, "Can't sleep. Might as well get up, huh?"

"Might as well," I agreed.

"Keep some coffee hot, will you?"

"Sure."

She went back to her room and dressed and then came and sat across the table from me. I poured her some coffee and she got a sweet roll from the breadbox.

"Eddie," she said.

"Yeah?"

"What time did Mom get home last night?"

"I don't know."

"You mean you didn't hear her come in at all?" She started to get up, like she was going to Mom's room to be sure she was there.

"She's home," I said. "I heard her come in. I just meant I didn't know what time it was. I didn't look at the clock."

"Pretty late, though?"

"I guess it was. I'd been asleep. She'll probably sleep till noon."

She nibbled at the roll thoughtfully. Always there'd be lipstick on the roll where she'd bitten it. I wondered why she bothered to put on lipstick before she ate breakfast.

"Eddie," she said. "I've got an idea."

"Yeah?"

"Mom drinks too much. If she keeps it up, well—"

There wasn't anything to say to that. I waited to see if there was any more coming. If not, it wasn't a particularly practical idea. I mean, there was nothing we could do about Mom's drinking.

Gardie looked at me with her eyes wide. "Eddie, there was a pint in her dresser drawer a couple of days ago. I took it and hid it and she never missed it. She must've forgot about it."

"Pour it out," I said.

"She'll buy more, Eddie. It costs a dollar forty-nine. And she'll just buy more."

"Then she'll buy more," I said. "So what?"

"Eddie, I'm going to *drink* it."

"You're crazy. My God, you're fourteen, and you—"

"I'm fifteen, Eddie. Next month. That's fifteen. And I have had drinks, on dates. I never got drunk, but—Listen, Eddie, don't you see?"

"Not with a telescope," I said. "You're crazy."

"Eddie, Pop drank too much, too."

"Leave Pop out of it," I told her. "That's over with. Anyway, what the hell's that got to do with your drinking? You mean you think you've got to carry on the family tradition, or something?"

"Don't be dumb, Eddie. What do you think would have stopped Pop drinking?"

I was getting a little mad at her for harping on that. Pop was out of this. Pop was six feet underground.

She said, "I'll tell you what might have stopped Pop, Eddie. If he'd seen you starting the same way. You were always goody-goody. He knew you'd never go haywire, the way he did. I mean, suppose you'd started coming home drunk, too, running with a wild gang—He might have stopped drinking, so you would. He loved you, Eddie. If he thought what he was doing was making you into a——"

"Can it," I said. "Damn it, Pop's dead and why bring up screwy ideas now?"

"Mom isn't dead. Maybe you don't think much of her, but she's my mother, Eddie."

I'd been dumb, sure. It actually took me that long to see what she was driving at.

I just sat there looking at her. There was a chance, maybe an off chance, that it would work. That if Gardie started going haywire that way, it would sort of wake Mom up. She'd lost Pop, but she still had Gardie and she sure as hell wouldn't want to see Gardie getting stinking drunk at fifteen.

Then I thought, the hell with it. That's no way of doing it.

But I had to give Gardie credit for thinking of it. She's been thinking about it, I could see.

"Nuts," I said. "You can't do it."

"The hell I can't, Eddie. I'm going to."

"You're not." But I thought, I can't stop her. She's thought this over and she's going to do it. I could maybe stop her now, but I can't stay around and watch her all the time.

"Now's a good time, Eddie," she said. "When she wakes up at noon with a hangover, she'll find me tight. You think she's going to like that?"

"She'll beat the hell out of you."

"How can she, when she does it herself? She wouldn't beat me anyway. She never did."

Maybe, I thought, it would be better if she had.

I said, "I don't want any part of it." I thought maybe I could get her mad. I said, "It's a gag anyway. You just want to get drunk to see what it's like."

She pushed her chair back. "I'm going to get the bottle. You can make like a goody-goody and take it away and break it. If you do, I'll go down on Clark Street and get drunk. I look older'n I am, and there are plenty of places where they'll buy a girl all the drinks she wants. And they won't be B-drinks."

Her heels clicked towards her room.

Get the hell out of this, Eddie, I told myself. You don't want any part of it. And she can and will get drunk on Clark Street if you stick your oar in. And probably end up at a whorehouse in Cicero. And like it.

I got up but I didn't go out.

I was on the spot. I couldn't stop her drinking, but I'd have to stick around to keep her out of trouble. When she hit a certain stage, she'd sure as hell want to go out. I couldn't let her do that. I was stuck with it.

She came back with the bottle. It had already been opened, she poured herself a drink.

She asked, "Have one, Eddie?"

I said, "I thought this was business."

"You could be sociable."

"I'm not," I told her.

She laughed and drank it down. She grabbed for a glass of water for a chaser, but she didn't choke or anything.

She poured another and then sat down.

She grinned at me. "Sure you don't want to come along?"

I said, "Nuts."

She laughed and drank the other one. She went into the living room and turned on the radio, monkeying with the dials until she got some music. It was good music for that time in the morning.

She said, "Come on, Eddie. Dance with me. It works faster if you dance."

"I don't want to dance."

"Goody-goody."

"Nuts," I said.

I saw it coming.

She took a few fancy pirouettes by herself, to the music, and then came back and sat down. She poured the third one.

"Not so fast," I said. "You can kill yourself guzzling that stuff fast when you're not used to it."

"I've drunk before. Not much, but some." She got another glass and poured some whisky in it. "Come on, Eddie, have just one. Please. It ain't nice to have to drink alone."

"All right," I said. "Just one. I mean it."

She'd picked up her glass and said, "Happy days," and I had to pick up mine and touch the rims. I took just a sip, but she downed hers.

She went back to the radio. She called, "Come on in here, Eddie. Bring the glasses and the bottle."

I went in and sat down. She sat down on the arm of my chair.

"Pour me another, Eddie. This is fun."

"Yeah," I said. I took a sip of my drink while she downed her fourth. She choked a little on that one.

"Eddie," she said, "please dance with me."

The music was good.

I said, "Cut it out, Gardie. Cut it out."

She got up and started to dance by herself to the music, swinging and dipping and swaying around the room.

She said, "Some day I'm going on the stage, Eddie. What do you think? How'm I doin'?"

"You dance swell," I told her.

"Bet I could strip-tease. Like Gypsy Rose. Watch." She reached behind her, as she danced, for the fastening of her dress.

I said, "Don't be a dope, Gardie. I'm your brother, remember?"

"You're not my brother. Anyway, what's that got to do with how I dance? How—"

She was having trouble with the catch. She danced near me. I reached out and grabbed her hand. I said, "Goddam it, Gardie, cut that out."

She laughed and leaned back against me. The pull on her wrist had brought her into my lap.

She said, "Kiss me, Eddie." Her lips were bright red, her body hot against mine. And then her lips were pressing against mine, without my doing anything about it.

I managed to stand up. I said, "Gardie, goddam it, stop. You're only a kid. We *can't*."

She pulled away and laughed a little. "All right, Eddie. All right. Let's have another drink, huh?"

I poured us two drinks. I handed her one. I said, "Here's to Mom, Gardie."

She said, "Okay, Eddie. Anything you say."

This time it was I that choked on it, and she laughed at me.

She took a few more dance steps. She said, "Pour me another, Eddie. Be back in a minute."

She weaved a little on the way through the door.

I poured two drinks and then went over to the radio and fiddled with it. I switched programmes and then switched back again. There wasn't anything else on but plays.

I didn't hear her come back till she said, "Eddie," and then I looked around.

The reason I hadn't heard her come back was that she was barefoot. She was stark naked.

She said, "Am I only a kid, Eddie?" She laughed a little. "Am I only a kid, huh?"

I quit fiddling with the radio. I shut it off.

I said, "You ain't a kid, Gardie. So let's kill the bottle first. Okay? Here's your drink."

I handed it to her and then I went out in the kitchen for water for chasers, and pretended I drank mine while I was out there, and came back with two more.

She said, "I feel—woozy."

"Here," I said. "This is good for it. Bottoms up, Gardie."

I drank that one with her. There was only about one shot left in the bottle; we must have been pouring really stiff ones.

She started to take a dance step towards me, and stumbled. I had to catch her, my arms around her and my hands on her.

I helped her to the sofa. I started back for the bottle. She said, "S'down, Eddie. S'dow. C'm—"

"Sure," I said, "sure. One more drink apiece left. Let's kill it, huh?"

Most of it went on the outside of her, but some got down. She giggled when I wiped off the whisky with my handkerchief.

"Feel woozy, E'ie. Woozy—"

"Close your eyes a minute," I said. "You'll be all right."

A minute was enough. She was all right.

I picked her up and carried her into her room. I found the bottoms of her pyjamas and got them on her, and then I closed the door.

I rinsed out the glasses and put the bottle out of sight in the step-on garbage can.

Then I got the hell out.

CHAPTER SIX

IT WAS ABOUT TWO O'CLOCK when I took the elevator at the Wacker to the twelfth floor, found Uncle Ambrose's room and knocked.

He looked at me closely as he let me in. He asked, "What's wrong, Ed? What you been doing?"

"Nothing," I said. "I've just been walking. Took a long walk."

"Nothing wrong? Where'd you go?"

"Nowhere," I said. "I just walked."

"Exercise?" .

"Cut it out," I said. "Let me alone."

"Sure, kid. I didn't mean to butt in. Sit down and relax."

"I thought we were going out to do something."

"Sure, we are. But there's no rush." He took out a crumpled pack of cigarettes. "Have one?"

"Sure."

We lighted up.

He stared at me through smoke. He said, "You're kind of fed up with everything, aren't you kid? I don't know exactly what set it off, but I might make a guess. One of your women threw a wingding, or maybe both of them. Was it you sobered up Madge for the funeral?"

I said, "You don't have to wear glasses, do you?"

He said, "Kid, Madge and Gardie are what they are. There's nothing you can do about it."

"It's not all Mom's fault," I said. "I guess she just can't help the way she is."

"It's never all anybody's fault, kid. You'll learn that. That goes for Wally. It goes for you. It isn't your fault you're what you are."

"What am I?"

"You're bitter. Black bitter. Not just because of Wally, either. I think it was before that. Kid, go over and take a look out of that window a minute."

His room was on the south side of the hotel. I went over and looked out. It was still foggy, grey. But you could see south to the squat, monstrous Merchandise Mart Building, and between the Wacker and it the ugly west near-north side. Mostly ugly old brick buildings hiding ugly lives.

"It's a hell of a view," I told him.

"That's what I meant, kid. When you look out of a window, when you look at anything, you know what you're seeing? Yourself.

A thing can look beautiful or romantic or inspiring only if the beauty or romance or inspiration is inside you. What you see is inside your head."

I said, "You talk like a poet, not a carney."

He chuckled. "I read a book once," he said. "Look, kid, don't try to label things. Words fool you. You call a guy a printer or a lush or a pansy or a truck driver and you think you've pasted a label on him. People are complicated; you *can't* label 'em with a word."

I was still standing at the window, but I'd turned around to face him. He got up off the bed and came over by me. He turned me around to look out the window again and stood there by me with his hand on my shoulder.

He said, "Look down there, kid. I want to show you another way of looking at it. The way that'll do you some good right now."

We stood there looking down out of the open window into the steaming streets.

He said, "Yeah, I read a book once. You've read this too, but maybe you never really looked at things the way they are, even if you know. That looks like something down there, doesn't it? Solid stuff, each chunk of it separate from the next one and air in between them.

"It isn't. It's just a mess of atoms whirling around and the atoms are just made up of electric charges, electrons, whirling around too, and there's space between them like there's space between the stars. It's a big mess of almost nothing, that's all. And there's no sharp line where the air stops and a building begins; you just think there is. The atoms get a little less far apart.

"And besides whirling, they vibrate back and forth, too. You think you hear noise, but it's just those awful-far-apart atoms wiggling a little faster.

"Look, there's a guy walking down Clark Street. Well, he isn't anything, either. He's just a part of the dance of the atoms, and he blends in with the sidewalk below him and the air around him."

He went back and sat down on the bed. He said, "Keep looking, kid. Get the picture. What you think you see is just bally, a front with the gimmicks all hidden if there are any gimmicks.

"A continuous mess of almost nothing, that's what's really there. Space between molecules. Enough solid, actual matter, if any, to make a chunk about the size of a—a soccer ball."

He chuckled. "Kid," he said. "You going to let a soccer ball kick you around?"

I kept standing there looking for another minute or so. When I turned around he was laughing at me, and I found myself grinning.

"Okay," I said. "Shall we go down and kick Clark Street around for a change?"

"Chicago Avenue. A spot near Orleans. We're going to scare hell out of a guy named Kaufman."

I said. "He's run bar in a tough neighbourhood for a lot of years. What kind of threat would scare a guy like that?"

"None. We're not going to threaten a damn thing. That's what'll scare him stiff. It's the one thing that will."

"I don't get it," I told him. "Maybe I'm dumb, but I don't get it."

"Come on," he said.

"What are we going to do?"

"Nothing. Not a damn thing. Just sit in his place."

I still didn't get it, but I could wait. We went down in the elevator.

As we crossed the lobby, he asked, "Can you use a new suit, Ed?"

"Sure, but I'd better not buy one now. I'm losing time off work."

"It's on me. You need a dark-blue, pin-stripe cut so it'll make you look older. You need the right kind of a hat. It's part of the job, kid, so don't squawk. You got to look like a gun punk."

"Okay," I said. "But I'll owe you for it. Someday I'll pay you."

We got the suit, and it cost forty bucks. That was nearly twice what I'd paid for my last one. Uncle Ambrose was particular about the style; we looked at quite a few before he found the one he wanted.

He told me, "That isn't too good a suit; it won't last very long. But while it's brand new, before it gets dry-cleaned, it looks like an expensive suit. Come on, we get a hat."

We got a hat, a dilly of a snap-brim. He wanted to buy me shoes, but I talked him into settling for a shine; the ones I had were nearly new and looked good once they were shined. We got a rayon shirt that looked like silk, and a snazzy tie.

Back at the hotel, I changed into the new stuff and took a gander at myself in the mirror on the bathroom door.

Uncle Ambrose said, "Wipe off that grin, you dope. It makes you look sweet sixteen."

I straightened out my face. "How's the hat look?"

"Swell. Where'd you get it?"

"Huh? Harzfeld's."

"Try again and think harder. You got it in Lake Geneva the last time I took you up there. We were a little hot then, or we thought we were. We holed out a week till Blane wired us the heat was off. Remember the hat-check girl at the roadhouse?"

"The little brunette?"

He nodded. "Coming back to you now, huh? Sure, she bought you that hat after yours blew out of the car that night. Why shouldn't she? You spent about three hundred bucks on her that week. Hell, you wanted to bring her back to Chi with you."

I said, "I still think I should have. Why didn't I?"

"I told you not to, see? And I'm the boss; get that through your head and keep it there. Kid, you'ld have fried two years ago if I didn't look out for you. I keep you from getting too big for your pants. Sure, I—God-dam it, get that grin off your mug!"

"Yeah, Chief. What would I have fried for?"

"The Burton Bank job for one thing. You're always too quick on the trigger. When that teller reached for the button, you could've shot his arm as easy as killing him; you were only a few feet away."

I said, "The bastard shouldn't reached."

"And the time I had you take care of Swann when he got out of line. What'd you do? Just plug him? No, you had to get fancy about it. Remember that?"

"He got funny. He asked for it."

He looked at me and shook his head. His voice changed. He said, "It ain't bad, Ed. But you're too relaxed. I want you stiff, jumpy. You've got a heater in that shoulder holster and it's loaded. The weight of it there won't let you forget it. Keep that heater on your mind, every minute."

"Sure," I said.

"And your eyes. Ever watched a guy's eyes after he's had about two reefers? And before he's smoked more than that?"

I nodded slowly.

He said, "Then you know what I mean. He's the king of the universe, and he's hot as a G string. But he's like a coiled spring, tied down by a thin thread. He can sit still with a kind of unholy calm, and still make you afraid to touch him with a ten-foot pole."

"I think I got it," I told him.

"Keep your eyes like that. When you look at a guy, you don't glare at him like you want to kill him. That's ham stuff. You just look *through* him like he wasn't there, like you don't give a damn whether you shoot him or not. Look at him like he was a telegraph pole."

"How about tone of voice?" I asked.

"Nuts to tone of voice. Keep your trap shut. Don't even talk to me, unless I ask you something. I'll do the talking and it won't be much."

He looked at his watch and got up off the bed. He said, "It's five o'clock, shank of the morning for this neighbourhood. Let's go."

"Will this take all evening?"

"Maybe longer."

I said, "I want to use your phone, then. It's kind of private. Will you go on down and wait for me in the lobby?"

He said, "Sure, kid," and went on out.

I called home. If Mom had answered I'd have hung up. I didn't want to talk to Mom before I found out what Gardie had told her.

But it was Gardie's voice.

I said, "This is Ed, Gardie. Is Mom around, or can you talk?"

"She went to the store. Oh, Eddie—did I—make an awful fool of myself?"

It was going to be all right.

I said, "Kind of, but let's forget it. You got tight, that's all. But no more, savvy? You try that again and I'll take a hairbrush to you."

She giggled a little. Or it might have been a giggle.

I said, "Does Mom know you drank that whisky?"

"No, Eddie. I woke up first. I felt like hell—I still don't feel so good. But I managed not to show it—Mom woke up feeling awful herself, so she didn't notice. I told her I had a headache."

"What happened to that bright idea about teaching her a lesson?"

"I forgot, Eddie. I clean forgot. I felt so lousy all I thought about was keeping out of Mom's way. I just couldn't have stood her bawling me out, or crying, or whatever she'd've done."

"Okay," I said. "So forget the idea permanently. *Both* ideas, if you know what I mean. You remember what you did when you were drunk?"

"N-not exactly, Eddie. What *did* I do?"

"Don't kid me," I said. "You remember all right."

Unmistakably, this time, it was a giggle.

I gave up. I said, "Listen, tell Mom I won't be home till late, probably, but not to worry. I'll be with Uncle Am. I might even stay with him over night. So long."

I hung up before she could ask any questions.

Going down in the elevator, I tried to get my mind back in the groove. Uncle Ambrose had been right in picking the clothes and the hat. I looked twenty-two or twenty-three in the elevator mirror, and I looked like I'd been around.

I stiffened up, and made my eyes hard.

My uncle nodded approvingly as I walked across the lobby toward him.

He said, "You'll do, kid. Damn if I'm not a little leary of you myself."

We walked north to Chicago Avenue and turned west. We went past the police station. I kept my eyes straight in front.

As we crossed diagonally over at Chicago and Orleans, heading for the Topaz beer sign, my uncle said, "All I want you to do is this, Ed. Don't talk. Watch Kaufman. Follow my leads."

"Sure," I said.

We went into the tavern. Kaufman was drawing beers for two men at the bar. There was a man and woman sitting in a booth at the side; they looked married. The two men at the bar looked a little drunk in a sleepy sort of way, like they'd been drinking beer all afternoon. They were together, but weren't talking.

Uncle Ambrose headed for a table at the back, sitting so he could face the bar. I pulled a chair to one side of the table, so I could face the same way.

I watched Kaufman.

He wasn't, I thought, particularly pleasant to look at. He was short and heavy-set, with long arms that looked powerful. He looked about forty or forty-five. He wore a clean white shirt with the sleeves rolled to the elbows, and his arms were hairy as a monkey's. His hair was slicked back and glossy, but he needed a shave. He still wore the thick-lensed glasses.

He rang up twenty cents on the register for the two beers he'd just drawn and then came around the end of the bar and approached our table.

I kept my eyes on him, studying him, weighing him.

He looked tough, like a guy able to handle himself in trouble. But then most bartenders in this part of town look like that; or they wouldn't be bartenders here.

He said, "What's it, gents?"

His eyes happened to fall on mine, and I locked them there. I remembered orders. I didn't move a muscle, not even a muscle of my face. But I thought, "You son of a bitch, I'd just as soon kill you as not."

Uncle Ambrose was saying, "White soda. Two glasses of plain white soda."

His eyes slid off mine and looked at my uncle. He looked doubtful, not knowing whether to take it for a joke and laugh, or not.

Uncle Ambrose didn't laugh. He said, "Two glasses of white soda."

He dropped a bill on the table.

Kaufman managed somehow to seem to shrug his shoulders without really doing it. He took the bill and went behind the bar. He came back with the two glasses and change.

"Anything for a wash?" he wanted to know.

Uncle Ambrose deadpanned him. He said, "When we want something else, we'll let you know."

Kaufman went back of the bar again.

We sat there and didn't do anything and didn't talk. Once in a long while Uncle Ambrose took a sip of his white soda.

The two men at the bar went out and another group, three this time, came in. We didn't pay any attention to them. We watched Kaufman; I don't mean we didn't take our eyes off him for a second, but in general we just sat there watching him.

You could see, after a while, that it began to puzzle him, and that he didn't like it a damn bit.

Two more men came in, and the couple sitting in the booth left.

At seven o'clock a bartender came on duty. A tall, skinny man who smiled a lot and showed a lot of gold teeth when he did. When he went behind the bar, Kaufman came over to our table.

"Two more white sodas," my uncle said.

Kaufman looked at him a moment, then he picked up the change my uncle put on the table and went behind the bar to refill our glasses. He came back and put them down without a word. Then he took off his apron, hung it on a hook and went out the back door of the tavern.

"Think he's going for the cops?"

My uncle shook his head. "He isn't that worried yet. He's going out to eat. Think that's a good idea?"

"Good Lord," I said. I just remembered that this was another day I'd practically gone without eating. Now that I thought of it, I was hungry enough to eat a cow.

We waited a few minutes longer and then went out the front way. We walked over to Clark Street and ate at the little chili joint a block south of Chicago. They make the best chili there of any place in town.

We took our time about eating. While we were drinking coffee, I asked, "We going back there tonight?"

"Sure. We'll get back by nine and stay till about twelve. He'll be getting jittery by then."

"Then what?"

"We help him jitter."

"Look," I said. "What if he does call copper? Yeah, there's nothing illegal about sitting a few hours over white soda, but if the cops get called, they'll want to ask questions."

"The cops are squared. Bassett's talked to the looie who'd get the call at the Chicago station. He'll tip off whatever coppers he sends in answer to the call, if he sends any."

I said, "Oh." I began to see about the hundred bucks. This was the first dividend, unless you counted that Bassett had said he'd canvass the buildings that had back porches on the alley. Maybe he'd have done that anyway, but squaring something like this was definitely in the line of extra service.

After we ate we went to a quiet little place off Clark Street on Ontario and had a beer apiece and a lot of conversation.

We talked about Pop mostly.

"He was a funny kid, Ed," Uncle Ambrose told me. "He was

two years younger than me, you know. He was wild as a colt. Well, I had itchy feet, too. I still have; that's why I'm a carney. You like to travel, Ed?"

"I think I would," I said. "I never had much chance up to now."

"Up to now? Hell, you're just a pup. But about Wally. He ran away from home when he was sixteen. That was the year our dad got a stroke and died suddenly; our mother had died three years before.

"I knew Wally'd write sooner or later, so I stuck around St. Paul until I got a letter from him, addressed to both me and Dad. He was in Petaluma, California. He owned a little newspaper there; he'd won it in a poker game."

"He never told me about that," I said.

My uncle chuckled. "He didn't have it long. He was gone by the time my wire went out in answer to his letter. I'd told him I was coming, but when I got there he was wanted by the police. Oh, nothing too serious; just a hell of a swell criminal libel action. He was too honest to run a newspaper. He'd come out with the flat, unvarnished truth about one of Petaluma's leading citizens. Probably just for the hell of it; anyway, that's what he told me later and I believed him."

He grinned at me. "It was a swell excuse for me to go on the road awhile, to look for him. I knew he'd head out of California, because the libel business wasn't something they were going to extradite him for, but he'd get out of the state. I picked up his trail in Phoenix, and I was just behind him several places before I ran into him in a gambling joint across the border from El Paso, in Juarez. Juarez was a wild and woolly spot in those days, kid. You should have seen it."

"I suppose he lost whatever he'd pulled out of the newspaper?"

"Huh? Oh, he'd lost that long before. He was working at the gambling joint. Dealing blackjack. He was fed up with Juarez by the time I got there, so he quit the dealing. He was picking up Mex and wanted me to head with him for Veracruz.

"Kid, that was a trip. Veracruz is a good twelve or thirteen hundred miles from Juarez and it took us four months to make it. We left Juarez with a stake of, I think, eighty-five bucks between us. But that changed into about four hundred bucks Mex, and while it wasn't much on the border, it made you rich when you got a hundred or so miles in, if you talked the lingo and didn't get yourself into the sucker joints.

"We were rich for half of that four months, nigger rich. Then in Monterrey we ran into some guys that were smarter than we were. We should have headed back for the border then, for Laredo, but we'd decided on Veracruz and we kept going. We got there on foot, in Mex clothes, what there was of them, and we hadn't had a peso between us in three weeks. We'd damn near forgotten how to talk English; we jabbered spik even to each other, to get better at it.

"We got jobs in Veracruz and straightened out. That's where your dad picked up linotype, Ed. A Spanish-language paper run by a German who had a Swedish wife and who'd been born in Burma. He needed a man who was fluent in both English and Spanish—he didn't speak much English himself—so he taught Wally how to run his linotype and the flat-bed press he printed the paper on."

I said, "I'll be damned."

"What now?"

I laughed a little. I said, "I took Latin in high school. Pop suggested Spanish when I started taking a language and said he could help me with it. I thought he remembered a little from having taken it in school himself. I never realized he could *talk* it."

Uncle Ambrose looked at me very seriously, as though he were thinking, and didn't say anything for a while.

I asked after a while, "Where did you go from Veracruz?"

"I went to Panama; he stayed in Veracruz for a while. There was something about Veracruz that he liked."

"Did he stay there long?"

"No," said my uncle shortly. He glanced up at the clock. "Come on, kid, we better get back to Kaufman's."

I looked at the clock too. I said, "We got time. You said we'd get back at nine. If there was something about Veracruz he liked, and he had a job, why didn't he stay there long?"

Uncle Ambrose looked at me for a moment and then his eyes twinkled a little. He said, "I don't suppose Wally would mind your knowing now."

"All right, give."

"He had a duel, and he won. The thing he liked about Veracruz was the wife of the German who ran the newspaper. The German challenged him to a duel, with Mausers, and he couldn't get out of it. He won the duel all right; hit the German in the shoulder and put him in the hospital. But Wally had to get out of there quick. And privately, in the cargo hold of a tramp steamer. I learned from him later what happened. They caught him four days out and he had to work his passage swabbing decks when he was so seasick he couldn't stand up. Wally never could stand the sea. But he couldn't jump ship till they docked for the first time. That was in Lisbon."

"You're kidding me," I said.

"Nope. Fact, Ed. He was in Spain awhile. Had a screwy idea he wanted to learn to be a matador, but he couldn't get an in; you got to start at that trade really young and have some pull even then. Besides, the picador part disgusted him."

"What's a picador?" I asked.

"The lancemen, on horseback. Horses get gored almost every fight. They fill 'em with sawdust and sew 'em so they can go back in. They won't live anyhow, once they're deeply gored, and so—Hell, skip it; I always hated that part of bullfighting myself. Last card I saw though, down in Juarez a few years ago, they pad the horses and that part's okay. A clean kill of the bull with the sword; that's all right. It's better than they do in the stockyards here, for that matter. They use a—"

"Let's stick to Pop," I suggested. "He was in Spain."

"Yeah. Well, he came back. We finally got in touch with one another through a friend back in St. Paul we both happened to write to. I was with a detective agency then—Wheeler's, out in L.A.—and Wally was in vaudeville. He used to be pretty good at juggling—oh, not a top act, even as jugglers go, but he was good with the Indian clubs. Good enough for a spot with a fair troupe. He ever juggle any lately?"

"No," I said. "No, he didn't."

"You got to keep up on something like that, or you lose it. But he was always good at anything with his hands. He used to be a swift on the linotype. Was he still?"

"Average speed is all," I said. I thought of something. "Maybe it was because he had arthritis in his hands and arms for a while, quite a few years ago. He couldn't work at all for a few months, and maybe that slowed him down from then on. That was while we were in Gary, just before we moved from Gary to Chicago."

Uncle Ambrose said, "He never told me that."

I asked, "Did you and he ever get together again, outside of visits, I mean?"

"Oh, sure. I was in dutch with the shamus outfit already, so I quit and Wally and I travelled together with a medicine show. He did juggling and stuff, in blackface."

"Can you juggle?"

"Me, no. Wally was the one who could use his hands. Me, I make with the mouth. I did spieling, and put on a vent act."

I must have looked pretty blank.

He grinned at me. "Ventriloquism, to you mooches. Come on, kid, we really got to move on. If you want the story of my life and Wally's, you can't have it in one sitting when we got a spot of work ahead. It's almost nine now."

I walked over to Kaufman's in a sort of a daze.

I'd never known that Pop had been anything but a linotype operator. I just couldn't think of him as a wild kid, bumming across

Mexico, having a duel, wanting to be a bullfighter in Spain, juggling with a medicine show, being part of a vaudeville troupe.

All that, I thought, and he died in an alley, drunk.

CHAPTER SEVEN

KAUFMAN'S PLACE WAS BUSIER. There were half a dozen men and two women at the bar, couples in two of the booths, and a pinochle game at a back table. The juke box was blaring.

Our table, though, was empty. We sat just as we had before. Kaufman was busy at the bar; he didn't see us come in or sit down.

He saw us, and met our eyes watching him, a minute or so later. He was pouring whiskey into a jigger glass in front of a man at the bar and the whiskey came up over the rim of the glass and made a little puddle on the varnished wood.

He rang up the sale, then came around the end of the bar and stood in front of us, hands on his hips and looking belligerent and undecided at the same time.

He pitched his voice low. "What do you guys want?"

Uncle Ambrose took it deadpan. There wasn't a trace of humour in his face or in his voice. He said, "Two white sodas."

Kaufman took his hands off his hips and wiped them slowly on his apron. His eyes went from my uncle's face to mine and I gave him the flat, level stare.

He didn't meet it long. He looked back at Uncle Ambrose.

He pulled out a chair and sat down. He said, "I don't want any trouble here."

Uncle Ambrose said, "We don't like trouble either. We don't want any. We wouldn't make any."

"You want *something*. Wouldn't it be a lot easier if you levelled?"

"About what?" my uncle asked.

The tavern-owner's lips went together tight for a second. He looked like he was going to get mad.

Then his voice was calmer than before. He said, "I've placed you. You were at the inquest on that guy that got slugged in an alley."

My uncle asked, "What guy?"

Kaufman took in a deep breath and let it out slowly. He said, "Yeah, I'm sure. You were in the back row, trying to keep outa sight. You a friend of this Hunter guy, or what?"

"What Hunter guy?"

Kaufman looked like he was going to get mad again, then he pulled in his horns.

He said, "Lemme save you trouble. Whatever you want, it ain't here. I ain't got it. I levelled with the coppers and at the inquest. I don't know a damn thing about it I didn't tell 'em. And you heard it; you was there."

My uncle didn't say anything. He took out a pack of cigarettes and handed it toward me. I took one, and he held it out to Kaufman. Kaufman ignored it.

Kaufman said, "It's all on the level. So what you coming in here for? What the hell do you want?"

Uncle Ambrose didn't bat an eyelash. He said, "White soda. Two glasses."

Kaufman stood up so suddenly that the chair he'd been sitting on went over backwards. Redness was spreading upward from his neck. He turned around and picked up the chair, pushing it back under the table carefully, as though its exact position there was a matter of importance.

He went back of the bar without saying another word.

A few minutes later the bartender, the tall skinny guy, brought our white sodas. He grinned cheerfully and my uncle grinned back. The little wrinkles of hell-with-it laughter were back around the corners of his eyes and he didn't look deadly at all.

Kaufman wasn't looking our way; he was busy at the other end of the bar.

"No Mickey?" Uncle Ambrose asked him.

"No Mickey," said the bartender. "You couldn't make a Mickey with plain white soda so it wouldn't taste."

"That's what I figured," said my uncle. He handed the slim guy a dollar bill. "Keep the change, Slim, for the baby's bank."

"Sure, thanks. Say, the kid was nuts about you, Am. Wants to know when you'll be out again."

"Soon, Slim. Better run along before his nibs sees us talking."

The bartender went back to the pinochle table to take their order.

I asked, "When did all this happen?"

"Last night. His evening off. Got his name and address from Bassett and went calling. He's on our side now."

"Another hundred bucks?"

My uncle shook his head. "There are guys you can buy, kid, and guys you can't. I managed to put a little silver in his kid's bank."

"Then that wasn't a gag about the kid's bank—I mean, about keeping the change out of the buck?"

"Hell, no. That's exactly where that change will go."

"I'll be damned," I said.

Kaufman was coming to the near end of the bar again, and I shut up and went back to watching him. He didn't look our way again.

We stayed there until a little after midnight. Then we got up and walked out.

When I got home, Mom and Gardie were asleep. There was a note from Mom asking me to wake her whenever I got up, because she wanted to start looking for a job.

I was tired, but I had trouble getting to sleep. I kept thinking about what I'd learned about Pop.

When he was my age, I thought, he'd owned and run a newspaper. He'd had a duel and shot a man. He'd had an affair with a married woman. He'd travelled across most of Mexico afoot and spoke Spanish like a native. He'd crossed the Atlantic and lived in Spain. He'd dealt blackjack in a border town.

When he was my age, I thought he'd been in vaudeville and was travelling with a medicine show.

I couldn't picture Pop in blackface. I couldn't picture any of the rest of it, either. I wondered what he'd looked like then.

But when I slept, finally, I didn't dream about Pop. I dreamed about me, and I was a matador in a bull ring in Spain. I had black grease paint on my face and a rapier in my hand. And, mixed up like dreams are mixed up, the bull was a real bull—a huge black bull—and yet he wasn't. Somehow, he was a tavern owner named Kaufman.

He came running at me and his horns were a yard long, with points as sharp as needles, and they gleamed in the sunlight, and I was scared, scared as hell. . . .

We went back to the tavern at three o'clock the next afternoon. Uncle Ambrose had learned that was about the time Kaufman came on. Slim went off duty then, and came back later in the evening when things got busy enough to need two men.

Kaufman was just tying on his apron, and Slim must have just left, when we walked into the place.

He just glanced at us casually, as though he expected us.

There wasn't anyone else there; just Kaufman and us. But there was something in the atmosphere, something besides the smell of beer and whisky.

There's going to be trouble, I thought.

I was scared, as scared as I'd been in my dream last night. I thought of it then, the dream.

We sat down at the table. The same table.

Kaufman came back. He said, "I don't want trouble. Why don't you guys move along?"

My uncle said, "We like it here."

"Okay," Kaufman said. He went back of the bar and came back with two glasses of white soda. My uncle gave him twenty cents.

He went back of the bar and started polishing glasses. He didn't look toward us. Once he dropped a glass and broke it.

A little later the door opened and two men came in.

They were big guys and they looked tough. One of them was an ex-pug; you could tell by his ears. He had a bullet head and shoulders like an ape. He had little pig eyes.

The other one looked small, standing by the big guy. But only by contrast; a second look told you he was five-eleven or so, and would go one-eighty stripped. He had a face like a horse.

They stopped just inside the door and looked the place over. Their eyes took in all the booths and saw they were empty. They looked everywhere except at us. My uncle moved in his chair, shifted his feet.

Then they went over to the bar.

Kaufman put two shot glasses in front of them and filled the glasses without their having said a word.

That was a give-away, if there'd been any need for one.

There was a growing cold feeling in the pit of my stomach. I wondered if my legs would wobble if I stood up.

I glanced out of the corner of my eye at Uncle Ambrose. His face was perfectly still, his lips weren't moving, but he was talking, just loud enough that I could hear him. It surprised me for a moment that his mouth didn't move, until I remembered the vent business.

He said, "Kid, I can handle this better alone. You go back to the can. There's a window; get out of it and scram. Right now; soon as they've had a drink, they'll make a play."

He was lying, I knew. Unless he was heeled there wasn't a way on earth he could handle this. And he wasn't heeled, any more than I was.

I thought, I'm the one that's supposed to be heeled. I'm the gun punk. I've got a new suit that looks like a hundred bucks and a new snap-brim hat. And I've got an imaginary thirty-eight automatic, with the safety catch off. It's in a shoulder holster on my left shoulder.

I stood up, and my legs weren't rubber.

I walked around back of Uncle Ambrose's chair and started for the door of the men's room, but I didn't go there. I stopped short right at the end of the bar, and stood there where I could watch up the bar, front and back.

I'd brought up my right hand and let it rest with the fingers just inside my coat, touching the butt of the thirty-eight automatic that wasn't there.

I didn't say anything; I just looked at them. I didn't tell them to keep their hands on the bar, but they kept them there.

I watched all three of them. Most of all I watched Kaufman's eyes. He'd have a gun back of the bar somewhere. I watched his eyes till I knew where it was. I couldn't see it from where I stood, but I knew now just where he kept it.

I asked, "You guys want anything?"

It was the horse-face one that answered. He said, "Not a thing, pal. Not a thing."

He turned his head to Kaufman. He said, "Nuts to you, George. For ten apiece we should play for keeps?"

I looked at Kaufman. I said, "It was a dirty trick, George. Maybe you should move up the bar a few steps."

He hesitated, and I let my hand slide another inch inside my coat.

He took three slow steps backwards.

I walked behind the bar and picked up his gun. It was a short-barrelled thirty-two revolver on a thirty-eight frame. A nice gun.

I swung out the cylinder and let the cartridges drop into dirty dishwater in one of the sinks built in back of the bar. I dropped the gun in after them.

I turned around to pick a bottle off the back bar. In the mirror I caught Uncle Ambrose's eye. He was sitting there at the table, grinning like a Cheshire cat. He winked at me.

The most expensive stuff I could see was a bottle of Teacher's Highland Cream.

"On the house, boys," I said. I poured them each a shot.

Horse-face grinned at me. He said, "You wouldn't want to give us our ten apiece outa the register, would you, pal? I figure we got it coming, from the dirty trick George played on us."

My uncle had stood up and was strolling over to the bar. He came in between Horse-face and the big guy. He looked tiny, standing there between them.

He said, "Let me," and took out his wallet. He took out two tens and gave one to each of the men on either side of him. He said, "You're right, fellas. I wouldn't want to see you rooked on this deal."

Horse-face stuffed the bill into his pants pocket. He said, "You're a right guy, mister. We'd just as soon earn this. Like us to?"

He looked at Kaufman, and the bigger guy looked at Kaufman, too. Kaufman started to get pale and took another step backwards.

"Nope," my uncle said. "We like George. We wouldn't want anything to happen to George. Give us another shot around, Ed."

I filled their glasses with the Highland Cream, and I put out two more shot glasses and solemnly put three-quarters of an ounce of white soda in each of them.

"Don't forget George," Uncle Ambrose said. "Maybe George will drink with us."

"Sure," I said.

I took a fifth shot glass and carefully filled it with white soda. I slid it along the bar towards Kaufman.

He didn't pick it up.

The other four of us drank.

Horse-face said, "You're sure you don't want us to—"

"Nope," my uncle said. "We like George. He's a nice guy when you get to know him. You boys better run along now. The copper on this beat'll be along soon. He might look in."

Horse-face said, "George wouldn't squawk," and he looked at Kaufman.

We had one more drink around, and then the two muscle-boys went out. It was very chummy.

My uncle grinned at me. He said, "You ring it up for George, Ed. You poured six shots of Scotch—figure it at fifty cents a shot. And five white sodas, counting George's." He put a five-dollar bill on the bar. "Ring up three-fifty."

"Right," I said. "We wouldn't want to be obligated to George."

I rang it up and gave Uncle Ambrose a dollar and a half change. I put the five in the register.

We went back to the table and sat down.

We sat there fully five minutes before Kaufman got the idea that it was all over and that we were going to make like it never happened.

At the end of that five minutes a man came in and wanted a beer. Kaufman drew it for him.

Then he came over to our table. He was still a little green about the gills.

He said, "Honest to God, I don't know anything about this Hunter guy's getting bumped off. Just what I told at the inquest."

Neither of us said anything.

Kaufman stood there for a moment, and then he went back of the bar again. He poured himself two fingers of whisky in a tumbler and drank it. It was the first drink I'd seen him take.

We sat there, straight through, until eight-thirty that evening.

A lot of customers came and went. Kaufman didn't take another drink, but he dropped and broke two glasses.

We didn't talk much walking back over Chicago Avenue. While we were eating, my uncle said, "You did swell, Ed. I—Hell, I'll be honest; I didn't think you had it in you."

I grinned at him. I said, "I'll be honest, too. I didn't think so either. Are we going back there tonight?"

"Nope. He's softened up pretty well right now, but we'll skip it till tomorrow. We'll take it from a different tack then. And maybe by tomorrow night we'll put the screws on him."

"You're sure he isn't on the level, that he's holding back something?"

"Kid, he's scared. He was scared at the inquest. I think he knows something; anyway, he's the only lead we got right now. Look, why don't you go home and turn in early? Get some sleep for a change."

"What are you doing?"

"I'm seeing Bassett at eleven. Nothing till then."

"I'll wait and see him too. I couldn't sleep."

"Uh-huh. After-effect. You put yourself in a tight spot back there. Your hand steady?"

I nodded. I said, "But my guts are shaking like a leaf. I was scared stiff, all the time I was doing it. I leaned against the end of the bar so I wouldn't fall over."

"You're probably right about not sleeping," he said, "but there's a couple of hours between now and eleven. How do you want to kill it?"

I said, "Maybe I'll drop in the Elwood Press. I want to pick up the cheques Pop and I have coming— half a week, no, better than half a week, three days is three-fifths of a week."

"Can you get them in the evening?"

"Sure, they're in the foreman's desk and the night foreman has a key. And I can get the stuff out of Pop's locker, and take it home."

"Uh-huh. And listen—there couldn't be any shop angle to your dad's being killed, could there?"

I said, "I don't see how. It's just a printing shop; I mean they don't run off any counterfeit money or anything."

"Well, keep your eyes and your brain open anyway. He have any enemies there? Everybody like him?"

"Yeah, everybody liked him. Oh, he didn't have really close friends there, but he got along all right. He and Bunny Wilson used to see a lot of each other. Not so much since Bunny got put on the night shift and Pop stayed on days. And there's Jake, the day-side foreman. He and Pop were fairly friendly."

"Uh-huh. Well, I'm meeting Bassett at the place on Grand Avenue where we saw him the other night. You be there around eleven if you want to join us."

"I'll be there," I said.

I walked around to the Elwood, on State Street up near Oak. It seemed funny to be going in there after dark, and not to be going to work.

I walked up the dimly lit stairs to the third floor and stood at the door of the composing room, looking in. There were the lino-types along the west side of the room, six of them. Bunny was setting type at the nearest one. There were operators at three of the others.

Pop's was vacant. Not because he wasn't there, I mean, but just because there are fewer operators on nights than there are machines and that one wasn't used. I stood there for a few minutes in the doorway, and nobody noticed me.

Then I saw Ray Metzner, the night foreman, walk across to his desk and I followed him and got there just as he sat down.

He looked up and said, "Hi Ed," and I said, "Hi," back and then both of us seemed stuck for something to say.

Bunny Wilson saw me then and came walking over. He said, "Coming back to work, Ed?"

"Pretty soon," I told him.

Ray Metzner was opening the locked drawer of the desk. He found the cheques and I stuck them in my pocket. He said "You sure look like a million bucks, Ed."

I'd forgotten how I was dressed; it embarrassed me a little, here.

Bunny said, "Look, kid, when you're ready to come back, why don't you ask them to put you on the night shift instead of days? We can use you here, can't we Ray?"

Metzner nodded. He said, "It's an idea, Ed. It's a good shift, pays a little more. And—you're learning keyboard, aren't you?"

I nodded.

He said, "You can get more practice, nights. I mean a couple of machines are always idle. Any time it's slack and we can spare you half an hour or so, you can go over and set for practice."

"I'll think about it," I said. "Maybe I'll do it."

I saw what they meant; I'd miss Pop more on the day side, where I was used to working with him. Maybe they were right, I thought. Anyway, they were nice guys.

"Well," I said, "I'm going back to the lockers; then I guess I'll run along. You got a master key that'll open Pop's, haven't you, Ray?"

"Sure," he said. He took it off his ring of keys and gave it to me.

Bunny said, "Fifteen minutes to lunch time, Ed. I'm going to have a sandwich and coffee down at the corner. Wait and have something with me."

"Just ate," I told him. "But sure, I'll have a cup of Java."

Metzner said, "Go ahead now, Bunny. I'll punch your card for you. I'd join you, but I bring my lunch."

We went back to the lockers. There wasn't anything I wanted out of mine. I opened Pop's. There wasn't anything in it except an old sweater, his line-gauge, and the little black suitcase.

The sweater wasn't worth taking home, but I didn't want to throw it away. I put it and the pica stick in my own locker and took the little suitcase. It was locked, so I didn't try to open it there.

When I got home, I'd find out what was in it. I'd always been mildly curious. It was just a dime-store type of cardboard case, about four inches thick and about twelve by eighteen inches. It had stood on end at the back of his locker ever since I'd been working at Elwood with him.

I'd asked him once what was in it and he'd said, "Just some old junk of mine, Ed, I don't want to leave around home. Nothing important." He hadn't volunteered anything beyond that and I hadn't asked again.

We went downstairs and to the little greasy spoon on the corner of State and Oak. We didn't talk much while he ate a sandwich and a piece of pie.

Then we lighted cigarettes and Bunny asked, "Have they—uh—got the guy yet? The guy that killed your dad?"

I shook my head.

"They don't—uh—They don't suspect anybody, do they, Ed?"

I looked at him.

It was such a hell of a funny way for him to say it. It took me maybe a minute to take that sentence apart and to see through it.

Then I said, "They don't suspect Mom, if that's what you mean, Bunny."

"I didn't mean—"

"Don't be a dope, Bunny. That's what you had to mean, asking it that way. Well, Mom didn't have anything to do with it."

"I know she didn't, Ed. That's what I—Oh, hell, I'm putting my foot in it worse all the time. I should have kept my trap shut completely. I haven't got brains enough to be subtle. I was trying to get information out of you without giving any, and it's going to be the other way around."

"All right, then," I said, "Give."

"Look, Ed, when a guy gets killed, they always suspect his wife unless she's in the clear. Don't make me explain why; they just do. Same when a woman's killed; they automatically suspect her husband first."

I said, "I guess maybe they would. But this was different; this was a straight holdup."

"Sure, but they'll investigate other angles, too. Just in case it isn't what it looks like, see? Well, I know where Madge—your mom—was between twelve and half past one, so she's in the clear. If she'd need an alibi, I could give her one. That's what I meant when I said I knew she didn't do it."

"Where did you see her?"

Bunny said, "I was having a drink or two Wednesday, my night off, and I called up your place about ten to see if Wally was around. And he—"

"I remember now," I said. "I answered the phone and told you he'd already gone out."

"Yeah. So I dropped in several places, thinking I might run into him. I didn't. Only about midnight I was in a place near Grand Avenue; I don't know the name of it. And Madge came in. Said she'd just decided to come down for a nightcap before she went to bed; that Wally hadn't come home yet."

I asked, "Was she mad about it, or anything?"

"I dunno, kid. She didn't seem to be, but you can't tell with a woman. Women are funny. Anyway we had a few drinks and talked, and it was about half past one when I walked her home and then went home myself. I know because I got home at a little before two o'clock.

I said, "It's a good alibi, if she needed one. Only she doesn't, Bunny. Say, was that why you came to the inquest? I wondered at the time why you were there."

"Sure. I wanted to know what time it happened. And everything. At the inquest they didn't even ask Madge whether she'd been in or out that evening. So I knew it was all right, up to then. Haven't they asked her?"

"Not that I know of," I told him. "It just didn't come up at all. I knew she'd been out, because she was still dressed that morning when I went in to wake up Pop, but—"

"Still dressed? Good Lord, Ed, why would she be—"

I wished now I'd kept my yap shut. I'd have to tell him now. I said, "She had a bottle at home and must have kept on drinking, waiting for Pop to come home. Only she went to sleep without undressing.

"Don't the cops know that?"

"I don't know, Bunny." I told him what had happened that morning. I said, "She was starting to get up when I left the place; I heard her. Well, if she changed dresses or had that one off and a bathrobe on when they came, they wouldn't know. If she answered the door the way she was when I left, well, they'd be pretty dumb if they didn't know."

"That's okay then," Bunny said. "If they don't know she was out at all, all right. If they—Well, you see what I mean."

"Sure," I said.

I was a little relieved myself, I found, to know where Mom had been that night and that there really wasn't anything to worry about.

Bunny tried again to lend me money when I left him.

When I went into the tavern, Uncle Ambrose was sitting alone in the booth we had occupied a few nights ago. It still lacked a few minutes of eleven o'clock.

He glanced at me, and then at the suitcase, and his eyes asked the question for him. I told him what it was.

He put it on the table in front of him and then started rummaging in his pockets. He came out with a paper clip and bent part of it straight, then put a little hook on the end.

"You don't mind, Ed?"

"Of course not," I told him. "Go ahead."

The lock was easy. He lifted the lid.

"I'll be damned," I said.

At first glance, it was a puzzling hodgepodge. Then one item after another began to make sense. They wouldn't have made sense to me before my uncle had told me some of the things Pop had done when he was younger.

There was a black, fuzzy wig, the kind that went with a minstrel's blackface make-up. Half a dozen bright-red balls about two and half inches in diameter, the size for juggling. A dagger, in a sheath of Spanish workmanship. A beautifully balanced single-shot target pistol. A black mantilla. A little clay figure of an Aztec idol.

There were other things. You couldn't take them all in at a glance.

There was a sheaf of papers with handwriting on them. There was something wrapped in tissue paper. There was a battered harmonica.

It was Pop's life, I thought, stuffed into a little suitcase. Anyway, one phase of his life. They were things he'd wanted to keep, but not to keep at home where they might have been kicked around or lost, or where he might have to answer questions about them.

A sound made me look up, and Bassett was standing there looking down. "Where'd this stuff come from?" he asked.

"Sit down," my uncle told him. He'd picked up one of the bright-red juggling balls and was looking at it like a man might look into a crystal. His eyes looked kind of funny. Not crying, exactly, but kind of not quite not-crying, either.

Without looking at either me or Bassett, he said, "Tell him, kid," and I told Bassett about the suitcase and where it had been.

Bassett reached over and picked up the sheaf of papers. He turned it around and said, "I'll be damned. It's Spanish."

"Looks like poetry," I said. "That way it's divided into lines. Uncle Am, did Pop ever write poetry in Spanish?"

He nodded without taking his eyes off the red ball.

Bassett was shuffling through the stack and a smaller paper fell out. A little rectangle of new crisp paper, about three by four inches. It was a printed form, but filled in with typewriting and a scribbled signature in ink.

Bassett was sitting next to me and I read it while he did.

It was a premium receipt from an insurance company, the Central Mutual. It was dated less than two months ago and was a quarterly premium receipt on a policy in the name of Wallace Hunter.

I looked at the amount and whistled. The policy was for five thousand bucks. A little notation under "Straight Life Policy" read "Double Indemnity." Ten thousand bucks—or is murder an accidental death?

The name of the beneficiary was shown, too. Mrs. Wallace Hunter.

Bassett cleared his throat and Uncle Ambrose looked up. Bassett passed the premium receipt across the table to him.

"Afraid it's all we need," he said. "A motive. She told me he didn't carry insurance."

Uncle Ambrose read it slowly. He said, "You're crazy. Madge didn't do it."

"She was out that night. She had a motive. She's lied on two counts. I'm sorry, Hunter, but—"

The bartender was standing by the table. He asked, "What's yours, gents?"

CHAPTER EIGHT

"LISTEN," I SAID, when the guy had taken our order and had left. "Mom couldn't have done it. She's got an alibi."

They both looked at me, and Uncle Am's left eyebrow went up half a pica.

I told them about Bunny.

I watched Bassett's face while I told it, but I couldn't tell anything. When I got done, he said, "Maybe. I'll look up the guy. Know where he lives?"

"Sure," I said. I gave him Bunny Wilson's address. "Gets off work at one-thirty in the morning. He might or might not go right home. I dunno."

"All right," he said. "I'll hold off till I talk to this Bunny guy. It might not mean anything, though. He's a friend of the family's—that means of hers, too. He could've stretched the hour a bit to do her a favour."

"Why would he?"

Bassett shrugged. The kind of a shrug that doesn't mean you don't know, but that it's nothing you want to talk about.

It told plenty. I said, "Listen, damn y—"

Uncle Am put his hand on my arm. He had a grip.

He said, "Shut up, Ed. Take yourself a walk around the block and cool down."

His grip got tight and it hurt.

He said, "Go ahead. I mean it."

Bassett got up to let me out of the booth, and I got up and went out fast. The hell with them I thought.

I went out and walked west on Grand.

It wasn't until I started to take out a cigarette that I found I had something in my hand. It was a round, red, rubber ball. Bright shiny red, one of the half dozen that had been in the suitcase.

I stopped by the staircase leading up to the el, and stared at the ball in my hand. Something was coming back to me. A vague picture of a man juggling some of them. I'd been a baby then. He was laughing and the bright balls were flashing in the lamplight of the nursery room in the Gary flat and I stopped crying to watch the whirling spheres.

Not once, but often. How old had I been? I remember I'd been walking, once at least, walking, reaching out for the bright balls, and he'd given me one to play with, and had laughed when I put it to my mouth to chew it.

I couldn't have been over three—not much over, anyway—the last time I'd seen them. I'd forgotten completely.

Only this ball in my hand, the size and the feel and the brightness of it, brought back the lost memory.

But the man, the juggler—I couldn't picture him at all.

Only laughter, and the bright flashing spheres.

I tossed it up and caught it, and it felt good. I wondered if I could learn to juggle six of them. I tossed it up again.

Somebody laughed and said, "Want some jacks?"

I caught the ball and put it in my pocket, and turned around.

It was Bobby Reinhart, the apprentice at Heiden's Mortuary, the guy who had identified Pop when he'd come to work on Thursday morning and found the body there. He was wearing a white Palm Beach suit that set off his darkish skin and his grease-slicked black hair.

He was grinning. It wasn't a nice grin. I didn't like it.

I said, "Did you say something?"

The grin faded out, and his face got ugly.

That was lovely. I just hoped he'd say something. I looked at his face and thought of him being with Gardie and I thought of his having seen Pop there in the mortuary and maybe working on the body, or watching while Heiden did, and—Oh, hell, if it had been somebody else, it would have been different. But when you don't like a guy to begin with, something like this happens, and you hate him.

He said, "What the hell are you getting—?" And he was reaching his right hand into the inside pocket of his Palm Beach coat.

Maybe he was reaching for a cigarette; I didn't know. He'd hardly have been reaching for a gun, out here in the open, even if there was nobody within half a block. But I didn't wait to find out. Maybe I was just looking for an excuse.

I grabbed him by the shoulder and whirled him around, and I had hold of his right wrist from behind, twisting it. He made a noise that was half-cursing, half-squawking, and something hit the concrete with a metallic clink.

I let go of his wrist and got the back of the collar of his coat. I jerked to keep him from stooping down, and as our shadows got out of the way, I could see the thing on the sidewalk was a set of brass knucks.

He gave a hell of a hard lunge to get away and the cloth of the coat tore in my hands. It ripped all the way down the back, and the right side of what was left of it fell down from his shoulder, and a notebook and a billfold fell out of the inside pocket.

He was backed up against the building now, and he looked

undecided. He wanted to take me apart, I could tell, but without those brass knucks, he knew he couldn't do it. And that torn coat was in his way.

He stood there, panting, ready if I came for him, not daring to try to pick up the things that had fallen from his coat, not willing to run away without them.

I gave the knucks a kick that sent them halfway across the street, and then took a step back. I said, "Okay, pick up your marbles and scram. Open your yap and I'll knock your teeth out."

His eyes said plenty, but his mouth didn't dare to. He came forward to get the stuff, and I looked down at it, and said. "*Wait a minute*," and reached down and picked up the billfold before he did.

It was Pop's wallet.

It was tooled leather, a nice one, and almost new. But there was a diagonal scratch across the polished leather. That scratch had been from the sharp corner of a hard-metal linotype slug. The wallet had happened to be lying on Pop's stand at the lino, and he'd let some slugs slide off a galley onto it. I'd been there.

I heard a car swinging in to the curb, and Bobby took a look past me and started running. I started after him, shoving the wallet into my pocket. A voice yelled "Hey—" The car started up again.

I caught him as he was trying to cut through a vacant lot, and was beating the hell out of him when the car and the squad coppers got there, and one of them got each of us. One caught my coat from in back, pulled me away from Bobby Reinhart, and slammed me alongside the face with the flat of his hand.

"Break it up, punks," he said. "Down to the station for you."

I wanted to kick out backward, but that wouldn't do any good.

I gulped air as we were headed for the squad car until I had enough of my mind back to talk, and then I started to talk fast.

"This isn't just a fight," I said. "This is part of a murder case. Bassett of Homicide is in a tavern two blocks east of here. Take us there; Bassett'll want this guy."

The copper that had me was running his hands over the outside of my pockets. He said. "Tell it down at the station."

The other one said, "There's a Homicide dick named Bassett. What case is it, kid?"

"My father," I said. "Wallace Hunter. Killed in an alley off Franklin Street last week."

He said, "There was a guy killed there." He looked at the copper that had me, and shrugged. He said. "We can look there. Two blocks. If it *is* a homicide case—"

We got in the car, and they didn't take any chances on us. They collared us again when they marched us into the tavern. It made quite a parade.

Bassett and Uncle Am were still in the booth. They looked up and neither of them showed any surprise.

The copper who knew Bassett beat me to the punch. He said, "We found these punks fighting. This one said you'd be interested. Are you?"

Bassett said, "I could be. You can let go of him, anyway. What is it, Ed?"

I took the wallet out of my pocket and tossed it on the table of the booth. I said, "Pop's wallet. This son of a bitch had it."

Bassett picked up the wallet and opened it. There were a few bills in it. One five and several singles. He looked at the identification card under the celluloid and then looked up at Bobby.

"Where'd you get it, Reinhart?" His voice was very mild and calm.

"Gardie Hunter. She gave it to me."

I heard Uncle Am let out a long breath that he'd been holding. He didn't look up at me. He kept his eyes on the wallet in Bassett's hand.

Bassett asked, "When was this?"

"Last night. Sure it had been her old man's. She said so."

Bassett folded the wallet back shut and put it carefully into his pocket. He took out a cigarette and lighted it.

Then he nodded to the squad-car men. He said, "Thanks a lot, boys. Look, I'd sort of like to keep track of Bobby here till I can check that story. Will you take him and book him on disorderly?"

"Okay."

"Who's on the desk tonight?"

"Norwald."

Bassett nodded. "I know him. Tell him I'll probably phone in pretty soon and tell him he can let Reinhart go." He took out the wallet again and handed Bobby the bills and identification from it. He said, "I guess we won't need these, son. The wallet's evidence, for a while."

Bobby looked around at me when they were taking him to the door.

I said, "Any time. Any place."

They took him out.

Bassett stood up. He said to Uncle Am, "Well, it was a nice try."

Uncle Am said. "You know it doesn't mean anything. About that wallet."

Bassett shrugged.

He turned to me. "Kid, 'fraid you can't sleep home tonight. You can bunk with your uncle, can't you?"

"Why," I asked.

"We'll have to do something we should have done right away.

Search the place. Find the insurance policy, and anything else we might find."

Uncle Am nodded. "He can stay with me."

Bassett went out. Uncle Am sat there and didn't say anything.

I said, "I guess I went off kind of half-cocked. I threw a monkey wrench in things."

He turned and looked at me. He said, "You look like hell. Go wash your face and straighten yourself out. I think you're going to have a mouse, too."

I said, "You ought to see the other guy."

That got a snort out of him, and I knew it was going to be all right with him. I went back to the washroom and cleaned up.

He asked, "How do you feel?"

"About that high," I said.

"I mean physically. Can you stay up all night?"

"If I can get up, I can stay up."

He said, "We've been piddling along. We've been kidding ourselves we've been investigating. We've been babes in the woods. We'd better start chopping down some trees."

"Swell," I said. "What's Bassett going to do—arrest Mom?"

"He's going to take her in for questioning. Gardie, too, now that wallet business came up. I had him talked out of it; he was going to give us another few days to crack Kaufman."

"He'll let them go when he's questioned them?"

"I don't know, kid. I don't know. If he finds that policy, maybe he won't. We got two kicks in the teeth tonight—that insurance receipt and the wallet. They both point the wrong way, but try to tell that to Bassett."

I had the red rubber ball in my hand again, playing with it. He reached over and took it from me and started squeezing it. Each time, it went almost flat. He had tremendously strong hands.

He said, "I wish we'd never found this stuff. It—Oh, hell, I can't explain. I just wish Wally hadn't kept it."

I said, "I think I know what you mean."

"He must have been a hell of a mess, Ed. I hadn't seen him in ten years. My God, what can happen to a guy in ten years—"

"Listen, Uncle Am," I said, "is there any way he could have done it himself? Hit himself with—say, with one of the bottles? Or—this sounds screwy except that he used you said, to juggle Indian clubs—thrown it up high and stood under it when it came down? I know it sounds crazy, but—"

"It doesn't, kid, except for one thing you don't know: Wally couldn't have killed himself. He had a—well, not exactly a phobia, but maybe you could call it a psychic block. He couldn't have killed himself. It wasn't fear of death—he might have wanted to die. I remember once when he did."

I said, "I don't see how you can be sure. Maybe he didn't want to badly enough, then."

He said, "It was on our trip through Mexico, south of Chihuahua. He was bitten by a Cugulla adder. We were alone, on a lonely road across wild country, not much more than a trail. We didn't have any first-aid stuff, and it wouldn't have mattered if we had. There isn't any antidote for a Cugulla bite. You die within two hours, and it's one of the worse and most painful deaths there is. It's unadulterated hell.

"His leg started swelling and hurting like hell right away. He had the only gun between us, and we—well, we said so long, and he tried to shoot himself. He simply couldn't—his reflexes wouldn't work. He begged me to do it. I—I don't know; I might have if it had got much worse, but we heard someone coming. It was a mestizo, riding an ancient burro.

"He said the snake wasn't a Cugulla—we'd shot it and it was lying there in the road. It was a local species that looked almost exactly like a Cugulla. And it was poisonous all right, but nothing like the real McCoy. We got Wally tied on the burro and packed him three miles to a medico in the next village, and we saved him, or the medico did."

I said, "But—"

"We had to stay there a month. That doc was a swell guy. I worked for him to help pay for us staying there while Wally was getting better, but evenings I read his books—mostly the ones on psychology and psychiatry. He had a flock of 'em, in English and Spanish.

"That's where I picked up a good start on what I know about stuff like that, and I've read a lot since—besides the practical angles you get working a mitt-camp. But, kid, we sort of psychoanalyzed, Wally and he had it. There are people who couldn't kill themselves—it's a physical and mental impossibility, no matter what. It's not too common, but it's not too rare either. It's an anti-suicide psychosis. And it's not something that would wear off or change as he got older."

I asked, "That's straight; you're not kidding me?"

"Not on any of it, kid."

He squeezed the rubber ball some more.

He said, "Kid, when we go in, you lean against the inside of the door. Don't say anything at all."

"Go in where?"

"Kaufman's room. He isn't married; he lives in a rooming house on LaSalle Street, a little north of Oak. He walks home. I've been there and I know the layout. We've monkeyed around with him too long. We'll write him off our books tonight, before things get too cold."

"Okay," I said. "When do we start?"

"He closes fairly early Monday night. Any time after one, he might get there. We'll have to leave pretty soon; it's after midnight now."

We had another drink, and then we left. We went by the Wacker and left Pop's suitcase there. Then we went north on Clark to Oak, and over to LaSalle.

My uncle picked a deep doorway on the west side of La Salle, just north of the corner, and we stood in there and waited. We waited almost an hour and only a few people went by.

Then Kaufman passed us. He didn't look in the doorway.

We waited till he was just past, and then stepped out and went up alongside him, one of us on either side.

He stopped as abruptly as if he'd run into a wall, but, one of us holding each of his arms, we started him walking again. I took a look at his face, and then didn't look again. It wasn't nice to look at. It was the face of a man who thinks he is dead, and who doesn't like it. It was just the colour of the sidewalk under our feet.

He said, "Listen, you guys, I—"

"We'll talk in your room," my uncle said.

We reached the doorway.

Uncle Ambrose let go of Kaufman's arm and went in first. He walked confidently down the hallway as though he knew where he was going. I remembered he said he'd been here before.

I walked third, behind Kaufman. Halfway down the hall, he lagged a bit. I touched the small of his back lightly with the end of my index finger and he jumped. He almost crowded Uncle Am, going up the stairs.

On the third floor, my uncle took a key from his pocket and opened the door of a room. He went on in and flicked the light.

We followed him and I closed the door and leaned against it.

My part in this was over, except for leaning against that door.

Kaufman said, "Listen, damn it, I—"

"Be quiet," my uncle told him. "Sit down." He gave the tavern keeper a very light push that sent him to a sitting position on the edge of the bed.

My uncle paid no more attention to him. He walked over to the dresser by the window. He reached around the end of it and pulled the window shade down flush with the sill.

Then he picked up the alarm clock on the dresser. It ticked loudly; the hands stood at nine minutes of two. He looked at his own wrist watch and adjusted the time to a quarter of two. He then gave each of the winding keys a few turns and then turned the button that turned the alarm band. He set it for two o'clock, pulled up the little lever that turned it on.

"Nice clock you have there," he said. "Hope it won't bother your neighbours if it goes off at two. We have to catch a train."

He opened the top left dresser drawer and reached in. His hand came out holding a little nickel-plated thirty-two revolver.

He said, "You won't mind if we borrow this a moment, will you, George?" He looked across the room at me. "Dangerous things, guns, kid. I've never owned one and never will. They get you in trouble faster'n anything."

"Yeah," I said.

He spun the cylinder, broke the gun, and snapped it shut. He said, "Kid, throw me that pillow."

I took the pillow from the bed and tossed it to him.

He held the gun in his right hand and bent the pillow around it with his left.

He leaned back against the dresser.

The clock ticked.

Kaufman was sweating. There were big drops on his forehead. He said, "You guys can't get away with this."

"With what?" my uncle asked him. He looked at me and grinned. He said, "Kid, you got any idea what this guy is talking about?"

I said, "Maybe he thinks we're threatening him."

My uncle looked surprised. "Why, we wouldn't do that. We like George."

The clock ticked again.

Kaufman took a handkerchief out of his pocket and wiped his forehead.

He said, "All right, shut that goddam alarm off. What do you want to know?"

I saw some of the tension go out of Uncle Am; I hadn't realized it was there until it left him. He said, "You know what we want to know, pal. Just tell it your own way."

"Does the name Harry Reynolds mean anything to you?"

Uncle Am said, "Just keep talking. It will."

"Harry Reynolds is a hood. He's dynamite. Three weeks ago he was in my place, sitting at the back with a couple guys, when this Wally Hunter comes in for a drink. There are a couple guys with Hunter, too."

"What kind of guys?"

"Just ordinary guys. Printers. A fat one and a little one. One I didn't know, but Hunter called him Jay. The other one had been in with Hunter before; his name is Bunny."

My uncle glanced at me, and I nodded. I knew who Jay would be.

Kaufman said, "They had just a drink around, and left, and one of the guys with Reynolds got up and left right after them, like he was going to follow them. Then this Reynolds comes over to the bar and asks me what the name of the guy who stood in the middle of the three of them was. I told him Wally Hunter."

My uncle asked, "Did he recognize the name?"

"Yeah. He got it. He hadn't been sure till I told him the name and then he was sure, all right. He asks me where this Hunter lives, and I say I don't know—which was the truth. He came in once in a while, maybe once a week, but I didn't know where he lived.

"So he lets it go at that, has a few more drinks and they leave.

"The next day he comes back. He says he wants to get in touch with Hunter about something and next time he comes in I should find out where he lives. And he gives me a phone number, too, and says the minute Hunter comes in I should call that number and say Hunter's there—but I shouldn't say anything to Hunter about it."

"What was the phone number?"

Kaufman said, "Wentworth three-eight-four-two. I was to leave a message if he wasn't there. Same if I found out Hunter's address from him; I was to call that number and leave the message."

"You say this was the next day?"

Kaufman nodded. He said, "I take it he sent one of the boys to follow Hunter home, but he lost him. So Reynolds came back to get it through me. He let me know what'd happen if I didn't—if he found out Hunter had been back and I hadn't let him know."

Uncle Am asked, "Did this Hunter come in again between that night and the night he was killed?"

"Nope, he didn't come in for two weeks after that. Till the night he was killed. And that night everything happened like I told at the inquest except that I called the number. Hell, I had to. Reynolds would've killed me if I hadn't."

"You talked to Reynolds personally?"

"No, nobody answered the phone when I called that number, I called twice, once a couple of minutes after Hunter came in, and again ten minutes after that. Nobody answered. I was damn glad. I didn't want to get mixed up in it any more'n I had to to keep Reynolds from burning me down. What's your angle in this?"

Uncle Am said, "Don't worry about our angle. We won't get you in trouble with Reynolds. What'd you tell Reynolds when you saw him?"

"I didn't see him since. He never came around. Hell, he wouldn't. He got in touch with Hunter some other way. He—or one of his boys—must've been following Hunter that night, waiting outside while he was in here. He must've been—"

The alarm went off and all three of us jumped. Uncle Am reached behind him and shut it off. He tossed the pillow back on the bed and put the little thirty-two on top of the dresser.

He asked, "Where does Harry Reynolds live?"

"I don't know. All I know is that phone number. Wentworth three-eight-four-two."

"What's his line?"

"Big-time stuff only. Banks, pay rolls, stuff like that. His brother's in stir, doing life, for a bank job."

My uncle shook his head sadly. He said, "George, you shouldn't get mixed up with people like that. Who were the other lugs who were with Reynolds the night he was in your place last—the night Wally Hunter came in?"

"One was called Dutch. A big guy. The other one was a little wop torpedo; I don't know his name. Dutch was the one followed Hunter out and lost him—I guess he lost him, or Reynolds wouldn't have had to come back the next day."

My uncle said, "That's all you can tell us, George? Now you've gone this far, the more the merrier—if you get what I mean."

Kaufman said, "I get what you mean. If I knew any more I'd tell you, all right. I hope you find him, now. You got a phone number. Just don't tell him where you got it."

"We won't, George. We won't tell anybody. We'll go now, and let you go to sleep." He started to the door, and I turned the knob to open it. He turned back to Kaufman a moment.

He said, "Listen, George, I'm pretending to play along with the cops on this; I may have to give them something. They can find Reynolds easier than we can if the phone number is a bust. But you keep that phone number under your hat. If Bassett comes around to see you, give him everything you gave me except the phone number. You were just to get Hunter's address, and Reynolds would come back for it. Only he didn't."

We went out and down the stairs, out into the clean night air.

I thought, we have a name now. We know who we're looking for. We got a name and a phone number. And this time we were up against the big time. Hoods; not mugs like Kaufman.

And we were going it by ourselves; Uncle Am wasn't giving Bassett that phone number.

Under the street light on Oak Street, Uncle Am looked at me. He asked, "Scared, kid?"

My throat was a little dry. I nodded.

He said, "So am I. Scared spitless. Shall we level with Bassett or shall we have some fun?"

I said, "Let's—try the fun."

CHAPTER NINE

THE COOL NIGHT AIR felt swell now. I'd been sweating. My collar felt tight and I loosened it and shoved my hat back on my head.

It was reaction again, but a different kind of reaction. I felt taller. I wasn't jittery, like after the night we'd been in at the tavern.

We walked south on Wells Street and we didn't say anything. We didn't have to. Somehow after what had happened, Uncle Am was a part of me and I was a part of him.

And I remembered that phrase again—*we're the Hunters*—and I thought, we're going to do it. The cops can't, but we can. I knew then that I hadn't really believed it before. I believed it now. I knew it now.

I was scared, yes, but it was a nice kind of afraidness—like when you read a good ghost story and it makes prickles run up and down your spine, but makes you like them.

We cut east on Chicago Avenue, and we went past the police station with the two blue lights by the door. I looked up the steps as we walked past it, and I didn't feel so good any more. Mom and Gardie would be having a tough time in there. Or had they taken them to the Homicide Bureau downtown?

But Mom hadn't done it. Bassett was way off on that.

We rounded the corner to Clark Street. Uncle Am asked, "Cup coffee, kid?"

"Sure," I said. "But are we going to call that number tonight? It's getting later."

"From now on it gets earlier," he said. "A few minutes won't matter."

We ordered a bowl of chili and coffee apiece, in the joint just north of Superior. We had our end of the counter to ourselves; two loud-voiced women down near the other end were arguing about somebody name Carey.

The chili was good, but it didn't taste good. I kept thinking about Mom. I thought, anyway they don't use a rubber hose on women.

Uncle Am said, "Think about something else, Ed."

"Sure. What?"

"Anything. What the hell." He looked around and his eye lit on the handbag one of the women had lying on the counter. "Think about handbags. Ever think about handbags?"

"No," I said. "Why should I?"

"Suppose you were a leather-goods designer. Then you'd be plenty interested. What's a handbag for? It's a substitute for pockets, that's all. A man has pockets, and a woman hasn't. Why? Because pockets—loaded ones—would spoil a woman's shape. She'd bulge in the wrong places, or too much in the right places. Wouldn't she?"

"I guess so," I said.

"Why, take handkerchiefs. Women do carry handkerchiefs in pockets sometimes, but little tiny ones, while a man carries big ones. And it isn't because they have any less snot in their noses than men do; it's because a big handkerchief would make a bulge. If they did carry big handkerchiefs, they'd carry them in pairs. But let's get back to handbags."

"Sure," I said, "Let's get back to handbags."

"The more a handbag holds the better it is and the smaller it looks, the better it is. Now, how would you design a handbag that would be big and look little? That would make a woman say, 'Golly, this bag holds more than you'd think'?"

"I don't know. How?"

"I think the approach would be empirical. You'd design a lot of 'em for looks and wait till you heard a woman say one of them holds more than you'd think. Then you'd study it to see why, and try to put the same thing in other bags. You might even reduce it to an equation. You know algebra. Ed?"

"Not intimately," I told him, "and the hell with handbags. They make me think of wallets. Was Bobby Reinhart telling the truth about Gardie giving it to him?"

"Sure, kid. If he was lying, he wouldn't tell one that could be checked on that easy. He'd say he found it, or something. But don't let it worry you."

"It does, though."

"My God, why? You don't think Gardie killed him, took the wallet and then gave it to Bobby, do you? Or that Madge killed him, left the wallet lying around loose, or gave it to Gardie, do you?"

I said, "I know neither of them did it, but it looks damn bad. How *did* Gardie get the wallet?"

"He didn't take it with him, that's all. Lots of guys leave their wallets home when they go out on a bender. They stick a few bucks in their pockets and leave their wallets safe at home. Gardie found it and glommed, onto the money in it, and didn't say anything. Even then it was dumb for her to give the wallet away—but if it was anything worse than that, she wouldn't have taken the chance. She'd have put the wallet in the incinerator."

"She should have, anyway," I said. "She's pretty damn dumb."

Uncle Am said, "I'm not so sure, kid. She'll get what she wants out of life. Most people do. Not all of them, but most people."

"Pop didn't," I said.

"No," Uncle Am said, "Wally didn't." He spoke slowly, as though he were choosing his words one at a time. "But there's a difference. Gardie is selfish; she won't mess up her life for the same reason. Wally messed up his. If she marries the wrong guy, she'd just walk out on him.

"Wally was the kind of guy who was loyal, kid, even to lost causes. He was also the kind of guy who should never have married at all. But your mother was a real woman, Ed, and he was happy with her. And she died before he got too restless, if you know what I mean. And Madge caught him on the rebound."

I said, "Mom is—oh, skip it." I realized that I was going to stick up for her out of loyalty. If I thought back about Mom and Pop, I remembered things, and Uncle Am was right. I was being soft, because she was in trouble now, and because she'd been different—a lot different—since Pop had died. But I shouldn't kid myself that would last.

Mom had been poison to him, and she'd have been poison to any man as decent as Pop was. Or had been, before she drove him to drink. And even his drinking had been quiet and not over quarrelsome.

I finished my chili and pushed the bowl aside.

Uncle Am said, "Not yet, kid. Let's have another cup of coffee." He ordered them. He said, "I'm trying to think out how best to handle talking to that phone number. I think best when I'm talking about something else. Let's talk about something else."

"Ladies' handbags?" I suggested.

He laughed. "They bored you, huh? Kid, that's because you don't know anything about them. The more you know about something, anything, the more interesting it is. I knew a leather-goods worker once; he could talk about handbags all night. Like a carney could talk about carnivals."

"Go ahead," I said, "I'd rather hear about carneys than about handbags. What's a blow?"

"Short for blow-off. It's a show for inside money, usually inside a freak show. I mean, say, you pay two bits to get into the freak show, and the spieler takes you around the platforms and then starts an inside bally for another two bits or more to see a special show on the inside, down at one end of the top. Why?"

I said, "I remember back at the carney you asked Hoagy to take over your ball game. He said he was sloughed and if Jake got a chance to use the blow after Springfield, he could get a cooch. What was he talking about?"

Uncle Am laughed. "You got a memory, kid."

"Yeah," I said. "I remember something out of tonight's talking, too. Wentworth three-eight-four-two. Have you got an angle yet?"

"Any minute now. Back to Hoagy. Hoagy's a sex spieler. The bally for the inside money at the freak-show top is a sex lecture with living models, for men only. Two bits each and money back if they're not satisfied."

"What do you mean, living models?" I asked.

"That's what pulls in the mooches. They want to know, too. Oh, he's got a nice spiel—but you could read it in any book on what a young man should know. And he does use living models, a couple girls in bathing suits. Discusses what types they are, as a reason for having them on the platform."

"Don't the mooches want their money back?"

"A few, a darned few. They get it, and so what? On a good night, he'll still take in a hundred bucks up and over the nut."

"What's the nut?"

"The overhead, kid. Say your expenses on a concession run thirty bucks a day; well, you're on the nut until you've taken in that much. The rest of it is profit; you're off the nut."

I drank the last of my coffee. I asked, "Why would a bank-robber have been looking for Pop?"

"I don't know, kid. We'll have to find out." He sighed and stood up. "Come on; let's start."

We walked down Clark Street to the Wacker and went up to his room.

He moved the chair out from the wall before he sat down. He said, "Stand behind me, Ed, and put your ear down to the receiver. I'll hold it a little out from my ear, and you can hear as well as I can. Use that memory of yours on what's said."

"Okay," I said. "What's the angle?"

"The hell with it. I'll ad lib. What I say depends on what they say."

"What if they say 'Hello'?" I asked him.

He chuckled. "I never thought of that. I'll wait and see."

He picked up the receiver and when he gave the number to the operator, his voice was different. It was low-pitched, gruff, with a completely different intonation. But I'd heard it before somewhere. It puzzled me for a second and then I placed it. He was imitating Hoagy's voice; we'd been talking about Hoagy and that had been the first voice he'd thought of to imitate. It was perfect.

I heard them ringing the number. I leaned closer, resting my weight on the chair back to put my ear as near the end of the receiver as I could.

It rang about three times and then a woman's voice said, "Hello."

It's funny, sometimes, how much you can tell—or anyway, guess—from a voice. Just one word, but you knew she was young, that she was pretty, and that she was smart. In all the senses of the word "smart." And just from the way she said that one word, you liked her.

My uncle said. "Who zis?"

"Claire. Wentworth three-eight-four-two."

"Howya, baby?" my uncle asked. "Member me? This's Sammy." He sounded very drunk.

"Afraid I don't," said the voice. It was considerably cooler now. "Sammy who?"

"G'wan, you r'member me," Uncle Am said, "*Sammy*. In at the bar th'other night. Look, Claire, I know 'sawful late to call you, 'nall that, but, honey, I jus' cleaned up a crap game. Took th' boys for two G's, an' it's burning a hole. Wanta see th' town, Chez Paree, the Medoc Club, n'everywhere. Want th' prettiest gal in Chi with me. Nothin' too good. Might even buy 'er a fur coat if she likes rabbit fur. How's 'bout can I come out 'n' getcha in a cab an' we'll go—"

"No," said the voice. The receiver clicked.

"Damn," said my uncle.

"It was a good try," I told him.

He put the receiver back on the phone. He said, "They don't pay off any more on good tries. Guess I'm not so hot as a Romeo. I should've let you try."

"Me? Lord, I don't know anything about women."

"That's what I mean. Hell, kid, you could have any woman you want. Take a look in the mirror."

I laughed, but I turned around to the mirror over the dresser.

I said, "I *am* getting a shiner. Damn Bobby Reinhart.'

Uncle Am grinned at me in the mirror. He said, "On you it looks romantic. Save it; don't put a steak on it. Well, now we try something that won't work."

He dialled a number and asked for the Wentworth exchange clerk. He asked her for the listing on three-eight-four-two. He waited a minute and then put the receiver down with an "Okay, thanks," that sounded discouraged.

"Unlisted number," he told me. "I thought it would be."

"So what do we do now?"

He sighed. "Work from the other end. Find out what's known about this Harry Reynolds. Bassett'll know something about him, or be able to dig it out of the morgue. Only thing is, I was hoping that phone number would give us an up on Bassett. Well, tomorrow we can try a couple more razzle-dazzles. We can be a phone-quiz radio programme giving a hundred-buck prize to whoever answers a phone number picked at random if he can tell us the capital of Illinois and his address. Or we can be—"

"Listen," I said, "I can get the listing on that phone number for you."

"Huh? How, kid? Those unlisted numbers are hard to get.'

"Bunny Wilson's sister-in-law, his brother's wife, works for the phone company, in the office where they handle those numbers. He found out one for Jake, the foreman at the plant, once. Just so we don't get his sister-in-law in trouble for it, he can get it for us.

"Kid, that's great. How soon could we get it?"

"If I can find Bunny tonight," I told him, "we can have it by tomorrow noon, I think. He could see his sister-in-law before she goes to work; then she could phone him when she goes out to lunch. She couldn't call from work, about that."

"Bunny got a phone?"

"His landlady has—but he can use it only daytimes. I can go over there, though. He lives on Halsted Street."

"He's home from work by now?"

"He should be. If he isn't, I'll wait."

"Okay, kid. We'll split up for a while, then. Here's ten bucks. Give it to Bunny to give his sister-in-law to buy herself a new hat or something. I'm going to hunt up Bassett and find out what gives on the inquisition. He'll go easier when I tell him we blew Kaufman open. Or maybe he's convinced by now that he was on the wrong street."

"Where'll we meet?"

"Come back here. I'll tell the desk clerk to give you my key if I'm not in. You run along; I'll try to find out where Bassett is by phone before I go chasing after him."

I walked down Grand, and was lucky enough to see an owl car coming, so it was only a few minutes before I got to Halsted and walked south to the place where Bunny roomed.

His light was off, which meant he was either out or asleep, but I went upstairs, anyway. This was important enough to wake him up about.

He was out; I knocked till I was sure.

I sat down on the stairs to wait, and then I remembered that he was usually careless about locking his door, and sure enough it was unlocked. So I went in and found a magazine to read.

When it got to be four o'clock I made coffee in his little kitchen-ette. I made it plenty strong.

He came home, stumbling up the stairs, just as I got the coffee made. He wasn't *too* drunk, just an edge on. But I got two cups of coffee down him before I told him what I wanted. I didn't give him the whole story, but enough of it that he knew why we needed the listing on that phone number.

He said, "Sure, Ed, sure. And t'hell with the ten bucks. She owes me a few favours."

I stuck it in his pocket and told him to give it to her anyway.

"Can you talk to her before she goes to work this morning?" I asked him.

"Sure, easy. She lives way out—gets up at five-thirty. I'll stay awake till I can phone her then. Then I'll set my alarm for eleven so I'll be awake when she phones me back. You can phone me any time after noon—I'll stick around till you do."

"That's swell, Bunny. Thanks."

"Skip it. You going home now?"

"Back to the Wacker."

"I'll walk part way with you." He looked at the clock. "Then by time I get back here, it'll be time for me to phone from the all-night drugstore on the corner."

We walked over Grand Avenue, over the bridge.

He said, "You're different lately, Ed. What's changed about you? You're different."

"I don't know," I said. "Maybe it's the new suit."

"Nope. Maybe you grew up, or something. Whatever it is, I like it. I—I think you could go places, Ed, if you want to. Not get stuck in a rut, like I am."

"You're not in a rut," I said. "I thought you were going to have a shop of your own."

"I don't know, Ed. Equipment costs like hell. I got a little saved, yeah, but when I think what it takes—Hell, if I had sense enough to stay sober I could save more, but I haven't. Here I am forty, and I got maybe half saved up for what I want to do. Rate I'm going, I'll be old before I even get started."

He laughed a little, bitterly. "Sometimes I feel like finding one of these big-time gambling games you hear about, where there's no limit, and betting my little bankroll on one blackjack hand quit win or lose. Then either I'd have enough or nothing. And nothing wouldn't be much worse than half enough. Maybe better."

"Better, how?"

"Then I could quit worrying about it. Then every time I spent a quarter for a shot of whisky or a dime for a glass of beer, it wouldn't hurt me. I'm not worried about going to hell, Ed, but I begrudge the money the ticket costs."

We walked in silence a little while and then he said, "It's my own fault, Ed. I got no kick coming, really. A guy can have anything he wants, damn near, if he wants it bad enough, if he's willing to give up other things to get it. Hell, on my income, and living alone, I could save thirty bucks a week, easy. I could have had enough money years ago. But I wanted fun out of life, too. Well, I've had it, so what the hell am I squawking about?"

We were almost to the el now and he said, "Well, guess I'll turn back here."

We stopped walking. I said, "Come up to the flat some afternoon, Bunny, or your next evening off. Mom—Mom hasn't got many friends. She'll be glad to see you."

"I'll do that, Ed. Thanks. Uh—say, how about having one drink with me? Across the street there."

I thought a minute, and then I said, "Sure, Bunny."

I didn't want the drink, really, but I could feel that, for some obscure reason, he really wanted me to drink with him. There was something in the way he said it.

We had it, just one, and then we parted in front of the tavern. I crossed over under the el and walked toward Clark Street.

I got to wondering about Mom and Gardie, whether they were home or not, so I turned north on Franklin and then cut through the alley back of our flat. When I got into the alley I could see our kitchen windows, and there was a light on in the kitchen.

I didn't know whether it was the police, still searching, or Mom home again, so I stood there and watched awhile until I saw Mom cross the window. She was still dressed, so I knew she hadn't been home long. I saw Gardie, too. Mom was going to and from the stove, and I guess they'd just got home and were getting something to eat before they turned in.

I didn't want to go upstairs. Bassett would have told Mom I was staying with Uncle Am and she wouldn't be wondering about me. She'd worry, maybe, if she knew I was still chasing around.

I walked on through the alley and over to Clark Street. The sky was turning light with dawn.

At the Wacker, I asked the desk clerk if a key had been left for me. It hadn't, so I knew Uncle Am was back.

Bassett was there with him. They'd swung out the writing table so one of them could sit on each side of it and they were playing cards. There was a bottle on the table between them. Bassett's eyes looked glassy.

Uncle Am asked, "Feel better with the tummy full, kid?"

I knew he was tipping me off what he'd told Bassett about where I was, so I knew the phone number was still a secret.

I said, "I ate three breakfasts. I'm set for all day now."

"Gin rummy," Uncle Am said. "Penny a point, so be quiet."

I sat down on the edge of the bed and watched the game. Uncle Am was winning; he had a lead of thirty points and two boxes. I looked at the paper they were scoring on and saw it was their third game; Uncle Am had taken the first two.

But Bassett won that hand. He took a long pull out of the bottle and turned around to face me while Uncle Am dealt the next hand. His eyes were owlishly wide. He said, "Ed, that sister of yours—somebody oughta—"

"Pick up your drink, Frank," my uncle said. "Let's get the game over with. I'll bring Ed up to date later."

Bassett picked up his cards. He dropped one of them and I got it for him. He finally got his hand arranged and took another pull at the bottle. It was a quart, and it was almost empty.

Bassett won that hand, too. But Uncle Am went gin on the next one and that put him over a hundred, and out.

Bassett said, "That's enough. Add 'em up. Jeez, I'm tired." He reached for his wallet.

Uncle Am said, "Skip it. It's about ten bucks for the three games; add 'em onto the expense account. Look, Frank, I'm going to get something to eat now. Whyn't you rest awhile? Ed might as well go home. When I get back, if you've gone to sleep, I'll wake you up."

Bassett's eyes were plenty glassy now, and half shut. All of a sudden the whisky was hitting him, and he was very drunk. He sat on the edge of the bed, swaying.

My uncle put the table back where it belonged. He looked at Bassett and grinned, and then gave him a slight push on his left shoulder. Bassett fell back and sideways and his head landed on the pillow.

Uncle Am picked up his feet and put them on the bed, too. He untied Bassett's shoes and took them off. He took off Bassett's shell-rimmed glasses and his hat and put them on the dresser. He loosened the detective's tie and opened the button at the collar of his shirt.

Bassett opened his eyes then. He said, "You son of a bitch."

"Sure," said my uncle, soothingly. "Sure, Frank."

We turned off the light and went out.

Going down in the elevator, I told him about Bunny and the phone number and that we could get the listing any time after noon.

He nodded. He said, "Bassett knows we're holding out something on him. He's a smart boy. I wouldn't put it past him to go see Kaufman himself and turn on a little heat."

I said, "You had Kaufman plenty scared. It'll take a bit of heat to crack him again. I think he's more scared of us now than he was of this Harry Reynolds." I thought a minute, then asked, "Say, what would we have done if that alarm clock *had* gone off before he broke?"

Uncle Am shrugged. "Looked pretty silly, I guess. How's about some breakfast—for real?"

"I could eat a cow," I told him.

We went to Thompson's at Clark and Chicago, and while we got outside ham and eggs, he told me what he'd learned from Bassett.

Gardie had admitted giving the billfold to the Reinhart boy. Her explanation had been just about what Uncle Am had suggested. Pop had an extra wallet—an old one. I'd known that. What I'd not known, and Gardie *had* known was that recently, whenever he'd gone out drinking, he'd left his good wallet and part of his money at home. He'd dropped it back of a row of books in the bookcase, and had taken only part of his money, in the old wallet.

I said, "I guess that would date from the time he got held up before. He lost his social security card and union card and everything and a good billfold. I guess he figured if he got held up again, or his pocket picked, he wouldn't lose anything but the money. It's plenty easy, I guess, to get rolled on Clark Street."

"Yeah," said Uncle Am. "Anyway, Gardie's seen him hide the wallet once, and knew about it. So she looked, and it was there in the bookcase, with twenty bucks left in it. She figured it wouldn't hurt anybody if she kept it."

I said, "Finders' keepers, sure. I don't mind that, that's what I figure she'd do, but why did she have to give the billfold away—and make me make a damn fool of myself? Oh, well, skip it. It was an off chance that I happened to see the billfold Reinhart was carrying. Did Bassett believe her?"

"After he'd looked in the bookcase. There was dust back of the books, and marks in the dust where the billfold had been, just where she'd said."

"And—about Mom?"

"I guess he pretty well convinced himself she didn't do it, kid. Even before I got hold of him and told him about the Reynolds angle. Also they searched the flat pretty thoroughly. They didn't find any insurance policy, or anything else of interest."

"What did Bassett know about Reynolds, if anything?"

"He knew *of* him. There is such a guy, and everything Kaufman told us about him fits with what Bassett knows. Bassett thinks there's a pick-up order out for the three of them—Harry Reynolds, Dutch, and the wop torpedo. Bassett'll look into it and get their names and histories. He thinks the three of 'em are wanted for bank robbery in Wisconsin. A recent one. Anyway, he's more interested now in that angle of the case than in heckling Madge."

"Did you get Bassett drunk on purpose tonight?"

"A man's like a horse, Ed. You can lead him to whisky but you can't make him drink. You didn't see me pouring any whisky down him, did you?"

"No," I admitted. "I didn't see you grabbing it away, either."

"You got a nasty suspicious mind," he said. "But just the same, we got the morning free. He'll sleep till noon, and we'll be ahead of him with the insurance company."

"Why do you care about that—now we got a lead on Reynolds."

"Kid, we don't know why this Reynolds was interested in your dad. I got a hunch if we find out the inside story of why Wally carried that much insurance—and kept it secret that he was carrying it—we might get an idea. I'd just as soon have some idea what it's all about before we go up against Reynolds. Also we can't make a move till we get the listing on that phone number, so what have we got to lose but sleep?"

"The hell with sleep," I said.

"Okay. You're young; you'll live through it. *I* ought to have more sense, but I guess I haven't. Shall we get some more coffee?"

I looked at Thompson's clock. I said, "We got over an hour before the offices open downtown. I'll go get the coffee, and then you can tell me more about what you and Pop did when you were together."

The hour went pretty quick.

CHAPTER TEN

THE CENTRAL MUTUAL turned out to be a moderate-sized branch office of a company whose headquarters were in St. Louis. It was a break for us; the smaller the office the more likely they were to remember Pop.

We asked for the manager and were taken into his office. Uncle Am did the talking and explained who we were.

The manager said, 'No, I don't recall him offhand, but I'll have our records checked. You say the policy hasn't turned up yet. That won't matter, if it's on our records, and paid up." He smiled, slightly, deprecatingly. "We're not a racket, you know. The policy is merely our client's record of a contract that exists and will be kept, whether or not his copy is lost or destroyed."

Uncle Am said, "I understand that. What we're interested in is whether you recall any circumstances about the policy—for instance, just why its existence was kept a secret from his family. He must have given a reason, some reason, to the agent who sold him the policy."

The manager said, "Just a minute." He went out into the general office and came back a few minutes later. He said, "The head clerk is looking up the file. He'll bring it in personally, and maybe he'll be able to recall the insured."

My uncle asked, "How unusual is it for a man to keep a policy secret that way?"

"It's not unique. It *is* highly unusual. The only other case I can recall offhand is that of a man who had a touch of persecution complex. He was afraid his relatives might do away with him if they knew he was insured. Yet, paradoxically, he loved them and wished to provide for them in case of his death. Uh–I didn't mean to imply that in this case—"

"Of course not," Uncle Am said.

A tall grey-haired man came into the office with a file folder in his hand. He said, "Here's the Wallace Hunter file, Mr. Bradbury. Yes, I recall him. Always came into the office to make his payments. There's a notation clipped to the file that no notices were to be sent out."

The manager took the file folder. He asked, "Ever talk to him, Henry? Ever ask him *why* the notices were not to be mailed for instance?"

The tall man shook his head. "No, Mr. Bradbury."

"All right, Henry."

The tall man went out.

The manager was leafing through the file. He said, "Yes, it's paid up. There are two small loans against it—made to meet premium payments. They'll be deducted from the face of the policy, but they won't amount to much." He turned another couple of pages. He said, "Oh, the policy wasn't sold from this office. It was transferred here from Gary, Indiana."

"Would they have any records on it there?"

"No, aside from a duplicate of this file at the main office in St. Louis, there are no other records. This file was transferred here from Gary at the time Mr. Hunter moved to Chicago. I see by the dates that was just a few weeks after the policy was taken out."

Uncle Am asked, "Would the policy itself show any details not given in that file?"

"No, the policy is a standard straight-life form, with the name and amount and date filled in. Pasted inside it is a photostatic copy of the application for the policy—but the original of that photostat is here in his file. You may see that if you wish."

He handed Uncle Am the file, opened to a form filled in with pen and ink, and I walked over behind Uncle Am's chair so I could read it over his shoulder. I made a mental note of the date of the application, and the signature of the agent who sold it—Paul B. Anderz.

Uncle Am asked, "Do you know if this agent, Anderz, is still working out of your Gary office?"

"No, I don't. We can write them and find out."

Uncle Am said, "Never mind, thanks anyway. You'll want a copy of the death certificate, of course?"

"Yes, before we can issue a cheque to the beneficiary. This young man's mother, I take it."

"His stepmother." Uncle Am handed back the folder and stood up. "Thanks a lot. Oh, by the way—was the policy paid quarterly?"

The manager did some leafing through the folder again. He said, "Yes, after the first payment. He paid a year's premium in advance with the original application."

Uncle Am thanked him again, and we left.

"Gary?" I asked.

"Yeah. We can get there on the el, can't we?"

"Less than an hour, I think." I thought for a minute. "Gosh, less than an hour from the Loop, and yet I never went back there after we left."

"Did Wally or Madge ever go back? For a visit, or anything?"

I thought, and then shook my head. "Not that I remember, I don't believe any of us ever went back there. Of course, I was only thirteen when we came from there to Chicago, but I think I'd remember."

"Tell me—wait, let's wait till we're on the train."

He didn't say any more till we had a seat on the Gary Express. Then he said, "All right, kid, let go. Relax, and tell me everything you can remember about Gary."

I said, "I went to Twelfth Street School. So did Gardie. I was in the eighth grade and she was in the fourth. When we left, I mean. We lived in a little frame house on Holman Street, three blocks from the school. The school had a band, and I wanted to get in it. They lent instruments and I borrowed a trombone. I was getting so I could read simple stuff on it, but Mom hated it. She called it 'that damn horn', and I had to go out in the woodshed to practice. Then when we came to Chicago we lived in a flat and I couldn't have practised even if Mom had liked it, so I—"

"Forget the trombone," Uncle Am said. "Get back to Gary."

I said, "We had a car part of the time, and part of the time we didn't. Pop worked at two or three different printing shops at one time or another. He was out of work for a while with arthritis in his arms and we went way in debt. I don't think we ever quite got out. I have a hunch we left so suddenly because we were running out on some of the debts we still had."

"You left suddenly?"

"It seems to me we did. I mean, I don't remember it being talked over. All of a sudden the van was there loading our furniture, and Pop had a job in Chicago and we had to leave right—Wait a minute—"

"Take your time, kid. I think you're getting at something. My God, Ed, what a sap I've been."

"You? How?"

He laughed. "I've been overlooking my best witness because I was too close to see him. Forget it. Get back to Gary."

I said, "I remember now. Something that was funny at the time, but I'd clean forgotten until I started talking about moving. I didn't know we were moving to Chicago until we got here. Pop said we were moving to Joliet; that's about twenty-five miles from Gary, same as Chicago, but west instead of northwest, and I remember telling all my kid friends we were going to Joliet—and then it turned out to be Chicago. Pop said he'd got a good job in Chicago and changed his mind about taking the one in Joliet. I remember, it seemed kind of funny to me, even then."

Uncle Am had his eyes closed. He said, "Go on, kid. Dig as deep as you can. You're doing swell."

"After we got to Chicago, we moved in right where we're still living. But Pop couldn't have been telling the truth about the job in Chicago, because he was around home the first few weeks after we came to Chi. Not all the time; but enough so I know he wasn't working. Then he got the job at Elwood Press."

"Back to Gary, kid. You keep ending up in Chicago."

"Well, we did," I said. "What do you want? The time Gardie had the mumps, or what?"

"I guess we can do without that. But keep on trying. Dig way down."

I said, "I remember vaguely something about a court. I can't remember what."

"Some creditor got a judgment against you?"

"That could be. I don't remember. I don't think Pop was working the last week or two we were in Gary. But I don't remember whether he'd lost a job or been laid off, or what. Say, that was the week he took all of us to the circus."

Uncle Am nodded. "And you sat in the reserved seats."

"Yeah, we—What made you say that?"

"Don't you see what you've been telling me, kid? Take what we learned at the insurance company this morning and use it as one piece of a jigsaw, use the little things you've been giving me as other pieces, and what do you get?"

I said, "We lammed out of Gary. We moved suddenly and without telling anybody where we were going. We even left a false trail. But it was just because we owed so much, wasn't it?"

"Kid, I'll bet you a buck. You figure out what stores you dealt with while you were there. You'll remember the grocery, anyway. Go round today and ask 'em—I'll bet you a buck Wally paid off everything he owed in cash before you left."

"How could he, if he was out of work? Hell, we were broke most of the time. And—Oh, oh."

"You begin to see it, Ed?"

"The insurance policy," I said. "It was about that time he took it out. And he paid a year's premium in cash, in advance. On five thousand, that'd run over a hundred bucks. And he'd have needed cash to pay for getting moved to Chicago, and paying rent on the new place."

"And," said Uncle Am, "living a few weeks without working in Gary and a few weeks before he started working in Chicago. And taking the whole kaboodle of you to the circus. Now that you're on the track, what can you add?"

I said, "Gardie and I got some new clothes to start school in Chicago. You'd win the buck, Uncle Am. He had a windfall, and it must have been at least three weeks before we left Gary. And if you're right that he'd have paid off debts out of it, it must have been—ummm—at least five hundred bucks, maybe even a thousand."

Uncle Am said, "I'll settle for it being a thousand. Wally'd have paid off those debts. He was funny that way. Well, kid, here comes Gary. We'll see what we can find out."

We went for a phone book right at the station, and first we looked up the office of the Central Mutual. Uncle Am went into the phone booth to call them.

He came out looking disappointed. He said, "Anderz isn't with 'em any more. He quit about three years ago. Last they'd heard of him he was in Springfield, Illinois."

I said, "That's pretty far—a hundred and fifty miles. But look, maybe he's got a phone in his own name. It's an unusual enough name; we could try."

Uncle Am said, "I don't think we'll even bother, kid. The more I think of it, the less I think of it. I mean, Wally wouldn't have told him anything. He wouldn't have told him where his windfall came from. He'd have had to give him some reason for not wanting the premium notices mailed to him, but I'll bet ten, five and even that it wouldn't be the real reason. I think we've got a better lead."

"Who?"

"You, Ed. I want you to do some more thinking. Do you remember how to get out to where you used to live?"

I nodded, "East End car; you catch it a block from here."

We rode out and I remembered the corner where we got off. Hardly a thing had changed. The same drugstore was on the corner there, and in the block and a half we had to walk from the car, hardly a building had changed.

The house was across the street. It was smaller than I remembered, and it was badly in need of paint. It couldn't have been painted since we'd lived there.

I said, "The fence is different. We used to have a higher one."

Uncle Am chuckled. He said, "Look at it again, kid."

I did, and it was an old fence all right. It made me feel funny to realize that I remembered that fence as being chest-high. It wasn't the fence that had changed; it was me.

We crossed the street.

I put my hand on the fence, and a big police dog came running out from the side of the house. It wasn't barking; it meant business. I pulled my hand back, and the dog didn't jump the fence. It stopped, growling.

I said, "Looks like I'm not welcome there any more."

We walked on past, slowly, the dog keeping pace with us inside the fence. I kept looking at the house. It was pretty much of a mess; the porch was sagging and the wooden steps were crooked and one of them was broken. The yard was littered with junk.

We kept on walking. The grocery down on the corner still had the same name on the window. I said, "Let's go in."

The man who came to wait on us looked familiar, but I got that funny feeling again. He was a little man; he should have been a big one. Outside of that, I recognized him, all right.

I asked for cigarettes and then said. "Remember me, Mr. Hagendorf? I used to live down the block."

He looked at me closely. After a few seconds he said "Not the Hunter boy, are you?"

"Yep," I said. "Ed Hunter."

He said, "I'll be damned." He put out his hand. "You moving back in the neighbourhood?"

"No," I told him. "But my uncle's moving near here. This is my uncle. Mr. Hagendorf, Ambrose Hunter. He's going to live near here. I thought I'd bring him in and introduce him to you."

Uncle Am shook hands with the grocer and said, "Yeah, Ed told me I ought to deal here. Thought I might open an account."

Hagendorf said, "We don't do much credit business but I guess it's all right." He grinned at me. He said, "Your dad sure got me in the red sometimes, but he paid it off before he left."

I said, "It was a pretty big bill, wasn't it?"

"High as it had ever been. Something over a hundred bucks; I forget exactly. But he paid it off, all right. How are things going in Joliet, Ed?"

"Pretty good," I told him. "Well, we'll be seeing you, Mr. Hagendorf."

We went out and I said, "You sure pick 'em, Uncle Am. Are you the seventh son of a seventh son? And thanks for being quick on the uptake in there. I thought if we could find out without coming right out and asking—"

"Sure. Well, kid—?"

I said, "You go on over to the car line. Wait for me by the drugstore."

Alone, I walked a couple of times around the block. I kept across the street from our house when I went by, so the dog wouldn't distract me by keeping pace along the fence. I hopped and leaned against a tree where I could watch the house, and see the windows of the upper front room where I'd slept, the windows of the dining room.

I wanted to cry, a little bit, but I swallowed the lump in my throat and let myself go back and remember things. I tried to keep my mind on the last month we'd been there.

One of those last weeks, it came to me, Pop hadn't been working, exactly. Yet he'd been gone. For a few days he'd been gone day and night, doing something. Not out of town, or was it? No.

I had it, and wondered why I hadn't remembered before. Maybe because, for some reason, it had never been talked about afterwards. It seemed to me that Pop had gone out of his way not to mention it again, now that I remembered.

I went over to where Uncle Am was waiting under the awning of the drugstore. There was a streetcar coming. I just nodded to him and we caught the car.

As we rode back downtown I told him. "Jury duty. Pop was on a jury a little while before we left."

"What kind of a case, kid?"

"I don't know. He never talked about it. We can look up in the files at a newspaper and see what was going on then. I guess that's why I forgot it; we never talked about it."

He looked at his watch. "We'll get downtown about noon. You can phone this Bunny Wilson about the listing first."

We got a lot of change so I could keep dropping coins if I had to; and I called Bunny. I made the call from a quiet hotel lobby and left the booth open so Uncle Am could hear.

Bunny said, "I got it for you, Ed. It's in the name of Raymond, Apartment Forty-three, Milan Towers. That's an apartment hotel on Ontario Street over between Michigan Boulevard and the Lake."

I said, "I think I know where it is. Thanks to hell and back, Bunny."

"Don't mention it, Ed. I wish I could help you more. If there's anything I can do, at all, let me know. I'll even take a night off work, any time you say. How you coming? Say, when Mrs. Horth called me just now she said it was long distance. Where you calling from?"

"Gary," I told him. "We came here to see a guy named Anderz who sold Pop that insurance policy."

"What policy, Ed?"

I forgot I hadn't told him about it. I told him, and he said, "I'll be damned, Ed. Well, that's good news for Madge. I was worried how she'd get along. That'll help out plenty, getting her started on her own. Did you see the guy you mentioned?"

"No, Anderz moved to Springfield. We aren't going to follow him. Probably wouldn't find out anything anyway. We're coming back. Well, thanks again and so long."

At the *Gary Times* office we got them to show us the back volume covering the date we were looking for.

It wasn't any hunt at all. It was on the front page. That was the week of the trial of Steve Reynolds for bank robbery. The trial had lasted three days and had ended in a verdict of guilty. He'd drawn life. One Harry Reynolds, his brother, had been a witness for the defence and had tried to alibi him. Obviously the alibi had not been believed, but for some reason not appearing in the newspapers, there hadn't been any prosecution for perjury.

The defence attorney had been Schweinberg, a notorious

mouthpiece for crooks who, I recalled, had been disbarred about a year ago.

There were photographs with the day-by-day accounts of the trial. One of Steven Reynolds. One of Harry. I studied them until I was sure I'd know them, especially Harry.

We finished and gave back the bound volume. We thanked them and left.

Uncle Am said, "I think we can go back to Chicago now Ed. We don't know the details, but we got enough. We guess most of the rest."

I asked, "What can't we guess?"

"Why he could wait three weeks after the trial before he lammed. Look, here's how I read it. Wally gets put on the Reynolds jury. This Schweinberg was disbarred for bribing jurors; that was his racket. Somehow he got to Wally and gave him a thousand bucks, more or less, to vote acquittal. He couldn't have hoped for anything more than to split the jury and get a mistrial, from the evidence.

"Wally took it—and crossed him. Wally had nerve, all right; he might have done that. Hell, he must have. He got about a thousand from somewhere. Right after the trial he uses part of it for an insurance policy—one big enough to carry Madge till you kids were through school. Then he lammed out of Gary and covered his trail so they couldn't find him. I don't know why he waited three weeks; there must have been something protected him for that long. Maybe they did hold Harry Reynolds for a while, intending him to get a stretch for perjury or as an accessory, then let him go. And with Harry loose, Wally would know he'd be gunned for."

I asked, "Do you suppose Mom knew about it?"

He shrugged his shoulders. "She must have known part of it. My guess is she didn't know much. We know he didn't tell her about the insurance policy he took out. Maybe she didn't know any of it. He could have told her he hit on a policy ticket to account for having extra dough. Maybe he let her think you were ducking Gary to run out on those old bills—he could have paid them without her knowing it."

I said, "It doesn't make sense, does it? He's honest enough to pay bills he *could* have run out on, since he was running anyway, but still he takes money from gangsters for a bribe—"

"Ah, that's the difference, kid. The way Wally'd figure it, it isn't dishonest to cheat a crook. Hell, I don't know if he was right or wrong about that; I don't care. It took plenty of guts to take dough for a thing like that and *not* deliver."

We didn't talk much, riding back to Chicago.

In the Loop, we transferred to a Howard Express and got off at Grand. I said, "I better go home and take a bath and put on clean clothes. I feel sticky."

Uncle Am nodded. He said, "Look, kid, we can't keep on forever without sleeping, either. You do that and take a nap, too. It's about two o'clock. Get a little sleep and come to the hotel around seven or eight. We'll take a look at the Milan Towers this evening, but we don't want to be dopey when we do it."

At our place, I went on upstairs and Uncle Am kept on over toward the Wacker.

The door was locked and I had to let myself in with my key. I was just as glad nobody was home. I had a bath and was in bed within twenty minutes. I set my alarm for seven.

When it went off and woke me up, there were voices in the living room. I put on the rest of my clothes and went out there. Mom and Gardie were home and Bunny was with them. They had just finished eating, and Mom said, "Hello, stranger," and wanted to know if I wanted to eat. I said I'd just get myself a cup and have coffee.

It got a cup and pulled up a chair. I couldn't get over looking at Mom. She'd been to a beauty parlour, and she sure looked different. She had on a black dress, a new one, but it made her look better than I'd ever seen her. She had on a little make-up, but not too much.

Gosh, I thought, she's really pretty when she's fixed up.

Gardie looked pretty good, too. But her face got a little sullen when she looked at me. I had a hunch she was holding it against me about the wallet business, and my little scrap with Bobby Reinhart.

Bunny said, "They're talking about going to Florida, Ed, as soon as they get the insurance money. I tell 'em they ought to stay here, where they got friends."

"Friends, nuts," Mom said. "Who outside of you Bunny? Ed, I hear you were in Gary this morning. Did you see the old place?"

I nodded. "Just from the outside."

Mom said, "It sure was a dump. This flat's bad enough, but it sure was a dump, in Gary."

I didn't say anything.

I put sugar and cream in the coffee Mom poured for me. It wasn't very hot so I drank it right down. I said, "I got to meet Uncle Am. I can't stay."

Bunny said, "Gee, Ed, we were counting on you to play some cards. When we found you were home, Madge looked at your clock and found you were going to wake up at seven. We thought you'd stick around."

I said, "Maybe I can bring Uncle Am back with me. I'll see."

I stood up. Gardie asked. "What are you going to do, Eddie? I don't mean now, I mean in general. You going back to work?"

"Sure," I said, "I'm going back to work. Why not?"

"I thought maybe you'd want to come to Florida with us, that's all. You don't, do you?"

I said, "I guess not."

She said, "The money's Mom's. I don't know if you know, but the policy was made out to her. It's hers."

Mom said, "Gardie!"

"I know that," I said "I don't want any of the money."

Mom said, "Gardie shouldn't of put it that way, Ed. But what she means is you've got a job and everything and I've got to finish putting her through school and—"

"It's all right, Mom," I told her. "Honest, I never even thought about wanting any of the money. I'm doing all right. Well, so long. So long, Bunny."

Bunny called out, "Wait a second, Ed," and joined me in the hall by the door. He pulled out a five-dollar bill. He said, "Bring your uncle over, Ed; I'd like to meet him. And bring some beer back with you. Out of this."

I didn't take the bill. I said, "Honest, Bunny, I can't. I'd like you to meet him, but some other time. We got something to do this evening. We're—well, you know what we're trying to do."

He shook his head slowly. He said, "There's no percentage in it, Ed. You ought to let it lay."

"Maybe," I said, "Maybe you're right, Bunny. But now we're started; well, we're going to see it through. It's goofy I guess, but that's the way it is."

"Then how about letting me help?"

"You did. You helped plenty, getting that listing for us. If anything else comes up, I'll let you know. Thanks a lot, Bunny."

At the hotel, I found Uncle Am shaving with an electric razor plugged in beside his bureau mirror.

He asked, "Get sleep?"

"Sure, lots of it." I took a look at his face in the mirror. It was a little puffy and his eyes were slightly red-rimmed. I said, "You didn't, did you?"

"I started to, and Bassett came around and woke me up. We took each other around for a drink and pumped each other."

"Dry?" I asked.

"I don't know how dry I got him—I think he's holding something back, but I don't know what. In fact, I wouldn't be surprised, Ed, if he's running a ring-tailed whizzer on us. But I can't figure where."

"And how did he do with you?"

"Not so bad. I told him about Gary, about the trial, about the extra dough Wally had—I gave him everything but the Milan Towers address and phone number. I got a hunch he's holding back something more important than that."

"As for instance?"

"I wish I knew, kid. Have you seen Madge?"

"She's going to Florida," I told him. "She and Gardie. Soon as they get the insurance."

He said, "I wish 'em luck. She'll land on her feet, kid. That money won't last her over a year, but she'll have another husband by then. She's still got her figure and—she was about six or seven years younger than Wally, if I remember right."

"She's thirty-six, I think."

Uncle Am said, "Bassett and I had a drink or two and then I got rid of him and there wasn't enough time left to sleep before you'd get here, so I went over and cased the Milan Towers. I made a start for us."

He came over and sat on the bed, leaned back against the pillow. He said, "There's a girl living alone in Apartment Forty-three. Name of Claire Raymond. Tasty dish, the bartender says. Her husband's away; the bartender thinks they're separated. He even thinks she got walked out on; but the rent's paid till the end of the month so she's staying there alone for that long anyway."

"Did you find out if—"

"Yeah, Raymond is Reynolds. He fits the description, anyway. And he'd been in the bar with a couple of friends that could be Dutch and Benny."

"Benny?"

"The wop torpedo. I got his name from Bassett; Bassett had looked up what the cops had on them and gave me some dope. Benny Rosso. Dutch's last name is Reagan, if you can figure that out. None of them has shown at the Milan for about a week—that'd be from a day or two before Wally's death."

"Figure that means anything?"

He yawned. "I wouldn't know. We'll have to ask 'em sometime. Well, I guess we might as well get going."

I said, "Relax a minute. I got to go down the hall."

"Okay, kid. Don't fall in."

I went down the hall, and when I came back he was sound asleep.

I stood there a minute, thinking. He'd been doing ninetenths of this by himself, with me playing tagalong. Didn't I have the brains or nerve to do something by myself for once? Especially when he needed sleep and I didn't.

I took a deep breath and let it out and said to myself, "Here goes nothing," and I turned out the light.

I got out without waking him up, and I headed for the Milan Towers.

CHAPTER ELEVEN

I SLOWED DOWN on the way, because it came to me I didn't know what I was going to do. It was pretty early in the evening, too, and I was hungry, so I stopped and ate. When I was through eating, I still didn't have any idea.

But I went on to the Milan Towers.

There was a cocktail bar in the corner of the building, connecting with the lobby. I went in and sat down at the bar. It was swanky as hell. I'd been going to order beer, but I'd have felt foolish ordering beer in a place like that.

I tilted my hat back a little and tried to feel tough.

"Rye," I told the bartender. I remembered George Raft, as Ned Beaumont in the movie, *The Glass Key*, always ordered rye. I tried to feel like George Raft had acted.

The bartender spun a shot expertly along the bar and filled it from an Old Overholt bottle. "Wash?"

"Plain water," I told him.

I got back thirty-five cents out of the dollar bill I put on the bar.

I thought, I don't have to be in any hurry to drink it. Without turning around, I studied the place, using the mirror back of the bar. I wondered, why do all bars have mirrors? I should think when a man's getting tight, the last thing he'd want to watch would be himself in a mirror. At least the ones who drink to get away from themselves.

In the mirror I could see through the door that led into the lobby of the hotel. I could see a clock in there. The dial of the clock was backwards in the mirror and it took me a little while to figure out that it was a quarter after nine.

At half-past nine, I thought, I'll do something. I don't know what, but I'll get started.

The first step will be to go out in the lobby and phone upstairs. But what am I going to say?

I wished now I'd either waked Uncle Am or waited for him. Maybe I was going to make a botch of things. Like I did taking a poke at Reinhart.

I looked around the place again in the mirror. Down at the other end of the bar a man sat alone. He looked like a successful business man. I thought, I wonder if he is? For all I know, he might be a gangster. And the little, dark, Italian fellow sitting alone over in the booth, might be a commission merchant, although he looked like a torpedo. He might even be Benny Rosso. I could ask him, but if he is, he's heeled and I'm not. And maybe he wouldn't tell me.

I took a sip of the rye and it tasted lousy, so I drank it down to get rid of it, and got hold of the chaser before I desecrated that sleek and shiny bar by exploding across it. I hoped nobody had noticed my lack of dignity in that dive for the water.

I looked at the backwards clock in the mirror and it looked like three thirty-one, so I figured out it was nine twenty-nine.

The bartender was coming back my way, but I shook my head at him. I wondered if he'd seen me almost choke on the drink. I felt silly, but I sat there one more minute and then I got up and started for the lobby door. I felt like my shirttail was hanging out and everybody was looking at it.

I was going to stutter into the phone and mess everything.

It was the juke box that saved me. It was between the bar and that door, against a square pillar in the middle of the room. It was bright and shiny and gaudy, even in that swanky bar-room. I stopped to look over the numbers on it and fished a nickel out of my pocket.

I picked a Benny Goodman out of the lot and dropped my nickel. I stood there watching the machine slide the platter out of the stack and bring down the needle.

I closed my eyes when it started to play and stood there taking in the introduction, not moving a muscle, but giving to the music with all of my body, with all of me, letting go inside.

Then I opened my eyes again and walked out into the lobby, riding on the high wail of the clarinet, drunk as a lord. Not from the rye.

I felt swell. I didn't feel like a kid, I didn't feel foolish, and my shirttail was in again. I could handle anything likely to happen and most things that were unlikely.

I stepped into the phone booth and dialed W–E–N–3–8–4–2. I heard the buzz of the phone ringing.

The click of the receiver and a girl's voice said, "Hello?" The voice I'd liked last night.

I said, "This is Ed, Claire."

"Ed who?"

"You don't know me. You've never met me. But I'm calling from the lobby downstairs. Are you alone?"

"Y-yes. Who *is* this?"

I asked, "Does the name Hunter mean anything to you?"

"Hunter? It doesn't."

I asked, "How about the name Reynolds?"

"Who *is* this?"

"I'd like to explain," I said. "May I come upstairs? Or would you meet me down in the bar for a drink?"

"Are you a friend of Harry's?"

"No."

"I don't know you," she said. "I don't see why I should see you."

I said, "That's the only way you'll get to know me."

"Do you *know* Harry?"

I said, "I'm an enemy of Harry's."

"Oh." It stalled her for a minute.

I said, "I'm coming upstairs. Open the door but leave the chain on it. If I don't look like a werewolf—or any other kind of wolf—maybe you'll unhook the chain."

I hung up before she could tell me not to. I thought I had her curious, enough so to let me in.

I didn't want to give her time to think it over, nor time to make a phone call. I didn't wait for an elevator; I hotfooted it up three flights of stairs.

She hadn't phoned anybody, because she was waiting at the door. There was a chain on it, all right, and she had the door open four inches on the chain and was standing there looking out. That way she could see me walking down the hall and get a better look than by opening it after I knocked.

She was young, and she was a knockout. Even through four inches of open door, I could see her. She was the kind of girl that could make you whistle twice.

I managed to get down the hall without stumbling on the carpet.

Her eyes stayed neutral, but she took the chain off the door when I got there. She opened it, and I went in. There wasn't anyone waiting back of the door with a sandbag, so I went on into the living room. It was a nice room except that it was a little like a movie set. There was a fireplace with brass andirons and a stand that held a dainty, shiny poker and shovel, but there'd never been a fire in the fireplace. There was a comfortable looking sofa in front of it. There were lamps and drapes and curtains and things; I can't describe it, but it was a nice room.

I walked to the front of the sofa and sat down. I held my hands out to the empty fireplace and rubbed them as though I were warming them.

I said, "It's a braw night. The snow is seven feet deep on the boulevard. My huskies gave out before I reached Ontario. The last mile I had to crawl on hand and knee." I rubbed my hands some more.

She stood there at the end of the sofa, looking down at me, arms akimbo. They were nice arms, for a sleeveless dress, and she was wearing a sleeveless dress.

She said, "I take it you're not in a hurry?"

I said, "I must catch a train a week from Wednesday."

She made a little noise that might have been a well-bred snort. She said, "I suppose we might as well have a drink then."

She bent down and opened the cabinet to the left of the fireplace and there was a row of bottles in it and a row of glasses. There were jiggers and stirring spoons and a shaker and—as God is my witness—there was a miniature freezing compartment at one side with three rubber trays of ice cubes.

I said, "What, no radio in it?"

"The other side of the fireplace. Radio-phono." I looked that way.

I said, "I'll bet you haven't any records."

"Do you want a drink, or don't you?"

I looked back at the row of bottles, and decided against anything mixed; I might be expected to mix it myself and not know how to do it. I said "Burgundy goes well with a maroon carpet. It doesn't make spots if you spill it."

"If that's all that worries you, you can have crème de menthe. The furnishings aren't mine."

"But you have to live with them."

"Not after next week."

I said. "Then to hell with Burgundy. We'll have crème de menthe. Anway me, I will."

She took a pair of tiny liqueur goblets from the top shelf and filled them from the crème de menthe bottle. She handed me one.

I saw a teakwood cigarette box on the mantel. I gave her one of her own cigarettes and lighted it for her, lighted one for myself and then sat down and took a sip of the liqueur. It tasted like peppermint candy and looked like green ink. I decided that I liked it.

She didn't sit down. She stood leaning back against the mantel, looking at me.

She was still neutral.

She had jet-black hair that managed to be sleek and wavy at the same time. She was slender, almost as tall as I. She had clear, calm eyes.

I said, "You're beautiful."

A corner of her mouth twitched a little bit. She asked, "Is that why you telephoned up, to tell me that?"

I said, "I didn't know it then, I'd never seen you. No, that wasn't why I wanted to talk to you."

"What do I have to do to get you started talking?"

"Liquor always helps," I said. "And I'm a sucker for music. Do you have any records?"

She took a deep drag on her cigarette and let the smoke out her nostrils, slowly. She said, "If I asked you how you got that black eye, I suppose you'd tell me you were bitten by a St. Bernard."

I said, "Nothing but the truth. A man hit me."

"Why?"

"He didn't like me."

"Did you hit him back?"

I said, "Yes."

She laughed. It was a full, honest laugh. She said, "I don't know whether you're crazy or not. I can't decide. What do you really want?"

I said, "Harry Reynold's address."

She frowned. "I don't have it. I don't know where he is. I don't care."

I said, "We were talking about phonograph records. Do you have—"

"Stop it. I want to know; why are you looking for Harry?"

I took a long breath and leaned forward, I said, "Last week a man was killed in an alley. He was my father, a printer. I'm an apprentice printer. I'm not as old as I look. My uncle is a carney. He and I are trying to find Harry Reynolds to turn him over to the police for killing my father. My uncle would be here with me, but he's asleep. He's a swell guy; you'd like him."

She said, "You do better in monosyllables. You were telling the truth about that black eye."

I said, "Then shall we try monosyllables again?"

She took another sip of the liqueur, watching me over the rim of the tiny glass.

"All right," she said. "What's your name?"

"Ed."

"Is that all of it? What's the rest?"

"Hunter," I told her. "That took two syllables. I tried to stick to Ed; it's all your fault."

"You really *are* looking for Harry? That's why you came here?"

"Yes."

"What do you want with him?"

"That'll take three syllables."

"Go ahead."

"To kill him."

"Who are you working for?"

"A man. His name wouldn't mean anything to you. If I thought it would, I'd tell you."

She said, "Your tongue isn't quite loose enough yet. We'll have to try more liquor." She refilled our glasses.

"And music," I told her, "soothes the savage breast. How about those records. If you have any."

She laughed again and walked across the room. She pulled aside some cretonne and there was a shelf of albums. "Who do you want, Ed? Most of them are here."

"Dorsey?"

"Both of them. Which Dorsey?"

"The trombone Dorsey."

She knew I meant Tommy. She took the records from one of the albums and put them in the phono, setting it for automatic.

She came and stood in front of me. "Who sent you here?"

I said, "It would be a nice line if I could say, 'Benny sent me'. But he didn't. I don't like Benny or Dutch any more than I like Harry. Nobody sent me, Claire, I just came."

She leaned over and touched both sides of my coat, where a shoulder holster would be. She straightened up, frowning. She said, "You haven't even got a—"

"Shut up," I said, "I want to hear Dorsey."

She shrugged, picked up her glass from the mantel, and sat down on the sofa, just far enough away to let me know I wasn't expected to make a pass. I didn't. I wanted to, but I didn't.

I waited till the phonograph finished the fourth record and quit.

Then I said, "What if there was money in it for you? For Harry's address, I mean."

She said, "I don't know it, Ed."

She turned and looked at me. She said, "Listen, this is the truth and I don't care if you believe it or not. I'm through with Harry and with—with everything he stands for. I've lived here two years now, and all I've got to show for it is enough money to get back home. Home is Indianapolis.

"I'm getting out of here and going back there, and I'm going to take a job and live in a hall bedroom, with one pillow on the bed. I can learn all over again how to live on twenty-five bucks a week. Or whatever. Maybe that sounds funny to you."

"Not particularly," I said. "But wouldn't a nest egg in the bank be a good start for turning over a new—"

"No, Ed. For two perfectly good reasons. First, a double-cross would be a hell of a start. Second, I don't know where Harry is, I haven't seen him for a week—almost two weeks. I don't even know if he's in Chicago. I don't care."

I said, "If that's the way it is—"

I got up and walked over to the shelf of albums. There was a book of old-timers there, featuring Jimmy Noone, Wang-Wang Blues, Wabash Blues—I'd heard a lot about Jimmy Noone, and I'd never heard one of his platters. I took the album over to the phono, figured out how to put it on, and stood watching till the first record got going. It was very, very swell stuff.

I held out my hand to Claire, and she stood up and came to me. We danced. The music was as blue as the crème de menthe had been green. Deep, deep blue. They don't play it like that any more. It got me.

It wasn't until the music stopped that I really realized I had Claire in my arms. And that she wasn't fighting to get out of them and that kissing her was going to be the most natural thing in the world.

It was. And it was there, in the silence between records, in the silence of that kiss, that we heard a key turning in the door.

She was out of my arms almost before I realized what the sound was.

She put a finger to her lips in a quick gesture of silence and then pointed toward a door that was ajar just to the left of the liquor cabinet. Then she whirled and started for the short hallway that led to the outer door of the apartment—the door in which the key had turned, the door that was opening by now.

I wasn't so slow, either. I got my glass and my cigarette off the mantel and my hat off the end of the sofa, and I was through the door she'd pointed to, all before she'd reached the doorway to the hall.

I was in a dark room. I pushed the door back as it had been, a few inches ajar.

I heard her voice say, "Dutch! What the hell do you mean by walking in here like—"

The phono started in again, on the second of the Jimmy Noone records, and I couldn't hear the rest. The record was Margie. "Margie, I'm always thinking of you, Margie—"

Through the crack of the door, I could see Claire crossing the room to shut it off. Her face was white with anger and her eyes—well, I'm glad they hadn't looked at me like that.

She shut if off, sharp. She said, "Goddam you, Dutch, did Harry give you that key or did you—"

"Now, Claire, climb off it. No, Harry didn't give me a key. You know damn well he wouldn't. *I* got this key, toots. I figured this angle a week ago."

"What angle? Skip it; I don't even want to know what you're talking about. Get out of here."

"Now, toots." He was farther into the room now. I saw him for the first time. I hadn't been able to tell anything by his voice except that he wasn't a soprano. I saw him now. He looked as big as the side of a house.

And if he was either Dutch or Irish, then I was a Hottentot. He looked like a Greek to me. A Greek or a Syrian or an Armenian. Maybe even Turkish or Persian or something. But how he got the last name of Reagan or the nickname Dutch, I wouldn't try to guess. He had swarthy skin, and if he'd been stripped, there would have been acres of it. He looked like a wrestler and walked as though he were muscle-bound.

"Now, toots," he said, "don't get up in the air like that. Take it easy. We got business to talk."

"Get *out* of here."

He stood there, smiling, turning his hat in his hands. His voice got softer.

He said, "You think I don't know Harry's crossing me? Me and Benny? Well, I'm not worried about Benny, but me, I don't like to be crossed. I'm going to explain that to Harry."

"I don't know what you're talking about."

"Don't you?" He took a fat cigar out of his breast pocket, put it between his puffy lips, and took his time lighting it with a silver lighter. He put his hat back on his head. He said again, "Don't you?"

Claire said, "I don't. And if you don't get out of here, I'll—"

"You'll what?" He chuckled. "You'll call copper? With forty G's, hot from Waupaca, in the joint? Don't make me laugh. Now listen careful, toots. First, I know the score. Harry pretended to break with you; he was smart, he did it *before* the Waupaca job. But like schlemiels, we let Harry take the stuff when we break up. Now where's Harry? I don't know, but I'll find out. And I know where the forty G's are. Here."

"You're crazy. You damn dumb—"

I'd been wrong in thinking he was muscle-bound. He just walked that way. His hand went out like a snake would strike and grabbed Claire's wrist. He jerked her to him and her back was against him, his arm holding her there, against his chest, pinning down both her arms.

His other hand clamped over her mouth.

His back was mostly toward me. I didn't know what I was going to do; I didn't know what I could do against a mountain of muscle like that, but I opened the door. I looked around for something. The only thing I could see was the lightweight poker by the phoney fireplace.

I started for it, walking quietly.

His voice hadn't changed a semitone in pitch. He kept on as though he was talking about the weather. He said, "Just a second, toots, I'll relax my hand over your yap enough to let you tell me yeah or no. One way to take the dough, you and me, toots, and Harry doesn't live here any more. Other way, well—you wouldn't like it."

I had hold of the poker now. My feet hadn't made any noise. Only, my God, it was a toy poker. It wasn't made to poke a fire or to hit a giant over the head with. It didn't have any heft. It would just make him mad.

The andirons were screwed down.

I remembered something I'd read. There's a jujitsu blow along the side of the neck, parallel to and just under the jawbone. It's given with the edge of the flat hand, and it can paralyse or even be fatal.

It was worth a try. I moved to just the right position, held the poker well back for a good swing.

I said, "Hold it, Dutch."

Plenty happened. He let go Claire with both hands, and turned his head at just the angle I'd figured he'd turn it, and I let go with the poker, a full arm swing. It hit on the dotted line that would have been there if his neck had been on a diagram.

Claire fell, and Dutch fell, and the double thud shook the Milan Towers. It really was a jar. It knocked Claire's crème de menthe glass off the mantel and it hit the tiles of the fireplace with a bright tinkle and a green splash. There were going to be spots on the maroon carpet after all.

My first thought was his gun. I didn't know if he was really out or for how long. It wasn't in a holster. It was a snub-nosed Police Positive revolver, in his side coat pocket.

Once I had it, I felt better. I could even hear what was going on, and what was going on was laughter. Claire was on her hands and knees trying to get up, and she was laughing like the devil. Slightly drunken laughter.

I didn't get it; she hadn't been drunk. It didn't sound like hysteria.

It wasn't. When she saw me looking at her, she stopped. She said, "Turn on the phonograph again, *quick*."

Then she started laughing again. Only it was just her mouth that was laughing. Her face was white; her eyes were scared. She got to her feet and staggered across the room, deliberately.

I didn't get it, I was dumb. But I can take orders; I got the phonograph going. She collapsed onto the sofa, sobbing, but sobbing quietly, very quietly.

The phonograph played, "Margie, I'm always thinking of you, Margie; you mean the world—"

Over it, she said, "Talk, Ed, Talk loudly. *Walk*, so they can hear you." She'd stopped sobbing, and brought her voice up in pitch. "Don't you *see*, you dope? a fall like that, a noise like that? It's either a murder or an accident—or a drunk falling down. If there's talking and walking and laughing after it, then they say, it was just a drunk. It there's dead quiet after a thud like that, they call the desk—"

"Sure," I said. I'd whispered it. I cleared my throat and said, "Sure," louder. Too loud. I didn't try it a third time.

I still had the gun in my hand. I shoved it in my pocket to get it out of the way, and went over to where Dutch still lay stretch out. I thought, My God, why is he still as that? He can't be dead from—

But he was. My hand inside his coat couldn't find any heartbeat, although I kept hunting. I didn't believe it. A trick blow like that, you read it in a book, but you don't really believe it would work. Not for you. For a jujitsu expert, yes, but not for you.

I'd been so scared that it wouldn't even faze him that I'd put my weight into it. It had worked. He was as dead as a mackerel.

I started laughing, and not to reassure the neighbours.

Claire came over and slapped my face and I stopped.

We went back to the sofa and sat down. I got hold of myself, and got cigarettes out for us. I got hold of myself, and when I struck a match and held it for us, my hand was steady.

She asked, "Want a drink, Ed?"

"No," I told her.

She said, "Neither do I."

The phonograph had changed records again. It started the Wang-Wang Blues. I got up and shut it off. If the neighbours under us or on either side were going to call copper or call the desk, they'd have done it by now.

I sat back down on the sofa. Claire put her hand in mine, and we sat there, not looking at each other, not talking, staring into a fireplace that didn't have a fire in it and never would have.

Anyway, looking at the fireplace, we didn't have to look at Dutch on the floor behind us.

But he was there. He didn't get up and leave. He never would. He wouldn't ever do anything. He was dead.

And his being there got bigger and bigger until it filled the room.

Claire's hand tightened convulsively in mine and she started sobbing again, very quietly.

CHAPTER TWELVE

I WAITED TILL SHE'D STOPPED CRYING and then I said, we've got to do something. We can call the police and tell them the truth; that's one thing. Another; we can scram out of here and let them find it whenever they do. The third would be tougher; we could put it somewhere else for them to find.

"We *can't* call the police, Ed. They'd find out Harry had been living here. They'd find out everything. They'd nail me as an accessory to every job he ever pulled. They'd—" Her face got white as a sheet. "Ed, they *did* take me along on one job, made me wait in the car and act as lookout. God, what a sap I was not to see he was deliberately fixing me up so I could never talk. The police know Dutch was on that job, and if—"

I said, "Could they identify you, and tie you in with that job?"

"I—I think they could."

I said, "Then we'd better not call them. But you're getting out of here, anyway, going back to Indianapolis. Couldn't you just leave tonight?"

"Yes, but—I'd be *wanted*. They could trace me when they found Dutch dead here. They could find out who I was and where I came from. I couldn't go back to Indianapolis; I'd have to go somewhere else. There'd be dodgers out for me. All the rest of my life, I'd be—"

I cut her short. "Okay," I said. "We can't call copper and we can't walk off and leave him. How could we get him out of here?"

"He's awful heavy, Ed. I don't know if we could do it, but there's a service elevator at the back of the hall that goes to a back door of the alley. And it's after midnight. But we'd need a car once we got him to the alley. And he's awful heavy, Ed. Do you think we could?"

I stood up and looked around till I saw the phone. I said, "I'll see what I can do, Claire. Wait."

I went over to the phone and called the Wacker and I gave Uncle Am's room number.

When his voice answered, I felt so relieved my knees got weak and I sat down in the chair by the phone table.

I said, "This is Ed, Uncle Am."

"You young squirt, what you mean walking off on me? I been waiting for you to call. I suppose you got yourself in a jam, huh?"

I said, "I suppose I did. I'm calling from—from the phone number we had."

"The hell. You're doing all right, kid. Or are you?"

"I don't know. It kind of depends on how you look at it. Listen, we need a car or a—"

He cut in, "Who's *we*?"

"Claire and I," I told him. "Listen, this call is through the hotel switchboard, isn't it?"

"Shall I call you back, kid?"

"It'd be an idea," I said.

The call came in five minutes. He said, "This is from a booth, Ed. Go ahead."

I said, "Claire and I were getting along, but we had company. A guy named Dutch. Dutch—uh—drank a bit too much and sort of passed out on us. We want to take him home without taking him through the front lobby. It'd be best if he wasn't found here. Now if somebody had a car and parked it in the alley back of here, by the service entrance, and then gave us a hand getting him down the service elevator—"

"Okay, kid. Would a taxi do?"

I said, "The driver might be worried about Dutch. He's pretty—uh—stiff, if you know what I mean."

Uncle Am said, "I guess I know what you mean. Okay, kid, hold the fort. The marines are coming."

I felt a hell of a lot better when I put down the phone and went back to the sofa beside Claire.

She gave me a funny kind of look. She said, "Ed, you called the guy *Uncle* Am. Is he really your uncle?"

I nodded.

She said, "That wild, screwy yarn you pulled about Harry killing your—your father last week and you and your uncle hunting him for that, only your uncle was asleep—wasn't that in with the seven-foot snow on Michigan Boulevard and the dog teams giving out and—"

I said, "It wasn't. It was the straight story. I told that first because I knew you wouldn't believe it, the way I put it. I didn't know where you stood then."

She put her hand in mine again. She said, "You should have told me."

"I did, didn't I? Listen, Claire, think hard. Did you ever hear Harry—or Dutch or Benny—mention the name, Hunter?"

"No, Ed. Not that I remember, anyway."

"How long have you known them?"

"Two years. I told you that."

I wanted to believe her. I wanted like hell to believe everything she'd told me. But I had to be sure.

I asked, "Did you ever hear the name Kaufman? George Kaufman?"

She didn't even hesitate. "Yes, about—I guess two or three weeks ago. Harry told me a man named Kaufman might call up this number and give me a message. He said the message could be an address, and I was to copy it down and give it to him. Or that it might be that someone Harry was interested in meeting was at the tavern Kaufman owned. And that if it was that the guy was there, I was to get in touch with Harry quick, if I knew where he was."

"Did Kaufman call?"

"No. Not any time I was here, anyway."

"Could anyone else have taken the message?"

"Harry might have—if it was over a week ago. There would have been times he was here and I was out. Nobody else could have, Ed, this man Harry wanted to meet if he came in Kaufman's—would it have been your father?"

I nodded. It checked; it fitted Kaufman's story like a glove, and proved that both he and Claire were telling the truth about it.

I asked her, "Know anything about Harry's brother, Steve?"

"Only that he's in jail. I think in Indiana. But that was before I met Harry. Ed, I *do* want a drink now. How about you? Can I mix you a Martini? Or would you rather have something else?"

I said, "A Martini would be swell."

When she stood up, she caught sight of herself in the mirror over the mantel. She gasped a little. She said, "I'll—I'll be back in a minute, Ed."

She went through the door behind which I'd hidden not so long ago, and I heard another door open and close and water running. She was feeling better, I knew. When a girl starts worrying about how she looks, she's feeling better.

She came back looking like a million bucks in crisp new currency.

She had a glass of ice cubes and a bottle of vermouth in her hands when the doorbell rang.

I said, "It's Uncle Am. I'll get it."

But I had my hand on the revolver in my coat pocket when I opened the door, on the chain.

It was Uncle Am. He was wearing a taxi-driver's cap, grinning. He said, "You phone for a cab?"

I unhooked the chain. "Yeah," I said. "Come on in. We got a little packing to do yet."

I closed the door behind him and looked in. He said, "Yeah, you've been doing all right. Wipe that lipstick off your mush and you'll look better, though. Where is it?"

We went into the living room. His eyebrows went up a little when he saw Claire. I saw his lips make the slight involuntary motion towards a whistle that men's lips often make when they look at something like Claire.

Then he turned his head a little and saw Dutch. He winced a little.

He said, "Kid, you should have told me to bring a derrick." He walked over and stood looking down. He said, "No blood, no marks. That's something, anyway. What'd you do, scare him to death?"

I said, "It was almost the other way round. Uncle Am, this is Claire."

She put out her hand and he took it. He said, "Even under the circumstances, it's a pleasure."

She said, "Thanks, Am. A Martini?"

She was already getting out a third glass. Uncle Am turned and looked at me and I knew what he was thinking. I said, "I'm all right. I had two thimblefuls of green ink, but that was several weeks ago. And one rye in the bar downstairs, but that was last year."

She finished the cocktails and handed one to each of us. I sipped mine. It tasted good; I liked it.

Uncle Am said, "How much have you told, Ed?"

"Enough," I told him. "Claire knows what the score is. She's on our team."

He said, "I hope you know what you're doing, Ed."

"I hope so, too," I told him.

"Well, you can tell me about it tomorrow. There's always another day."

I said, "There's the rest of tonight."

He grinned. He said, "I doubt it. Well, let's get going. Think you can manage half of our drunken friend?"

"I can try."

He turned to Claire. "The cab is in the alley, outside the service door. But it's locked; I came in the front way. You got a key?"

"It opens from the inside. And we can put a piece of cardboard so the catch of the lock will stay back and we can get in again. The elevator will be at the first floor. I think I can run it; I'll go down now and bring it up to the fourth—"

"No," Uncle Am said. "Elevators are noisy—especially ones that aren't supposed to be in use in the middle of the night. We'll get him down those back stairs. You just stay ahead of us so we don't run into anybody. If you see anybody, speak to 'em; we'll hear your voice and stop to wait."

She nodded.

Uncle Am took Dutch's shoulders and I took his feet. He was just too heavy for us to try walking him between us like an ambulating drunk. We'd have to carry him and take our chances.

We got him through the hall and down the stairs. It wasn't a job I'd want to do regularly.

We got all the breaks. The door was like Claire had said it would be. There wasn't anyone around the alley. We got him into the cab, jack-knifed on the floor of the back seat, and put over him a blanket Claire had brought down for the purpose.

I sat down and wiped the sweat off my forehead. Uncle Am did, too.

Then he got in behind the wheel and Claire and I got in back.

He said, "Any choice of a final resting place?"

I said, "There's an alley off Franklin—No, skip it; that's the *last* place we'd want to put him."

Claire said, "I know where he used to live, up to a few weeks ago. An apartment building on Division. If we left him in the alley back of there—"

"Smart girl," Uncle Am said. "If there's a tie-in between who he is and where he's found, it'll look like he's been dropped off there. It'll focus the investigation away from the Milan."

He slid the car into gear.

We came out of the alley on Fairbanks, went north to Erie and cut over Erie to the boulevard. We stayed in the heavy traffic of the boulevard north to Division Street.

Claire gave him the address and ten minutes later we were rid of Dutch. We didn't waste any time getting out of there.

We hadn't talked any at all. We still didn't talk until we were lost in the boulevard traffic again, heading south. Somewhere a big clock struck two.

Claire was very quiet in a corner of the back seat, with my arm around her.

Uncle Am said, "You still got the gun, kid?"

"Yeah, I got it."

He pulled into the alley, stopped the cab right where it had been before. He said, "Stay in here, you two. Ed give me the gun and I'll case the joint. If you had company before, there could be someone waiting there. Claire, give me the key."

I wanted to go up with him, but he wouldn't let me.

It was very, very quiet.

Claire said, "Kiss me, Ed."

A little later she said, "I'm taking an early train tomorrow, Ed. I'd—I'd be afraid there alone. Will you stay, and take me to the train?"

I said, "Chicago is big. Can't you go somewhere else in Chicago, for a while, anyway? Until this is all over?"

"No, Ed. And you've got to promise that you'll never come to Indianapolis looking for me. I won't give you my address. Tomorrow morning's got to be good-bye. For good."

I wanted to argue, but down inside I knew she was right, I don't know how I knew it, but I did.

Uncle Am was opening the door of the taxi. He said, "Break it up, you two. Here's the gun and the key, Ed. Listen, you don't know what that gun's been used for. Keep it tonight, but get rid of it before you come back to the Wacker. And without your prints on it."

I said, "I'm not that dumb, Uncle Am."

"Sometimes I wonder, kid. But you'll grow out of it. When'll I see you again? Around noon?"

"I guess so."

Claire said, "Won't you come up for a drink, Am?"

We were getting out of the cab. Uncle Am opened the front door and slid into the driver's seat. He said, "I guess not, kids. This taxi and cap are costing me twenty-five bucks an hour and I've had 'em two hours now. That's a little rich for my blood."

He stepped on the starter of the taxi and then leaned out of the window. He said, "God bless you, my children. Don't do anything I wouldn't do."

He drove off.

We stood there a little while, hand in hand, in the warm summer night, in the darkness of the alley.

Claire said. "It's nice tonight."

I said, "It's going to be nicer."

"Yes, it's going to be nicer, Ed."

She leaned against me a little. I let go her hand and put my arms around her. I kissed her.

After a minute she said, "Shall we go in out of the snow?"

We went in out of the snow.

When I woke up, Claire was dressed already, and was packing a suitcase. I looked at the little electric clock on the bedstand and it was only ten o'clock.

She smiled at me and said, "Morning, Eddie."

I asked, "Is it still snowing out?"

"No, it's all through snowing. I was just going to wake you. There's a train at eleven-fifteen. We'll have to hurry, if we're going to eat any breakfast."

She went to a closet for another suitcase.

I got up, took a quick shower, and dressed. She'd finished packing by then. She said, "We'll have to settle for coffee and doughnuts at the station. There's only an hour now."

"Had I better phone for a cab?"

"There's a stand out in front. At this time of morning, we can get one."

I took the two suitcases and she took the overnight bag and a small package that I saw was stamped for mailing. She saw me glance at it and said, "Birthday present for a friend of mine; I should have mailed it two days ago. Remind me, on the way."

I didn't give a damn about birthday presents. I walked to the door and then turned around, with my back toward it and put down the suitcases.

I held out my arms, but she didn't come. She shook her head slowly. "No, Ed. No good-byes, please. Last night was good-bye for us. And you mustn't ever look for me; you mustn't ever try to follow me."

"Why not, Claire?"

"You'll know why, Ed, when you've had time to think things out. You'll know I'm right. Your uncle will know; maybe he can tell you. I can't."

"But—"

"How old are you, Ed? Really? Twenty?"

"Almost nineteen."

"I'm twenty-nine, Ed. Don't you see that—"

I said, "Yeah, you're practically dying of old age. Your arteries are hardening. Your—"

"Ed, you don't see what I mean. Twenty-nine isn't old, no, but it's not young any more, either, for a woman. And—Ed, I was lying to you last night about the job and the hall bedroom and all that. When a woman's used to good things and money, she can't go back, Ed. Not unless she's stronger than I am. *I'm* not going back to that, Ed."

"You mean you're going to find yourself another mug like Harry?"

"Not like Harry, no, I have learned that much. A guy with money, but not earned *that* way. I've learned that much in Chicago. Especially last night when Dutch—I'm glad you were here, Eddie."

I said, "Maybe I understand a little. But why can't we—"

"How much do you make, Eddie, as a printer? Do you see?"

"Okay," I said.

I picked up the suitcases and went out. We got a taxi at the stand in front of the hotel, and started for the Dearborn Station.

In the taxi, Claire sat very straight, but I happened to notice that there were tears in her eyes.

I don't know whether it made me feel better or worse. Better, I guess, about last night, and worse about her. I was all mixed up, inside, something like the time Mom had fooled me by being so nice to me, when I came home from going to the carney to get Uncle Am.

I thought, why can't women be consistent? Why can't they be good or bad, and make up their minds which? I thought, I guess most of us are that way, good and bad mixed up, but women are worse and they change back and forth faster. They go to almost absurd lengths of being nice to you, or being nasty.

Claire said, "Five years from now, you'll hardly remember me, Ed."

"I'll remember you," I said.

We crossed Van Buren, under the el, and we were through the Loop, only two blocks from the station.

She said, "Kiss me once more, Ed—if—if you still want to, after I told you the truth."

I still wanted to, and I did. My arms were still around her when the cab stopped. The little package she'd been holding slid to the floor as she moved and I picked it up and handed it to her. I noticed the address and the name.

I said, "If I hit a million-dollar jackpot, I'll get in touch with you through your girl friend in Miami."

"Don't try, Ed, either for me or for any jackpots. Stick to your job and to being what you are. And don't come in the station with me. Here comes a redcap for my bags."

"But you said—"

"It's almost train time, Ed. *Please* stay in the cab. Mama knows best. Good-bye."

The redcap was picking up the bags and starting away with them.

"Good-bye," I said.

The cabby asked, "Back to the Milan Towers?" and I said, "Yeah," watching Claire walk away from me. She didn't turn around to look back. She stopped at the mailbox outside the door and mailed the package, and didn't turn around at all as she went into the door of the Dearborn Station.

My cab was pulling away from the curb, but I was still looking out. That's how I happened to notice the dark little man get out of the cab that had been right behind mine at the curb, and walk rapidly into the station.

Something bothered me; he looked familiar but I couldn't think where I'd seen him.

We were pulling across the street, turning north into Dearborn Street. I told the driver, "I didn't mean to tell you back to the Milan. I want to go to the Wacker on Clark Street."

He nodded and kept going.

We slowed for a stop light on the next corner, and suddenly I remembered where I'd seen the guy who'd gotten out of the cab behind us. It had been yesterday evening in the bar of the Milan Towers. And he'd been Italian, and I'd thought he looked like a torpedo. I'd wondered if he'd been Benny Rosso—

"Stop," I told the driver. "Let me out here, quick."

He finished crossing the street and pulled to a stop along the line of cars at the curb. He said, "Anything you say, mister. Just make up your mind."

I fumbled a couple of singles out of my wallet and gave them to him. I didn't wait for change. I was out of the cab, running back toward the station. I could get back there quicker on foot than by having the cab go on around the block and wait for lights at every corner.

But it was an awfully long block from Harrison back to Polk. I almost got run down by a car crossing in front of the station, but I kept on running until I was inside the doors.

I stopped running then, and walked fast through the station, looking around. I'd never realized what an enormous place it was. I didn't see Claire and I didn't see the man who might have been following her.

I made two fast circuits of the station and I hadn't seen them, either of them: I hurried up to the information desk. I asked, "Which track is the Indianapolis train on, if it hasn't left?"

"Isn't loading yet. It doesn't pull in until twelve-five."

"The eleven-fifteen," I said. "Has it pulled out already?"

"There's no eleven-fifteen for Indianapolis, sir."

I looked up at the clock; it was fourteen after eleven already. I asked, "What eleven-fifteen trains *are* there?"

"Two of them; the St. Louis Flyer on Track Six, and Number Nineteen on Track One—Ft. Wayne, Columbus, Charleston—"

I turned away.

It was hopeless; two long trains leaving in one minute. I probably wouldn't be able to reach one of them, certainly not both. I didn't have enough money left to buy a fare even to Ft. Wayne.

I looked up and saw the gateman closing the iron gate marked Track Five.

A last desperate chance, I thought. The redcap; if I could find the redcap who took—I looked around and there were a dozen redcaps in sight, in different parts of the station. They didn't all look alike, but I realized I hadn't even looked at the one that had taken her bags. I'd been looking at Claire.

One was walking past me, and I grabbed his arm. I asked, "Did you take two suitcases and an overnight bag for a lady, alone, from a taxi just a little while ago?"

He pushed his cap back and scratched his head. He said, "Well, I mighta. What train?"

"That's what I want to know. It was fifteen minutes ago."

"I—I put a lady on the St. Louie 'bout that long ago, I guess. I don't rightly 'member if she had jest two suitcases and a bag. I—I think there was a violin case, suh."

I said, "Okay, skip it," and gave him a dime. There wouldn't be any use trying to talk to every redcap in the place. By the time I got the right one, he wouldn't remember anyway.

I thought, she might not have been taking a train at all, for all I know. She wouldn't let me come into the station with her. She lied about where she was going, maybe she was lying about the rest of it. Maybe she went out the other door of the station or something.

I sat down on a bench and talked myself into being mad instead of worried. I might have been ten miles off in thinking the guy who got out of the cab had been the same man I'd seen in the Milan. I didn't know our cab had been followed. And if it *was* the guy, it wasn't any more than a wild guess that he'd been following our cab and that he was Rosso. Every Italian in Chicago could be a gunsel named Rosso.

Only I couldn't get mad at Claire.

Sure she'd given me the runaround, but she'd told me she was doing it. She'd told me why.

After last night, I though, I could never be really mad at Claire. And when I'm married and settled down and have kids and grand-kids, I thought, there'd always be just a little bit of love left over for my memory of her.

I got out before I made an ass of myself by starting to bawl or something. I walked over to South Clark and caught a street car north.

CHAPTER THIRTEEN

I KNOCKED IN THE DOOR of Uncle Am's room and his voice called out, "Come on in," and I did.

He was still in bed.

I asked him, "Did I wake you up, Uncle Am?"

"No, kid, I been awake half an hour or so. I been lying here thinking."

"Claire's gone," I said. "She left town—I think."

"What do you mean, you think?"

I sat down on the edge of the bed. Uncle Am doubled the pillow under his head to raise it up, and he said, "Tell me about it, Ed. Not the personal passages. Skip those, but tell me everything that gal told you about Harry Reynolds, and what happened about Dutch last night, and what happened this morning. Just start at the beginning, from the time you left here yesterday evening.

I told him. When I got through he said, "My God, kid, you've got a memory. But don't you see the holes in it?"

"What holes? You mean Claire changed her story about herself, yeah, but what's that got to do with what we're working on?"

"I don't know, kid. Maybe nothing. I feel old this morning, this afternoon, whatever it is. I feel like we've been chasing our tails and getting nowhere. Hell, maybe you got more sense than I have. I don't know. I'm worried about Bassett."

"Has he been around?"

"No, that's what worries me. Part of what worries me. Something's wrong, and I don't know what."

"How do you mean, Uncle Am?"

"I don't know how to put it. You're nuts on music; let me put it this way. There's a sour note somewhere in a chord, and you can't find it. You sound each note by itself and it's right, and then you listen to the chord again and it's sour. It's not a major or a minor or a diminished seventh. It's a noise."

"Can't you come closer to saying what instrument it is?"

"It's not the trombone, kid. Not you. But listen, kid, it's in my bones; somebody's putting something over on us. I don't know what. I think it's Bassett, but I don't know what."

I said, "Then let's not worry about it. Let's go ahead."

"Go ahead and do what?"

I opened my mouth, then closed it again. He grinned at me.

He said, "Kid, you're starting to grow up. It's time you learned something.

"What?" I asked.

"When you kiss a woman, wipe off the lipstick."

I wiped it off and grinned back at him. I said, "I'll try to remember, Uncle Am. What are we going to do today?"

"Got any ideas?"

"I guess not."

"Neither have I. Let's take the day off and go slumming down in the Loop. Let's see a movie and then have a good dinner and then go take in a floor show. Yeah, we'll pick one with a good band if there are any. Let's take the day and evening off and get our perspective back."

It was a funny time, that afternoon and evening. We went places, and we enjoyed ourselves, but we didn't. There was a feeling about it like the quietness of the air while the barometer drops before a storm. Even I could feel it. Uncle Am was uneasy like a man waiting for something and not knowing what he's waiting for. For the first time since I'd known him, he was a little crabby. And three times he called the Homicide Department to try to get Bassett, and Bassett wasn't there.

But we didn't talk about it. We talked about the show we saw, and the band, and he told me more about the carney. We didn't talk about Pop at all.

About midnight we called it a day and broke up. I went home. I still felt uneasy. Maybe it was partly the heat. The hot wave was coming back. It was a sultry night and it was going to be hot as the hinges tomorrow.

Mom called out from her room. "That you, Ed?" When I answered, she slipped on a bathrobe and came out. She must have just turned in; she hadn't been asleep yet.

She said, "I'm glad you came home for a change, Ed. I wanted to talk with you."

"What is it, Mom?"

"I was in to the insurance company today. I took them the certificate, and they're putting it through, but the cheque's got to come from St. Louis and they say it'll be a few days yet. And I'm broke, Ed. Have you got any money?"

"Just a couple of bucks, Mom. I've got twenty-some dollars in that savings account I started."

"Could you lend it to me, Ed? I'll give it back as soon as the insurance cheque comes through."

"Sure, Mom. Anyway, I'll lend you twenty of it. I'd like to keep the few odd dollars myself. I'll draw it out tomorrow. If you need more than that, I'll bet Bunny could lend you some."

"Bunny was here this evening awhile, but I didn't want to bother him about it. He's worried; his sister in Springfield's going to have an operation early next week. A pretty bad one; he's going to take off work next week and go there, he thinks."

"Oh," I said.

"But if you can give me twenty, Ed, that'll do all right. The man said the cheque'll be only a few days."

"Okay, Mom. I'll go to the bank first thing tomorrow. 'Night."

I went in and went to bed in my room. It felt funny. I mean, it seemed like I was going back there after having been away for years. It didn't seem like home or anything, though. It was just a familiar room. I wound the clock, but I didn't set it to go off.

Somewhere outside, a clock struck one and I remembered it was Wednesday night. I thought, just about this time a week ago Pop was getting killed.

Somehow it seemed a lot longer time than that. It seemed a year, almost; so much had happened since then. It had only been a week. But I thought too: I've got to go back to work. I can't keep on staying away from work much longer. It's been a week. Next Monday I'll have to go back. Yet going back to work I thought, would be even stranger than coming back to this room to sleep.

I tried not to think about Claire, and finally I went to sleep.

It was almost eleven when I woke. I dressed and went out to the kitchen. Gardie had gone out somewhere. Mom was making coffee; she looked like she'd just got up.

She said, "There's nothing in the house. If you want to go to the bank now, will you bring some eggs and some bacon back with you, Ed?"

I said "Sure" and went out to the bank and got stuff for breakfast on the way back. Mom cooked it and we'd just about finished eating when the phone rang. I answered it, and it was Uncle Am.

"You up, Ed?"

"Just finished breakfast."

He said, "I finally got Bassett—or he got me. He called up a few minutes ago. He's coming round right away. Something's going to break, Ed. He sounded like the cat that ate the canary."

"I'm coming over," I said. "Leave in a few minutes."

I went back to the table and picked up my coffee to finish it without sitting down. I told Mom I had to meet Uncle Am right away.

She said, "I forgot, Ed. When Bunny was here last night, he wanted to see you, and because he didn't know when or where he could get in touch with you, he left a note. Something in connection with his going down-state next week."

"Where is it?"

"I think I put it on the sideboard, in the living room."

I got it on my way out and read it going down the stairs. Bunny had written: "I guess Madge told you why I'm going to Springfield this week-end. You said a guy named Anderz who had sold insurance in Gary had moved to Springfield, and you'd wanted to see him. Want me to look him up while I'm there and interview him for you? If you do, let me know before Sunday, and tell me what questions to ask."

I stuffed the note into my pocket. I'd ask Uncle Am, but he'd said he didn't think the insurance agent would be able to tell us anything. Still, it might be worth a try if Bunny was going anyway.

When I got there, Bassett was just ahead of me. He was sitting on the bed. His eyes looked more tired and washed-out than I'd ever seen them. His clothes looked like they'd been slept in, and yet he looked like he himself needed sleep. He had a flat bottle in his pocket, wrapped in brown paper, twisted above the cork.

My uncle grinned at me. He looked cheerful.

He said, "Hi, kid, shut the door. Frank here is about ready to explode with news, but I told him to hold it till you were here."

It was hot and stuffy in the hotel room. I tossed my hat on the bed, loosened my collar and sat down on the writing desk.

Bassett said, "We got the gang you been looking for. We got Harry Reynolds. We got Benny Rosso, Dutch Reagan is dead. Only—"

"Only," my uncle cut in, "none of 'em killed Wally Hunter."

Bassett had opened his mouth to go on. He closed it again and looked at Uncle Am. Uncle Am grinned at him. He said, "Obvious, my dear Bassett. What else bright and cheerful could you have been going to say with that tone of voice and that look on your ugly mug? You've been letting us pull chestnuts out of the fire for you."

"Nuts," Bassett said, "You didn't get near Harry Reynolds. You never saw him. Did you?"

Uncle Am shook his head. "You're right. We didn't."

Bassett said, "I gave you more credit, Am. I figured you for a smart guy. When you found out Harry'd been interested in your brother and started out after Harry, I gave you rope. I thought you'd lead us to him, maybe."

"But we didn't."

"Nope, you didn't. You disappointed me, Am. You never got to first base. *We* found him. Look, Am, the minute you brought up that gang, I knew you were in the clear. Maybe it was a dirty trick not to tell you, but they were wanted for the bank job in Waupaca, Wisconsin. They'd been identified by Waupaca witnesses. The reward was posted for them. And the Waupaca job was the evening your brother was killed."

Uncle Am said, "Sweet of you, Frank. You got my hundred bucks, and you get the reward, too. Or do you?"

"I don't, damn it. I wasn't the one that got 'em. If it makes you any happier, Am, I been tooken too. Nobody gets the reward on Dutch; he's cold meat. Benny was caught out of the state, and who got Reynolds? The beat coppers!"

"Did you lose much, I hope?"

"Half a G on each of them. They haven't got the Waupaca money yet. Forty grand. There's a ten-per-cent reward on that. Four G's." He licked his lips. "But hell, it'll turn up in a safe-deposit vault somedays on a routine check. There's no lead I can follow on it."

"That's nice," said Uncle Am. "How's about my hundred bucks back? I'm getting low on cash." He opened his wallet and looked into it. "I got only a hundred left out of four hundred I came here with."

"Nuts," said Bassett. "I rode along with you guys; I gave you your money's worth. I told you everything I was going to do."

Uncle Am said, "I'll bet you give it back."

"You'll *bet*?"

"Twenty bucks," Uncle Am said. He took out his wallet again, pulled a twenty out of it. He handed it to me. He said, "The kid'll hold stakes. Twenty says you'll give me that hundred bucks back voluntarily, of your own free will, today."

Bassett looked at him and then at me. His eyes were half closed hooded. He said, "I should never bet a man at his own game. But—" He took out a twenty and handed it to me.

Uncle Am grinned. He said, "Now how about a drink out of that bottle?"

Bassett took it out of his pocket and opened it. Uncle Am took a long drink and then I took a sip for sociability. Bassett took a long pull and then put the bottle on the floor by the bed.

Uncle Am leaned back against the wall, next to where I sat at the desk. He said, "How did the gang get caught?"

"What's the difference?" Bassett asked. "I told you none of 'em—"

"Sure, but we're curious. Tell us."

Bassett shrugged. "Dutch was found dead early this morning at dawn, in an alley back of Division. They found Reynolds fast asleep in the building Dutch was back of. Dutch was right under his window.

I leaned forward, and Uncle Am took my arm and pulled me back. He kept hold of my arm.

"How do you figure it?" he asked Bassett.

"Reynolds didn't, that's for sure. Probably Benny. Reynolds would never leave the corpse under his own window. But the whole gang was double-crossing each other. Reynold's woman—we find she lived at the Milan Towers—crossed the whole bunch of them."

"Who was that?" Uncle Am asked.

"A dame who went by the name of Claire Redmond in Chicago. We think her right name was Elsie Coleman. She came from Indianapolis. According to reports, she was quite a looker."

Uncle Am squeezed my arm tight. His grip said, "Steady, kid." Out loud he asked very casually. "Was?"

"She's dead, too," Bassett said, "Benny killed her last night, and got caught on the spot. It was on a train, in Georgia. We got a long-distance call from there this morning. Benny sang plenty when they caught him cold with a shiv in the dame."

"And the burden of his song?"

Bassett said, "He followed her from Chicago. He and Dutch each figured she had the mazuma and that she and Harry were figuring to cross them. Meanwhile, they must've crossed each other. Benny must have killed Dutch, because he left Dutch's body where it would lead to Harry Reynolds getting caught. Only he doesn't admit that, or hasn't yet."

"You got side-tracked, Frank," Uncle Am said. "Why'd he knife this Elsie-Claire Coleman-Redmond?"

"He thought she was lamming with the dough. Maybe he was right; I don't know. Anyway, he was following her. She had a compartment on the train. Some time during the night he got in and was searching for the hay. She woke up and yelled and he knifed her. But there happened to be a couple marshals in the car. They nailed him before he could get out of the compartment. But the dough wasn't there."

Uncle Am said, "Hand me the bottle, Frank. I'll have another sip of that mountain dew."

Bassett picked it up and handed it over. He said, "Mountain dew, hell. That's good Scotch."

Uncle Am drank and handed it back. He said, "So what now, Frank. What are you going to do now?"

Bassett shrugged. "I don't know. Keep the case on the records. Go to work on something else. Ever occur to you, Am, that maybe this was just a straight holdup-slugging after all, and that we'll never get the guy who did it?"

Uncle Am said, "No, Frank, that never occurred to me."

Bassett took another pull at the bottle. It was half empty already. He said, "Then you're nuts. Am. Listen, if it was anything else, then Madge did it. Incidentally, the insurance company's holding that cheque till I give them the green light. But I guess the only reason I stalled is I haven't seen this Wilson guy yet. Maybe I'll see him now and get it over with."

He got up, went over to the wash basin. He said, "I'm dirty as a pig. I better clean up a little before I go out again."

He turned on the water. I said to Uncle Am, "Bunny left a note. He's going to Springfield Sunday. He says—here—" I'd found the note by then and handed it to him. He read it and handed it back.

I said, "Shall we have him see the guy?"

Uncle Am shook his head slowly.

He looked at Bassett and took in a long breath and let it out slowly. Bassett was wiping his hands on the towel. He put his glasses in a case in his pocket and rubbed his eyes.

He said, "Well—"

"About that hundred bucks," Uncle Am said, "How would you like to know where to put your hands on that forty grand from Waupaca? Would you pay a hundred bucks to know, even if you had to go out of town to get it?"

"I'll pay a hundred to get four grand, sure. But you're kidding me. How the hell would you know?"

"Pay the hundred bucks," Uncle Am said.

"You're crazy. How could you know?"

"I don't know," Uncle Am said. "But I know a guy who does. And I'll guarantee it."

Bassett stared at him awhile, then his wallet came slowly out of his pocket. He took out five twenties and gave them to Uncle Am. "If this is a runaround, Am—"

Uncle Am said, "Tell him, kid."

Bassett's eyes switched to me. I said. "The money was mailed in Chicago a few minutes after eleven o'clock yesterday. Claire sent it on ahead of her. It was addressed to Elsie Cole, General Delivery, Miami."

Bassett's lips moved, but he didn't say anything I could hear.

I said, "I guess you win your bet, Uncle Am." I handed him the two twenties I had, and he put them in his wallet with the ones Bassett had given him.

Uncle Am said, "Don't take it so hard, Frank. We'll do you one more favour. We'll go over to Bunny Wilson's with you. I've never met the guy."

Bassett came out of it slowly.

CHAPTER FOURTEEN

IT WAS HOT AS THE Sahara Desert and getting hotter every minute as we walked over Grand Avenue. I took off my coat and carried it, and then I took off my hat and carried that, too. I looked at Uncle Am alongside of me and he didn't even look warm. He was wearing a suit coat, a vest, and a hat. There must be a trick to looking as cool as that, I thought.

We crossed the bridge and there wasn't even a breath of breeze off the water.

At Halsted, we went south a block and a half and turned in at the door of Bunny's rooming house. We climbed the stairs and knocked on the door of his room.

Inside I could hear the bed creak. He shuffled to the door in slippers and opened it a crack, then wider when he recognized me.

"Hi," he said. "I was just going to get up. Come in." We all went in.

Bassett leaned against the inside of the door. Uncle Am and I went over and sat down on the bed. The room was like an oven and I loosened my tie and unbuttoned the top button of my shirt. I hoped we wouldn't be here long.

Uncle Am was staring at Bunny with a funny look on his face. He looked puzzled, almost bewildered.

I said, "Bunny, this is my Uncle Am. And this is Mr. Bassett, the police detective working on Pop's case."

I looked at Bunny and couldn't see anything to be puzzled about. He had on a faded dressing gown over whatever he'd been sleeping in, if anything. He needed a shave and his hair was mussed, and he'd obviously had a few drinks the night before. But not enough for a heavy hangover.

Bunny said, "Glad to know you, Bassett. And you, Am. Ed's talked about you a lot."

I said, "My uncle's a little screwy, but he's a good guy."

Bunny got up and walked over to the dresser and I saw there was a bottle there and some glasses. He said, "Will you gentlemen have a—"

Bassett interrupted. He said, "Later, Wilson. Sit down a minute first. I want to check up on that alibi you gave Madge Hunter. I let it go because of another angle. But I want to know now if you can prove what time it was you—"

Uncle Am said, "Shut up, Bassett."

Bassett turned to look at him. His eyes got hot with sudden anger. He said, "Goddam you, Hunter, you stay out of my way or I'll—"

He was taking a step toward the bed, but he stopped when he saw that my uncle wasn't paying any attention to him, none at all. He was still staring at Bunny, with that funny look on his face.

Uncle Am said, "I don't get it, Bunny. You're not what I thought you'd be. You don't look like a killer. But you killed Wally. Didn't you?"

There was a silence you could have cut in chunks.

A long silence.

It stretched out and lasted until it became an answer in itself.

My uncle asked quietly, "You've got the policy here?"

Bunny nodded. He said, "Yeah. In the top drawer there."

Bassett seemed to wake up. He went over to the dresser and pulled open the drawer. He reached under some shirts and groped around. His hand came out with a thick envelope of the type they keep insurance policies in.

He stared at it. He said, "Maybe I'm dumb. How could *he* collect on this? Madge is the beneficiary, ain't she?"

Uncle Ambrose said, "He was planning to marry Madge. He knew she liked him and that she'd be looking for another husband pretty soon. Her type always marries again—she wouldn't have wanted to go back to being a waitress when a guy with a good job like Bunny's wants to support her. And she isn't so young any more and—well, I don't have to draw a diagram, do I?"

Bassett said, "You mean he didn't know about that premium receipt and thought Madge wouldn't know about the policy until after he'd married her? But how'd he account for having hidden the policy?"

Uncle Am said, "He wouldn't have to. After they're married he could pretend to find it somewhere among some stuff of Wally's. And Madge would let him use it for starting his own printing shop; he could talk her into that, because that way it would give them an income for life."

Bunny nodded. "She was always at Wally to get ambitious that way," he said. "But Wally didn't want to."

Uncle Am took off his hat and wiped sweat from his forehead. He didn't look so cool any more. He said, "Bunny, I still don't get it. Unless—Bunny, whose ideas was this? Yours—or Wally's?"

Bunny said. "His. Honest. He *wanted* me to kill him, or I'd never even have thought of it. He kept dogging me. I don't mean he ever came right out and said 'Kill me, pal,' but after I took to going around with him and he found out I needed money for my shop, and that I liked Madge and she liked me, he kept *at* me."

Bassett asked, "How do you mean, kept at you?"

"Well, he told me where he kept the policy—in his locker at work, and said nobody else knew about it. He'd say, 'Madge likes you, Bunny. If anything ever happens to me—' Hell, he worked out the whole thing. He told me that *if* something happened to him, it'd be better for Madge if she didn't know about the policy right away, that if she got the money direct she'd head for California or somewhere and blow it in, and he wished he could fix it so she wouldn't know she had the money coming until she was safely married to some guy who could invest it for her."

Bassett said, "But man, that wasn't suggesting you *kill* him. He just said if he died."

Bunny shook his head. "That was what he said, but not what he meant. He told me he wished he had the nerve to kill himself, but that he didn't. That anybody'd be doing him a favour—"

Bassett asked, "What happened that night?"

"Just like I told Ed, up to half past twelve. I took Madge home then, instead of half past one. Afterwards, I figured she wouldn't have known what time it was and if I said one-thirty I'd be protecting both of us.

"I'd given up looking for Wally by then. I knew where there was an all-night poker game on Chicago Avenue over near the river. I was walking up Orleans Street and was almost to Chicago when I met Wally coming the other way. Heading home with four bottles of beer. He was pretty tight.

"He insisted I walk home with him. He gave me one of the bottles to carry. One. He picked the darkest alley to cut through. The street light was out at the other end of it. He quit talking when we started through it. He walked a little ahead of me, and then he took off his hat and carried it in his hand—and, well, he *wanted* me to do it, and if I did I could have Madge and my own shop like I've always wanted and—well, I did."

Bassett asked. "Then why did you—

My uncle said to him, "Shut up, copper. You've got all you need. Let the guy alone. I understand the whole thing now."

He walked over to the dresser and poured some drinks out of the bottle. He looked at me, but I shook my head. He stopped at three drinks and gave the stiffest one to Bunny.

Bunny stood up to drink it. He gulped it down and started for the bathroom door. He was almost there when Bassett seemed to realize what was happening. He yelled, "Hey, don't—" and started across the room to grab the knob of the closing door before it could lock on the inside.

My uncle stumbled into Bassett, and the bathroom door's bolt slid home with a click.

Bassett said, "Goddam it, he's gonna—"

"Sure, Frank," my uncle said. "You got any better ideas? Come on, Ed, let's get out of here."

I wanted out quick, too.

I almost had to run to keep up with him after we were downstairs and out on the sidewalk.

We walked fast, under the blazing afternoon sun. We walked for blocks before he seemed to realize I was there with him.

He slowed down. He looked at me and grinned.

He said, "Weren't we a couple of marks, kid? Going hunting for wolves and catching a rabbit?"

"I wish now we'd never gone hunting."

He said, "So do I. My fault, kid. When I saw that note an hour ago I knew Bunny did it, but I couldn't guess why. I'd never met him, and—Hell, why should I excuse myself? I should have gone to see him alone. But no, I had to grandstand and go along with Bassett."

I asked, "How did the note—? Oh-oh. I see it now, now that I know there's something to see. He spelled the name right; that's what you mean, isn't it?"

Uncle Am nodded. "Anderz. He'd heard it over the phone from you, and you didn't spell it for him. He'd have written it 'Anders' if he hadn't read it on the insurance policy he said he didn't know existed."

I said, "I read the note and didn't see it."

My uncle didn t seem to hear me. He said, "I knew it wasn't suicide. I told you about that psychological quirk of Wally's—he *couldn't* have committed suicide. But I never dreamed he'd gone downhill to where he'd pull a stunt like that. I guess—well, if that's what life did to him, Ed, it's just as well. To play a trick like that on Bunny—"

"He thought he was doing Bunny a favour."

"Let's hope so. He should have known better."

I asked, "How long do you think he'd been planning this?"

"He took out that policy five years ago in Gary. He took that bribe from Reynolds to vote for his brother's acquittal, and then he voted for conviction. He must have figured the Reynolds gang would kill him for that.

"But either something happened to change his mind, that time, or he lost his nerve. He scrammed out of Gary and covered his trail. He couldn't have known Reynolds was here in Chicago, or he wouldn't have bothered with Bunny. He could have gone to Reynolds and had the job done cheaper."

"You mean for five years he's wanted to—"

"He must have kept it in mind, Ed. He kept up the policy, once he had it. Maybe he decided to ride it out until you were through school, started in a good job. Maybe he started working on Bunny about the time you started to work at the Elwood. My God."

We were waiting for lights to change, and I saw we were waiting to cross Michigan Boulevard. We'd walked plenty far, farther than I'd realized.

The lights said, "Walk," and we went across.

My uncle said, "Want a beer, kid?"

I said, "I'll take a Martini. Just one."

"Then I'll give you one in style, Ed. Come on, I'll show you something."

"What?"

"The world without a little red fence around it."

We walked north two blocks on the east side of Michigan Boulevard to the Allerton Hotel. We went in, and there was a special elevator. We rode up a long time, I don't know how many floors, but the Allerton is a tall building.

The top floor was a very swanky cocktail bar. The windows were open and it was cool there. Up as high as that, the breeze was a cool breeze and not something out of a blast furnace.

We took a table by a window on the south side, looking out toward the Loop. It was beautiful in the bright sunshine. The tall, narrow buildings were like fingers reaching toward the sky. It was like something out of a science-fiction story. You couldn't quite believe it, even looking at it.

"Ain't it something, kid?"

"Beautiful as hell," I said. "But it's a clipjoint."

He grinned. The little laughing wrinkles were back in the corners of his eyes.

He said, "It's a fabulous clipjoint, kid. The craziest things can happen in it, and not all of them are bad."

I nodded. I said, "Like Claire."

"Like your bluffing down Kaufman's loogans. Like the swat between the eyes you gave Bassett telling him where the Waupaca money is. He'll spend the rest of his life wondering how you knew."

He chuckled. "Kid, a few days ago you were a bit startled because at your age Wally had fought a duel and had an affair with an editor's wife. You ain't doing so bad yourself, kid. I'm a bit older than you and I've never yet killed a bank robber with a twelve-ounce poker, nor slept with a gun-moll."

"But it's over now," I said. "I've got to go back to work. You going back to the carney?"

"Yeah. And you're going to be a printer?"

"I guess so," I said. "Why not?"

"No reason at all. It's a good trade. Better than being a carney. There's no security in that. You make money sometimes, but you spend it. You live in tents like goddam Bedouins. You never have a home. The food is lousy and when it rains you go nuts. It's a hell of a life."

I felt disappointed. I wasn't going with him, of course, but I'd wanted him to want me to. It was silly, but that's the way it was.

He said, "Yeah, it's a hell of a life, kid. But if you're crazy enough to want to try it, I'd sure like to show you the ropes. You could get along; you've got what it takes."

"Thanks," I said, "But—well—"

"Okay," he said. "I wouldn't talk you into it. I'm going to send a wire to Hoagy and then go back to the Wacker to pack up."

"So long," I said.

We shook hands. He went off and I sat down at the table again and looked out.

The waitress came back and wanted to know if I wanted anything else and I told her I didn't.

I sat there until the shadows of the monstrous buildings got long and the light blue of the lake got darker. The cool breeze came in the open window.

Then I got up, and I was scared as hell that he'd gone without me. I found a phone booth and called the Wacker. I got his room and he was still there.

"It's Ed," I said. "I'm going along."

"I was waiting for you. You took a little longer than I thought."

"I'll rush home and pack a suitcase," I said. "Then shall I meet you at the depot?"

"Kid, we're going back by rattler. I'm broke. Just got a few bucks left for eats on the way."

"Broke?" I asked. "You can't be broke. You had two hundred dollars only a few hours ago."

He laughed. "It's an art, Ed. I told you a carney's money didn't last long. Listen, I'll meet you at Clark and Grand in an hour. We'll catch a streetcar out to where we can grab a freight."

I hurried home and packed. I was both glad and sorry that Mom and Gardie were out. I left a note for them.

Uncle Am was already at the corner when I got there. He had his suitcase and a trombone case, a new one.

He chuckled when he saw how I looked at it. He said, "A going-away present, kid. With a carney, you can learn to play it. With a carney, the more noise you make, the better, and some day you'll play yourself out of the carney. Harry James's first job was with a circus band."

He wouldn't let me open the case there. We got our streetcar and rode away out. Then we walked to a freight yard and cut across tracks.

He said, "We're bums now, kid. Ever eat a mulligan? We'll make one tomorrow. Tomorrow night we'll be with the carney."

A train was making up. We found an empty boxcar and got in. It was dusk now, and dim inside the car, but I opened the trombone case.

I let out a low whistle and something seemed to come up in my throat and stick there. I knew what had happened to just about all of Uncle Am's two hundred dollars.

It was a professional trombone, about the best one you can get. It was gold-plated and burnished so bright you could have used it for a mirror, and it was a feather-weight model. It was the kind of a tram that Teagarden or Dorsey would use.

It was out of this world.

I took it out of the case reverently and put it together. The feel and balance of it were wonderful.

From the trombone playing I'd done in the Gary school, I still remembered the positions for the C-scale. One-seven-four-three—

I put it to my lips and blew till I found the first note. It was fuzzy and sloppy, but that was me, not the trombone. Carefully I worked my way up the scale.

The engine highballed and the jerks of the couplings came along the train toward us and past us, like a series of firecrackers in a bunch. The car started moving slowly. I felt my way back down the scale again, getting more confident with each note. It wasn't going to take me long to be playing it.

Then somebody yelled "Hey!" and I looked and saw my serenade had brought us trouble. A brakeman was trotting alongside the car. He yelled, "Get the hell outa there," and put his hands on the floor of the car to vault inside.

My uncle said, "Give me the horn, kid," and took it out of my hands. He went near the door and put the horn to his lips and blew a godawful Bronx cheer of a note—a down-sliding, horrible-sounding note—as he pushed the slide out towards the brakie's face.

The brakie cussed and let go. He ran alongside a few more steps and then the train was going too fast and he lost ground and dropped behind us.

My uncle handed me back the trombone. We were both laughing.

I managed to stop, and I put the mouthpiece to my lips again. I blew and I got a clear note—a clear, beautiful-as-hell, ringing, resonant tone that was just dumb luck for me to have hit without years of practice.

And then the tone split and it was worse than the horribly bad note Uncle Am had just played for the brakeman.

Uncle Am started laughing, and I tried to blow again but I couldn't because I was laughing too.

For a minute or so we got to laughing at each other, and got worse, and couldn't stop. That's the way the rattler took us out of Chicago, both of us laughing like a couple of idiots.